GREAT BOOKS OF THE WESTERN WORLD

GREAT BOOKS
OF THE WESTERN WORLD
ROBERT MAYNARD HUTCHINS, *EDITOR IN CHIEF*

24.

RABELAIS

GARGANTUA AND PANTAGRUEL

BY FRANÇOIS RABELAIS

Translated by SIR THOMAS URQUHART
and PETER MOTTEUX

WILLIAM BENTON, *Publisher*

ENCYCLOPÆDIA BRITANNICA, INC.

CHICAGO · LONDON · TORONTO

BIOGRAPHICAL NOTE
François Rabelais, c. 1495–1553

Rabelais was born at Chinon in Touraine somewhere between 1483 and 1500; 1495 is the year most frequently given. His father is thought to have owned a small estate called La Devinière and to have been a vine-grower, and an apothecary, or a tavern-keeper, or a lawyer.

An indistinct allusion in his work has been interpreted to mean that Rabelais, when about nine, was sent to the convent of Seuilly to be made a monk. He is supposed to have been educated at La Baumette, near Angers, where he was at school with the brothers Du Bellay and Geoffroy d'Estissac, who were his influential friends in later life. He was ordained a priest at the Franciscan monastery of Fontenay-le-Comte, and by 1519 had attained a position of sufficient importance to sign deeds for the community. He also continued his studies, especially Greek, for he was soon in correspondence with the famous Humanist, Guillaume Budé. One of these letters reveals that his ardor for the new studies caused trouble with his superiors, and for a brief period his library of Greek books was confiscated. In 1524, through the influence of D'Estissac, who had become Bishop of Maillezais, Rabelais obtained permission to transfer from the Franciscan to the Benedictine order, and he moved to Maillezais, a learned and hospitable retreat, where he lived and studied for the next six years.

In 1530 Rabelais exchanged his Benedictine robes for those of a secular priest and, as he put it, "wandered for sometime about the world." For a time the Du Bellays provided him with an abode near their own château of Langey. Later that same year he went to the University of Montpellier, where he entered the faculty of medicine. In less than two months he received a bachelor's degree and in 1531 was lecturing publicly on Galen and Hippocrates. With this period at Montpellier are associated his appearance as an actor in the farce, *The Man Who Married a Dumb Wife,* and the composition of a fish sauce in imitation of the ancient *garum,* which he sent to the famous scholar, Étienne Dolet.

In 1532 Rabelais moved to Lyons, then the center of an unusually enlightened society. Although acting as physician to the Hôtel Dieu, he appears to have devoted most of his time to literature. During the year of his arrival he edited the medical *Epistles* of Giovanni Manardi, the *Aphorisms* of Hippocrates, and the *Ars Parva* of Galen. It was also probably at this time that he first began to think of writing about Gargantua and Pantagruel. Both seem to have been names of popular giants in the Middle Ages, and in 1532 at Lyons a short burlesque was published entitled, *Les Grandes et inestimables chroniques du grand et énorme géant Gargantua,* which Rabelais may have edited. Within a year he wrote and published his first *Pantagruel,* which constitutes the second book of the completed work. In 1533, as well, Rabelais issued the *Pantagrueline Prognostication* and the first of the series of *Almanacs* he compiled annually until 1550. The Pantagruel literature he signed with the anagrammatic pseudonym of "Alcofribas Nasier."

Rabelais resumed his wanderings in 1534 when his friend, Jean du Bellay, who had become Bishop of Paris, passed through Lyons on an embassy to Rome and engaged him as physician. Although this first visit to Rome was of short duration, Rabelais edited Marliani's *Topographia Antiquae Romae* and dedicated it to his patron upon his return to Lyons. The following year he brought out *Gargantua* and again joined Du Bellay, who was traveling to Rome to be made a Cardinal. While in Rome, Rabelais filed a petition for absolution from violation of his monastic vows. There had been some irregularity in his leaving the Benedictines to become a secular priest, and, furthermore, both *Pantagruel* and *Gargantua* had been condemned by the Sorbonne almost immediately upon publication. While waiting for the absolution, Rabelais made a collection of flowers and herbs which he sent to his friend, D'Estissac. Early in 1536 he received the bull of absolution which freed him from ecclesiastical censure, entitled him to return to the Benedictines when he chose, and allowed him to practise medicine, provided that he did not make use of the scalpel and cautery and did not work for gain. Upon his return to France he became a canon of St. Maur and continued his work in medicine. In 1537 he publicly demonstrated an anatomical dissection and took his doctor's degree at Montpellier, where he lectured upon a "very ancient" Greek text of Hippocrates.

Through his association with the Du Bellays, Rabelais was appointed to a diplomatic office at the conference between Francis I and Charles V in 1538. Following that, he entered the service of Guillaume du Bellay, the elder brother of his former patron, who was the leading diplomat of Francis I and at that time governor of Piedmont. He remained with the elder Du Bellay until his death in 1543 and during some of that time was employed in collecting manuscripts in Italy for the king's library. In 1545 he was allowed to print his book, to which a third volume was now added, "avec privilège du roi."

Despite the official sanction, the third book was also banned by the Sorbonne, and the following year Rabelais appears to have gone into something like voluntary exile by accepting the position of city physician in Metz. Shortly after the death of Francis I, he again joined Jean du Bellay in Rome. While there, in 1549, he wrote an account of the festivals held to celebrate the birth of a second son to the new king, Henry II. This account, known as the *Sciomachie*, was dedicated to the powerful Cardinal de Guise. Rabelais, feeling perhaps that he now had such strong supporters that he need not fear the Sorbonne authorities, returned to France and was presented with the livings of Saint Martin de Meudon and Saint Christophe de Jambet, although there is no evidence that he was ever active at either benefice. In 1552 he published the fourth volume of his work. The Sorbonne censured it, and the parliament suspended its sale, taking advantage of the king's absence from Paris. But it was soon relieved of the suspension. In January, 1553 Rabelais resigned his ecclesiastical positions because of ill health. He died, it is said, on April 9.

CONTENTS

CONTENTS

CONTENTS

BOOK ONE

THE INESTIMABLE LIFE OF THE GREAT GARGANTUA,
FATHER OF PANTAGRUEL, HERETOFORE COMPOSED
BY M. ALCOFRIBAS,[1] ABSTRACTOR OF THE QUINTESSENCE,
A BOOK FULL OF PANTAGRUELISM

TO THE READERS

Good friends, my readers, who peruse this book,
Be not offended, whilst on it you look:
Denude yourselves of all deprav'd affection,
For it contains no badness nor infection:
'Tis true that it brings forth to you no birth
Of any value, but in point of mirth;
Thinking therefore how sorrow might your mind
Consume, I could no apter subject find;
One inch of joy surmounts of grief a span;
Because to laugh is proper to the man.

THE AUTHOR'S PROLOGUE

Most noble and illustrious drinkers, and you thrice precious pockified blades (for to you, and none else do I dedicate my writings), Alcibiades, in that dialogue of Plato's which is entitled *The Banquet,* whilst he was setting forth the praises of his schoolmaster Socrates (without all question the prince of philosophers), amongst other discourses to that purpose said that he resembled the Sileni. Sileni of old were little boxes, like those we now may see in the shops of apothecaries, painted on the outside with wanton toyish figures, as harpies, satyrs, bridled geese, horned hares, saddled ducks, flying goats, thiller harts, and other such counterfeited pictures, at pleasure, to excite people unto laughter, as Silenus himself, who was the foster-father of good Bacchus, was wont to do; but within those capricious caskets called Sileni were carefully preserved and kept many rich and fine drugs, such as balm, ambergreese, amomon, musk, civet, with several kinds of precious stones, and other things of great price. Just such another thing was Socrates: for to have eyed his outside, and esteemed of him by his exterior

appearance, you would not have given the peel of an onion for him, so deformed he was in body, and ridiculous in his gesture. He had a sharp pointed nose, with the look of a bull, and countenance of a fool; he was in his carriage simple, boorish in his apparel, in fortune poor, unhappy in his wives, unfit for all offices in the commonwealth, always laughing, tippling, and merry, carousing to every one, with continual gibes and jeers, the better by those means to conceal his divine knowledge. Now, opening this box you would have found within it a heavenly and inestimable drug, a more than human understanding, an admirable virtue, matchless learning, invincible courage, inimitable sobriety, certain contentment of mind, perfect assurance, and an incredible disregard of all that for which men commonly do so much watch, run, sail, fight, travel, toil, and turmoil themselves.

Whereunto (in your opinion) doth this little flourish of a preamble tend? For so much as you, my good disciples, and some other jolly fools of ease and leisure, reading the pleasant titles of some books, of our invention, as *Gargantua, Pantagruel, Whippot,* the

[1] *Alcofribas Nasier,* anagram of François Rabelais.

1

Dignity of Codpieces, of Pease and Bacon, with a commentary, &c., are too ready to judge that there is nothing in them but jests, mockeries, lascivious discourse, and recreative lies; because the outside (which is the title) is usually, without any farther inquiry, entertained with scoffing and derision. But truly it is very unbeseeming to make so slight account of the works of men, seeing yourselves avouch that it is not the habit that makes the monk, many being monasterially accoutred, who inwardly are nothing less than monachal; and that there are of those that wear Spanish caps who have but little of the valour of Spaniards in them. Therefore is it, that you must open the book, and seriously consider of the matter treated in it. Then shall you find that it containeth things of far higher value than the box did promise; that is to say, that the subject thereof is not so foolish, as by the title at the first sight it would appear to be.

And put the case, that in the literal sense you meet with purposes merry and solacious enough, and consequently very correspondent to their inscriptions, yet must not you stop there as at the melody of the charming Syrens, but endeavour to interpret that in a sublimer sense, which possibly you intended to have spoken in the jollity of your heart. Did you ever pick the lock of a cupboard to steal a bottle of wine out of it? Tell me truly, and, if you did, call to mind the countenance which then you had. Or, did you ever see a dog with a marrow-bone in his mouth,—the beast of all others, says Plato, *lib.* 2, *De Republica,* the most philosophical? If you have seen him, you might have remarked with what devotion and circumspectness he wards and watcheth it: with what care he keeps it: how fervently he holds it: how prudently he gobbets it: with what affection he breaks it: and with what diligence he sucks it. To what end all this? What moveth him to take all these pains? What are the hopes of his labour? What doth he expect to reap thereby? Nothing but a little marrow. True it is, that this little is more savoury and delicious than the great quantities of other sorts of meat, because the marrow (as Galen testifieth, 3, *Facult. Nat.* and, 11, *De Usu Partium*) is a nourishment most perfectly elaboured by nature.

In imitation of this dog, it becomes you to be wise to smell, feel, and have in estimation, these fair, goodly books, stuffed with high conceptions, which though seemingly easy in the pursuit, are in the cope and encounter somewhat difficult. And then, like him, you must, by a sedulous lecture, and frequent meditation, break the bone, and suck out the marrow; that is, my allegorical sense, or the things I to myself propose to be signified by these Pythagorical symbols; with assured hope, that in so doing, you will at last attain to be both well-advised and valiant by the reading of them: for, in the perusal of this treatise, you shall find another kind of taste, and a doctrine of a more profound and abstruse consideration, which will disclose unto you the most glorious doctrines and dreadful mysteries, as well in what concerneth our religion, as matters of the public state and life economical.

Do you believe, upon your conscience that Homer, whilst he was couching his *Iliads* and *Odysses,* had any thought upon those allegories, which Plutarch, Heraclides Ponticus, Eustathius, Cornutus, squeezed out of him, and which Politian filched again from them? If you trust it, with neither hand nor foot do you come near to my opinion, which judgeth them to have been as little dreamed of by Homer, as the gospel sacraments were by Ovid, in his *Metamorphosis;* though a certain gulligut friar, and true bacon-picker would have undertaken to prove it, if, perhaps, he had met with as very fools as himself, and as the proverb says, "a lid worthy of such a kettle."

If you give any credit thereto, why do not you the same to these jovial new Chronicles of mine? Albeit, when I did dictate them, I thought thereof no more than you, who possibly were drinking the whilst, as I was. For in the composing of this lordly book, I never lost nor bestowed any more, nor any other time, than what was appointed to serve me for taking of my bodily refection, that is, whilst I was eating and drinking. And, indeed, that is the fittest and most proper hour, wherein to write these high matters and deep sentences: as Homer knew very well, the paragon of all philologues, and Ennius, father of the Latin poets, as Horace calls him, although a certain sneaking jobbernol alleged that his verses smelled more of the wine than oil.

So saith a Turlupin or a new start-up grub of my books; but a turd for him. The fragrant odour of the wine, oh! how much more dainty, pleasant, laughing, celestial, and delicious it is, than that smell of oil! and I will glory as much when it is said of me, that I have spent more on wine than oil, as did Demosthenes, when it was told him, that his expense on oil was greater than on wine. I truly hold it for an honour and praise to be called and reputed a frolic Gaulter and a Robin Goodfellow; for under this name am I welcome in all choice companies of Pantagruelists. It was upbraided to Demosthenes, by an envious, surly knave, that his *Orations* did smell like the sarpler, or wrapper of a foul and filthy oil vessel. For this cause interpret you all my deeds and sayings, in the perfectest sense; reverence the cheese-like brain that feeds you with these faire billevezees and trifling jollities, and do what lies in you to keep me always merry. Be frolic now, my lads, cheer up your hearts, and joyfully read the rest, with all the ease of your body and profit of your reins. But hearken, joltheads, you viedazes, or dickens take ye, remember to drink a health to me for the favour again, and I will pledge you instantly, *Tout ares-metys.*

❧❦❧

CHAPTER 1

Of the Genealogy and Antiquity of Gargantua

I MUST refer you to the great Chronicle of Pantagruel for the knowledge of that genealogy and antiquity of race by which Gargantua is come unto us. In it you may understand more at large how the giants were born in this world, and how from them by a direct line issued Gargantua, the father of Pantagruel: and do not take it ill, if for this time I pass by it, although the subject be such, that the oftener it were remembered, the more it would please your worshipful Seniorias; according to which you have the authority of Plato in *Philebo* and *Gorgias;* and of Flaccus, who says that there are some kinds of purposes (such as these are without doubt) which, the frequentlier they be repeated, still prove the more delectable.

Would to God every one had as certain knowledge of his genealogy since the time of the ark of Noah until this age. I think many are at this day emperors, kings, dukes, princes, and popes on the earth, whose extraction is from some porters and pardon-pedlars; as on the contrary, many are now poor wandering beggars, wretched and miserable, who are descended of the blood and lineage of great kings and emperors, occasioned, as I conceive it, by the transport and revolution of kingdoms and empires, from the Assyrians to the Medes, from the Medes to the Persians, from the Persians to the Macedonians, from the Macedonians to the Romans, from the Romans to the Greeks, from the Greeks to the French.

And to give you some hint concerning myself, who speak unto you, I cannot think but I am come of the race of some rich king or prince in former times; for never yet saw you any man that had a greater desire to be a king, and to be rich, than I have, and that only that I may make good cheer, do nothing, nor care for anything, and plentifully enrich my friends, and all honest and learned men. But herein do I comfort myself, that in the other world I shall be so, yea, and greater too than at this present I dare wish. As for you, with the same or a better conceit consolate yourselves in your distresses, and drink fresh if you can come by it.

To return to our wethers, I say, that by the sovereign gift of heaven, the antiquity and genealogy of Gargantua hath been reserved for our use more full and perfect than any other except that of the Messias, whereof I mean not to speak; for it belongs not unto my purpose, and the devils, that is to say, the false accusers and dissembled gospellers, will therein oppose me. This genealogy was found by John Andrew, in a meadow, which he had near the pole-arch under the olive tree, as you go to Narsay: where, as he was making a cast up of some ditches, the diggers with their mattocks struck against a great brazen tomb, and unmeasurably long, for they could never find the end thereof, by reason that it entered too far within the sluices of Vienne. Opening this tomb in a certain place thereof, sealed on the top with the mark of a goblet, about which was written in Hetrurian letters, HIC BIBITUR, they found nine flagons, set in such order as they used to rank their skittles in Gascony, of which that which was placed in the middle had under it a big, fat, great, grey, pretty, small, mouldy, little pamphlet, smelling stronger, but no better than roses. In that book, the said genealogy was found written all at length, in a chancery hand, not in paper, not in parchment, nor in wax, but in the bark of an elm tree; yet so worn with the long tract of time, that hardly could three letters together be there perfectly discerned.

I, though unworthy, was sent for thither, and with much help of those spectacles, whereby the art of reading dim writings, and letters that do not clearly appear to the sight, is practised, as Aristotle teacheth it; did translate the book, as you may see in your Pantagruelising, that is to say, in drinking stiffly to your own heart's desire, and reading the dreadful and horrific acts of Pantagruel. At the end of the book there was a little treatise, entituled the *Antidoted Fanfreluches;* or, a *Galimatia* of extravagant conceits. The rats and moths, or (that I may not lie) other wicked beasts, had nibbled off the beginning: the rest I have hereto subjoined, for the reverence I bear to antiquity.

CHAPTER 2

The Antidoted Fanfreluches: or, a Galimatia of extravagant conceits found in an ancient Monument

No sooner did the Cymbrians' overcommer
Pass through the air to shun the dew of
    summer,
But at his coming straight great tubs were
    fill'd,
With pure fresh butter down in showers
    distill'd:
Wherewith when water'd was his grandam
    heigh,
Aloud he cried, fish it, sir, I pray;
Because his beard is almost all bewray'd;
Or, that he would hold to'm a scale he pray'd.

To lick his slipper, some told was much
    better,
Than to gain pardons, and the merit greater.
In th'interim a crafty chuff approaches,
From the depth issued, where they fish for
    roaches;
Who said, Good sire, some of them let us
    save,
The eel is here, and in this hollow cave
You'll find, if that our looks on it demur,
A great waste in the bottom of his fur.

To read this chapter when he did begin,
Nothing but a calf's horns were found
    therein;
I feel, quoth he, the mitre which doth hold

My head so chill, it makes my brain take cold.
Being with the perfume of a turnip warm'd,
To stay by chimney hearths himself he arm'd,
Provided that a new thill-horse they made
Of every person of a hair-brain'd head.

They talked of the bunghole of Saint
    Knowles,
Of Gilbathar and thousand other holes,
If they might be reduc'd t' a scarry stuff,
Such as might not be subject to the cough:
Since ev'ry man unseemly did it find,
To see them gaping thus at ev'ry wind:
For, if perhaps they handsomely were clos'd,
For pledges they to men might be expos'd.

In this arrest by Hercules the raven
Was flayed at her [his] return from Lybia
    haven.
Why am not I, said Minos, there invited?
Unless it be myself, not one's omitted:
And then it is their mind, I do no more
Of frogs and oysters send them any store:
In case they spare my life and prove but
    civil,
I give their sale of distaffs to the devil.

To quell him comes Q. B. who limping frets
At the safe pass of trixy crackarets;
The boulter, the grand Cyclops' cousin, those
Did massacre, whilst each one wip'd his nose:
Few ingles in this fallow ground are bred,
But on a tanner's mill are winnowed.
Run thither all of you, th' alarms sound clear,
You shall have more than you had the last
    year.

Short while thereafter was the bird of Jove
Resolv'd to speak, though dismal it should
    prove;
Yet was afraid, when he saw them in ire,
They should o'erthrow quite flat, down dead,
    th' empire.
He rather chus'd the fire from heaven to
    steal,
To boats where were red-herrings put to sale;
Than to be calm 'gainst those who strive to
    brave us,
And to the Massorets fond words enslave us.

All this at last concluded gallantly,
In spite of Até and her hern-like thigh,
Who, sitting, saw Penthesilea ta'en,
In her old age, for a cresse-selling quean.
Each one cried out, thou filthy collier toad,
Doth it become thee to be found abroad?

Thou hast the Roman standard filch'd away,
Which they in rags of parchment did display.

Juno was born, who under the rainbow,
Was a bird-catching with her duck below:
When her with such a grievous trick they
    plyed,
That she had almost been bethwacked by it.
The bargain was, that, of that throat-full, she
Should of Proserpina have two eggs free;
And if that she thereafter should be found,
She to a hawthorn hill should be fast bound.

Seven months thereafter lacking twenty-two,
He, that of old did Carthage town undo,
Did bravely midst them all himself advance,
Requiring of them his inheritance;
Although they justly made up the division,
According to the shoe-welt-laws decision,
By distributing store of brews and beef
To these poor fellows that did pen the brief.

But th' year will come, sign of a Turkish bow,
Five spindles yarn'd and three pot-bottoms
    too,
Wherein of a discourteous king the dock
Shall pepper'd be under an hermit's frock.
Ah! that for one she hypocrite you must
Permit so many acres to be lost!
Cease, cease, this vizard may become
    another,
Withdraw yourselves unto the serpent's
    brother.

'Tis in times past that he who is shall reign
With his good friends in peace now and
    again.
No rash nor heady prince shall then rule
    crave,
Each good will its arbitrement shall have;
And the joy, promised of old as doom
To the heaven's guests, shall in its beacon
    come.
Then shall the breeding mares, that
    benumb'd were,
Like royal palfreys ride triumphant there.

And this continue shall from time to time,
Till Mars be fettered for an unknown crime;
Then shall one come, who others will sur-
    pass,
Delightful, pleasing, matchless, full of grace.
Cheer up your hearts, approach to this repast,
All trusty friends of mine; for he's deceas'd
Who would not for a world return again.
So highly shall time past be cry'd up then.

He who was made of wax shall lodge each
    member
Close by the hinges of a block of timber.
We then no more shall master, master, whoot
The swagger, who th' alarum bell holds out;
Could one seize on the dagger which he
    bears,
Heads would be free from tingling in the ears,
To baffle the whole storehouse of abuses;
And thus farewell Apollo and the Muses.

CHAPTER 3

*How Gargantua was carried eleven months
in his Mother's Belly*

GRANGOUSIER was a good fellow in his time,
and notable jester; he loved to drink neat, as
much as any man that then was in the world,
and would willingly eat salt meat. To this
intent he was ordinarily well furnished with
gammons of bacon, both of Westphalia,
Mayence and Bayonne, with store of dried
neat's tongues, plenty of links, chitterlings
and puddings, in their season; together with
salt beef and mustard, a good deal of hard
rows of powdered mullet called botargos,
great provision of sausages, not of Bolonia
(for he feared the Lombard Boccone), but of
Bigorre, Longaulnay, Brene, and Rouargue.
In the vigour of his age he married Gargamelle, daughter to the King of the Parpail-
lons, a jolly pug, and well-mouthed wench.
These two did oftentimes do the two-backed
beast together, joyfully rubbing and frotting
their bacon against one another, in so far,
that at last she became great with child of a
fair son, and went with him unto the eleventh
month; for so long, yea longer, may a woman
carry her great belly, especially when it is
some masterpiece of nature, and a person
predestinated to the performance, in his due
time, of great exploits. As Homer says, that
the child, which Neptune begot upon the
Nymph, was borne a whole year after the
conception, that is in the twelfth month. For,
as Aulus Gellius saith, *lib.* 3 ,this long time
was suitable to the majesty of Neptune, that
in it the child might receive his perfect form.
For the like reason Jupiter made the night,
wherein he lay with Alcmena, last forty-eight
hours, a shorter time not being sufficient for
the forging of Hercules, who cleansed the
world of the monsters and tyrants, wherewith
it was opprest. My masters, the ancient Pantagruelists, have confirmed that which I say,
and withal declared it to be not only possible,

but also maintained the lawful birth and legitimation of the infant born of a woman in the eleventh month after the decease of her husband. Hypocrates, *lib. De Alimento.* Plinius, *lib.* 7. *cap.* 5. Plautus, in his *Cistellaria.* Marcus Varro in his Satyre inscribed *The Testament,* alleging to this purpose the authority of Aristotle. Censorinus, *lib. De Die Natali.* Arist. *lib.* 7. *cap.* 3 and 4. *De Natura Animalium.* Gellius, *lib.* 3. *cap.* 16. Servius, in his exposition upon this verse of Virgil's *Eclogues, Matri longa decem,*[1] &c. and a thousand other fools, whose number hath been increased by the lawyers *ff. de suis, et legit. l. intestato. paragrapho. fin.* and *in Auth. de restitut. et ea quæ parit in xi mense.*[2] Moreover upon these grounds they have foisted in their Robidilardick, or Lapiturolive law. *Gallus ff. de lib. et posth. l. sept. ff. de stat. hom.*[3] and some other laws, which at this time I dare not name. By means whereof the honest widows may without danger play at the close-buttock game with might and main, and as hard as they can for the space of the first two months after the decease of their husbands. I pray you, my good lusty springal lads, if you find any of these females, that are worth the pains of untying the cod-piece-point, get up, ride upon them, and bring them to me; for, if they happen within the third month to conceive, the child shall be heir to the deceased, if, before he died, he had no other children, and the mother shall pass for an honest woman.

When she is known to have conceived, thrust forward boldly, spare her not, whatever betide you, seeing the paunch is full. As Julia, the daughter of the Emperor Octavian, never prostituted herself to her belly-bumpers, but when she found herself with child, after the manner of ships that receive not their steersman, till they have their ballast and lading. And if any blame them for this their rataconniculation and reiterated lechery upon their pregnancy and big-belliedness, seeing beasts, in the like exigent of their fulness, will never suffer the male-masculant to encroach them, their answer will be, that those are beasts, but they are women, very well skilled in the pretty vales, and small fees of the pleasant trade and mysteries of superfetation: as Populia heretofore answered, according to the relation of Macrobius, *lib.* 2. *Saturnal.* If the devil would not have them to bag, he must ring hard the spigot, and stop the bung-hole.

CHAPTER 4

How Gargamelle, being great with Gargantua, did eat a huge deal of tripes

THE occasion and manner how Gargamelle was brought to bed, and delivered of her child, was thus: and, if you do not believe it, I wish your bum-gut may fall out, and make an escapade. Her bum-gut, indeed, or fundament escaped her in an afternoon, on the third day of February, with having eaten at dinner too many godebillios. Godebillios are the fat tripes of coiros. Coiros are beeves fattened at the cratch in ox stalls, or in the fresh guimo meadows. Guimo meadows are those, that for their fruitfulness may be mowed twice a year. Of those fat beeves they had killed three hundred sixty-seven thousand and fourteen, to be salted at Shrove-tide, that in the entering of the spring they might have plenty of powdered beef, wherewith to season their mouths at the beginning of their meals, and to taste their wine the better.

They had abundance of tripes, as you have heard, and they were so delicious, that every one licked his fingers. But as the devil would have it, for all men could do, there was no possibility to keep them long in that relish; for in a very short while they would have stunk, which had been an indecent thing. It was therefore concluded, that they should be all of them gulched up, without losing anything. To this effect they invited all the burghers of Sainais, of Suillé, of the Roche-Clermaud, of Vaugaudry, without omitting the Coudray Monpensier, the Gué de Véde, and other their neighbours, all stiff drinkers, brave fellows, and good players at nine-pins. The good man Grangousier took great pleasure in their company, and commanded there should be no want, nor pinching for anything. Nevertheless he bid his wife eat sparingly, because she was near her time, and that these tripes were no very commendable meat. They would fain, said he, be at the chewing of ordure, that would eat the case wherein it was. Notwithstanding these admonitions, she did eat sixteen quarters, two bushels, three pecks, and a pipkin full. O the fair fecality, wherewith she swelled, by the ingrediency of such shitten stuff!

After dinner they all went out in a hurle, to the grove of the willows, where, on the green grass, to the sound of the merry flutes, and pleasant bagpipes, they danced so gallantly, that it was a sweet and heavenly sport to see them so frolic.

CHAPTER 5

How they chirped over their cups

THEN did they fall upon the chat of victuals, and some belly furniture to be snatched at in the very same place. Which purpose was no sooner mentioned, but forthwith began flagons to go, gammons to trot, goblets to fly, great bowls to ting, glasses to ring. Draw, reach, fill, mix, give it me without water. So my friend, so, whip me off this glass neatly, bring me hither some claret, a full weeping glass till it run over. A cessation and truce with thirst. Ha, thou false fever, wilt thou not be gone? By my figgins, godmother, I cannot as yet enter in the humour of being merry, nor drink so currently as I would. You have catch'd a cold, gammer? Yea, forsooth, sir. By the belly of Sanct Buff, let us talk of our drink: I never drink but at my hours, like the Pope's mule. And I never drink but in my breviary, like a fair father guardian. Which was first, thirst or drinking? Thirst, for who in the time of innocence would have drunk without being athirst? Nay, sir, it was drinking; for *privatio præsupponit habitum*.[4] I am learned, you see: *Fœcundi calices quem non fecere disertum?*[5] We poor innocents drink but too much without thirst. Not I truly, who am a sinner, for I never drink without thirst, either present or future. To prevent it, as you know, I drink for the thirst to come. I drink eternally. This is to me an eternity of drinking, and drinking of eternity. Let us sing, let us drink, and tune up our roundlays. Where is my funnel? What, it seems I do not drink but by an attorney? Do you wet yourselves to dry, or do you dry to wet you? Pish, I understand not the rhetoric (theoric I should say), but I help myself somewhat by the practice. Beast, enough! I sup, I wet, I humect, I moisten my gullet, I drink, and all for fear of dying. Drink always and you shall never die. If I drink not, I am a ground dry, gravelled and spent. I am stark dead without drink, and my soul ready to fly into some marsh amongst frogs: the soul never dwells in a dry place, drought kills it. O you butlers, creators of new forms, make me of no drinker a drinker, perenity and everlastingness of sprinkling, and bedewing me through these my parched and sinewy bowels. He drinks in vain, that feels not the pleasure of it. This

entereth into my veins, the pissing tool and urinal vessels shall have nothing of it. I would willingly wash the tripes of the calf, which I appareled this morning. I have pretty well now ballasted my stomach, and stuffed my paunch. If the papers of my bonds and bills could drink as well as I do, my creditors would not want for wine when they come to see me, or, when they are to make any formal exhibition of their rights to what of me they can demand. This hand of yours spoils your nose. O how many other such will enter here before this go out! What, drink so shallow? It is enough to break both girds and pettrel. This is called a cup of dissimulation, or flaggonal hypocrisy.

What difference is there between a bottle and a flagon? Great difference; for the bottle is stopped and shut up with a stopper, but the flagon with a vice. Bravely and well played upon the words! Our fathers drank lustily, and emptied their cans. Well cacked, well sung! Come, let us drink: will you send nothing to the river? Here is one going to wash the tripes. I drink no more than a sponge. I drink like a Templar Knight. And I, *tanquam sponsus*.[6] And I, *sicut terra sine aqua*.[7] Give me a synonymon for a gammon of bacon. It is the compulsory of drinkers: it is a pully. By a pully-rope wine is let down into the cellar and by a gammon into the stomach. Hey! now boys, hither, some drink, some drink. There is no trouble in it. *Respice personam, pone pro duo, bus non est in usu*.[8] If I could get up as well as I can swallow down, I had been long ere now very high in the air.

Thus became Tom Toss-pot rich; thus went in the tailor's stitch. Thus did Bacchus conquer Inde; thus Philosophy, Melinde. A little rain allays a great deal of wind; long tippling breaks the thunder. But, if there came such liquor from my ballock, would you not willingly thereafter suck the udder whence it issued? Here page, fill! I prythee, forget me not, when it comes to my turn, and I will enter the election I have made of thee into the very register of my heart. Sup, Guillot, and spare not, there is somewhat in the pot. I appeal from thirst, and disclaim its jurisdiction. Page, sue out my appeal in form. This remnant in the bottom of the glass must follow its leader. I was wont heretofore to drink out all, but now I leave nothing. Let us not make too much haste; it is requisite we carry all along with us. Hey day, here are tripes fit for our sport, and, in earnest, excellent godebillios of the dun ox (you know) with the black streak. O, for God's sake, let us lash them soundly, yet thriftily. Drink, or I will—. No, no, drink, I beseech you. Sparrows will not eat unless you bob them on the tail, nor can I drink if I be not fairly spoke to. The concavities of my body are like another hell for their capacity. *Lagonædatera.* There is not a corner, nor cuniburrow in all my body, where this wine doth not ferret out my thirst. Ho, this will bang it soundly. But this shall banish it utterly. Let us wind our horns by the sound of flagons and bottles, and cry aloud, that whoever hath lost his thirst come not hither to seek it. Long clysters of drinking are to be voided without doors. The great God made the planets, and we make the platters neat. I have the word of the gospel in my mouth, *Sitio.*[9] The stone called Asbestos is not more unquenchable than the thirst of my paternity. Appetite comes with eating, says Angeston, but the thirst goes away with drinking. I have a remedy against thirst, quite contrary to that which is good against the biting of a mad dog. Keep running after a dog, and he will never bite you; drink always before the thirst, and it will never come upon you. There I catch you, I awake you. Argus had a hundred eyes for his sight, a butler should have (like Briareus) a hundred hands wherewith to fill us wine indefatigably. Hey now, lads, let us moisten ourselves, it will be time to dry hereafter. White wine here, wine, boys! Pour out all in the name of Lucifer, fill here, you, fill and fill (peascods on you) till it be full. My tongue peels. *Lans tringue;* to thee countryman, I drink to thee, good fellow, comrade to thee, lusty, lively! Ha, la, la, that was drunk to some purpose, and bravely gulped over. *O lachryma Christi,* it is of the best grape? I' faith, pure Greek, Greek! O the fine white wine! upon my conscience, it is a kind of taffatas wine; hin, hin, it is of one ear, well wrought, and of good wool. Courage, comrade; up thy heart, Billy! We will not be beasted at this bout, for I have got one trick. *Ex hoc in hoc.*[10] There is no enchantment, nor charm there, every one of you hath seen it. My apprenticeship is out, I am a free man of this trade. I am prester Macé, Prish, Brum! I should say, master *passé.* O the drinkers, those that are a-dry, O poor thirsty souls! Good page, my friend, fill me here some, and crown the wine, I pray thee. *À la Cardinale! Natura abhorret vac-*

uum.[11] Would you say that a fly could drink in this? This is after the fashion of Switzerland. Clear off, neat, *supernaculum!*[12] Come, therefore, blades, to this divine liquor, and celestial juice, swill it over heartily, and spare not! It is a decoction of nectar and ambrosia.

CHAPTER 6
How Gargantua was born in a strange manner

WHILST they were on this discourse and pleasant tattle of drinking, Gargamelle began to be a little unwell in her lower parts; whereupon Grangousier arose from off the grass, and fell to comfort her very honestly and kindly, suspecting that she was in travail, and told her, that it was best for her to sit down upon the grass under the willows, because she was likely very shortly to see young feet, and that therefore it was convenient she should pluck up her spirits, and take a good heart of new at the fresh arrival of her baby; saying to her withal, that although the pain was somewhat grievous to her, it would be but of short continuance, and that the succeeding joy would quickly remove that sorrow, in such sort that she should not so much as remember it. On with a sheep's courage, quoth he. Dispatch this boy, and we will speedily fall to work for the making of another. Ha! said she, so well as you speak at your own ease, you that are men! Well then, in the name of God, I'll do my best, seeing that you will have it so; but would to God that it were cut off from you! What, said Grangousier? Ha, said she, you are a good man indeed, you understand it well enough. What, my member? said he. By the goat's blood, if it please you, that shall be done instantly; cause bring hither a knife. Alas, said she, the Lord forbid, and pray Jesus to forgive me! I did not say it from my heart, therefore let it alone, and do not do it neither more nor less any kind of harm for my speaking so to you. But I am like to have work enough to do to-day, and all for your member, yet God bless you and it.

Courage, courage, said he, take you no care of the matter, let the four foremost oxen do the work. I will yet go drink one whiff more, and if, in the mean time, any thing befal you, that may require my presence, I will be so near to you, that, at the first whistling in your fist, I shall be with you forthwith. A little while after she began to groan, lament, and cry. Then suddenly came the midwives from all quarters, who groping her below, found some peloderies, which was a certain filthy stuff, and of a taste truly bad enough. This they thought had been the child, but it was her fundament that was slipt out with the mollification of her straight entrail, which you call the bum-gut, and that merely by eating of too many tripes, as we have showed you before. Whereupon an old ugly trot in the company, who had the repute of an expert she-physician, and was come from Brisepaille, near to Saint Genou, three score years before, made her so horrible a restrictive and binding medicine, and whereby all her larris, arse-pipes, and conduits were so oppilated, stopped, obstructed, and contracted, that you could hardly have opened and enlarged them with your teeth, which is a terrible thing to think upon; seeing the devil at the mass at Saint Martin's was puzzled with the like task, when with his teeth he had lengthened out the parchment whereon he wrote the tittle tattle of two young mangy whores. By this inconvenience the cotyledons of her matrix were presently loosened, through which the child sprung up and leaped, and so, entering into the hollow vein, did climb by the diaphragm even above her shoulders, where the vein divides itself into two, and from thence taking his way towards the left side, issued forth at her left ear. As soon as he was born, he cried not as other babes use to do, miez, miez, miez, but with a high, sturdy, and big voice shouted about, Some drink, some drink, some drink, as inviting all the world to drink with him. The noise hereof was so extremely great, that it was heard in both the countries at once, of Beauce and Bibarois. I doubt me, that you do not thoroughly believe the truth of this strange nativity. Though you believe it not, I care not much: but an honest man, and of good judgment, believeth still what is told him, and that which he finds written.

Is this beyond our law, or our faith; against reason or the Holy Scripture? For my part, I find nothing in the sacred Bible that is against it. But tell me, if it had been the will of God, would you say that he could not do it? Ha, for favour sake, I beseech you, never cmberlucock or impulregafize your spirits with these vain thoughts and idle conceits; for I tell you, it is not impossible with God; and, if he pleased, all women henceforth should bring forth their children at the ear. Was not Bacchus engendered out of the very thigh of Jupiter? Did not Roquetaillade come out of his mother's heel, and Crocmoush from the slipper of his nurse? Was not Minerva born of the brain, even through the ear of Jove? Adonis, of the bark of a myrrh tree; and Castor and Pollux of the doupe of that egg which was laid and hatched by Leda? But you would wonder more, and with far greater amazement, if I should now present you with that chapter of Plinius, wherein he treateth of strange births, and contrary to nature, and yet am I not so impudent a liar as he was. Read the seventh book of his *Natural History*, chap. 3, and trouble not my head any more about this.

CHAPTER 7

After what manner Gargantua had his name given him, and how he tippled, bibbed, and curried the can

THE good man Grangousier, drinking and making merry with the rest, heard the horrible noise which his son had made as he entered into the light of this world, when he cried out, Some drink, some drink, some drink; whereupon he said in French *Que grand tu as et souple le gousier!* [13] that is to say, How great and nimble a throat thou hast. Which the company hearing said, that verily the child ought to be called Gargantua; because it was the first word that after his birth his father had spoke, in imitation, and at the example, of the ancient Hebrews; whereunto he condescended, and his mother was very well pleased therewith. In the mean while, to quiet the child, they gave him to drink *à tirelarigot*, that is, till his throat was like to crack with it; then was he carried to the font, and there baptized, according to the manner of good Christians.

Immediately thereafter were appointed for him seventeen thousand nine hundred and thirteen cows of the towns of Pautille and Brehemond, to furnish him with milk in ordinary, for it was impossible to find a nurse sufficient for him in all the country, considering the great quantity of milk that was requisite for his nourishment; although there were not wanting some doctors of the opinion of Scotus, who affirmed that his own mother gave him suck, and that she could draw out of her breasts one thousand four hundred two pipes, and nine pails of milk at every time.

Which indeed is not probable, and this point hath been found duggishly scandalous and offensive to tender ears, for that it savoured a little of heresy. Thus was he handled for one year and ten months; after which time, by the advice of physicians, they began to carry him, and then was made for him a fine little cart drawn with oxen, of the invention of Jan Denio, wherein they led him hither and thither with great joy; and he was worth the seeing, for he was a fine boy, had a burly physiognomy, and almost ten chins. He cried very little, but beshit himself every hour; for, to speak truly of him, he was wonderly phlegmatic in his posteriors, both by reason of his natural complexion, and the accidental disposition which had befallen him by his too much quaffing of the Septembral juice. Yet without a cause did not he sup one drop; for if he happened to be vexed, angry, displeased, or sorry, if he did fret, if he did weep, if he did cry, and what grievous quarter soever he kept, in bringing him some drink, he would be instantly pacified, reseated in his own temper, in a good humour again, and as still and quiet as ever. One of his governesses told me (swearing by her fig), how he was so accustomed to this kind of way, that, at the sound of pints and flagons, he would on a sudden fall into an ecstasy, as if he had then tasted of the joys of paradise; so that they, upon consideration of this, his divine complexion, would every morning, to cheer him up, play with a knife upon the glasses, on the bottles with their stopples, and on the pottle-pots with their lids and covers, at the sound whereof he became gay, did leap for joy, would loll and rock himself in the cradle, then nod with his head, monocordising with his fingers, and barytonising with his tail.

CHAPTER 8

How they apparelled Gargantua

BEING of this age, his father ordained to have clothes made to him in his own livery, which was white and blue. To work then went the tailors, and with great expedition were clothes made, cut, and sewed, according to the fashion that was then in request. I find by the ancient records or pancarts, to be seen in the chamber of accounts, or Court of the Exchequer at Montsoreau, that he was accoutred in manner as followeth. To make him every shirt of his were taken up nine hundred ells of Chatelerauld linen, and two hundred for the gussets, in manner of cushions, which they put under his arm-pits. His shirt was not gathered nor plaited, for the plaiting of shirts was not found out, till the seamstresses (when the point of their needles was broken) began to work and occupy with the tail. There were taken up for his doublet, eight hundred and thirteen ells of white satin, and for his points fifteen hundred and nine dogs' skins and a half. Then was it that men began to tie their breeches to their doublets, and not their doublets to their breeches: for it is against nature, as hath most amply been showed by Ockam upon the exponibles of Master Hautechaussade.

For his breeches were taken up eleven hundred and five ells and a third of white broad cloth. They were cut in the form of pillars, chamfered, channelled, and pinked behind, that they might not overheat his reins: and were, within the panes, puffed out with the lining of as much blue damask as was needful; and remark, that he had very good leg-harness, proportionable to the rest of his stature.

For his codpiece were used sixteen ells and a quarter of the same cloth, and it was fashioned on the top like unto a triumphant arch most gallantly fastened with two enamelled clasps, in each of which was set a great emerald, as big as an orange; for, as says Orpheus, *lib. De Lapidibus*, and Plinius, *libro ultimo*, it hath an erective virtue and comfort and comfortative of the natural member. The exiture, out-jecting or out-standing of his codpiece, was of the length of a yard, jagged and pinked, and withal bagging, and strutting out with the blue damask lining, after the manner of his breeches. But had you seen the fair embroidery of the small needle-work pearl, and the curiously interlaced knots, by the goldsmith's art set out and trimmed with rich diamonds, precious rubies, fine torquoises, costly emeralds, and Persian pearls, you would have compared it to a fair Cornucopia, or horn of abundance, such as you see in antiques, or as Rhea gave to the two nymphs, Amalthea and Ida, the nurses of Jupiter.

And, like to that horn of abundance, it was still gallant, succulent, droppy, sappy, pithy, lively, always flourishing, always fructifying, full of juice, full of flower, full of fruit, and all manner of delight. I avow God, it would have done one good to have seen him, but I will tell you more of him in the book which I have made, Of the Dignity of Codpieces. One thing I will tell you, that, as it was both long and large, so was it well furnished and victualled within, nothing like unto the hypocritical codpieces of some fond wooers, and wench-courters, which are stuffed only with wind, to the great prejudice of the female sex.

For his shoes were taken up four hundred and six ells of blue crimson velvet, and were very neatly cut by parallel lines, joined in uniform cylinders. For the soling of them were made use of eleven hundred hides of brown cows, shapen like the tail of a keeling.

For his coat were taken up eighteen hundred ells of blue velvet, dyed in grain, embroidered in its borders with fair gilliflowers, in the middle decked with silver pearl intermixed, with plates of gold, and stores of pearls, hereby showing, that in his time he would prove an especial good fellow, and singular whip-can.

His girdle was made of three hundred ells and a half of silken serge, half white and half blue, if I mistake it not. His sword was not of Valentia, nor his dagger of Saragossa, for his father could not endure these *hidalgos borrachos maranisados como diablos:* but he had a fair sword made of wood, and the dagger of boiled leather, as well painted and gilded as any man could wish.

His purse was made of the cod of an elephant, which was given him by Her Pracontal, proconsul of Lybia.

For his gown were employed nine thousand six hundred ells, wanting two thirds, of blue velvet as before, all so diagonally pearled, that by true perspective issued thence an unnamed colour, like that you see in the necks of turtle-doves or turkey-cocks, which wonderfully rejoiced the eyes of the beholders. For his bonnet or cap were taken up three hundred two ells and a quarter of white velvet, and the form thereof was wide and round, of the bigness of his head; for his father said, that the caps of the Marrabaise fashion, made like the cover of a pasty, would one time or other bring a mischief on those that wore them. For his plume, he wore a fair great blue feather, plucked from an Onocrontal of the country of Hircania the wild, very prettily hanging down over his right ear. For the jewel or broach which in his cap he carried, he had in a cake of gold, weighing three score and eight marks, a fair piece enamelled, wherein was pourtrayed a man's body with two heads, looking towards one another, four arms, four feet, two arses,

such as Plato, *in Symposio,* says was the mystical beginning of man's nature; and about it was written in Ionic letters, Ἀγαπη οὐ ζητει τα ἑαυτης, or rather Ἀνὴρ καὶ γυνὴ ζυγᾶδα ἄνθρωπος ἰδιαίτατα that is *Vie et Mulier junction propiisime homo.*[14]

To wear about his neck, he had a golden chain, weighing twenty-five thousand and sixty-three marks of gold, the links thereof being made after the manner of great berries, amongst which were set in work green jaspers, engraven, and cut dragon-like, all environed with beams and sparks, as King Nicepsos of old was wont to wear them: and it reached down to the very bust of the rising of his belly, whereby he reaped great benefit all his life-long, as the Greek physicians know well enough. For his gloves were put in work sixteen otters' skins, and three of the loupgarous or men-eating wolves, for the bordering of them: and of this stuff were they made, by the appointment of the Cabalists of Sanlouand. As for the rings which his father would have him to wear, to renew the ancient mark of nobility, he had on the forefinger of his left hand a carbuncle as big as an ostrich's egg, enchased very daintily in gold of the fineness of a Turkey seraph. Upon the middle finger of the same hand, he had a ring made of four metals together, of the strangest fashion that ever was seen; so that the steel did not crash against the gold, nor the silver crush the copper. All this was made by Captain Chappuys, and Alcofribas his good agent. On the medical finger of his right hand, he had a ring made spireways, wherein was set a perfect baleu ruby, a pointed diamond, and a Physon emerald, of an inestimable value. For Hans Carvel, the King of Melinda's jeweller, esteemed them at the rate of three score nine millions eight hundred ninety-four thousand and eighteen French crowns of Berry, and at so much did the Foucres of Augsburg prize them.

CHAPTER 9

The Colours and Liveries of Gargantua

GARGANTUA's colours were white and blue, as I have showed you before, by which his father would give us to understand, that his son to him was a heavenly joy; for the white did signify gladness, pleasure, delight, and rejoicing, and the blue, celestial things. I know well enough, that, in reading this, you laugh at the old drinker, and hold this exposition of colours to be very extravagant, and utterly disagreeable to reason, because white is said to signify faith, and blue, constancy. But without moving, vexing, heating or putting you in a chafe (for the weather is dangerous,), answer me, if it please you; for no other compulsory way of arguing will I use towards you, or any else; only now and then I will mention a word or two of my bottle. What is it that induceth you; what stirs you up to believe, or who told you, that white signifieth faith, and blue constancy? An old paltry book, say you, sold by the hawking pedlars and ballad-mongers, entitled *The Blazon of Colours*. Who made it? Whoever it was, he was wise in that he did not set his name to it. But, besides, I know not what I should rather admire in him, his presumption or his sottishness. His presumption and overweening, for that he should without reason, without cause, or without any appearance of truth, have dared to prescribe, by his private authority, what things should be denotated and signified by the colour: which is the custom of tyrants, who will have their will to bear sway instead of equity, and not of the wise and learned, who, with the evidence of reason, satisfy their readers. His sottishness and want of spirit, in that he thought, that without any other demonstration or sufficient argument, the world would be pleased to make his blockish and ridiculous impositions the rule of their devices. In effect, according to the proverb, "To a shitten tail fails never ordure," he hath found, it seems, some simple ninny in those rude times of old, when the wearing of high round bonnets was in fashion, who gave some trust to his writings, according to which they carved and engraved their apophthegms and mottos, trapped and caparisoned their mules and sumpter-horses, apparelled their pages, quartered their breeches, bordered their gloves, fringed the curtains and valances of their beds, painted their ensigns, composed songs, and, which is worse, played many deceitful jugglings, and unworthy base tricks undiscoveredly, amongst the very chastest matrons. In the like darkness and mist of ignorance are wrapped up these vain-glorious courtiers, and name-transposers, who, going about in their impresas to signify *esperance* [*espoir,*] (that is, hope) have pourtrayed a sphere; and bird's pennes for pains; l'Ancholie (which is the flower colombine) for melancholy; a horned moon or crescent, to show the increasing or rising of one's fortune; a

bench rotten and broken, to signify bankrupt; *non* and a corslet for *non dur habit* (otherwise *non durabit,* it shall not last); *un lit sans ciel,* that is, a bed without a tester, for *un licentié,* a graduated person, as, bachelor in divinity, or utter barrister-at-law; which are equivocals so absurd and witless, so barbarous and clownish, that a fox's tail should be fashioned to the neck-piece of, and a vizard made of a cow's-turd given to, every one that henceforth should offer, after the restitution of learning, to make use of any such fopperies in France.

By the same reasons (if reasons I should call them, and not ravings rather, and idle triflings about words) might I cause paint a pannier, to signify that I am in pain—a mustard-pot, that my heart tarries much for it—one pissing upwards for a bishop—the bottom of a pair of breeches for a vessel full of farthings—a codpiece for the office of the clerks of the sentences, decrees or judgments, or rather, (as the English bears it,) for the tail of a cod-fish—and a dog's turd, for the dainty turret, wherein lies the heart of my sweetheart.

Far otherwise did heretofore the sages of Egypt, when they wrote by letters, which they called Hieroglyphics, which none understood who were not skilled in the virtue, property and nature of the things represented by them. Of which Orus Apollo hath in Greek composed two books, and Polyphilus, in his *Dream of Love,* set down more. In France you have a taste of them in the device or impresa of my Lord Admiral which was carried before that time by Octavian Augustus. But my little skiff along these unpleasant gulfs and shoals will sail no further, therefore must I return to the port from whence I came. Yet do I hope one day to write more at large of these things, and to show both by philosophical arguments and authorities, received and approved of, by and from all antiquity, what, and how many colours there are in nature, and what may be signified by every one of them, if God save the mould of my cap, which is my best wine-pot, as my grandam said.

CHAPTER 10

Of that which is signified by the colours white and blue

THE white therefore signifieth joy, solace, and gladness, and that not at random, but upon just and very good grounds: which you may perceive to be true, if, laying aside all prejudicate affections, you will but give ear to what presently I shall expound unto you.

Aristotle saith, that, supposing two things contrary in their kind, as good and evil, virtue and vice, heat and cold, white and black, pleasure and pain, joy and grief,—and so of others,—if you couple them in such manner, that the contrary of one kind may agree in reason with the contrary of the other, it must follow by consequence, that the other contrary must answer to the remnant opposite to that wherewith it is conferred. As for example, virtue and vice are contrary in one kind, so are good and evil. If one of the contraries of the first kind be consonant to one of those of the second, as virtue and goodness, for it is clear that virtue is good, so shall the other two contraries, which are evil and vice, have the same connexion, for vice is evil.

This logical rule being understood, take these two contraries, joy and sadness, then these other two, white and black, for they are physically contrary. If so be, then, that black do signify grief, by good reason then should white import joy. Nor is this signification instituted by human imposition, but by the universal consent of the world received, which philosophers call *Jus Gentium*, the Law of Nations, or an uncontrollable right of force in all countries whatsoever. For you know well enough, that all people, and all languages and nations, except the ancient Syracusans, and certain Argives, who had cross and thwarting souls, when they mean outwardly to give evidence of their sorrow, go in black; and all mourning is done with black. Which general consent is not without some argument, and reason in nature, the which every man may by himself very suddenly comprehend, without the instruction of any; and this we call the law of nature. By virtue of the same natural instinct, we know that by white all the world hath understood joy, gladness, mirth, pleasure, and delight. In former times, the Thracians and Grecians did mark their good, propitious, and fortunate days with white stones, and their sad, dismal, and unfortunate ones with black. Is not the night mournful, sad, and melancholy? It is black and dark by the privation of light. Doth not the light comfort all the world? And it is more white than anything else. Which to prove, I could direct you to the book of Laurentius Valla against Bartolus; but an Evangelical testimony I hope will content you. In *Matth.* 17, it is said, that at the transfiguration of our Lord, *Vestimenta ejus facta sunt alba sicut lux,* his apparel was made white like the light. By which lightsome whiteness he gave his three apostles to understand the Idea and Figure of the eternal joys; for by the light are all men comforted, according to the word of the old woman, who, although she had never a tooth in her head, was wont to say, *Bona lux.*[15] And *Tobit, chap.* 5, after he had lost his sight, when Raphael saluted him, answered, what joy can I have, that do not see the light of heaven? In that colour did the angels testify the joy of the whole world, at the resurrection of our Saviour, *John* 20, and at his Ascension, *Acts* 1. With the like colour of vesture did St. John the Evangelist, *Apoc.* 4. 7, see the faithful clothed in the heavenly and blessed Jerusalem.

Read the ancient, both Greek and Latin, histories, and you shall find, that the town of Alba, (the first pattern of Rome,) was founded, and so named by reason of a white sow that was seen there. You shall likewise find in those stories, that when any man, after he had vanquished his enemies, was, by a decree of the senate, to enter into Rome triumphantly, he usually rode in a chariot drawn by white horses: which, in the Ovatian Triumph, was also the custom; for by no sign or colour would they so significantly express the joy of their coming, as by the white. You shall there also find, how Pericles, the general of the Athenians, would needs have that part of his army, unto whose lot befel the white beans, to spend the whole day in mirth, pleasure, and ease, whilst the rest were a-fighting. A thousand other examples and places could I allege to this purpose, but that it is not here where I should do it.

By understanding hereof, you may resolve one problem, which Alexander Aphrodiseus hath accounted unanswerable, why the lion who, with his only cry and roaring, affrights all beasts, dreads and feareth only a white cock? For, as Proclus saith, *libro De Sacrificio et Magia,* it is because the presence, or the virtue of the sun, which is the organ and promptuary of all terrestrial and siderial light, doth more symbolise and agree with a white cock, as well in regard of that colour, as of his property and specifical quality, than with a lion. He saith furthermore, that devils have been often seen in the shape of lions, which, at the sight of a white cock, have pres-

ently vanished. This is the cause why *Galli*
(so are the Frenchmen called, because they
are naturally as white as milk, which the
Greeks call *Gala*) do willingly wear in their
caps white feathers, for by nature they are of
a candid disposition, merry, kind, gracious,
and well-beloved, and for their cognizance
and arms have the whitest flower of any, the
Flower de luce, or Lily.

If you demand, how, by white, nature
would have us understand joy and gladness?
I answer, that the analogy and uniformity is
thus. For, as the white doth outwardly disperse and scatter the rays of the sight, whereby the optic spirits are manifestly dissolved,
according to the opinion of Aristotle in his
problems and perspective treatises; as you
may likewise perceive by experience when
you pass over mountains covered with snow,
how you will complain that you cannot see
well; as Xenophon writes to have happened
to his men, and as Galen very largely declareth, *lib.* 10. *De Usu Partium:* just so the heart
with excessive joy is inwardly dilated, and
suffereth a manifest resolution of the vital
spirits, which may go so far on, that it may
thereby be deprived of its nourishment, and
by consequence of life itself, by this peri-
charie or extremity of gladness, as Galen
saith, *lib.* 12, *Method. lib.* 5, *de Locis Affec-
tis,* and *lib.* 2, *De Symptomatum Causis.* And
as it hath come to pass in former times, witness Marcus Tullius, *lib.* 1. *Quæst Tuscul.*
Verrius, Aristotle, Titus Livius, in his relation
of the battle of Cannæ, Plinius, *lib.* 7. *cap.* 32
and 34, A. Gellius, *lib.* 3. *c.* 15, and many other writers,—to Diagoras the Rhodian, Chilon,
Sophocles, Dionysius the tyrant of Sicily, Phi-
lippides, Philemon, Polycrates, Philistion, M.
Juventi, and others who died with joy. And
as Avicen speaketh, in 2 *canon et lib. De Vi-
rib. Cordis,* of the saffron, that it doth so rejoice the heart, that, if you take of it excessively, it will by a superfluous resolution and di-
lation deprive it altogether of life. Here peruse Alex. Aphrodiseus, *lib.* 1. *Probl. cap.* 19,
and that for a cause. But what? It seems I
am entered further into this point than I intended at the first. Here, therefore, will
I strike sail, referring the rest to that book
of mine, which handleth this matter to the
full. Meanwhile, in a word I will tell you,
that blue doth certainly signify heaven and
heavenly things, by the very same tokens
and symbols, that white signifieth joy and
pleasure.

CHAPTER 11
Of the youthful age of Gargantua

GARGANTUA, from three years upwards unto
five, was brought up and instructed in all convenient discipline, by the commandment of
his father; and spent that time like the other
little children of the country, that is, in drinking, eating, and sleeping: in eating, sleeping,
and drinking: and in sleeping, drinking, and
eating. Still he wallowed and rolled himself
up and down in the mire and dirt: he blurred
and sullied his nose with filth; he blotted and
smutched his face with any kind of scurvy
stuff; he trod down his shoes in the heel; at
the flies he did often times yawn, and ran very
heartily after the butterflies, the empire
whereof belonged to his father. He pissed in
his shoes, shit in his shirt, and wiped his nose
on his sleeve; he did let his snot and snivel fall
in his pottage, and dabbled, paddled and
slobbered every where; he would drink in his
slipper, and ordinarily rub his belly against a
pannier. He sharpened his teeth with a top,
washed his hands with his broth, and combed
his head with a bowl. He would sit down betwixt two stools, and his arse to the ground;
would cover himself with a wet sack, and
drink in eating of his soup. He did eat his
cake sometimes without bread, would bite in
laughing, and laugh in biting. Oftentimes did
he spit in the basin, and fart for fatness, piss
against the sun, and hide himself in the water
for fear of rain. He would strike out of the
cold iron, be often in the dumps, and frig and
wriggle it. He would flay the fox, say the
ape's pater-noster, return to his sheep, and
turn the hogs to the hay. He would beat the
dogs before the lion, put the plough before
the oxen, and claw where it did not itch. He
would pump one to draw somewhat out of
him, by griping all would hold fast nothing,
and always eat his white bread first. He shoed
the geese, tickled himself to make himself
laugh, and was cook-ruffin in the kitchen:
made a mock at the gods, would cause sing
Magnificat[16] at Matins, and found it very convenient so to do. He would eat cabbage, and
shite beets; knew flies in a dish of milk, and
would make them lose their feet. He would
scrape paper, blur parchment, then run away
as hard as he could. He would pull at the
kid's leather, or vomit up his dinner, then
reckon without his host. He would beat the
bushes without catching the birds, thought
the moon was made of green cheese, and that

bladders are lanterns. Out of one sack he would take two moultures or fees for grinding; would act the ass's part to get some bran, and of his fist would make a mallet. He took the cranes at the first leap, and would have the mail-coats to be made link after link. He always looked a gift horse in the mouth, leaped from the cock to the ass, and put one ripe between two green. By robbing Peter he paid Paul, he kept the moon from the wolves, and hoped to catch larks if ever the heavens should fall. He did make of necessity virtue, of such bread such pottage, and cared as little for the peeled as for the shaven. Every morning he did cast up his gorge, and his father's little dogs eat out of the dish with him, and he with them. He would bite their ears, and they would scratch his nose; he would blow in their arses, and they would lick his chaps.

But hearken, good fellows, the spigot ill betake you, and whirl round your brains, if you do not give ear! this little lecher was always groping his nurses and governesses, upside down, arsiversy, topsiturvy, harri bourriquet, with a Yacco haick, hyck gio! handling them very rudely in jumbling and tumbling them to keep them going; for he had already begun to exercise the tools, and put his codpiece in practice. Which codpiece, or braguette, his governesses did every day deck up and adorn with fair nosegays, curious rubies, sweet flowers, and fine silken tufts, and very pleasantly would pass their time in taking you know what between their fingers, and dandling it, till it did revive and creep up to the bulk and stiffness of a suppository, or street magdaleon, which is a hard rolled up salve spread upon leather. Then did they burst out in laughing, when they saw it lift up its ears, as if the sport had liked them. One of them would call it her pillicock, her fiddle-diddle, her staff of love, her tickle-gizzard, her gentle-titler. Another, her sugar-plum, her kingo, her old rowley, her touch-trap, her flap dowdle. Another again, her branch of coral, her placket-racket, her Cyprian sceptre, her titbit, her bob-lady. And some of the other women would give these names, my Roger, my cockatoo, my nimble-wimble, bush-beater, claw-buttock, eves-dropper, pick-lock, pioneer, bully-ruffin, smell-smock, trouble-gusset, my lusty live sausage, my crimson chitterlin, rump-splitter, shove-devil, down right to it, stiff and stout, in and to, at her again, my coney-borrow-ferret, wily-beguiley, my pretty rogue. It belongs to me, said one. It is mine, said the other. What, quoth a third, shall I have no share in it? By my faith, I will cut it then. Ha, to cut it, said the other, would hurt him. Madam, do you cut little children's things? Were his cut off, he would be then *Monsieur sans queue*, the curtailed master. And that he might play and sport himself after the manner of the other little children of the country, they made him a fair weather whirl jack, of the wings of the windmill of Myrebalais.

CHAPTER 12

Of Gargantua's Wooden Horses

AFTERWARDS, that he might be all his lifetime a good rider, they made to him a fair great horse of wood, which he did make leap, curvet, yerk out behind, and skip forward, all at a time: to pace, trot, rack, gallop, amble, to play the hobby, the hackney gelding: go the gate of the camel, and of the wild ass. He made him also change his colour of hair, as the Monks of Coultibo (according to the variety of their holidays) use to do their clothes, from bay brown, to sorrel, daple-grey, mouse-dun, deer-colour, roan, cow-colour, gin-gioline, skued colour, piebald, and the colour of the savage elk.

Himself of a huge big post made a hunting nag, and another for daily service of the beam of a wine-press: and of a great oak made up a mule, with a foot-cloth, for his chamber. Besides this, he had ten or twelve spare horses, and seven horses for post; and all these were lodged in his own chamber, close by his bed-side. One day the Lord of Breadinbag came to visit his father in great bravery, and with a gallant train: and at the same time, to see him, came likewise the Duke of Freemeale, and the Earl of Wetgullet. The house truly for so many guests at once was somewhat narrow, but especially the stables; whereupon the steward and harbinger of the said Lord Breadinbag, to know if there were any other empty stable in the house, came to Gargantua, a little young lad, and secretly asked him where the stables of the great horses were, thinking that children would be ready to tell all. Then he led them up along the stairs of the castle, passing by the second hall unto a broad great gallery, by which they entered into a large tower, and as they were going up at another pair of stairs, said the harbinger to the steward,— This child deceives us, for the stables are never on the top of the house. You may be mistaken, said the steward, for I know some places at Lyons, at the Basmette, at Chaisnon, and elsewhere, which have their stables at the very tops of the houses; so it may be, that behind the house there is a way to come to this ascent. But I will question with him further. Then said he to Gargantua, my pretty little boy, whither do you lead us? To the stable, said he, of my great horses. We are almost come to it, we have but three stairs to go up at. Then leading them along another great hall, he brought them into his chamber, and, closing the door, said unto them, this is the stable you ask for, this is my gennet, this is my gelding, this is my courser, and this is my hackney, and laid on them with a great lever. I will bestow upon you, said he, this Frizeland horse, I had him from Francfort, yet will I give him you; for he is a pretty little nag, and will go very well, with a tessel of goshawks, half a dozen of spaniels, and a brace of grey-hounds: thus are you king of the hares and partridges for all this winter. By St. John, said they, now we are paid, he hath gleeked us to some purpose, bobbed we are now for ever. I deny it, said he, he was not here above three days. Judge you now, whether they had most cause, either to hide their heads for shame, or to laugh at the jest. As they were going down again thus amazed, he asked them, will you have a whimwham? What is that, said they? It is, said he, five turds to make you a muzzle. To-day, said the steward, though we happen to be roasted, we shall not be burnt, for we are pretty well quipped and larded in my opinion. O my jolly dapper boy, thou has given us a gudgeon, I hope to see thee pope before I die. I think so, said he, myself; and then shall you be a puppy, and this gentle popinjay a perfect papelard, that is, dissembler. Well, well, said the harbinger. But, said Gargantua, guess how many stitches there are in my mother's smock. Sixteen, quoth the harbinger. You do not speak Gospel, said Gargantua, for there is sent before, and sent behind, and you did reckon them ill, considering the two under holes. When, said the harbinger? Even then, said Gargantua, when they made a shovel of your nose to take up a quarter of dirt, and of your throat a funnel, wherewith to put it into another vessel, because the bottom of the old one was out. Cocksbod, said the steward, we have met with a prater. Farewell, master tatler, God keep you, so goodly are the words

which you come out with, and so fresh in your mouth, that it had need to be salted.

Thus going down in great haste, under the arch of the stairs they let fall the great lever, which he had put upon their backs; whereupon Gargantua said, what a devil! you are, it seems, but bad horsemen, that suffer your bilder to fail you, when you need him most. If you were to go from hence to Cahusac, whether had you rather ride on a gosling, or lead a sow in a leash? I had rather drink, said the harbinger. With this they entered into the lower hall, where the company was, and relating to them this new story, they made them laugh like a swarm of flies.

CHAPTER 13

How Gargantua's wonderful understanding became known to his Father Grangousier, by the invention of a torchecul or wipe-breech

ABOUT the end of the fifth year, Grangousier, returning from the conquest of the Canarians, went by the way to see his son Gargantua. There was he filled with joy, as such a father might be at the sight of such a child of his: and whilst he kissed and embraced him, he asked many childish questions of him about divers matters, and drank very freely with him and with his governesses, of whom in great earnest he asked, amongst other things, whether they had been careful to keep him clean and sweet? To this Gargantua answered, that he had taken such a course for that himself, that in all the country there was not to be found a cleanlier boy than he. How is that, said Grangousier? I have, answered Gargantua, by a long and curious experience, found out a means to wipe my bum, the most lordly, the most excellent, and the most convenient that ever was seen. What is that, said Grangousier, how is it? I will tell you by and by, said Gargantua. Once I did wipe me with a gentlewoman's velvet mask, and found it to be good; for the softness of the silk was very voluptuous and pleasant to my fundament. Another time with one of their hoods, and in like manner that was comfortable. At another time with a lady's neckerchief, and after that I wiped me with some earpieces of hers made of crimson satin, but there was such a number of golden spangles in them (turdy round things, a pox take them) that they fetched away all the skin off my tail with a vengeance. Now I wish St. Anthony's fire burn the bum-gut of the goldsmith that made them, and of her that wore them! This hurt I cured by wiping myself with a page's cap, garnished with a feather after the Switzers' fashion.

Afterwards, in dunging behind a bush, I found a March-cat, and with it I wiped my breech, but her claws where so sharp that they scratched and exulcerated all my perinee. Of this I recovered the next morning thereafter, by wiping myself with my mother's gloves, of a most excellent perfume and scent of the Arabian Benin. After that I wiped me with sage, with fennel, with anet, with marjorum, with roses, with gourd-leaves, with beets, with colewort, with leaves of the vine-tree, with mallows, wool-blade, which is a tail-scarlet, with lettuce and with spinage leaves. All this did very great good to my leg. Then with mercury, with pursly, with nettles, with comfrey, but that gave me the bloody flux of Lombardy, which I healed by wiping me with my braguette. Then I wiped my tail in the sheets, in the coverlet, in the curtains, with a cushion, with arras hangings, with a green carpet, with a table cloth, with a napkin, with a handkerchief, with a combing cloth; in all which I found more pleasure than do the mangy dogs when you rub them. Yea, but, said Grangousier, which torchecul did you find to be the best? I was coming to it, said Gargantua, and by and by shall you hear the *tu autem*,[17] and know the whole mystery and knot of the matter. I wiped myself with hay, with straw, with thatch-rushes, with flax, with wool, with paper, but,

Who his foul tail with paper wipes,
Shall at his ballocks leave some chips.

What, said Grangousier, my little rogue, hast thou been at the pot, that thou dost rhyme already? Yes, yes, my lord the king, answered Gargantua, I can rhyme gallantly, and rhyme till I become hoarse with rheum. Hark, what the privy says to the skiters:

Shittard
Squittard
Crakard
Turdous,
Thy bung
Hath flung
Some dung
On us:
Filthard
Cackard
Stinkard,
St. Anthony's fire seize on thy toane,
If thy
Dirty
Dounby
Thou do not wipe, ere
thou be gone.

Will you have any more of it? Yes, yes, answered Grangousier. Then said Gargantua,

A ROUNDELAY

In shitting yesterday I did know
The sess I to my arse did owe:
The smell was such came from that slunk,
That I was with it all bestunk:
O had but then some brave Signor
Brought her to me I waited for,
In shitting!
I would have cleft her water-gap,
And join'd it close to my flip-flap,
Whilst she had with her fingers guarded
My foul nockandrow, all bemerded
In shitting.

Now say that I can do nothing! By the Merdi, they are not of my making, but I heard them of this good old grandam, that you see here, and ever since have retained them in the budget of my memory.

Let us return to our purpose, said Grangousier. What, said Gargantua, to skite? No, said Grangousier, but to wipe our tails. But, said Gargantua, will not you be content to pay a puncheon of Breton wine, if I do not blank and gravel you in this matter, and put you to a non-plus? Yes truly, said Grangousier.

There is no need of wiping one's tail, said Gargantua, but when it is foul; foul it cannot be, unless one have been a skiting; skite then we must, before we wipe our tails. O my pretty little waggish boy, said Grangousier, what an excellent wit thou hast? I will make thee very shortly proceed doctor in the jovial quirks of gay learning and that, by G—, for thou hast more wit than age. Now, I prythee, go on in this torcheculatife, or wipe-bummatory discourse, and by my beard, I swear, for one puncheon, thou shalt have threescore pipes, I mean of the good Breton wine, not that which grows in Britain, but in the good country of Verron. Afterwards I wiped my bum, said Gargantua, with a kerchief, with a pillow, with a pantoufle, with a pouch, with a pannier, but that was a wicked and unpleasant torchecul; then with a hat. Of hats, note, that some are shorn, and others shaggy, some velveted, others covered with taffities, and others with satin. The best of all these is the shaggy hat, for it makes a very neat abstersion of the fecal matter.

Afterwards I wiped my tail with a hen, with a cock, with a pullet, with a calf's skin, with a hare, with a pigeon, with a cormorant, with an attorney's bag, with a montero, with a coif, with a falconer's lure. But, to conclude, I say and maintain, that of all torcheculs, arsewisps, bumfodders, tail napkins, bung-hole cleansers, and wipe-breeches, there is none in the world comparable to the neck of a goose, that is well downed, if you hold her neck betwixt your legs. And believe me therein upon mine honour, for you will thereby feel in your knuckle a most wonderful pleasure, both in regard of the softness of the said down, and of the temperate heat of the goose, which is easily communicated to the bum-gut, and the rest of the inwards, in so far as to come even to the regions of the heart and brains. And think not, that the felicity of the heroes and demigods in the Elysian fields consisteth either in their Asphodele, Ambrosia, or Nectar, as our old women here used to say; but in this, according to my judgment, that they wipe their tails with the neck of a goose, holding her head betwixt their legs, and such is the opinion of Master John of Scotland, alias Scotus.

CHAPTER 14

How Gargantua was taught Latin by a Sophister

THE good man Grangousier having heard this discourse, was ravished with admiration, considering the high reach, and marvellous understanding of his son Gargantua, and said to his governesses, Philip King of Macedon knew the wit of his son Alexander, by his skilful managing of a horse; for his horse Bucephalus was so fierce and unruly, that none durst adventure to ride him, after that he had given to his riders such devilish falls, breaking the neck of this man, the other man's leg, braining one, and putting another out of his jaw-bone. This by Alexander being considered, one day in the hippodrome, (which was a place appointed for the breaking and managing of great horses,) he perceived that the fury of the horse proceeded merely from the fear he had of his own shadow, whereup-

on getting on his back, he run him against the sun, so that the shadow fell behind, and by that means tamed the horse, and brought him to his hand. Whereby his father, knowing the divine judgment that was in him, caused him most carefully to be instructed by Aristotle, who at that time was highly renowned above all the philosophers of Greece. After the same manner I tell you, that by this only discourse, which now I have here had before you with my son Gargantua, I know that his understanding doth participate of some divinity, and that if he be well taught, and have that education which is fitting, he will attain to a supreme degree of wisdom. Therefore will I commit him to some learned man, to have him indoctrinated according to his capacity, and will spare no cost. Presently they appointed him a great sophister-doctor, called Master Tubal Holophernes, who taught him his A. B. C. so well, that he could say it by heart backwards; and about this he was five years and three months. Then read he to him Donat, le Facet, Theodolet, and Alanus *in Parabolis*. About this he was thirteen years, six months, and two weeks. But you must remark, that in the meantime he did learn to write in Gothic characters, and that he wrote all his books,—for the art of printing was not then in use,—and did ordinarily carry a great pen and inkhorn, weighing about seven thousand quintals, (that is seven hundred thousand pounds weight,) the pencase whereof was as big and as long as the great pillar of Enay, and the horn was hanging to it in great iron chains, it being of the wideness of a tun of merchant ware. After that he read unto him the book, *De Modis Significandi,* with the commentaries of Hurtbise, of Fasquin, of Tropdieux, of Gaulhaut, of John Calf, of Bilonio, of Berlinguandus, and a rabble of others; and herein he spent more than eighteen years and eleven months, and was so well versed in it, that, to try masteries in school disputes with his condisciples, he would recite it by heart backwards; and did sometimes prove on his finger ends to his mother, *quod de modis significandi non erat scientia.*[18] Then did he read to him the compost, for knowing the age of the moon, the seasons of the year, and tides of the sea, on which he spent sixteen years and two months, and that justly at the time that his said Preceptor died of the French pox, which was in the year one thousand four hundred and twenty. Afterwards he got an old coughing fellow to teach him, named Master Jobelin Bridé, or muzzled dolt, who read unto him Hugutio, Hebrard's *Grecisme*, the *Doctrinal*, the *Parts*, the *Quid est*, the *Supplementum*, Marmotret, *De Moribus in mensa servandis*; Seneca *De Quatuor Virtutibus Cardinalibus*; Passavantus *cum Commento*, and *Dormi Securè*,[19] for the holidays, and some other of such like meally stuff, by reading whereof he became as wise as any we ever since baked in an oven.

CHAPTER 15

How Gargantua was put under other Schoolmasters

AT the last his father perceived, that indeed he studied hard, and that, although he spent all his time in it, he did nevertheless profit nothing, but which is worse, grew thereby foolish, simple, doted and blockish, whereof making a heavy regret to Don Philip of Marays, Viceroy or depute King of Papeligosse, he found that it were better for him to learn nothing at all, than to be taught such like books, under such schoolmasters; because their knowledge was nothing but brutishness, and their wisdom but blunt foppish toys, serving only to bastardise good and noble spirits, and to corrupt all the flower of youth. That it is so, take, said he, any young boy of this time, who hath only studied two years; if he have not a better judgment, a better discourse, and that expressed in better terms than your son, with a completer carriage and civility to all manner of persons, account me for ever hereafter a very clounch, and bacon slicer of Brene. This pleased Grangousier very well, and he commanded that it should be done. At night at supper, the said Des Marays brought in a young page of his, of Ville-gouges, called Eudemon, so neat, so trim, so handsome in his apparel, so spruce, with his hair in so good order, and so sweet and comely in his behaviour, that he had the resemblance of a little angel more than of a human creature. Then he said to Grangousier, do you see this young boy? He is not as yet full twelve years old. Let us try, if it please you, what difference there is betwixt the knowledge of the doting Mateologians of old time, and the young lads that are now. The trial pleased Grangousier, and he commanded the page to begin. Then Eudemon, asking leave of the Viceroy his master so to do, with his cap in his hand, a clear and open countenance, beautiful and ruddy lips, his eyes steady, and his looks fixed upon Gargantua, with a youthful modesty, standing up straight on his feet, began very gracefully to commend him; first, for his virtue and good manners; secondly, for his knowledge; thirdly, for his nobility; fourthly, for his bodily accomplishments; and, in the fifth place, most sweetly exhorted him to reverence his father with all due observancy, who was so careful to have him well brought up. In the end he prayed him, that he would vouchsafe to admit of him amongst the least of his servants; for other favour at that time desired he none of heaven, but that he might do him some grateful and acceptable service. All this was by him delivered with such proper gestures, such distinct pronunciation, so pleasant a delivery, in such exquisite fine terms, and so good Latin, that he seemed rather a Gracchus, a Cicero, an Æmilius of the time past, than a youth of this age. But all the countenance that Gargantua kept was, that he fell to crying like a cow, and cast down his face, hiding it with his cap, nor could they possibly draw one word from him, no more than a fart from a dead ass. Whereat his father was so grievously vexed that he would have killed Master Jobelin, but the said Des Marays withheld him from it by fair persuasions, so that at length he pacified his wrath. Then Grangousier commanded he should be paid his wages, that they should whittle him up soundly, like a sophister, with good drink, and then give him leave to go to all the devils in hell. At least said he, to-day shall it not cost his host much, if by chance he should die as drunk as an Englishman. Master Jobelin being gone out of the house, Grangousier consulted with the Viceroy what schoolmaster they should choose for him, and it was betwixt them resolved that Ponocrates, the tutor of Eudemon, should have the charge, and that they should go altogether to Paris, to know what was the study of the young men of France at that time.

CHAPTER 16

How Gargantua was sent to Paris, and of the huge Great Mare that he rode on; how she destroyed the Ox-Flies of the Beauce

IN the same season Fayoles, the fourth King of Numidia, sent out of the country of Africa to Grangousier, the most hideous great mare that ever was seen, and of the strangest form, for you know well enough how it is said, that

Africa always is productive of some new thing. She was as big as six elephants, and had her feet cloven into fingers, like Julius Cæsar's horse, with slouch-hanging ears, like the goats in Languedoc, and a little horn on her buttock. She was of a burnt sorel hue, with a little mixture of daple grey spots, but above all she had a horrible tail; for it was little more or less, than every whit as great as the steeple-pillar of St. Mark, besides Langes: and squared as that is, with tuffs, and en-nicroches or hair-plaits wrought within one another, no otherwise than as the beards are upon the ears of corn.

If you wonder at this, wonder rather at the tails of the Scythian rams, which weighed above thirty pounds each, and of the Surian sheep, who need, if Tenaud say true, a little cart at their heels to bear up their tail, it is so long and heavy. You female lechers in the plain countries have no such tails. And she was brought by sea in three carricks and a brigantine into the harbour of Olone in Thalmondois. When Grangousier saw her, "Here is," said he, "what is fit to carry my son to Paris. So now, in the name of God, all will be well. He will in times coming be a great scholar. If it were not, my masters, for the beasts, we should live like clerks. The next morning, after they drunk, you must understand, they took their journey; Gargantua, his pedagogue Ponocrates, and his train, and with them Eudemon the young page. And because the weather was fair and temperate, his father caused to be made for him a pair of dun boots; Babin calls them buskins. Thus did they merrily pass their time in travelling on their high way, always making good cheer, and were very pleasant till they came a little above Orleans, in which place there was a forest of five-and-thirty leagues long, and seventeen in breadth, or thereabouts. This forest was most horribly fertile and copious in dorflies, hornets, and wasps, so that it was a very purgatory for the poor mares, asses, and horses. But Gargantua's mare did avenge herself handsomely of all the outrages therein committed upon beasts of her kind, and that by a trick whereof they had no suspicion. For as soon as ever they were entered into the said forest, and that the wasps had given the assault, she drew out and unsheathed her tail, and therewith skirmishing, did so sweep them, that she overthrew all the wood alongst and athwart, here and there, this way and that way, longwise and sidewise, over and un-

der, and felled every where the wood with as much ease, as the mower doth the grass, in such sort that never since hath there been there, neither wood, nor dorflies: for all the country was thereby reduced to a plain champagne field. Which Gargantua took great pleasure to behold, and said to his company no more but this, "*Je trouve beau ce*," I find this pretty; whereupon that country hath been ever since that time called Beauce. But all the breakfast the mare got that day, was but a little yawning and gaping, in memory whereof the gentlemen of Beauce do as yet to this day break their fast with gaping, which they find to be very good, and do spit the better for it. At last they came to Paris, where Gargantua refreshed himself two or three days, making very merry with his folks, and inquiring what men of learning there were then in the city, and what wine they drank there.

CHAPTER 17

How Gargantua paid his welcome to the Parisians, and how he took away the great Bells of Our Lady's Church

SOME few days after that they had refreshed themselves, he went to see the city, and was beheld of every body there with great admiration; for the people of Paris are so sottish, so badot, so foolish and fond by nature, that a juggler, a carrier of indulgences, a sumpter-horse, or mule with cymbals, or tinkling bells, a blind fiddler in the middle of a cross lane, shall draw a greater confluence of people together, than an Evangelical preacher. And they pressed so hard upon him, that he was constrained to rest himself upon the towers of Our Lady's Church. At which place, seeing so many about him, he said with a loud voice, I believe that these buzzards will have me to pay them here my welcome hither, and my *Proficiat.*[20] It is but good reason. I will now give them their wine, but it shall be only in sport. Then smiling, he untied his fair braguette, and drawing out his mentul into the open air, he so bitterly all-to-be-pissed them, that he drowned two hundred and sixty thousand four hundred and eighteen, besides the women and little children. Some, nevertheless, of the company escaped this piss-flood by mere speed of foot, who, when they were at the higher end of the university, sweating, coughing, spitting, and out of breath, they began to swear and curse, some in good hot earnest, and others in jest. *Carimari, cari-mara: golynoly, golynolo.* By my sweet Sanctesse, we are washed in sport, a sport truly to laugh at;—in French, *Par ris,* for which that city hath been ever since called Paris, whose name formerly was Leucotia, as Strabo testifieth, *lib. quarto,* from the Greek word λευκότης whiteness,—because of the white thighs of the ladies of that place. And forasmuch as, at this imposition of a new name, all the people that were there swore every one by the Sancts of his parish, the Parisians, which are patched up of all nations, and all pieces of countries, are by nature both good jurors, and good jurists, and somewhat overweening; whereupon Joanninus de Barrauco, *libro De Copiositate Reverentiarum,*[21] thinks that they are called Parisians, from the Greek word παρρησία which signifies boldness and liberty of speech.

This done, he considered the great bells, which were in the said towers, and made them sound very harmoniously. Which whilst he was doing, it came into his mind, that they would serve very well for tingling Tantans, and ringing Campanels, to hang about his mare's neck, when she should be sent back to his father, as he intended to do, loaded with Brie cheese, and fresh herring. And indeed he forthwith carried them to his lodging. In the meanwhile there came a master beggar of the friars of St. Anthony, to demand in his canting way the usual benevolence of some hoggish stuff, who, that he might be heard afar off, and to make the bacon he was in quest of shake in the very chimnies, made account to filch them away privily. Nevertheless, he left them behind very honestly, not for that they were too hot, but that they were somewhat too heavy for his carriage. This was not he of Bourg, for he was too good a friend of mine.

All the city was risen up in sedition, they being, as you know, upon any slight occasion, so ready to uproars and insurrections, that foreign nations wonder at the patience of the kings of France who do not by good justice restrain them from such tumultuous courses, seeing the manifold inconveniences which thence arise from day to day. Would to God, I knew the shop wherein are forged these divisions and factious combinations, that I might bring them to light in the confraternities of my parish! Believe for a truth, that the place wherein the people gathered together, were thus sulphured, hopurymated, moiled, and bepissed, was called Nesle, where then

was, but now is no more, the Oracle of Leucetia. There was the case proposed, and the inconvenience showed of the transporting of the bells. After they had well ergoted pro and con, they concluded in Baralipton,[22] that they should send the oldest and most sufficient of the faculty unto Gargantua, to signify unto him the great and horrible prejudice they sustain'd by the want of those bells. And notwithstanding the good reasons given in by some of the university, why this charge was fitter for an orator than a sophister, there was chosen for this purpose our Master Janotus de Bragmardo.

CHAPTER 18

How Janotus de Bragmardo was sent to Gargantua, to recover the Great Bells

MASTER Janotus, with his hair cut round like a dish *à la Cæsarine,* in his most antic accoutrement liripipionated with a graduate's hood, and, having sufficiently antidoted his stomach with oven marmalades, that is, bread and holy water of the cellar, transported himself to the lodging of Gargantua, driving before him three red muzzled beadles, and dragging after him five or six artless masters, all thoroughly bedraggled with the mire of the streets. At their entry Ponocrates met them, who was afraid, seeing them so disguised, and thought they had been some maskers out of their wits, which moved him to inquire of one of the said artless masters of the company, what this mummery meant? It was answered him, that they desired to have their bells restored to them. As soon as Ponocrates heard that, he ran in all haste to carry the news unto Gargantua, that he might be ready to answer them, and speedily resolve what was to be done. Gargantua being advertised hereof, called apart his schoolmaster Ponocrates, Philotimus steward of his house, Gymnastes his esquire, and Eudemon, and very summarily conferred with them, both of what he should do, and what answer he should give. They were all of opinion that they should bring them unto the goblet-office, which is the buttery, and there make them drink like roysters, and line their jackets soundly. And that this cougher might not be puft up with vain glory, by thinking the bells were restored at his request, they sent, whilst he was chopining and plying the pot, for the major of the city, the rector of the faculty, and the vicar of the church, unto whom they resolved to deliver the bells, before the sophister had propounded his commission. After that, in their hearing, he should pronounce his gallant oration, which was done; and they being come, the sophister was brought in full hall, and began as followeth, in coughing.

CHAPTER 19

The Oration of Master Janotus de Bragmardo, for the recovery of the Bells

HEM, hem, gud-day, sirs, gud-day. *Et vobis,* my masters. It were but reason that you should restore to us our bells; for we have great need of them. Hem, hem, aihfuhash. We have often-times heretofore refused good money for them of those of London, in Cahors, yea and those of Bourdeaux in Brie, who would have brought them for the substantific quality of the elementary complexion, which is intronificated in the terrestreity of their quidditative nature, to extraneize the blasting mists, and whirlwinds upon our vines, indeed not ours, but these round about us. For if we lose the piot and liquor of the grape, we lose all, both sense and law. If you restore them unto us at my request, I shall gain it by six baskets full of sausages, and a fine pair of breeches, which will do my legs a great deal of good, or else they will not keep their promise to me. Ho by gob, *Domine,* a pair of breeches is good, *et vir sapiens non abhorrebit eam.*[23] Ha, ha, a pair of breeches is not so easily got; I have experience of it myself. Consider, *Domine,* I have been these eighteen days in matagrabolising this brave speech. *Reddite quæ sunt Cæsaris, Cæsari, et quæ sunt Dei, Deo. Ibi jacet lepus.*[24] By my faith, *Domine,* if you will sup with me in *cameris,* by cox body, *charitatis, nos faciemus bonum cherubin. Ego occidi unum porcum, et ego habet bonum vino.*[25] but of good wine we cannot make bad Latin. Well, *de parte Dei date nobis bellas nostras.*[26] Hold, I give you in the name of the faculty a *Sermones de Utino,* that *utinam*[27] you will give us our bells. *Vultis etiam pardonos? Per diem vos habebitis, et nihil payabitis.*[28]

O Sir, *Domine, bellagivaminor nobis;* verily, *est bonum urbis.*[29] They are useful to everybody. If they fit your mare well, so do they do our faculty; *quæ comparata est jumentis insipientibus, et similis facta est eis, Psalmo nescio quo.*[30] Yet did I quote it in my notebook, *et est unum bonum Achilles,*[31] a good

defending argument. Hem, hem, hem, haikhash! For I prove unto you that you should give me them. *Ego sic argumentor. Omnis bella bellabilis in bellerio bellando, bellans bellativo, bellare facit, bellabiliter bellantes. Parisius habet bellas. Ergo gluc.*[32] Ha, ha, ha. This is spoken to some purpose. It is *in tertio primæ,* in *Darii,*[33] or elsewhere. By my soul, I have seen the time that I could play the devil in arguing, but now I am much failed, and henceforward want nothing but a cup of good wine, a good bed, my back to the fire, my belly to the table, and a good deep dish. *Hei, Domine,* I beseech you, *in nomine Patris, Filii, et Spiritus Sancti,* Amen, to restore unto us our bells: and God keep you from evil, and our Lady from health, *qui vivit et regnat per omnia sæcula sæculorum,* Amen. Hem, hashchehhawksash, qzrchremhemhash.

Verum enim vero, quandoquidem, dubio procul. Edepol, quoniam, ita certe, meus deus fidius,[34] a town without bells is like a blind man without a staff, an ass without a crupper, and a cow without cymbals. Therefore be assured, until you have restored them unto us, we will never leave crying after you, like a blind man that hath lost his staff, braying like an ass without a crupper, and making a noise like a cow without cymbals. A certain Latinisator, dwelling near the hospital, said once, producing the authority of one Taponus,—I lie, it was one Pontanus the secular poet,—who wished those bells had been made of feathers, and the clapper of a foxtail, to the end that they might have begot a chronicle in the bowels of his brain, when he was about the composing of his carminiformal lines. But

or

> *nac petetin petetac,*
> *tic, torche lorgne,*

> *rot kipipur kipipot,*
> *put pantse malf,*

he was declared an heretic. We make them as of wax. And no more saith the deponent. *Valete et plaudite. Calepinus recensui.*[35]

CHAPTER 20

How the Sophister carried away his cloth, and how he had a Suit in Law against the other Masters

THE sophister had no sooner ended, but Ponocrates and Eudemon burst out into a laughing so heartily, that they had almost split with it, and given up the ghost, in rendering their souls to God: even just as Crassus did, seeing a lubberly ass eat thistles; and as Philemon, who, for seeing an ass eat those figs which were provided for his own dinner, died with force of laughing. Together with them Master Janotus fell a laughing too as fast as he could, in which mood of laughing they continued so long, that their eyes did water by the vehement concussion of the substance of the brain, by which these lachrymal humidities, being prest out, glided through the optic nerves, and so to the full represented Democritus Heraclitising, and Heraclitus Democritising.

When they had done laughing, Gargantua consulted with the prime of his retinue, what should be done. There Ponocrates was of opinion, that they should make this fair orator drink again; and seeing he had showed them more pastime, and made them laugh more than a natural fool could have done, that they should give him ten baskets full of sausages, mentioned in his pleasant speech, with a pair of hose, three hundred great billets of logwood, five and twenty hogsheads of wine, a good large down bed, and a deep capacious dish, which he said were necessary for his old age. All this was done as they did appoint: only Gargantua, doubting that they could not quickly find out breeches fit for his wearing, because he knew not what fashion would best become the said orator, whether the martingal fashion of breeches, wherein is a spunghole with a draw-bridge, for the more easy caguing: or the fashion of the mariners, for the greater solace and comfort of his kidneys: or that of the Switzers, which keeps warm the *bedondaine* or belly-tabret: or round breeches with strait cannions, having in the seat a piece like a cod's tail, for fear of over-heating his reins. All which considered, he caused to be given him seven ells of white cloth for the linings. The wood was carried by the porters, the masters of arts carried the sausages and the dishes, and Master Janotus himself would carry the cloth. One of the said Masters, called Jousse Bandouille, showed him that it was not seemly nor decent for one of his condition to do so, and that therefore he should deliver it to one of them. Ha, said Janotus, Baudet, Baudet, or Blockhead, Blockhead, thou dost not conclude *in modo et figura.* For lo, to this end serve the suppositions, and *parva logicalia. Pannus, pro quo supponit? Confusè,* said Bandouille, *et distributivè.* I do not ask thee, said Janotus, blockhead, *quomodo supponit,* but *pro quo?* It is blockhead, *pro tibiis* meis, and therefore I will carry it, *egomet sicut suppositum portat appositum.*[36] So did he carry it away very close and covertly, as Patelin, the buffoon, did his cloth. The best was, that when this cougher, in a full act or assembly held at the Mathurins, had with great confidence required his breeches and sausages, and that they were flatly denied him, because he had them of Gargantua, according to the informations thereupon made, he showed them that this was gratis, and out of his liberality, by which they were not in any sort quit of their promises. Notwithstanding this, it was answered him, that he should be content with reason, without expectation of any other bribe there. Reason, said Janotus? We use none of it here. Unlucky traitors, you are not worth the hanging. The earth beareth not more arrant villains than you are. I know it well enough; halt not before the lame. I have practised wickedness with you. By God's rattle I will inform the king of the enormous abuses that are forged here and carried underhand by you, and let me be a leper, if he do not burn you alive like bougres, traitors, heretics, and seducers, enemies to God and virtue.

Upon these words they framed articles against him: he on the other side warned them to appear. In sum, the process was retained by the Court, and is there as yet. Hereupon the magisters made a vow, never to decrott themselves in rubbing off the dirt of either their shoes or clothes: Master Janotus with his adherents vowed never to blow or snuff their noses, until judgment were given by a definitive sentence.

By these vows do they continue unto this time both dirty and snotty; for the Court hath not garbled, sifted, and fully looked into all the pieces as yet. The judgment or decree shall be given out and pronounced at the next Greek Calends, that is, never. As you know that they do more than nature, and contrary to their own articles. The articles of Paris maintain, that to God alone belongs infinity, and nature produceth nothing that is immortal; for she putteth an end and period to all things by her engendered, according to the saying, *Omnia orta cadunt,*[37] &c. But these thick mist-swallowers make the suits in law depending before them both infinite and immortal. In doing whereof, they have given occasion to, and verified the saying of Chilo the Lacedæmonian, consecrated to the Oracle at Delphos, that misery is the inseparable companion of law-suits; and that suitors are miserable; for sooner shall they attain to the end of their lives, than to the final decision of their pretended rights.

CHAPTER 21

The Study of Gargantua, according to the discipline of his Schoolmasters and Sophisters

THE first day being thus spent, and the bells put up again in their own place, the citizens of Paris, in acknowledgment of this courtesy, offered to maintain and feed his mare as long as he pleased, which Gargantua took in good part, and they sent her to graze in the forest of Biere. I think she is not there now. This done, he with all his heart submitted his study to the discretion of Ponocrates; who for the beginning appointed that he should do as he was accustomed, to the end he might understand by what means, in so long time, his old masters had made him so sottish and ignorant. He disposed therefore of his time in such fashion, that ordinarily he did awake between eight and nine a clock, whether it was day or not, for so had his ancient governors ordained, alleging that which David saith, *Vanum est vobis ante lucem surgere.*[38] Then did he tumble and toss, wag his legs, and wallow in the bed some time, the better to stir up and rouse his vital spirits, and appareled himself according to the season: but willingly he would wear a great long gown of thick frieze, furried with fox skins. Afterwards he combed his head with an Alman comb, which is the four fingers and the thumb. For his preceptor said, that to comb himself other ways, to wash and make himself neat, was to lose time in this world. Then he dunged, pist, spued, belched, cracked, yawned, spitted, coughed, yexed, sneezed, and snotted himself like an arch-deacon, and to suppress the dew and bad air, went to breakfast, having some good fried tripe, fair rashers on the coals, excellent gammons of bacon, store of fine minced meat, and a great deal of sippit brewis, made-up of the fat of the beef-pot, laid upon bread, cheese, and chopped parsley stewed together. Ponocrates showed him, that he ought not eat so soon after rising out of his bed, unless he had performed some exercise beforehand. Gargantua answered, what! have not I sufficiently well exercised myself? I have wallowed and rolled myself six or seven turns in my bed, before I rose. Is not that enough? Pope Alexander did so, by the advice of a Jew his physician, and lived till his dying day in despite of his enemies. My first masters have used me to it, saying that to breakfast made a good memory, and therefore they drank first. I am very well after it, and dine but the better. And Master Tubal, who was the first licenciate at Paris, told me, that it was not enough to run a pace, but to set forth betimes: so doth not the total welfare of our humanity depend upon perpetual drinking in a ribble rabble, like ducks, but on drinking early in the morning; *unde versus,*

To rise betimes is no good hour,
To drink betimes is better sure.

After he had thoroughly broke his fast, he went to church, and they carried him in a great basket, a huge impantoufled or thick covered breviary, weighing, what in grease, clasps, parchment, and cover, little more or less than eleven hundred and six pounds. There he heard six and twenty or thirty masses. This while, to the same place came his orison-mutterer impaletocked, or lapped up about the chin, like a tufted whoop, and his breath antidoted with the store of the vine-tree-sirup. With him he mumbled all his kiriels, and dunsicals breborions, which he so curiously thumbed and fingered, that there fell not so much as one grain to the ground. As he went from the church, they brought him, upon a dray drawn with oxen, a confused heap of *Pater-nosters* and *Aves* of Sanct Claude, every one of them being of the bigness of a hat-block; and thus walking through the cloisters, galleries or garden, he said more in turning them over, than sixteen hermits would have done. Then did he study some paltry half hour with his eyes fixed upon his book; but as the comic saith, his mind was in the kitchen. Pissing then a full urinal, he sat down at table; and because he was naturally phlegmatic, he began his meal with some dozens of gammons, dried neat's tongues, hard rows of mullet, called botargos, andouilles, or sausages, and such other forerunners of wine. In the mean while, four of his folks did cast into his mouth one after another continually mustard by whole shovels full. Immediately after that, he drank a horrible draught of white-wine for the ease of his kidneys. When that was done, he ate according to the season meat agreeable to his appetite, and then left off eating when his belly began to strout, and was like to crack for fulness. As for his drinking, he had neither end nor rule. For he was wont to say that the limits and bounds of drinking were, when the cork of the shoes of him that drinketh swelleth up half a foot high.

CHAPTER 22

The games of Gargantua

THEN blockishly mumbling with a set on countenance a piece of scurvy grace, he washed his hands in fresh wine, picked his teeth with the foot of a hog, and talked jovially with his attendants. Then the carpet being spread, they brought plenty of cards, many dice, with great store and abundance of checkers and chessboards.

There he played

At flusse
At primero
At the beast
At the rifle
At trump
At the prick and spare not
At the hundred
At the peeny
At the unfortunate woman
At the fib
At the pass ten
At one and thirty
At post and pair, or even and sequence
At three hundred
At the unlucky man
At the last couple in hell
At the hock
At the surly
At the lanskenet
At the cuckoo
At puff, or let him speak that hath it
At take nothing and throw out
At the marriage
At the frolic or jackdaw
At the opinion
At who doth the one, and doth the other

At the sequences
At the ivory bundles
At the tarots
At losing load him
At he's gulled and esto
At the torture
At the handruff
At the click
At honours
At love
At the chess
At Reynard the fox
At the squares
At the cowes
At the lottery
At the chance or mumchance
At three dice or maniest bleaks
At the tables
At nivinivinack
At the lurch
At doublets or queen's game
At the failie
At the French trictrac
At the long tables or ferkeering
At feldown
At tods body
At needs must
At the dames or draughts

At bob and mow
At *primus secundus*
At mark-knife
At the keys
At span-counter
At even or odd
At cross or pile
At ball and huckle-bones
At ivory balls
At the billiards
At bob and hit
At the owl
At the charming of the hare
At pull yet a little
At trudgepig
At the magatipes
At the horn
At the flowered or shrovtide ox
At the madge-owlet
At pinch without laughing
At prickle me tickle me
At the unshoing of the ass
At the cocksess
At hari hohi
At I set me down
At earlie beardie
At the old mode
At draw the spit
At put out
At gossip lend me your sack
At the ramcod ball
At thrust out the harolt
At Marseil figs
At nicknamrie
At stick and hole
At boke or him, or flaying the fox
At the branching it
At the cat selling
At trill madam, or grapple my lady
At blow the coal
At the re-wedding
At the quick and dead judge
At unoven the iron
At the false clown

At the flints, or at the nine stones
At to the crutch hulch back
At the sanct is found
At hinch, pinch and laugh not
At the leek
At bumdockdousse
At the loose gig
At the hoop
At the sow
At belly to belly
At the dales or straths
At the twigs
At the quoits
At I'm for that
At tilt at weekie
At nine pins
At the cock quintin
At tip and hurle
At the flat bowles
At the veere and tourn
At rogue and ruffian
At bumbatch touch
At the mysterious trough
At the short bowls
At the dapple-grey
At cock and crank it
At break pot
At my desire
At twirly whirlytril
At the rush bundles
At the short staff
At the whirling gigge
At hide and seek, or are you all hid
At the picket
At the blank
At the pilferers
At the caveson
At prison bars
At have at the nuts
At cherry-pit
At rub and rice
At whip-top
At the casting top
At the hobgoblins
At the O wonderful
At the soilie smutchy
At fast and loose
At scutchbreech
At the broom-besom

At St. Cosme I come to adore thee
At the lusty brown boy
At I take you napping
At fair and softly passeth Lent
At the forked oak
At truss
At the wolf's tail
At bum to buss or nose in breech
At Geordie give me my lance
At swaggy, waggy, or shoggy-shou
At stook and rook, shear and threave
At the birch
At the musse
At the dilly dilly darling
At ox moudy
At purpose in purpose
At nine less
At blind-man-buff
At the fallen bridges
At bridled nick
At the white at buts
At thwack swinge him
At apple, pear, and plum
At mumgi
At the toad
At cricket
At the pounding stick
At jack and the box
At the queens
At the trades
At heads and points
At the vine-tree hug
At black be thy fall
At ho the distaffe

At Joanne Thomson
At the boulting cloth
At the oat's seed
At greedy glutton
At the Moorish dance
At feebie
At the whole frisk and gambole
At battabum, or riding the wild mare
At Hinde the Plowman
At the good mawkin
At the dead beast
At climb the ladder Billy
At the dying hog
At the salt doup
At the pretty pigeon
At barley break
At the bavine
At the bush leap
At crossing
At bo-peep
At the hardit arsepursey
At the harrower's nest
At forward hey
At the fig
At gunshot crack
At mustard peel
At the gome
At the relapse
At jog breech, or prick him forward
At knockpate
At the Cornish chough
At the crane dance
At slash and cut
At bobbing, or flirt on the nose
At the larks
At filipping

After he had thus well played, revelled, past and spent his time, it was thought fit to drink a little, and that was eleven glassfuls the man, and, immediately after making good cheer again, he would stretch himself upon a fair bench, or a good large bed, and there sleep two or three hours together, without thinking or speaking any hurt. After he was awakened he would shake his ears a little. In the meantime they brought him fresh wine. Then he drank better than ever. Ponocrates showed him, that it was an ill diet to drink so after sleeping. It is, answered Gargantua, the very life of the patriarchs and holy fathers; for naturally I sleep salt, and my sleep hath been to me instead of so many gammons of bacon. Then began he to study a little, and out came the *patenotres* or rosary of beads, which the better and more formally to despatch, he got up on an old mule, which had served nine kings, and so mumbling with his mouth, nodding and doddling his head, would go see a coney ferreted or caught in a gin. At his return he went into the kitchen, to know what roast meat was on the spit, and what otherwise was to be drest for supper. And supped very well upon my conscience, and commonly did invite some of his neighbours that were good drinkers, with whom carousing and drinking merrily, they told stories of all sorts from the old to the new. Amongst others, he had for domestics the Lords of Fou, of Gourville, of Griniot, and of Marigny. After supper were brought in upon the place the fair wooden gospels, and the books of the four kings, that is to say, many pairs of tables and cards; or the fair flusse, one, two, three; or all to make short work; or else they went to see the wenches thereabouts, with little small banquets, intermixed with collations and reer-suppers. Then did he sleep without unbridling, until eight o'clock in the next morning.

CHAPTER 23

How Gargantua was instructed by Pono-crates, and in such sort disciplinated, that he lost not one hour of the day

WHEN Ponocrates knew Gargantua's vicious manner of living, he resolved to bring him up in another kind; but for a while he bore with him, considering that nature cannot endure such a change, without great violence. Therefore to begin his work the better, he requested a learned physician of that time, called Master Theodorus, seriously to perpend, if it were possible, how to bring Gargantua unto a better course. The said physician purged him canonically with Anticyrian-hellebore, by which medicine he cleansed all the alteration, and perverse habitude of his brain. By this means also Ponocrates made him forget all that he had learned under his ancient preceptors, as Timotheus did to his disciples, who had been instructed under other musicians. To do this better, they brought him into the company of learned men, which were there, in whose imitation he had a great desire and affection to study otherwise, and to improve his parts. Afterwards he put himself into such a road and way of studying that he lost not any one hour in the day, but employed all his time in learning, and honest knowledge. Gargantua awak'd, then about four o'clock in the morning. Whilst they were in rubbing of him, there was read unto him some chapter of the Holy Scripture aloud and clearly, with a pronunciation fit for the matter, and hereunto was appointed a young page born in Basché, named Anagnostes. According to the purpose and argument of that lesson, he oftentimes gave himself to worship, adore, pray, and send up his supplications to that good God, whose word did show his majesty and marvellous judgment. Then went he into the secret places to make excretion of his natural digestions. There his master repeated what had been read, expounding unto him the most obscure and difficult points. In returning, they considered the face of the sky, if it was such as they had observed it the night before, and into what signs the sun was entering, as also the moon for that day. This done, he was appareled, combed, curled, trimmed and perfumed, during which time they repeated to him the lessons of the day before. He himself said them by heart, and upon them would ground some practical cases concerning the estate of man, which he would prosecute sometimes two or three hours, but ordinarily they ceased as soon as he was fully clothed. Then for three good hours he had a lecture read unto him. This done, they went forth, still conferring of the substance of the lecture, either unto a field near the university called the Brack, or unto the meadows where they played at the ball, the long-tennis, and at the pile trigone, most gallantly exercising their bodies, as formerly they had done their minds. All their play was but in liberty, for they left off when they pleased, and that was commonly when they did sweat over all their body, or were otherwise weary. Then were they very well wiped and rubbed, shifted their shirts, and walking soberly, went to see if dinner was ready. Whilst they stayed for that, they did clearly and eloquently pronounce some sentences that they had retained of the lecture. In the meantime Master Appetite came, and then very orderly sat they down at table. At the beginning of the meal, there was read some pleasant history of the warlike actions of former times, until he had taken a glass of wine. Then, if they thought good, they continued reading, or began to discourse merrily together; speaking first of the virtue, propriety, efficacy and nature of all that was served in at that table; of bread, of wine, of water, of salt, of fleshes, fishes, fruits, herbs, roots, and of their dressing. By means whereof, he learned in a little time all the passages competent for this, that were to be found in Pliny, Athenæus, Dioscorides, Julius Pollux, Galen, Porphyrius, Oppian, Polybius, Heliodorus, Aristotle, Ælian, and others. Whilst they talked of these things, many times, to be the more certain, they caused the very books to be brought to the table, and so well and perfectly did he in his memory retain the things above said, that in that time there was not a physician that knew half so much as he did. Afterwards they conferred of the lessons read in the morning, and, ending their repast with some conserve or marmalade of quinces, he picked his teeth with mastic tooth-pickers, washed his hands and eyes with fair fresh water, and gave thanks unto God in some fine canticks, made in praise of the divine bounty and munificence. This done, they brought in cards, not to play, but to learn a thousand pretty tricks, and new inventions, which were all grounded upon arithmetic. By this means he fell in love with that numerical science, and every day after dinner and supper he passed his time in it as pleasantly, as he was wont to do at cards and dice: so that at last he understood so well both the theory and practical part thereof, that Tunstal the Englishman, who had written very largely of that purpose, confessed that verily in comparison of him he had no skill at all. And not only in that, but in the other mathematical sciences, as geometry, astronomy, music, &c. For in waiting on the concoction, and attending the digestion of his food, they made a thousand pretty instruments and geometrical figures, and did in some measure practice the astronomical canons.

After this they recreated themselves with singing musically, in four or five parts, or upon a set theme or ground at random, as it best pleased them. In matter of musical instruments, he learned to play upon the lute, the virginals, the harp, the Allman flute with nine holes, the violin, and the sackbut. This hour thus spent, and digestion finished, he did purge his body of natural excrements, then betook himself to his principal study for three hours together, or more, as well to repeat his matutinal lectures, as to proceed in the book wherein he was, as also to write handsomely, to draw and form the antique and Roman letters. This being done, they went out of their house, and with them a young gentleman of Touraine, named the Esquire Gymnast, who taught him the art of riding. Changing then his clothes, he rode a Naples courser, Dutch roussin, a Spanish gennet, a barbed or trapped steed, then a light fleet horse, unto whom he gave a hundred carieres, made him go the high saults, bounding in the air, free a ditch with a skip, leap over a stile or pale, turn short in a ring both to the right and left hand. There he broke not his lance; for it is the greatest foolery in the world to say, I have broken ten lances at tilts or in fight. A carpenter can do even as much. But it is a glorious and praiseworthy action, with one lance to break and overthrow ten enemies. Therefore with a sharp, stiff, strong, and well-steeled lance, would he usually force up a door, pierce a harness, beat down a tree, carry away the ring, lift up a cuirassier saddle, with the mail-coat and gauntlet. All this he did in complete arms from head to foot. As for the prancing flourishes, and smacking popisms, for the better cherishing of the horse, commonly used in riding, none did them better than he. The voltiger of Ferrara was but as an ape compared to him. He was singularly skilful in leaping nimbly from one horse to another without putting foot to ground, and these horses were called desultories. He could likewise from either side, with a lance in his hand, leap on horseback without stirrups, and rule the horse at his pleasure without a bridle, for such things are useful in military engagements. Another day he exercised the battle-axe, which he so dexterously wielded, both in the nimble, strong, and smooth management of that weapon, and that in all the feats practiceable by it, that he passed knight of arms in the field, and at all essays.

Then tossed he the pike, played with the two-handed sword, with the back sword, with the Spanish tuck, the dagger, poniard, armed, unarmed, with a buckler, with a cloak, with a target. Then would he hunt the hart, the roebuck, the bear, the fallow deer, the wild boar, the hare, the pheasant, the partridge and the bustard. He played at the balloon, and made it bound in the air, both with fist and foot. He wrestled, ran, jumped, not at three steps and a leap, called the hops, nor at *clochepied,* called the hare's leap, nor yet at the *Almanes;* for, said Gymnast, these jumps are for the wars altogether unprofitable, and of no use: but at one leap he would skip over a ditch, spring over a hedge, mount six paces upon a wall, ramp and grapple after this fashion up against a window, of the full height of a lance. He did swim in deep waters on his belly, on his back, sideways, with all his body, with his feet only, with one hand in the air, wherein he held a book, crossing thus the breadth of the River Seine, without wetting, and dragging along his cloak with his teeth, as did Julius Cæsar; then with the help of one hand he entered forcibly into a boat, from whence he cast himself again headlong into the water, sounded the depths, hollowed the rocks, and plunged into the pits and gulfs. Then turned he the boat about, governed it, led it swiftly or slowly with the stream and against the stream, stopped it in his course, guided it with one hand, and with the other laid hard about him with a huge great oar, hoisted the sail, hied up along the mast by the shrouds, ran upon the edge of the decks, set the compass in order, tackled the bowlines, and steered the helm. Coming out of the water, he ran furiously up against a hill, and with the same alacrity and swiftness ran down again. He climbed up trees like a cat, leaped from the one to the other like a squirrel. He did pull down the great boughs and branches, like another Milo; then with two sharp well-steeled daggers, and two tried bodkins, would be run up by the wall to the very top of a house like a rat; then suddenly come down from the top to the bottom with such an even composition of members, that by the fall he would catch no harm.

He did cast the dart, throw the bar, put the stone, practise the javelin, the boar spear or partisan, and the halbert. He broke the strongest bows in drawing, bended against his breast the greatest cross-bows of steel, took his aim by the eye with the hand-gun, and shot well, traversed and planted the cannon, shot at but-marks, at the papgay from below upwards, or to a height from above downwards; or to a descent; then before him sidewise, and behind him, like the Parthians. They tied a cable-rope to the top of a high tower, by one end whereof hanging near the ground he wrought himself with his hands to the very top; then upon the same tract came down so sturdily and firm that you could not on a plain meadow have run with more assurance. They set up a great pole fixed upon two trees. There would he hang by his hands, and with them alone, his feet touching at nothing, would go back and fore along the aforesaid rope with so great swiftness, that hardly could one overtake him with running; and then, to exercise his breast and lungs, he would shout like all the devils in hell. I heard him once call Eudemon from St. Victor's gate to Montmartre. Stentor never had such a voice at the siege of Troy. Then for the strengthening of his nerves or sinews, they made him two great sows of lead, each of them weighing eight thousand and seven hundred quintals, which they called Alteres. Those he took up from the ground, in each hand one, then lifted them up over his head, and held them so without stirring three quarters of an hour or more, which was an inimitable force. He fought at barriers with the stoutest and most vigorous champions; and when it came to the cope, he stood so sturdily on his feet, that he abandoned himself unto the strongest, in case they could remove him from his place, as Milo was wont to do of old. In whose imitation likewise he held a pomegranate in his hand, to give it unto him that could take it from him. The time being thus bestowed, and himself rubbed, cleansed, wiped, and refreshed with other clothes, he returned fair and softly; and passing through certain meadows, or other grassy places, beheld the trees and plants, comparing them with what is written of them in the books of the ancients, such as Theophrast, Dioscorides, Marinus, Pliny, Nicander, Macer, and Galen, and carried home to the house great handfuls of them, whereof a young page called Rizotomos had charge; together with little mattocks, pickaxes, grubbing hooks, cabbies, pruning knives, and other instruments requisite for herborising. Being come to their lodging, whilst supper was making ready, they repeated certain passages of that which had been read, and then sat down at table. Here remark, that his dinner was sober and thrifty, for he did then eat only to prevent the gnawings of his stomach, but his supper was copious and large; for he took then as much as was fit to maintain and nourish him; which indeed is the true diet prescribed by the art of good and sound physic,

although a rabble of loggerheaded physicians, muzzled in the brabbling shop of sophisters, counsel the contrary. During that repast was continued the lesson read at dinner as long as they thought good: the rest was spent in good discourse, learned and profitable. After that they had given thanks, he set himself to sing vocally, and play upon harmonious instruments, or otherwise passed his time at some pretty sports, made with cards and dice, or in practising the feats of legerdemain with cups and balls. There they staid some nights in frolicking thus, and making themselves merry till it was time to go to bed; and on other nights they would go make visits unto learned men, or to such as had been travellers in strange and remote countries. When it was full night before they retired themselves, they went unto the most open place of the house to see the face of the sky, and there beheld the comets, if any were, as likewise the figures, situations, aspects, oppositions and conjunctions of both the fixed stars and planets.

Then with his master did he briefly recapitulate, after the manner of the Pythagoreans, that which he had read, seen, learned, done and understood in the whole course of that day.

Then prayed they unto God the Creator, in falling down before him, and strengthening their faith towards him, and glorifying him for his boundless bounty; and, giving thanks unto him for the time that was past, they recommended themselves to his divine clemency for the future. Which being done, they went to bed, and betook themselves to their repose and rest.

CHAPTER 24

How Gargantua spent his time in rainy weather

If it happened that the weather were any thing cloudy, foul, and rainy, all the forenoon was employed, as before specified, according to custom, with this difference only, that they had a good clear fire lighted, to correct the distempers of the air. But after dinner, instead of their wonted exercitations, they did abide within, and, by way of Apotherapie, did recreate themselves in bottling up of hay, in cleaving and sawing of wood, and in threshing sheaves of corn at the barn. Then they studied the art of painting or carving; or brought into use the antique play of tables, as

Leonicus hath written of it, and as our good friend Lascaris playeth at it. In playing they examined the passages of ancient authors, wherein the said play is mentioned, or any metaphor drawn from it. They went likewise to see the drawing of metals, or the casting of great ordnance: how the lapidaries did work, as also the goldsmiths and cutters of precious stones. Nor did they omit to visit the alchymists, money-coiners, upholsterers, weavers, velvet-workers, watch-makers, looking-glass-framers, printers, organists, and other such kind of artificers, and, every where giving them somewhat to drink, did learn and consider the industry and invention of the trades. They went also to hear the public lectures, the solemn commencements, the repetitions, the acclamations, the pleadings of the gentle lawyers, and sermons of Evangelical preachers. He went through the halls and places appointed for fencing, and there played against the masters themselves at all weapons, and showed them by experience, that he knew as much in it as, yea more than, they. And, instead of herborising, they visited the shops of druggists, herbalists, and apothecaries, and diligently considered the fruits, roots, leaves, gums, seeds, the grease and ointments of some foreign parts, as also how they did adulterate them. He went to see jugglers, tumblers, mountebanks and quacksalvers, and considered their cunning, their shifts, their summer-saults and smooth tongues especially of those of Chauny in Picardy, who are naturally great praters, and brave givers of fibs, in matter of green apes.

At their return they did eat more soberly at supper than at other times, and meats more dessicative and extenuating; to the end that the intemperate moisture of the air, communicated to the body by a necessary confinity, might by this means be corrected, and that they might not receive any prejudice for want of their ordinary bodily exercise. Thus was Gargantua governed, and kept on in this course of education, from day to day profiting, as you may understand such a young man of his age may, of a pregnant judgment, with good discipline well continued. Which, although at the beginning it seemed difficult, became a little after so sweet, so easy, and so delightful, that it seemed rather the recreation of a king than the study of a scholar. Nevertheless Ponocrates, to divert him from this vehement intension of the spirits, thought fit, once in a month, upon some fair and clear day to go out of the city betimes in the morning, either towards Gentilly, or Boulogne, or to Montrouge, or Charanton-bridge, or to Vanves, or St. Clou, and there spend all the day long in making the greatest cheer that could be devised, sporting, making merry, drinking healths, playing, singing, dancing, tumbling in some fair meadow, unnestling of sparrows, taking of quails, and fishing for frogs and crabs. But although that day was past without books or lecture, yet was it not spent without profit; for in the said meadows they usually repeated certain pleasant verses of Virgil's agriculture, of Hesiod, and of Politian's husbandry; would set a broach some witty Latin epigrams, then immediately turned them into roundelays and songs for dancing in the French language. In their feasting, they would sometimes separate the water from the wine that was therewith mixed, as Cato teacheth, *De Re Rustica*, and Pliny with an ivy cup would wash the wine in a basin full of water, then take it out again with a funnel as pure as ever. They made the water go from one glass to another, and contrived a thousand little automatory engines, that is to say, moving of themselves.

CHAPTER 25

How there was a great Strife and Debate raised betwixt the Cake-Bakers of Lerné, and those of Gargantua's country, whereupon were waged great wars

AT that time, which was the season of vintage, in the beginning of harvest, when the country shepherds were set to keep the vines, and hinder the starlings from eating up the grapes, as some cake-bakers of Lerné happened to pass along in the broad highway, driving into the city ten or twelve horses loaded with cakes, the said shepherds courteously entreated them to give them some for their money, as the price then ruled in the market. For here it is to be remarked, that it is a celestial food to eat for breakfast, hot fresh cakes with grapes, especially the frail clusters, the great red grapes, the muscadine, the verjuice grape, and the luskard, for those that are costive in their belly; because it will make them gush out, and squirt the length of a hunter's staff, like the very tap of a barrel; and oftentimes, thinking to let a squib, they did all-to-besquatter and conskite themselves, whereupon they are commonly called the vintage thinkers. The bunsellers or cake-makers were in nothing inclinable to their request; but, (which was worse,) did injure them most outrageously, calling them brattling gabblers, licorous gluttons, freckled bittors, mangy rascals, shite-a-bed scoundrels, drunken roysters, sly knaves, drowsy loiterers, slapsauce fellows, slabber-degullion druggels, lubbardly louts, cozening foxes, ruffian rogues, paultry customers, sychophant-varlets, drawlatch hoydons, flouting milksops, jeering companions, staring clowns, forlorn snakes, ninny lobcocks, scurvy sneaksbies, fondling fops, base loons, saucy coxcombs, idle lusks, scoffing braggards, noddy meacocks, blockish grutnols, doddipol joltheads, jobbernol goosecaps, foolish loggerheads, flutch calf-lollies, grouthead gnat-snappers, lob-dotterels, gaping changelings, codshead loobies, woodcock slangams, ninnie-hammer fly-catchers, noddie-peak simpletons, turdy-gut, shitten shepherds, and other such like defamatory epithets; saying further that it was not for them to eat of these dainty cakes, but might very well content themselves with the coarse unraunged bread, or to eat of the great brown household loaf. To which provoking words, one amongst them, called Forgier, an honest fellow of his person, and a notable springal, made answer very calmly thus. How long is it since you have got horns, that you are become so proud? Indeed formerly you were wont to give us some freely, and will you not now let us have any for our money? This is not the part of good neighbours, neither do we serve you thus, when you come hither to buy our good corn, whereof you make your cakes and buns. Besides that, we would have given you to the bargain some of our grapes, but, by his zounds, you may chance to repent it, and possibly have need of us at another time, when we shall use you after the like manner, and therefore remember it. Then Marquet, a prime man in the confraternity of the cake-bakers, said unto him, Yea, sir, thou art pretty well crest-risen this morning, thou didst eat yesternight too much mullet and bolymong. Come hither, sirrah, come hither, I will give thee some cakes. Whereupon Forgier dreading no harm, in all simplicity went towards him, and drew a sixpence out of his leather satchel, thinking that Marquet would have sold him some of his cakes. But instead of cakes, he gave him with his whip such a rude lash overthwart the legs, the marks of the whipcord knots were apparent in them, then would have fled away;

but Forgier cried out as loud as he could, O murder, murder, help, help, help! and in the mean time threw a great cudgel after him, which he carried under his arm, wherewith he hit him in the coronal joint of his head, upon the crotaphic artery of the right side thereof, so forcibly, that Marquet fell down from his mare, more like a dead than a living man. Meanwhile the farmers and country swains that were watching their walnuts near to that place, came running with their great poles and long staves, and laid such load on these cake-bakers, as if they had been to thrash upon green rye. The other shepherds and shepherdesses, hearing the lamentable shout of Forgier, came with their slings and slackies following them, and throwing great stones at them, as thick as if it had been hail. At last they overtook them, and took from them about four or five dozen of their cakes. Nevertheless they paid for them the ordinary price, and gave them over and above one hundred eggs, and three baskets full of mulberries. Then did the cake-bakers help to get up to his mare, Marquet, who was most shrewdly wounded, and forthwith returned to Lerné, changing the resolution they had to go to Pareille, threatening very sharp and boisterously the cowherds, shepherds, and farmers, of Sevillé and Sinays. This done, the shepherds and shepherdesses made merry with these cakes and fine grapes, and sported themselves together at the sound of the pretty small pipe, scoffing and laughing at those vain glorious cake-bakers, who had that day met with a mischief for want of crossing themselves with a good hand in the morning. Nor did they forget to apply to Forgier's leg some fair great red medicinal grapes, and so handsomely dressed it and bound it up, that he was quickly cured.

CHAPTER 26

How the inhabitants of Lerné, by the commandment of Picrochole, their King, assaulted the shepherds of Gargantua unexpectedly and on a sudden

THE cake-bakers, being returned to Lerné, went presently, before they did either eat or drink, to the capitol, and there before their King, called Picrochole, the third of that name, made their complaint, showing their panniers broken, their caps all crumpled, their coats torn, their cakes taken away, but, above all, Marquet most enormously wounded, saying, that all that mischief was done by the shepherds and herdsmen of Grangousier, near the broad highway beyond Sevillé. Picrochole incontinent grew angry and furious; and, without asking any further what, how, why, or wherefore, commanded the *ban* and *arriere ban* to be sounded throughout all his country, that all his vassals of what condition soever should, upon pain of the halter, come in the best arms they could, unto the great place before the castle, at the hour of noon, and the better to strengthen his design, he caused the drum to be beat about the town. Himself, whilst his dinner was making ready, went to see his artillery mounted upon the carriage, to display his colours, and set up the great royal standard, and loaded wains with store of ammunition both for the field and the belly, arms and victuals. At dinner he despatched his commissions, and by his express edict my Lord Shagrag was appointed to command the vanguard, wherein were numbered sixteen thousand and fourteen harquebussiers or firelocks, together with thirty thousand and eleven volunteer adventurers. The great Torquedillon, master of the horse, had the charge of the ordnance, wherein were reckoned nine hundred and fourteen brazen pieces, in cannons, double cannons, basilisks, serpentines, culverins, bombards or murtherers, falcons, bases or passevolans, spiroles and other sorts of great guns. The rearguard was committed to the Duke of Scrapegood. In the main battle was the king, and the princes of his kingdom. Thus being hastily furnished, before they would set forward, they sent three hundred light horsemen under the conduct of Captain Swillwind, to discover the country, clear the avenues, and see whether there was any ambush laid for them. But, after they had made diligent search, they found all the land round about in peace and quiet, without any meeting or convention at all; which Picrochole understanding commanded that every one should march speedily under his colours. Then immediately in all disorder, without keeping either rank or file, they took the fields one amongst another, wasting, spoiling, destroying and making havoc of all wherever they went, not sparing poor nor rich, privileged nor unprivileged places, church nor laity, drove away oxen and cows, bulls, calves, heifers, wethers, ewes, lambs, goats, kids, hens, capons, chickens, geese, ganders, goslings, hogs, swine, pigs and such like; beating down the walnuts, plucking the grapes, tearing the hedges, shaking the fruit-trees, and committing such incomparable abuses, that the like abomination was never heard of. Nevertheless, they met with none to resist them, for every one submitted to their mercy, beseeching them, that they might be dealt with courteously, in regard that they had always carried themselves as became good and loving neighbours; and that they had never been guilty of any wrong or outrage done unto them, to be thus suddenly surprised, troubled and disquieted, and that if they would not desist, God would punish them very shortly. To which expostulations and remonstrances no other answer was made, but that they would teach them to eat cakes.

CHAPTER 27

How a monk of Sevillé saved the close of the Abbey from being ransacked by the Enemy

So much they did, and so far they went pillaging and stealing, that at last they came to Sevillé, where they robbed both men and women, and took all they could catch: nothing was either too hot or too heavy for them. Although the plague was there in the most part of all their houses, they nevertheless entered everywhere, then plundered and carried away all that was within, and yet for all this not one of them took any hurt, which is a most wonderful case. For the curates, vicars, preachers, physicians, chirurgeons and apothecaries, who went to visit, to dress, to cure, to heal, to preach unto, and admonish those that were sick, were all dead with the infection; and these devilish robbers and murderers caught never any harm at all. Whence comes this to pass, my masters? I beseech you think upon it. The town being thus pillaged, they went unto the abbey with a horrible noise and tumult, but they found it shut and made fast against them. Whereupon the body of the army marched forward towards a pass or ford called the *Gué de Véde,* except seven companies of foot, and two hundred lancers, who, staying there, broke down the walls of the close, to waste, spoil and make havoc of all the vines and vintage within that place. The monks (poor devils) knew not in that extremity to which of all their sancts they should vow themselves. Nevertheless, at all adventures they rang the bells *ad capitulum capitulantes.*[39] There it was decreed, that they should make a fair procession, stuffed with good lectures, prayers, and litanies *contra hostium insidias*,[40] and jolly responses *pro pace*.[41]

There was then in the abbey a claustral monk, called Friar John of the funnels and gobbets, in French, *des Entommeures,* young, gallant, frisk, lusty, nimbly, quick, active, bold, adventurous, resolute, tall, lean, wide-mouthed, long-nosed, a fair despatcher of morning prayers, unbridler of masses, and runner over vigils; and, to conclude summarily in a word, a right monk, if ever there was any, since the monking world monked a monkery: for the rest, a clerk even to the teeth in matter of breviary. This monk, hearing the noise that the enemy made within the inclosure of the vineyard, went out to see what they were doing; and perceiving that they were cutting and gathering the grapes, whereon was grounded the foundation of all their next year's wine, returned unto the quire of the church where the other monks were, all amazed and astonished like so many bell-melters. Whom when he heard sing, *im, im, pe, ne, ne, ne, ne, nene, tum, ne num, num, ini, i mi, co, o, no, o, o, neno, ne, no, no, no, rum, nenum, num:* It is well shit, well sung, said he. By the virtue of God, why do not you sing, Panniers farewell, vintage is done? The devil snatch me, if they be not already within the middle of our close, and cut so well both vines and grapes that, by God's body, there will not be found for these four years to come so much as a gleaning in it. By the belly of Sanct James, what shall we poor devils drink the while? Lord God! *da mihi potum*.[42] Then said the prior of the convent: —What should this drunken fellow do here, let him be carried to prison for troubling the divine service. Nay, said the monk, the wine service, let us behave ourselves so, that it be not troubled; for you yourself, my lord prior, love to drink of the best, and so doth every honest man. Never yet did a man of worth dislike good wine, it is a monastical apophthegm. But these responses that you chant here, by G—, are not in season. Wherefore is it, that our devotions were instituted to be short in the time of harvest and vintage, and long in the advent and all the winter? The late friar, Macé Pelosse, of good memory, a true zealous man, (or else I give myself to the devil,) of our religion, told me, and I remember it well, how the reason was, that in this season we might press and make the wine, and in winter whiff it up. Hark you, my mas-

ters, you that love the wine, Cop's body, follow me; for Sanct Anthony burn me as freely as a faggot, if they get leave to taste one drop of the liquor, that will not now come and fight for relief of the vine. Hog's belly, the goods of the church! Ha, no, no. What the devil, Sanct Thomas of England was well content to die for them; if I died in the same cause, should not I be a sanct likewise? Yes. Yet shall not I die there for all this, for it is I that must do it to others and send them a packing.

As he spake this, he threw off his great monk's habit, and laid hold upon the staff of the cross, which was made of the heart of a sorb-apple-tree, it being the length of a lance, round, of a full gripe, and a little powdered with lilies called *flower de luce,* the workmanship whereof was almost all defaced and worn out. Thus went he out in a fair long-skirted jacket, putting his frock scarfwise athwart his breast, and in this equipage, with his staff, shaft, or truncheon of the cross, laid on so lustily, brisk, and fiercely upon his enemies, who without any order, or ensign, or trumpet, or drum, were busied in gathering the grapes of the vineyard. For the cornets, guidons, and ensign-bearers had laid down their standards, banners, and colours by the wall-sides: the drummers had knocked out the heads of their drums on one end, to fill them with grapes: the trumpeters were loaded with great bundles of bunches, and huge knots of clusters: in sum, every one of them was out of array, and all in disorder. He hurried, therefore, upon them so rudely, without crying gare or beware, that he overthrew them like hogs, tumbled them over like swine, striking athwart and alongst, and by one means or other laid so about him, after the old fashion of fencing, that to some he beat out their brains, to others he crushed their arms, battered their legs, and bethwacked their sides till their ribs cracked with it. To others again he unjointed the spondyles or knuckles of the neck, disfigured their chaps, gashed their faces, made their cheeks hang flapping on their chin, and so swinged and belammed them, that they fell down before him like hay before a mower. To some others he spoiled the frame of their kidneys, marred their backs, broke their thigh-bones, pushed in their noses, poached out their eyes, cleft their mandibules, tore their jaws, dash'd in their teeth into their throat, shook asunder their omoplates or shoulder blades, sphacelated their shins, mortified their shanks, inflamed their ankles, heaved off of the hinges their ishies, their sciatica or hip-gout, dislocated the joints of their knees, squattered into pieces the boughts or pestles of their thighs, and so thumped, mawled and belaboured them everywhere, that never was corn so thick and threefold thrashed upon by ploughmen's flails, as were the pitifully disjoined members of their mangled bodies, under the merciless baton of the cross. If any offered to hide himself amongst the thickest of the vines, he laid him squat as a flounder, bruised the ridge of his back, and dashed his reins like a dog. If any thought by flight to escape, he made his head to fly in pieces by the lambduidal commissure, which is a seam in the hinder part of the skull. If any one did scramble up into a tree, thinking there to be safe, he rent up his perinee, and impaled him in at the fundament. If any of his old acquaintance happened to cry out, ha, Friar John, my friend, Friar John, quarter, quarter, I yield myself to you, to you I render myself! So thou shalt, said he, and must, whether thou wouldst or no, and withal render and yield up thy soul to all the devils in hell, then suddenly gave them dronos, that is, so many knocks, thumps, raps, dints, thwacks and bangs, as sufficed to warn Pluto of their coming, and despatch them a going. If any was so rash and full of temerity as to resist him to his face, then was it he did show the strength of his muscles, for without more ado he did transpierce him, by running him in at the breast, through the mediastine and the heart. Others, again, he so quashed and bebumped, that, with a sound bounce under the hollow of their short ribs, he overturned their stomachs so that they died immediately. To some, with a smart souse on the epigaster, he would make their midriff swag, then, redoubling the blow, gave them such a home-push on the navel, that he made their puddings to gush out. To others through their ballocks he pierced their bum-gut, and left not bowel, tripe, nor entral in their body, that had not felt the impetuosity, fierceness, and fury of his violence. Believe, that it was the most horrible spectacle that ever one saw. Some cried unto Sanct Barbe, others to St. George. O the holy Lady Nytouch, said one, the good Sanctesse. O our Lady of Succours, said another, help, help! Others cried, Our Lady of Cunaut, of Loretto, of Good Tidings, on the other side of the water St. Mary Over. Some

vowed a pilgrimage to St. James, and others to the holy handkerchief at Chamberry, which three months after that burnt so well in the fire, that they could not get one thread of it saved. Others sent up their vows to St. Cadouin, others to St. John d'Angly, and to St. Eutropius of Xaintes. Others again invoked St. Mesmes of Chinon, St. Martin of Candes, St. Clouaud of Sinays, the holy relics of Laurezay, with a thousand other jolly little sancts and santrels. Some died without speaking, others spoke without dying; some died in speaking, others spoke in dying. Others shouted as loud as they could, Confession, confession, *confiteor, miserere, in manus!* So great was the cry of the wounded, that the Prior of the Abbey with all his monks came forth, who, when they saw these poor wretches so slain amongst the vines, and wounded to death, confessed some of them. But whilst the priests where busied in confessing them, the little monkitos ran all to the place where Friar John was, and asked him, wherein he would be pleased to require their assistance? To which he answered, that they should cut the throats of those he had thrown down upon the ground. They presently, leaving their outer habits and cowls upon the rails, began to throttle and make an end of those whom he had already crushed. Can you tell with what instruments they did it? With fair gullies, which are little haulchbacked demi-knives, the iron tool whereof is two inches long, and the wooden handle one inch thick, and three inches in length, wherewith the little boys in our country cut ripe walnuts in two, while they are yet in the shell, and pick out the kernel, and they found them very fit for the expediting of wezand-slitting exploits. In the mean time Friar John, with his formidable baton of the cross, got to the breach which the enemies had made, and there stood to snatch up those that endeavoured to escape. Some of the monkitos carried the standards, banners, ensigns, guidons, and colours into their cells and chambers, to make garters of them. But when those that had been shriven would have gone out at the gap of the said breach, the sturdy monk quashed and felled them down with blows, saying, These men have had confession and are penitent souls, they have got their absolution and gained the pardons: they go into paradise as straight as a sickle, or as the way is to Faye, (like Crookedlane at Eastcheap). Thus by his prowess and valour were discomfited all those of the army that entered into the close of the abbey unto the number of thirteen thousand six hundred twenty and two, besides the women and little children, which is always to be understood. Never did Maugis the Hermit bear himself more valiantly with his bourdon or pilgrim's staff against the Saracens, of whom is written in the *Acts* of the four sons of Haymon, than did this monk against his enemies with the staff of the cross.

CHAPTER 28

How Picrochole stormed and took by assault the Rock Clermond, and of Grangousier's unwillingness and aversion from the undertaking of war

WHILST the monk did thus skirmish, as we have said, against those which were entered within the close, Picrochole in great haste passed the ford of *Véde,*—a very especial pass,—with all his soldiery, and set upon the rock Clermond, where there was made him no resistance at all: and, because it was already night, he resolved to quarter himself and his army in that town, and to refresh himself of his pugnative choler. In the morning he stormed and took the bulwarks and castle, which afterwards he fortified with rampiers, and furnished with all ammunition requisite, intending to make his retreat there, if he should happen to be otherwise worsted; for it was a strong place, both by art and nature, in regard of the stance and situation of it. But let us leave them there, and return to our good Gargantua, who is at Paris very assiduous and earnest at the study of good letters, and athletical exercitations, and to the good old man Grangousier his father, who after supper warmeth his ballocks by a good, clear, great fire, and, waiting upon the broiling of some chesnuts, is very serious in drawing scratches on the hearth, with a stick burnt at the one end, wherewith they did stir up the fire, telling to his wife and the rest of the family pleasant old stories and tales of former times.

Whilst he was thus employed, one of the shepherds which did keep the vines, named Pillot, came towards him, and to the full related the enormous abuses which were committed, and the excessive spoil that was made by Picrochole, King of Lerné, upon his lands and territories, and how he had pillaged, wasted, and ransacked all the country, except the inclosure at Sevillé, which Friar John *des Entommeures,* to his great honour, had preserved; and that at the same present time the said king was in the rock Clermond, and there, with great industry and circumspection, was strengthening himself and his whole army. Halas, halas, alas, said Grangousier, what is this, good people? Do I dream, or is it true that they tell me? Picrochole, my ancient friend of old time, of my own kindred and alliance, comes he to invade me? What moves him? What provokes him? What sets him on? What drives him to it? Who hath given him this counsel? Ho, ho, ho, ho, ho, my God, my Saviour, help me, inspire me, and advise me what I shall do! I protest, I swear before thee, so be thou favourable to me, if ever I did him or his subjects any damage or displeasure, or committed any the least robbery in his country; but, on the contrary, I have succoured and supplied him with men, money, friendship, and counsel, upon any occasion, wherein I could be steadable for the improvement of his good. That he hath therefore at this nick of time so outraged and wronged me, it cannot be but by the malevolent and wicked spirit. Good God thou knowest my courage, for nothing can be hidden from thee. If perhaps he be grown mad, and that thou hast sent him hither to me for the better recovery and re-establishment of his brain, grant me power and wisdom to bring him to the yoke of thy holy will by good discipline. Ho, ho, ho, ho, my good people, my friends, and my faithful servants, must I hinder you from helping me? Alas, my old age required henceforward nothing else but rest, and all the days of my life I have laboured for nothing so much as peace; but now I must, I see it well, load with arms my poor, weary and feeble shoulders, and take in my trembling hand the lance and horseman's mace, to succour and protect my honest subjects. Reason will have it so; for by their labour am I entertained, and with their sweat am I nourished, I, my children and my family. This notwithstanding, I will not undertake war, until I have first tried all the ways and means of peace; that I resolve upon.

Then assembled he his counsel, and proposed the matter as it was indeed. Whereupon it was concluded, that they should send some discreet man unto Picrochole, to know wherefore he had thus suddenly broken the peace, and invaded those lands unto which he had no right nor title. Furthermore, that they should send for Gargantua, and those under his command, for the preservation of the country, and defence now at need. All this pleased Grangousier very well, and he commanded that so it should be done. Presently therefore he sent Basque, his lackey, to fetch Gargantua with all diligence, and wrote to him as followeth.

CHAPTER 29

The tenor of the Letter which Grangousier wrote to his Son Gargantua

THE fervency of thy studies did require, that I should not in a long time recall thee from that philosophical rest thou now enjoyest, if the confidence reposed in our friends and ancient confederates had not at this present disappointed the assurance of my old age. But seeing such is my fatal destiny, that I should be now disquited by those in whom I trusted most, I am forced to call thee back to help the people and goods, which by the right of nature belong unto thee. For even as arms are weak abroad, if there be not counsel at home, so is that study and counsel unprofitable, which in a due and convenient time is not by virtue executed and put in effect. My deliberation is not to provoke, but to appease—not to assault, but to defend—not to conquer, but to preserve my faithful subjects and hereditary dominions, into which Picrochole is entered in a hostile manner without any ground or cause, and from day to day pursueth his furious enterprise with that height of insolence that is intolerable to free-born spirits. I have endeavoured to moderate his tyrannical choler, offering him all that which I thought might give him satisfaction; and oftentimes have I sent lovingly unto him, to understand wherein, by whom, and how he found himself to be wronged. But of him could I obtain no other answer, but a mere defiance, and that in my lands he did pretend only to the right of a civil correspondency and good behaviour, whereby I knew that the eternal God hath left him to the disposure or his own free will and sensual appetite,—which cannot choose but be wicked, if by divine grace it be not continually guided,—and to contain him within his duty, and to bring him to know himself, hath sent him hither to me by a grievous token. Therefore, my beloved son, as soon as thou canst, upon sight of these letters, repair hither with all diligence to succour not me so much, which nevertheless by natural piety thou oughtest to do, as thine own people, which by reason thou mayest save and preserve. The exploit shall be done with as little effusion of blood as may be. And, if possible, by means far more expedient, such as military policy, devices and stratagems of war, we shall save all the souls, and send them home as merry as crickets unto their own houses. My dearest son, the peace of Jesus Christ, our Redeemer be with thee. Salute from me Ponocrates, Gymnastes, and Eudemon. The twentieth of September.

THY FATHER, GRANGOUSIER

CHAPTER 30

How Ulrich Gallet was sent unto Picrochole

THE letters being dictated, signed, and sealed, Grangousier ordained that Ulrich Gallet, Master of the Requests, a very wise and discreet man, of whose prudence and sound judgment he had made trial in several difficult and debateful matters, [should] go unto Picrochole, to show what had been decreed amongst them. At the same hour departed the good man Gallet, and, having passed the ford, asked at the miller that dwelt there, in what condition Picrochole was: who answered him, that his soldiers had left neither cock nor hen, that they were retired and shut up into the rock Clermond, and that he would not advise him to go any further for fear of the scouts, because they were enormously furious. Which he easily believed, and therefore lodged that night with the miller.

The next morning he went with a trumpeter to the gate of the castle, and required of the guards he might be admitted to speak with the king of somewhat that concerned him. These words being told unto the king, he would by no means consent that they should open the gate; but, getting upon the top of the bulwark, said unto the ambassador, What is the news, what have you to say? Then the ambassador began to speak as followeth.

CHAPTER 31

The Speech made by Gallet to Picrochole

THERE cannot arise amongst men a juster cause of grief, than when they receive hurt and damage, where they may justly expect for favour and good will; and not without cause though without reason, have many, after they had fallen into such a calamitous accident, esteemed this indignity less supportable than the loss of their own lives, in such sort, that if they have not been able by force of arms, nor any other means, by reach of wit or subtilty, to correct it, they have fallen into desperation, and utterly deprived themselves of this light. It is therefore no wonder if King Grangousier, my master, be full of high displeasure, and much disquieted in mind upon thy outrageous and hostile coming: but truly it would be a marvel, if he were not sensible of, and moved with the incomparable abuses and injuries perpetrated by thee and thine upon those of his country, towards whom there hath been no example of inhumanity omitted. Which in itself is to him so grievous, for the cordial affection, wherewith he hath always cherished his subjects, that more it cannot be to any mortal man; yet in this, above human apprehension, is it to him the more grievous, that these wrongs and sad offences hath been committed by thee and thine, who, time out of mind, from all antiquity, thou and thy predecessors, have been in a continual league and amity with him, and all his ancestors; which, even until this time, you have, as sacred, together inviolably preserved, kept and entertained so well that not he and his only, but the very barbarous nations of the Poictevins, Bretons, Manceaux, and those that dwell beyond the isles of the Canaries, and that of Isabella, have thought it as easy to pull down the firmament, and to set up the depths above the clouds, as to make a breach in your alliance; and have been so afraid of it in their enterprises, that they have never dared to provoke, incense, or indamage the one for fear of the other. Nay, which is more, this sacred league hath so filled the world, that there are few nations at this day inhabiting throughout all the continent and isles of the ocean, who have not ambitiously aspired to be received into it, upon your own covenants and conditions, holding your joint confederacy in as high esteem as their own territories and dominions, in such sort, that from the memory of man, there hath not been either prince or league so wild and proud, that durst have offered to invade, I say not your countries, but not so much as those of your confederates. And if, by rash and heady counsel, they have attempted any new design against them, as soon as they heard the name and title of your alliance, they have suddenly desisted from their enterprises. What rage and madness, therefore, doth now incite thee, all old alliance infringed, all amity trod under foot, and all right violated, thus in a hostile manner to invade his country, without having been by him or his in any thing prejudiced, wronged or provoked? Where is faith? Where is law? Where is reason? Where is humanity? Where is the fear of God? Dost thou think that these atrocious abuses are hidden from the Eternal Spirit, and the supreme God, who is the just rewarder of all our undertakings? If thou so think, thou deceivest thyself; for all things shall come to pass, as in his incomprehensible judgment he hath appointed. Is it thy fatal destiny, or influences of the stars, that would put an end to thy so long enjoyed ease and rest? For that all things have their end and period, so as that, when they are come to the superlative point of their greatest height, they are in a trice tumbled down again, as not being able to abide long in that state. This is the conclusion and end of those who cannot by reason and temperance moderate their fortunes and prosperities. But if it be predestinated that thy happiness and ease must now come to an end, must it needs be by wronging my king; him by whom thou wert established? If thy house must come to ruin, should it therefore in its fall crush the heels of him that set it up? The matter is so unreasonable, and so dissonant from common sense, that hardly can it be conceived by human understanding, and [it will remain] altogether incredible unto strangers till by the certain and undoubted effects thereof it be made apparent, that nothing is either sacred or holy to those, who having emancipated themselves from God and reason, do merely follow the perverse affections of their own depraved nature. If any wrong had been done by us to thy subjects and dominions—if we had favoured thy ill-willers—if we had not assisted thee in thy need—if thy name and reputation had been wounded by us—or, to speak more truly, if the calumniating spirit, tempting to induce thee to evil, had, by false illusions and deceitful fantasies, put into thy conceit the impression of a thought, that we had done unto thee any thing unworthy of our ancient correspondence and friendship, thou oughtest first to have inquired out the truth, and afterwards by a seasonable warning to admonish us thereof; and we should have so satisfied thee, according to thine own heart's desire, that thou shouldest have had occasion to be contented. But, O eternal God, what is thy enterprise? Wouldest thou, like a perfidious tyrant, thus spoil and lay waste my master's kingdom? Hast thou found him so silly and blockish, that he would not, or so destitute of men and money, of counsel and skill in military discipline, that he cannot withstand thy unjust invasion? March hence presently, and to-morrow, some time of the day, retreat into thine own country, without doing any kind of violence or disorderly act by the way; and pay with all a thousand besans of gold, (which, in English money, amounted to five thousand pounds) for reparation of the damages thou hast done in his country. Half thou shalt pay to-morrow, and the other half at the ides of May next coming, leaving with us in the meantime, for hostages, the Dukes of Turnbank, Lowbuttock and Smalltrash, together with the Prince of Itches, (Scrubbado) and Viscount of Snatchbit.

CHAPTER 32

How Grangousier, to buy peace, caused the Cakes to be restored

WITH that the good man Gallet held his peace, but Picrochole to all his discourse answered nothing but, "Come and fetch them; come and fetch them; they have ballocks fair and soft; they will knead and provide some cakes for you." Then returned he to Grangousier, whom he found upon his knees, bare-headed, crouching in a little corner of his cabinet, and humbly praying unto God, that he would vouchsafe to assuage the choler of Picrochole, and bring him to the rule of reason without proceeding by force. When the good man came back, he waked him, Ha, my friend, my friend, what news do you bring me? There is neither hope nor remedy, said Gallet: the man is quite out of his wits, and forsaken of God. Yea, but, said Grangousier, my friend, what cause doth he pretend for his outrages? He did not show me any cause at all, said Gallet, only that in a great anger he spoke some words of cakes. I cannot tell, if they have done any wrong to his cake-bakers. I will know, said Grangousier, the matter thoroughly, before I resolve any more upon what is to be done. Then sent he to learn concerning that business, and found by true information, that his men had taken violently some cakes from Picrochole's people, and that Marquet's head was broken with a slacky or

short cudgel: that, nevertheless, all was well, and that the said Marquet had first hurt Forgier with a stroke of his whip athwart the legs. And it seemed good to his whole counsel, that he should defend himself with all his might. Notwithstanding all this, said Grangousier, seeing the question is but about a few cakes, I will labour to content him; for I am very unwilling to wage war against him. He inquired then what quantity of cakes they had taken away, and understanding, that it was but some four or five dozen, he commanded five cart-loads of them to be baked that same night; and that there should be one full of cakes made with fine butter, fine yolks of eggs, fine saffron, and fine spice, to be bestowed upon Marquet unto whom likewise he directed to be given seven hundred thousand and three Philips, (that is, at three shillings the piece, one hundred and five thousand pounds, nine shillings of English money,) for reparation of his losses and hinderances, and for satisfaction of the chirurgeon that had dressed his wound; and furthermore settled upon him and his for ever in freehold, the apple orchard called *La Pomardière*. For the conveyance and passing of all which was sent Gallet, who by the way as they went, made them gather near the willow-trees, great store of boughs, canes, and reeds, wherewith all the carriers were enjoined to garnish and deck their carts, and each of them to carry one in his hand, as himself likewise did, thereby to give all men to understand, that they demanded by peace, and that they came to buy it.

Being come to the gate, they required to speak with Picrochole from Grangousier. Picrochole would not so much as let them in, nor go to speak with them, but sent them word that he was busy, and that they should deliver their mind to Captain Touquedillon, who was then planting a piece of ordnance upon the wall. Then said the good man unto him, My Lord, to ease you of all this labour, and to take away all excuses why you may not return unto our former alliance, we do here presently restore unto you the cakes upon which the quarrel arose. Five dozen did our people take away: they were well paid for: we love peace so well that we restore unto you five cart-loads, of which this cart shall be for Marquet, who doth most complain. Besides, to content him entirely, here are seven hundred thousand and three Philips, which I deliver to him, and, for the losses he may pretend to have sustained, I resign for ever the farm of the Pomardiere, to be possessed in fee-simple by him and his, for ever, without the payment of any duty, or acknowledgment of homage, fealty, fine, or service whatsoever, and here is the tenor of the deed. And, for God's sake, let us live henceforward in peace, and withdraw yourselves merrily into your own country from within this place, unto which you have no right at all, as yourselves must needs confess, and let us be good friends as before. Touquedillon related all this to Picrochole, and more and more exasperated his courage, saying to him; These clowns are afraid to some purpose. By G—, Grangousier conskites himself for fear, the poor drinker. He is not skilled in warfare, nor hath he any stomach for it. He knows better how to empty the flagons,—that is his art. I am of opinion, that it is fit we send back the carts and the money, and for the rest, that very speedily we fortify ourselves here, then prosecute our fortune. But what! Do they think to have to do with a ninny-whoop, to feed you thus with cakes? You may see what it is. The good usage, and great familiarity which you have had with them heretofore, hath made you contemptible in their eyes. *Ungenton purget pungentom rustius unget.*[43]

Ça, ça, ça, said Picrochole, by St. James you have given a true character of them. One thing I will advise you, said Touquedillon. We are here but badly victualled, and furnished with mouth-harness very slenderly. If Grangousier should come to besiege us I would go presently, and pluck out of all your soldiers' heads and mine own all the teeth, except three to each of us, and with them alone we should make an end of our provision but too soon. We shall have, said Picrochole, but too much sustenance and feeding stuff. Come we hither to eat or to fight? To fight, indeed, said Touquedillon; yet from the paunch comes the dance, and where famine rules, force is exiled. Leave off your prating, said Picrochole, and forthwith seize upon what they have brought. Then took they money and cakes, oxen and carts, and sent them away without speaking one word, only that they would come no more so near, for a reason that they would give them the morrow after. Thus without doing any thing returned they to Grangousier, and related the whole matter unto him, subjoining that there was no hope left to draw them to peace, but by sharp and fierce wars.

CHAPTER 33

How some Statesmen of Picrochole, by hairbrained counsel, put him in extreme danger

THE carts being unloaded, and the money and cakes secured, there came before Picrochole the Duke of Smalltrash, the Earl of Swashbuckler, and Captain Durtaille, who said unto him, Sir, this day we make you the happiest, the most warlike and chivalrous prince that ever was, since the death of Alexander of Macedonia. Be covered, be covered, said Picrochole. Grammercie, said they, we do but our duty. The manner is thus. You shall leave some captain here to have the charge of this garrison, with a party competent for keeping of the place, which, besides its natural strength, is made stronger by the rampiers and fortresses of your devising. Your army you are to divide into two parts, as you know very well how to do. One part thereof shall fall upon Grangousier and his forces. By it shall he be easily at the very first shock routed, and then shall you get money by heaps, for the clown hath store of ready coin. Clown we call him, because a noble and generous prince hath never a penny, and that to hoard up treasure is but a clownish trick. The other part of the army in the mean time shall draw towards Onys, Xaintonge, Angoumois and Gascony. Then march to Perigourt, Medos, and Elanes, taking wherever you come, without resistance, towns, castles, and forts: afterwards to Bayonne, St. John de Luz, to Fuentarabia, where you shall seize upon all the ships, and coasting along Gallicia and Portugal, shall pillage all the maritime places, even unto Lisbon, where you shall be supplied with all necessaries befitting a conqueror. By copsodie, Spain will yield, for they are but a race of loobies. Then are you to pass by the Straits of Gibraltar, where you shall erect two pillars more stately than those of Hercules, to the perpetual memory of your name, and the narrow entrance there shall be called the Picrocholinal sea.

Having passed the Picrocholinal Sea, behold, Barbarossa yields himself your slave. I will, said Picrochole, give him fair quarter and spare his life. Yea, said they, so that he be content to be christened. And you shall conquer the kingdoms of Tunis, of Hippo, Argier, Bomine, Corone, yea all Barbary. Furthermore, you shall take into your hands

Majorca, Minorca, Sardinia, Corsica, with the other islands of the Ligustic and Balearian Seas. Going along on the left hand, you shall rule all Gallia Narbonensis, Provence, the Allobrogians, Genua, Florence, Lucca, and then God b'w'ye Rome. [Our poor Monsieur the pope dies now for fear.] By my faith, said Picrochole, I will not then kiss his pantofle.

Italy being thus taken, behold Naples, Calabria, Apulia, and Sicily all ransacked, and Malta too. I wish the pleasant Knights heretofore of Rhodes would but come to resist you, that we might see their urine. I would, said Picrochole, very willingly go to Loretto. No, no, said they, that shall be at our return. From thence we will sail eastwards, and take Candia, Cyprus, Rhodes, and the Cyclade Islands, and set upon the Morea. It is ours, by St. Trenian. The Lord preserve Jerusalem; for the great Soldan is not comparable to you in power. I will then, said he, cause Solomon's Temple to be built. No, said they, not yet, have a little patience, stay a while, be never too sudden in your enterprises. Can you tell what Octavian Augustus said? *Festina lenté.*[44] It is requisite that you first have the Lesser Asia, Caria, Lycia, Pamphylia, Cilicia, Lydia, Phrygia, Mysia, Bithynia, Carazia, Satalia, Samagaria, Castamena, Luga, Savasta, even unto Euphrates. Shall we see, said Picrochole, Babylon and Mount Sinai? There is no need, said they, at this time. Have we not hurried up and down, travelled and toiled enough, in having transfreted and past over the Hircanian Sea, marched along the two Armenias, and the three Arabias? Ay, by my faith, said he, we have played the fools, and are undone. Ha, poor souls! What's the matter, said they? What shall we have, said he, to drink in these deserts? For Julian Augustus with his whole army died there for thirst, as they say. We have already, said they, given order for that. In the Syriac Sea you have nine thousand and fourteen great ships laden with the best wines in the world. They arrived at port Joppa. There they found two and twenty thousand camels, and sixteen hundred elephants, which you shall have taken at one hunting about Sigelmes, when you entered into Lybia; and, besides this, you had all the Mecca caravan. Did not they furnish you sufficiently with wine? Yes, but, said he, we did not drink it fresh. By the virtue, said they, not of a fish, a valiant man, a conqueror, who pretends and aspires to the monarchy of the world, cannot always have his ease. God be thanked, that you and your men are come safe and sound unto the banks of the River Tigris. But, said he, what doth that part of our army in the meantime, which overthrows that unworthy swill-pot Grangousier? They are not idle, said they. We shall meet with them by and by. They shall have won you Brittany, Normandy, Flanders, Hainhault, Brabant, Artois, Holland, Zealand; they have passed the Rhine over the bellies of the Switzers and Lanskenets, and a party of these hath subdued Luxemburg, Lorrain, Champaigne, and Savoy, even to Lyons, in which place they have met with your forces returning from the naval conquests of the Mediterranean Sea; and have rallied again in Bohemia, after they had plundered and sacked Suevia, Wirtemberg, Bavaria, Austria, Moravia, and Styria. Then they set fiercely together upon Lubeck, Norway, Swedeland, Riga, Denmark, Gitland, Greenland, the Sterlins, even unto the Frozen Sea. This done, they conquered the isles of Orkney, and subdued Scotland, England and Ireland. From thence sailing through the sandy sea, and by the Sarmates, they have vanquished and overcome Prussia, Poland, Lithuania, Russia, Wallachia, Transylvania, Hungary, Bulgaria, Turquieland, and are now at Constantinople. Come, said Picrochole, let us go join with them quickly, for I will be Emperor of Trebezonde also. Shall we not kill all these dogs, Turks and Mahometans? What a devil should we do else, said they? And you shall give their goods and lands to such as shall have served you honestly. Reason, said he, will have it so, that is but just. I give unto you Caramania, Suria, and all Palestine. Ha, sir, said they, it is out of your goodness; grammercie, we thank you. God grant you may always prosper. There was there present at that time an old gentleman well experienced in the wars, a stern soldier, and who had been in many great hazards, named Echephron, who, hearing this discourse, said, I do greatly doubt that all this enterprise will be like the tale or interlude of the pitcher full of milk, wherewith a shoemaker made himself rich in conceit: but, when the pitcher was broken, he had not whereupon to dine. What do you pretend by these large conquests? What shall be the end of so many labours and crosses? Thus it shall be, said Picrochole, that when we are returned, we shall sit down, rest, and be merry. But, said Echephron, if by chance you should never come back, for the voyage is long and dangerous, were it not better for us to take our rest now, than unnecessarily to expose ourselves to so many dangers? O, said Swashbuckler by G—, here is a good dotard, come, go hide ourselves in the corner of a chimney, and there let us spend the whole time of our life amongst ladies, in threading pearls, or spinning, like Sardanaplus. He, that nothing ventures, hath neither horse nor mule, says Solomon. He, who adventureth too much, said Echephron, loseth both horse and mule, as answered Malchon. Enough, said Picrochole, go forward. I fear nothing but that these devilish legions of Grangousier, whilst we are in Mesopotamia, will come on our backs, and charge up our rear. What course shall we then take? What shall be our remedy? A very good one, said Durtaille; a pretty little commission, which you must send unto the Muscovites, shall bring you into the field in an instant four hundred and fifty thousand choice men of war. O that you would but make me your Lieutenant-General, I should for the lightest faults of any inflict great punishments. I fret, I charge, I strike, I take, I kill, I slay, I play the devil. On, on, said Picrochole, make haste, my lads, and let him that loves me follow me.

CHAPTER 34

How Gargantua left the city of Paris to succour his country, and how Gymnast encountered with the enemy

In this same very hour Gargantua, who was gone out of Paris, as soon as he had read his father's letters, coming upon his great mare, had already passed the Nunnery-bridge, himself, Ponocrates, Gymnast, and Eudemon, who all three, the better to enable them to go along with him, took post-horses. The rest of his train came after him by even journeys at a slower pace, bringing with them all his books and philosophical instruments. As soon as he had alighted at Parillé, he was informed by a farmer of Gouguet, how Picrochole had fortified himself within the rock Clermond, and had sent Captain Tripet with a great army to set upon the wood of Vede and Vaugaudry, and that they had already plundered the whole country, not leaving cock nor hen, even as far as to the wine-press of Billard. These strange and almost incredible news of the enormous abuses, thus committed over all the land, so affrighted Gargantua, that he knew not what to say nor do. But Ponocrates counselled to go unto the Lord of Vauguyon, who at all times had been their friend and confederate, and that by him they should be better advised in their business. Which they did incontinently, and found him very willing and fully resolved to assist them, and therefore was of opinion, that they should send some one of his company, to scout along and discover the country, to learn in what condition and posture the enemy was, that they might take counsel, and proceed according to the present occasion. Gymnast offered himself to go. Whereupon it was concluded, that for his safety, and the better expedition, he should have with him some one that knew the ways, avenues, turnings, windings, and rivers thereabout. Then away went he and Prelingot, the equerry or gentleman of Vauguyon's horse, who scouted and espied as narrowly as they could upon all quarters without any fear. In the meantime Gargantua took a little refreshment, ate somewhat himself, the like did those who were with him, and caused to give to his mare a picotine of oats, that is, threescore and fourteen quarters and three bushels. Gymnast and his comrade rode so long, that at last they met with the enemy's forces, all scattered and out of order, plundering, stealing, robbing, and pillaging all they could lay their hands on. And, as far off as they could perceive him, they ran thronging upon the back of one another in all haste towards him, to unload him of his money, and untruss his portmanteaus. Then cried he out unto them, My masters, I am a poor devil, I desire you to spare me. I have yet one crown left. Come, we must drink it, for it is *aurum potabile*,[45] and this horse here shall be sold to pay my welcome. Afterwards take me for one of your own, for never yet was there any man that knew better how to take, lard, roast and dress, yea, by G—, to tear asunder and devour a hen, than I that am here: and for my *Proficiat* I drink to all good fellows. With that he unscrewed his borracho, (which was a great Dutch leathern bottle,) and without putting in his nose drank very honestly. The marroufle rogues looked upon him, opening their throats a foot wide, and putting out their tongues like greyhounds, in hopes to drink after him: but Captain Tripet, in the very nick of that their expectation, came running to him to see who it was. To him Gymnast offered his bottle, saying, Hold captain, drink boldly and spare not; I have been thy taster, it is wine of *La Faye Monjau*. What! said Tripet, this fellow gybes and flouts us? Who art thou? said Tripet. I am, said Gymnast, a poor devil (*pauvre diable*). Ha, said Tripet, seeing thou art a poor devil, it is reason that thou shouldest be permitted to go whithersoever thou wilt, for all poor devils pass every where without toll or tax. But it is not the custom of poor devils to be so well mounted; therefore, Sir Devil, come down, and let me have your horse, and if he do not carry me well, you, Master Devil, must do it: for I love a life that such a devil as you should carry me away.

CHAPTER 35

How Gymnast very souply and cunningly killed Captain Tripet, and others of Picrochole's Men

WHEN they heard these words, some amongst them began to be afraid, and blest themselves with both hands, thinking indeed that he had been a devil disguised, insomuch that one of them, named Good John, captain of the trained bands of the country bumpkins, took his psalter out of his codpiece, and cried out aloud, *Hagios ho Theos*.[46] If thou be of God, speak, if thou be of the other spirit, avoid hence, and get thee going. Yet he went not away: which words being heard by all the soldiers that were there, divers of them being a little inwardly terrified, departed from the place. All this did Gymnast very well remark and consider, and therefore making as if he would have alighted from off his horse, as he was poising himself on the mounting side, he most nimbly, with his short sword by his thigh, shifting his foot in the stirrup, performed the stirrup leather feat, whereby, after the inclining of his body downwards, he forthwith launched himself aloft in the air, and placed both his feet together on the saddle, standing upright with his back turned towards the horse's head. Now, said he, my case goes backward. Then suddenly, in the same very posture wherein he was, he fetched a gambol upon one foot, and turning to the left hand, failed not to carry his body perfectly round, just into its former stance, without missing one jot. Ha, said Tripet, I will not do that at this time, and not without cause. Well, said Gymnast, I have failed, I will undo this leap. Then, with a marvellous strength and agility, turning towards the right hand, he fetched another frisking gambol, as before, which done, he set his right hand thumb up-

on the hind bow of the saddle, raised himself up, and sprung in the air; poising and upholding his whole body upon the muscle and nerve of the said thumb, and so turned and whirled himself about three times. At the fourth, reversing his body, and overturning it upside down, and foreside back, without touching any thing, he brought himself betwixt the horse's two ears, springing with all his body into the air, upon the thumb of his left hand, and in that posture, turning like a windmill, did most actively do that trick which is called the miller's pass. After this, clapping his right hand flat upon the middle of the saddle, he gave himself such a jerking swing, that he thereby seated himself upon the crupper, after the manner of gentlewomen sitting on horseback. This done, he easily past his right leg over the saddle, and placed himself like one that rides in croup. But, said he, it were better for me to get into the saddle; then putting the thumbs of both hands upon the crupper before him, and thereupon leaning himself, as upon the only supporters of his body, he incontinently turned heels over head in the air, and straight found himself betwixt the bows of the saddle in a good settlement. Then with a summer-sault springing into the air again, he fell to stand with both his feet close together upon the saddle, and there made above a hundred frisks, turns, and demi-pommads, with his arms held out across, and in so doing cried out aloud, I rage, I rage, devils, I am stark mad; devils, I am mad; hold me, devils, hold me, hold, devils, hold, hold!

Whilst he was thus vaulting, the rogues in great astonishment said to one another, By cocks death he is a goblin or a devil thus disguised,—*Ab hoste maligno libera nos, Domine*,[47]—and ran away in a full flight, as if they had been routed, looking now and then behind them, like a dog that carrieth away a goose-wing in his mouth. Then Gymnast, spying his advantage, alighted from his horse, drew his sword, and laid on great blows upon the thickest, and highest-crested among them, and overthrew them in great heaps, hurt, wounded, and bruised, being resisted by nobody, they thinking he had been a starved devil, as well in regard of his wonderful feats in vaulting, which they had seen, as for the talk Tripet had with him, calling him poor devil. Only Tripet would have traitorously cleft his head with his horseman's sword, or lansquenet fauchion; but he was well armed, and felt nothing of the blow, but the weight of the stroke. Whereupon turning suddenly about, he gave Tripet a home-thrust, and upon the back of that, whilst he was about to ward his head from a slash, he ran him in at the breast with a hit, which at once cut his stomach, the fifth gut called the colon, and the half of his liver, wherewith he fell to the ground, and in falling gushed forth above four pottles of pottage, and his soul mingled with the pottage.

This done, Gymnast withdrew himself, very wisely considering that a case of great adventure and hazard should not be pursued unto its utmost period, and that it becomes all cavaliers modestly to use their good fortune without troubling or stretching it too far. Wherefore, getting to horse, he gave him the spur, taking the right way unto Vauguyon, and Prelingot with him.

CHAPTER 36

How Gargantua demolished the Castle at the Ford of Vede, and how they passed the Ford

As soon as he came, he related the estate and condition wherein they had found the enemy, and the stratagem which he alone had used against all their multitude, affirming that they were but rascally rogues, plunderers, thieves, and robbers, ignorant of all military discipline, and that they might boldly set forward unto the field; it being an easy matter to fell and strike them down like beasts. Then Gargantua mounted his great mare, accompanied as we have said before, and finding in his way a high and great tree, which commonly was called by the name of St. Martin's tree, because heretofore St. Martin planted a pilgrim's staff there, which in tract of time grew to that height and greatness, said, This is that which I lacked: this tree shall serve me both for a staff and lance. With that he pulled it up easily, plucked off the boughs, and trimmed it at his pleasure. In the meantime his mare pissed to ease her belly, but it was in such abundance, that it did overflow the country seven leagues, and all the piss of that urinal flood ran glib away towards the ford of Vede, wherewith the water was so swollen, that all the forces the enemy had there were with great horror drowned, except some who had taken the way on the left hand towards the hills. Gargantua, being come to the place of the wood of Vede, was informed by Eudemon, that there was some remainder of the enemy within the castle, which to know, Gargantua cried out as loud as he was able. Are you there, or are you not there? If you be there, be there no more; and if you are not there, I have no more to say. But a ruffian gunner, whose charge was to attend the portcullis over the gate, let fly a cannon-ball at him, and hit him with that shot most furiously on the right temple of his head, yet did him no more hurt, than if he had but cast a prune or kernel of a wine-grape at him. What is this, said Gargantua; do you throw at us grape-kernels here? The vintage shall cost you dear; thinking indeed that the bullet had been the kernel of a grape, or raisin-kernel.

Those who were within the castle, being till then busy at the pillage, when they heard this noise, ran to the towers and fortresses, from whence they shot at him above nine thousand and five-and-twenty falcon-shot and harquebusades, aiming all at his head, and so thick did they shoot at him, that he cried out, Ponocrates, my friend, these flies here are like to put out mine eyes; give me a branch of those willow-trees to drive them away, thinking that the bullets and stones shot out of the great ordnance had been but dun-flies. Ponocrates looked and saw that there were no other flies, but great shot which they had shot from the castle. Then was it that he rushed with his great tree against the castle, and with mighty blows overthrew both towers and fortresses, and laid all level with the ground, by which means all that were within were slain and broken in pieces. Going from thence, they came to the bridge at the mill, where they found all the ford covered with dead bodies so thick that they had choked up the mill, and stopped the current of its water, and these were those that were destroyed in the urinal deluge of the mare. There they were at a stand, consulting how they might pass without hindrance by these dead carcasses. But Gymnast said, if the devils have passed there, I will pass well enough. The devils have passed there, said Eudemon, to carry away the damned souls. By St. Rhenian! said Ponocrates, then by necessary consequence he shall pass there. Yes, yes, said Gymnast, or I shall stick in the way. Then, setting spurs to his horse, he passed through freely, his horse not fearing, nor being any thing affrighted at the sight of the dead bodies; for he had accustomed him, according to the doctrine of Ælian, not to fear armour, nor the carcasses of dead men; and that not by killing men as Diomedes did the Thracians, or as Ulysses did in throwing the corpses of his enemies at his horse's feet, as Homer saith, but by putting a Jack a-lent amongst his hay, and making him go over it ordinarily, when he gave him his oats. The other three followed him very close, except Eudemon only, whose horse's foreright or far forefoot sank up to the knee in the paunch of a great fat chuff, who lay there upon his back drowned, and could not get it out. There was he pestered, until Gargantua, with the end of his staff, thrust down the rest of the villain's tripes into the water, whilst the horse pulled out his foot; and, which is a wonderful thing in hippiatrie, the said horse was thoroughly cured of a ringbone which he had in that foot, by this touch of the burst guts of that great looby.

CHAPTER 37

How Gargantua, in combing his Head, made the great Cannon Balls fall out of his Hair

BEING come out of the river of Vede, they came very shortly after to Grangousier's castle, who waited for them with great longing. At their coming they were entertained with many congies, and cherished with embraces. Never was seen a more joyful company, for *Supplementum Supplementi Chronicorum*[48] saith, that Gargamelle died there with joy; for my part, truly I cannot tell, neither do I care very much for her, nor for any body else. The truth was, that Gargantua, in shifting his clothes, and combing his head with a comb, which was nine hundred feet long of the Jewish cane measure, and whereof the teeth were great tusks of elephants, whole and entire, he made fall at every rake about seven balls of bullets, at a dozen the ball, that stuck in his hair, at the razing of the castle of the wood of Vede. Which his father Grangousier seeing, thought they had been lice, and said unto him, What, my dear son, hast thou brought us this far some short-winged hawks of the college of Montague? I did not mean that thou shouldest reside there. Then answered Ponocrates, My sovereign lord, think not that I have placed him in that lousy college, which they call Montague; I had rather have put him amongst the grave-diggers of Sanct Innocent, so enormous is the cruelty and villany that I have known there: for the galley-slaves are far better used amongst the Moors

and Tartars, the murderers in the criminal dungeons, yea, the very dogs in your house, than are the poor wretched students in the aforesaid college. And if I were King of Paris, the devil take me if I would not set it on fire, and burn both principal and regents, for suffering this inhumanity to be exercised before their eyes. Then, taking up one of these bullets, he said, These are cannon-shot, which your son Gargantua hath lately received by the treachery of your enemies, as he was passing before the wood of Vede.

But they have been so rewarded, that they are all destroyed in the ruin of the castle, as were the Philistines by the policy of Samson, and those whom the tower of Silohim slew, as it is written in the thirteenth of Luke. My opinion is, that we pursue them whilst the luck is on our side; for occasion hath all her hair on her forehead; when she is past, you may not recall her,—she hath no tuft whereby you can lay hold on her, for she is bald in the hinder part of her head, and never returneth again. Truly, said Grangousier, it shall not be at this time; for I will make you a feast this night, and bid you welcome.

This said, they made ready supper, and, of extraordinary, besides his daily fare, were roasted sixteen oxen, three heifers, two and thirty calves, three score and three fat kids, four score and fifteen wethers, three hundred farrow pigs souced in sweet wine or musk, eleven score partridges, seven hundred snipes and woodcocks, four hundred Loudun and Cornwall capons, six thousand pullets, and as many pigeons, six hundred crammed hens, fourteen hundred leverets, or young hares and rabbits, three hundred and three buzzards, and one thousand and seven hundred cockerels. For venison, they could not so suddenly come by it, only eleven wild boars, which the Abbot of Turpenay sent, and eighteen fallow deer, which the Lord of Gramount bestowed; together with seven score pheasants, which were sent by the Lord of Essars; and some dozens of queests, cushats, ring-doves, and woodculvers; river fowl, teals, and awteals, bitterns, courtes, plovers, francolins, briganders, tyrasons, young lapwings, tame ducks, shovelers, woodlanders, herons, moor hens, criels, storks, canepetiers, oranges, flamans, which are phœnicopters, or crimson-winged sea-fowls, terrigoles, turkeys, arbens, coots, solan-geese, curlews, termagants, and water-wagtails, with a great deal of cream, curds, and fresh cheese, and store of soup, pottages, and brewis with great variety. Without doubt there was meat enough, and it was handsomely dressed by Snapsauce, Hotchpot, and Brayver-juice, Grangousier's cooks. Jenkin Trudg-apace and Clean-glass were very careful to fill them drink.

CHAPTER 38

How Gargantua did eat up six Pilgrims in a sallad

THE story requireth, that we relate that which happened unto six pilgrims, who came from Sebastian near to Nantes: and who for shelter that night, being afraid of the enemy, had hid themselves in the garden upon the chichling peas, among the cabbages and lettuces. Gargantua finding himself somewhat dry, asked whether they could get any lettuce to make him a sallad; and hearing that there were the greatest and fairest in the country, for they were as great as plum-trees, or as walnut-trees, he would go thither himself, and brought thence in his hand what he thought good, and withal carried away the six pilgrims, who were in so great fear, that they did not dare to speak nor cough. Washing them, therefore, first at the fountain, the pilgrims said one to another softly, What shall we do? We are almost drowned here amongst these lettuce, shall we speak? But if we speak he will kill us for spies. And, as they were thus deliberating what to do, Gargantua put them with the lettuce into a platter of the house, as large as the huge tun of the White Friars of the Cistertian order; which done, with oil, vinegar, and salt, he ate them up, to refresh himself a little before supper, and had already swallowed up five of the pilgrims, the sixth being in the platter, totally hid under a lettuce, except his bourbon or staff that appeared, and nothing else. Which Grangousier seeing, said to Gargantua, I think that is the horn of a shell snail, do not eat it. Why not, said Gargantua, they are good all this month: which he no sooner said, but, drawing up the staff, and therewith taking up the pilgrim, he ate him very well, then drank a terrible draught of excellent white wine. The pilgrims, thus devoured, made shift to save themselves as well as they could, by drawing their bodies out of the reach of the grinders of his teeth, but could not escape from thinking they had been put in the lowest dungeon of a prison. And when Gargantua whiffed the great draught, they thought to have drowned in his mouth, and the flood of wine had almost carried them away into the gulf of his stomach. Nevertheless, skipping with their bourbons, as St. Michael's palmers use to do, they sheltered themselves from the danger of that inundation under the banks of his teeth. But one of them by chance, groping or sounding the country with his staff, to try whether they were in safety or no, struck hard against the cleft of a hollow tooth, and hit the mandibulary sinew or nerve of the jaw, which put Gargantua to very great pain, so that he began to cry for the rage that he felt. To ease himself therefore of his smarting ache, he called for his tooth-picker, and rubbing towards a young walnut-tree, where they lay skulking, unnestled you my gentlemen pilgrims.

For he caught one by the legs, another by the scrip, another by the pocket, another by the scarf, another by the band of the breeches, and the poor fellow that had hurt him with the bourbon, him he hooked to him by the codpiece, which snatch nevertheless did him a great deal of good, for it pierced unto him a pocky botch he had in the groin, which grievously tormented him ever since they were past Ancenis. The pilgrims thus dislodged, ran away athwart the plain a pretty fast pace, and the pain ceased, even just at the time when by Eudemon he was called to supper, for all was ready. I will go then, said he, and piss away my misfortune; which he did do in such a copious measure, that, the urine taking away the feet from the pilgrims, they were carried along with the stream unto the bank of a tuft of trees. Upon which, as soon as they had taken footing, and that for their self-preservation they had run a little out of the road, they on a sudden fell all six, except Fourniller, into a trap that had been made to take wolves by a train, out of which, nevertheless, they escaped by the industry of the said Fourniller, who broke all the snares and ropes. Being gone from thence, they lay all the rest of that night in a lodge near unto Coudray, where they were comforted in their miseries by the gracious words of one of their company, called Sweer-to-go, who showed them, that this adventure had been foretold by the Prophet David, in the Psalms.—*Quum exsurgerent homines in nos, fortè vivos deglutissent nos;* when we were eaten in the sallad, with salt, oil, and vinegar. *Quum irasceretur furor eorum in nos, forsitan aqua absorbuisset nos;* when he drank the great draught. *Tor-*

rentem pertransivit anima nostra; when the stream of his water carried us to the thicket. *Forsitan pertransisset anima nostra aquam intolerabilem;* that is, the water of his urine, the flood whereof, cutting our way, took our feet from us. *Benedictus Dominus, qui non dedit nos in captionem dentibus eorum. Anima nostra sicut passer, erepta est de laqueo venantium;* when we fell into the trap. *Laqueus contritus est,* by Fourniller, *et nos liberati sumus. Adjutorium nostrum,* &c.[49]

CHAPTER 39

How the Monk was feasted by Gargantua, and of the jovial discourse they had at supper

WHEN Gargantua was set down at table, after all of them had somewhat stayed their stomachs by a snatch or two of the first bits eaten heartily, Grangousier began to relate the source and cause of the war, raised between him and Picrochole; and came to tell, how Friar John of the Funnels had triumphed at the defence of the close of the abbey, and extolled him for his valour above Camillus, Scipio, Pompey, Cæsar, and Themistocles. Then Gargantua desired that he might be presently sent for, to the end that with him they might consult of what was to be done. Whereupon, by a joint consent, his steward went for him, and brought him along merrily, with his staff of the cross, upon Grangousier's mule. When he was come, a thousand huggings, a thousand embracements, a thousand good days were given. Ha, Friar John, my friend, Friar John, my brave cousin, Friar John from the devil! Let me clip thee, my heart, about the neck; to me an armsful. I must gripe thee, my ballock, till thy back crack with it. Come, my cod, let me coll thee till I kill thee. And Friar John, the gladdest man in the world, never was man made welcomer, never was any more courteously and graciously received than Friar John. Come, come, said Gargantua, a stool here close by me at this end. I am content, said the monk, seeing you will have it so. Some water, page; fill, my boy, fill, it is to refresh my liver. Give me some, child, to gargle my throat withal. *Deposita cappà,*[50] said Gymnast, let us pull off this frock. Ho, by G—, gentlemen, said the monk, there is a chapter *in Statutis Ordinis,*[51] which opposeth my laying of it down. Pish! said Gymnast, a fig for your chapter! This frock breaks both your shoulders, put it off. My friend, said the

monk, let me alone with it; for, by G—, I'll drink the better that it is on. It makes all my body jocund. If I should lay it aside, the waggish pages would cut to themselves garters out of it as I was once served at Coulaines. And, which is worse, I shall lose my appetite. But if in this habit I sit down at table, I will drink, by G—, both to thee and to thy horse, and so, courage, frolic, God save the company! I have already supped, yet will I eat never a whit the less for that: for I have a paved stomach, as hollow as a butt of malvasie, or St. Benedictus' boot, and always open like a lawyer's pouch. Of all fishes, but the tench, take the wing of a partridge, or the thigh of a nun. Doth not he die like a good fellow that dies with a stiff catso? Our prior loves exceedingly the white of a capon. In that, said Gymnast, he doth not resemble the foxes: for of the capons, hens, and pullets, which they carry away, they never eat the white. Why, said the monk? Because, said Gymnast, they have no cooks to dress them; and, if they be not competently made ready, they remain red and not white; the redness of meats being a token that they have not got enough of the fire, whether by boiling, roasting, or otherwise, except shrimps, lobsters, crabs, and cray-fishes, which are cardinalised with boiling. By God's feast gazers, said the monk, the porter of our abbey, then, hath not his head well boiled, for his eyes are as red as a mazer made of an alder-tree. The thigh of this leveret is good for those that have the gout. To the purpose of the trowel,—what is the reason, that the thighs of a gentlewoman are always fresh and cool? This problem, said Gargantua, is neither in Aristotle, in Alexander Aphrodiseus, nor in Plutarch. There are three causes, said the monk, by which that place is naturally refreshed. *Primo,* because the water runs all along it. *Secundo,* because it is a shady place, obscure and dark, upon which the sun never shines. And thirdly, because it is continually flabbelled, blown upon and aired by the northwinds of the hole arstic, the fan of the smock, and flipflap of the codpiece. And lusty, my lads. Some bousing liquor, Page! So! crack, crack, crack, O how good is God, that gives us of this excellent juice! I call him to witness, if I had been in the time of Jesus Christ, I would have kept him from being taken by the Jews in the garden of Olivet. And the devil fail me, if I should have failed to cut off the hams of those gentlemen Apostles, who ran away so basely after they had well supped, and left their good master in the lurch. I hate that man worse than poison that offers to run away, when he should fight and lay stoutly about him. Oh that I were but King of France for fourscore or a hundred years! By G—, I should whip like curtail-dogs these runaways of Pavia. A plague take them, why did they not choose rather to die there, than to leave their good prince in that pinch and necessity? Is it not better and more honourable to perish in fighting valiantly than to live in disgrace by a cowardly running away? We are like to eat no great store of goslings this year, therefore, friend, reach me some of that roasted pig there.

Diavolo, is there no more must? No more sweet wine? *Germinavit radix Jesse.*[52] *Je renie ma vie, j'enrage de soif;* I renounce my life I rage for thirst. This wine is none of the worst. What wine drink you at Paris? I give myself to the devil, if I did not once keep open house at Paris for all comers six months together. Do you know Frair Claud of the High Kilderkins? Oh the good fellow that he is! But I do not know what fly hath stung him of late, he is become so hard a student. For my part, I study not at all. In our abbey we never study for fear of the mumps, which disease in horses is called the mourning in the chine. Our late abbot was wont to say, that it is a monstrous thing to see a learned monk. By G—, master, my friend. *Magis magnos clericos non sunt magis magnos sapientes.*[53] You never saw so many hares as there are this year. I could not any where come by a goss-hawk, nor tassel of falcon. My Lord Belloniere promised me a lanner, but he wrote to me not long ago, that he was become pursy. The partridges will so multiply henceforth, that they will go near to eat up our ears. I take no delight in the stalking-horse; for I catch such cold, that I am like to founder myself at that sport. If I do not run, toil, travel, and trot about, I am not well at ease. True it is, that in leaping over the hedges and bushes, my frock leaves always some of its wool behind it. I have recovered a dainty greyhound; I give him to the devil, if he suffer a hare to escape him. A groom was leading him to my Lord Huntlittle, and I robbed him of him. Did I ill? No, Friar John, said Gymnast, no, by all the devils that are, no! So, said the monk, do I attest these same devils so long as they last, or rather, virtue G—, what could that gouty limpard have done with so fine a

dog? By the body of G—, he is better pleased, when one presents him with a good yoke of oxen. How now, said Ponocrates, you swear, Friar John; it is only said the monk, but to grace and adorn my speech. They are colours of a Ciceronian rhetoric.

CHAPTER 40

Why Monks are the outcasts of the World; and wherefore some have bigger Noses than others

By the faith of a Christian, said Eudemon, I do wonderfully dote, and enter in a great ecstasy, when I consider the honesty and good fellowship of this monk; for he makes us here all merry. How is it, then, that they exclude the monks from all good companies, calling them feast-troublers, marrers of mirth, and disturbers of all civil conversation, as the bees drive away the drones from their hives? *Ignavum fucos pecus,* said Maro, *à præsepibus arcent.*[54] Hereunto, answered Gargantua, there is nothing so true, as that the frock and cowl draw to them the opprobries, injuries, and maledictions of the world, just as the wind called *Cecias,* attracts the clouds. The peremptory reason is, because they eat the ordure and excrements of the world, that is to say the sins of the people, and, like dung-chewers, and excrementitious eaters, they are cast into the privies and secessive places, that is, the convents and abbeys, separated from political conversation, as the jakes and retreats of a house are. But if you conceive, how an ape in a family is always mocked, and provokingly incensed, you shall easily apprehend how monks are shunned of all men, both young and old. The ape keeps not the house as a dog doth; he draws not in the plough as the ox; he yields neither milk nor wool as the sheep; he carrieth no burthen as a horse doth. That which he doth, is only to conskite, spoil, and defile all, which is the cause wherefore he hath of men mocks, frumperies and bastonadoes.

After the same manner a monk; I mean those lither, idle, lazy monks, doth not labour and work, as do the peasant and artificer; doth not ward and defend the country, as doth the man-of-war; cureth not the sick and diseased, as the physician doth; doth neither preach nor teach, as do the Evangelical doctors and school-masters; doth not import commodities and things necessary for the commonwealth, as the merchant doth. Therefore is it, that by and of all men they are hooted at, hated and abhorred. Yea, but, said Grangousier, they pray to God for us. Nothing less, answered Gargantua. True it is, that with a tingle tangle jangling of bells they trouble and disquiet all their neighbours about them. Right, said the monk; a mass, a matin, a vesper well rung is half said. They mumble out great store of legends and psalms, by them not at all understood: they say many *Pater-Nosters,* interlarded with *Ave-Maries,* without thinking upon, or apprehending the meaning of what it is they say, which truly I call mocking of God, and not prayers. But so help them God, as they pray for us, and not for being afraid to lose their victuals, their manchets, and good fat pottage. All true Christians, of all estates and conditions, in all places, and at all times, send up their prayers to God, and the Mediator prayeth and intercedeth for them, and God is gracious to them. Now such a one is our good Friar John, therefore every man desireth to have him in his company. He is no bigot or hypocrite, he is not torn and divided betwixt reality and appearance, no wretch of a rugged and peevish disposition, but honest, jovial, resolute, and a good fellow. He travels, he labours, he defends the oppressed, comforts the afflicted, helps the needy, and keeps the close of the abbey. Nay, said the monk, I do a great deal more than that; for, whilst we are despatching our matins and anniversaries in the quire, I make withal some cross-bow strings, polish glass-bottles and bolts; I twist lines and weave purse nets, wherein to catch coneys. I am never idle. But now, hither come, some drink, some drink here! Bring the fruit. These chesnuts are of the wood of Estrox, and with good new wine are able to make you a fine cracker and composer of bum-sonnets. You are not as yet, it seems, well-moistened in this house with the sweet wine and must. By G—, I drink to all men freely, and at all fords like a proctor, or promoter's horse. Friar John, said Gymnast, take away the snot that hangs at your nose. Ha, ha, said the monk, am not I in danger of drowning, seeing I am in water even to the nose? No, no, *Quare? Quia,*[55] though some water come out from thence, there never goes in any; for it is well antidoted with pot-proof armour, and sirrup of the vine-leaf.

O my friend, he that hath winter-boots made of such leather may boldly fish for oysters, for they will never take water. What is the cause, said Gargantua, that Friar John hath such a fair nose? Because, said Grangousier, that God would have it so, who frameth us in such form, and for such end, as is most agreeable with his divine will, even as a potter fashioneth his vessels. Because, said Ponocrates, he came with the first to the fair of noses, and therefore made choice of the fairest and the greatest. Pish, said the monk, that is not the reason of it, but, according to the true monastical philosophy, it is because my nurse had soft teats, by virtue whereof, whilst she gave suck, my nose did sink in as in so much butter. The hard breasts of nurses make children short-nosed. But hey, gay, *Ad formam nasi cognoscitur ad te levavi.*[56] I never eat any confections, page, whilst I am at the bibbery. Item, bring me rather some toasts.

CHAPTER 41

How the Monk made Gargantua sleep, and of his hours and breviaries

SUPPER being ended, they consulted of the business in hand, and concluded that about midnight they should fall unawares upon the enemy, to know what manner of watch and ward they kept, and that in the mean while they should take a little rest, the better to refresh themselves. But Gargantua could not sleep by any means, on which side soever he turned himself. Whereupon the monk said to him, I never sleep soundly but when I am at sermon or prayers. Let us therefore begin, you and I, the seven penitential psalms, to try whether you shall not quickly fall asleep. The conceit pleased Gargantua very well, and, beginning the first of these psalms, as soon as they came to the words, *Beati quorum,* they fell asleep both the one and the other. But the monk, for his being formerly accustomed to the hour of claustral matins, failed not to awake a little before midnight, and being up himself, awaked all the rest, in singing aloud, and with a full clear voice, the song,

> Awake, O Reinian, Ho, awake!
> Awake, O Reinian, Ho!
> Get up, you no more sleep must take,
> Get up, for we must go.

When they were all roused and up, he said, My masters, it is a usual saying, that we begin matins with coughing, and supper with drinking. Let us now, in doing clean contrarily, begin our matins with drinking, and at night before supper we shall cough as hard as we can. What, said Gargantua, to drink so soon after sleep? This is not to live according to the diet and prescript rule of the physicians, for you ought first to scour and cleanse your stomach of all its superfluities and excrements. O well physicked, said the monk; a hundred devils leap into my body, if there be not more old drunkards than old physicians! I have made this paction and covenant with my appetite, that it always lieth down, and goes to bed with myself, for to that I every day give very good order, then the next morning it also riseth with me, and gets up when I am awake. Mind you your charges, gentlemen, or tend your cures as much as you will. I will get me to my drawer, in terms of falconry, my tiring. What drawer or tiring do you mean, said Gargantua? My breviary, said the monk, for just as the falconers, before they feed their hawks, do make them draw at a hen's leg, to purge their brains of phlegm, and sharpen them to a good appetite, so, by taking this merry little breviary in the morning, I scour all my lungs, and am presently ready to drink.

After what manner, said Gargantua, do you say these fair hours and prayers of yours? After the manner of Whipfield, said the monk, by three psalms, and three lessons, or nothing at all, he that will. I never tie myself to hours, prayers, and sacraments: for they are made for the man, and not the man for them. Therefore is it, that I make my prayers in fashion of stirrup-leathers; I shorten or lengthen them when I think good. *Brevis oratio penetrat cœlos et longa potatio evacuat scyphos.*[57] Where is that written? By my faith, saith Ponocrates, I cannot tell, my pillicock, but thou art more worth than gold. Therein, said the monk, I am like you: but, *venite, apotemus.*[58] Then made they ready store of carbonadoes, or rashers on the coals, and good fat soups, or brewis with sippets; and the monk drank what he pleased. Some kept him company, and the rest did forbear, for their stomachs were not as yet opened. Afterwards every man began to arm and befit himself for the field. And they armed the monk against his will; for he desired no other armour for back and breast, but his frock, nor any other weapon in his hand, but the staff of the cross. Yet at their pleasure was he completely armed *cap-a-pie,* and mounted upon one of the best horses in the kingdom, with a good slashing shable by his side, together with Gargantua, Ponocrates, Gymnast, Eudemon, and five and twenty more of the most resolute and adventurous of Grangousier's house, all armed at proof with their lances in their hands, mounted like St. George, and every one of them having a harquebusier behind him.

CHAPTER 42

How the Monk encouraged his fellow-champions, and how he hanged upon a tree

THUS went out those valiant champions on their adventure, in full resolution to know what enterprise they should undertake, and what to take heed of, and look well to, in the day of the great and horrible battle. And the monk encouraged them, saying, My children, do not fear nor doubt, I will conduct you safely. God and Sanct Benedict be with us! If I had strength answerable to my courage, by's death, I would plume them for you like ducks. I fear nothing but the great ordnance; yet I know of a charm by way of prayer, which the sub-sexton of our abbey taught me, that will preserve a man from the violence of guns, and all manner of fire-weapons and engines; but it will do me no good, because I do not believe it. Nevertheless, I hope my staff of the cross shall this day play devilish pranks amongst them. By G—, whoever of our party shall offer to play the duck, and shrink when blows are a dealing, I give myself to the devil, if I do not make a monk of him in my stead, and hamper him within my frock, which is a sovereign cure against cowardice. Did you never hear of my Lord Meurles's greyhound, which was not worth a straw in the fields? He put a frock about his neck: by the body of G—, there was neither hare nor fox that could escape him, and, which is more, he lined all the bitches in the country, though before that he was feeble-reined, and *de frigidis et maleficiatis.*[59]

The monk uttering these words in choler, as he passed under a walnut-tree, in his way towards the causey, he broached the vizor of his helmet on the stump of a great branch of the said tree. Nevertheless, he set his spurs so fiercely to the horse, who was full of metal, and quick on the spur, that he bounded forwards, and the monk, going about to ungrapple his vizor, let go his hold of the bridle, and so hanged by his hand upon the bough, whilst his horse stole away from under him.

By this means was the monk left, hanging on the walnut-tree, and crying for help, murder, murder, swearing also that he was betrayed. Eudemon perceived him first, and calling Gargantua said, Sir, come and see Absalom hanging. Gargantua being come, considered the countenance of the monk, and in what posture he hanged; wherefore he said to Eudemon, You were mistaken in comparing him to Absalom; for Absalom hung by his hair, but this shaveling monk hangeth by the ears. Help me, said the monk, in the devil's name, is this a time for you to prate? You seem to me to be like the decretalist preachers, who say, that whosoever shall see his neighbour in the danger of death, ought, upon pain of trisulk excommunication, rather choose to admonish him to make his confession to a priest, and put his conscience in the state of peace, than otherwise to help and relieve him.

And therefore when I shall see them fallen into a river, and ready to be drowned, I shall make them a fair long sermon, *de contemptu mundi, et fuga seculi;*[60] and when they are stark dead, shall then go to their aid and succour in fishing after them. Be quiet, said Gymnast, and stir not, my minion. I am now coming to unhang thee, and to set thee at freedom, for thou art a pretty little gentle *monachus. Monachus in claustro non valet ova duo; sed quando est extra bene valet triginta.*[61] I have seen above five hundred hanged, but I never saw any have a better countenance in his dangling and pendilatory swagging. Truly, if I had so good a one, I would willingly hang thus all my lifetime. What said the monk, have you almost done preaching? Help me, in the name of God, seeing you will not in the name of the other spirit, or, by the habit which I wear, you shall repent it, *tempore et loco prælibatis.*[62]

Then Gymnast alighted from his horse, and, climbing up the walnut-tree, lifted up the monk with one hand by the gussets of his armour under the arm-pits, and with the other undid his vizor from the stump of the broken branch, which done, he let him fall to the ground and himself after. As soon as the monk was down, he put off all his armour, and threw away one piece after another about the field, and, taking to him again his staff of the cross, remounted up to his horse, which Eudemon had caught in his running away. Then went they on merrily, riding along on the high way.

CHAPTER 43

How the Scouts and Fore-Party of Picrochole were met with by Gargantua, and how the Monk slew Captain Draw-forth and then was taken Prisoner by his Enemies

PICROCHOLE, at the relation of those who had escaped out of the broil and defeat, wherein Tripet was untriped, grew very angry that the devils should have so run upon his men, and held all that night a counsel of war, at which Rashcalf and Touchfaucet concluded his power to be such, that he was able to defeat all the devils of hell, if they should come to jostle with his forces. This Picrochole did not fully believe, though he doubted not much of it. Therefore sent he under the command and conduct of the Count Draw-forth, for discovering of the country, the number of sixteen horsemen, all well mounted upon light horses for skirmish, and thoroughly besprinkled with holy water; and every one for their field-mark or cognizance had the sign of a star in his scarf, to serve at all adventures, in case they should happen to encounter with devils; that by the virtue, as well of that Gregorian water, as of the stoles which they wore, they might make them disappear and vanish.

In this equipage they made an excursion upon the country, till they came near to the Vauguyon, which is the valley of Guyon, and to the Hospital, but could never find any body to speak unto; whereupon they returned a little back, and took occasion to pass above the aforesaid Hospital, to try what intelligence they could come by in those parts. In which resolution riding on, and by chance in a pastoral lodge, or shepherd's cottage near to Coudray, hitting upon the six pilgrims, they carried them way-bound and manacled, as if they had been spies, for all the exclamations, adjurations, and requests that they could make. Being come down from thence towards Sevillé, they were heard by Gargantua, who said then unto those that were with him, Comrades and fellow soldiers, we have here met with an encounter, and they are ten times in number more than we. Shall we charge them or no? What a devil, said the monk, shall we do else? Do you esteem men by their number, rather than by their valour and prowess? With this he cried out, Charge, devils, charge! Which when the enemies heard, they thought certainly that they had been very devils, and therefore even then began all of them to run away as hard as they could drive, Draw-forth only excepted, who immediately settled his lance on its rest, and therewith hit the monk with all his force on the very middle of his breast, but, coming against his horrific frock, the point of the iron, being with the blow either broke off or blunted, it was in matter of execution, as if you had struck against an anvil with a little wax-candle.

Then did the monk, with his staff of the cross, give him such a sturdy thump and whirret betwixt his neck and shoulders, upon the acromion bone, that he made him lose both sense and motion, and fall down stone dead at his horse's feet; and, seeing the sign of the star which he wore scarfwise, he said unto Gargantua, These men are but priests, which is but the beginning of a monk; by St. John, I am a perfect monk, I will kill them to you like flies. Then ran he after them at a swift and full gallop, till he overtook the rear, and felled them down like tree-leaves, striking athwart and along and every way. Gymnast presently asked Gargantua if they should pursue them? To whom Gargantua answered, By no means; for, according to right military discipline, you must never drive your enemy unto despair, for that such a strait doth multiply his force, and increase his courage, which was before broken and cast down; neither is there any better help, or outgate of relief for men that are amazed, out of heart, toiled, and spent, than to hope for no favour at all. How many victories have been taken out of the hands of the victors by the vanquished, when they would not rest satisfied with reason, but attempt to put all to the sword, and totally to destroy their enemies, without leaving so much as one to carry home news of the defeat of his fellows. Open, therefore, unto your enemies all the gates and ways, and make to them a bridge of silver rather than fail, that you may be rid of them. Yea, but, said Gymnast, they have the monk. Have they the monk? said Gargantua. Upon mine honour then it will prove to their cost. But to prevent dangers, let us not yet retreat, but halt here quietly, as in an ambush; for I think I do already understand the policy and judgment of our enemies. They are truly more directed by chance and mere fortune, than by good advice and counsel. In the mean while, whilst these made a stop under the walnut-trees, the monk pursued on the chase, charging all he overtook, and giving

quarter to none, until he met with a trooper, who carried behind him one of the poor pilgrims, and there would have rifled him. The pilgrim, in hope of relief at the sight of the monk, cried out, Ha, my Lord Prior, my good friend, my Lord Prior, save me, I beseech you, save me! Which words being heard by those that rode in the van, they instantly faced about, and seeing there was nobody but the monk that made this great havoc and slaughter among them, they loaded him with blows as thick as they use to do an ass with wood. But of all this he felt nothing, especially when they struck upon his frock, his skin was so hard. Then they committed him to two of the marshal's men to keep, and, looking about, saw nobody coming against them, whereupon they thought that Gargantua and his party were fled. Then was it that they rode as hard as they could towards the walnut-trees to meet with them, and left the monk there all alone, with his two foresaid men to guard him. Gargantua heard the noise and neighing of the horses, and said to his men, Comrades, I hear the track and beating of the enemy's horsefeet, and withal perceive that some of them come in a troop and full body against us. Let us rally and close here, then set forward in order, and by this means we shall be able to receive their charge, to their loss and our honour.

CHAPTER 44

How the Monk rid himself of his Keepers, and how Picrochole's Forlorn Hope was defeated

THE monk, seeing them break off thus without order, conjectured that they were to set upon Gargantua and those that were with him, and was wonderfully grieved that he could not succour them. Then considered he the countenance of the two keepers in whose custody he was, who would have willingly run after the troops to get some booty and plunder, and were always looking towards the valley unto which they were going. Farther, he syllogized, saying, These men are but badly skilled in matters of war, for they have not required my parole, neither have they taken my sword from me. Suddenly hereupon he drew his brackmard or horseman's sword, wherewith he gave the keeper which held him on the right side, such a sound slash, that he cut clean through the jugular veins, and the sphagitid or transparent arteries of the neck, with the fore-part of the throat called the gargareon, even unto the two adenes, which are throat-kernels; and, redoubling the blow, he opened the spinal marrow betwixt the second and third vertebræ. There fell down that keeper stark dead to the ground. Then the monk, reining his horse to the left, ran upon the other, who, seeing his fellow dead, and the monk to have the advantage of him, cried with a loud voice, Ha, my Lord Prior, quarter, I yield, my Lord Prior, quarter, quarter, my good friend, my Lord Prior. And the monk cried likewise, My Lord Posterior, my friend, my Lord Posterior, you shall have it upon your *posteriorums*. Ha, said the keeper, my Lord Prior, my minion, my gentle Lord Prior, I pray God make you an Abbot. By the habit, said the monk, which I wear, I will here make you a Cardinal. What! do you use to pay ransoms to religious men? You shall therefore have by and by a red hat of my giving. And the fellow cried, Ha, my Lord Prior, my Lord Prior, my Lord Abbot that shall be, my Lord Cardinal, my Lord all! Ha, ha, hes, no my Lord Prior, my good little Lord the Prior, I yield, render and deliver myself up to you. And I deliver thee, said the monk, to all the devils in hell. Then at one stroke he cut off his head, cutting his scalp upon the temple-bones, and lifting up in the upper part of the skull the two triangulary bones called sincipital, or the two bones bregmatis, together with the sagittal commissure or dart-like seam which distinguisheth the right side of the head from the left, as also a great part of the coronal or fore-head bone, by which terrible blow likewise he cut the two meninges or films which enwrap the brain, and made a deep wound in the brain's two posterior ventricles, and the cranium or skull abode hanging upon his shoulders by the skin of the pericranium behind, in form of a doctor's bonnet, black without and red within. Thus fell he down also to the ground stark dead.

And presently the monk gave his horse the spur, and kept the way that the enemy held, who had met with Gargantua and his companions in the broad highway, and were so diminished of their number, for the enormous slaughter that Gargantua had made with his great tree amongst them, as also Gymnast, Ponocrates, Eudemon, and the rest, that they began to retreat disorderly and in great haste, as men altogether affrighted and troubled in both sense and understanding; and, as if they had seen the very proper species and form of death before their eyes; or rather, as when you see an ass with a brizze or gadbee under his tail, or fly that stings him, run hither and thither without keeping any path or way, throwing down his load to the ground, breaking his bridle and reins, and taking no breath nor rest, and no man can tell what ails him, for they see not anything touch him. So fled these people destitute of wit, without knowing any cause of flying, only pursued by a panic terror, which in their minds they had conceived. The monk, perceiving that their whole intent was to betake themselves to their heels, alighted from his horse, and got upon a big large rock, which was in the way, and with his great brackmard sword laid such load upon those runaways, and with main strength fetching a compass with his arm without feigning or sparing, slew and overthrew so many, that his sword broke in two pieces. Then thought he within himself that he had slain and killed sufficiently, and that the rest should escape to carry news. Therefore, he took up a battle axe of those that lay there dead, and got upon the rock again, passing his time to see the enemy thus flying, and to tumble himself amongst the dead bodies, only that he suffered none to carry pike, sword, lance, nor gun with him, and those who carried the pilgrims bound he made to alight, and gave their horses unto the said pilgrims, keeping them there with him under the hedge, and also Touchfaucet, who was then his prisoner.

CHAPTER 45

How the Monk carried along with him the Pilgrims, and of the good words that Grangousier gave them

THIS skirmish being ended, Gargantua retreated with his men, excepting the monk, and about the dawning of the day they came unto Grangousier, who in his bed was praying unto God for their safety and victory. And seeing them all safe and sound, he embraced them lovingly, and asked what was become of the monk? Gargantua answered him, that without doubt the enemies had the monk. Then have they mischief and ill luck, said Grangousier, which was very true. Therefore is it a common proverb to this day, to give a man the monk, or as in French, *luy bailler le moyne*, when they would express the doing unto one a mischief. Then commanded he a good breakfast to be provided for their refreshment. When all was ready, they called Gargantua, but he was so aggrieved that the monk was not to be heard of, that he would neither eat nor drink. In the meanwhile, the monk comes, and from the gate of the outer court cries out aloud, Fresh wine, fresh wine, Gymnast my friend! Gymnast went out and saw that it was Friar John, who brought along with him six pilgrims and Touchfaucet prisoners; whereupon Gargantua likewise went forth to meet him, and all of them made him the best welcome that possibly they could, and brought him before Grangousier, who asked him of all his adventures. The monk told him all, both how he was taken, how he rid himself of his keepers, of the slaughter he had made by the way, and how he had rescued the pilgrims, and brought along with him Captain Touchfaucet. Then did they altogether fall to banqueting most merrily. In the meantime Grangousier asked the pilgrims what countrymen they were, whence they came, and whither they went? Sweer-to-go in the name of the rest answered, My sovereign lord, I am of Saint Genou in Berry, this man is of Palau, this other is of Onzay, this of Argy, this of St. Nazarand, and this man of Villebrenin. We come from St. Sebastian near Nantes, and are now returning, as we best may, by easy journeys. Yea, but said Grangousier, what went you to do at Saint Sebastian? We went, said Sweer-to-go, to offer up unto that Sanct our vows against the plague. Ah, poor men, said Grangousier, do you thing that the plague comes from St. Sebastian? Yes, truly, answered Sweer-to-go, our preachers tell us so indeed. But it is so, said Grangousier, do the false prophets teach you such abuses. Do they thus blaspheme the Sancts and holy men of God, as to make them like unto the devils, who do nothing but hurt unto mankind,—as Homer writeth, that the plague was sent into the camp of the Greeks by Apollo, and as the poets feign a great rabble of Vejoves and mischievous gods. So did a certain Cafard or dissembling religionary preach at Sinay, that Saint Antony sent the fire into men's legs, that St. Eutropius made men hydropic, St. Gildas, fools, and that St. Genou made them goutish. But I punished him so exemplarily, though he called me heretic for it, that since that time no such hypocritical rogue durst set his foot within my territories. And truly I wonder that your king should suffer them in their sermons to publish such scandalous doctrine in his dominions; for they deserve to be chastised with greater severity than those who, by magical art, or any other device, have brought the pestilence into a country. The pest killeth but the bodies, but such abominable impostors empoison our very souls. As he spoke these words, in came the monk very resolute, and asked them, whence are you, you poor wretches? Of Saint Genou, said they. And how, said the monk, does the Abbot Gulligut the good drinker, and the monks, what cheer make they? By G— body, they'll have a fling at your wives, and breast them to some purpose, whilst you are upon your roaming rant and gadding pilgrimage. Hin, hen, said Sweer-to-go, I am not afraid of mine, for he that shall see her by day will never break his neck to come to her in the night-time. Yea, marry, said the monk, now you have hit it. Let her be as ugly as ever was Proserpina, she will once, by the Lord G—, be overturned, and get her skin-coat shaken, if there dwell any monks near to her; for a good carpenter will make use of any kind of timber. Let me be peppered with the pox, if you find not all your wives with child at your return; for the very shadow of the steeple of an abbey is fruitful. It is, said Gargantua, like the water of Nilus in Egypt, if you believe Strabo and Pliny, *lib.* 7, *cap.* 3. What virtue will there be, then, said the monk, in their bullets of concupiscence, their habits, and their bodies?

Then said Grangousier, Go your ways poor men, in the name of God the Creator, to whom I pray to guide you perpetually, and henceforward be not so ready to undertake these idle and unprofitable journeys. Look to your families, labour every man in his vocation, instruct your children, and live as the good Apostle St. Paul directeth you: in doing whereof, God, his angels and sancts, will guard and protect you, and no evil or plague at any time shall befal you. Then Gargantua led them into the hall to take their refection; but the pilgrims did nothing but sigh, and said to Gargantua, O how happy is that land which hath such a man for their lord! We have been more edified and instructed by the talk which he had with us, than by all the sermons that ever were preached in our town. This is, said Gargantua, that which Plato saith, *lib.* 5, *De Republ.,* That those commonwealths are happy, whose rulers philosophise, and whose philosophers rule. Then caused he their wallets to be filled with victuals, and their bottles with wine, and gave unto each of them a horse to ease them upon the way, together with some pence to live by.

CHAPTER 46

How Grangousier did very kindly entertain Touchfaucet his Prisoner

TOUCHFAUCET was presented unto Grangousier, and by him examined upon the enterprise and attempt of Picrochole, what it was he could pretend to, or aim at, by the rustling stir and tumultuary coil of this his sudden invasion. Whereunto he answered, that his end and purpose was to conquer all the country, if he could, for the injury done to his cakebakers. It is too great an undertaking, said Grangousier; and, as the proverb is, He that gripes too much, holds fast but little. The time is not now as formerly, to conquer the kingdoms of our neighbour princes, and to build up our own greatness upon the loss of our nearest Christian brother. This imitation of the ancient Herculeses, Alexanders, Hannibals, Scipios, Cæsars, and other such heroes, is quite contrary to the profession of the gospel of Christ, by which we are commanded to preserve, keep, rule, and govern every man his own country and lands, and not in a hostile manner to invade others; and that which heretofore the Barbarians and Saracens called prowess and valour, we now call robbing, thievery, and wickedness. It would have been more commendable in him to have contained himself within the bounds of his own territories, royally governing them, than to insult and domineer in mine, pillaging and plundering every where like a most unmerciful enemy; for, by ruling his own with discretion, he might have increased his greatness, but by robbing me, he cannot escape destruction. Go your ways in the name of God, prosecute good enterprises, show your king what is amiss, and never counsel him with regard unto your own particular profit, for the public loss will swallow up the private benefit. As for your ransom, I do freely remit it to you, and will that your arms and horse be restored to you; so should good neighbours do, and ancient friends, seeing this our difference is not properly war. As Plato, *lib.* 5, *De Repub.* would not have it called war but sedition, when the Greeks took up arms against one another, and that, therefore, when such combustions should arise amongst them, his advice was to behave themselves in the managing of them with all discretion and modesty. Although you call it war, it is but superficial, it entereth not into the closet and inmost cabinet of our hearts. For neither of us hath been wronged in his honour, nor is there any question betwixt us in the main, but only how to redress, by the by, some petty faults, committed by our men,—I mean, both yours and ours, which, although you knew, you ought to let pass; for these quarrelsome persons deserve rather to be contemned than mentioned, especially seeing I offered them satisfaction according to the wrong. God shall be the just judge of our variances, whom I beseech, by death rather to take me out of this life, and to permit my goods to perish and be destroyed before mine eyes, than that by me or mine he should in any sort be wronged. These words uttered, he called the monk, and before them all thus spoke unto him. Friar John, my good friend, is it you that took prisoner the Captain Touchfaucet here present? Sir, said the monk, seeing himself is here, and that he is of the years of discretion, I had rather you should know it by his confession than by any words of mine. Then said Touchfaucet, My sovereign lord, it is he indeed that took me, and I do therefore most freely yield myself his prisoner. Have you put him to any ransom? said Grangousier to the monk. No, said the monk, of that I take no care. How much would you have for having taken him? Nothing, nothing, said the monk, I am not swayed by that, nor do I regard it. Then Grangousier commanded that, in presence of Touchfaucet, should be delivered to the monk for taking him the sum of threescore and two thousand saluts, (in English money, fifteen thousand and five hundred pounds,) which was done, whilst they made a collation or little banquet to the said Touchfaucet, of whom Grangousier asked, If he would stay with him, or if he loved rather to return to his king? Touchfaucet answered, that he was content to take whatever course he would advise him to. Then, said Grangousier, return unto your king, and God be with you.

Then he gave him an excellent sword of a Vienne blade, with a golden scabbard wrought with vine branch-like flourishes, of fair goldsmith's work, and a collar or neckchain of gold, weighing seven hundred and two thousand merks (at eight ounces each), garnished with precious stones of the finest sort, esteemed at a hundred and sixty thousand ducats, and ten thousand crowns more, as an honourable donative by way of present. After this talk Touchfaucet got to his horse, and Gargantua for his safety allowed him the guard of thirty men at arms, and six score archers to attend him under the conduct of Gymnast, to bring him even unto the gate of the rock Clermond, if there were need. As soon as he was gone, the monk restored unto Grangousier the three-score and two thousand saluts, which he had received, saying, Sir, it is not as yet the time for you to give such gifts,—stay till this war be at an end, for none can tell what accidents may occur, and war, begun without good provision of money before-hand for going through with it, is but as a breathing of strength, and blast that will quickly pass away. Coin is the sinews of war. Well then, said Grangousier, at the end I will content you by some honest recompense, as also all those who shall do me good service.

CHAPTER 47

How Grangousier sent for his Legions, and how Touchfaucet slew Rashcalf, and was afterwards executed by the command of Picrochole

ABOUT this same time those of Besse, of the Old Market, of St. James' Bourg, of the Drag-gage, of Parillé, of the Rivers, of the rocks of St. Pol, of the Vaubreton, of Pautillé, of the Brehemont, of Clainbridge, of Cravant, of Grandmont, of the town at the Badgerholes, of Huymes, of Segré, of Husse, of St. Lovant, of Panzoust, of the Coldraux, of Verron, of Coulaines, of Chose, of Varenes, of Bourgueil, of the Bouchard Island, of the Croullay, of Narsay, of Cande, of Montsoreau, and other bordering places, sent ambassadors unto Grangousier, to tell him that they were advised of the great wrongs which Picrochole had done him, and in regard of their ancient confederacy, offered him what assistance they could afford, both in men, money, victuals, and ammunition, and other necessaries for war. The money, which by the joint agreement of them all was sent unto him, amounted to six score and fourteen millions two crowns and a half of pure gold. The forces wherewith they did assist him, did consist of fifteen thousand cuirassiers, two and thirty thousand light horsemen, four score and nine thousand dragoons, and a hundred and forty thousand volunteer adventurers. These had with them eleven thousand and two hundred cannons, double cannons, long pieces of artil-

lery called basilisks, and smaller sized ones, known by the name of spirols, besides the mortar-pieces and granadoes. Of pioneers they had seven and forty thousand, all victualled and paid for six months and four days of advance. Which offer Gargantua did not altogether refuse, nor wholly accept of; but, giving them hearty thanks, said, that he would compose and order the war by such a device, that there should not be found great need to put so many honest men to trouble in the managing of it; and therefore was content at that time to give order only for bringing along the legions, which he maintained in his ordinary garrison towns of the Deviniere, of Chavigny, of Gravot, and of the Quinquenais, amounting to the number of two thousand cuirassiers, three score and six thousand foot soldiers, six and twenty thousand dragoons, attended by two hundred pieces of great ordnance, two and twenty thousand pioneers, and six thousand light horsemen, all drawn up in troops, so well befitted and accommodated with their commissaries, sutlers, farriers, harness-makers, and other such like necessary members in a military camp; so fully instructed in the art of warfare, so perfectly knowing and following their colours, so ready to hear and obey their captains, so nimble to run, so strong at their charging, so prudent in their adventures, and every day so well disciplined, that they seemed rather to be a concert of organ-pipes, or mutual concord of the wheels of a clock, than an infantry and cavalry, or army of soldiers.

Touchfaucet immediately after his return presented himself before Picrochole, and related unto him at large all that he had done and seen, and at last endeavoured to persuade him with strong and forcible arguments to capitulate and make an agreement with Grangousier, whom he found to be the honestest man in the world; saying further, that it was neither right nor reason thus to trouble his neighbours, of whom they never received any thing but good. And in regard of the main point, that they should never be able to go through stitch with that war, but to their great damage and mischief: for the forces of Picrochole were not so considerable, but that Grangousier could easily overthrow them.

He had not well done speaking, when Rashcalf said out aloud, Unhappy is that prince, which is by such men served, who are so easily corrupted, as I know Touchfaucet is. For I see his courage so changed, that he had willingly joined with our enemies to fight against us and betray us, if they would have received him; but, as virtue is of all, both friends and foes, praised and esteemed, so is wickedness soon known and suspected, and although it happen the enemies do make use thereof for their profit, yet have they always the wicked and the traitors in abomination.

Touchfaucet, being at these words very impatient, drew out his sword, and therewith ran Rashcalf through the body, a little under the nipple of his left side, whereof he died presently, and pulling back his sword out of his body, said boldly, So let him perish, that shall a faithful servant blame. Picrochole incontinently grew furious, and seeing Touch-faucet's new sword and his scabbard so richly diapered with flourishes of most excellent workmanship, said, Did they give thee this weapon so feloniously therewith to kill before my face my so good friend Rashcalf? Then immediately commanded he his guard to hew him in pieces, which was instantly done, and that so cruelly, that the chamber was all dyed with blood. Afterwards he appointed the corpse of Rashcalf to be honourably buried, and that of Touchfaucet to be cast over the walls into the ditch.

The news of these excessive violences were quickly spread through all the army; whereupon many began to murmur against Picrochole, in so far that Pinchpenny said to him, My sovereign lord, I know not what the issue of this enterprise will be. I see your men much dejected, and not well resolved in their minds, by considering that we are here very ill provided of victuals, and that our number is already much diminished by three or four sallies. Furthermore, great supplies and recruits come daily in to your enemies: but we so moulder away, that, if we be once besieged, I do not see how we can escape a total destruction. Tush, pish, said Picrochole, you are like the Melun eels, you cry before they come to you. Let them come, let them come, if they dare.

CHAPTER 48

How Gargantua set upon Picrochole within the Rock Clermond and utterly defeated the Army of the said Picrochole

GARGANTUA had the charge of the whole army, and his father Grangousier stayed in his castle, who, encouraging them with good words, promised great rewards unto those that should do any notable service. Having thus set forward, as soon as they had gained the pass at the ford of Vede, with boats and bridges speedily made, they passed over in a trice. Then considering the situation of the town, which was on a high and advantageous place, Gargantua thought fit to call his council and pass that night in deliberation upon what was to be done. But Gymnast said unto him, My sovereign lord, such is the nature and complexion of the French, that they are worth nothing but at the first push. Then they are more fierce than devils. But if they linger a little, and be wearied with delays, they will prove more faint and remiss than women. My opinion is, therefore, that now presently after your men have taken breath, and some small refection, you give order for a resolute assault, and that we storm them instantly. His advice was found very good, and for effectuating thereof he brought forth his army into the plain field, and placed the reserves on the skirt or rising of a little hill. The monk took along with him six companies of foot, and two hundred horsemen well armed, and with great diligence crossed the marsh, and valiantly got upon the top of the green hillock even unto the highway which leads to Loudun. Whilst the assault was thus begun, Picrochole's men could not tell what was best, to issue out and receive the assailants, or keep within the town and not to stir. Himself in the meantime, without deliberation, sallied forth in a rage with the cavalry of his guard, who were forthwith received and royally entertained with great cannon-shot that fell upon them like hail from the high grounds, on which the artillery was planted. For which purpose the Gargantuists betook themselves unto the valleys, to give the ordnance leave to play and range with the larger scope.

Those of the town defended themselves as well as they could, but their shot passed over without doing any hurt at all. Some of Picrochole's men, that had escaped our artillery, set most fiercely upon our soldiers, but prevailed little; for they were all let in betwixt the files, and there knocked down to the ground, which their fellow-soldiers seeing, they would have retreated, but the monk having seized upon the pass, by which they were to return, they run away and fled in all the disorder and confusion that could be imagined.

Some would have pursued after them, and followed the chase, but the monk withheld them, apprehending that in their pursuit the pursuers might lose their ranks, and so give occasion to the besieged to sally out of the town upon them. Then staying there some space, and none coming against him, he sent the Duke Phrontist, to advise Gargantua to advance towards the hill upon the left hand, to hinder Picrochole's retreat at that gate; which Gargantua did with all expedition, and sent thither four brigades under the conduct of Sebast, which had no sooner reached the top of the hill, but they met Picrochole in the teeth, and those that were with him scattered.

Then charged they upon them stoutly, yet were they much damaged by those that were upon the walls, who galled them with all manner of shot, both from the great ordnance, small guns, and bows. Which Gargantua perceiving, he went with a strong party to their relief, and with his artillery began to thunder so terribly upon that canton of the wall, and so long, that all the strength within the town, to maintain and fill up the breach, was drawn thither. The monk, seeing that quarter which he kept besieged void of men and competent guards, and in a manner altogether naked and abandoned, did most magnanimously on a sudden lead up his men towards the fort, and never left it till he had got up upon it, knowing, that such as come to the reserve in a conflict bring with them always more fear and terror, than those that deal about them with their hands in the fight.

Nevertheless he gave no alarm till all his soldiers had got within the wall, except the two hundred horsemen, whom he left without to secure his entry. Then did he give a most horrible shout, so did all those who were with him, and immediately thereafter, without resistance, putting to the edge of the sword the guard that was at that gate, they opened it to the horsemen, with whom most furiously they altogether ran towards the east gate, where all the hurly burly was, and coming close upon them in the rear, overthrew all their forces.

The besieged, seeing that the Gargantuists had won the town upon them, and that they were like to be secure in no corner of it, submitted themselves unto the mercy of the monk, and asked for quarter, which the monk very nobly granted to them, yet made them lay down their arms; then, shutting them up within churches, gave order to seize upon all the staves of the crosses, and placed men at the doors to keep them from coming forth.

Then, opening the east gate, he issued out to succour and assist Gargantua. But Picrochole, thinking it had been some relief coming to him from the town, adventured more forwardly than before, and was upon the giving of a most desperate home-charge, when Gargantua cried out, Ha, Friar John, my friend, Friar John, you are come in a good hour. Which unexpected accident so affrighted Picrochole and his men, that, giving all for lost, they betook themselves to their heels, and fled on all hands. Gargantua chased them till they came near to Vaugaudry, killing and slaying all the way, and then sounded the retreat.

CHAPTER 49

How Picrochole in his flight fell into great misfortunes, and what Gargantua did after the Battle

PICROCHOLE, thus in despair, fled towards the Bouchard Island, and in the way to Riviere his horse stumbled and fell down, whereat he on a sudden was so incensed, that he with his sword without more ado killed him in his choler; then, not finding any that would remount him, he was about to have taken an ass at the mill that was thereby; but the miller's men did so baste his bones, and so soundly bethwack him, that they made him both black and blue with strokes; then, stripping him of all his clothes, gave him a scurvy old canvas jacket wherewith to cover his nakedness. Thus went this poor choleric wretch, who passing the water at Port-Huaux, and relating his misadventurous disasters, was foretold by an old Lourpidon hag, that his kingdom should be restored to him at the coming of the Cocklicranes. What is become of him since we cannot certainly tell, yet was I told that he is now a porter at Lyons, as testy and pettish in humour as ever he was before, and would be always, with great lamentation, inquiring at all strangers of the coming of the Cocklicranes, expecting assuredly, according to the old woman's prophecy, that at their coming he shall be re-established in his kingdom. The first thing Gargantua did after his return into the town was to call the muster-toll of his men, which when he had done he found that there were very few either killed or wounded, only some few foot of Captain Tolmere's company, and Ponocrates, who was shot with a musket-ball through the doublet. Then he caused them all at and in their several posts and divisions to take a little refreshment, which was very plenteously provided for them in the best drink and victuals that could be had for money, and gave order to the treasurers and commissaries of the army, to pay for and defray that repast, and that there should be no outrage at all, nor abuse committed in the town, seeing it was his own. And furthermore commanded, that immediately after the soldiers had done with eating and drinking for that time sufficiently, and to their own hearts' desire, a gathering should be beaten, for bringing them altogether, to be drawn upon the piazza before the castle, there to receive six months' pay completely. All which was done. After this, by his direction, were brought before him in the said place all those that remained of Picrochole's party, unto whom, in the presence of the princes, nobles, and officers of his court and army, he spoke as followeth.

CHAPTER 50

Gargantua's speech to the vanquished

OUR forefathers and ancestors of all times have been of this nature and disposition, that, upon the winning of a battle, they have chosen rather, for a sign and memorial of their triumphs and victories, to erect trophies and monuments in the hearts of the vanquished by clemency, than by architecture in the lands which they had conquered. For they did hold in greater estimation the lively remembrance of men, purchased by liberality, than the dumb inscription of arches, pillars, and pyramids, subject to the injury of storms and tempests, and to the envy of every one. You may very well remember of the courtesy, which by them was used towards the Bretons, in the battle of St. Aubin of Cormier, and at the demolishing of Partenay. You have heard, and hearing admire, their gentle comportment towards those at the barriers of Spaniola, who had plundered, wasted, and ransacked the maritime borders of Olone and Thalmondois. All this hemisphere of the world was filled with the praises and congratulations which yourselves and your fathers made, when Alpharbal King of Canarre, not satisfied with his own fortunes, did most furiously invade the land of Onyx, and with cruel piracies molest all the Armorick Islands, and confine regions of Brittany. Yet was he in a set naval fight justly taken and vanquished by my father, whom God preserve and pro-

tect. But what? Whereas other kings and emperors, yea those who entitle themselves catholics, would have dealt roughly with him, kept him a close prisoner, and put him to an extreme high ransom, he entreated him very courteously, lodged him kindly with himself in his own palace, and out of his incredible mildness and gentle disposition sent him back with a safe conduct, laden with gifts, laden with favours, laden with all offices of friendship. What fell out upon it? Being returned into his country, he called a parliament, where all the princes and states of his kingdom being assembled, he showed them the humanity which he had found in us, and therefore wished them to take such course by way of compensation therein, as that the whole world might be edified by the example, as well of their honest graciousness to us, as of our gracious honesty towards them. The result hereof was, that it was voted and decreed by an unanimous consent, that they should offer up entirely their lands, dominions, and kingdoms, to be disposed of by us according to our pleasure.

Alpharbal in his own person presently returned with nine thousand and thirty-eight great ships of burden, bringing with him the treasures, not only of his house and royal lineage, but almost of all the country besides. For he embarking himself to set sail with a west-north-east wind, every one in heaps did cast into the ship gold, silver, rings, jewels, spices, drugs, and aromatical perfumes, parrots, pelicans, monkeys, civet-cats, black-spotted weasels, porcupines, &c. He was accounted no good mother's son, that did not cast in all the rare and precious things he had.

Being safely arrived, he came to my said father, and would have kissed his feet. That action was found too submissively low, and therefore was not permitted, but in exchange he was most cordially embraced. He offered his presents; they were not received, because they were too excessive: he yielded himself voluntarily a servant and vassal, and was content his whole posterity should be liable to the same bondage; this was not accepted of, because it seemed not equitable: he surrendered, by virtue of the decree of his great parliamentary council, his whole countries and kingdoms to him, offering the deed and conveyance, signed, sealed, and ratified, by those that were concerned in it; this was altogether refused, and the parchments cast into the fire. In end, this free good will and simple

meaning of the Canarrines wrought such ten-
derness in my father's heart, that he could not
abstain from shedding tears, and wept, most
profusely; then, by choice words very congruously adapted, strove in what he could to
diminish the estimation of the good offices
which he had done them, saying, that any
courtesy he had conferred upon them was not
worth a rush, and what favour soever he had
showed them, he was bound to do it. But so
much the more did Alpharbal augment the
repute thereof. What was the issue? Whereas
for his ransom in the greatest extremity of rigour, and most tyrannical dealing, could not
have been exacted above twenty times a hundred thousand crowns, and his eldest sons
detained as hostages, till that sum had been
paid, they made themselves perpetual tributaries, and obliged to give us every year two
millions of gold at four and twenty carats
fine. The first year we received the whole
sum of two millions; the second year of their
own accord they paid freely to us three and
twenty hundred thousand crowns; the third
year, six and twenty hundred thousand; the
fourth year, three millions, and do so increase
it always out of their own good will, that we
shall be constrained to forbid them to bring
us any more. This is the nature of gratitude
and true thankfulness. For time, which
gnaws and diminisheth all things else, aug-
ments and increaseth benefits; because a noble action of liberality, done to a man of reason, doth grow continually, by his generous
thinking of it, and remembering it.

Being unwilling therefore any way to degenerate from the hereditary mildness and
clemency of my parents, I do now forgive
you, deliver you from all fines and imprison-
ments, fully release you, set you at liberty,
and every way make you as frank and free as
ever you were before. Moreover, at your going out of the gate, you shall have every one
of you three months' pay to bring you home
into your houses and families, and shall have
a safe convoy of six hundred cuirassiers and
eight thousand foot under the conduct of Alexander, esquire of my body, that the club-
men of the country may not do you any injury. God be with you! I am sorry from my
heart that Picrochole is not here; for I would
have given him to understand that this war
was undertaken against my will, and without
any hope to increase either my goods or renown. But seeing he is lost, and that no man
can tell where, nor how he went away, it is

my will that this kingdom remain entire to
his son; who, because he is too young, he not
being yet full five years old, shall be brought
up and instructed by the ancient princes, and
learned men of the kingdom. And because a
realm, thus desolate, may easily come to ruin,
if the covetousness and avarice of those, who
by their places are obliged to administer justice in it, be not curbed and restrained, I or-
dain and will have it so, that Ponocrates be
overseer and superintendent above all his
governors, with whatever power and authority is requisite thereto, and that he be continually with the child, until he find him able
and capable to rule and govern by himself.

Now I must tell you, that you are to understand how a too feeble and dissolute facility
in pardoning evil-doers giveth them occasion
to commit wickedness afterwards more readily, upon this pernicious confidence of receiving favour. I consider, that Moses, the meek-
est man that was in his time upon the earth,
did severely punish the mutinous and seditious people of Israel. I consider likewise, that
Julius Cæsar, who was so gracious an emper-
or, that Cicero said of him, that his fortune
had nothing more excellent than that he
could, and his virtue nothing better, than that
he would always save and pardon every man;
he, notwithstanding all this, did in certain
places most rigorously punish the authors of
rebellion. After the example of these good
men, it is my will and pleasure, that you deliver over unto me, before you depart hence,
first, that fine fellow Marquet, who was the
prime cause, origin, and ground-work of this
war, by his vain presumption and overweening: secondly, his fellow cake-bakers, who
were neglective in checking and reprehend-
ing his idle hair-brained humour in the instant time: and lastly, all the counsellors, captains, officers, and domestics of Picrochole
who have been incendiaries or fomenters of
the war, by provoking, praising, or counsel-
ling him to come out of his limits thus to
trouble us.

CHAPTER 51

*How the victorious Gargantuists were recom-
pensed after the Battle*

WHEN Gargantua had finished his speech,
the seditious men whom he required were delivered up unto him, except Swashbuckler,
Durtaille, and Smalltrash, who ran away six
hours before the battle,—one of them as far as

to Lainielneck at one course, another to the valley of Vire, and the third even unto Logroine, without looking back, or taking breath by the way,—and two of the cake-bakers who were slain in the fight. Gargantua did them no other hurt, but that he appointed them to pull at the presses of his printing-house, which he had newly set up. Then those who died there he caused to be honourably buried in Blacksoille-valley, and Burnhag-field, and gave order that the wounded should be dressed and had care of in his great hospital or *Nosocome*. After this, considering the great prejudice done to the town and its inhabitants, he reimbursed their charges, and repaired all the losses that by their confession upon oath could appear they had sustained; and, for their better defence and security in times coming against all sudden uproars and invasions, commanded a strong citadel to be built there with a competent garrison to maintain it. At his departure he did very graciously thank all the soldiers of the brigades that had been at this overthrow, and sent them back to their winter-quarters in their several stations, and garrisons; the decumane legion only excepted, whom in the field on that day he saw do some great exploit, and their captains also, whom he brought along with himself unto Grangousier.

At the sight and coming of them, the good man was so joyful, that it is not possible fully to describe it. He made them a feast the most magnificent, plentiful, and delicious that ever was seen since the time of the King Ashuerus. At the taking up of the table he distributed amongst them his whole cupboard of plate, which weighed eight hundred thousand and fourteen besants of gold, in great antique vessels, huge pots, large basins, big tasses, cups, goblets, candlesticks, comfit-boxes and other such plate, all of pure massy gold besides the precious stones, enamelling, and workmanship, which by all men's estimation was more worth than the matter of the gold. Then unto every one of them out of his coffers caused he to be given the sum of twelve hundred thousand crowns ready money. And, further, he gave to each of them for ever and in perpetuity, unless he should happen to decease without heirs, such castles and neighbouring lands of his as were most commodious for them. To Ponocrates he gave the rock Clermond; to Gymnast the Coudray; to Eudemon, Monpensier; Rivau, to Tolmere; to Ithibolle, Montsaureau; to Acamas, Cande; Varenes, to Chironacte; Gravot, to Sebaste; Quinquenais, to Alexander; Ligre, to Sophrone, and so of his other places.

CHAPTER 52

How Gargantua caused to be built for the Monk the Abbey of Theleme

THERE was left only the monk to provide for, whom Gargantua would have made Abbot of Sevillé, but he refused it. He would have given him the Abbey of Bourgueil, or of Sanct Florent, which was better, or both, if it pleased him; but the monk gave him a very peremptory answer, that he would never take upon him the charge nor government of monks. For how shall I be able, said he, to rule over others, that have not full power and command of myself? If you think I have done you, or may hereafter do you any acceptable service, give me leave to found an abbey after my own mind and fancy. The motion pleased Gargantua very well, who thereupon offered him all the country of Theleme by the River of Loire, till within two leagues of the great forest of Port-Huaut. The monk then requested Gargantua to institute his religious order contrary to all others. First then, said Gargantua, you must not build a wall about your convent, for all other abbeys are strongly walled and mured about. See, said the monk, and not without cause, where there is *mur* before, and *mur* behind, there is store of murmur, envy, and mutual conspiracy. Moreover, seeing there are certain convents in the world, whereof the custom is, if any women come in, I mean chaste and honest women, they immediately sweep the ground which they have trod upon; therefore was it ordained, that if any man or woman, entered into religious orders, should by chance come within this new abbey, all the rooms should be thoroughly washed and cleansed through which they had passed. And because in all other monasteries and nunneries all is compassed, limited, and regulated by hours, it was decreed that in this new structure there should be neither clock nor dial, but that according to the opportunities and incident occasions, all their hours should be disposed of; for, said Gargantua, the greatest loss of time that I know, is to count the hours. What good comes of it? Nor can there be any greater dotage in the world than for one to guide and direct his courses by the sound of a bell, and not by his own judgment and discretion.

Item, Because at that time they put no women into nunneries, but such as were either purblind, blinkards, lame, crooked, ill-favoured, mis-shapen, fools, senseless, spoiled, or corrupt; nor encloistered any men, but those that were either sickly, subject to defluxions, ill-bred louts, simple sots, or peevish trouble-houses. But to the purpose, said the monk. A woman that is neither fair nor good, to what use serves she? To make a nun of, said Gargantua. Yea, said the monk, to make shirts and smocks. Therefore was it ordained, that into this religious order should be admitted no women that were not fair, well-featured, and of a sweet disposition; nor men that were not comely, personable, and well conditioned.

Item, Because in the convents of women, men come not but underhand, privily, and by stealth; it was therefore enacted, that in this house there shall be no women in case there be not men, nor men in case there be not women.

Item, Because both men and women, that are received into religious orders after the expiring of their noviciat or probation year, were constrained and forced perpetually to stay there all the days of their life; it was therefore ordered, that all whatever, men or women, admitted within this abbey, should have full leave to depart with peace and contentment, whensoever it should seem good to them so to do.

Item, for that the religious men and women did ordinarily make three vows, to wit, those of chastity, poverty, and obedience; it was therefore constituted and appointed, that in this convent they might be honourably married, that they might be rich, and live at liberty. In regard of the legitimate time of the persons to be initiated, and years under and above which they were not capable of reception, the women were to be admitted from ten till fifteen, and the men from twelve till eighteen.

CHAPTER 53

How the Abbey of the Thelemites was built and endowed

FOR the fabric and furniture of the abbey, Gargantua caused to be delivered out in ready money seven and twenty hundred thousand, eight hundred and one and thirty of those golden rams of Berry, which have a sheet stamped on the one side, and a flow-ered cross on the other; and for every year until the whole work were completed, he allotted threescore nine thousand crowns of the sun, and as many of the seven stars, to be charged all upon the receipt of the custom. For the foundation and maintenance thereof for ever, he settled a perpetual fee-farm-rent of three and twenty hundred, threescore and nine thousand, five hundred and fourteen rose nobles, exempted from all homage, fealty, service, or burden whatsoever, and payable every year at the gate of the abbey; and of this, by letters patent passed a very good grant. The architecture was in a figure hexagonal, and in such a fashion, that in every one of the six corners there was built a great round tower of threescore feet in diameter, and were all of a like form and bigness. Upon the north-side ran along the river of Loire, on the bank whereof was situated the tower called Arctic. Going towards the east, there was another called Calaer,—the next following Anatole,—the next Mesembrine,—the next Hesperia, and the last Criere. Every tower was distant from the other the space of three hundred and twelve paces. The whole edifice was every where six stories high, reckoning the cellars under ground for one. The second was arched after the fashion of a basket-handle, the rest were sealed with pure wainscot, flourished with Flanders fret-work, in the form of the foot of a lamp, and covered above with fine slates, with an indorsement of lead, carrying the antique figures of little puppets, and animals of all sorts, notably well suited to one another, and gilt, together with the gutters, which jetting without the walls from betwixt the cross bars in a diagonal figure, painted with gold and azure, reached to the very ground, where they ended into great conduit-pipes, which carried all away unto the river from under the house.

This same building was a hundred times more sumptuous and magnificent than ever was Bonnivet, Chambourg, or Chantilly; for there were in it nine thousand three hundred and two and thirty chambers, every one whereof had a withdrawing room, a handsome closet, a wardrobe, an oratory, and neat passage, leading into a great and spacious hall. Between every tower, in the midst of the said body of building, there was a pair of winding, such as we now call lanthorn stairs, whereof the steps were part of porphyry, which is a dark red marble, spotted with white, part of Numidian stone, which is a kind of yellowishly-streaked marble upon various colours, and part of serpentine marble, with light spots on a dark green ground, each of those steps being two and twenty feet in length, and three fingers thick, and the just number of twelve betwixt every rest, or, as we now term it, landing place. In every resting place were two fair antique arches where the light came in: and by those they went into a cabinet, made even with, and of the breadth of the said winding, and the re-ascending above the roofs of the house ending conically in a pavilion. By that vize or winding, they entered on every side into a great hall, and from the halls into the chambers. From the Arctic tower unto the Criere, were the fair great libraries in Greek, Latin, Hebrew, French, Italian and Spanish, respectively distributed in their several cantons, according to the diversity of these languages. In the midst there was a wonderful scalier or winding-stair, the entry whereof was without the house, in a vault or arch, six fathoms broad. It was made in such symmetry and largeness, that six men at arms with their lances in their rests might together in a breast ride all up to the very top of all the palace. From the tower Anatole to the Mesembrine were fair spacious galleries, all covered over and painted with the ancient prowesses, histories and descriptions of the world. In the midst thereof there was likewise such another ascent and gate, as we said there was on the river-side. Upon that gate was written in great antique letters that which followeth.

CHAPTER 54

The Inscription set upon the great Gate of Theleme

HERE enter not vile bigots, hypocrites,
Externally devoted apes, base snites,
Puft up, wry-necked beasts, worse than the Huns,
Or Ostrogots, forerunners of baboons:
Cursed snakes, dissembling varlets, seeming sancts,
Slipshop caffards, beggars pretending wants,
Fat chuffcats, smell-feast knockers, doltish gulls,
Out-strouting cluster-fists, contentious bulls,
Fomenters of divisions and debates,
Elsewhere, not here, make sale of your deceits.
Your filthy trumperies

Stuffed with pernicious lies,
(Not worth a bubble)
Would only trouble
Our earthly paradise,
Your filthy trumperies.

Here enter not attorneys, barristers,
Nor bridle-champing law-practitioners;
Clerks, commissaries, scribes, nor pharisees,
Wilful disturbers of the people's ease:
Judges, destroyers, with an unjust breath,
Of honest men, like dogs, ev'n unto death.
Your salary is at the gibbet-foot:
Go drink there! for we do not here fly out
On those excessive courses, which may draw
A waiting on your courts by suits in law.
Law-suits, debates, and wrangling
Hence are exil'd, and jangling.
Here we are very
Frolic and merry,
And free from all entangling,
Law-suits, debates, and wrangling.

Here enter not base pinching usurers,
Pelf-lickers, everlasting gatherers.
Gold-graspers, coin-grippers, gulpers of mists,
With harpy-griping claws, who, though your chests
Vast sums of money should to you afford,
Would ne'ertheless add more unto that hoard,
And yet not be content,—you clunchfists dastards,
Insatiable fiends, and Pluto's bastards,
Greedy devourers, chichy sneakbill rogues,
Hell-mastiffs gnaw your bones, you rav'nous dogs.
You beastly-looking fellows,
Reason doth plainly tell us,
That we should not
To you allot
Room here, but at the gallows,
You beastly-looking fellows.

Here enter not fond makers of demurs
In love adventures, peevish jealous curs,
Sad pensive dotards, raisers of garboyles,
Hags, goblins, ghosts, firebrands of household broils,
Nor drunkards, liars, cowards, cheaters, clowns,
Thieves, cannibals, faces o'ercast with frowns,
Nor lazy slugs, envious, covetous,
Nor blockish, cruel, nor too credulous,—
Here mangy, pocky folks shall have no place,

No ugly lusks, nor persons of disgrace.
  Grace, honour, praise, delight,
  Here sojourn day and night.
    Sound bodies lin'd
    With a good mind,
  Do here pursue with might
  Grace, honour, praise, delight.

Here enter you, and welcome from our
  hearts,
All noble sparks, endow'd with gallant parts.
This is the glorious place, which bravely shall
Afford wherewith to entertain you all.
Were you a thousand, here you shall not
  want
For any thing: for what you'll ask we'll grant.
Stay here you lively, jovial, handsome, brisk,
Gay, witty, frolic, cheerful, merry, frisk,
Spruce, jocund, courteous, furtherers of
  trades,
And in a word, all worthy, gentle blades.
    Blades of heroic breasts
    Shall taste here of the feasts,
      Both privily
      And civilly
    Of the celestial guests,
    Blades of heroic breasts.

Here enter you, pure, honest, faithful, true,
Expounders of the Scriptures old and new.
Whose glosses do not blind our reason, but
Make it to see the clearer, and who shut
Its passages from hatred, avarice,
Pride, factions, covenants, and all sort of vice.
Come, settle here a charitable faith,
Which neighbourly affection nourisheth.
And whose light chaseth all corrupters hence,
Of the blest word, from the aforesaid sense.
    The Holy Sacred Word,
    May it always afford
      T' us all in common,
      Both man and woman,
    A spiritual shield and sword,
    The Holy Sacred Word.

Here enter you all ladies of high birth,
Delicious, stately, charming, full of mirth,
Ingenious, lovely, miniard, proper, fair,
Magnetic, graceful, splendid, pleasant, rare,
Obliging, sprightly, virtuous, young,
  solacious,
Kind, neat, quick, feat, bright, compt, ripe,
  choice, dear, precious.
Alluring, courtly, comely, fine, complete.
Wise, personable, ravishing, and sweet,
Come joys enjoy. The Lord celestial

Hath given enough, wherewith to please us
all.
    Gold give us, God forgive us,
    And from all woes relieve us;
      That we the treasure
      May reap of pleasure,
    And shun whate'er is grievous,
    Gold give us, God forgive us.

CHAPTER 55

What manner of dwelling the Thelemites had

IN the middle of the lower court there was a stately fountain of fair alabaster. Upon the top thereof stood the three Graces, with their cornucopias, or horns of abundance, and did jet out the water at their breasts, mouth, ears, eyes, and other open passages of the body. The inside of the buildings in this lower court stood upon great pillars of Cassydony stone, and Porphyry marble, made archwise after a goodly antique fashion. Within those were spacious galleries, long and large, adorned with curious pictures, the horns of bucks and unicorns; with rhinoceroses, water-horses, called hippopotames; the teeth and tusks of elephants, and other things well worth the beholding. The lodging of the ladies, for so we may call those gallant women, took up all from the tower Arctic unto the gate Mesembrine. The men possessed the rest. Before the said lodging of the ladies, that they might have their recreation, between the two first towers, on the outside, were placed the tilt-yard, the barriers or lists for tournaments, the hippodrome or riding court, the theatre or public play-house, and natatory or place to swim in, with most admirable baths in three stages, situated above one another, well furnished with all necessary accommodation, and store of myrtle-water. By the river-side was the fair garden of pleasure, and in the midst of that the glorious labyrinth. Between the two other towers were the courts for the tennis and the baloon. Towards the tower Criere stood the orchard full of all fruit-trees, set and ranged in a quincuncial order. At the end of that was the great park, abounding with all sort of venison. Betwixt the third couple of towers were the butts and marks for shooting with a snap-work gun, an ordinary bow for common archery, or with a cross bow. The office-houses were without the tower Hesperia, of one story high. The stables were beyond the offices, and before them stood the falconry, managed by ostrich-keepers and falconers, very expert in the art, and it was yearly supplied and furnished by the Candians, Venetians, Sarmates, now called Moscoviters, with all sorts of most excellent hawks, eagles, gerfalcons, goshawks, sacres, lanners, falcons, sparhawks, merlins, and other kinds of them, so gentle and perfectly well manned, that, flying of themselves sometimes from the castle for their own disport, they would not fail to catch whatever they encountered. The venery, where the beagles and hounds were kept, was a little farther off, drawing towards the park.

All the halls, chambers, and closets or cabinets were richly hung with tapestry, and hangings of divers sorts, according to the variety of the seasons of the year. All the pavements and floors were covered with green cloth. The beds were all embroidered. In every back-chamber or withdrawing room there was a looking-glass of pure crystal set in a frame of fine gold, garnished all about with pearls, and was of such greatness, that it would represent to the full the whole lineaments and proportion of the person that stood before it. At the going out of the halls, which belong to the ladies' lodgings, were the perfumers and trimmers, through whose hands the gallants past when they were to visit the ladies. Those sweet artificers did every morning furnish the ladies' chambers with the spirit of roses, orange-flower-water, and angelica; and to each of them gave a little precious casket vapouring forth the most odoriferous exhalations of the choicest aromatical scents.

CHAPTER 56

How the Men and Women of the religious order of Theleme were apparelled

THE ladies of the foundation of this order were apparelled after their own pleasure and liking. But, since that of their own accord and free will they have reformed themselves, their accoutrement is in manner as followeth. They wore stockings of scarlet crimson, or ingrained purple dye, which reached just three inches above the knee, having a list beautified with exquisite embroideries, and rare incisions of the cutter's art. Their garters were of the colour of their bracelets, and circled the knee a little both over and under. Their shoes, pumps and slippers were either of red, violet, or crimson velvet, pinked and jagged like lobster wadles.

Next to their smock they put on the pretty kirtle or vasquin of pure silk camblet: above that went the taffaty or tabby vardingale, of white, red, tawny grey, or of any other colour. Above this taffaty petticoat they had another of cloth of tissue, or brocade, embroidered with fine gold, and interlaced with needlework, or as they thought good, and according to the temperature and disposition of the weather, had their upper coats of satin, damask, or velvet, and those either orange, tawny, green, ash-coloured, blue, yellow, bright red, crimson, or white, and so forth; or had them of cloth of gold, cloth of silver, or some other choice stuff, enriched with purple, or embroidered according to the dignity of the festival days and times wherein they wore them.

Their gowns being still correspondent to the season, were either of cloth of gold frizzled with a silver-raised work; of red satin, covered with gold purl; of tabby, or taffaty, white, blue, black, tawny, &c., of silk serge, silk camblet, velvet, cloth of silver, silver tissue, cloth of gold, gold wire, figured velvet, or figured satin, tinselled and overcast with golden threads, in divers variously purfled draughts.

In the summer, some days, instead of gowns, they wore light handsome mantles, made either of the stuff of the aforesaid attire, or like Moresco rugs, of violet velvet frizzled, with a raised work of gold upon silver purl, or with a knotted cordwork, of gold embroidery, every where garnished with little Indian pearls. They always carried a fair panache, or plume of feathers, of the colour of their muff, bravely adorned and tricked out with glistering spangles of gold. In the winter time, they had their taffaty gowns of all colours, as above named, and those lined with the rich furrings of hind-wolves, or speckled linxes, black spotted weasels, martlet skins of Calabria, sables, and other costly furs of an inestimable value. Their beads, rings, bracelets, collars, carcanets, and neck-chains were all of precious stones, such as carbuncles, rubies, baleus, diamonds, sapphires, emeralds, turquoises, garnets, agates, beryles, and excellent margarites. Their head-dressing also varied with the season of the year, according to which they decked themselves. In winter it was of the French fashion; in the spring, of the Spanish; in summer, of the fashion of Tuscany, except only upon the holy days and Sundays, at which times they were accoutred in the French mode, because they accounted it more honourable, and better befitting the garb of a matronal pudicity.

The men were apparelled after their fashion. Their stockings were of tamine or of cloth-serge, of white, black, scarlet, or some other ingrained colour. Their breeches were of velvet, of the same colour with their stockings, or very near, embroidered and cut according to their fancy. Their doublet was of cloth of gold, of cloth of silver, of velvet, satin, damask, taffaties, &c., of the same colours, cut, embroidered, and suitably trimmed up in perfection. The points were of silk of the same colours, the tags were of gold well enamelled. Their coats and jerkins were of cloth of gold, cloth of silver, gold, tissue or velvet embroidered, as they thought fit. Their gowns were every whit as costly as those of the ladies. Their girdles were of silk, of the colour of their doublets. Every one had a gallant sword by his side, the hilt and handle whereof were gilt, and the scabbard of velvet, of the colour of his breeches, with a chape of gold, and pure goldsmith's work. The dagger of the same. Their caps or bonnets were of black velvet, adorned with jewels and buttons of gold. Upon that they wore a white plume most prettily and minion-like parted by so many rows of gold spangles, at the end whereof hung dangling in a more sparkling resplendency fair rubies, emeralds, diamonds, &c., but there was such a sympathy betwixt the gallants and the ladies, that every day they were apparelled in the same livery. And that they might not miss, there were certain gentlemen appointed to tell the youths every morning what vestments the ladies would on that day wear; for all was done according to the pleasure of the ladies. In these so handsome clothes, and habiliments so rich, think not that either one or other of either sex did waste any time at all; for the masters of the wardrobes had all their raiments and apparel so ready for every morning, and the chamber-ladies were so well skilled, that in a trice they would be dressed, and completely in their clothes from head to foot. And, to have those accoutrements with the more conveniency, there was about the wood of Theleme a row of houses of the extent of half a league, very neat and cleanly, wherein dwelt the goldsmiths, lapidaries, jewellers, embroiderers, tailors, gold-drawers, velvet-weavers, tapestry-makers, and upholsterers, who wrought there every one in his own trade, and all for the aforesaid jolly friars and nuns of the new stamp. They were furnished with matter and stuff from the hands of the Lord Nausiclete, who every year brought them seven ships from the Perlas and Cannibal Islands, laden with ingots of gold, with raw silk, with pearls and precious stones. And if any margarites, called unions [pearls], began to grow old, and lose somewhat of their natural whiteness and lustre, those by their art they did renew, by tendering them to eat to some pretty cocks, as they use to give casting unto hawks.

CHAPTER 57

How the Thelemites were governed, and of their manner of living

ALL their life was spent not in laws, statutes, or rules, but according to their own free will and pleasure. They rose out of their beds when they thought good: they did eat, drink, labour, sleep, when they had a mind to it, and were disposed for it. None did awake them, none did offer to constrain them to eat, drink, nor to do any other thing; for so had Gargantua established it. In all their rule, and strictest tie of their order, there was but this one clause to be observed.

DO WHAT THOU WILT.

Because men that are free, well-born, well-bred, and conversant in honest companies, have naturally an instinct and spur that prompteth them unto virtuous actions, and withdraws them from vice, which is called honour. Those same men, when by base subjection and constraint they are brought under and kept down, turn aside from that noble disposition, by which they formerly were inclined to virtue, to shake off and break that bond of servitude, wherein they are so tyrannously enslaved; for it is agreeable with the nature of man to long after things forbidden, and to desire what is denied us.

By this liberty they entered into a very laudable emulation, to do all of them what they saw did please one. If any of the gallants or ladies should say, Let us drink, they would all drink. If any one of them said, Let us play, they all played. If one said, Let us go a walking into the fields, they went all. If it were to go a hawking or a hunting, the ladies mounted upon dainty well-paced nags, seated in a stately palfrey saddle, carried on their lovely fists, miniardly begloved every one of them, either a sparhawk, or a laneret, or a merlin, and the young gallants carried the other kinds of hawks. So nobly were they taught, that there was neither he nor she amongst them, but could read, write, sing, play upon several musical instruments, speak five or six several languages, and compose in them all very quaintly, both in verse and prose. Never were seen so valiant knights, so noble and worthy, so dexterous and skilful both on foot and a horseback, more brisk and lively, more nimble and quick, or better handling all manner of weapons than were there. Never were seen ladies so proper and handsome, so miniard and dainty, less forward, or more ready with their hand, and with their needle, in every honest and free action belonging to that sex, than were there. For this reason, when the time came, that any man of the said abbey, either at the request of his parents, or for some other cause, had a mind to go out of it, he carried along with him one of the ladies, namely her whom he had before that chosen for his mistress, and they were married together. And if they had formerly in Theleme lived in good devotion and amity, they did continue therein and increase it to a greater height in their state of matrimony: and did entertain that mutual love till the very last day of their life, in no less vigour and fervency, than at the very day of their wedding.

Here must not I forget to set down unto you a riddle, which was found under the ground, as they were laying the foundation of the abbey, engraven in a copper plate, and it was thus as followeth.

CHAPTER 58

A Prophetical Riddle

Poor mortals, who wait for a happy day,
Cheer up your hearts, and hear what I shall say;
If it be lawful firmly to believe,
That the celestial bodies can us give
Wisdom to judge of things that are not yet;
Or if from heaven such wisdom we may get,
As may with confidence make us discourse
Of years to come, their destiny and course;
I to my hearers give to understand,
That this next winter, though it be at hand,
Yea and before, there shall appear a race
Of men, who, loth to sit still in one place,
Shall boldly go before all people's eyes,
Suborning men of divers qualities,
To draw them unto covenants and sides,

In such a manner, that whate'er betides,
They'll move you, if you give them ear, no doubt,
With both your friends and kindred to fall out.
They'll make a vassal to gain-stand his lord,
And children their own parents; in a word,
All reverence shall then be banished,
No true respect to other shall be had.
They'll say that every man should have his turn,
Both in his going forth, and his return;
And hereupon there shall arise such woes,
Such jarrings, and confused to's and fro's,
That never was in history such coils
Set down as yet, such tumults and garboyles.
Then shall you many gallant men see by
Valour stirr'd up, and youthful fervency,
Who, trusting too much in their hopeful time,
Live but a while, and perish in their prime.
Neither shall any, who this course shall run,
Leave off the race which he hath once begun,
Till they the heavens with noise by their contention
Have fill'd, and with their steps the earth's dimension.
Then those shall have no less authority,
That have no faith, than those that will not lie;
For all shall be governed by a rude,
Base, ignorant, and foolish multitude;
The veriest lout of all shall be their judge,
A horrible and dangerous deluge!
Deluge I call it, and that for good reason,
For this shall be omitted in no season;
Nor shall the earth of this foul stir be free,
Till suddenly you in great store shall see
The waters issue out, with whose streams the
Most moderate of all shall moisten'd be,
And justly too; because they did not spare
The flocks of beasts that innocentest are,
But did their sinews, and their bowels take,
Not to the gods a sacrifice to make,
But usually to serve themselves for sport:
And now consider, I do you exhort,
In such commotions so continual,
What rest can take the globe terrestrial?
Most happy then are they, that can it hold,
And use it carefully as precious gold,
By keeping it in goal, whence it shall have
No help but him, who being to it gave.
And to increase his mournful accident,
The sun, before it set in th' occident,
Shall cease to dart upon it any light,
More than in an eclipse, or in the night,—
So that at once its favour shall be gone

And liberty with it be left alone.
And yet, before it come to ruin thus,
Its quaking shall be as impetuous
As Ætna's was, when Titan's sons lay under,
And yield, when lost, a fearful sound like
   thunder.
Inarimé did not more quickly move,
When Typheus did the vast huge hills
   remove,
And for despite into the sea them threw.
   Thus shall it then be lost by ways not few,
And changed suddenly, when those that have
   it
To other men that after come shall leave it.
Then shall it be high time to cease from this
So long, so great, so tedious exercise;
For the great waters told you now by me,
Will make each think where his retreat shall
   be;
And yet, before that they be clean dispers't,
You may behold in th' air, where nought was
   erst.
The burning heat of a great flame to rise,
Lick up the water, and the enterprise.
   It resteth after those things to declare,
That those shall sit content, who chosen are,
With all good things, and with celestial
   manne,
And richly recompensed every man:
The others at the last all stripp'd shall be,
That after this great work all men may see
How each shall have his due. This is their lot;
O he is worthy praise that shrinketh not.

No sooner was this enigmatical monument read over, but Gargantua, fetching a very deep sigh, said unto those that stood by, It is not now only, I perceive, that people called to the faith of the gospel, and convinced with the certainty of evangelical truths, are persecuted. But happy is that man that shall not be scandalized, but shall always continue to the end, in aiming at that mark, which God by his dear Son hath set before us, without being distracted or diverted, by his carnal affections and depraved nature.

The monk then said, What do you think in your conscience is meant and signified by this riddle? What? said Gargantua,—the progress and carrying on of the divine truth. By St. Goderan, said the monk, that is not my exposition. It is the style of the prophet Merlin. Make upon it as many grave allegories and glosses as you will, and dote upon it you and the rest of the world as long as you please: for my part, I can conceive no other meaning in it, but a description of a set at tennis in dark and obscure terms. The suborners of men are the makers of matches, which are commonly friends. After the two chases are made, he that was in the upper end of the tennis-court goeth out, and the other cometh in. They believe the first, that saith the ball was over or under the line. The waters are the heats that the players take till they sweat again. The cords of the rackets are made of the guts of sheep or goats. The globe terrestrial is the tennis-ball. After playing, when the game is done, they refresh themselves before a clear fire, and change their shirts; and very willingly they make all good cheer, but most merrily those that have gained. And so, farewell.

BOOK TWO

PANTAGRUEL, KING OF THE DIPSODES, WITH HIS HEROIC ACTS AND PROWESSES, COMPOSED BY M. ALCOFRIBAS

THE AUTHOR'S PROLOGUE

MOST illustrious and thrice valorous champions, gentlemen, and others, who willingly apply your minds to the entertainment of pretty conceits, and honest harmless knacks of wit; you have not long ago seen, read, and understood the great and inestimable Chronicle of the huge and mighty giant Gargantua, and, like upright faithfullists, have firmly believed all to be true that is contained in them, and have very often passed your time with them amongst honourable ladies and gentlewomen, telling them fair long stories, when you were out of all other talk, for which you are worthy of great praise and sempiternal memory. And I do heartily wish that every man would lay aside his own business, meddle no more with his profession nor trade, and throw all affairs concerning himself behind his back, to attend this wholly, without distracting or troubling his mind with any thing else, until he have learned them without book; that if by chance the art of printing should cease, or in case that in time to come all books should perish, every man might truly teach them unto his children, and deliver them over to his successors and survivors from hand to hand, as a religious cabala; for there is in it more profit, than a rabble of great pocky loggerheads are able to discern, who surely understand far less in these little merriments, than the fool Raclet did in the Institutions of Justinian.

I have known great and mighty lords, and of those not a few, who, going a deer-hunting, or a hawking after wild ducks, when the chase had not encountered with the blinks, that were cast in her way to retard her course, or that the hawk did but plain and smoothly fly without moving her wings, perceiving the prey, by force of flight, to have gained bounds of her, have been much chafed and vexed, as you understand well enough; but

the comfort unto which they had refuge, and that they might not take cold, was to relate the inestimable deeds of the said Gargantua. There are others in the world,—these are no flimflam stories, nor tales of a tub,—who, being much troubled with the toothache, after they had spent their goods upon physicians, without receiving at all any ease of their pain, have found no more ready remedy than to put the said Chronicles betwixt two pieces of linen cloth made somewhat hot, and so apply them to the place that smarteth, synapising them with a little powder of projection, otherwise called *doribus*.[1]

But what shall I say of those poor men that are plagued with the pox and the gout? O how often have we seen them, even immediately after they were anointed and thoroughly greased, till their faces did glister like the key-hole of a powdering tub, their teeth dance like the jacks of a pair of little organs or virginals, when they are played upon, and that they foamed from their very throats like a boar, which the mongrel mastiff hounds have driven in, and overthrown amongst the toils,—what did they then? All their consolation was to have some page of the said jolly book read unto them. And we have seen those who have given themselves to a hundred puncheons of old devils, in case that they did not feel a manifest ease and assuagement of pain at the hearing of the said book read, even when they were kept in a purgatory of torment; no more nor less than women in travail use to find their sorrow abated, when the life of St. Margarite is read unto them. Is this nothing? Find me a book in any language, in any faculty or science whatsoever, that hath such virtues, properties, and prerogatives, and I will be content to pay you a quart of tripes. No, my masters, no, it is peerless, incomparable, and not to be matched; and this

68

am I resolved for ever to maintain even unto the fire *exclusivè*.[2] And those that will pertinaciously hold the contrary opinion, let them be accounted abusers, predestinators, impostors, and seducers of the people. It is very true, that there are found in some gallant and stately books, worthy of high estimation, certain occult and hid properties; in the number of which are reckoned Whippot, Orlando Furioso, Robert the Devil, Fierabras, William without Fear, Huon of Bourdeaux, Monteville, and Matabrune: but they are not comparable to that which we speak of, and the world hath well known by infallible experience the great emolument and utility which it hath received by this Gargantuine Chronicle; for the printers have sold more of them in two months' time, than there will be bought of Bibles in nine years.

I therefore, your humble slave, being very willing to increase your solace and recreation yet a little more, do offer you for a present another book of the same stamp, only that it is a little more reasonable and worthy of credit than the other was. For think not, unless you wilfully err against your knowledge, that I speak of it as the Jews do of the Law. I was not born under such a planet, neither did it ever befal me to lie, or affirm a thing for true that was not. I speak of it like a lusty frolic Onocrotarie, I should say Crotenotarie of the martyrised lovers, and Croquenotarie of love. *Quod vidimus testamur.*[3] It is of the horrible and dreadful feats and prowesses of Pantagruel, whose menial servant I have been ever since I was a page, till this hour, that by his leave I am permitted to visit my cow-country, and to know if any of my kindred there be alive.

And therefore, to make an end of this Prologue, even as I give myself to an hundred thousand panniers-full of fair devils, body and soul, tripes and guts, in case that I lie so much as one single word in this whole history; after the like manner, St. Anthony's fire burn you, Mahoom's disease whirl you, the squinance with a stitch in your side, and the wolf in your stomach truss you, the bloody flux seize upon you, the cursed sharp inflammations of wild fire, as slender and thin as cow's hair strengthened with quicksilver, enter into your fundament, and like those of Sodom and Gomorrha, may you fall into sulphur, fire, and bottomless pits, in case you do not firmly believe all that I shall relate unto you in this present Chronicle.

CHAPTER 1

Of the original and antiquity of the great Pantagruel

IT will not be an idle nor unprofitable thing, seeing we are at leisure, to put you in mind of the fountain and original source, whence is derived unto us the good Pantagruel. For I see that all good historiographers have thus handled their chronicles, not only the Arabians, Barbarians, and Latins, but also the gentle Greeks, who were eternal drinkers. You must therefore remark, that at the beginning of the world,—I speak of a long time, it is above forty quarantains, or forty times forty nights, according to the supputation of the ancient Druids,—a little after that Abel was killed by his brother Cain, the earth, imbrued with the blood of the just, was one year so exceeding fertile in all those fruits which it usually produces to us, and especially in medlars, that ever since, throughout all ages, it hath been called the year of the great medlars; for three of them did fill a bushel. In it the Calends were found by the Grecian almanacks. There was that year nothing of the month of March in the time of Lent, and the middle of August was in May. In the month of October, as I take it, or at least September, that I may not err, for I will carefully take heed of that, was the week so famous in the Annals, which they call the week of the three Thursdays; for it had three of them by means of their irregular leap-years, called Bissextiles, occasioned by the sun's having tripped and stumbled a little towards the left hand, like a debtor afraid of serjeants, coming right upon him to arrest him: and the moon varied from her course above five fathom, and there was manifestly seen the motion of trepidation in the firmament of the fixed stars, called Aplanes, so that the middle Pleiade, leaving her fellows, declined towards the equinoctial, and the star named Spica left the constellation of the Virgin to withdraw herself towards the Balance, known by the name of

Libra; which are cases very terrible, and matters so hard and difficult, that astrologians cannot set their teeth in them; and indeed their teeth had been pretty long if they could have reached thither.

However, account you it for a truth, that every body did most heartily eat of those medlars, for they were fair to the eye, and in taste delicious. But even as Noah, that holy man, to whom we are so much beholding, bound, and obliged, for that he planted to us the vine, from whence we have that nectarian, delicious, precious, heavenly, joyful, and deific liquor, which they call *piot* or tiplage, was deceived in the drinking of it, for he was ignorant of the great virtue and power thereof; so likewise the men and women of that time did delight much in the eating of that fair great fruit, but divers and very different accidents did ensue thereupon; for there fell upon them all in their bodies a most terrible swelling, but not upon all in the same place, for some were swollen in the belly, and their belly strouted out big like a great tun; of whom it is written *Ventrem omnipotentem;*[4] who were all very honest men, and merry blades. And of this race came St. Fatgulch, and Shrove-Tuesday. Others did swell at the shoulders, who in that place were so crump and knobby, that they were therefore called Montifers, which is as much as to say Hill-carriers, of whom you see some yet in the world, of divers sexes and degrees. Of this race came Æsop, some of whose excellent words and deeds you have in writing. Some other puffs did swell in length by the member, which they call the labourer of nature, in such sort that it grew marvellous long, fat, great, lusty, stirring, and crest-risen, in the antique fashion, so that they made use of it as of a girdle, winding it five or six times about their waist: but if it happened the aforesaid member to be in good case, spooming with a full sail, bunt fair before the wind, then to have seen those strouting champions, you would have taken them for men that had their lances settled on their rest, to run at the ring or tilting whintam [quintain]. Of these, believe me, the race is utterly lost and quite extinct, as the women say; for they do lament continually, that there are none extant now of those great, &c. You know the rest of the song. Others did grow in matter of ballocks so enormously, that three of them would well fill a sack, able to contain five quarters of wheat.

From them are descended the ballocks of Lorraine, which never dwell in codpieces but fall down to the bottom of the breeches. Others grew in the legs, and to see them you would have said they had been cranes, or the reddish-long-billed-stork-like-scrank-legged sea-fowls, called flamans, or else men walking upon stilts or scatches. The little grammar schoolboys, known by the name of Grimos, called those leg-grown slangams, iambics, in allusion to the French word Jambe, which signifieth a leg. In others, their nose did grow so, that it seemed to be the beak of a limbeck, in every part thereof most variously diapered with the twinkling sparkles of crimson-blisters budding forth, and purpled with pimples all enamelled with thick-set wheals of a sanguine colour, bordered with gules: and such have you seen the canon, or prebend Panzoult, and Woodenfoot the physician of Angiers. Of which race there were few that liked the ptisane, but all of them were perfect lovers of the pure septembral juice. Naso and Ovid had their extraction from thence, and all those of whom it is written, *Ne reminiscaris.*[5] Others grew in ears, which they had so big, that out of one would have been stuff enough got to make a doublet, a pair of breeches, and a jacket, whilst with the other they might have covered themselves as with a Spanish cloak; and they say, that in Bourbonnois this race remaineth yet. Others grew in length of body, and of those came the giants, and of them Pantagruel.

And the first was Chalbroth,
Who begat Sarabroth,
Who begat Faribroth,
Who begat Hurtali, that was a brave eater of pottage, and reigned in the time of the flood;
Who begat Nembroth,
Who begat Atlas, that with his shoulders kept the sky from falling;
Who begat Goliah,
Who begat Erix, that invented the hocus-pocus plays of legerdemain,
Who begat Titius,
Who begat Eryon,
Who begat Polyphemus,
Who begat Cacus,
Who begat Etion, the first man who ever had the pox, for not drinking fresh in summer as Bartachin witnesseth;

Who begat Enceladus,
Who begat Ceus,
Who begat Tiphœus,
Who begat Alœus,
Who begat Othus,
Who begat Ægeon,
Who begat Briareus, that had a hundred hands;
Who begat Porphyrio,
Who begat Adamastor,
Who begat Anteus,
Who begat Agatho,
Who begat Porus, against whom fought Alexander the Great;
Who begat Aranthas,
Who begat Gabbara, that was the first inventor of the drinking of healths;
Who begat Goliah of Secondille,
Who begat Offot, that was terribly well nosed for drinking at the barrelhead;
Who begat Artachæus,
Who begat Oromedon,
Who begat Gemmagog, the first inventor of Poulan shoes, which are open on the foot, and tied over the instep with a latchet;
Who begat Sisyphus,
Who begat the Titans, of whom Hercules was born,
Who begat Enay, the most skilful man that ever was, in matter of taking the little worms (called cirons) out of the hands;
Who begat Fierabras, that was vanquished by Oliver, Peer of France, and Roland's camerad;
Who begat Morgan, the first in the world that played at dice with spectacles;
Who begat Fracassus, of whom Merlin Coccaius hath written, of him was born Ferragus;
Who begat Hapmouche, the first that ever invented the drying of neats' tongues in the chimney; for, before that, people salted them, as they do now gammons of bacon;
Who begat Bolivorax,
Who begat Longis,
Who begat Gayoffo, whose ballocks were of popular, and his pendulum of the servise, or sorb-apple tree;
Who begat Maschefain,
Who begat Brusleter,
Who begat Angoulevent,
Who begat Galehault, the inventor of flagons;
Who begat Mirelangaut,
Who begat Galaffre,

Who begat Falourdin,
Who begat Roboast,
Who begat Sortibrant of Conimbres,
Who begat Brushant of Mommiere,
Who begat Bruyer that was overcome by Ogier the Dane, Peer of France;
Who begat Mabrun,
Who begat Foustanon,
Who begat Haquelebac,
Who begat Vitdegrain,
Who begat Grangousier,
Who begat Gargantua,
Who begat the noble Pantagruel my master.

I know that reading this passage, you will make a doubt within yourselves, and that grounded upon very good reasons, which is this,—how is it possible that this relation can be true, seeing at the time of the flood all the world was destroyed, except Noah, and seven persons more with him in the ark, into whose number Hurtali is not admitted? Doubtless the demand is well made, and very apparent, but the answer shall satisfy you, or my wit is not rightly caulked. And, because I was not at that time to tell you any thing of my own fancy, I will bring unto you the authority of the Massorets, good honest fellows, true ballockeering blades, and exact Hebraical bagpipers, who affirm, that verily the said Hurtali was not within the ark of Noah, neither could he get in, for he was too big, but he sat astride upon it, with one leg on the one side, and another on the other, as little children use to do on their woodenhorses: or as the great bull of Berne, which was killed at Marinian did ride for his hackney the great murdering piece called the Canonpevier, a pretty beast of a fair and pleasant amble without all question.

In that posture, he, after God, saved the said ark from danger, for with his legs he gave it the brangle that was needful, and with his foot turned it whither he pleased, as a ship answereth her rudder. Those that were within sent him up victuals in abundance by a chimney, as people very thankfully acknowledging the good that he did them. And sometimes they did talk together as Icaromenippus did to Jupiter, according to the report of Lucian. Have you understood all this well? Drink then one good draught without water, for if you believe it not;—no truly do I not, quoth she.

CHAPTER 2

*Of the Nativity of the most dread and re-
doubted Pantagruel*

GARGANTUA at the age of four hundred fourscore forty and four years begat his son Pantagruel, upon his wife named Badebec,
daughter to the king of the Amaurots in
Utopia, who died in child-birth; for he was so
wonderfully great and lumpish, that he could
not possibly come forth in the light of the
world without thus suffocating his mother.
But that we may fully understand the cause
and reason of the name of Pantagruel, which
at his baptism was given him, you are to remark that in that year there was so great
drought over all the country of Africa, that
there past thirty and six months, three weeks,
four days, thirteen hours, and a little more,
without rain, but with a heat so vehement,
that the whole earth was parched and withered by it. Neither was it more scorched and
dried up with heat in the days of Elijah, than
it was at that time; for there was not a tree to
be seen, that had either leaf or bloom upon it.
The grass was without verdure or greenness,
the rivers were drained, the fountains dried
up, the poor fishes abandoned and forsaken
by their proper element, wandering and crying upon the ground most horribly. The birds
did fall down from the air for want of moisture and dew, wherewith to refresh them.
The wolves, foxes, harts, wild-boars, fallow-
deer, hares, coneys, weasels, brocks, badgers,
and other such beasts, were found dead in the
fields with their mouths open. In respect of
men, there was the pity, you should have seen
them lay out their tongues like hares that
have been run six hours. Many did throw
themselves into the wells. Others entered
within a cow's belly to be in the shade; those
Homer calls *Alibantes*.[6] All the country was
idle, and could do no virtue. It was a most
lamentable case to have seen the labour of
mortals in defending themselves from the vehemency of this horrific drought; for they had
work enough to do to save the holy water in
the churches from being wasted; but there
was such order taken by the counsel of my
Lords the Cardinals, and of our holy Father,
that none did dare to take above one lick.
Yet, when any one came into the church, you
should have seen above twenty poor thirsty
fellows hang upon him that was the distribu-
tor of the water, and that with a wide open
throat, gaping for one little drop, like the rich
glutton in Luke, that might fall by, lest anything should be lost. O how happy was he in
that year, who had a cool cellar under
ground, well plenished with fresh wine!

The philosopher reports in moving the
question,—Wherefore is it that the sea-water
is salt?—that at the time when Phœbus gave
the government of his resplendent chariot to
his son Phaëton, the said Phaëton, unskilful in
the art, and not knowing how to keep the
ecliptic line betwixt the two tropics of the latitude of the sun's course, strayed out of his
way, and came so near the earth, that he dried
up all the countries that were under it, burning a great part of the heavens, which the
philosophers call the *via lactea*,[7] and the huff-
snuffs, St. James's-way; although the most
coped, lofty, and high-crested poets affirm
that to be the place where Juno's milk fell,
when she gave suck to Hercules. The earth at
that time was so excessively heated, that it
fell into an enormous sweat, yea such a one as
made it sweat out the sea, which is therefore
salt, because all sweat is salt; and this you
cannot but confess to be true, if you will taste
of your own, or of those that have the pox,
when they are put into sweating, it is all one
to me.

Just such another case fell out this same
year: for on a certain Friday, when the whole
people were bent upon their devotions, and
had made goodly processions, with store of litanies, and fair preachings, and beseeching
of God Almighty, to look down with his eye of
mercy upon their miserable and disconsolate
condition, there was even then visibly seen
issue out of the ground great drops of water,
such as fall from a puff-bagged man in a top
sweat, and the poor hoydons began to rejoice,
as if it had been a thing very profitable unto
them; for some said that there was not one
drop of moisture in the air, whence they
might have any rain, and that the earth did
supply the default of that. Other learned men
said, that it was a shower of the Antipodes, as
Seneca saith in his fourth book *Quæstionum
naturalium,* speaking of the source and spring
of *Nilus.* But they were deceived; for, the procession being ended, when every one went
about to gather of this dew, and to drink of it
with full bowls, they found that it was nothing but pickle, and the very brine of salt, more
brackish in taste than the saltest water of the
sea. And because in that very day Pantagruel
was born, his father gave him that name; for
Panta in Greek is as much as to say all, and

Gruel, in the Hagarene language, doth signify thirsty; inferring thereby, that at his birth the whole world was a-dry and thirsty, as likewise foreseeing that he would be some day supreme lord and sovereign of the thirsty thrapples, which was shown to him at that very same hour by a more evident sign. For when his mother Badebec was in the bringing of him forth, and that the midwives did wait to receive him, there came first out of her belly three score and eight tregeneers, that is, salt-sellers, every one of them leading in a halter, a mule heavy laden with salt; after whom issued forth nine dromedaries, with great loads of gammons of bacon, and dried neats' tongues on their backs. Then followed seven camels loaded with links and chitterlings, hogs' puddings, and sausages. After them came out five great wains, full of leeks, garlick, onions, and chibots, drawn with five-and-thirty strong cart-horses, which was six for every one besides the thiller. At the sight hereof the said midwives were much amazed; yet some of them said, Lo, here is good provision, and indeed, we need it; for we drink but lazily, as if our tongues walked on crutches, and not lustily like Lansman Dutches. Truly this is a good sign, there is nothing here but what is fit for us, these are the spurs of wine that set it a-going. As they were tattling thus together after their own manner of chat, behold, out comes Pantagruel all hairy like a bear, whereupon one of them inspired with a prophetical spirit, said, This will be a terrible fellow, he is born with all his hair, he is undoubtedly to do wonderful things, and, if he live, he shall have age.

CHAPTER 3

Of the grief wherewith Gargantua was moved at the decease of his Wife Badebec

WHEN Pantagruel was born, there was none more astonished and perplexed than was his father Gargantua; for, of the one side, seeing his wife Badebec dead, and on the other side his son Pantagruel born, so fair and so great, he knew not what to say, nor what to do. And the doubt that troubled his brain was to know whether he should cry for the death of his wife, or laugh for the joy of his son. He was *hinc and indè*[8] choaked with sophistical arguments, for he framed them very well *in modo et figura,*[9] but he could not resolve them, remaining pestered and entangled by this means, like a mouse caught in a trap, or kite

snared in a gin. Shall I weep, said he? Yes, for why? My so good wife is dead, who was the most this, the most that, that was ever in the world. Never shall I see her, never shall I recover such another, it is unto me an inestimable loss! O my good God, what had I done that thou shouldest thus punish me? Why didst thou not take me away before her? Seeing for me to live without her is but to languish. Ah Badebec, Badebec, my minion, my dear heart, my sugar, my sweeting, my honey, my little coney,—yet it had in circumference full six acres, three rods, five poles, four yards, two feet, one inch and a half of good woodland measure,—my tender peggy, my codpiece darling, my bob and hit, my slipshoe-lovie, never shall I see thee! Ah, poor Pantagruel, thou hast lost thy good mother, thy sweet nurse, thy well-beloved lady! O false death, how injurious and despiteful hast thou been to me! How malicious and outrageous have I found thee in taking her from me, my well-beloved wife, to whom immortality did of right belong!

With these words he did cry like a cow; but on a sudden fell a laughing like a calf, when Pantagruel came into his mind. Ha, my little son, said he, my childilolly, fedlifondy, dandlichucky, my ballocky, my pretty rogue! O how jolly thou art, and how much I am bound to my gracious God, that hath been pleased to bestow on me a son, so fair, so spriteful, so lively, so smiling, so pleasant, and so gentle! Ho, ho, ho, ho, how glad I am! Let us drink, ho, and put away melancholy! Bring of the best, rinse the glasses, lay the cloth, drive out these dogs, blow this fire, light candles, shut that door there, cut this bread in sippets for brewis, send away these poor folks in giving them what they ask, hold my gown. I will strip myself into my doublet, *(én cuerpo,)* to make the gossips merry, and keep them company.

As he spake this, he heard the litanies and the *mementos* of the priests that carried his wife to be buried, upon which he left the good purpose he was in, and was suddenly ravished another way, saying, Lord God, must I again contrist myself? This grieves me. I am no longer young, I grow old, the weather is dangerous; I may perhaps take an ague, then shall I be foiled, if not quite undone. By the faith of a gentleman, it were better to cry less, and drink more. My wife is dead, well, by G—, *(da jurandi)*[10] I shall not raise her again by my crying: she is well, she is in

Paradise, at least, if she be no higher: she prayeth to God for us, she is happy, she is above the sense of our miseries, nor can our calamities reach her. What though she be dead, must not we also die? The same debt which she hath paid, hangs over our heads; nature will require it of us, and we must all of us some day taste of the same sauce. Let her pass then, and the Lord preserve the survivors; for I must now cast about how to get another wife. But I will tell you what you shall do, said he to the midwives; in France called wise women (where be they? good folks, I cannot see them). Go you to my wife's interment, and I will the while rock my son; for I find myself somewhat altered and distempered, and should otherwise be in danger of falling sick; but drink one draught first, you will be the better for it, believe me upon mine honour. They at his request went to her burial and funeral obsequies. In the meanwhile poor Gargantua, staying at home, and willing to have somewhat in remembrance of her to be engraven upon her tomb, made this epitaph, in the manner as followeth:

Dead is the noble Badebec,
Who had a face like a rebec;
A Spanish body, and a belly
Of Switzerland; she died, I tell ye,
In child-birth. Pray to God, that her
He pardon wherein she did err.
Here lies her body, which did live
Free from all vice, as I believe,
    And did decease at my bed-side,
    The year and day in which she died.

CHAPTER 4

Of the Infancy of Pantagruel

I FIND by the ancient historiographers and poets, that divers have been born in this world after very strange manners, which would be too long to repeat: read therefore the seventh chapter of Pliny, if you have so much leisure. Yet have you never heard of any so wonderful as that of Pantagruel; for it is a very difficult matter to believe, how, in the little time he was in his mother's belly, he grew both in body and strength. That which Hercules did was nothing when in his cradle he slew two serpents, for those serpents were but little and weak, but Pantagruel, being yet in the cradle, did far more admirable things, and more to be amazed at. I pass by here the relation of how at every one of his

meals he supped up the milk of four thousand six hundred cows, and how, to make him a skillet to boil his milk in, there were set to work all the braziers of Saumure in Anjou, of Villedieu in Normandy, and of Bramont in Lorraine. And they served in this whitepot-meat to him in a huge great bell, which is yet to be seen in the city of Bourges in Berry, near the palace, but his teeth were already so well grown, and so strengthened with vigour, that of the said bell he bit off a great morsel, as very plainly doth appear to this hour.

One day in the morning, when they would have made him suck one of his cows,—for he never had any other nurse, as the history tells us,—he got one of his arms loose from the swaddling-bands, wherewith he was kept fast in the cradle, laid hold on the said cow under the left fore ham, and grasping her to him, ate up her udder and half of her paunch, with the liver and the kidneys, and had devoured all up, if she had not cried out most horribly, as if the wolves had held her by the legs, at which noise company came in, and took away the said cow from Pantagruel. Yet could they not so well do it, but that the quarter whereby he caught her was left in his hand, of which quarter he gulped up the flesh in a trice, even with as much ease as you would eat a sausage, and that so greedily with desire of more, that, when they would have taken away the bone from him, he swallowed it down whole, as a cormorant would do a little fish; and afterwards began fumblingly to say, Good, good, good—for he could not yet speak plain—giving them to understand thereby, that he had found it very good, and that he did lack but so much more. Which when they saw that attended him, they bound him with great cable-ropes, like those that are made at Tain, for the carriage of salt to Lyons: or such as those are, whereby the great French ship rides at anchor in the road of Newhaven in Normandy. But on a certain time, a great bear, which his father had bred, got loose, came towards him, began to lick his face, for his nurses had not thoroughly wiped his chaps, at which unexpected approach being on a sudden offended, he as lightly rid himself of those great cables, as Samson did of the hawser ropes wherewith the Philistines had tied him, and, by your leave, takes me up my lord the bear, and tears him to you in pieces like a pullet, which served him for a gorgeful or good warm bit for that meal.

Whereupon Gargantua, fearful lest the

PANTAGRUEL

child should hurt himself, caused four great
chains of iron to be made to bind him, and so
many strong wooden arches unto his cradle,
most firmly stocked and morticed in huge
frames. Of those chains you have got one at
Rochelle, which they draw up at night betwixt the two great towers of the haven. Another is at Lyons,—a third at Angiers,—and
the fourth was carried away by the devils to
bind Lucifer, who broke his chains in those
days, by reason of a cholic that did extraordi-
narily torment him, taken with eating a serjeant's soul fried for his breakfast. And therefore you may believe that which Nicholas de
Lyra saith upon that place of the Psalter,
where it is written, *Et Og regem Basan,*[11] that
the said Og, being yet little, was so strong
and robustious, that they were fain to bind
him with chains of iron in his cradle. Thus
continued Pantagruel for a while very calm
and quiet, for he was not able so easily to
break those chains, especially having no room
in the cradle to give a swing with his arms.
But see what happened once upon a great
holiday that his father Gargantua made a
sumptuous banquet to all the princes of his
court. I am apt to believe, that the menial officers of the house were so imbusied in waiting each on his proper service at the feast,
that nobody took care of poor Pantagruel,
who was left *à reculorum,*[12] behind-hand, all
alone and as forsaken. What did he? Hark
what he did, good people. He strove and es-
sayed to break the chains of the cradle with
his arms, but could not, for they were too
strong for him. Then did he keep with his feet
such a stamping stir, and so long, that at last
he beat out the lower end of his cradle, which
notwithstanding was made of a great post five
foot in square; and, as soon as he had gotten
out his feet, he slid down as well as he could
till he had got his soles to the ground, and
then with a mighty force he rose up, carrying
his cradle upon his back, bound to him like a
tortoise that crawls up against a wall; and, to
have seen him you would have thought it had
been a great carrick of five hundred ton upon
one end. In this manner he entered into the
great hall where they were banqueting, and
that very boldly, which did much affright the
company; yet, because his arms were tied in,
he could not reach anything to eat, but with
great pain stooped now and then a little, to
take with the whole flat of his tongue some
good lick, good bit, or morsel. Which when
his father saw, he saw well enough that they

had left him without giving him anything
to eat, and therefore commanded that he
should be loosed from the said chains, by the
counsel of the princes and lords there present. Besides that, also, the physicians of Gargantua said, that, if they did thus keep him in
the cradle, he would be all his life-time subject to the stone. When he was unchained,
they made him to sit down, where, after he
had fed very well, he took his cradle, and
broke it into more than five hundred thousand pieces with one blow of his fist, that he
struck in the midst of it, swearing that he
would never come into it again.

CHAPTER 5

*Of the acts of the noble Pantagruel in his
    youthful age*

THUS grew Pantagruel from day to day, and
to every one's eye waxed more and more in all
his dimensions, which made his father to rejoice by a natural affection. Therefore caused
he to be made for him, whilst he was yet little, a pretty cross-bow, wherewith to shoot at
small birds, which now they call the great
cross-bow at Chantelle. Then he sent him to
the school to learn, and to spend his youth in
virtue. In the prosecution of which design he
came first to Poictiers, where, as he studied
and profited very much, he saw that the scholars were oftentimes at leisure, and knew not
how to bestow their time, which moved him
to take such compassion on them, that one
day he took from a long ledge of rocks, called
there Passelourdin, a huge great stone, of
about twelve fathom square, and fourteen
handfuls thick, and with great ease set it upon four pillars in the midst of a field, to no
other end, but that the said scholars, when
they had nothing else to do, might pass their
time in getting up on that stone, and feast it
with store of gammons, pasties, and flagons,
and carve their names upon it with a knife; in
token of which deed till this hour the stone is
called the lifted stone. And in remembrance
hereof there is none entered into the register
and matricular book of the said university, or
accounted capable of taking any degree
therein, till he have first drunk in the Caballine fountain of Croustelles, passed at Passelourdin, and got up upon the lifted stone.
    Afterwards, reading the delectable Chron-
icles of his Ancestors, he found that Geoffrey of Lusinian, called Geoffrey with the
great tooth, grandfather to the cousin-in-law

of the eldest sister of the aunt of the son-in-law of the uncle of the good daughter of his stepmother, was interred at Maillezais; therefore one day he took *campos,* (which is a little vacation from study to play a while,) that he might give him a visit as unto an honest man. And going from Poictiers with some of his companions, they passed by Legugé, visiting the noble Abbot Ardillon: then by Lusignan, by Sansay, by Celles, By Colonges, by Fontenay le Comte, saluting the learned Tiraqueau, and from thence arrived at Maillezais, where he went to see the sepulchre of the said Geoffrey with the great tooth; which made him somewhat afraid, looking upon the picture, whose lively draughts did set him forth in the representation of a man in extreme fury, drawing his great Malchus faulchion half-way out of his scabbard. When the reason hereof was demanded, the canons of the said place told him, that there was no other cause of it, but that *Pictoribus atque poetis,* &c.;[13] that is to say, that painters and poets have liberty to paint and devise what they list after their own fancy. But he was not satisfied with their answer, and said, He is not thus painted without a cause, and I suspect that at his death there was some wrong done him, whereof he requireth his kindred to take revenge. I will inquire further into it, and then do what shall be reasonable. Then he returned not to Poictiers, but would take a view of the other Universities of France. Therefore, going to Rochelle, he took shipping and arrived at Bordeaux, where he found no great exercise, only now and then he would see some mariners and lightermen a wrestling on the quay or strand by the river side. From thence he came to Thoulouse, where he learned to dance very well, and to play with the two-handed sword, as the fashion of the scholars of the said University is to bestir themselves in games, whereof they may have their hands full: but he stayed not long there, when he saw that they did cause burn their regents alive, like red herrings, saying, Now God forbid that I should die this death! for I am by nature sufficiently dry already, without heating myself any further.

He went then to Montpellier, where he met with the good wives of Mirevaux, and good jovial company withal, and thought to have set himself to the study of physic; but he considered that that calling was too troublesome and melancholic, and that physicians did smell of glisters like old devils. Therefore he resolved he would study the laws; but seeing that there were but three scauld, and one bald-pated legist in that place, he departed from thence, and in his way made the bridge of Guard, and the amphitheatre of Nismes, in less than three hours, which nevertheless seems to be a more divine than human work. After that he came to Avignon, where he was not above three days before he fell in love; for the women there take great delight in playing at the close-buttock game, because it is papal ground. Which his tutor and pedagogue Epistemon perceiving, he drew him out of that place, and brought him to Valence in the Dauphiny, where he saw no great matter of recreation, only that the lubbards of the town did beat the scholars, which so incensed him with anger, that when, upon a certain very fair Sunday, the people being at their public dancing in the streets, and one of the scholars offering to put himself into the ring to partake of that sport, the foresaid lubberly fellows would not permit him the admittance into their society, he taking the scholar's part, so belaboured them with blows, and laid such load upon them, that he drove them all before him, even to the brink of the river Rhone, and would have there drowned them, but that they did squat to the ground like moles, and there lay close a full half league under the river. The hole is to be seen there yet.

After that he departed from thence, and in three strides and one leap, came to Angiers, where he found himself very well, and would have continued there some space, but that the plague drove them away. So from thence he came to Bourges, where he studied a good long time, and profited very much in the faculty of the laws, and would sometimes say, that the books of the civil law were like unto a wonderfully precious, royal, and triumphant robe of gold, edged with dirt; for in the world are no goodlier books to be seen, more ornate, nor more eloquent than the texts of the *Pandects,* but the bordering of them, that is to say, the gloss of Accursius, is so scurvy, vile, base, and unsavoury, that it is nothing but filthiness and villany.

Going from Bourges, he came to Orleans, where he found store of swaggering scholars that made him great entertainment at his coming, and with whom he learned to play at tennis so well, that he was a master at that game. For the students of the said place make a prime exercise of it; and sometimes they carried him unto Cupid's houses of commerce, (in that city termed islands, because of their being most ordinarily environed with other houses, and not contiguous to any), there to recreate his person at the sport of poussevant, which the wenches of London call the ferkers in and in. As for breaking his head with over much study, he had an especial care not to do it in any case, for fear of spoiling his eyes. Which he the rather observed, for that it was told him by one of his teachers, there called regents, that the pain of the eyes was the most hurtful thing of any to the sight. For this cause when he one day was made a licentiate, or graduate in law, one of the scholars of his acquaintance, who of learning had not much more than his burden, though instead of that he could dance very well, and play at tennis, made the blazon and device of the licentiates in the said university, saying,

> So you have in your hand a racket,
> A tennis-ball in your cod-placket,
> A Pandect law in your cap's tippet,
> And that you have the skill to trip it
> In a low dance, you will be allowed
> The grant of the licentiate's hood.

CHAPTER 6

How Pantagruel met with a Limosin, who affected to speak in learned phrase

UPON a certain day, I know not when, Pantagruel walking after supper with some of his fellow-students without that gate of the city, through which we enter on the road to Paris, encountered with a young spruce-like scholar that was coming upon the very same way, and, after they had saluted one another, asked him thus, My friend, from whence comest thou now? The scholar answered him, From alme, inclyte and celebrate academy, which is vocitated Lutetia. What is the meaning of this? said Pantagruel to one of his men. It is, answered he, from Paris. Thou comest from Paris, then? said Pantagruel, and how do you spend your time there, you my masters the students of Paris? The scholar answered, We transfretate the Sequane at the dilucul and crepuscul: we deambulate by the compites and quadrives of the urb; we despumate the Latial verbocination;[14] and, like verisimilary amorabonds, we captat the benevolence of the omnijugal, omniform, and omnigenal fœminine sex. Upon certain diecules we invisat the lupanares, and in a venerian ecstasy

inculcate our veretres into the penitissime recesses of the pudends of these amicabilissimes meretricules. Then do we cauponisate[15] in the meritory taberns of the Pineapple, the Castle, the Magdalene, and the Mule, goodly vervecine spatules perforaminated with petrocile.[16] And if by fortune there be rarity, or penury of pecune in our marsupies,[17] and that they be exhausted of ferruginean metal, for the shot we demit our codices, and oppignerat[18] our vestiments, whilst we prestolate[19] the coming of the Tabellaries[20] from the penates and patriotic lares. To which Pantagruel answered, What devilish language is this? by the Lord, I think thou art some kind of heretic. My lord, no, said the scholar; for libentissimally, as soon as it illucesceth any minutule slice of the day, I demigrate into one of these so well architected minsters, and, there, irrorating myself with fair lustral water, I mumble off little parcels of some missic precation of our sacrificuls, and, submurmurating my horary precules, I elave and absterge my anime from its nocturnal inquinations. I revere the olympicols. I latrially venere the supernal astripotent. I dilige and redame my proxims. I observe the decalogical precepts, and, according to the facultatule of my vires, I do not discede from them one late unguicule. Nevertheless it is veriform, that because *Mammona* doth not supergurgitate anything in my loculs, that I am somewhat rare and lent to supererogate the elemosynes to those egents, that hostially queritate their stipe.[21]

Prut, tut, said Pantagruel, what doth this fool mean to say? I think he is upon the forging of some diabolical tongue, and that enchanter-like he would charm us. To whom one of his men said, Without doubt, sir, this fellow would counterfeit the language of the Parisians, but he doth only flay the Latin, imagining by so doing that he doth highly Pindarize it in most eloquent terms, and strongly conceiteth himself to be therefore a great orator in the French, because he disdaineth the common manner of speaking. To which Pantagruel said, It is true. The scholar answered, My worshipful lord, my genie is not apt nate to that which this flagitious nebulon saith, to excoriate the cuticle of our vernacular Gallic, but viceversally I gnave opere, and by veles and rames enite to locupletate it with the Latinicome redundance.[22] By G—, said Pantagruel, I will teach you to speak. But first come hither, and tell me whence thou art? To this the scholar answered, The primeval origin of my aves and ataves was indigenary of the Lemovick regions, where requiesceth the corpor of the hagiotat St. Martial.[23] I understand thee very well, said Pantagruel. When all comes to all, thou art a Limosin, and thou wilt here by thy affected speech counterfeit the Parisians. Well now, come hither, I must show thee a new trick, and handsomely give thee the combfeat. With this he took him by the throat, saying to him, Thou flayest the Latin,—by St. John, I will make thee flay the fox, for I will now flay thee alive. Then began the poor Limosin to cry, Haw, gwid Maaster, haw, Laord, my halp and St. Marshaw, haw, I'm worried. Haw, my thropple, the bean of my cragg is bruck! Haw, for Gaud's seck, lawt my lean, Maaster; waw, waw, waw. Now, said Pantagruel, thou speakest naturally, and so let him go, for the poor Limosin had totally bewrayed and thoroughly conshit his breeches, which were not deep and large enough, but round strait cannoned gregs, having in the seat a piece like a keeling's tail, and therefore in French called, *de chausses a queüe de merlus.* Then, said Pantagruel, St. Alipantin, what civette! Fie! to the devil with this turnip-eater, How he stinks! and so let him go. But this hug of Pantagruel's was such a terror to him all the days of his life, and took such deep impression in his fancy, that very often, distracted with sudden affrightments, he would startle and say that Pantagruel held him by the neck. Besides that it procured him a continual drought and desire to drink, so that after some few years he died of the death Roland, in plain English called thirst, a work of divine vengeance, showing us that which saith the philosopher, and Aulus Gellius, that it becometh us to speak according to the common language; and that we should, as said Octavian Augustus, strive to shun all strange and unknown words with as much heedfulness and circumspection, as pilots of ships use to avoid the rocks and banks in the sea.

CHAPTER 7

How Pantagruel came to Paris, and of the choice books of the Library of St. Victor

AFTER that Pantagruel had studied very well at Orleans, he resolved to see the great University at Paris; but, before his departure, he was informed, that there was a huge big bell at St. Anian, in the said town of Orleans, under the ground, which had been there above two hundred and fourteen years, for it was so great that they could not by any device get it so much as above the ground, although they used all the means that are found in Vitruvius *De Architectura,* Albertus *De Re Ædificatoria,* Euclid, Theon, Archimedes, and Hero *De Ingeniis:* for all that was to no purpose. Wherefore, condescending heartily to the humble request of the citizens and inhabitants of the said town, he determined to remove it to the tower that was erected for it. With that he came to the place where it was, and lifted it out of the ground with his little finger, as easily as you would have done a hawk's bell, or bell-weather's tingle tangle; but, before he would carry it to the foresaid tower or steeple appointed for it, he would needs make some music with it about the town, and ring it along all the streets, as he carried it in his hand, wherewith all the people were very glad. But there happened one great inconveniency, for with carrying it so, and ringing it about the streets, all the good Orleans wine turned instantly, waxed flat, and was spoiled, which nobody there did perceive till the night following; for every man found himself so altered, and a-day with drinking these flat wines, that they did nothing but spit, and that as white as Maltha cotton, saying, We have got the Pantagruel, and our very throats are salted. This done, he came to Paris with his retinue. And at his entry every one came out to see him—as you know well enough, that the people of Paris is sottish by nature, by B flat, and B sharp,—and beheld him with great astonishment, mixed with no less fear, that he would carry away the palace into some other country *à remotis,*[24] and far from them, as his father formerly had done the great peal bells at Our Lady's church, to tie about his mare's neck. Now after he had stayed there a pretty space, and studied very well in all the seven liberal arts, he said it was a good town to live in, but not to die; for that the grave-digging rogues of St. Innocent used in frosty nights to warm their bums with dead men's bones. In his abode there he found the library of St. Victor, a very stately and magnificent one, especially in some books which were there, of which followeth the Repertory and Catalogue, *Et primo:*

The two-horse tumbrel of Salvation.
The Codpiece of the Law.

The Slippers or Pantofles of the Decretals.

The Pomegranate of Vice.

The Clew-bottom of Theology.

The Duster or Foxtail-flap of Preachers, composed by Turlupin.

The Churning Ballock of the Valiant.

The Henbane of the Bishops.

Marmotretus *De baboonis et apis, cum Commento Dorbellis.*

Decretum Universitatis Parisiensis super Gorgiasitate Muliercularum ad Placitum.[25]

The Apparition of Sanct Geltrude to a Nun of Poissy, being in travail, at the bringing forth of a child.

Ars Honestè Fartandi in Societate,[26] *per Marcum Ortuinum.*

The Mustard-pot of Penance.

The Gamashes, *alias* the Boots of Patience.

Formicarium Artium.[27]

De brodiorum Usu, et Honestate Chopinandi, per Sylvestrem Prioratem[28] *Jacobinum.*

The Cuckold in Court.

The Frail of the Scriveners.

The Marriage-packet.

The Crucible of Contemplation.

The Flimflams of the Law.

The Goad of Wine.

The Spur of Cheese.

Decrotatorium Scholarium.[29]

Tartaretus De Modo Cacandi.[30]

The Bravades of Rome.

Bricot *De Differentiis Browsarum.*[31]

The Tail-piece-Cushion, or Close-breech of Discipline.

The Cobbled Shoe of Humility.

The Trivet of good Thoughts.

The Kettle of Magnanimity.

The Cavilling Intanglements of Confessors.

The Curate's rap over the Knuckles.

Reverendi patris fratris Lubini, provincialis Bavardiæ, De gulpendis Lardslicionibus, libri tres.[32]

Pasquilli Doctoris Marmorei, De Capreolis cum Artichoketa Comedendis tempore Papali ab Ecclesia interdicto.[33]

The Invention of the Holy Cross, personated by six wily Priests.

The Spectacles of Pilgrims bound for Rome.

Majoris De Modo Faciendi Puddinos.[34]

The Bagpipe of the Prelates.

Beda De Optimitate Triparum.[35]

The Complaint of the Barristers upon the reformation of Comfites.

The Furred Cat of the Solicitors and Attornies.

Of Peas and Bacon, *cum Commento.*

The Small Vales or Drinking Money of the Indulgences.

Præclarissimi juris utriusque Doctoris Maistre Pillotti, &c., Scrapfarthingi De Botchandis Glossæ Accursianæ Triflis Repetitio Enucidiluculidissima.[36]

Stratagemata Francharchieri de Baniolet.[37]

Franctopinus or Churlbumpkinus, De Re Militari cum Figuris Tevoti.[38]

De Usu et Utilitate Flayandi Equos et Equas, authore Magistro nostro de Quebecu.[39]

The Sauciness of Country-Stewards.

M. N. Rostocostojambedanesse De Mustarda Post Prandium Servienda, libri quatuordecim, apostilati per M. Vaurillonis.[40]

The *Couillage* or Wench-tribute of Promoters.

Jabolenus De Cosmographia Purgatorii.[41]

Quæstio Subtilissima, utrum Chimæra in vacuo bombinans possit comedere secundas intentiones; et fuit debatuta per decem hebdomadas in Consilio Constantiensi.[42]

The Bridle-champer of the Advocates.

Smutchudlamenta Scoti.[43]

The Rasping and Hard-scraping of the Cardinals.

De Calcaribus Removendis, Decades undecim, per M. Albericum de Rosata.[44]

Ejusdem De Castrametandis Criminibus libri tres.[45]

The entrance of Anthony *de Leve* into the territories of Brazil.

Marforii, bacalarii cubantis Romæ, De Peelandis aut Unskinnandis Blurrandisque Cardinalium Mulis.[46]

The said Author's Apology against those who allege that the Pope's mule doth eat but at set times.

Prognosticatio quæ incipit, Silvii Triquebille, balata per M. N.,[47] the deep dreaming gull Sion.

Boudarini Episcopi De Emulgentiarum Profectibus Enneades novem, cum privilegio Papali ad triennium, et postea non.[48]

The Shitabrenna of the Maids.

The Bald Arse or Peeled Breech of the Widows.

The Cowl or Capouch of the Monks.

The Mumbling Devotion of the Cœlestine Friars.

The Passage-toll of Beggarliness.

The Teeth-chatter or Gum-didder of Lubberly Lusks.

The Paring-shovel of the Theologues.

The Drenching-horn of the Masters of Arts.

The scullions of Olcam the Uninitiated Clerk.

Magistri N. Lickdishetis, De Garbellisifta-tionibus Horarum Canonicarum, libri qua-draginta.[49]

Arsiversitatorium Confratriarum, incerto au-thore.[50]

The Rasher of Cormorants and Ravenous Feeders.

The Rammishness of the Spaniards supercoquelicanticked by Friar Inigo.

The Muttering of Pitiful Wretches.

Dastardismus Rerum Italicarum, authore Magistro Burnegad.[51]

R. Lullius De Batisfolagiis Principum.[52]

Calibistratorium Caffardiæ, authore M. Ja-cobo Hocstraten hereticometra.[53]

Codtickler, De Magistro nostrandorum Ma-gistro nostratorumque Beuvetis, libri octo galantissimi.[54]

The Crackarades of Bullists or stone-throwing Engines, Contrepate Clerks, Scriveners, Brief-writers, Rapporters, and Papal Bull-de-spatchers, lately compiled by Regis.

A perpetual Almanack for those that have the gout and the pox.

Manera sweepandi fornacellos per Mag. Ec-cium.[55]

The Shable, or Scimetar of Merchants.

The Pleasures of the Monachal Life.

The Hodge-podge of Hypocrites.

The History of the Hobgoblins.

The Ragamuffianism of the pensionary maimed soldiers.

The Gulling Fibs and counterfeit Shows of Commissaries.

The Litter of Treasurers.

The *Juglingatorium* of Sophisters.

Antipericatametanaparbeugedamphicribra-tiones Toordicantium.

The Periwinkle of Ballard-makers.

The Push-forward of the Alchemists.

The Niddy-noddy of the Satchel-loaded Seekers, by Friar Blindfastatis.

The Shackles of Religion.

The Racket of Swaggerers.

The Leaning-stock of old age.

The Muzzle of Nobility.

The Ape's *Paternoster*.

The Crickets and Hawks bells of Devotion.

The Pot of the Ember weeks.

The Mortar of the politic life.

The Flap of the Hermits.

The Riding-hood or Monterg of the Penitentiaries.

The Trictrac of the Knocking Friars.

Blockheadodus, De vitá et honestate braga-dochiorum.[56]

Lyrippii Sorbonici Moralisationes, per M. Lupoldum.[57]

The Carrier-horse bells of Travellers.

The Bibbings of the tippling Bishops.

Tarrabalationes Doctorum Coloniensium ad-versus Reuchlin.[58]

The Cymbals of Ladies.

The Dungers' Martingale.

Whirlingfriskorum Chasemarkerorum per Fratrem Crackwoodloguetis.

The Clouted Patches for a Stout Heart.

The Mummery of the Racket-keeping Robin-good-fellows.

Gerson, De Auferibilitate Papæ ab Ecclesia.[59]

The Catalogue of the Nominated and Graduated Persons.

Jo. Dytebrodii, De Terribilitate Excommuni-cationum libellulus Acephalos.[60]

Ingeniositas Invocandi Diabolos et Diabolas, per M. Guingolphum.[61]

The Hotch-potch or Gallimaufry of the perpetually begging Friars.

The Morris-dance of the Heretics.

The Whinings of Cajetan.

Muddisnout Doctoris Cherubici, De Origine Roughfootedarum, et Wryneckedorum Ritibus, libri septem.

Sixty-nine fat Breviaries.

The Night-Mare of the five orders of Beggars.

The Skinnery of the new Start-ups, extracted out of the fallow-butt, incornifistibulated and plodded upon in the angelic sum.

The Raver and idle Talker in cases of Conscience.

The Fat Belly of the Presidents.

The Baffling Flowter of the Abbots.

Sutoris Adversus quendam qui vocaverat eum Slabsauceatorem et quod Slabsaucea-tores non sunt damnati ab Ecclesia.[62]

Cacatorium Medicorum.[63]

The Chimney-Sweeper of Astrology.

Campi clysteriorum per § C.[64]

The bumsquibcracker of Apothecaries.

The Kissbreech of Chirurgery.

Justinianus De White-leperotis Tollendis.[65]

Antidotarium Animæ.[66]

Merlinus Coccaius, De Patria Diabolorum.[67]

The practice of Iniquity, by Cleuraunes Sadden.

Of which library some books are already printed, and the rest are now at the press, in this noble city of Tubingen.

CHAPTER 8

How Pantagruel, being at Paris, received letters from his Father Gargantua, and the copy of them

PANTAGRUEL studied very hard, as you may well conceive, and profited accordingly; for he had an excellent understanding, and notable wit, together with a capacity in memory, equal to the measure of twelve oil budgets, or butts of olives. And, as he was there abiding one day, he received a letter from his father in manner as followeth:

MOST DEAR SON, Amongst the gifts, graces, and prerogatives with which the sovereign plasmator God Almighty hath endowed and adorned human nature at the beginning, that seems to me most singular and excellent, by which we may in a moral estate attain to a kind of immortality, and in the course of this transitory life perpetuate our name and seed, which is done by a progeny issued from us in the lawful bonds of matrimony. Whereby that in some measure is restored unto us, which was taken from us by the sin of our first parents, to whom it was said, that, because they had not obeyed the commandment of God their Creator, they should die; and by death should be brought to nought that so stately frame and plasmature, wherein the man at first had been created.

But by this means of seminal propagation, there continueth in the children what was lost in the parents; and in the grand-children that which perished in their fathers, and so successively until the day of the last judgment, when Jesus Christ shall have rendered up to God the Father his kingdom in a peaceable condition, out of all danger and contamination of sin; for then shall cease all generations and corruptions, and the elements leave off their continual transmutations, seeing the so much desired peace shall be attained unto and enjoyed, and that all things shall be brought to their end and period. And, therefore, not without just and reasonable cause do I give thanks to God my Saviour and Preserver, for that he hath enabled me to see my bald old age reflourish in thy youth; for when, at his good pleasure, who rules and governs all things, my soul shall leave this mortal habitation, I shall not account myself wholly to die, but to pass from one place unto another, considering that, in and by thee, I continue in my visible image living in the world, visiting and conversing with people of honour, and other my good friends, as I was wont to do. Which conversation of mine, although it was not without sin, (because we are all of us trespassers, and therefore ought continually to beseech his divine majesty to blot our transgressions out of his memory,) yet was it by the help and grace of God, without all manner of reproach before men.

Wherefore, if those qualities of the mind but shine in thee, wherewith I am endowed, as in thee remaineth the perfect image of my body, thou wilt be esteemed by all men to be the perfect guardian and treasure of the immortality of our name. But, if otherwise, I shall truly take but small pleasure to see it, considering that the lesser part of me, which is the body, would abide in thee, and the best, to wit, that which is the soul, and by which our name continues blessed amongst men, would be degenerate and abastardized. This I do not speak out of any distrust that I have of thy virtue, which I have heretofore already tried, but to encourage thee yet more earnestly to proceed from good to better. And that which I now write unto thee is not so much that thou shouldest live in this virtuous course, as that thou shouldest rejoice in so living and having lived, and cheer up thyself with the like resolution in time to come; to the prosecution and accomplishment of which enterprise and generous undertaking thou mayest easily remember how that I have spared nothing, but have so helped thee as if I had no other treasure in this world, but to see thee once in my life completely well bred and accomplished, as well in virtue, honesty, and valour, as in all liberal knowledge and civility, and so to leave thee after my death as a mirror representing the person of me thy father, and if not so excellent, and such indeed as I do wish thee, yet such is my desire.

But although my deceased father of happy memory, Grangousier, had bent his best endeavours to make me profit in all perfection and political knowledge, and that my labour and study was fully correspondent to, yea, went beyond his desire, nevertheless, as thou mayest well understand, the time then was not so proper and fit for learning as it is at present, neither had I plenty of such good masters as thou hast had. For that time was darksome, obscured with clouds of ignorance, and savouring a little of the infelicity and calamity of the Goths, who had, wherever they set footing, destroyed all good literature, which in my age hath by the divine goodness been restored unto its former light and dignity, and that with such amendment and increase of knowledge, that now hardly should I be admitted unto the first form of the little grammar-school boys. I say, I, who in my youthful days was, and that justly, reputed the most learned of that age, Which I do not speak in vain boasting, although I might lawfully do it in writing unto thee,—in verification whereof thou hast the authority of Marcus Tullius in his book *Of Old Age,* and the sentence of Plutarch, in the book intituled, *How a man may praise himself without envy:* —but to give thee an emulous encouragement to strive yet further.

Now it is, that the minds of men are qualified with all manner of discipline and the old sciences revived, which for many ages were extinct. Now it is, that the learned languages are to their pristine purity restored, *viz.,* Greek, without which a man may be ashamed to account himself a scholar, Hebrew, Arabic, Chaldæan, and Latin. Printing likewise is now in use, so elegant and so correct, that better cannot be imagined, although it was found out but in my time by divine inspiration, as by a diabolical suggestion on the other side, was the invention of ordnance. All the world is full of knowing men, of most learned schoolmasters, and vast libraries; and it appears to me as a truth, that neither in Plato's time, nor Cicero's, nor Papinian's, there was ever such conveniency for studying, as we see at this day there is. Nor must any adventure henceforward to come in public or present himself in company, that hath not been pretty well polished in the shop of Minerva. I see robbers, hangmen, free-booters, tapsters, ostlers, and such like, of the very rubbish of the people, more learned now than the doctors and preachers were in my time.

What shall I say? The very women and children have aspired to this praise and celestial manna of good learning. Yet so it is, that at the age I am now of, I have been constrained to learn the Greek tongue,—which I contemned not like Cato, but had not the leisure in my younger years to attend the study of it,—and I take much delight in the reading of Plutarch's *Morals,* the pleasant *Dialogues* of Plato, the *Monuments* of Pausanias, and the *Antiquities* of Athenæus, in waiting on

the hour wherein God my Creator shall call me, and command me to depart from this earth and transitory pilgrimage. Wherefore, my son, I admonish thee to employ thy youth to profit as well as thou canst, both in thy studies and in virtue. Thou art at Paris, where the laudable examples of many brave men may stir up thy mind to gallant actions, and hast likewise, for thy tutor and pedagogue the learned Epistemon, who by his lively and vocal documents may instruct thee in the arts and sciences.

I intend, and will have it so, that thou learn the languages perfectly; first of all, the Greek, as Quintilian will have it; secondly, the Latin; and then the Hebrew, for the Holy Scripture-sake; and then the Chaldee and Arabic likewise, and that thou frame thy style in Greek in imitation of Plato; and for the Latin, after Cicero. Let there be no history which thou shalt not have ready in thy memory;—unto the prosecuting of which design, books of cosmography will be very conducible, and help thee much. Of the liberal arts of geometry, arithmetic and music, I gave thee some taste when thou wert yet little, and not above five or six years old. Proceed further in them, and learn the remainder if thou canst. As for astronomy, study all the rules thereof. Let pass, nevertheless, the divining and judicial astrology, and the art of Lullius, as being nothing else but plain abuses and vanities. As for the civil law, of that I would have thee to know the texts by heart, and then to confer them with philosophy.

Now, in matter of the knowledge of the works of nature, I would have thee to study that exactly; that so there be no sea, river, nor fountain, of which thou dost not know the fishes; all the fowls of the air; all the several kinds of shrubs and trees, whether in forest or orchards; all the sorts of herbs and flowers that grow upon the ground; all the various metals that are hid within the bowels of the earth; together with all the diversity of precious stones, that are to be seen, in the orient and south parts of the world. Let nothing of all these be hidden from thee. Then fail not most carefully to peruse the books of the Greek, Arabian, and Latin physicians, not despising the Talmudists and Cabalists; and by frequent anatomies, get thee the perfect knowledge of that other world, called the microcosm, which is man. And at some of the hours of the day apply thy mind to the study of the Holy Scriptures; first, in Greek, the

New Testament, with the Epistles of the Apostles; and then the Old Testament in Hebrew, in brief, let me see thee an abyss, and bottomless pit of knowledge: for from henceforward, as thou growest great and becomest a man, thou must part from this tranquillity and rest of study, thou must learn chivalry, warfare, and the exercises of the field, the better thereby to defend my house and our friends, and to succour and protect them at all their needs, against the invasion and assaults of evil doers.

Furthermore, I will that very shortly thou try how much thou hast profited, which thou canst not better do, than by maintaining publicly theses and conclusions in all arts, against all persons whatsoever, and by haunting the company of learned men, both at Paris and otherwhere. But because, as the wise man Solomon saith, Wisdom entereth not into a malicious mind, and that knowledge without conscience is but the ruin of the soul; it behoveth thee to serve, to love, to fear God, and on him to cast all thy thoughts and all thy hope, and, by faith formed in charity, to cleave unto him, so that thou mayst never be separated from him by thy sins. Suspect the abuses of the world. Set not thy heart upon vanity, for this life is transitory, but the Word of the Lord endureth for ever. Be serviceable to all thy neighbours, and love them as thyself. Reverence thy preceptors; shun the conversation of those whom thou desirest not to resemble; and receive not in vain the graces which God hath bestowed upon thee. And, when thou shalt see that thou hast attained to all the knowledge that is to be acquired in that part, return unto me, that I may see thee, and give thee my blessing before I die. My son, the peace and grace of our Lord be with thee, Amen.

Thy father, GARGANTUA.

From Utopia *the 17th day of the month of March.*

These letters being received and read, Pantagruel plucked up his heart, took a fresh courage to him, and was inflamed with a desire to profit in his studies more than ever, so that if you had seen him, how he took pains, and how he advanced in learning, you would have said that the vivacity of his spirit amidst the books was like a great fire amongst dry wood, so active it was, vigorous, and indefatigable.

CHAPTER 9

How Pantagruel found Panurge, whom he loved all his life-time

ONE day as Pantagruel was taking a walk without the city, towards St. Anthony's abbey, discoursing and philosophating with his own servants, and some other scholars, he met with a young man of very comely stature, and surpassing handsome in all the lineaments of his body, but in several parts thereof most pitifully wounded; in such bad equipage in matter of his apparel, which was but tatters and rags, and every way so far out of order, that he seemed to have been a-fighting with mastiff dogs, from whose fury he had made an escape, or, to say better, he looked, in the condition wherein he then was, like an applegatherer of the country of Perche.

As far off as Pantagruel saw him, he said to those that stood by, Do you see that man there, who is a coming hither upon the road from Charenton-bridge? By my faith, he is only poor in fortune; for I may assure you, that by his physiognomy it appeareth, that nature hath extracted him from some rich and noble race, and that too much curiosity hath thrown him upon adventures, which possibly have reduced him to this indigence, want, and penury. Now as he was just amongst them, Pantagruel said unto him, Let me entreat you, friend, that you may be pleased to stop here a little, and answer me to that which I shall ask you, and I am confident you will not think your time ill bestowed; for I have an extreme desire, according to my ability, to give you some supply in this distress, wherein I see you are; because I do very much commiserate your case, which truly moves me to great pity. Therefore, my friend, tell me, who you are? Whence you come? Whither you go? What you desire? And what your name is? The companion answered him in the German tongue, thus:

"Junker, Gott geb euch glück und heil zuvor. Lieber Junker, ich lasz euch wissen, das da ihr mich von fragt, ist ein arm und erbärmlich Ding, und wer viel darvon zu sagen, welches euch verdrüssig zu hören, und mir zu erzelen wer, wiewol die Poeten und Oratorn vorzeiten haben gesagt in ihren Sprüchen und Sentenzen, das die gedechtnus des elends und armuths vorlängst erlitten ist eine grosse lust." My friend, said Pantagruel, I have no skill in that gibberish of yours, therefore, if you would have us to understand you, speak

to us in some other language. Then did the drole answer him thus:

"*Albarildim gotfano dechmin brin alabo dordio falbroth ringuam albaras. Nin portzadikin almucatin milko prin alelmin en thoth dalheben ensouim: kuthim al dum alkatim nim broth dechoth porth min michais im endoth, pruch dalmaisoulum hol moth danfrihim lupaldas im voldemoth. Nin hur diavosth mnarbotim dalgousch palfrapin duch im scoth pruch galeth dal chinon, min foulchrich al conin brutathem doth dal prin.*" Do you understand none of this? said Pantagruel to the company. I believe, said Epistemon, that this is the language of the Antipodes, and such a hard one, that the devil himself knows not what to make of it. Then, said Pantagruel, Gossip, I know not if the walls do comprehend the meaning of your words, but none of us here doth so much as understand one syllable of them. Then said my blade again:

"*Signor mio, vio vedete per essempio, che la cornamusa non suona mai, s'ella non ha il ventre pieno. Cosi io parimente non vi saprei contare le mie fortune, se prima il tribulato ventre non ha la solita refettione. Al quale è adviso che le mani et li denti habbiano perso il loro ordine naturale et del tutto annichilati.*" To which Epistemon answered, As much of the one as of the other, and nothing of either, Then said Panurge:

"Lord, if you be so virtuous of intelligence, as you be naturally releaved to the body, you should have pity of me. For nature hath made us equal, but fortune hath some exalted, and others deprived; nevertheless is virtue often deprived, and the virtuous men despised; for before the last end none is good." Yet less, said Pantagruel. Then said my jolly Panurge:

"*Jona andie guaussa goussy etan beharda er remedio beharde versela ysser landa. Anbat es otoy y es nausu ey nessassust gourray proposian ordine den. Non yssena bayta facheria egabe gen herassy badia sadassu noura assia. Aran hondavan gualde cydassu naydassuna, Estou oussyc eg vinan soury hein er darstura eguy harm. Genicoa plasar vadu.*" Are you there, said Eudemon, Genicoa? To this said Carpalim, St. Trinian's rammer unstitch your bum, for I had almost understood it. Then answered Panurge:

"*Prust frest frinst sorgdmand strochdi drhds pag brlelang Gravot Chavigny Pomardiere rusth pkaldracg Deviniere pres Nays. Couille kalmuch monach drupp del muepplist*

rincq drlnd dodelb up drent loch minc stz rinq jald de vins ders cordelis bur jocst stzampenards." Do you speak Christian, said Epistemon, or the buffoon language, otherwise called Patelinois? Nay, it is the puzlatory tongue, said another, which some call Lanternois. Then said Panurge:

"*Heere, ik ken spreeke anders geen tael dan kersten taele: my dunkt noghtans, al en seg ik u niet een wordt, mynen noot verklaert genoegh wat ik begeere: geeft my uyt bermhertigheyt yets, waar van ik gevoet magh zyn.*" To which answered Pantagruel, As much of that. Then said Panurge:

"*Señor, de tanto hablar yo soy cansado, por que yo suplico a vuestra reverentia que mire a los preceptos evangelicos, para que ellos movan vuestra reverentia a lo que es de conscientia; y si ellos non bastaren, para mover vuestra reverentia a piedad, yo suplico que mire a la piedad natural, la qual yo creo que le movera como es de razon: y con esso non digo mas.*" Truly, my friend, said Pantagruel, I doubt not but you can speak divers languages; but tell us that which you would have us to do for you in some tongue, which you conceive we may understand. Then said the companion:

"*Min Herre, endog ieg med ingen tunge talede, ligesom bærn, oc uskellige creatuure: Mine klædebon oc mit legoms magerhed uduiser alligeuel klarlig huad ting mig best behof gioris, som er sandelig mad oc dricke: Huorfor forbarme dig ofuer mig, oc befal at giue mig noguet, af huilchet ieg kand styre min giæendis mage, ligeruiis som mand Cerbero en suppe forsetter: Saa skalt du lefue længe oc lycksalig.*" I think really, said Eusthenes, that the Goths spoke thus of old, and that, if it pleased God, we would all of speak so with our tails. Then again said Panurge:

"*Adon, scalom lecha: im ischar harob hal hebdeca bimeherah thithen li kikar lehem: chanchat ub laah al Adonai cho nen ral.*" To which answered Epistemon, At this time have I understood him very well; for it is the Hebrew tongue most rhetorically pronounced. Then again said the gallant:

"*Despota tinyn panagathe, dioti sy my ouk artodotis? horas gar limo analiscomenon eme athlion, ke en to metaxy me ouk eleis oudamos, zetis de par emou ha ou chre. Ke homos philologi pantes homologousi tote logous te ke remata peritta hyparchin, opote pragma afto pasi delon esti. Entha gar anakei monon logi isin, hina pragmata (hon peri am-*

phisbetoumen), me prosphoros epiphenete." What? said Carpalim, Pantagruel's footman, It is Greek, I have understood him. And how? has thou dwelt any while in Greece? Then said the drole again:

"Agonou dont oussys vous dedagnez algarou: nou den farou zamist vous mariston ulbrou, fousques voubrol tant bredaguez moupreton den goulhoust, daguez daguez non cropys fost pardonnoflist nougrou. Agou paston tol nalprissys hourtou los echatonous, prou dhouquys brol pany gou den bascrou noudous caguons goulfren goul oustaroppassou." Methinks I understand him, said Pantagruel; for either it is the language of my country of Utopia, or sounds very like it. And, as he was about to have begun some argument the companion said:

"Jam toties vos per sacra, perque deos deasque omneis obtestatus sum, ut si qua vos pietas permovet, egestatem meam solaremini, nec hilum proficio clamans et ejulans. Sinite, quæso, sinite, viri impii, quo me fata vocant abire; nec ultra vanis vestris interpellationibus obtundatis, memores veteris illius adagii, quo venter famelicus auriculis carere dicitur."[68] Well, my friend, said Pantagruel, but cannot you speak French? That I can do, Sir, very well, said the companion, God be thanked. It is my natural language and mother tongue; for I was born and bred in my younger years in the garden of France, to wit, Touraine. Then said, Pantagruel, tell us what is your name, and from whence you are come: for, by my faith, I have already stamped in my mind such a deep impression of love towards you, that, if you will condescend unto my will, you shall not depart out of my company, and you and I shall make up another couple of friends, such as Æneas and Achates were. Sir, said the companion, my true and proper Christian name is Panurge, and now I come out of Turkey, to which country I was carried away prisoner at that time, when they went to Metelin with a mischief. And willingly would I relate unto you my fortunes, which are more wonderful than those of Ulysses were; but, seeing that it pleaseth you to retain me with you, I most heartily accept of the offer, protesting never to leave you, should you go to all the devils in hell. We shall have therefore more leisure at another time, and a fitter opportunity wherein to report them; for at this present I am in a very urgent necessity to feed, my teeth are sharp, my belly empty, my throat dry, and my stomach fierce and burning, all is ready. If you will but set me to work, it will be as good as a balsamum for sore eyes to see me gulch and raven it. For God's sake, give order for it. Then Pantagruel commanded that they should carry him home, and provide him good store of victuals; which being done, he ate very well that evening, and, capon-like, went early to bed, then slept until dinner-time the next day, so that he made but three steps and one leap from the bed to the board.

CHAPTER 10

How Pantagruel equitably decided a controversy, which was wonderfully obscure and difficult, whereby he was reputed to have a most admirable judgment

PANTAGRUEL, very well remembering his father's letter and admonitions, would one day make trial of his knowledge. Thereupon in all the *Carrefours*, that is, throughout all the four quarters, streets, and corners of the city, he set up Conclusions, to the number of nine thousand seven hundred and sixty-four, in all manner of learning, touching in them the hardest doubts that are in any science. And first of all, in the Fodder-street he held dispute against all the regents or fellows of colleges, artists or masters of arts, and orators, and did so gallantly, that he overthrew them, and set them all upon their tails. He went afterwards to the Sorbonne, where he maintained argument against all the theologians or divines, for the space of six weeks, from four o'clock in the morning until six in the evening, except an interval of two hours to refresh themselves, and take their repast. And at this were present the greatest part of the lords of the court, the masters of requests, presidents, counsellors, those of the accompts, secretaries, advocates and others: as also the sheriffs of the said town, with the physicians and professors of the canon-law. Amongst which, it is to be remarked, that the greatest part were stubborn jades, and in their opinions obstinate; but he took such course with them, that for all their *ergos* and fallacies, he put their backs to the wall, gravelled them in the deepest questions and made it visibly appear to the world, that compared to him, they were but monkeys, and a knot of muffled calves. Whereupon every body began to keep a bustling noise, and talk of his so marvellous knowledge, through all degrees of persons in both sexes, even to the very laundresses, brokers, roastmeat-sellers, penknife-makers and others, who, when he past along in the street, would say, This is he! In which he took delight, as Demosthenes the prince of Greek orators did, when an old crouching wife, pointing at him with her fingers, said, That is the man.

Now at this same very time there was a process or suit in law depending in court between two great lords, of which one was called my Lord Kissbreech, plaintiff of one side, and the other my Lord Suckfist, defendant of the other; whose controversy was so high and difficult in law, that the court of parliament could make nothing of it. And, therefore, by the commandment of the king there were assembled four of the greatest and most learned of all the parliaments of France, together with the great counsel, and all the principal regents of the universities, not only of France, but of England also and Italy, such as Jason, Philippus Decius, Petrus de Petronibus, and a rabble of other old Rabbinists; who being thus met together, after they had thereupon consulted for the space of six and forty weeks, finding that they could not fasten their teeth in it, nor with such clearness understand the case, as that they might in any manner of way be able to right it, or to take up the difference betwixt the two aforesaid parties, it did so grievously vex them, that they most villanously conshit themselves for shame. In this great extremity one amongst them, named Du Douhet, the learnedest of all, and more expert and prudent than any of the rest, whilst one day they were thus at their wit's end, all-to-be-dunced and philogrobolized in their brains, said unto them. We have been here, my masters, a good long space, without doing any thing else than trifle away both our time and money, and can nevertheless find neither brim nor bottom in this matter, for, the more we study about it, the less we understand therein, which is a great shame, and disgrace to us, and a heavy burden to our consciences, yea, such, that in my opinion we shall not rid ourselves of it without dishonour unless we take some other course; for we do nothing but doat in our consultations.

See, therefore, what I have thought upon. You have heard much talking of that worthy personage named Master Pantagruel, who hath been found to be learned above the capacity of this present age, by the proofs he gave in those great disputations, which he held publicly against all men. My opinion is, that we send for him, to confer with him about this business; for never any man will compass the bringing of it to an end, if he do it not.

Hereunto all the counsellors and doctors willingly agreed, and, according to that their result, having instantly sent for him, they intreated him to be pleased to canvas the process, and sift it thoroughly, that, after a deep search and narrow examination of all the points thereof, he might forthwith make the report unto them, such as he shall think good in true and legal knowledge. To this effect they delivered into his hands the bags wherein were the writs and pancarts concerning that suit, which for bulk and weight were almost enough to load four great *couillard* or stoned asses. But Pantagruel said unto them, Are the two lords, between whom this debate and process is, yet living? It was answered him, Yes. To what a devil, then, said he, serve so many paltry heaps, and bundles of papers and copies which you give me? Is it not better to hear their controversy from their own mouths, whilst they are face to face before us, than to read these vile fopperies, which are nothing but trumperies, deceits, diabolical cozenages of Cepola, pernicious slights and subversions of equity? For I am sure, that you, and all those through whose hands this process hath past, have by your devices added what you could to it *pro et contra* in such sort, that, although their difference perhaps was clear and easy enough to determine at first, you have obscured it, and made it more intricate, by the frivolous, sottish, unreasonable and foolish reasons and opinions of Accursius, Baldus, Bartolus, de Castro, de Imola, Hippolytus, Panormo, Bertachin, Alexander, Curtius, and those other old mastiffs, who never understood the least law of the Pandects, they being but mere blockheads and great tithe-calves, ignorant of all that which was needful for the understanding of the laws; for, as it is most certain, they had not the knowledge either of the Greek or Latin tongue, but only of the Gothic and Barbarian. The laws, nevertheless, were first taken from the Greeks, according to the testimony of Ulpian, *L. poster. De Origine Juris*, which we likewise may perceive, by that all the laws are full of Greek words and sentences. And then we find that they are reduced into a Latin style, the most elegant and ornate that whole language is able to afford, without excepting that of any that ever wrote therein, nay, not of Sallust, Varro, Cicero, Seneca, Titus Livius, nor Quintilian. How, then, could these old dotards be able to understand aright the text of the laws, who never in their time had looked upon a good Latin book, as doth evidently enough appear by the rudeness of their style, which is fitter for a chimney-sweeper, or for a cook or a scullion, than for a juris-consult and doctor in the laws?

Furthermore, seeing the laws are excerpted out of the middle of moral and natural philosophy, how should these fools have understood it, that have, by G—, studied less in philosophy than my mule? In respect of human learning, and the knowledge of antiquities and history, they were truly laden with those faculties as a toad is with feathers. And yet of all this the laws are so full, that without it they cannot be understood, as I intend more fully to show unto you in a peculiar treatise, which on that purpose I am about to publish. Therefore, if you will that I make any meddling in this process, first, cause all these papers to be burned; secondly, make the two gentlemen come personally before me, and, afterwards, when I shall have heard them, I will tell you my opinion freely, without any feignedness or dissimulation whatsoever.

Some amongst them did contradict this motion, as you know that in all companies there are more fools than wise men, and that the greater part always surmounts the better, as saith Titus Livius, in speaking of the Carthaginians. But the aforesaid Du Douhet held the contrary opinion, maintaining that Pantagruel had said well, and what was right, in affirming that these records, bills of inquests, replies, rejoinders, exceptions, depositions, and other such diableries of truth-intangling writs, were but engines wherewith to overthrow justice, and unnecessarily to prolong such suits as did depend before them; and that, therefore, the devil would carry all away to hell, if they did not take another course, and proceeded not in times coming according to the prescripts of evangelical and philosophical equity. In fine, all the papers were burned, and the two gentlemen summoned and personally convented. At whose appearance before the court, Pantagruel said unto them, Are you they who have this great difference betwixt you? Yes, my lord, said they. Which of you, said Pantagruel, is the plaintiff? It is I, said my Lord Kissbreech. Go to, then my friend, said he, and relate your matter unto me from point to point, according to the real truth, or else, by cock's body, if I find you to lie so much as in one word, I will make you shorter by the head, and take it from off your shoulders, to show others, by your example, that in justice and judgment men ought to speak nothing but the truth. Therefore take heed you do not add nor impair anything in the narration of your case. Begin.

CHAPTER 11

How the Lords of Kissbreech and Suckfist did plead before Pantagruel without an Attorney

THEN began Kissbreech in manner as followeth: My Lord, it is true, that a good woman of my house carried eggs to the market to sell. Be covered, Kissbreech, said Pantagruel. Thanks to you, my Lord, said the Lord Kissbreech; but to the purpose. There passed betwixt the two tropics the sum of three pence towards the zenith and a halfpenny, forasmuch as the Riphæan mountains had been that year oppressed with a great sterility of counterfeit gudgeons, and shows without substance, by means of the babbling tattle, and fond fibs, seditiously raised between the gibble-gabblers, and Accursian gibberish-mongers, for the rebellion of the Switzers, who had assembled themselves to the full number of the bum-bees, and myrmidons, to go ahandsel-getting on the first day of the new year, at that very time when they give brewis to the oxen, and deliver the key of the coals to the country-girls, for serving in of the oats to the dogs. All the night long they did nothing else, keeping their hands still upon the pot, but dispatch bulls a-foot, and bulls a-horseback, to stop the boats; for the tailors and seamsters would have made of the stolen shreds and clippings a goodly sagbut to cover the face of the ocean, which then was great with child of a potful of cabbage, according to the opinion of the hay-bundle-makers. But the physicians said, that by the urine they could discern no manifest sign of the bustard's pace, nor how to eat double-tongued mattocks with mustard, unless the lords and gentlemen of the court should be pleased to give by b. mol. express command to the pox, not to run about any longer, in gleaning up of coppersmiths and tinkers; for the jobbernolls had already a pretty good beginning in their dance of the British jig, called the *estrindore,* to a perfect diapason, with one foot in the fire, and their head in the middle, as good man Ragot was wont to say.

Ha, my masters, God moderates all things, and disposeth of them at his pleasure, so that against unlucky fortune a carter broke his frisking whip, which was all the wind instrument he had. This was done at his return from a little paltry town, even then when Master Antitus of Cresseplots was licentiated, and had passed his degrees in all dullery and blockishness, according to this sentence of the canonists, *Beati dunces, quoniam ipsi stumblaverunt.*[69] But that which makes Lent to be so high, by St. Fiacre of Bry, is for nothing else, but that Pentecost never comes, but to my cost; yet, on afore there, ho! a little rain stills a great wind; and we must think so, seeing that the sergeant hath propounded the matter so far above my reach, that the clerks and secondaries could not with the benefit thereof lick their fingers, feathered with ganders, so orbicularly as they were wont in other things to do. And we do manifestly see, that every one acknowledgeth himself to be in the error, wherewith another hath been charged, reserving only those cases whereby we are obliged to take an ocular inspection in a perspective glass of these things, towards the place in the chimney, where hangeth the sign of the wine of forty girths, which have been always counted very necessary for the number of twenty pannels and pack-saddles of the bankrupt protectionaries of five years respite. Howsoever, at least, he, that would not let fly the fowl before the cheesecakes, ought in law to have discovered his reason why not, for the memory is often lost in the wayward shoeing. Well, God keep Theobal Mitain from all danger. Then said Pantagruel, Hold there! Ho! my friend, soft and fair, speak at leisure, and soberly, without putting yourself in choler. I understand the case,—go on. Now then, my lord, said Kissbreech, the foresaid good woman, saying her *Gaudez* and *Audi nos,* could not cover herself with a treacherous back-blow, ascending by the wounds and passions of the privileges of the universities, unless by the virtue of a warming-pan she had angelically fomented every part of her body, in covering them with a hedge of garden-beds: then giving in a swift unavoidable thrust very near to the place where they sell the old rags, whereof the painters of Flanders make great use, when they are about neatly to clap on shoes on grasshoppers, locusts, *cigals* and such like fly-fowls, so strange to us, that I am wonderfully astonished why the world doth not lay, seeing it is so good to hatch.

Here the Lord of Suckfist would have interrupted him and spoken somewhat, whereupon Pantagruel said unto him, St! by St. Anthony's belly, doth it become thee to speak without command? I sweat here with the extremity of labour and exceeding toil I take to understand the proceeding of your mutual difference, and yet thou comest to trouble and disquiet me. Peace, in the devil's name, peace. Thou shalt be permitted to speak thy bellyful, when this man hath done, and no sooner. Go on, said he to Kissbreech, speak calmly, and do not overheat yourself with too much haste.

In perceiving, then, said Kissbreech, that the pragmatical sanction did make no mention of it, and that the holy Pope to every one gave liberty to fart at his own ease, if that the blankets had no streaks, wherein the liars were to be crossed with a ruffian like crew, and the rainbow being newly sharpened at Milan to bring forth larks, gave his full consent that the good woman should tread down the heel of the hip-gut pangs, by virtue of a solemn protestation put in by the little testiculated or codsted fishes, which, to tell the truth, were at that time very necessary for understanding the syntax and construction of old boots. Therefore John Calf, her cousin gervais once removed, with a log, from the woodstock, very seriously advised her not to put herself into the hazard of quagswagging in the lee, to be scoured with a buck of linen clothes, till first she had kindled the paper. This counsel she laid hold on, because he desired her to take nothing, and throw out, for *Non de ponte vadit, qui cum sapientia cadit.*[70] Matters thus standing, seeing the masters of the chamber of accompts, or members of that committee, did not fully agree amongst themselves in casting up the number of the Almany whistles, whereof were framed those *Spectacles for Princes,* which have been lately printed at Antwerp, I must needs think that it makes a bad return of the writ, and that the adverse party is not to be believed *in sacer verbo dotis*.[71] For that having a great desire to obey the pleasure of the king, I armed myself from toe to top with belly furniture, of the soles of good venison-pasties, to go see how my grape-gathers and vintagers had pinked and cut full of small holes their high coped-caps, to lecher it the better, and play at in and in. And indeed the time was very dangerous in coming from the fair, in so far that many trained bow-men were cast at the muster, and quite rejected, although the chimney-tops were high enough, according to the proportion of the windgalls in the legs of horses, or of the malanders, which in the esteem of expert farriers is no better disease, or else the story of Ronypatifam, or Lamibaudichon, interpreted by some to be the tale of a tub, or of a roasted horse, savours of apocrypha, and is not an authentic history. And by this means there was that year great abundance, throughout all the country of Artois, of tawny buzzing beetles, to the no small profit of the gentlemen-great-stick-faggot-carriers, when they did eat without disdaining the cocklicranes, till their belly was like to crack with it again. As for my own part, such is my Christian charity towards my neighbours, that I could wish from my heart every one as good a voice, it would make us play the better at the tennis and the baloon. And truly, my Lord, to express the real truth without dissimulation, I cannot but say, that those petty subtile devices, which are found out in the etymologizing of pattens, would descend more easily into the river of Seine, to serve for ever at the millers' bridge upon the said water, as it was heretofore decreed by the king of the Canarians, according to the sentence or judgment given thereupon, which is to be seen in the registry and records within the clerk's office of this house.

And therefore, my Lord, I most humbly require, that by your Lordship there may be said and declared upon the case what is reasonable, with costs, damages, and interest. Then said Pantagruel, My friend is this all you have to say? Kissbreech answered yes, my Lord, for I have told you all the *tu autem*,[72] and have not varied at all upon mine honour in so much as one single word. You then, said Pantagruel, my Lord of Suckfist, say what you will, and be brief, without omitting, nevertheless, anything that may serve to the purpose.

CHAPTER 12

How the Lord of Suckfist pleaded before Pantagruel

THEN began the Lord Suckfist in manner as followeth. My Lord, and you my masters, if the iniquity of men were as easily seen in categorical judgment, as we can discern flies in a milk-pot, the world's four oxen had not been so eaten up with rats, nor had so many ears upon the earth been nibbled away so scurvily. For although all that my adversary hath spoken be of a very soft and downy truth, in so much as concerns the letter and history of the *factum*,[73] yet nevertheless, the crafty slights, cunning subtilties, sly cozenages, and little troubling intanglements are hid under the rose-pot, the common cloak and cover of all fraudulent deceits.

Should I endure, that, when I am eating my pottage equal with the best, and that without either thinking or speaking any manner of ill, they rudely come to vex, trouble, and perplex my brains with that antique proverb, which saith:

He that will in his pottage drink
When he is dead shall not see one wink.

And, good lady, how many great captains have we seen in the day of battle, when in open field the sacrament was distributed in luncheons of the sanctified bread of the confraternity, the more honestly to nod their heads, play on the lute, and crack with their tails, to make pretty little platform leaps, in keeping level by the ground? But now the world is unshackled from the corners of the packs of Leicester. One flies out lewdly and becomes debauched, another, likewise, five, four, and two, and that at such random, that, if the court take not some course therein, it will make as bad a season in matter of gleaning this year, as ever it made, or it will make goblets. If any poor creature go to the stoves to illuminate his muzzle with a cowshard, or to buy winter-boots, and that the sergeants passing by, or those of the watch, happen to receive the decoction of a clyster, or the fecal matter of a close-stool, upon their rustling-wrangling-clutter-keeping masterships, should any because of that make bold to clip the shillings and testers, and fry the wooden dishes? Sometimes, when we think one thing, God does another; and when the sun is wholly set, all beasts are in the shade.

Let me never be believed again, if I do not gallantly prove it by several people that have seen the light of the day.

In the year thirty and six, buying a Dutch curtail, which was a middle-sized horse, both high and short, of a wool good enough, and dyed in grain, as the goldsmiths assured me, although the notary put an &c. in it, I told really, that I was not a clerk of so much learning as to snatch at the moon with my teeth; but, as for the butter-firkin, where Vulcanian deeds and evidences were sealed, the rumour was, and the report thereof went current, that salt-beef will make one find the way to the wine without a candle, though it were hid in the bottom of a collier's sack, and that, with his drawers on he were mounted on a barbed horse furnished with a fronstal, and such arms, thighs, and leg-pieces as are requisite for the well frying and broiling of a swaggering sauciness. Here is a sheep's head, and it is well they make a proverb of this, that it is good to see black cows in burnt wood, when one attains to the enjoyment of his love. I had a consultation upon this point with my masters the clerks, who for resolution concluded in *frisesomorum*,[74] that there is nothing like to mowing in the summer, and sweeping clean away in water, well garnished with paper, ink, pens, and penknives of Lyons upon the river of Rhone; *dolopym dolopof, tarabin tarabas, tut, prut, pish:* for, incontinently after that armour begins to smell of garlick, the rust will go near to eat the liver, not of him that wears it; and then do they nothing else but withstand others' courses, and wryneckedly set up their bristles against one another, in lightly passing over their afternoon's sleep; and this is that which maketh salt so dear. My Lords, believe not when the said good woman had with bird-lime caught the shovelar fowl, the better before a serjeant's witness to deliver the younger son's portion to him, that the sheep's pluck or hog's haslet, did lodge and shrink back in the usurer's purses, or that there could be anything better to preserve one from the cannibals, than to take a rope of onions, knit with three hundred turnips, and a little of a calf's chaldern of the best alloy that the alchymists have provided, and that they daub and do over with clay, as also calcinate and burn to dust these pantofles, muff in muff out, *mouflin mouflard,* with the fine sauce of the juice of the rabble rout, whilst they hide themselves in some petty moldwharp-hole, saving always the little slices of bacon. Now, if the dice will not favour you with any other throw but ambes-ace, and the chance of three at the great end, mark well the ace, then take me your dame, settle her in a corner of the bed, and whisk me her up drille trille, there, there, *troureloura la la;* which when you have done, take a hearty draught of the best, *despicando grenovillibus,*[75] in despite of the frogs, whose fair coarse bebuskined stockings shall be set apart, for the little green geese, or mued goslings, which, fattened in a coop, take delight to sport themselves at the wag-tail game, waiting for the beating of the metal, and heating of the wax by the slavering drivellers of consolation.

Very true it is, that the four oxen which are in debate, and whereof mention was made, were somewhat short in memory. Nevertheless, to understand the game aright, they feared neither the cormorant nor mallard of Savoy, which put the good people of my country in great hope that their children some time should become very skilful in algorism. Therefore is it, that by a law rubric and special sentence thereof, that we cannot fail to take the wolf, if we make our hedges higher than the wind-mill, whereof somewhat was spoken by the plaintiff. But the great devil did envy it, and by that means put the High Dutch far behind, who played the devils in swilling down and tippling at the good liquor, *trink, meen herr, trink,* by two of my table men in the corner-point I have gained the lurch. For it is not probable, nor is there any appearance of truth in this saying, that at Paris upon a little bridge the hen is proportionable, and were they as copped and high-crested as marish whoops, if veritably they did not sacrifice the printer's pumpet-balls at Moreb, with a new edge set upon them by text letters, or those of a swift-writing hand, it is all one to me, so that the head-band of the book breed not moths or worms in it. And put the case, that at the coupling together of the buck-hounds, the little puppies should have waxed proud, before the notary could have given an account of the serving of his writ by the cabalistic art, it will necessarily follow, under correction of the better judgment of the court, that six acres of meadow ground of the greatest breadth will make three buts of fine ink, without paying ready money; considering that, at the funeral of King Charles, we might have had the fathom in open market for one and two, that is, deuce ace. This I may affirm with a safe conscience, upon my oath of wool.

And I see ordinarily in all good bag-pipes, that, when they go to the counterfeiting of the chirping of small birds, by swinging a broom three times about a chimney, and putting his name upon record, they do nothing but bend a cross-bow backwards, and wind a horn, if perhaps it be too hot, and that, by making if fast to a rope he was to draw, immediately after the sight of the letters, the cows were restored to him. Such another sentence after the homeliest manner was pronounced in the seventeenth year, because of the bad government of Louzefougarouse, whereunto it may please the Court to have regard. I desire to be rightly understood; for truly, I say not, but that in all equity, and with an upright conscience, those may very well be dispossessed, who drink holy water, as one would do a weaver's shuttle, whereof suppositories are made to those that will not resign, but on the terms of ell and tell, and giving of one thing for another. *Tunc,* my Lords, *quid juris pro minoribus?*[76] For the common custom of the Salic law is such, that the first incendiary or fire-brand of sedition, that flays the cow and wipes his nose in a full concert of music, without blowing in the cobbler's stitches, should in the time of the nightmare sublimate the penury of his member by moss gathered when people are like to founder themselves at the mass at midnight, to give the estrapade to these white-wines of Anjou, that do gambetta, neck to neck, after the fashion of Brittany, concluding as before with costs, damages, and interests.

After that the Lord of Suckfist had ended, Pantagruel said to the Lord of Kissbreech, My friend, have you a mind to make any reply to what is said? No, my lord, answered Kissbreech; for I have spoke all I intended, and nothing but the truth. Therefore, put an end, for God's sake, to our difference, for we are here at great charge.

CHAPTER 13

How Pantagruel gave judgment upon the difference of the two Lords

THEN Pantagruel, rising up, assembled all the presidents, counsellors, and doctors that were there, and said unto them, Come now, my masters, you have heard, *vivæ vocis oraculo,*[77] the controversy that is in question; what do you think of it? They answered him, We have indeed heard it, but have not understood the devil so much as one circumstance of the case; and therefore we beseech you, *unâ voce,*[78] and in courtesy request you that you would give sentence as you think good, and *ex nunc prout ex tunc,*[79] we are satisfied with it, and do ratify it with our full consents. Well, my masters, said Pantagruel, seeing you are so well pleased, I will do it: but I do not truly find the case so difficult as you make it. Your paragraph *Caton,* the law *Frater,* the law *Gallus,* the law *Quinque pedum,* the law *Vinum,* the law *Si Dominus,* the law *Mater,* the law *Prætor,* the law *Venditor;* and a great *Pomponius,* the law *Fundi,* the law *Emptor,* the law *Praetor,* the law *Venditor;* and a great many others, are far more intricate in my opinion. After he had spoke this, he walked a turn or two about the hall, plodding very profoundly, as one may think; for he did groan like an ass, whilst they girth him too hard, with the very intensiveness of considering how he was bound in conscience to do right to both parties, without varying or accepting of persons. Then he returned, sat down, and began to pronounce sentence as followeth:

"Having seen, heard, calculated, and well-considered of the difference between the Lords of Kissbreech and Suckfist, the Court saith unto them, that in regard of the sudden quaking, shivering, and hoariness of the flickermouse, bravely declining from the estival solstice, to attempt by private means the surprisal of toyish trifles in those, who are a little unwell for having taken a draught too much, through the lewd demeanour and vexation of the beetles, that inhabit the diarodal climate of an hypocritical ape on horseback, bending a cross-bow backwards, the plaintiff truly had just cause to calfet, or with oakum, to stop the chinks of the galleon, which the good woman blew up with wind, having one foot shod and the other bare, reimbursing and restoring to him, low and stiff in his conscience, as many bladder-nuts and wild pistachios as there is of hair in eighteen cows, with as much for the embroiderer, and so much for that. He is likewise declared innocent of the case privileged from the Knapdardies, into the danger whereof it was thought he had incurred; because he could not jocundly, and with fulness of freedom, untruss and dung, by the decision of a pair of gloves perfumed with the scent of bum-gunshot, at the walnut tree taper, as is usual in his country of Mirebalais. Slacking, therefore, the top-sail, and letting go the boulin with the brazen bullets, wherewith the mariners did by way of protestation bake in paste-meat, great store of pulse interquilted with the dormouse, whose hawk-bells were made with a puntinaria, after the manner of Hungary or Flanders lace, and which his brother-in-law carried in a pannier, lying near to three chevrons or bordered gules, whilst he was clean out of heart, drooping and crest-fallen by the too narrow sifting, canvassing, and curious examining of the matter, in the angularly dog-hole of nasty scoundrels, from whence we shoot at the vermiformal popinjay with the flap made of a foxtail.

"But in that he chargeth the defendant, that he was a botcher, cheese-eater, and trimmer of man's flesh embalmed, which in the arsiversy swagfall tumble was not found true, as by the defendant was very well discussed.

"The Court, therefore, doth condemn and amerce him in three porringers of curds, well cemented and closed together, shining like pearls, and cod-pieced after the fashion of the country, to be paid unto the said defendant about the middle of August in May. But on the other part, the defendant shall be bound to furnish him with hay and stubble, for stopping the caltrops of his throat, troubled and impulregafized, with gabardines garbled shufflingly, and friends as before, without costs and for cause."

Which sentence being pronounced, the two parties departed, both contented with the decree, which was a thing almost incredible. For it never came to pass since the great rain, nor shall the like occur in thirteen jubilees hereafter, that two parties, contradictorily contending in judgment, be equally satisfied and well pleased with the definitive sentence. As for the counsellors, and other doctors in the law, that were there present, they were all so ravished with admiration at the more than human wisdom of Pantagruel, which they did most clearly perceive to be in him, by his so accurate decision of this so difficult and thorny cause, that their spirits, with the extremity of the rapture, being elevated above the pitch of actuating the organs of the body, they fell into a trance and sudden ecstasy, wherein they stayed for the space of three long hours, and had been so as yet in that condition, had not some good people

fetched store of vinegar and rosewater to bring them again unto their former sense and understanding, for the which God be praised everywhere. And so be it.

CHAPTER 14

How Panurge related the manner how he escaped out of the hands of the Turks

THE great wit and judgment of Pantagruel was immediately after this made known unto all the world by setting forth his praises in print, and putting upon record this late wonderful proof he hath given thereof amongst the Rolls of the Crown, and Registers of the Palace, in such sort, that everybody began to say, that Solomon, who by a probable guess only, without any further certainty, caused the child to be delivered to its own mother, showed never in his time such a master-piece of wisdom, as the good Pantagruel hath done. Happy are we, therefore, that have him in our country. And, indeed, they would have made him thereupon master of the requests, and president in the court: but he refused all, very graciously thanking them for their offer. For, said he, there is too much slavery in these offices, and very hardly can they be saved that do exercise them, considering the great corruption that is amongst men. Which makes me believe, if the empty seats of angels be not filled with other kind of people than those, we shall not have the final judgment these seven thousand sixty and seven jubilees yet to come, and so Cusanus will be deceived in his conjecture. Remember that I have told you of it, and given you fair advertisement in time and place convenient.

But, if you have any hogsheads of good wine, I willingly will accept of a present of that. Which they very heartily did do, in sending him of the best that was in the city, and he drank reasonably well, but poor Panurge bibbed and bowsed of it most villanously, for he was as dry as a red-herring, as lean as a rake, and, like a poor, lank, slender cat, walked gingerly as if he had trod upon eggs. So that by some one being admonished in the midst of his draught of a large deep bowl, full of excellent claret, with these words,—Fair and softly, gossip, you suck as if you were mad. I give thee to the devil, said he, thou hast not found here thy little tippling sippers of Paris, that drink no more than the little bird called a spink or chaffinch, and never take in their beak full of liquor, till they be bobbed on the tails after the manner of the sparrows. O companion, if I could mount up as well as I can get down, I had been long ere this above the sphere of the moon with Empedocles. But I cannot tell what a devil this means. This wine is so good and delicious, that, the more I think thereof, the more I am athirst. I believe that the shadow of my master Pantagruel engendereth the altered and thirsty men, as the moon doth the catarrhs and defluxions. At which word the company began to laugh, which Pantagruel perceiving, said, Panurge, what is that which moves you to laugh so? Sir, said he, I was telling them that these devilish Turks are very unhappy, in that they never drink one drop of wine, and that though there were no other harm in all Mahomet's *Alcoran,* yet for this one base point of abstinence from wine, which therein is commanded, I would not submit myself unto their law. But now tell me, said Pantagruel, how you escaped out of their hands. By G—, sir, said Panurge, I will not lie to you in one word.

The rascally Turks had broached me upon a spit all larded like a rabbit, for I was so dry and meagre, that, otherwise, of my flesh they would have made but very bad meat, and in this manner began to roast me alive. As they were thus roasting me, I recommended myself unto the divine grace, having in my mind the good St. Lawrence, and always hoped in God that he would deliver me out of this torment. Which came to pass, and that very strangely. For, as I did commit myself with all my heart unto God, crying, Lord God, help me, Lord God, save me, Lord God, take me out of this pain and hellish torture, wherein these traitorous dogs detain me for my sincerity in the maintenance of thy law! the roaster or turn-spit fell asleep by the divine will, or else by the virtue of some good Mercury, who cunningly brought Argus into a sleep for all his hundred eyes. When I saw that he did no longer turn me in roasting, I looked upon him, and perceived that he was fast asleep. Then took I up in my teeth a firebrand by the end where it was not burned, and cast it into the lap of my roaster, and another did I throw as well as I could under a field-couch, that was placed near to the chimney, wherein was the straw-bed of my master turn-spit. Presently the fire took hold in the straw, and from the straw to the bed, and from the bed to the loft, which was planked and sealed with fir, after the fashion of the foot of a lamp. But the best was, that the fire which I had cast into the lap of my poultry roaster burned all his groin, and was beginning to seize upon his cullions, when he became sensible of the danger, for his smelling was not so bad, but that he felt it sooner than he could have seen daylight. Then suddenly getting up, and in a great amazement running to the window, he cried out to the streets as high as he could, *Dal baroth, dal baroth, dal baroth,* which is as much as to say Fire, fire, fire. Incontinently turning about, he came straight towards me, to throw me quite into the fire, and to that effect had already cut the ropes, wherewith my hands were tied, and was undoing the cords from off my feet, when the master of the house hearing him cry fire, and smelling the smoke from the very street where he was walking with some other Bashaws and Mustaphas, ran with all the speed he had to save what he could, and to carry away his jewels. Yet such was his rage, before he could well resolve how to go about it, that he caught the broach whereon I was spitted, and therewith killed my roaster stark dead, of which wound he died there for want of regimen or otherwise; for he ran him in with the spit a little above the naval, towards the right flank, till he pierced the third lappet of his liver, and, the blow slanting upwards from the midriff or diaphragm, through which it had made penetration, the spit passed athwart the pericardium, or capsule of his heart, and came out above at his shoulders, betwixt the spondyls or turning joints of the chine of the back, and the left homoplat, which we call the shoulder-blade.

True it is, for I will not lie, that, in drawing the spit out of my body, I fell to the ground near unto the andirons, and so by the fall took some hurt, which indeed had been greater, but that the lardons, or little slices of bacon, wherewith I was stuck, kept off the blow. My bashaw then seeing the case to be desperate, his house burnt without remission, and all his goods lost, gave himself over unto all the devils in hell, calling upon some of them by their names, Grilgoth, Astaroth, Rappalus, and Gribouillis, nine several times. Which when I saw, I had above five penny worth of fear, dreading that the devils would come even then to carry away this fool, and, seeing me so near him, would perhaps snatch me up too. I am already, thought I, half roasted, and my lardons will be the cause of my mischief; for these devils are very liquorous of lardons, according to the authority which you have of the philosopher Jamblicus, and Murmault, in the *Apology* of Bossutis, adulterated *pro magistros nostros*. But for my better security I made the sign of the cross, crying, *Hagios, athanatos ho Theos*,[80] and none came. At which my rogue bashaw, being very much aggrieved, would, in transpiercing his heart with my spit, have killed himself, and to that purpose had set it against his breast, but it could not enter, because it was not sharp enough. Whereupon I, perceiving that he was not like to work upon his body the effect which he intended, although he did not spare all the force he had to thrust it forward, came up to him and said, Master Bugrino, thou dost here but trifle away thy time, or rashly lose it, for thou wilt never kill thyself as thou doest. Well, thou mayest hurt or bruise somewhat within thee, so as to make thee languish all thy life-time most pitifully amongst the hands of the chirurgeons; but, if thou wilt be counselled by me, I will kill thee clear outright, so that thou shalt not so much as feel it, and trust me, for I have killed a great many others, who have found themselves very well after it. Ha, my friend, said he, I prithee do so, and for thy pains I give thee my budget; take, here it is, there are six hundred seraphs in it and some fine diamonds, and most excellent rubies. And where are they, said Epistemon? By St. John, said Panurge, they are a good way hence, if they always keep going. But where is the last year's snow? This was the greatest care that Villon the Parisian poet took. Make an end, said Pantagruel, that we may know how thou didst dress they bashaw. By the faith of an honest man, said Panurge, I do not lie in one word. I swaddled him in a scurvy swathel-binding, which I found lying there half burnt, and with my cords tied him royster-like both hand and foot, in such sort that he was not able to wince; then past my spit through his throat, and hanged him thereon, fastening the end thereof at two great hooks or cramp-irons, upon which they did hang their halberds; and then, kindling a fair fire under him, did flame you up my Milourt, as they use to do dry herrings in a chimney. With this, taking his budget, and a little javelin that was upon the aforesaid hooks, I ran away a fair gallop-rake, and God he knows how I did smell my shoulder of mutton.

When I came down into the street, I found every body came to put out the fire with store of water, and seeing me so half-roasted, they did naturally pity my case, and threw all their water upon me, which, by a most joyful refreshing of me, did me very much good. Then did they present me with some victuals, but I could not eat much, because they gave me nothing to drink but water after their fashion. Other hurt they did me none, only one little villanous Turkey knob-breasted rogue came thiefteously to snatch away some of my lardons, but I gave him such a sturdy thump and sound rap on the fingers with all the weight of my javelin, that he came no more the second time. Shortly after this, there came towards me a pretty young Corinthian wench, who brought me a box full of conserves, of round Mirabolan plums, called emblicks, and looked upon my poor robin with an eye of great compassion, as it was flea-bitten and pinked with the sparkles of the fire from whence it came, for it reached no farther in length, believe me, than my knees. But note, that this roasting cured me entirely of a sciatica, whereunto I had been subject above seven years before, upon that side, which my roaster, by falling asleep, suffered to be burnt.

Now, whilst they were busy about me, the fire triumphed, never ask how? For it took hold on above two thousand houses, which one of them espying cried out, saying, By Mahoom's belly, all the city is on fire, and we do nevertheless stand gazing here, without offering to make any relief. Upon this every one ran to save his own; for my part, I took my way towards the gate. When I was got upon the knap of a little hillock, not far off, I turned me about as did Lot's wife, and, looking back, saw all the city burning in a fair fire, whereat I was so glad, that I had almost beshit myself for joy. But God punished me well for it. How? said Pantagruel. Thus, said Panurge; for when with pleasure I beheld his jolly fire, jesting with myself, and saying,— Ha! poor flies, ha! poor mice, you will have a bad winter of it this year, the fire is in your reeks, it is in your bed-straw,—out came more than six, yea more than thirteen hundred and eleven dogs, great and small, altogether out of the town, flying away from the fire. At the first approach they ran all upon me, being carried on by the scent of my lecherous half-roasted flesh, and had even then devoured me in a trice, if my good angel had not well inspired me with the instruction of a remedy, very sovereign against the toothache.

And wherefore, said Pantagruel, wert thou afraid of the toothache, or pain of the teeth? Wert thou not cured of thy rheums? By Palm Sunday, said Panurge, is there any greater pain of the teeth, than when the dogs have you by the legs? But on a sudden, as my good angel directed me, I thought upon my lardons, and threw them into the midst of the field amongst them. Then did the dogs run, and fight with one another at fair teeth, which should have the lardons. By this means they left me, and I left them also bustling with, and hairing one another. Thus did I escape frolic and lively, grammercy roast-meat and cookery.

CHAPTER 15

How Panurge showed a very new way to build the Walls of Paris

PANTAGRUEL, one day to refresh himself of his study, went a walking towards St. Marcel's suburbs, to see the extravagancy of the Gobeline building, and to taste of their spiced bread. Panurge was with him, having always a flagon under his gown, and a good slice of gammon of bacon; for without this he never went, saying, that it was as a yeoman of the guard to him, to preserve his body from harm. Other sword carried he none: and, when Pantagruel would have given him one, he answered, that he needed none, for that it would but heat his milt. Yea, but, said Epistemon, if thou shouldst be set upon, how wouldst thou defend thyself? With great brodkin blows, answered he, provided thrusts were forbidden. At their return, Panurge considered the walls of the city of Paris, and in derision said to Pantagruel, See what fair walls are here? O how strong they are, and well fitted to keep geese in a mew or coop to fatten them! By my beard they are competently scurvy for such a city as this is; for a cow with one fart would go near to overthrow above six fathoms of them. O my friend, said Pantagruel, dost thou know what Agesilaus said, when he was asked, Why the great city of Lacedæmon was not inclosed with walls? Lo here, said he, the walls of the city! in showing them the inhabitants and citizens thereof, so strong, so well-armed, so expert in military discipline; signifying thereby, that there is no wall but of bones, and that towns and cities cannot have a surer wall, nor better fortification, than the prowess and virtue of the citizens and inhabitants. So is this

city so strong, by the great number of warlike people that are in it, that they care not for making any other walls. Besides, whosoever would go about to wall it, as Strasburg, Orleans, or Ferrara, would find it almost impossible, the cost and charges would be so excessive. Yea, but, said Panurge, it is good, nevertheless, to have an outside of stone, when we are invaded by our enemies, were it but to ask, Who is below there? As for the enormous expense, which you say would be needful for undertaking the great work of walling this city about, if the gentlemen of the town will be pleased to give me a good rough cup of wine, I will show them a pretty, strange, and new way, how they may build them good cheap. How? said Pantagruel. Do not speak of it, then, answered Panurge, and I will tell it you. I see that the *sine quo nons, callibistris,* or *contrapunctums* of the women of this country are cheaper than stones. Of them should the walls be built, ranging them in good symmetry by the rules of architecture and placing the largest in the first ranks, then sloping downwards ridgeways, like the back of an ass. The middlesized ones must be ranked next, and last of all the least and smallest. This done, there must be a fine little interlacing of them, like points of diamonds, as is to be seen in the great tower of Bourges, with a like number of the *nudinnudos, nilnisistandos,* and stiff bracmards, that dwell in amongst the claustral codpieces. What devil were able to overthrow such walls? There is no metal like it to resist blows, in so far that, if culverin-shot should come to graze upon it, you would incontinently see distil from thence the blessed fruit of the great pox, as small as rain. Beware, in the name of the devils, and hold off. Furthermore, no thunderbolt or lightning would fall upon it. For, why? They are all either blest or consecrated. I see but one inconveniency in it. Ho, ha, ha, ha! said Pantagruel, and what is that? It is, that the flies would be so liquorish of them, that you would wonder, and they would quickly gather there together, and there leave their ordure and excretions, and so all the work would be spoiled. But see how that might be remedied; they must be wiped and made rid of the flies with fair fox-tails, or good great *viedazes,* which are ass-pizzles, of Provence. And to this purpose I will tell you, as we go to supper, a brave example set down by *Frater Lubinus, Libro de compotationibus mendicantium.*[81]

In the time that the beasts did speak, which is not yet three days since, a poor lion, walking through the forest of Bieure, and saying his own little private devotions, past under a tree, where there was a roguish collier gotten up to cut down wood, who, seeing the lion, cast his hatchet at him, and wounded him enormously in one of his legs, whereupon the lion halting, he so long toiled and turmoiled himself in roaming up and down the forest to find help, that at last he met with a carpenter, who willingly looked upon his wound, cleansed it as well as he could, and filled it with moss, telling him that he must wipe his wound well, that the flies might not do their excrements in it, whilst he should go search for some yarrow or millefoil, commonly called the carpenter's herb. The lion being thus healed, walked along in the forest; at what time a sempiternous crone and old hag was picking up and gathering some sticks in the said forest, who, seeing the lion coming towards her, for fear fell down backwards, in such sort, that the wind blew up her gown, coats, and smock, even as far as above her shoulders. Which the lion, perceiving, for pity ran to see, whether she had taken any hurt by the fall; thereupon, considering her how do you call it, said, O poor woman, who hath thus wounded thee? Which words, when he had thus spoken, he espied a fox, whom he called to come to him, saying, Gossip Reynard, ha, hither, hither, and for cause! When the fox was come, he said unto him, My gossip and friend, they have hurt this good woman here between the legs most villanously, and there is a manifest solution of continuity. See how great a wound it is, even from the tail up to the navel, in measure four, nay full five handfulls and a-half. This is the blow of an hatchet, I doubt me, it is an old wound; and therefore that the flies may not get into it, wipe it lustily well and hard, I prithee, both within and without; thou hast a good tail, and long. Wipe, my friend, wipe, I beseech thee, and in the meanwhile I will go get some moss to put into it; for thus ought we to succour and help one another. Wipe it hard, thus, my friend, wipe it well, for this wound must be often wiped, otherwise the party cannot be at ease. Go to, wipe well, my little gossip, wipe, God hath furnished thee with a tail, thou hast a long one, and of a bigness proportionable, wipe hard, and be not weary. A good wiper, who, in wiping contin-

ually, wipeth with his wipard, by wasps shall never be wounded. Wipe, my pretty minion, wipe my little bully, I will not stay long. Then went he to get store of moss; and, when he was a little way off, he cried out in speaking to the fox thus, Wipe well still, gossip, wipe, and let it never grieve thee to wipe well, my little gossip, I will put thee into service to be wiper to Don Pedro de Castille, wipe, only wipe, and no more. The poor fox wiped as hard as he could, here and there, within and without; but the false old trot did so fizzle and foist, that she stunk like a hundred devils, which put the poor fox to a great deal of illease, for he knew not to what side to turn himself, to escape the unsavoury perfume of this old woman's postern blasts. And whilst to that effect he was shifting hither and thither, without knowing how to shun the annoyance of those unwholesome gusts, he saw that, behind, there was yet another hole, not so great as that which he did wipe, out of which came this filthy and infectious air. The lion at last returned, bringing with him of moss more than eighteen packs would hold, and began to put into the wound, with a staff which he had provided for that purpose, and had already put in full sixteen packs and a half, at which he was amazed. What a devil? said he, this wound is very deep, it would hold above two cart loads of moss. The fox, perceiving this, said unto the lion, O gossip lion, my friend, I pray thee, do not put in all thy moss there, keep somewhat, for there is here another little hole, that stinks like five hundred devils; I am almost choked with the smell thereof, it is so pestiferous and impoisoning.

Thus must these walls be kept from the flies, and wages allowed to some for wiping of them. Then said Pantagruel, How dost thou know that the privy parts of women are at such a cheap rate? For in this city there are many virtuous, honest, and chaste women besides the maids. *Et ubi prenus?*[82] said Panurge. I will give you my opinion of it, and that upon certain and assured knowledge. I do not brag, that I have bum-basted four hundred and seventeen, since I came into this city, though it be but nine days ago; but this very morning I met with a good fellow, who in a wallet, such as Æsop's was, carried two little girls, of two or three years old at the most, one before, and the other behind. He demanded alms of me, but I made him answer, that I had more cods than pence. Afterwards I asked him, Good man, these two girls, are they maids? Brother, said he, I have carried them thus these two years, and in regard of her that is before, whom I see continually, in my opinion she is a virgin; nevertheless, I will not put my finger in the fire for it; as for her that is behind, doubtless I can say nothing.

Indeed, said Pantagruel, thou art a gentle companion, I will have thee to be apparelled in my livery. And therefore caused him to be clothed most gallantly according to the fashion that then was, only that Panurge would have the codpiece of his breeches three feet long, and in shape square, not round; which was done, and was well worth the seeing. Oftentimes was he wont to say, that the world had not yet known the emolument and utility that is in wearing great codpieces; but time would one day teach it them, as all things have been invented in time. God keep from hurt, said he, the good fellow whose long codpiece or braguet hath saved his life! God keep from hurt him, whose long braguet hath been worth to him in one day one hundred threescore thousand and nine crowns! God keep from hurt him, who by his long braguet hath saved a whole city from famine! And, by God, I will make a book of the commodity of long braguets, when I shall have more leisure. And indeed he composed a fair great book with figures; but it is not printed as yet that I know of.

CHAPTER 16

Of the qualities and conditions of Panurge

PANURGE was of a middle stature, not too high nor too low, and had somewhat an aquiline nose, made like the handle of a razor. He was at that time five and thirty years old, or thereabouts, fine to gild like a leaden dagger, —for he was a notable cheater and conycatcher,—he was a very gallant and proper man of his person, only that he was a little lecherous, and naturally subject to a kind of disease, which at that time they called lack of money,—it is an incomparable grief, yet, notwithstanding, he had threescore and three tricks to come by it at his need, of which the most honourable and most ordinary was in manner of thieving, secret purloining, and filching, for he was a wicked lewd rogue, a cozener, drinker, roysterer, rover, and a very dissolute and debauched fellow, if there were

any in Paris; otherwise, and in all matters else, the best and most virtuous man in the world; and he was still contriving some plot, and devising mischief against the serjeants and the watch.

At one time he assembled three or four especial good hacksters and roaring boys; made them in the evening drink like Templars, afterwards led them till they came under St. Genevieve, or about the college of Navarre, and, at the hour that the watch was coming up that way, which he knew by putting his sword upon the pavement, and his ear by it, and, when he heard his sword shake, it was an infallible sign that the watch was near at that instant,—then he and his companions took a tumbrel or dungcart, and gave it the brangle, hurling it with all their force down the hill, and so overthrew all the poor watchmen like pigs, and then ran away upon the other side; for in less than two days he knew all the streets, lanes, and turnings in Paris, as well as his *Deus det*.[83]

At another time he laid in some fair place where the said watch was to pass, a train of gunpowder, and, at the very instant that they went along, set fire to it, and then made himself sport to see what good grace they had in running away, thinking that St. Anthony's fire had caught them by the legs. As for the poor masters of arts, he did prosecute them above all others. When he encountered with any of them upon the street, he would never fail to put some trick or other upon them, sometimes putting the bit of a fried turd in their graduate hoods, at other times pinning on little foxtails, or hare-ears behind them, or some such other roguish prank. One day that they were appointed all to meet in the Fodder-street, (Sorbonne,) he made a Borbonnesa tart, or filthy and slovenly compound, made of store of garlick, of *assafœtida*, of *castoreum*, of dog's turds very warm, which he steeped, tempered, and liquefied in the corrupt matter of pocky boils, and pestiferous botches; and, very early in the morning, therewith anointed all the pavement, in such sort, that the devil could not have endured it, which made all these good people there to lay up their gorges, and vomit what was upon their stomachs before all the world, as if they had flayed the fox; and ten or twelve of them died of the plague, fourteen became lepers, eighteen grew lousy, and above seven and twenty had the pox, but he did not care a button for it.

He commonly carried a whip under his gown, wherewith he whipped without remission the pages, whom he found carrying wine to their masters, to make them mend their pace. In his coat he had about six and twenty little fobs and pockets always full, one with some lead-water, and a little knife as sharp as a glover's needle, wherewith he used to cut purses: another with some kind of bitter stuff, which he threw into the eyes of those he met: another with clotburs, penned with little geese's or capons' feathers, which he cast upon the gowns and caps of honest people, and often made them fair horns, which they wore about all the city, sometimes all their life. Very often also upon the women's French hoods would he stick in the hind-part somewhat made in the shape of a man's member. In another, he had a great many little horns full of fleas and lice, which he borrowed from the beggars of St. Innocent, and cast them with small canes or quills to write with, into the necks of the daintiest gentlewomen that he could find, yet, even in the church; for he never seated himself above in the choir, but always sat in the body of the church amongst the women, both at mass, at vespers, and at sermon. In another, he used to have good store of hooks and buckles, wherewith he would couple men and women together, that sat in company close to one another, but especially those that wore gowns of crimson taffaties, that, when they were about to go away, they might rend all their gowns. In another, he had a squib furnished with tinder, matches, stones to strike fire, and all other tackling necessary for it. In another, two or three burning glasses, wherewith he made both men and women sometimes mad, and in the church put them quite out of countenance; for he said, that there was but an antistrophe, or little more difference than of a literal inversion between a woman, *folle à la messe* and *molle à la fesse;* that is, foolish at the mass, and of a pliant buttock.

In another, he had a good deal of needles and thread, wherewith he did a thousand little devilish pranks. One time, at the entry of the palace unto the great hall, where a certain grey friar or cordelier was to say mass to the counsellors, he did help to apparel him, and put on his vestments; but in the accoutreing of him, he sewed on his alb, surplice or stole, to his gown and shirt, and then withdrew himself, when the said lords of the court, or counsellors came to hear the said mass. But when it came to the *Ite, missa est,*[84] that the poor *Frater* would have laid by his stole or surplice, as the fashion then was, he plucked off withal both his frock and shirt, which were well sewed together, and thereby stripping himself up to the very shoulders, showed his *bel vedere* to all the world, together with his Don Cypriano, which was no small one, as you may imagine. And the friar still kept hauling, but so much the more did he discover himself, and lay open his back-parts, till one of the lords of the court said, How now, what's the matter? will this fair father make us here an offering of his tail to kiss it? Nay, St. Anthony's fire kiss it for us! From henceforth it was ordained that the poor fathers should never disrobe themselves any more before the world, but in their vestry-room, or sextry, as they call it, especially in the presence of women, lest it should tempt them to the sin of longing and inordinate desire. The people then asked, why it was, the friars had so long and large genitories? The said Panurge resolved the problem very neatly, saying, That which makes asses to have such great ears, is, that their dams did put no biggins on their heads, as d'Alliaco mentioneth in his *Suppositions.* By the like reason, that which makes the genitories or generation-tools of those fair fraters so long, is, for that they wear no bottomed breeches, and therefore their jolly member, having no impediment, hangeth dangling at liberty, as far as it can reach, with a wiggle-waggle down to their knees, as women carry their Paternoster beads. And the cause wherefore they have it so correspondingly great is, that in this constant wig-wagging the humours of the body descend into the said member. For, according to the legists, agitation and continual motion is cause of attraction.

Item, he had another pocket full of itching powder, called stone-allum, whereof he would cast some into the backs of those women whom he judged to be most beautiful and stately, which did so ticklishly gall them, that some would strip themselves in the open view of the world, and others dance like a cock upon hot embers, or a drumstick on a tabour. Others again ran about the streets, and he would run after them. To such as were in the stripping vein he would very civilly come to offer his attendance, and cover them with his cloak, like a courteous and very gracious man.

Item, in another he had a little leather bottle full of old oil, wherewith, when he saw any man or woman in a rich new handsome suit, he would grease, smutch, and spoil all the best parts of it under colour and pretence of touching them, saying, this is good cloth, this is good satin, good taffaties: Madam, God give you all that your noble heart desireth! You have a new suit, pretty sir;—and you a new gown, sweet mistress, God give you joy of it, and maintain you in all prosperity! And with this would lay his hand upon their shoulder, at which touch such a villanous spot was left behind, so enormously engraven to perpetuity in the very soul, body and reputation, that the devil himself could never have taken it way. Then upon his departing, he would say, Madam, take heed you do not fall, for there is a filthy great hole before you, whereinto if you put your foot, you will quite spoil yourself.

Another he had all full of euphorbium, very finely pulverised. In that powder did he lay a fair handkerchief, curiously wrought, which he had stolen from a pretty sempstress of the palace, in taking away a louse from off her bosom, which he had put there himself, and, when he came into the company of some good ladies, he would trifle them into a discourse of some fine workmanship of bone-lace, and then immediately put his hand into their bosom, asking them, And this work, is it of Flanders, or of Hainault? and then drew out his handkerchief, and said, Hold, hold, hold, look what work here is, it is of Foutignan or of Fontarabia,—and, shaking it hard at their nose, made them sneeze for four hours without ceasing. In the meanwhile he would fart like a horse, and the women would laugh and say, How now, do you fart, Panurge? No, no, Madam, said he, I do but tune my tail to the plain song of the music, which you make with your nose. In another he had a picklock, a pelican, a cramp-iron, a crook and some other iron tools, wherewith there was no door nor coffer which he could not pick open. He had another full of little cups, wherewith he played very artificially, for he had his fingers to his hand, like those of Minerva or Arachne, and had heretofore cried treacle. And when he changed a teston, cardecu, or any other piece of money, the changer had been more subtle than a fox, if Panurge had not at every time made five or six sols, (that is some six or seven pence,) vanish away invisibly, openly and manifestly, without making any hurt or lesion, whereof the changer should have felt nothing but the wind.

CHAPTER 17

How Panurge gained the pardons, and married the old Women, and of the suit in Law which he had at Paris

ONE day I found Panurge very much out of countenance, melancholic, and silent, which made me suspect that he had no money, whereupon I said unto him, Panurge, you are sick, as I do very well perceive by your physiognomy, and I know the disease. You have a flux in your purse; but take no care. I have yet seven pence half-penny, that never saw father nor mother, which shall not be wanting, no more than the pox in your necessity. Whereunto he answered me, Well, well,—for money, one day I shall have but too much; for I have a philosopher's stone, which attracts money out of men's purses, as the adamant doth iron. But will you go with me to gain the pardons? said he. By my faith, said I, I am no great pardon-taker in this world,—if I shall be any such in the other, I cannot tell; yet let us go, in God's name, it is but one farthing more or less. But, said he, lend me then a farthing upon interest. No, no, said I, I will give it you freely and from my heart. *Grates vobis dominos,*[85] said he.

So we went along, beginning at St. Gervase, and I got the pardons at the first box only, for in those matters very little contenteth me. Then did I say my suffrages, and the prayers of St. Brigid; but he gained them at all the boxes, and always gave money to every one of the pardoners. From thence we went to our Lady's church, to St. John's, to St. Anthony's, and so to the other churches, where there was a bank of pardons. For my part, I gained no more of them; but he at all the boxes kissed the relics, and gave at every one. To be brief, when we were returned, he brought me to drink at the castle-tavern, and there he showed me ten or twelve of his little bags full of money, at which I blest myself, and made the sign of the cross, saying, Where have you recovered so much money in so little time? Unto which he answered me, that he had taken it out of the basins of the pardons. For in giving them the first farthing, said he, I put it in with such slight of hand, and so dexterously, that it appeared to be a three-pence, thus with one hand I took three-pence, nine-pence, or six-pence at the least, and with the other as much, and so through all the churches where we have been. Yea, but said I, you damn yourself like a snake, and are withal a thief and sacrilegious person. True, said he, in your opinion, but I am not of that mind; for the pardoners do give me it, when they say unto me, in presenting the relics to kiss, *Centuplum accipies,* that is, that for one penny I should take a hundred; for *accipies* is spoken according to the manner of the Hebrews, who use the future tense instead of the imperative, as you have in the law, *Diliges Dominum;* that is, *Dilige.* Even so, when the pardon-bearer says to me, *Centuplum accipies,* his meaning is *Centuplum accipe;* and so doth Rabbi Kimy, and Rabbi Aben Ezra expound it, and all the Massorets, *et ibi Bartholus.*[86] Moreover, Pope Sixtus gave me fifteen hundred francs of yearly pension, which in English money is a hundred and fifty pounds, upon his ecclesiastical revenues and treasure, for having cured him of a cankerous botch, which did so torment him, that he thought to have been a cripple by it all his life. Thus I do pay myself at my own hand, for otherwise I get nothing, upon the said ecclesiastical treasure. Ho, my friend, said he, if thou didst know what advantage I made, and how well I feathered my nest, by the pope's bull of the crusade, thou wouldest wonder exceedingly. It was worth to me above six thousand florins; in English coin six hundred pounds. And what a devil is become of them? said I; for of that money thou hast not one half-penny. They returned from whence they came, said he; they did no more but change their master.

But I employed at least three thousand of them, that is, three hundred pounds English, in marrying,—not young virgins; for they find but too many husbands,—but great old sempiternous trots, which had not so much as one tooth in their heads; and that out of the consideration I had, that these good old women had very well spent the time of their youth in playing at the close-buttock-game to all comers, serving the foremost first, till no man would have any more dealing with them. And by G—, I will have their skincoat shaken once yet before they die. By this means, to one I gave a hundred florins, to another six score, to another three hundred, according to that they were infamous, detestable, and abominable. For, by how much the more honourable and execrable they were, so much the more must I needs have given them, otherwise the devil would not have jum'd them. Presently I went to some great and fat woodporter, or such like, and did myself make the match. But, before I did show him the old hags, I made a fair muster to him of the crowns, saying, Good fellow, see what I will give thee, if thou wilt but condescend to duffle, dinfredaille, or lecher it one good bout. Then began the poor rogues to gape like old mules, and I caused to be provided for them a banquet, with drink of the best, and store of spiceries, to put the old women in rut and heat of lust. To be short, they occupied all like good souls; only, to those that were horribly ugly and ill-favoured, I caused their head to be put within a bag to hide their face.

Besides all this, I have lost a great deal in suits of law. And what law-suits couldest thou have? said I; thou hast neither house nor lands. My friend, said he, the gentlewomen of this city had found out, by the instigation of the devil of hell, a manner of high-mounted bands, and neckerchiefs for women, which did so closely cover their bosoms, that men could no more put their hands under. For they had put the slit behind, and those neckcloths were wholly shut before, whereat the poor sad contemplative lovers were much discontented. Upon a fair Tuesday, I presented a petition to the court, making myself a party against the said gentlewomen, and showing the great interest that I pretended therein, protesting that by the same reason, I would cause the codpiece of my breeches to be sewed behind, if the court would not take order for it. In sum, the gentlewomen put in their defences, showed the grounds they went upon, and constituted their attorney for the prosecuting of the cause. But I pursued them so vigorously, that by a sentence of the court it was decreed those high neckcloths should be no longer worn, if they were not a little cleft and open before; but it cost me a good sum of money. I had another very filthy and beastly process against the dung-farmer called Master Fifi and his deputies, that they should no more read privily the pipe, puncheon, nor quart of *Sentences;* but in fair full day, and that in the Fodder schools, in face of the Arrian sophisters; where I was ordained to pay the charges, by reason of some clause mistaken in the relation of the sergeant. Another time I framed a complaint to the court against the mules of the presidents, counsellors, and others, tending to this purpose, that, when in the lower court of the palace they left them to champ on their bridles, some bibs were made for them by the counsellors' wives, that with their drivelling they might not spoil the pavement; to the end that the pages of the palace might play upon it with their dice, or at the game of coxbody, at their own ease, without spoiling their breeches at the knees. And for this I had a fair decree; but it cost me dear. Now reckon up what expense I was at in little banquets, which from day to day I made to the pages of the palace. And to what end? said I. My friend, said he, thou hast no pastime at all in this world. I have more than the king, and if thou wilt join thyself with me, we will do the devil together. No, no, said I, by St. Adauras, that will I not, for thou wilt be hanged one time or other. And thou, said he, wilt be interred some time or other. Now, which is most honourable, the air or the earth? Ho, grosse pecore!

Whilst the pages are at their banqueting, I keep their mules, and to some one I cut the stirrup-leather of the mounting side, till it hung by a thin strap or thread, that when the great puff-buts of the counsellor or some other hath taken his swing to get up, he may fall flat on his side like a porker, and so furnish the spectators with more than a hundred francs' worth of laughter. But I laugh yet further, to think how at his homecoming the master-page is to be whipped like green rye, which makes me not to repent what I have bestowed in feasting them. In brief, he had, as I said before, threescore and three ways to acquire money, but he had two hundred and fourteen to spend it, besides his drinking.

CHAPTER 18

How a great Scholar of England would have argued against Pantagruel, and was overcome by Panurge

IN that same time, a certain learned man, named Thaumast, hearing the fame and renown of Pantagruel's incomparable knowledge, came out of his own country of England with an intent only to see him, to try thereby, and prove, whether his knowledge in effect was so great as it was reported to be. In this resolution, being arrived at Paris, he went forthwith unto the house of the said Pantagruel, who was lodged in the palace of St. Denys, and was then walking in the garden thereof with Panurge, philosophizing after the fashion of the Peripatetics. At his first entrance he startled and was almost out of his wits for fear, seeing him so great, and so tall. Then did he salute him courteously as the manner is, and said unto him, Very true it is, saith Plato, the prince of philosophers, that,

if the image and knowledge of wisdom were corporeal and visible to the eyes of mortals, it would stir up all the world to admire her. Which we may the rather believe, that the very bare report thereof, scattered in the air, if it happen to be received into the ears of men, who, for being studious, and lovers of virtuous things, are called philosophers, doth not suffer them to sleep nor rest in quiet, but so pricketh them up, and sets them on fire, to run unto the place where the person is, in whom the said knowledge is said to have built her temple, and uttered her oracles. As it was manifestly shown unto us in the queen of Sheba, who came from the utmost borders of the East and Persian sea, to see the order of Solomon's house, and to hear his wisdom; in Anarcharsis, who came out of Scythia, even unto Athens, to see Solon; in Pythagoras, who travelled far to visit the memphitical vaticinators; in Plato, who went a great way off to see the magicians of Egypt, and Architas of Tarentum; in Apollonius Tyaneus, who went as far as unto Mount Caucasus, passed along the Scythians, the Massagetes, the Indians, and sailed over the great river Phison, even to the Brachmans to see Hiarchas; as likewise unto Babylon, Chaldea, Media, Assyria, Parthia, Syria, Phœnicia, Arabia, Palestina, and Alexandria, even unto Æthiopia, to see the Gymnosophists. The like example have we of Titus Livius, whom to see and hear, divers studious persons came to Rome, from the confines of France and Spain. I dare not reckon myself in the number of those so excellent persons, but well would be called studious, and a lover, not only of learning, but of learned men also. And indeed, having heard the report of your so inestimable knowledge, I have left my country, my friends, my kindred, my house, and am come thus far, valuing as nothing the length of the way, the tediousness of the sea, nor strangeness of the land, and that only to see you, and to confer with you about some passages in philosophy, of geomancy, and of the cabalistic art, whereof I am doubtful, and cannot satisfy my mind; which if you can resolve, I yield myself unto you for a slave henceforward, together with all my posterity; for other gift have I none, that I can esteem a recompence sufficient for so great a favour. I will reduce them into writing, and to-morrow publish them to all the learned men in the city, that we may dispute publicly before them.

But see in what manner I mean that we

shall dispute. I will not argue *pro et contra,* as do the sottish sophisters of this town, and other places. Likewise I will not dispute after the manner of the academics by declamation; nor yet by numbers, as Pythagoras was wont to do, and as Picus de la Mirandula did of late at Rome. But I will dispute by signs only, without speaking, for the matters are so abstruse, hard, and arduous, that words proceeding from the mouth of man will never be sufficient for unfolding of them to my liking. May it, therefore, please your magnificence to be there, it shall be at the great hall of Navarre, at seven o'clock in the morning. When he had spoke these words, Pantagruel very honourably said unto him, Sir, of the graces that God hath bestowed upon me, I would not deny to communicate unto any man to my power. For whatever comes from him is good, and his pleasure is, that it should be increased, when we come amongst men worthy and fit to receive this celestial manna of honest literature. In which number, because that in this time, as I do already very plainly perceive, thou holdest the first rank, I give thee notice, that at all hours thou shalt find me ready to condescend to every one of thy requests, according to my poor ability; although I ought rather to learn of thee, than thou of me. But, as thou hast protested, we will confer of thy doubts together, and will seek out the resolution, even unto the bottom of that undrainable well, where Heraclitus says the truth lies hidden. And I do highly commend the manner of arguing which thou hast proposed, to wit, by signs without speaking; for by this means thou and I shall understand one another well enough, and yet shall be free from that clapping of hands, which these blockish sophisters make, when any of the arguers hath gotten the better of the argument. Now to-morrow I will not fail to meet thee at the place and hour that thou hast appointed, but let me entreat thee, that there be not any strife or uproar between us, and that we seek not the honour and applause of men, but the truth only. To which Thaumast answered, The Lord God maintain you in his favour and grace, and, instead of my thankfulness to you, pour down his blessings upon you, for that your highness and magnificent greatness hath not disdained to descend to the grant of the request of my poor baseness. So farewell till-tomorrow! Farewell, said Pantagruel.

Gentlemen, you that read this present discourse, think not that ever men were more elevated and transported in their thoughts, than all this night were both Thaumast and Pantagruel; for the said Thaumast said to the keeper of the house of Cluny, where he was lodged, that in all his life he had never known himself so dry as he was that night. I think, said he, that Pantagruel held me by the throat. Give order, I pray you, that we may have some drink, and see that some fresh water be brought to us, to gargle my palate. On the other side, Pantagruel stretched his wits as high as he could, entering into very deep and serious meditations, and did nothing all that night but dote upon, and turn over the book of Beda, *De Numeris et signis;* Plotin's book, *De Inenarrabilibus;* the book of Proclus, *De Magia;* the book of Artemidorus, περὶ Ὀνειροκριτικῶν; of Anaxagoras, περὶ Σημείων; Dinarius, περὶ Ἀφάτων; the books of Philistion; Hipponax, περὶ Ἀνεκφωνητῶν, and a rabble of others, so long that Panurge said unto him:

My lord, leave all these thoughts and go to bed; for I perceive your spirits to be so troubled by a too intensive bending of them, that you may easily fall into some quotidian fever with this so excessive thinking and plodding. But, having first drunk five and twenty or thirty good draughts, retire yourself and sleep your fill, for in the morning I will argue against and answer my master the Englishman, and, if I drive him not *ad metam non loqui,*[87] then call me knave. Yea, but, said he, my friend Panurge, he is marvellously learned, how wilt thou be able to answer him? Very well, answered Panurge; I pray you talk no more of it, but let me alone. Is any man so learned as the devils are? No, indeed, said Pantagruel, without God's especial grace. Yet for all that, said Panurge, I have argued against them, gravelled and blanked them in disputation, and laid them so squat upon their tails, that I made them look like monkies. Therefore, be assured, that to-morrow I will make this vain-glorious Englishman to skite vinegar before all the world. So Panurge spent the night with tippling amongst the pages, and played away all the points of his breeches at *primus et secundus,* and at peck point, in French called *La Vergette.* Yet, when the appointed time was come, he failed not to conduct his master Pantagruel to the appointed place, unto which, believe me, there was neither great nor small in Paris but came, thinking with themselves that this devilish Pantagruel, who had overthrown and vanquished in dispute all these doting fresh-water sophisters, would now get full payment and be tickled to some purpose. For this Englishman is a terrible bustler, and horrible coil-keeper. We will see who will be the conqueror, for he never met with his match before.

Thus all being assembled, Thaumast staid for them; and then, when Pantagruel and Panurge came into the hall, all the school-boys, professors of arts, senior-sophisters, and bachelors, began to clap their hands, as their scurvy custom is. But Pantagruel cried out with a loud voice, as if it had been the sound of a double cannon, saying, Peace, with a devil to you, peace! By G—, you rogues, if you trouble me here, I will cut off the heads of every one of you. At which words they remained all daunted and astonished like so many ducks, and durst not so much as cough, although they had swallowed fifteen pounds of feathers. Withal, they grew so dry with this only voice, that they laid out their tongues a full half foot beyond their mouths, as if Pantagruel had salted all their throats. Then began Panurge to speak, saying to the Englishman, Sir, are you come hither to dispute contentiously in those propositions you have set down, or otherwise but to learn and know the truth? To which answered Thaumast, Sir, no other thing brought me hither but the great desire I had to learn, and to know, that of which I have doubted all my life long, and have neither found book nor man able to content me in the resolution of those doubts which I have proposed. And, as for disputing contentiously, I will not do it, for it is too base a thing, and therefore leave it to those sottish sophisters, who, in their disputes do not search for the truth, but for contradiction only and debate. Then, said Panurge, If I who am but a mean and inconsiderable disciple of my master, my lord Pantagruel, content and satisfy you in all and everything, it were a thing below my said master, wherewith to trouble him. Therefore is it fitter that he be chairman, and sit as a judge and moderator of our discourse and purpose, and give you satisfaction in many things, wherein perhaps I shall be wanting in your expectation. Truly, said Thaumast, it is very well said, Begin then. Now you must note, that Panurge had set at the end of his long codpiece a pretty tuft of red silk, as also of white, green, and blue, and within it had put a fair orange.

CHAPTER 19

How Panurge put to a non-plus the Englishman, that argued by signs

EVERYBODY then taking heed and hearkening with great silence, the Englishman lift up on high into the air his two hands severally, clenching in all the tops of his fingers together, after the manner, which, *à la Chinonnese*, they call the hen's arse, and struck the one hand on the other by the nails four several times. Then he, opening them, struck the one with the flat of the other, till it yielded a clashing noise, and that only once. Again, in joining them as before, he struck twice, and afterwards four times in opening them. Then did he lay them joined, and extended the one towards the other, as if he had been devoutly to send up his prayers unto God. Panurge suddenly lifted up in the air his right hand, and put the thumb thereof into the nostril of the same side, holding his four fingers straight out, and closed orderly in a parallel line to the point of his nose, shutting the left eye wholly, and making the other wink with a profound depression of the eyebrows and eyelids. Then lifted he up his left hand, with hard wringing and stretching forth his four fingers, and elevating his thumb, which he held in a line directly correspondent to the situation of his right hand, with the distance of a cubit and a half between them. This done, in the same form he abased towards the ground both the one and the other hand. Lastly, he held them in the midst, as aiming right at the Englishman's nose. And if Mercury,—said the Englishman. There Panurge interrupted him, and said, You have spoken, Mask.

Then made the Englishman this sign. His left hand all open he lifted up into the air, then instantly shut into his fist the four fingers thereof, and his thumb extended at length he placed upon the gristle of his nose. Presently after, he lifted up his right hand all open, and all open abased and bent it downwards, putting the thumb thereof in the very place where the little finger of the left hand did close in the fist, and the four right hand fingers he softly moved in the air. Then contrarily he did with the right hand what he had done with the left, and with the left what he had done with the right.

Panurge, being not a whit amazed at this, drew out into the air his trismegist codpiece with the left hand, and with his right drew forth a truncheon of a white ox-rib, and two pieces of wood of a like form, one of black ebony, and the other of incarnation Brazil, and put them betwixt the fingers of that hand in good symmetry; then knocking them together, made such a noise as the lepers of Brittany use to do with their clappering clickets, yet better resounding, and far more harmonious, and with his tongue contracted in his mouth did very merrily warble it, always looking fixedly upon the Englishman. The divines, physicians, and chirurgeons, that were there, thought that by this sign he would have inferred that the Englishman was a leper. The counsellors, lawyers, and decretalists conceived that, by doing this, he would have concluded some kind of mortal felicity to consist in leprosy, as the Lord maintained heretofore.

The Englishman for all this was nothing daunted, but, holding up his two hands in the air, kept them in such form, that he closed the three master fingers in his fist, and passing his thumbs through his indical, or foremost and middle fingers, his auriculary or little fingers remained extended and stretched out, and so presented he them to Panurge. Then joined he them so, that the right thumb touched the left, and the left little finger touched the right. Hereat Panurge, without speaking one word, lifted up his hands and made this sign.

He put the nail of the forefinger of his left hand to the nail of the thumb of the same, making in the middle of the distance as it were a buckle, and of his right hand shut up all the fingers into his fist, except the forefinger, which he often thrust in and out through the said two others of the left hand. Then stretched he out the forefinger, and middle finger or medical of his right hand, holding them asunder as much as he could, and thrusting them toward Thaumast. Then did he put the thumb of his left hand upon the corner of his left eye, stretching out all his hand like the wing of a bird, or the fin of a fish, and, moving it very daintily this way and that way, he did as much with his right hand upon the corner of his right eye. Thaumast began then to wax somewhat pale, and to tremble, and made him this sign.

With the middle finger of his right hand he struck against the muscle of the palm or pulp, which is under the thumb. Then put he the forefinger of the right hand in the like buckle of the left, but he put it under and not over, as Panurge did. Then Panurge knocked one hand against another, and blowed in his palm, and put again the forefinger of his right hand into the overture or mouth of the left, pulling it often in and out. Then held he out his chin, most intentively looking upon Thaumast. The people there, who understood nothing in the other signs, knew very well that therein he demanded, without speaking a word to Thaumast—What do you mean by that? In effect, Thaumast then began to sweat great drops, and seemed to all the spectators a man strangely ravished in high contemplation. Then he bethought himself, and put all the nails of his left hand against those of his right, opening his fingers as if they had been semicircles, and with this sign lifted up his hands as high as he could. Whereupon Panurge presently put the thumb of his right hand under his jaws, and the little finger thereof in the mouth of the left hand, and in this posture made his teeth to sound very melodiously, the upper against the lower. With this Thaumast, with great toil and vexation of spirit, rose up, but in rising he let a great baker's fart, for the bran came after; and pissing withal very strong vinegar, stunk like all the devils in hell. The company began to stop their noses; for he had conshited himself with mere anguish and perplexity. Then lifted he up his right hand, clenching it in such sort, that he brought the ends of all his fingers to meet together, and his left hand he laid flat upon his breast. Whereat Panurge drew out his long cod-piece with his tuft, and stretched it forth a cubit and a half, holding it in the air with his right hand, and with his left took out his orange, and, casting it up into the air seven times, at the eighth he hid it in the fist of his right hand, holding it steadily up on high, and then began to shake his fair cod-piece, showing it to Thaumast.

After that, Thaumast began to puff up his two cheeks like a player on a bagpipe, and blew as if he had been to puff up a pig's bladder. Whereupon Panurge put one finger of his left hand in his nockandrow, by some called St. Patrick's hole, and with his mouth sucked in the air, in such a manner as when one eats oysters in the shell, or when we sup up our broth. This done, he opened his mouth somewhat, and struck his right hand flat upon it, making therewith a great and a deep sound, as if it came from the superficies of the midriff, through the trachean artery, or pipe of the lungs; and this he did for sixteen times: but Thaumast did always keep blowing like a goose. Then Panurge put the fore-finger of his right hand into his mouth, pressing it very hard to the muscles thereof; then he drew it out, and withal made a great noise, as when little boys shoot pellets out of the pot-cannons made of the hollow sticks of the branch of an elder tree, and he did it nine times.

Then Thaumast cried out, Ha, my Masters, a great secret. With this he put in his hand up to the elbow, then drew out a dagger that he had, holding it by the point downwards. Whereat Panurge took his long codpiece, and shook it as hard as he could against his thighs; then put his two hands intwined in manner of a comb upon his head, laying out his tongue as far as he was able, and turning his eyes in his head, like a goat that is ready to die. Ha, I understand, said Thaumast, but what? making such a sign that he put the haft of his dagger against his breast, and upon the point thereof the flat of his hand, turning in a little the ends of his fingers. Whereat Panurge held down his head on the left side, and put his middle finger into his right ear, holding up his thumb bolt upright. Then he crost his two arms upon his breast, and coughed five times, and at the fifth time he struck his right foot against the ground. Then he lift up his left arm, and closing all his fingers into his fist, held his thumb against his forehead, striking with his right hand six times against his breast. But Thaumast, as not content therewith, put the thumb of his left hand upon the top of his nose, shutting the rest of his said hand, whereupon Panurge set his two master-fingers upon each side of his mouth, drawing it as much as he was able, and widening it so, that he showed all his teeth, and with his two thumbs plucked down his two eyelids very low, making therewith a very ill-favoured countenance, as it seemed to the company.

CHAPTER 20

How Thaumast relateth the virtues and knowledge of Panurge

THEN Thaumast rose up, and, putting off his cap, did very kindly thank the said Panurge, and with a loud voice said unto all the people that were there—My lords, gentlemen and others, at this time may I to some good purpose speak that evangelical word, *Et ecce plus quàm Salomon hic!*[88] You have here in your presence in incomparable treasure, that is, my lord Pantagruel, whose great renown

hath brought me hither, out of the very heart of England, to confer with him about the insoluble problems, both in magic, alchemy, the cabala, geomancy, astrology and philosophy, which I had in my mind. But at present I am angry even with fame itself, which I think was envious to him, for that it did not declare the thousandth part of the worth that indeed is in him. You have seen how his disciple only hath satisfied me, and hath told me more than I asked of him. Besides, he hath opened unto me, and resolved other inestimable doubts, wherein I can assure you he hath to me discovered the very true well, fountain, and abyss of the encyclopaedia of learning; yea, in such a sort, that I did not think I should ever have found a man that could have made his skill appear in so much as the first elements of that, concerning which we disputed by signs, without speaking either word or half word. But, in fine, I will reduce into writing that which we have said and concluded, that the world may not take them to be fooleries, and will thereafter cause them to be printed, that every one may learn as I have done, Judge, then, what the master had been able to say, seeing the disciple hath done so valiantly; *Non est discipulus super magistrum.*[89] Howsoever, God be praised, and I do very humbly thank you, for the honour that you have done us at this act. God reward you for it eternally! The like thanks gave Pantagruel to all the company, and going from thence, he carried Thaumast to dinner with him: and I believe that they drank as much as their skins could hold, or, as the phrase is, with unbuttoned bellies, (for in that age they made fast their bellies with buttons, as we do now the collars of our doublets or jerkins.) even till they neither knew where they were, nor whence they came. Blessed Lady, how they did carouse it, and pluck, as we say, at the kid's leather; and flagons to trot, and they to toot, Draw, give, page, some wine here, reach hither, fill with a devil, so! There was not one but did drink five-and-twenty or thirty pipes. Can you tell how? Even *sicut terra sine aqua;*[90] for the weather was hot, and, besides that, they were very dry. In matter of the exposition of the propositions set down by Thaumast, and the signification of the signs, which they used in their disputation, I would have set them down for you, according to their own relation, but I have been told that Thaumast made a great book of it, imprinted at London, wherein he hath set down all, without omitting anything, and, therefore, at this time I do pass by it.

CHAPTER 21

How Panurge was in love with a Lady of Paris

PANURGE began to be in great reputation in the city of Paris, by means of this disputation, wherein he prevailed against the Englishman, and from thenceforth made his codpiece to be very useful to him. To which effect he had it pinked with pretty little embroideries after the Romanesca fashion. And the world did praise him publicly, in so far that there was a song made of him, which little children did use to sing, when they were to fetch mustard. He was withal made welcome in all companies of ladies and gentlewomen, so that at last he became presumptuous, and went about to bring to his lure one of the greatest ladies in the city. And, indeed, leaving a rabble of long prologues and protestations, which ordinarily these dolent contemplative lent-lovers make, who never meddle with the flesh, one day he said unto her, Madam, it would be a very great benefit to the commonwealth, delightful to you, honourable to your progeny, and necessary for me, that I cover you for the propagating of my race; and believe it, for experience will teach it you. The lady at this word thrust him back above a hundred leagues, saying, You mischievous fool, is it for you to talk thus unto me? Whom do you think you have in hand? Be gone, never to come in my sight again; for, if one thing were not, I would have your legs and arms cut off. Well, said he, that were all one to me, to want both legs and arms, provided you and I had but one merry bout together, at the brangle-buttock-game; for here within is,—showing her his long codpiece,— Master John Thursday, who will play you such an antic, that you shall feel the sweetness thereof even to the very marrow of your bones. He is a gallant, and doth so well know how to find out all the corners, creeks, and ingrained inmates in your carnal trap, that after him there needs no broom, he'll sweep so well before, and leave nothing to his followers to work upon. Whereunto the lady answered, Go, villain, go. If you speak to me one such word more, I will cry out, and make you to be knocked down with blows. Ha, said he, you are not so bad as you say,—no, or else I am deceived in your physiognomy. For sooner

shall the earth mount up into the heavens, and the highest heavens descend into the hells, and all the course of nature be quite perverted, than that, in so great beauty and neatness as in you is, there should be one drop of gall or malice. They say, indeed, that hardly shall a man ever see a fair woman, that is not also stubborn. Yet that is spoke only of those vulgar beauties; but yours is so excellent, so singular, and so heavenly, that I believe nature hath given it you as a paragon, and master-piece of her art, to make us know what she can do, when she will employ all her skill, and all her power. There is nothing in you but honey, but sugar, but a sweet and celestial manna. To you it was, to whom Paris ought to have adjudged the golden apple, not to Venus, no, nor to Juno, nor to Minerva, for never was there so much magnificence in Juno, so much wisdom in Minerva, nor so much comeliness in Venus, as there is in you. O heavenly gods and goddesses; How happy shall that man be to whom you will grant the favour to embrace her, to kiss her, to rub his bacon with her's! By G—, that shall be I, I know it well; for she loves me already her belly full, I am sure of it; and so was I predestinated to it by the fairies. And, therefore, that we lose no time, put on, thrust out your gammons!—and would have embraced her, but she made as if she would put out her head at the window, to call her neighbours for help. Then Panurge on a sudden ran out, and, in his running away, said, Madam, stay here till I come again, I will go call them myself, do not you take so much pains. Thus went he away, not much caring for the repulse he had got, nor made he any whit the worse cheer for it. The next day he came to the church, at the time she went to mass. At the door he gave her some of the holy water, bowing himself very low before her, Afterwards he kneeled down by her very familiarly, and said unto her, Madam, know that I am so amorous of you, that I can neither piss nor dung for love. I do not know, lady, what you mean, but if I should take any hurt by it, how much you would be to blame! Go, said she, go, I do not care, let me alone to say my prayers. Ay, but, said he, equivocate upon this; *à Beaumont le viconte*. I cannot, said she. It is, said he, *à beau con le vit mont*. And upon this, pray to God to give you that which your noble heart desireth, and I pray you give me these patenotres. Take them, said she, and trouble me no longer. This done, she would have taken off her patenotres, which were made of a kind of yellow stone called Cestrin, and adorned with great spots of gold, but Panurge nimbly drew out one of his knives, wherewith he cut them off very handsomely, and while he was going away to carry them to the brokers, he said to her, Will you have my knife? No, no, said she. But, said he, to the purpose. I am at your commandment, body and goods, tripes and bowels.

In the meantime, the lady was not very well content with the want of her patenotres, for they were one of her implements to keep her countenance by in the church; then thought with herself, this bold flouting roister is some giddy, fantastical light-headed fool of a strange country. I shall never recover my patenotres again. What will my husband say? He will no doubt be angry with me. But I will tell him, that a thief hath cut them off from my hands in the church, which he will easily believe, seeing the end of the riband left at my girdle. After dinner Panurge went to see her, carrying in his sleeve a great purse full of palace-crowns, called counters, and began to say unto her, Which of us two loveth other best, you me, or I you? Whereunto she answered, As for me, I do not hate you; for, as God commands, I love all the world. But to the purpose, said he; are you not in love with me? I have, said she, told you so many times already, that you should talk so no more to me, and, if you speak of it again, I will teach you, that I am not one to be talked unto dishonestly. Get you hence packing, and deliver me my patenotres, that my husband may not ask me for them.

How now, madam, said he, your patenotres? Nay, by mine oath, I will not do so, but I will give you others. Had you rather have them of gold well enamelled in great round knobs, or after the manner of love-knots, or, otherwise, all massive, like great ingots, or, if you had rather have them of ebony, of jacinth, or of grained gold, with the marks of fine torquoises, or fair topazes, marked with fine sapphires, or of baleu rubies, with great marks of diamonds of eight and twenty squares? No, no, all this is too little. I know a fair bracelet of fine emeralds, marked with spotted ambergris, and at the buckle a Persian pearl as big as an orange. It will not cost above five-and-twenty thousand ducats. I will make you a present of it, for I have ready coin enough, and withal he made a noise with his counters as if they had been French crowns.

Will you have a piece of velvet, either of the violet colour, or of crimson dyed in grain, or a piece of broached or crimson satin? Will you have chains, gold, tablets, rings? You need no more but say, Yes,—so far as fifty thousand ducats may reach, it is but as nothing to me. By the virtue of which words he made the water come in her mouth: but she said unto him, No, I thank you, I will have nothing of you. By G—, said he, but I will have somewhat of you; yet shall it be that which shall cost you nothing, neither shall you have a jot the less, when you have given it. Hold, (showing his long cod-piece,) this is Master John Goodfellow, that asks for lodging,—and with that would have embraced her, but she began to cry out, yet not very loud. Then Panurge put off his counterfeit garb, changed his false visage, and said unto her, You will not then otherwise let me do a little? A turd for you! You do not deserve so much good, nor so much honour; but, by G—, I will make the dogs ride you; and with this he ran away as fast as he could, for fear of blows, whereof he was naturally fearful.

CHAPTER 22

How Panurge served a Parisian Lady a trick that pleased her not very well

Now you must note, that the next day was the great festival of Corpus Christi, called the *Sacre,* wherein all women put on their best apparel, and on that day the said lady was clothed in a rich gown of crimson satin, under which she wore a very costly white velvet petticoat.

The day of the eve, called the vigil, Panurge searched so long of one side and another, that he found a hot or salt bitch, which, when he had tied her with his girdle, he led to his chamber, and fed her very well all that day and night. In the morning thereafter he killed her, and took that part of her which the Greek geomancers know, and cut it into several pieces, as small as he could. Then carrying it away as close as might be, he went to the place where the lady was to come along, to follow the procession, as the custom is upon the said holy day; and, when she came in, Panurge sprinkled some holy water on her, saluting her very courteously. Then, a little while after she had said her petty devotions, he sat down close by her upon the same bench, and gave her this roundelay, in writing, in manner as followeth.

A ROUNDELAY

For this one time, that I to you my love
Discovered, you did too cruel prove,
To send me packing, hopeless, and so soon,
Who never any wrong to you had done,
In any kind of action, word, or thought;
So that, if my suit lik'd you not, you ought
T' have spoke more civilly, and to this sense,
My friend be pleased to depart from hence,
    For this one time.
What hurt do I, to wish you to remark
With favour and compassion, how a spark
Of your great beauty hath inflam'd my heart
With deep affection, and that, for my part,
I only ask, that you with me would dance
The brangle gay in feats of dalliance,
    For this one time.

And, as she was opening this paper to see
what it was, Panurge very promptly and
lightly scattered the drug that he had upon
her in divers places, but especially in the
plaits of her sleeves, and of her gown. Then
said he unto her, Madam, the poor lovers are
not always at ease. As for me, I hope that
those heavy nights, those pains and troubles,
which I suffer for love of you, shall be deduction to me of so much pain in purgatory; yet,
at the least, pray to God to give me patience
in my misery. Panurge had no sooner spoke
thus, but all the dogs that were in the church
came running to this lady with the smell of
the drugs that he had stewed upon her, both
small and great, big and little, all came, laying out their member, smelling to her, and
pissing every where upon her, it was the
greatest villany in the world. Panurge made
the fashion of driving them away; then took
his leave of her, and withdrew himself into
some chapel or oratory of the said church, to
see the sport; for these villanous dogs did
compiss all her habiliments, and left none of
her attire unbesprinkled with their staling, in
so much that a tall greyhound pissed upon
her head, others in her sleeves, others on her
crupper-piece, and the little ones pissed upon
her pattens; so that all the women that were
round about her had much ado to save her.
Whereat Panurge very heartily laughing, he
said to one of the lords of the city, I believe
that same lady is hot, or else that some greyhound hath covered her lately. And when he
saw that all the dogs were flocking about her,
yarring at the retardment of their access to
her, and every way keeping such a coil with
her, as they were wont to do about a proud or

salt bitch, he forthwith departed from thence,
and went to call Pantagruel, not forgetting,
in his way along all the streets, through which
he went, where he found any dogs, to give
them a bang with his foot, saying, Will you
not go with your fellows to the wedding?
Away, hence, avaunt, avaunt, with a devil
avaunt! And, being come home, he said to
Pantagruel, Master I pray you, come and see
all the dogs of the country, how they are assembled about a lady, the fairest in the city,
and would duffle and line her. Whereunto
Pantagruel willingly condescended, and saw
the mystery, which he found very pretty and
strange. But the best was at the procession,
in which were seen above six hundred thousand and fourteen dogs about her, which did
very much trouble and molest her, and whithersoever she past, those dogs that came
afresh, tracing her footsteps, followed her at
her heels, and pissed in the way wherever her
gown had touched. All the world stood gazing at this spectacle, considering the countenance of those dogs, who, leaping up, got
about her neck, and spoiled all her gorgeous
accoutrements, for the which she could find
no remedy, but to retire unto her house,
which was a palace. Thither she went, and
the dogs after her; she ran to hide herself,
but the chambermaids could not abstain from
laughing. When she was entered into the
house, and had shut the door upon herself, all
the dogs came running, of half a league
round, and did so well bepiss the gate of her
house, that there they made a stream with
their urine, wherein a duck might have very
well swam, and it is the same current that
now runs at St. Victor, in which Gobelin
dyeth scarlet, by the specifical virtue of these
piss-dogs, as our master Doribus did heretofore preach publicly. So may God help you, a
mill would have ground corn with it. Yet not
so much as those of Basacle at Toulouse.

CHAPTER 23

How Pantagruel departed from Paris, hearing
* news that the Dipsodes had invaded the*
* land of the Amaurots; and the cause*
* wherefore the leagues are so short in*
* France*

A LITTLE while after, Pantagruel heard news,
that his father Gargantua had been translated
into the Land of the Fairies by Morgue, as
heretofore were Ogier and Arthur; as also,
that, the report of the translation being

spread abroad, that the Dipsodes had issued out beyond their borders, with inroads, had wasted a great part of Utopia, and at that very time had besieged the great city of the Amaurots. Whereupon, departing from Paris, without bidding any man farewell, for the business required diligence, he came to Rouen.

Now Pantagruel in his journey, seeing that the leagues of that little territory about Paris called France, were very short, in regard of those of other countries, demanded the cause and reason of it from Panurge, who told him a story which Marotus of the Lac, *monachus,* set down in the *Acts of the Kings of Canarre,* saying, that in old times countries were not distinguished into leagues, miles, furlongs, nor parasanges, until that King Pharamond divided them, which was done in manner as followeth. The said king chose at Paris, a hundred fair, gallant, lusty, brisk young men, all resolute and bold adventurers in Cupid's duels, together with a hundred comely, pretty, handsome, lovely, and well complexioned wenches of Picardy; all of which he caused to be well entertained, and highly fed, for the space of eight days. Then, having called for them, he delivered to every one of the young men his wench, with store of money to defray their charges, and this injunction besides, to go unto divers places here and there. And, wheresoever they should biscot and thrum their wenches, that they setting a stone there, it should be counted for a league. Thus went away those brave fellows and sprightly blades most merrily, and because they were fresh, and had been at rest, they very often jummed and franfreuchled at almost every field's end, and this is the cause why the leagues about Paris are so short. But when they had gone a great way, and were now as weary as poor devils, all the oil in their lamps being almost spent they did not chink and duffle so often, but contented themselves, (I mean for the men's part,) with one scurvy, paltry bout in a day, and this is that which makes the leagues in Brittany, Delanes, Germany, and other more remote countries so long. Other men give other reasons for it, but this seems to me of all others the best. To which Pantagruel willingly adhered. Parting from Rouen, they arrived at Honfleur, where they took shipping, Pantagruel, Panurge, Epistemon, Eusthenes, and Carpalim.

In which place, waiting for a favourable wind, and caulking their ship, he received from a lady of Paris, whom he had formerly kept, and entertained a good long time, a letter directed on the outside thus,—To the best beloved of the fair women, and least loyal of the valiant men.

                              P.N.T.G.R.L.

CHAPTER 24

A Letter which a Messenger brought to Pantagruel from a Lady of Paris, together with the exposition of a Posy written in a gold ring

WHEN Pantagruel had read the superscription, he was much amazed, and therefore demanded of the said messenger the name of her that had sent it. Then opened he the letter, and found nothing written in it, nor otherwise inclosed, but only a gold ring, with a square table diamond. Wondering at this, he called Panurge to him, and showed him the case. Whereupon Panurge, told him, that the leaf of paper was written upon, but, with such cunning and artifice, that no man could see the writing at the first sight. Therefore, to find it out, he set it by the fire, to see if it was made with sal ammoniac soaked in water. Then put he it into the water, to see if the letter was written with the juice of tithymalle. After that he held it up against the candle, to see if it was written with the juice of white onions.

Then he rubbed one part of it with the oil of nuts, to see if it were written with the lee of a fig-tree, and another part of it with the milk of a woman giving suck to her eldest daughter, to see if it was written with the blood of red toads, or green earth frogs. Afterwards he rubbed one corner with the ashes of a swallow's nest, to see if it were not written with the dew that is found within the herb alcakengy, called the winter-cherry. He rubbed, after that, one end with ear-wax, to see if it were not written with the gall of a raven. Then did he dip it into vinegar, to try if it was not written with the juice of the garden spurge. After that he greased it with the fat of a bat or flitter-mouse, to see if it was not written with the sperm of a whale, which some call ambergris. Then put it very fairly into a basin full of fresh water, and forthwith took it out, to see whether it was written with stone-allum. But after all experiments, when he perceived that he could find out nothing, he called the messenger and asked him, Good fellow, the lady that sent thee hither, did she not give thee a staff to bring with thee? thinking that it had been according to the conceit, whereof Aulus Gellius maketh mention. And the messenger answered him, No, Sir. Then Panurge would have caused his head to be shaven, to see whether the lady had written upon his bald pate, with the hard lye whereof soap is made; that which she meant; but, perceiving that his hair was very long, he forbore, considering that it could not have grown to so great a length in so short a time.

Then he said to Pantagruel, Master, by the virtue of G—, I cannot tell what to do or say in it. For, to know whether there be anything written upon this or no, I have made use of a good part of that which Master Francisco di Nianto, the Tuscan, sets down, who had written the manner of reading letters that do not appear; that which Zoroaster published, *Peri Grammaton Acriton;* and Calphurnius Bassus, *De Literis Illegibilibus.* But I can see nothing, nor do I believe that there is anything else in it than the ring. Let us, therefore, look upon it. Which when they had done, they found this in Hebrew written within, *Lama sabachthani;* whereupon they called Epistemon, and asked him what that meant? To which he answered, that they were Hebrew words, signifying, Wherefore hast thou forsaken me? Upon that Panurge suddenly replied, I know the mystery. Do you see this diamond? It is a false one. This, then, is the exposition of that which the lady means, *Diamant faux,* that is, false lover, why hast thou forsaken me? Which interpretation Pantagruel presently understood, and withal remembering, that at his departure, he had not bid the lady farewell, he was very sorry, and would fain have returned to Paris, to make his peace with her. But Epistemon put him in mind of Æneas's departure from Dido, and the saying of Heraclitus of Tarentum, That, the ship being at anchor, when need requireth, we must cut the cable rather than lose time about untying of it—and that he should lay aside all other thoughts, to succour the city of his nativity, which was then in danger. And, indeed, within an hour after that, the wind arose at the north-north-west, wherewith they hoisted sail, and put out, even into the main sea, so that within few days, passing by Porto Sancto, and by the Madeiras, they went ashore in the Canary islands. Parting from thence, they passed by Capo-bianco, by Senega, by Capo-verde, by Gambra, by Sagres, by Melli, by the Cap di Buona Speranza, and set ashore again in the kingdom of Melinda. Parting from thence, they sailed away with a tramontane or northerly wind, passing by Meden, by Uti, by Uden, by Gelasem, by the Isles of the Fairies, and along the kingdom of Achory, till at last they arrived at the port of Utopia, distant from the city of the Amaurots three leagues and somewhat more.

When they were ashore, and pretty well refreshed, Pantagruel said, Gentlemen, the city is not far from hence, therefore were it not amiss, before we set forward, to advise well what is to be done, that we be not like the Athenians, who never took counsel until after the fact. Are you resolved to live and die with me? Yes, Sir, said they all, and be as confident of us as of your own fingers. Well, said he, there is but one thing that keeps my mind in great doubt and suspense, which is this, that I know not in what order nor of what number the enemy is, that layeth siege to the city; for, if I were certain of that, I should go forward, and set on with the better assurance. Let us, therefore, consult together, and bethink ourselves by what means we may come to this intelligence. Whereunto they all said, Let us go thither and see, and stay you here for us; for this very day, without further respite, do we make account to bring you a certain report thereof.

Myself, said Panurge, will undertake to enter into their camp, within the very midst of their guards, unespied by their watch, and merrily feast and lecher it at their cost, without being known of any, to see the artillery and the tents of all the captains, and thrust myself in with a grave and magnific carriage, amongst all their troops and companies, without being discovered. The devil would not be able to peck me out with all his circumventions, for I am of the race of Zopyrus.

And I, said Epistemon, know all the plots and stratagems of the valiant captains, and warlike champions of former ages, together with all the tricks and subtleties of the art of war. I will go, and, though I be detected and revealed, I will escape, by making them believe of you whatever I please, for I am of the race of Sinon.

I, said Eusthenes, will enter and set upon them in their trenches, in spite of their sentries, and all their guards; for I will tread upon their bellies, and break their legs and arms, yea, though they were every bit as strong as the devil himself, for I am of the race of Hercules.

And I, said Carpalim, will get in there, if the birds can enter, for I am so nimble of body, and light withal, that I shall have leaped over their trenches, and ran clean through all their camp, before that they perceive me; neither do I fear shot, nor arrow, nor horse, how swift soever, were he the Pegasus of Perseus or Pacolet, being assured that I shall be able to make a safe and sound escape before them all, without any hurt. I will undertake to walk upon the ears of corn, or grass in the meadows, without making either of them do so much as bow under me, for I am of the race of Camilla the Amazon.

CHAPTER 25

How Panurge, Carpalim, Eusthenes, and Epistemon, the Gentlemen Attendants of Pantagruel, vanquished and discomfited six hundred and three-score Horsemen very cunningly

As he was speaking this, they perceived six hundred and three-score light horsemen, gallantly mounted, who made an outride thither, to see what ship it was that was newly arrived in the harbour, and came in a full gallop to take them if they had been able. Then said Pantagruel, My lads, retire yourselves into the ship, here are some of our enemies coming apace, but I will kill them here before you like beasts, although they were ten times so many; in the meantime, withdraw yourselves, and take your sport at it. Then answered Panurge, No, Sir, there is no reason that you should do so, but, on the contrary, retire you unto the ship, both you and the rest, for I will alone here discomfit them; but we must not linger, come, set forward. Whereunto the others said, It is well advised, Sir, withdraw yourself, and we will help Panurge here, so shall you know what we are able to do. Then said Pantagruel, Well, I am content, but, if that you be too weak, I will not fail to come to your assistance. With this Panurge took two great cables of the ship, and tied them to the kempstock or capstan which was on the deck towards the hatches, and fastened them in the ground, making a long circuit, the one further off, the other within that. Then said he to Epistemon, Go aboard the ship, and, when I give you a call, turn about the capstan upon the orlop diligently, drawing unto you the two cable ropes; and said to Eusthenes, and to Carpalim, My bullies, stay you here, and offer yourselves freely to your enemies. Do as they bid you, and make as if you would yield unto them, but take heed that you come not within the compass of the ropes,—be sure to keep yourselves free of them. And presently he went aboard the ship, and took a bundle of straw, and a barrel of gunpowder, strewed it round about the compass of the cords, and stood by with a brand of fire, or match lighted in his hand. Presently came the horsemen with great fury, and the foremost ran almost home to the ship, and, by reason of the slipperiness of the bank, they fell, they and their horses, to the number of four and forty; which the rest seeing, came on, thinking that resistance had been made them at their arrival. But Panurge said unto them, My masters, I believe that you have hurt yourselves, I pray you pardon us, for it is not our fault, but the slipperiness of the sea-water, that is always unctuous; we submit ourselves to your good pleasure. So said likewise his two other fellows, and Epistemon that was upon the deck. In the meantime Panurge withdrew himself, and seeing that they were all within the compass of the cables, and that his two companions were retired, making room for all those horses which came in a crowd, thronging upon the neck of one another to see the ship, and such as were in it, cried out on a sudden to Epistemon, Draw, draw! Then began Epistemon to wind about the capstan, by doing whereof the two cables so entangled and impestered the legs of the horses, that they were all of them thrown down to the ground easily, together with their riders. But they seeing that, drew their swords, and would have cut them; whereupon Panurge set fire to the train, and there burnt them all up like damned souls, both men and horses, not one escaping save one alone, who being mounted on a fleet Turkey courser, by mere speed in flight got himself out of the circle of the ropes. But when Carpalim perceived him, he ran after him, with such nimbleness and celerity, that he overtook him in less than a hundred paces; then leaping close behind him upon the crupper of his horse, clasped him in his arms, and brought him back to the ship.

This exploit being ended, Pantagruel was

very jovial, and wondrously commended the industry of these gentlemen, whom he called his fellow-soldiers, and made them refresh themselves, and feed well and merrily upon the sea-shore, and drink heartily with their bellies upon the ground, and their prisoner with them, whom they admitted to that familiarity: only that the poor devil was somewhat afraid that Pantagruel would have eaten him up whole, which, considering the wideness of his mouth, and capacity of his throat, was no great matter for him to have done; for he could have done it as easily as you would eat a small comfit, he showing no more in his throat than would a grain of millet-seed in the mouth of an ass.

CHAPTER 26

How Pantagruel and his Company were weary in eating still salt meats; and how Carpalin went a hunting to have some venison

THUS as they talked and chatted together, Carpalim said, And by the belly of St. Quenet, shall we never eat any venison? This salt meat makes me horribly dry. I will go and fetch you a quarter of one of those horses which we have burned; it is well roasted already. As he was rising up to go about it, he perceived under the side of a wood a fair great roe-buck, which came out of his fort, as I conceive, at the sight of Panurge's fire. Him did he pursue and run after with as much vigour and swiftness, as if it had been a bolt out of a cross-bow, and caught him in a moment; and whilst he was in his course, he with his hands took in the air four great bustards, seven bitterns, six and twenty grey partridges, two and thirty red-legged ones, sixteen pheasants, nine woodcocks, nineteen herons, two and thirty cushats and ring-doves; and with his feet killed ten or twelve leverets and rabbits, which were then at relief, and pretty big withal, eighteen rails in a knot together, with fifteen young wild boars, two little beavers, and three great foxes. So, striking the kid with his falchion athwart the head, he killed him, and, bearing him on his back, he in his return took up his hares, rails, and young wild boars, and as far off as he could be heard, cried out, and said Panurge, my friend, vinegar, vinegar! Then the good Pantagruel, thinking he had fainted, commanded them to provide him some vinegar; but Panurge knew well that there was some

good prey in hands, and forthwith showed unto noble Pantagruel, how he was bearing upon his back a fair roe-buck, and all his girdle bordered with hares. Then immediately did Epistemon make, in the name of the nine muses, nine antique wooden spits, Eusthenes did help to flay, and Panurge placed two great cuirassier saddles in such sort, that they served for andirons, and, making their prisoner to be their cook, they roasted their venison by the fire, wherein the horsemen were burned; and, making great cheer with a good deal of vinegar, the devil a one of them did forbear from his victuals,—it was a triumphant and incomparable spectacle to see how they ravened and devoured. Then said Pantagruel, Would to God, every one of you had two pairs of little anthem or sacring bells, hanging at your chin, and that I had at mine the great clocks of Rennes, of Poictiers, of Tours, and of Cambray, to see what a peal they would ring with the wagging of our chaps. But, said Panurge, it were better we thought a little upon our business, and by what means we might get the upper hand of our enemies. That is well remembered said Pantagruel. Therefore spoke he thus to the prisoner, My friend, tell us here the truth, and do not lie to us at all, if thou wouldest not be flayed alive, for it is I that eat the little children. Relate unto us, at full the order, the number, and the strength of the army. To which the prisoner answered, Sir, know for a truth that in the army there are three hundred giants, all armed with armour of proof, and wonderful great. Nevertheless, not fully so great as you, except one that is their head, named Loupgarou, who is armed from head to foot with Cyclopical anvils. Furthermore, one hundred threescore and three thousand foot, all armed with the skins of hobgoblins, strong and valiant men; eleven thousand four hundred men at arms or cuirassiers; three thousand six hundred double cannons, and harquebusiers without number; fourscore and fourteen thousand pioneers; one hundred and fifty thousand whores, fair like goddesses (that is for me, said Panurge,) whereof some are Amazons, some Lionnoises, others Parisiennes, Tourangelles, Angevines, Poictevines, Normands, and High Dutch—there are of them of all countries, and all languages.

Yea, but, said Pantagruel, is the king there? Yes, Sir, said the prisoner, he is there in person, and we call him Anarchus, King of the Dipsodes, which is as much as to say thirsty people, for you never saw men more thirsty, nor more willing to drink; and his tent is guarded by the giants. It is enough said Pantagruel, Come, brave boys, are you resolved to go with me? To which Panurge answered, God confound him that leaves you! I have already bethought myself how I will kill them all like pigs, and so that the devil one leg of them shall escape. But I am somewhat troubled about one thing. And what is that? said Pantagruel. It is, said Panurge how I shall be able to set forward to the justling and bragmardising of all the whores that be there this afternoon, in such sort, that there escape not one unbumped by me, breasted and jummed after the ordinary fashion of man and woman in the Venetian conflict. Ha, ha, ha, ha, said Pantagruel.

And Carpalim said, The devil take these sink-holes, if, by G—, I do not bumbast some one of them. Then said Eusthenes, What, shall not I have any, whose spaces, since we came from Rouen, were never so well wound up, as that my needle could mount to ten or eleven o'clock, till now, that I have it hard, stiff, and strong, like a hundred devils? Truly, said Panurge, thou shalt have of the fattest, and of those that are most plump, and in the best case.

How now, said Epistemon, every one shall ride, and I must lead the ass? the devil take him that will do so. We will make use of the right of war, *Qui potest capere, capiat.*[91] No, no, said Panurge, but tie thine ass to a crook, and ride as the world doth. And the good Pantagruel laughed at all this, and said unto them, You reckon without your host. I am much afraid, that, before it be night, I shall see you in such taking, that you will have no great stomach to ride, but more like to be rode upon, with sound blows of pike and lance. *Baste,* said Epistemon, enough of that! I will not fail to bring them to you, either to roast or boil, to fry or put in paste. They are not so many in number as were in the army of Xerxes, for he had thirty hundred thousand fighting men, if you will believe Herodotus and Trogus Pompeius, and yet Themistocles with a few men overthrew them all. For God's sake, take you no care for that. Cobsminny, cobsminny, said Panurge, my codpiece alone shall suffice to overthrow all the men: and my St. Sweephole, that dwells within it, shall lay all the women squat upon their backs. Up then, my lads, said Pantagruel, and let us march along.

CHAPTER 27

How Pantagruel set up one trophy in memorial of their valour, and Panurge another in remembrance of the Hares. How Pantagruel likewise with his Farts begat little Men, and with his Fisgs little women: and how Panurge broke a great Staff over two glasses

BEFORE we depart hence said Pantagruel, in remembrance of the exploit that you have now performed, I will in this place erect a fair trophy. Then every man amongst them, with a fair joy, and fine little country songs, set up a huge big post, whereunto they hanged a great cuirassier saddle, the fronstal of a barbed horse, bridle-bosses, bully-pieces for the knees, stirrup-leathers, spurs, stirrups, a coat of mail, a corslet tempered with steel, a battle-axe, a strong, short, and sharp horseman's sword, a gantlet, a horseman's mace, gushet-armour for the arm-pits, leg-harness, and a gorget, with all other furniture needful for the decoration of a triumphant arch, in sign of a trophy. And, then Pantagruel, for an eternal memorial, wrote this victorial Ditton, as followeth:

Here was the prowess made apparent of
Four brave and valiant champions of proof,
Who, without any arms but wit, at once,
Like Fabius, or the two Scipios,
Burnt in a fire six hundred and threescore
Crablice, strong rogues ne'er vanquished before.
By this each King may learn, Rook, Pawn, and Knight,
That slight is much more prevalent than might.

For victory,
As all men see,
Hangs on the ditty
Of that committee,
Where the great God
Hath his abode.

Nor doth he to it strong and great men give,
But to his elect, as we must believe;
Therefore shall be obtain wealth and esteem,
Who through faith doth put his trust in him.

Whilst Pantagruel was writing these foresaid verses, Panurge halved and fixed upon a great stake the horns of a roe-buck, together with the skin, and the right forefoot thereof, the ears of three leverets, the chine of a cony, the jaws of a hare, the wings of two bustards, the feet of four quest-doves, a bottle or *borracho* full of vinegar, a horn wherein to put salt, a wooden spit, a larding stick, a scurvy kettle full of holes, dripping pan to make sauce in, an earthen salt-cellar, and a goblet of Beauvois. Then, in imitation of Pantagruel's verses and trophy, wrote that which followeth:

Here four brave topers sitting on their bums,
With flagons, nobler noise than drums,
Carous'd it, bous'd it, toss'd the liquor,
Each seem'd a Bacchus-priest, or vicar:
Hares, conies, bustards, pigs were brought
    'em,
With jugs and pipkins strew'd about 'em;
For trophy-spoils to each good fellow,
That is hereafter to be mellow.

> In every creed,
> 'Tis on all hands agreed,
> And plainly confest;
>   When the weather is hot,
>   That we stick to the pot,
> And drink o' the best.

First note, that in your bill of fare,
Sauce he provided for the rare.
But vinegar the most extol;
'Tis of an hare the very soul.

Then said Pantagruel, Come, my lads, let us begone, we have staid here too long about our victuals; for very seldom doth it fall out, that the greatest eaters do the most martial exploits. There is no shadow like that of flying colours, no smoke like that of horses, no clattering like that of armour. At this Epistemon began to smile, and said, There is no shadow like that of the kitchen, no smoke like that of pasties, and clattering like that of goblets. Unto which answered Panurge, There is no shadow like that of curtains, no smoke like that of women's breasts, and no clattering like that of ballocks. Then forthwith rising up he gave a fart, a leap, and a whistle, and most joyfully cried out aloud, Ever live Pantagruel! When Pantagruel saw that, he would have done as much; but with the fart that he let, the earth trembled nine leagues about, wherewith and with the corrupted air, he begot above three and fifty thousand little men, ill-favoured dwarfs, and with one fisg that he

let, he made as many little women, crouching down, as you shall see in divers places, which never grow but like cows' tails, downwards, or, like the Limosin radishes, round. How now, said Panurge, are your farts so fertile and fruitful? By G—, here be brave farted men, and fisgued women, let them be married together, they will beget fine hornets and dorflies. So did Pantagruel, and called them pygmies. Those he sent to live in an island thereby, where since that time they are increased mightily. But the cranes make war with them continually, against which they do most courageously defend themselves; for these little ends of men and dandiprats, (whom in Scotland they call whiphandles, and knots of a tar-barrel,) are commonly very testy and choleric: the physical reason whereof is, because their heart is near their turd.

At this time, Panurge took two drinking glasses that were there, both of one bigness, and filled them with water up to the brim, and set one of them upon one stool, and the other upon another, placing them about five feet from one another. Then he took the staff of a javelin, about five feet and a half long, and put it upon the two glasses, so that the two ends of the staff did come just to the brims of the glasses. This done, he took a great stake or billet of wood, and said to Pantagruel, and to the rest, My Masters, behold how easily we shall have the victory over our enemies; for, just as I shall break this staff here upon these glasses, without either breaking or crazing of them, nay, which is more, without spilling one drop of the water that is within them, even so shall we break the heads of our Dipsodes, without receiving any of us any wound, or loss in our person or goods. But, that you may not think there is any witchcraft in this, hold, said he to Eusthenes, strike upon the midst as hard as thou canst with this log. Eusthenes did so, and the staff broke in two pieces, and not one drop of water fell out of the glasses. Then, said he, I know a great many such other tricks, let us now therefore march boldly, and with assurance.

CHAPTER 28

How Pantagruel got the Victory very strangely over the Dipsodes, and the Giants

AFTER all this talk, Pantagruel took the prisoner to him, and sent him away, saying, Go thou unto thy king in his camp, and tell him tidings of what thou hast seen, and let him resolve to feast me to-morrow about noon; for as soon as my galleys shall come, which will be to-morrow at furthest, I will prove unto him by eighteen hundred thousand fighting men, and seven thousand giants, all of them greater than I am, that he hath done foolishly and against reason, thus to invade my country. Wherein Pantagruel feigned that he had an army at sea. But the prisoner answered, that he would yield himself to be his slave, and that he was content never to return to his own people, but rather with Pantagruel to fight against them, and for God's sake besought him, that he might be permitted so to do. Whereunto Pantagruel would not give consent, but commanded him to depart thence speedily, and be gone, as he had told him, and to that effect gave him a box full of euphorbium, together with some grains of the black cameleon thistle, steeped into *aqua vitæ*, and made up into the condiment of a wet sucket, commanding him to carry it to his king, and say unto him, that, if he were able to eat one ounce of that without drinking after it, he might then be able to resist him, without any fear or apprehension of danger.

The prisoner then besought him with joint hands, that in the hour of the battle he would have compassion upon him. Whereat Pantagruel said unto him, After that thou hast delivered all unto the king, put thy whole confidence in God, and he will not forsake thee; because, although for my part I be mighty, as thou mayest see, and have an infinite number of men in arms, I do nevertheless trust neither in my force nor in mine industry, but all my confidence is in God my protector, who doth never forsake those that in him do put their trust and confidence. This done, the prisoner requested him, that he would be contented with some reasonable composition for his ransom. To which Pantagruel answered, that his end was not to rob nor ransom men, but to enrich them, and reduce them to total liberty. Go thy way, said he, in the peace of the living God, and never follow evil company, lest some mischief befal thee. The prisoner being gone, Pantagruel said to his men, Gentlemen, I have made this prisoner believe that we have an army at sea, as also, that we will not assault them till to-morrow at noon, to the end that they, doubting

of the great arrival of our men, may spend this night in providing and strengthening themselves, but in the meantime my intention is, that we charge them about the hour of the first sleep.

Let us leave Pantagruel here with his apostles, and speak of King Anarchus and his army. When the prisoner was come, he went unto the king, and told him how there was a great giant come, called Pantagruel, who had overthrown, and made to be cruelly roasted, all the six hundred and nine and fifty horsemen, and he alone escaped to bring the news. Besides that, he was charged by the said giant to tell him, that the next day, about noon, he must make a dinner ready for him, for at that hour he was resolved to set upon him. Then did he give him that box wherein were those comfitures. But, as soon as he had swallowed down one spoonful of them, he was taken with such a heat in the throat, together with an ulceration in the flap of the top of the windpipe, that his tongue peeled with it, in such sort, that, for all they could do unto him, he found no ease at all, but by drinking only without cessation; for as soon as ever he took the goblet from his head, his tongue was on fire, and therefore they did nothing but still pour in wine into his throat with a funnel. Which when his captains, bashaws, and guard of his body did see, they tasted of the same drugs, to try whether they were so thirst-procuring and alterative or no. But it so befel them as it had done their king, and they plied the flagon so well, that the noise ran throughout all the camp, how the prisoner was returned,—that the next day they were to have an assault,—that the king and his captains did already prepare themselves for it, together with his guards, and that with carousing lustily, and quaffing as hard as they could. Every man, therefore, in the army began to tipple, ply the pot, swill, and guzzle it as fast as they could. In sum, they drunk so much, and so long, that they fell asleep like pigs, all out of order throughout the whole camp.

Let us now return to the good Pantagruel, and relate how he carried himself in this business. Departing from the place of the trophies, he took the mast of their ship in his hand like a pilgrim's staff, and put within the top of it two hundred and seven and thirty puncheons of white wine of Anjou, the rest was of Rouen, and tied up to his girdle the bark all full of salt, as easily as the Lanskennets carry their little panniers, and so set onward on his way with his fellow soldiers. When he was come near to the enemy's camp, Panurge said unto him, Sir, if you would do well, let down this white wine of Anjou from the scuttle of the mast of the ship, that we may all drink thereof, like Bretons.

Hereunto Pantagruel very willingly consented, and they drank so neat, that there was not so much as one poor drop left, of two hundred and seven and thirty puncheons, except one *boracho* or leathern bottle of Tours, which Panurge filled for himself, for he called that his *vademecum,* and some scurvy lees of wine in the bottom, which served him instead of vinegar. After they had whittled and curried the can pretty handsomely, Panurge gave Pantagruel to eat some devilish drugs, compounded of lithotripton, which is a stone-dissolving ingredient, nephrocatarticon, that purgeth the reins, the marmalade of quinces, called codiniac, a confection of cantharides, which are green flies breeding on the tops of olive trees, and other kinds of diuretic or piss-procuring simples. This done, Pantagruel said to Carpalim, Go into the city, scrambling like a cat up against the wall, as you can well do, and tell them, that now presently they come out, and charge their enemies as rudely as they can, and, having said so, come down, taking a lighted torch with you, wherewith you shall set on fire all the tents and pavilions in the camp, then cry as loud as you are able with your great voice, and then come away from thence. Yea, but, said Carpalim, were it not good to cloy all their ordnance? No, no, said Pantagruel, only blow up all their powder. Carpalim obeying him, departed suddenly, and did as he was appointed by Pantagruel, and all the combatants came forth that were in the city, and, when he had set fire in the tents and pavilions, he passed so lightly through them, and so highly and profoundly did they snort and sleep, that they never perceived him. He came to the place where their artillery was, and set their munition on fire. But here was the danger. The fire was so sudden, that poor Carpalim had almost been burnt. And, had it not been for his wonderful agility, he had been fried like a roasting pig. But he departed away so speedily, that a bolt or arrow out of a crossbow could not have had a swifter motion. When he was clear of their trenches, he shouted aloud, and cried out so dreadfully, and with

such amazement to the hearers, that it seemed all the devils of hell had been let loose. At which noise the enemies awaked, but can you tell how? Even no less astonished than are monks at the ringing of the first peal to matins, which in Lusonnois is called *Rubballock.*

In the meantime Pantagruel began to sow the salt that he had in his bark, and, because they slept with an open gaping mouth, he filled all their throats with it, so that these poor wretches were by it made to cough like foxes, crying, Ha, Pantagruel, how thou addest greater heat to the firebrand that is in us! Suddenly Pantagruel had will to piss, by means of the drugs which Panurge had given him, and pissed amidst the camp so well and so copiously, that he drowned them all, and there was a particular deluge, ten leagues round about, of such considerable depth, that the history saith, if his father's great mare had been there, and pissed likewise, it would undoubtedly have been a more enormous deluge than that of Deucalion; for she did never piss, but she made a river, greater than is either the Rhone, or the Danube. Which those that were come out of the city seeing, said, They are all cruelly slain, see how the blood runs along. But they were deceived in thinking Pantagruel's urine had been the blood of their enemies; for they could not see but by the light of the fire of the pavilions, and some small light of the moon.

The enemies, after that they were awaked, seeing on one side the fire in the camp, and on the other the inundation of the urinal deluge, could not tell what to say, nor what to think. Some said, that it was the end of the world, and the final judgment, which ought to be by fire. Others, again thought that the sea-gods, Neptune, Proteus, Triton, and the rest of them, did persecute them, for that indeed they found it to be like sea-water and salt.

O who were able now condignly to relate how Pantagruel did demean himself against the three hundred giants? O my Muse, my Calliope, my Thalia, inspire me at this time, restore unto me my spirits; for this is the logical bridge of asses! Here is the pitfall, here is the difficulty, to have ability enough to express the horrible battle that was fought. Ah, would to God that I had now a bottle of the best wine that ever those drank, who shall read this so veridical history.

CHAPTER 29

How Pantagruel discomfited the three hundred Giants armed with free-stone, and Loupgarou their Captain

THE giants seeing all their camp drowned, carried away their King Anarchus upon their backs, as well as they could, out of the fort, as Æneas did his father Anchises, in the time of the conflagration of Troy. When Panurge perceived them, he said to Pantagruel, Sir, yonder are the giants coming forth against you, lay on them with your mast gallantly like an old fencer; for now is the time that you must show yourself a brave man and an honest. And for our part we will not fail you. I myself will kill to you a good many boldly enough; for why, David killed Goliath very easily, and then this great lecher Eusthenes, who is stronger than four oxen, will not spare himself. Be of good courage, therefore and valiant, charge amongst them with point and edge, and by all manner of means. Well, said Pantagruel, of courage I have more than for fifty francs, but let us be wise, for Hercules first never undertook against two. That is well cacked, well scummered, said Panurge, do you compare yourself with Hercules? You have, by G—, more strength in your teeth, and more scent in your bum, than ever Hercules had in all his body and soul. So much is a man worth as he esteems himself. Whilst they spake these words, behold Loupgarou was come with all his giants, who, seeing Pantagruel in a manner alone, was carried away with temerity and presumption, for hopes that he had to kill the good man. Whereupon he said to his companions the giants, You wenchers of the low country, by Mahoom, if any of you undertake to fight against these men here, I will put you cruelly to death. It is my will, that you let me fight single. In the meantime you shall have good sport to look upon us.

Then all the other giants retired with their king, to the place where the flagons stood, and Panurge and his comrades with them, who counterfeited those that have had the pox, for he writhed about his mouth, shrunk up his fingers, and with a harsh and hoarse voice said unto them, I forsake —od, fellow-soldiers, if I would have it to be believed, that we make any war at all. Give us somewhat to eat with you, while you masters fight against one another. To this the king and giants jointly condescended, and accordingly made them to banquet with them. In the

meantime Panurge told them the follies of Turpin, the examples of St. Nicholas, and the tale of a tub. Loupgarou then set forward towards Pantagruel, with a mace all of steel, and that of the best sort, weighing nine thousand seven hundred quintals, and two quarterons, at the end whereof were thirteen pointed diamonds, the least whereof was as big as the greatest bell of Our Lady's church at Paris,—there might want perhaps the thickness of a nail, or at most, that I may not lie, of the back of those knives which they call cut-lugs or ear-cutters, but for a little off or on, more or less, it is no matter,—and it was enchanted in such sort, that it could never break, but contrarily all, that it did touch, did break immediately. Thus, then, as he approached with great fierceness and pride of heart, Pantagruel, casting up his eyes to heaven, recommended himself to God with all his soul, making such a vow as followeth.

O thou Lord God, who hast always been my protector, and my saviour, thou seest the distress wherein I am at this time. Nothing brings me hither but a natural zeal, which thou hast permitted unto mortals, to keep and defend themselves, their wives and children, country and family, in case thy own proper cause were not in question, which is the faith; for in such a business thou wilt have no coadjutors, only a catholic confession and service of thy word, and hast forbidden us all arming and defence. For thou art the Almighty, who in thine own cause, and where thine own business is taken in hand, canst defend it far beyond all that we can conceive, thou who hast thousand thousands of hundreds of millions of legions of angels, the least of which is able to kill all mortal men, and turn about the heavens and earth at his pleasure, as heretofore it very plainly appeared in the army of Sennacherib. If it may please thee, therefore, at this time to assist me, as my whole trust and confidence is in thee alone, I vow unto thee, that in all countries whatsoever, wherein I shall have any power or authority, whether in this of Utopia, or elsewhere, I will cause thy holy gospel to be purely, simply, and entirely preached, so that the abuses of a rabble of hypocrites and false prophets, who by human constitutions, and depraved inventions, have impoisoned all the world, shall be quite exterminated from about me.

This vow was no sooner made, but there was heard a voice from heaven, saying, *Hoc fac et vinces:* that is to say, Do this, and thou shalt overcome. Then Pantagruel seeing that Loupgarou with his mouth wide open was drawing near to him, went against him boldly, and cried out as loud as he was able, Thou diest, villain, thou diest! purposing by his horrible cry to make him afraid, according to the discipline of the Lacedæmonians. Withal, he immediately cast at him out of his bark, which he wore at his girdle, eighteen cags, and four bushels of salt, wherewith he filled both his mouth, throat, nose, and eyes. At this Loupgarou was so highly incensed, that, most fiercely setting upon him, he thought even with a blow of his mace to have beat out his brains. But Pantagruel was very nimble, and had always a quick foot, and a quick eye, and therefore, with his left foot did he step back one pace, yet not so nimbly, but that the blow, falling upon the bark, broke it in four thousand, four score and six pieces, and threw all the rest of the salt about the ground. Pantagruel, seeing that, most gallantly displayed the vigour of his arms, and according to the art of the axe, gave him with the great end of his mast a home-thrust a little above the breast; then, bringing along the blow to the left side, with a slash struck him between the neck and shoulders. After that, advancing his right foot, he gave him a push upon the couillons, with the upper end of his said mast, wherewith breaking the scuttle, on the top thereof, he spilt three or four puncheons of wine that were left therein.

Upon that, Loupgarou thought that he had pierced his bladder and that the wine that came forth had been his urine. Pantagruel, being not content with this, would have doubled it by a side-blow; but Loupgarou, lifting up his mace, advanced one step upon him, and with all his force would have dashed it upon Pantagruel, wherein, to speak the truth, he so sprightfully carried himself, that, if God had not succoured the good Pantagruel, he had been cloven from the top of his head to the bottom of his milt. But the blow glanced to the right side, by the brisk nimbleness of Pantagruel, and his mace sank into the ground above threescore and thirteen feet, through a huge rock, out of which the fire did issue greater than nine thousand and six tons. Pantagruel, seeing him busy about plucking out his mace, which stuck in the ground between the rocks, ran upon him, and would have clean cut off his head, if by mischance his mast had not touched a little against the stock of Loupgarou's mace, which

was enchanted, as we have said before. By this means his mast broke off about three handfuls above his hand, whereat he stood amazed like a bell-founder, and cried out, Ah, Panurge, where art thou? Panurge, seeing that, said to the king and the giants, by G—, they will hurt one another if they be not parted. But the giants were as merry as if they had been at a wedding. Then Carpalim would have risen from thence to help his master; but one of the giants said unto him, by Golfarin the nephew of Mahoom, if thou stir hence, I will put thee in the bottom of my breeches, instead of a suppository, which cannot choose but do me good. For in my belly I am very costive, and cannot well cagar without gnashing my teeth, and making many filthy faces. Then Pantagruel, thus destitute of a staff, took up the end of his mast, striking athwart and alongst upon the giant, but he did him no more hurt than you would do with a filip upon a smith's anvil. In the meantime Loupgarou was drawing his mace out of the ground, and, having already plucked it out, was ready therewith to have struck Pantagruel, who, being very quick in turning, avoided all his blows, in taking only the defensive part in hand, until on a sudden he saw, that Loupgarou did threaten him with these words, saying, Now villain, will not I fail to chop thee as small as minced meat, and keep thee henceforth from ever making any more poor men athirst! Then, without any more ado, Pantagruel struck him such a blow with his foot against the belly, that he made him fall backwards, his heels over his head, and dragged him thus along at flay-buttock above a flight-shot. Then Loupgarou cried out, bleeding at the throat, Mahoom, Mahoom, Mahoom, at which noise all the giants arose to succour him. But Panurge said unto them, Gentlemen, do not go, if you will believe me; for our master is mad, and strikes athwart and alongst, he cares not where; he will do you a mischief. But the giants made no account of it, seeing that Pantagruel had never a staff.

And when Pantagruel saw those giants approach very near unto him, he took Loupgarou by the two feet, and lift up his body like a pike in the air, wherewith it being harnished with anvils, he laid such heavy load amongst those giants armed with freestone, that, striking them down as a mason doth little knobs of stones, there was not one of them that stood before him, whom he threw not flat to the ground. And by the breaking of this stony armour there was made such a horrible rumble, as put me in mind of the butter-tower of St. Stephen's at Bourges, when it melted before the sun. Panurge, with Carpalim and Eusthenes, did cut in the meantime the throats of those that were struck down, in such sort, that there escaped not one. Pantagruel to any man's sight was like a mower, who with his scythe, which was Loupgarou, cut down the meadow-grass, to wit, the giants; but, with this fencing of Pantagruel's, Loupgarou lost his head, which happened when Pantagruel struck down one whose name was Riflandouille, or Pudding-plunderer, who was armed *cap-a-pie* with Grison-stones, one chip whereof splintering abroad cut off Epistemon's neck clean and fair. For otherwise the most part of them were but lightly armed with a kind of sandy brittle stone, and the rest with slates. At last, when he saw that they were all dead, he threw the body of Loupgarou, as hard as he could, against the city, where falling like a frog upon his belly, in the great piazza thereof, he with the said fall killed a singed he-cat, wet she-cat, a farting duck, and a bridled goose.

CHAPTER 30

How Epistemon, who had his head cut off, was finely healed by Panurge, and of the news which he brought from the Devils, and of the damned People in Hell

THIS gigantal victory being ended, Pantagruel withdrew himself to the place of the flagons, and called for Panurge and the rest, who came unto him safe and sound, except Eusthenes, whom one of the giants had scratched a little in the face, whilst he was about the cutting of his throat, and Epistemon, who appeared not at all. Whereat Pantagruel was so aggrieved, that he would have killed himself. But Panurge said unto him, Nay, Sir, stay a while, and we will search for him amongst the dead, and find out the truth of all. Thus as they went seeking after him, they found him stark dead, with his head between his arms all bloody. Then Eusthenes cried out, Ah, cruel death! hast thou taken from me the perfectest amongst men? At which words Pantagruel rose up with the greatest grief that ever any man did see, and said to Panurge, Ha, my friend, the prophecy of your two glasses, and the javelin staff, was a great deal too deceitful. But Panurge answered, My dear bullies all, weep not one

drop more, for, he being yet all hot, I will make him as sound as ever he was. In saying this, he took the head, and held it warm foregainst his codpiece, that the wind might not enter into it. Eusthenes and Carpalim carried the body to the place where they had banqueted, not out of any hope that ever he would recover, but that Pantagruel might see it.

Nevertheless Panurge gave him very good comfort, saying, If I do not heal him, I will be content to lose my head, which is a fool's wager. Leave off, therefore, crying, and help me. Then cleansed he his neck very well with pure white wine, and, after that, took his head, and into it synapised some powder of diamerdis, which he always carried about him in one of his bags. Afterwards he anointed it with I know not what ointment, and set it on very just, vein against vein, sinew against sinew, and spondyl against spondyl, that he might not be wry-necked,—for such people, he mortally hated. This done, he gave it round about some fifteen or sixteen stitches with a needle, that it might not fall off again, then on all sides, and everywhere, he put a little ointment on it, which he called resuscitative.

Suddenly Epistemon began to breathe, then opened his eyes, yawned, sneezed, and afterwards let a great household fart. Whereupon Panurge said, Now, certainly, he is healed,—and therefore gave him to drink a large full glass of strong white wine, with a sugared toast. In this fashion was Epistemon finely healed, only that he was somewhat hoarse for above three weeks together, and had a dry cough of which he could not be rid, but by the force of continual drinking. And now he began to speak, and said, that he had seen the devil, had spoken with Lucifer familiarly, and had been very merry in hell, and in the Elysian fields, affirming very seriously before them all, that the devils were boon companions and merry fellows. But, in respect of the damned, he said he was very sorry, that Panurge had so soon called him back into this world again; for, said he, I took wonderful delight to see them. How so? said Pantagruel. Because they do not use them there, said Epistemon, so badly as you think they do. Their estate and condition of living is but only changed after a very strange manner; for I saw Alexander the Great there, mending and patching on clouts upon old breeches and stockings, and thus got a very poor living.

Xerxes was a crier of mustard.
Romulus, a salter, and patcher of pattens.
Numa, a nailsmith.
Tarquin, a porter.
Piso, a clownish swain.
Sylla, a ferryman.
Cyrus, a cowherd,
Themistocles, a glass-maker.
Epaminondas, a maker of mirrors or looking-glasses.
Brutus and Cassius, surveyors or measurers of land.
Demosthenes, a vine-dresser.
Cicero, a fire-kindler.
Fabius, a threader of beads.
Artaxerxes, a rope-maker.
Æneas, a miller.
Achilles was a scald-pated maker of hay-bundles.
Agamemnon, a lick-box.
Ulysses, a hay-mower.
Nestor, a deer-keeper or forester.
Darius, a gold-finder, or jakes-farmer.
Ancus Martius, a ship-trimmer.
Camillus, a foot-post.
Marcellus, a sheller of beans.
Drusus, a taker of money at the doors of play-houses.
Scipio Africanus, a crier of lee in a wooden-slipper.
Asdrubal, a lantern-maker.
Hannibal, a kettle-maker and seller of egg shells.
Priamus, a seller of old clouts.
Lancelot of the Lake was a flayer of dead horses.
All the Knights of the Round Table, were poor day-labourers, employed to row over the rivers of Cocytus, Phlegeton, Styx, Acheron, and Lethe, when my lords the devils had a mind to recreate themselves upon the water, as in the like occasion are hired the boatmen at Lyons, the gondoliers of Venice, and oars of London. But with this difference, that these poor knights have only for their fare a bob or flirt on the nose, and, in the evening, a morsel of coarse mouldy bread.
Trajan was fisher of frogs.
Antoninus, a lackey.
Commodus, a bagpiper.
Pertinax, a peeler of walnuts.
Lucullus, a maker of rattles and hawks' bells.
Justinian, a pedlar.
Hector, a snap-sauce scullion.
Paris, was a poor beggar.

Cambyses, a mule driver.
Nero, a base blind fiddler, or player on that instrument which is called a wind-broach. Fierabras was his serving-man, who did him a thousand mischievous tricks, and would make him eat of the brown bread, and drink of the turned wine, when himself did both eat and drink of the best.
Julius Cæsar and Pompey were boat-wrights and tighters of ships.
Valentine and Orson did serve in the stoves of hell, and were sweat-rubbers in hot houses.
Giglan and Gawain were poor swine-herds.
Geoffrey with the great tooth, was a tinder-maker and seller of matches.
Godfrey de Bullion, a hood maker.
Jason was a bracelet-maker.
Don Pietro de Castille, a carrier of indulgences.
Morgante, a beer-brewer.
Huon of Bordeaux, a hooper of barrels.
Pyrrhus, a kitchen-scullion.
Antiochus, a chimney-sweeper.
Octavian, a scraper of parchment.
Nerva, a mariner.
Pope Julius was a crier of pudding-pies, but he left off wearing there his great buggerly beard.
John of Paris was a greaser of boots.
Arthur of Britain, an ungreaser of caps.
Perce-Forest, a carrier of fagots.
Pope Boniface the Eighth, a scummer of pots.
Pope Nicholas the Third, a maker of paper.
Pope Alexander, a rat-catcher.
Pope Sixtus, an anointer of those that have the pox.

What, said Pantagruel, have they the pox there too? Surely, said Epistemon, I never saw so many: there are there, I think, above a hundred millions, for believe, that those who have not had the pox in this world, must have it in the other.

Cotsbody, said Panurge, then I am free; for I have been as far as the hole of Gibraltar, reached unto the outmost bounds of Hercules, and gathered of the ripest.

Ogier the Dane, was a furbisher of armour.
The King Tigranes, a mender of thatched houses.
Galien Restored, a taker of moldwarps.
The four sons of Aymon were all tooth-drawers.

Pope Calixtus was a barber of a woman's *sine qua non.*

Pope Urban, a bacon-picker.

Melusina was a kitchen drudge-wench.

Matabrune, a laundress.

Cleopatra, a crier of onions.

Helen, a broker for chamber-maids.

Semiramis, the beggars' lice-killer.

Dido did sell mushrooms.

Penthesilea sold cresses.

Lucretia was an ale-house keeper.

Hortensia, a spinstress.

Livia, a grater of verdgrease.

After this manner, those, that had been great lords and ladies here, got but a poor scurvy wretched living there below. And, on the contrary, the philosophers and others, who in this world had been altogether indigent and wanting, were great lords there in their turn. I saw Diogenes there strut it out most pompously, and in great magnificence, with a rich purple gown on him, and a golden sceptre in his right hand. And which is more, he would now and then make Alexander the Great mad, so enormously would he abuse him, when he had not well patched his breeches; for he used to pay his skin with sound bastinadoes. I saw Epictetus there most gallantly apparelled after the French fashion, sitting under a pleasant arbour, with store of handsome gentlewomen, frolicking, drinking, dancing, and making good cheer, with abundance of crowns of the sun. Above the lattice were written these verses for his device:

To leap and dance, to sport and play,
　And drink good wine both white and
　　brown,
Or nothing else do all the day,
　But tell bags full of many a crown.

When he saw me, he invited me to drink with him very courteously, and I being willing to be entreated, we tippled and chopined together most theologically. In the meantime came Cyrus to beg one farthing of him for the honour of Mercury, therewith to buy a few onions for his supper. No, no, said Epictetus, I do not use in my alms-giving to bestow farthings. Hold, thou varlet, there's a crown for thee, be an honest man. Cyrus was exceeding glad to have met with such a booty; but the other poor rogues, the kings that are there below, as Alexander, Darius, and oth-

ers, stole it away from him by night. I saw Pathelin the treasurer of Rhadamanthus, who, in cheapening the pudding-pies that Pope Julius cried, asked him how much a dozen? Three blanks, said the pope. Nay, said Pathelin, three blows with a cudgel. Lay them down here, you rascal, and go fetch more. The poor pope went away weeping, who, when he came to his master the pie-maker, told him that they had taken away his pudding-pies. Whereupon his master gave him such a sound lash with an eel-skin, that his own would have been worth nothing to make bag-pipe-bags of. I saw Master John *Le Maire* there personate the pope, in such fashion, that he made all the poor kings and popes of this world kiss his feet; and, taking great state upon him, gave them his benediction, saying, Get the pardons, rogues, get the pardons, they are good and cheap. I absolve you of bread and pottage, and dispense with you to be never good for anything. Then, calling Caillet and Triboulet to him, he spake these words, My lords the cardinals, dispatch their bulls, to wit, to each of them a blow with a cudgel upon the reins. Which, accordingly, was forthwith performed. I heard Master Francis Villon ask Xerxes, How much the mess of mustard? A farthing, said Xerxes. To which the said Villon answered, The pox take thee for a villain! As much of square-eared wheat is not worth half that price, and now thou offerest to enhance the price of victuals. With this be pissed in his pot, as the mustard-makers of Paris used to do. I saw the trained bow-man of the bathing tub, known by the name of the *Franc archer de Baignolet*, who, being one of the trustees of the Inquisition, when he saw Perce-Forest making water against a wall, on which was painted the fire of St. Anthony, declared him heretic, and would have caused him to be burnt alive, had it not been for Morgante, who for his *Proficiat* and other small fees, gave him nine tuns of beer.

Well, said Pantagruel, reserve all these fair stories for another time, only tell us how the usurers are there handled. I saw them, said Epistemon, all very busily employed in seeking of rusty pins, and old nails in the kennels of the streets, as you see poor wretched rogues do in this world. But the quintal, or hundred weight, of this old iron ware is there valued but at the price of a cantle of bread, and yet they have but a very bad dispatch and riddance in the sale of it. Thus the poor misers are sometimes three whole weeks without eating one morsel or crumb of bread, and yet work both day and night, looking for the fair to come. Nevertheless, of all this labour, toil, and misery, they reckon nothing, so cursedly active they are in the prosecution of that their base calling, in hopes, at the end of the year, to earn some scurvy penny by it.

Come, said Pantagruel, let us now make ourselves merry one bout, and drink my lads, I beseech you, for it is very good drinking all this month. Then did they uncase their flagons by heaps and dozens, and with their leaguer provision made excellent good cheer. But the poor King Anarchus could not all this while settle himself towards any fit of mirth; whereupon Panurge said, Of what trade shall we make my lord the king here, that he may be skilful in the art, when he goes thither to sojourn amongst all the devils of hell? Indeed, said Pantagruel, that was well advised of thee. Do with him what thou wilt, I give him to thee. Grammercy, said Panurge, the present is not to be refused, and I love it from you.

CHAPTER 31

How Pantagruel entered into the city of the Amaurots, and how Panurge married King Anarchus to an old lantern-carrying hag, and made him a crier of green sauce

AFTER this wonderful victory, Pantagruel sent Carpalim unto the city of the Amaurots, to declare and signify unto them, how the King Anarchus was taken prisoner, and all the enemies of the city overthrown. Which news when they heard, all the inhabitants of the city came forth to meet him in good order, and with a great triumphant pomp, conducting him with a heavenly joy into the city, where innumerable bon-fires were kindled, through all the parts thereof, and fair round tables, which were furnished with store of good victuals, set out in the middle of the streets. This was a renewing of the golden age in the time of Saturn, so good was the cheer which then they made.

But Pantagruel, having assembled the whole senate, and common council-men of the town, said My masters, we must now strike the iron whilst it is hot. It is, therefore, my will that, before we frolic it any longer, we advise how to assault and take the whole kingdom of the Dipsodes. To which effect, let those that will go with me to provide themselves against to-morrow after drinking; for

then will I begin to march. Not that I need any more men than I have, to help me to conquer it; for I could make it as sure that way as if I had it already, but I see this city is so full of inhabitants, that they can scarce turn into the streets. I will, therefore, carry them as a colony in Dipsody, and will give them all that country, which is fair, wealthy, fruitful, and pleasant, above all other countries in the world, as many of you can tell, who have been there heretofore. Every one of you, therefore, that will go along, let him provide himself as I have said. This counsel and resolution being published in the city, the next morning there assembled in the piazza, before the palace, to the number of eighteen hundred fifty-six thousand and eleven, besides women and little children. Thus began they to march straight into Dipsody, in such good order as did the people of Israel, when they departed out of Egypt, to pass over the Red Sea.

But, before we proceed any further in this purpose, I will tell you how Panurge handled his prisoner the King Anarchus; for, having remembered that which Epistemon had related, how the kings and rich men in this world were used in the Elysian fields, and how they got their living there by base and ignoble trades, he, therefore, one day apparelled his king in a pretty little canvass doublet, all jagged and pinked like the tippet of a light horseman's cap, together with a pair of large mariner's breeches, and stockings without shoes,—For, said he, they would but spoil his sight,—and a little peach-coloured bonnet, with a great capon's feather in it—I lie, for I think he had two—and a very handsome girdle of a sky colour and green, (in French called *pers et vert*) saying, that such a livery did become him well, for that he had always been perverse, and, in this plight bringing him before Pantagruel, said unto him, Do you know this roister? No, indeed, said Pantagruel. It is, said Panurge, my lord the king of the three batches, or thread-bare sovereign. I intend to make him an honest man. These devilish kings, which we have here, are but as so many calves, they know nothing, and are good for nothing but to do a thousand mischiefs to their poor subjects, and to trouble all the world with war for their unjust and detestable pleasure. I will put him to a trade, and make him a crier of green sauce. Go to, begin and cry, Do you lack any green sauce? and the poor devil cried. That is too low, said Panurge, then took him by the ear, saying

Sing higher in *ge, sol, re, ut*. So, so, poor dev-il, thou hast a good throat: thou wert never so happy as to be no longer king. And Panta-gruel made himself merry with all this; for I dare boldly say, that he was the best little gaffer that was to be seen between this and the end of a staff. Thus was Anarchus made a good crier of green sauce. Two days thereaf-ter, Panurge married him with an old lantern-carrying hag, and he himself made the wed-ding with fine sheep's-heads, brave haslets with mustard, gallant salligots with garlic, of which he sent five horse-loads unto Panta-gruel, which he ate up all, he found them so appetising. And for their drink, they had a kind of small well-watered wine, and some fine sorb-apple cider. And to make them dance, he hired a blind man, that made music to them with a wind-broach.

After dinner he led them to the palace, and shewed them to Pantagruel, and said, point-ing to the married woman, You need not fear that she will crack. Why? said Pantagruel. Because, said Panurge, she is well slit and broke up already. What do you mean by that? said Pantagruel. Do not you see, said Pa-nurge, that the chesnuts which are roasted in the fire, if they be whole, they crack as if they were mad; and, to keep them from cracking, they make an incision in them, and slit them. So this new bride is in her lower parts well slit before, and, therefore, will not crack behind.

Pantagruel gave them a little lodge near the lower street, and a mortar of stone where-in to bray and pound their sauce, and in this manner did they do their little business, he being as pretty a crier of green sauce, as ever was seen in the country of Utopia. But I have been told since, that his wife doth beat him like plaster, and the poor sot dares not defend himself, he is so simple.

CHAPTER 32

How Pantagruel with his tongue covered a whole Army, and what the Author saw in his Mouth

THUS as Pantagruel with all his army had en-tered into the country of the Dipsodes, every one was glad of it, and incontinently rendered themselves unto him, bringing him out of their own good wills the keys of all the cities where he went, the Almirods only excepted, who, being resolved to hold out against him, made answer to his heralds, that they would

not yield but upon very honourable and good conditions.

What? said Pantagruel, do they ask any better terms, than the hand at the pot, and the glass in their fist? Come, let us go sack them, and put them all to the sword. Then did they put themselves in good order, as be-ing fully determined to give an assault, but by the way, passing through a large field, they were overtaken with a great shower of rain, whereat they began to shiver and trem-ble, to crowd, press, and thrust close to one another. When Pantagruel saw that, he made their captains tell them that it was nothing, and that he saw well above the clouds, that it would be nothing but a little dew; but how-soever, that they should put themselves in or-der, and he would cover them. Then did they put themselves in a close order, and stood as near to each other as they could, and Panta-gruel drew out his tongue only half-ways, and covered them all, as a hen doth her chickens. In the meantime I, who relate to you these so veritable stories, hid myself under a burdock-leaf, which was not much less in largeness than the arch of the bridge of Montrible, but, when I saw them thus covered, I went to-wards them to shelter myself likewise; which I could not do, for that they were so, as the saying is, *At the yard's end there is no cloth left*. Then, as well as I could, I got upon it, and went along full two leagues upon his tongue, and so long marched, that at last I came into his mouth. But, oh gods and god-desses, what did I see there! Jupiter confound me with his trisulk lightning if I lie! I walked there as they do in Sophie, at Constantinople, and saw there great rocks, like the mountains in Denmark—I believe that those were his teeth. I saw also fair meadows, large forests, great and strong cities, not a jot less than Lyons or Poictiers. The first man I met there was a good honest fellow planting coleworts, whereat being very much amazed, I asked him, My friend, what dost thou make here? I plant coleworts, said he. But how, and where-with, said I? Ha, Sir, said he, every one can-not have his ballocks as heavy as a mortar, neither can we be all rich. Thus do I get my poor living, and carry them to the market to sell in the city which is here behind. Jesus! said I, is there here a new world? Sure, said he, it is never a jot new, but it is commonly reported, that, without this, there is an earth, whereof the inhabitants enjoy the light of a sun and moon, and that it is full of, and replenished with, very good commodities; but yet this is more ancient than that. Yea, but, said I, my friend, what is the name of that city, whither thou carriest thy coleworts to sell? It is called Aspharage, said he, and all the in-dwellers are Christians, very honest men, and will make you good cheer. To be brief, I resolved to go thither. Now, in my way, I met with a fellow that was lying in wait to catch pigeons, of whom I asked, My friend, from whence come these pigeons? Sir, said he, they come from the other world. Then I thought, that, when Pantagruel yawned, the pigeons went into his mouth in whole flocks, thinking that it had been a pigeon-house.

Then I went into the city, which I found fair, very strong, and seated in a good air; but at my entry the guard demanded of me my pass or ticket. Whereat I was much astonished, and asked them, My masters, is there any danger of the plague here? O Lord, said they, they die hard by here so fast, that the cart runs about the streets. Good God, said I, and where? Whereunto they answered, that it was in Larynx and Pharynx, which are two great cities, such as Rouen and Nantes, rich and of great trading. And the cause of the plague was by a stinking and infectious exhalation, which lately vapoured out of the abismes, whereof there have died above two and twenty hundred and threescore thousand and sixteen persons within this sevennight. Then I considered, calculated, and found, that it was an unsavoury breathing, which came out of Pantagruel's stomach, when he did eat so much garlic, as we have aforesaid.

Parting from thence, I passed amongst the rocks, which were his teeth, and never left walking, till I got up on one of them; and there I found the pleasantest places in the world, great large tennis-courts, fair galleries, sweet meadows, store of vines, and an infinite number of banqueting summer outhouses in the fields, after the Italian fashion, full of pleasure and delight, where I stayed full four months, and never made better cheer in my life as then. After that I went down by the hinder teeth to come to the chaps. But in the way I was robbed by thieves in a great forest, that is in the territory towards the ears. Then, after a little further travelling, I fell upon a pretty petty village,—truly I have forgot the name of it,—where I was yet merrier than ever, and got some certain money to live by.

Can you tell how? By sleeping. For there they hire men by the day to sleep, and they get by it sixpence a day, but they than can snore hard get at least ninepence. How I had been robbed in the valley, I informed the senators, who told me, that, in very truth, the people of that side were bad livers, and naturally thievish, whereby I perceived well, that as we have with us the countries Cisalpine and Transalpine, that is, be-hither and beyond the mountains, so have they there the countries Cidentine and Tradentine, that is, behither and beyond the teeth. But it is far better living on this side, and the air is purer. There I began to think, that it is very true, which is commonly said, that one half of the world knoweth not how the other half liveth; seeing none before myself had ever written of that country, wherein are above five and twenty kingdoms inhabited, besides deserts, and a great arm of the sea. Concerning which, I have composed a great book intituled *The History of the Gorgians*, because they dwell in the gorge of my master Pantagruel.

At last I was willing to return, and, passing by his beard, I cast myself upon his shoulders, and from thence slid down to the ground, and fell before him. As soon as I was perceived by him, he asked me, Whence comest thou, Alcofribas? I answered him, Out of your mouth, my lord! And how long hast thou been there? said he. Since the time, said I, that you went against the Almirods. That is about six months ago, said he. And wherewith didst thou live? What didst thou drink? I answered, My lord, of the same that you did, and of the daintiest morsels that passed through your throat I took toll. Yea, but, said he, where didst thou shite? In your throat, my lord, said I. Ha, ha, thou art a merry fellow, said he. We have with the help of God conquered all the land of the Dipsodes; I will give thee the *Chastelleine,* or Lairdship of Salmigondin. Grammercy, my lord, said I, you gratify me beyond all that I have deserved of you.

CHAPTER 33

How Pantagruel became sick, and the manner how he was recovered

AWHILE after this the good Pantagruel fell sick, and had such an obstruction in his stomach, that he could neither eat nor drink: and, because mischief seldom comes alone, a hot piss seized on him, which tormented him more than you would believe. His physicians nevertheless helped him very well, and with store of lenitives and diuretic drugs made him piss away his pain. His urine was so hot, that since that time it is not yet cold, and you have of it in divers places of France, according to the course that it took, and they are called the hot baths, as

At Coderets.
At Limous.
At Dast.
At Balleruc.
At Neric.
At Bourbennensy, and elsewhere in Italy.
At Mongros.
At Appone.
At Sancto Petro de Padua.
At St. Helen.
At Casa Nuova.
At St. Bartolomeo, in the county of Boulogne.
At the Porrette, and a thousand other places.

And I wonder much at a rabble of foolish philosophers and physicians, who spend their time in disputing, whence the heat of the said waters cometh, whether it be by reason of borax, or sulphur, or alum, or salt-petre, that is within the mine. For they do nothing but dote, and better were it for them to rub their arse against a thistle, than to waste away their time in thus disputing of that, whereof they know not the original; for the resolution is easy, neither need we to inquire any further, than that the said baths came by a hot piss of the good Pantagruel.

Now, to tell you, after what manner he was cured of his principal disease, I let pass how for a minorative, or gentle potion, he took four hundred pound weight of colophoniac scammony, six score and eighteen cart loads of cassia, an eleven thousand and nine hundred pound weight of rhubarb, besides other confused jumblings of sundry drugs. You must understand, that by the advice of the physicians it was ordained, that what did offend his stomach should be taken away; and, therefore, they made seventeen great balls of copper, each whereof was bigger than that which is to be seen on the top of St. Peter's needle at Rome, and in such sort, that they did open in the midst, and shut with a spring. Into one of them entered one of his men, carrying a lantern and a torch lighted, and so Pantagruel swallowed him down like a little pill. Into seven others went seven country fellows, having every one of them a shovel on

his neck. Into nine others entered nine wood-carriers, having each of them a basket hung at his neck, and so were they swallowed down like pills. When they were in his stomach, every one undid his spring, and came out of their cabins. The first whereof was he that carried the lantern, and so they fell more than half a league into a most horrible gulf, more stinking and infectious than ever was Mephitis, or the marshes of the Camerina, or the abominably unsavoury lake of Sorbonne, whereof Strabo maketh mention. And had it not been, that they had very well antidoted their stomach, heart, and wine-pot, which is called the noddle, they had been altogether suffocated and choked with these detestable vapours. O what a perfume! O what an evaporation wherewith to bewray the masks or mufflers of young mangy queans. After that, with groping and smelling they came near to the fecal matter and the corrupted humours. Finally, they found a *montjoy* or heap of ordure and filth. Then fell the pioneers to work to dig it up, and the rest with their shovels filled the baskets; and, when all was cleansed, every one retired himself into his ball.

This done, Pantagruel enforcing himself to a vomit very easily brought them out, and they made no more show in his mouth, than a fart in yours. But, when they came merrily out of their pills, I thought upon the Grecians coming out of the Trojan horse. By this means was he healed, and brought into his former state and convalescence; and of these brazen pills, or rather copper balls, you have one at Orleans, upon the steeple of the Holy Cross Church.

CHAPTER 34

The conclusion of this present Book, and the excuse of the Author

Now, my masters, you have heard a beginning of the horrific history of my lord and master Pantagruel. Here will I make an end of the first book. My head aches a little, and I perceive that the registers of my brain are somewhat jumbled and disordered with the septembral juice. You shall have the rest of the history at Frankfort mart next coming, and there shall you see, how Panurge was married and made a cuckold within a month after his wedding: how Pantagruel found out the philosopher's stone, the manner how he found it, and the way how to use it: how he passed over the Caspian mountains, and how he sailed through the Atlantic sea, defeated the Cannibals, and conquered the isles of Pearls, how he married the daughter of the King of India, called Presthan, how he fought against the devil, and burnt up five chambers of hell, ransacked the great black chamber, threw Proserpina into the fire, broke five teeth to Lucifer, and the horn that was in his arse. How he visited the regions of the moon, to know whether indeed the moon were not entire and whole, or if the women had three quarters of it in their heads, and a thousand other little merriments all veritable. These are brave things truly. Good night, gentlemen. *Perdonate mi,* and think not so much upon my faults, that you forget your own.

If you say to me, master, it would seem, that you were not very wise in writing to us these flimflam stories, and pleasant fooleries; I answer you, that you are not much wiser to spend your time in reading them. Nevertheless, if you read them to make yourselves merry, as in manner of pastime I wrote them, you and I both are far more worthy of pardon, than a great rabble of squint-minded fellows, dissembling and counterfeit saints, demure lookers, hypocrites, pretended zealots, tough friars, buskin monks, and other such sects of men, who disguise themselves like maskers to deceive the world. For, whilst they give the common people to understand,

that they are busied about nothing but contemplation and devotion in fastings, and maceration of their sensuality,—and that only to sustain and aliment the small frailty of their humanity,—it is so far otherwise, that, on the contrary, God knows, what cheer they make: *Et Curios simulant, sed Bacchanalia vivunt.*[92] You may read it in great letters in the colouring of their red snouts, and gulching bellies as big as a tun, unless it be when they perfume themselves with sulphur. As for their study, it is wholly taken up in reading of Pantagruelin books, not so much to pass the time merrily, as to hurt some one or other mischievously, to wit, in articling, sole articling, wry-neckifying, buttock-stirring, ballocking, and diabliculating, that is calumniating. Wherein they are like unto the poor rogues of a village, that are busy in stirring up and scraping in the ordure and filth of little children, in the season of cherries and guinds, and that only to find the kernels, that they may sell them to the druggists, to make thereof pomander oil. Fly from these men, abhor and hate them as much as I do, and upon my faith you will find yourselves the better for it. And if you desire to be good Pantagruelists, that is to say, to live in peace, joy, health, making yourselves always merry; never trust those men that always peep out at one hole.

BOOK THREE

TREATING OF THE HEROIC DEEDS AND SAYINGS
OF THE GOOD PANTAGRUEL

FRANCIS RABELAIS

To the Spirit of the Queen of Navarre

Abstracted soul, ravish'd with ecstasies,
Gone back, and now familiar in the skies,
Thy former host, thy body, leaving quite,
Which to obey thee always took delight,—
Obsequious, ready,—now from motion free,
Senseless, and, as it were in apathy,
Would'st thou not issue forth, for a short space,
From that divine, eternal heavenly place,
To see the third part, in this earthy cell.
Of the brave acts of good Pantagruel?

THE AUTHOR'S PROLOGUE

Good people, most illustrious drinkers, and you thrice precious gouty gentlemen, did you ever see Diogenes the cynic philosopher? If you have seen him, you then had your eyes in your head, or I am very much out of my understanding and logical sense. It is a gallant thing to see the clearness of (wine, gold,) the sun. I'll be judged by the blind-born, so renowned in the sacred Scriptures, who, having at his choice to ask whatever he would from him who is Almighty, and whose word in an instant is effectually performed, asking nothing else but that he might see. *Item,* you are not young, which is a competent quality for you to philosophize more than physically on wine, (*en vin*) not in vain (*en vain*) and henceforwards to be of the Bacchic Council; to the end that opining there, you may give your opinion faithfully of the substance, colour, excellent odour, eminency, propriety, faculty, virtue, and effectual dignity of the said blessed and desired liquor.

If you have not seen him, as I am easily induced to believe that you have not, at least you have heard some talk of him. For through the air, and the whole extent of this hemisphere of the heavens, hath his report and fame, even until this present time, remained very memorable and renowned. Then all of you are derived from the Phrygian blood, if I be not deceived. If you have not so many crowns as Midas had, yet have you something, I know not what, of him, which the Persians of old esteemed more of in all their otacusts, and which was more desired by the Emperor Antoninus; and gave occasion thereafter to the Basilisco at Rohan to be surnamed Goodly Ears. If you have not heard of him, I will presently tell you a story to make your wine relish. Drink then,—so, to the purpose. Hearken now whilst I give you notice, to the end that you may not, like infidels, be by your simplicity abused, that in his time he was a rare philosopher, and the cheerfullest of a thousand. If he had some imperfection, so have you, as have we; for there is nothing, but God, that is perfect. Yet so it was, that by Alexander the Great, although he had Aristotle for his instructor and domestic, was he held in such estimation, that he wished, if he had not been Alexander, to have been Diogenes the Sinopian.

When Philip King of Macedon enterprised the siege and ruin of Corinth, the Corin-

127

thians having received certain intelligence by their spies, that he with a numerous army in battle array was coming against them, were all of them, not without cause, most terribly afraid; and therefore were not neglective of their duty, in doing their best endeavours to put themselves in a fit posture to resist his hostile approach and defend their own city.

Some from the fields brought into the fortified places their moveables, cattle, corn, wine, fruit, victuals, and other necessary provision.

Others did fortify and rampire their walls, set up little fortresses, bastions, squared ravelins, digged trenches, cleansed countermines, fenced themselves with gabions, contrived platforms, emptied casemates, barricaded the false brays, erected the cavalliers, repaired the contrescarpes plaistered the courtines, lengthened ravelins, stopped parapets, mortaised barbacans, new-pointed the portcullices, fastened the herses, sarasinesks, and cataracts, placed their sentries, and doubled their patrol. Every one did watch and ward, and none was exempted from carrying the basket. Some polished corselets, varnished backs and breasts, cleaned the headpieces, mail-coats, brigandines, salades, helmets, morions, jacks, gushets, gorgets, hoguines, brassars, and cuissards, corselets, haubergeons, shields, bucklers, targets, greves, gantlets and spurs. Others made ready bows, slings, crossbows, pellets, catapults, migraines or fire-balls, firebrands, balists, scorpions, and other such warlike engines, expugnatory, and destructive to the helepolides. They sharpened and prepared spears, staves, pikes, brown bills, halberts, long hooks, lances, zagayes, quarterstaves, eel-spears, partisans, troutstaves, clubs, battle-axes, maces, darts, dartlets, glaves, javelins, javelots, and truncheons. They set edges upon scimetars, cutlasses, badelaire, back-swords, tucks, sapiers, bayonets, arrow-heads, dags, daggers, mandousians, poniards, whynyards, knives, skenes sables, chippin knives and raillons.

Every man exercised his weapon, every man scoured off the rust from his natural hanger: nor was there a woman amongst them, though never so reserved, or old, who made not her harness to be well furbished; as you know the Corinthian women of old were reputed very courageous combatants.

Diogenes seeing them all so warm at work, and himself not employed by the magistrates in any business whatsoever, he did very seri-

ously, for many days together, without speaking one word, consider, and contemplate the countenances of his fellow-citizens.

Then on a sudden, as if he had been roused up and inspired by a martial spirit, he girded his cloak, scarf-wise, about his left arm, tucked up his sleeves to the elbow, trussed himself like a clown gathering apples, and giving to one of his old acquaintance his wallet, books, and opistographs, away went he out of town towards a little hill or promontory of Corinth, called Craneum, and there on the strand, a pretty level place, did he roll his jolly tub, which served him for a house to shelter him from the injuries of the weather; there, I say in great vehemency of spirit, did he turn it, veer it, wheel it, frisk it, jumble it, shuffle it, huddle it, tumble it, hurry it, jolt it, justle it, overthrow it, evert it, invert it, subvert it, overturn it, beat it, thwack it, bump it, batter it, knock it, thrust it, push it, jerk it, shock it, shake it, toss it, throw it, overthrow it, upside down, topsiturvy, arsiversy, tread it, trample it, stamp it, tap it, ting it, ring it, tingle it, towl it, sound it, resound it, stop it, shut it, unbung it, close it, unstopple it, And then again in a mighty bustle he bandied it, slubbered it, hacked it, whitled it, wayed it, darted it, hurled it, staggered it, reeled it, swinged it, brangled it, tottered it, lifted it, heaved it, transformed it, transfigured it, transposed it, transplaced it, reared it, raised it, hoised it, washed it, dighted it, cleansed it, rinced it, nailed it, settled it, fastened it, shackled it, fettered it, levelled it, blocked it, tugged it, tewed it, carried it, bedashed it, bewrayed it, parched it, mounted it, broached it, nicked it, notched it, bespattered it, decked it, adorned it, trimmed it, garnished it, gaged it, furnished it, bored it, pierced it, trapped it, rumbled it, slid it down the hill, and precipitated it from the very height of the Craneum; then from the foot to the top, (like another Sisyphus with his stone,) bore it up again, and every way so banged it and belaboured it, that it was ten thousand to one he had not struck the bottom of it out.

Which when one of his friends had seen, and asked him why he did so toil his body, perplex his spirit, and torment his tub? the philosopher's answer was, That, not being employed in any other charge by the Republic, he thought it expedient to thunder and storm it so tempestuously upon his tub, that, amongst a people so fervently busy and earnest at work, he alone might not seem a loitering slug and lazy fellow. To the same purpose may I say of myself,

> Though I be rid from fear,
> I am not void of care.

For perceiving no account to be made of me towards the discharge of a trust of any great concernment, and considering that through all the parts of this most noble kingdom of France, both on this and on the other side of the mountains, every one is most diligently exercised and busied,—some in the fortifying of their own native country, for its defence,—others in the repulsing of their enemies by an offensive war; and all this with a policy so excellent, and such admirable order, so manifestly profitable for the future, whereby France shall have its frontiers most magnifically enlarged, and the French assured of a long and well-grounded peace, that very little withholds me from the opinion of good Heraclitus, which affirmeth war, to be the father of all good things; and therefore do I believe that war is in Latin called *Bellum,* and not by antiphrasis, as some patchers of old rusty Latin would have us to think, because in war there is little beauty to be seen; but absolutely and simply, for that in war appeareth all that is good and graceful, and that by the wars is purged out all manner of wickedness and deformity. For proof whereof the wise and pacific Solomon could no better represent the unspeakable perfection of the divine wisdom, than by comparing it to the due disposure and ranking of an army in battle array, well provided and ordered.

Therefore, by reason of my weakness and inability, being reputed by my compatriots unfit for the offensive part of warfare; and, on the other side, being no way employed in matter of the defensive, although it had been but to carry burdens, fill ditches, or break clods, either whereof had been to me indifferent, I held it not a little disgraceful to be only an idle spectator of so many valorous, eloquent, and warlike persons, who in the view and sight of all Europe act this notable interlude or tragi-comedy, and not exert myself, and contribute thereto this nothing, my all, which remained for me to do. In my opinion, little honour is due to such as are mere lookers on, liberal of their eyes, and of their strength parsimonious; who conceal their crowns, and hide their silver; scratching their head with one finger like grumbling puppies,

gaping at the flies like tithe calves; clapping down their ears like Arcadian asses at the melody of musicians, who with their very countenances in the depth of silence express their consent to the *Prosopopeia.*[1] Having made this choice and election, it seemed to me that my exercise therein would be neither unprofitable nor troublesome to any, whilst I should thus set agoing my Diogenical tub, which is all that is left me safe from the shipwreck of my former misfortunes.

At this dingle dangle wagging of my tub, what would you have me to do? By the Virgin that tucks up her sleeve, I know not as yet. Stay a little, till I suck up a draught of this bottle; it is my true and only Helicon; it is my Caballine Fountain; it is my sole enthusiasm. Drinking thus, I meditate, discourse, resolve, and conclude. After that the epilogue is made, I laugh, I write, I compose, and drink again. Ennius drinking wrote, and writing drank. Æschylus, if Plutarch in his *Symposiacs* merit any faith, drank composing, and drinking composed. Homer never wrote fasting, and Cato never wrote till after he had drank. These passages I have brought before you, to the end you may not say that I live without the example of men well praised, and better prized. It is good and fresh enough, even as if you would say, it is entering upon the second degree. God, the good God of Sabaoth, that is to say, the God of armies, be praised for it eternally! If you after the same manner would take one great draught, or two little ones, whilst you have your gown about you, I truly find no kind of inconvenience in it, provided you send up to God for all some small scantling of thanks.

Since then my luck or destiny is such as you have heard,—for it is not for every body to go to Corinth,—I am fully resolved to be so little idle and unprofitable, that I will set myself to serve the one and the other sort of people. Amongst the diggers, pioneers, and rampart-builders, I will do as did Neptune and Apollo, at Troy, under Laomedon, or as did Renault of Montauban in his latter days: I will serve the masons, I will set on the pot to boil for the bricklayers: and whilst the minced meat is making ready at the sound of my small pipe, I will measure the muzzle of the missing dotards. Thus did Amphion with the melody of his harp found, build, and finish the great and renowned city of Thebes.

For the use of the warriors I am about to broach off a new barrel to give them a taste,

(which by two former volumes of mine, if by
the deceitfulness and falsehood of printers,
they had not been jumbled, marred, and
spoiled, you would have very well relished,)
and draw unto them, of the growth of our
own trippery pastimes, a gallant third part of
a gallon, and consequently a jolly cheerful
quart of Pantagruelic sentences, which you
may lawfully call, if you please, Diogenical;
and shall have me, seeing I cannot be their
fellow-soldier, for their faithful butler, refreshing and cheering, according to my little
power, their return from the alarms of the enemy; as also for an indefatigable extoller of
their martial exploits and glorious achievements. I shall not fail therein, par *lapathium
acutum*[2] *de Dieu;* if Mars fail not in Lent,
which the cunning lecher, I warrant you, will
be loth to do.

I remember nevertheless to have read, that
Ptolemy, the son of Lagus, one day amongst
the many spoils and booties, which by his
victories he had acquired, presenting to the
Egyptians, in the open view of the people, a
Bactrian camel all black, and a party-coloured slave, in such sort, as that the one half
of his body was black, and the other white,
not in partition of breadth by the diaphragm,
as was that woman consecrated to the Indian
Venus, whom the Tyanean philosopher did
see between the River Hydaspes and Mount
Caucasus, but in a perpendicular dimension of
altitude; which were things never before that
seen in Egypt. He expected by the show of
these novelties to win the love of the people.
But what happened thereupon? At the production of the camel they were all affrighted,
and offended at the sight of the party-coloured man,—some scoffed at him as a detestable monster brought forth by the error of nature,—in a word, of the hope which he had to
please these Egyptians, and by such means
to increase the affection which they naturally
bore him, he was altogether frustrated and
disappointed; understanding fully by their
deportments, that they took more pleasure
and delight in things that were proper, handsome, and perfect, than in misshapen, monstrous, and ridiculous creatures. Since which
time he had both the slave and the camel
in such dislike, that very shortly thereafter,
either through negligence, or for want of
ordinary sustenance, they both tipt over
the perch.

This example putteth me in a suspense between hope and fear, misdoubting that, for

the contentment which I aim at, I will but
reap what shall be most distasteful to me: my
cake will be dough, and for my Venus I shall
have but some deformed puppy; instead of
serving them, I shall but vex them, and offend
them whom I propose to exhilarate; resembling, in this dubious adventure, Euclion's
cock, so renowned by Plautus in his *Pot,* and
by Ausonius in his *Griphon,* and by divers
others; which cock, for having by his scraping
discovered a treasure, had his hide well curried. Put the case I get no anger by it, though
formerly such things fell out, and the like may
occur again. Yet by Hercules, it will not. So
I perceive in them all, one and the same specifical form, and the like individual proprie-
ties, which our ancestors called Pantagruelism; by virtue whereof they will bear with
any thing that floweth from a good, free, and
loyal heart. I have seen them ordinarily take
good will in part of payment, and remain satisfied therewith, when one was not able to do
better. Having dispatched this point, I return
to my barrel.

Up, my lads, to this wine, spare it not!
Drink boys, and trowl it off at full bowls! If
you do not think it good, let it alone. I am
not like those officious and importunate sots,
who by force, outrage, and violence, constrain an easy good-natured fellow to whiffle,
quaff, carouse, and what is worse. All honest
tipplers, all honest gouty men, all such as are
a-dry, coming to this little barrel of mine,
need not drink thereof, if it please them not;
but if they have a mind to it, and that the
wine prove agreeable to the tastes of their
worshipful worships, let them drink, frankly,
freely, and boldly, without paying any thing,
and welcome. This is my decree, my statute,
and ordinance. And let none fear there shall
be any want of wine, as at the marriage of
Cana in Galilee; for how much soever you
shall draw forth at the faucet, so much shall
I tun in at the bung. Thus shall the barrel remain inexhaustible; it hath a lively spring
and perpetual current. Such was the beverage contained within the cup of Tantalus,—
which was figuratively represented amongst
the Brachman sages. Such was in Iberia the
mountain of salt, so highly written of by Cato. Such was the branch of gold consecrated
to the subterranean goddess, which Virgil
treats of so sublimely. It is a true cornucopia
of merriment and raillery. If at any time it
seem to you to be emptied to the very lees,
yet shall it not for all that be drawn wholly

dry. Good hope remains there at the bottom, as in Pandora's box; and not despair, as in the leaky tubs of the Danaids. Remark well what I have said, and what manner of people they be whom I do invite; for, to the end that none be deceived, I , in imitation of Lucilius, who did protest that he wrote only to his own Tarentines and Consentines, have not pierced this vessel for any else, but you, honest men, who are drinkers of the first edition, and gouty blades of the highest degree. The great dorophages, bribemongers, have on their hands occupation enough, and enough on the hooks for their venison. There may they follow their prey; here is no garbage for them. You pettifoggers, garblers, and masters of chicanery, speak not to me, I beseech you, in the name of, and for the reverence you bear to, the four hips that engendered you, and to the quickening peg, which at that time conjoined them. As for hypocrites, much less; although they were all of them unsound in body, pockified, scurvy, furnished with unquenchable thirst, and insatiable eating. And

wherefore? Because, indeed, they are not of good but of evil, and of that evil from which we daily pray to God to deliver us. And albeit we see them sometimes counterfeit devotion, yet never did old ape make pretty moppet. Hence, mastiffs, dogs in a doublet, get you behind, aloof, villains, out of my sunshine; curs, to the devil! Do you jog hither, wagging your tails, to pant at my wine, and bepiss my barrel? Look, here is the cudgel which Diogenes, in his last will ordained to be set by him after his death, for beating away, crushing the reins, and breaking the backs of these bustuary hobgoblins, and Cerberian hell-hounds. Pack you hence, therefore, you hypocrites, to your sheep, dogs; get you gone, you dissemblers, to the devil! Hay! What! are you there yet? I renounce my part of Papimanie, if I snap you, Grr, Grrr, Grrrrr. Avant, Avant! Will you not be gone? May you never shit till you be soundly lashed with stirrup leather, never piss but by the strappado, nor be otherwise warmed than by the bastinado.

CHAPTER 1

How Pantagruel transported a Colony of Utopians into Dipsody

PANTAGRUEL having wholly subdued the land of Dipsody, transported thereunto a colony of Utopians to the number of 9,876,543,210, men besides the women and little children, artificers of all trades, and professors of all sciences, to people, cultivate, and improve that country, which otherwise was ill inhabited, and in the greatest part thereof but a mere desert and wilderness; and he did transport them not so much for the excessive multitude of men and women, which were in Utopia multiplied, for number, like grasshoppers upon the face of the land. You understand well enough, nor is it needful, further, to explain it to you, that the Utopian men had so rank and fruitful genitories, and that the Utopian women carried matrixes so ample, so gluttonous, so tenaciously retentive, and so architectonically cellulated, that at the end of every ninth month seven children at the least, what male what female, were brought forth by every married woman, in imitation of the people of Israel in Egypt, if Anthony

de Lyra be to be trusted. Nor yet was this transplantation made so much for the fertility of the soil, the wholesomeness of the air, or commodity of the country of Dipsody, as to retain that rebellious people within the bounds of their duty and obedience, by this new transport of his ancient and most faithful subjects, who, from all time out of mind, never knew, acknowledged, owned, or served any other sovereign lord but him; and who likewise, from the very instant of their birth, as soon as they were entered into this world, had, with the milk of their mothers and nurses, sucked in the sweetness, humanity, and mildness of his government, to which they were all of them so nourished and habituated, that there was nothing surer, than that they would sooner abandon their lives than swerve from this singular and primitive obedience naturally due to their prince, whithersoever they should be dispersed or removed.

And not only should they, and their children successively descending from their blood, be such, but also would keep and maintain in this same fealty, and obsequious observance, all the nations lately annexed to his empire; which so truly came to pass, that therein he was not disappointed of his intent. For if the Utopians were, before their transplantation thither, dutiful and faithful subjects, the Dipsodes, after some few days conversing with them, were every whit as, if not more, loyal than they; and that by virtue of I know not what natural fervency incident to all human creatures at the beginning of any labour wherein they take delight: solemnly attesting the heavens, and supreme intelligences, of their being only sorry, that no sooner unto their knowledge had arrived the great renown of the good Pantagruel.

Remark therefore here, honest drinkers, that the manner of preserving and retaining countries newly conquered in obedience, is not, as hath been the erroneous opinion of some tyrannical spirits to their own detriment and dishonour, to pillage, plunder, force, spoil, trouble, oppress, vex, disquiet, ruin, and destroy the people, ruling, governing, and keeping them in awe with rods of iron; and, in a word, eating and devouring them, after the fashion that Homer calls an unjust and wicked king, Δημό βορον, that is to say, a devourer of his people.

I will not bring you to this purpose the testimony of ancient writers. It shall suffice to put you in mind of what your fathers have seen thereof, and yourselves too, if you be not very babes. New-born, they must be given suck to, rocked in a cradle, and dandled. Trees newly planted must be supported, under-propped, strengthened, and defended against all tempests, mischiefs, injuries, and calamities. And one lately saved from a long and dangerous sickness, and new upon his recovery, must be forborn, spared, and cherished, in such sort that they may harbour in their own breasts this opinion, that there is not in the world a king or prince, who does not desire fewer enemies, and more friends. Thus Osiris, the great king of the Egyptians, conquered almost the whole earth, not so much by force of arms, as by easing the people of their troubles, teaching them how to live well, and honestly giving them good laws, and using them with all possible affability, courtesy, gentleness, and liberality. Therefore was he by all men deservedly entitled, The Great King Euergetes, that is to say, Benefactor, which style he obtained by virtue of the command of Jupiter to one Pamyla.

And in effect, Hesiod, in his *Hierarchy*, placed the good demons, (call them angels if you will, or Genii,) as intercessors, and mediators betwixt the gods and men, they being of a degree inferior to the gods, but superior to men. And for that through their hands the riches and benefits we get from heaven are dealt to us, and that they are continually doing us good, and still protecting us from evil, he saith, that they exercise the offices of kings; because to do always good, and never ill, is an act most singularly royal.

Just such another was the emperor of the universe, Alexander the Macedonian. After this manner was Hercules sovereign possessor of the whole continent, relieving men from monstrous oppressions, exactions, and tyrannies; governing them with discretion, maintaining them in equity and justice, instructing them with seasonable policies and wholesome laws, convenient for and suitable to the soil, climate, and disposition of the country, supplying what was wanting, abating what was superfluous, and pardoning all that was past, with a sempiternal forgetfulness of all preceding offences; as was the amnesty of the Athenians, when by the prowess, valour, and industry of Thrasybulus the tyrants were exterminated; afterwards at Rome by Cicero set forth, and renewed under the emperor Aurelian. These are the philtres, allurements, ïynges, inveiglements, baits, and enticements of love, by the means whereof that may be peaceably retained, which was painfully acquired. Nor can a conqueror reign more happily, whether he be a monarch, emperor, king, prince, or philosopher, than by making his justice to second his valour. His valour shows itself in victory and conquest; his justice will appear in the good will and affection of the people, when he maketh laws, publisheth ordinances, establisheth religion, and doth what is right to every one, as the noble poet Virgil writes of Octavian Augustus.

> —— *Victorque volentes*
> *Per populos dat jura.*[3]

Therefore is it that Homer in his *Iliads* calleth a good prince and great king Κοσμή-τορα λαῶν, that is, The ornament of the people.

Such was the consideration of Numa Pompilius, the second king of the Romans, a just politician and wise philosopher, when he ordained that to the god Terminus, on the day of his festival called Terminales, nothing should be sacrificed that had died; teaching us thereby, that the bounds, limits, and frontiers of kingdoms should be guarded, and preserved in peace, amity, and meekness, without polluting our hands with blood and robbery. Who doth otherwise, shall not only lose what he hath gained, but also be loaded with this scandal and reproach, that he is an unjust and wicked purchaser, and his acquests perish with him; *Juxta illud, male parta, male dilabuntur.*[4] And although during his whole lifetime he should have peaceable possession thereof, yet, if what hath been so acquired moulder away in the hands of his heirs, the same opprobry, scandal, and imputation will be charged upon the defunct, and his memory remain accursed for his unjust and unwarrantable conquest; *Juxta illud, de male quæsitis vix guadet tertius hæres.*[5]

Remark, likewise, gentlemen, you gouty feoffees, in this main point worthy of your observation, how by these means Pantagruel of one angel made two, which was a contingency opposite to the council of Charlemaine, who made two devils of one, when he transplanted the Saxons into Flanders, and the Flemings into Saxony. For, not being able to keep in such subjection the Saxons, whose dominion he had joined to the empire, but that ever and anon they would break forth into open rebellion, if he should casually be drawn into Spain, or other remote kingdoms, he caused them to be brought unto his own country of Flanders, the inhabitants whereof did naturally obey him, and transported the Hainaults and Flemings, his ancient loving subjects, into Saxony, not mistrusting their loyalty, now that they were transplanted into a strange land. But it happened that the Saxons persisted in their rebellion and primitive obstinacy; and the Flemings dwelling in Saxony did imbibe the stubborn manners and conditions of the Saxons.

CHAPTER 2

How Panurge was made Laird of Salmygondin in Dipsodie, and did waste his Revenue before it came in

WHILST Pantagruel was giving order for the government of all Dipsodie, he assigned to Panurge the Lairdship of Salmygondin, which was yearly worth 6,789,106,789 rials of certain rent, besides the uncertain revenue of the locusts and periwinkles, amounting, one year with another, to the value of 2,435,-768, or 2,435,769 French crowns of Berry.

Sometimes it did amount to 1,234,554,321 seraphs when it was a good year, and that locusts and periwinkles were in request; but that was not every year.

Now his worship, the new laird, husbanded this his estate so providently well and prudently, that in less than fourteen days he wasted and dilapidated all the certain and uncertain revenue of his lairdship for three whole years. Yet did not he properly dilapidate it, as you might say, in founding of monasteries, building of churches, erecting of colleges, and setting up of hospitals, or casting his bacon flitches to the dogs; but spent it in a thousand little banquets and jolly collations, keeping open house for all comers and goers; yea, to all good fellows, young girls, and pretty wenches; felling timber, burning the great logs for the sale of the ashes, borrowing money beforehand, buying dear, selling cheap, and eating his corn, as it were, whilst it was but grass.

Pantagruel, being advertised of this his lavishness, was in good sooth no way offended at the matter, angry nor sorry; for I once told you, and again tell it you, that he was the best, little, great goodman that ever girded a sword to his side. He took all things in good part, and interpreted every action to the best sense. He never vexed nor disquieted himself with the least pretence of dislike to any thing, because he knew that he must have most grossly abandoned the divine mansion of reason, if he had permitted his mind to be never so little grieved, afflicted, or altered at any occasion whatsoever. For all the goods that the heaven covereth, and that the earth containeth, in all their dimensions of height, depth, breath, and length, are not of so much worth, as that we should for them disturb or disorder our affections, trouble or perplex our senses or spirits.

He only drew Panurge aside, and then, making to him a sweet remonstrance and mild admonition, very gently represented before him in strong arguments, That, if he should continue in such an unthrifty course of living, and not become a better *mesnagier,* it would prove altogether impossible for him, or at least hugely difficult at any time to make him rich. Rich! answered Panurge, Have you fixed your thoughts there? Have you undertaken the task to enrich me in this world? Set your mind to live merrily in the name of God and good folks, let no other cark nor care be harboured within the sacro-sanctified domicile of your celestial brain. May the calmness and tranquillity thereof be never incommoded with, or overshadowed by any frowning clouds of sullen imaginations and displeasing annoyance. For if you live joyful, merry, jocund, and glad, I cannot be but rich enough. Everybody cries up thrift, thrift, and good husbandry. But many speak of Robin Hood that never shot in his bow, and talk of that virtue of mesnagery, who know not what belongs to it. It is by me that they must be advised. From me, therefore, take this advertisement and information, that what is imputed to me for a vice hath been done in imitation of the university and parliament of Paris, places in which is to be found the true spring and source of the lively idea of Pantheology, and all manner of justice. Let him be counted an heretic that doubteth thereof, and doth not firmly believe it. Yet they in one day eat up their bishop, or the revenue of the bishopric—is it not all one?—for a whole year; yea, sometimes for two. This is done on the day he makes his entry, and is installed. Nor is there any place for an excuse; for he cannot avoid it, unless he would be hooted at and stoned for his parsimony.

It hath been also esteemed an act flowing from the habit of the four cardinal virtues. Of prudence in borrowing money before hand; for none knows what may fall out. Who is able to tell if the world shall last yet three years? But although it should continue longer, is there any man so foolish, as to have the confidence to promise himself three years?

What fool so confident to say,
That he shall live one other day?

Of commutative justice, in buying dear, I say upon trust, and selling goods cheap, that is, for ready money. What says Cato in his Book of *Husbandry* to this purpose? The father of a family, says he, must be a perpetual seller; by which means it is impossible but ther of a family, says he, must be a perpetual vendible ware enough still ready for sale.

Of distributive justice it doth partake, in giving entertainment to good,—remark,— good,—and gentle fellows, whom fortune had shipwrecked, like Ulysses, upon the rock of a hungry stomach with provision of sustenance: and likewise to good and young—remark, good and young—wenches. For, according to the sentence of Hippocrates, Youth is impatient of hunger, chiefly if it be vigorous, lively, frolic, brisk, stirring, and bouncing. Which wanton lasses willingly and heartily devote themselves to the pleasure of honest men; and are in so far both Platonic and Ciceronian, that they do acknowledge their being born into this world not to be for themselves alone, but that in their proper persons their country may claim one share and their friends another.

The virtue of fortitude appears therein, by the cutting down and overthrowing of the great trees, like a second Milo making havoc of the dark forest, which did serve only to furnish dens, caves, and shelter to wolves, wild boars and foxes, and afford receptacles, withdrawing corners, and refuges to robbers, thieves, and murderers, lurking holes and skulking places for cut-throat assassinators, secret obscure shops for coiners of false money, and safe retreats for heretics; laying woods even and level with the plain champagne fields and pleasant heathy ground, at the sound of the hautboys and bag-pipes playing reeks with the high and stately timber, and preparing seats and benches for the eve of the dreadful day of judgment.

I gave thereby proof of my temperance in eating my corn whilst it was but grass, like an hermit feeding upon sallets and roots, that, so affranchising myself from the yoke of sensual appetites to the utter disclaiming of their sovereignty, I might the better reserve somewhat in store, for the relief of the lame, blind, cripple, maimed, needy, poor, and wanting wretches.

In taking this course I save the expense of the weed-grubbers, who gain money,—of the reapers in harvest-time, who drink lustily, and without water,—of gleaners, who will expect their cakes and bannocks,—of threshers, who leave no garlic, scallions, leeks, nor onions in our gardens, by the authority of Thestilis in Virgil,—and of the millers, who are generally thieves—and of the bakers, who are little better. Is this small saving or frugality? Besides the mischief and damage of the field-mice, the decay of barns, and the destruction usually made by weasels and other vermin.

Of corn in the blade you may make good green sauce, of a light concoction and easy digestion, which recreates the brain, and exhilarates the animal spirits, rejoiceth the sight, openeth the appetite, delighteth the taste, comforteth the heart, tickleth the tongue, cheereth the countenance, striking a fresh and lively colour, strengthening the muscles, tempers the blood, disburdens the midriff, refresheth the liver, disobstructs the spleen, easeth the kidneys, suppleth the reins, quickens the joints of the back, cleanseth the urine-conduits, dilates the spermatic vessels, shortens the cremasters, purgeth the bladder, puffeth up the genitories, correcteth the prepuce, hardens the nut and rectifies the member. It will make you have a current belly to trot, fart, dung, piss, sneeze, cough, spit, belch, spew, yawn, snuff, blow, breathe, snort, sweat, and set taut your Robin, with a thousand other rare advantages. I understand you very well, says Pantagruel; you would thereby infer, that those of a mean spirit and shallow capacity have not the skill to spend much in a short time. You are not the first in whose conceit that heresy hath entered. Nero maintained it, and above all mortals admired most his uncle Caius Caligula, for having, in a few days, by a most wonderfully pregnant invention, totally spent all the goods and patrimony which Tiberius had left him.

But, instead of observing the sumptuous supper-curbing laws of the Romans,—to wit, the Orchia, the Fannia, the Didia, the Licinia, the Cornelia, the Lepidiana, the Antia, and of the Corinthians,—by the which they were inhibited, under pain of great punishment, not to spend more in one year than their annual revenue did amount to, you have offered up the oblation of Protervia, which was with the Romans such a sacrifice as the paschal lamb was amongst the Jews, wherein all that was eatable was to be eaten, and the remainder to be thrown into the fire, without reserving any thing for the next day. I may very justly say of you, as Cato did of Albidius, who after that he had by a most extravagant expense wasted all the means and possessions he had to one only house, he fairly set it on fire, that he might the better say, *Consummatum est.*[6] Even just as since his time St. Thomas Aquinas did, when he had eaten up the whole lamprey, although there was no necessity in it.

CHAPTER 3

How Panurge praiseth the Debtors and Borrowers

BUT, quoth Pantagruel, when will you be out of debt? At the next ensuing term of the Greek kalends, answered Panurge, when all the world shall be content, and that it be your fate to become your own heir. The Lord forbid that I should be out of debt, as if, indeed, I could not be trusted. Who leaves not some leaven over night, will hardly have paste the next morning.

Be still indebted to somebody or other, that there may be somebody always to pray for you; that the giver of all good things may grant unto you a blessed, long, and prosperous life; fearing, if fortune should deal crossly with you, that it might be his chance to come short of being paid by you, he will always speak good of you in every company, ever and anon purchase new creditors unto you; to the end, that through their means you may make a shift by borrowing from Peter to pay Paul, and with other folk's earth fill up his ditch. When of old in the regions of the Gauls, by the institution of the Druids, the servants, slaves, and bondsmen were burned quick at the funerals and obsequies of their lords and masters, had not they fear enough, think you, that their lords and masters should die? For, perforce, they were to die with them for company. Did not they incessantly send up their supplications to their great god Mercury, as likewise unto Dis the Father of Wealth, to lengthen out their days, and preserve them long in health? Were not they very careful to entertain them well, punctually to look unto them, and to attend them faithfully and circumspectly? For, by those means, were they to live together at least unto the hour of death. Believe me, your creditors, with a more fervent devotion, will beseech Almighty God to prolong your life, they being of nothing more afraid than that you should die; for that they are more concerned for the sleeve than the arm, and love silver better than their own lives. As it evidently appeareth by the usurers of Landerousse, who not long since hanged themselves, because the price of corn and wines was fallen, by the return of a gracious season. To this Pantagruel answering nothing, Panurge went on his discourse, saying, truly, and in good sooth, Sir, when I ponder my destiny aright, and think well upon it, you put me shrewdly to my plunges, and have me at a bay in twitting me with the reproach of my debts and creditors. And, yet did I, in this only respect and consideration of being a debtor, esteem myself worshipful, reverend, and formidable. For against the opinion of most philosophers, that, of nothing ariseth nothing, yet, without having bottomed on so much as that which is called the First Matter, did I out of nothing become such a maker and creator that I have created,—what?—a gay number of fair and jolly creditors. Nay, creditors, I will maintain it, even to the very fire itself exclusively, are fair and goodly creatures. Who lendeth nothing is an ugly and wicked creature, and an accursed imp of the infernal Old Nick. And there is made—what? Debts. A thing most precious and dainty, of great use and antiquity. Debts, I say, surmounting the number of syllables which may result from the combinations of all the consonants, with each of the vowels heretofore projected, reckoned and calculated by the noble Xenocrates. To judge of the perfection of debtors by the numerosity of their creditors is the readiest way for entering into the mysteries of practical arithmetic.

You can hardly imagine how glad I am, when every morning I perceive myself environed and surrounded with brigades of creditors, humble, fawning, and full of their reverences. And whilst I remark, that as I look more favourably upon, and give a cheerfuller countenance to one than to another, the fellow thereupon buildeth a conceit that he shall be the first dispatched, and the foremost in the date of payment; and he valueth my smiles at the rate of ready money. It seemeth unto me, that I then act and personate the god of the Passion of Saumure, accompanied with his angels and cherubims.

These are my flatterers, my soothers, my claw-backs, my smoothers, my parasites, my saluters, my givers of good morrows and perpetual orators; which makes me verily think, that the supremest height of heroic virtue, described by Hesiod, consisteth in being a debtor, wherein I held the first degree in my commencement. Which dignity, though all human creatures seem to aim at, and aspire thereto, few, nevertheless, because of the difficulties in the way, and incumbrances of hard passages, are able to reach it; as is easily perceivable by the ardent desire and vehement longing harboured in the breast of every one, to be still creating more debts, and new creditors.

Yet doth it not lie in the power of every one to be a debtor. To acquire creditors is not at the disposure of each man's arbitrament. You nevertheless would deprive me of this sublime felicity. You ask me, when I will be out of debt. Well, to go yet further on, and possibly worse in your conceit, may Saint Bablin, the good saint, snatch me, if I have not all my life-time held debt to be as an union or conjunction of the heavens with the earth, and the whole cement whereby the race of mankind is kept together; yea, of such virtue and efficacy, that, I say, the whole progeny of Adam would very suddenly perish without it. Therefore, perhaps, I do not think amiss, when I repute it to be the great soul of the universe, which, according to the opinion of the Academics, vivifyeth all manner of things. In confirmation whereof, that you may the better believe it to be so, represent unto yourself, without any prejudice of spirit, in a clear and serene fancy, the idea and form of some other world than this; take, if you please, and lay hold on the thirtieth of those which the philosopher Metrodorus did enumerate, wherein it is to be supposed there is no debtor or creditor, that is to say, a world without debts.

There amongst the planets will be no regular course, all will be in disorder. Jupiter, reckoning himself to be nothing indebted unto Saturn, will go near to detrude him out of his sphere, and with the Homeric chain will be like to hang up the Intelligencies, Gods, Heavens, Demons, Heroes, Devils, Earth, and Sea, together with the other elements. Saturn no doubt combining with Mars will reduce that so disturbed world into a chaos of confusion.

Mercury then would be no more subjected to the other planets; he would scorn to be any longer their Camillus, as he was of old termed in the Hetrurian tongue. For it is to be imagined that he is no way a debtor to them.

Venus will be no more venerable, because she shall have lent nothing. The moon will remain bloody and obscure. For to what end should the sun impart unto her any of his light? He owed her nothing. Nor yet will the sun shine upon the earth, nor the stars send down any good influence, because the terrestrial globe hath desisted from sending up their wanted nourishment by vapours and exhalation, wherewith Heraclitus said, the Stoics proved, Cicero maintained, they were cherished and alimented. There would likewise be in such a world no manner of symbolization, alteration, nor transmutation amongst the elements; for the one will not esteem itself obliged to the other, as having borrowed nothing at all from it. Earth then will not become water, water will not be changed into air, of air will be made no fire, and fire will afford no heat unto the earth; the earth will produce nothing but monsters, Titans, giants; no rain will descend upon it, nor light shine thereon; no wind will blow there, nor will there be in it any summer or harvest. Lucifer will break loose, and issuing forth of the depth of hell, accompanied with his furies, fiends, and horned devils, will go about to un-nestle and drive out of heaven all the gods, as well of the greater as of the lesser nations. Such a world without lending will be no bet-ter than a dog-kennel, a place of contention and wrangling, more unruly and irregular than that of the rector of Paris; a devil of an hurly-burly, and more disordered confusion, than that of the plagues of Doüay. Men will not then salute one another; it will be but lost labour to expect aid or succour from any, or to cry fire, water, murder, for none will put to their helping hand. Why? He lent no mon-ey, there is nothing due to him. Nobody is concerned in his burning, in his shipwreck, in his ruin, or in his death; and that because he hitherto had lent nothing, and would never thereafter have lent any thing. In short, Faith, Hope, and Charity would be quite banished from such a world,—for men are born to relieve and assist one another; and in their stead should succeed and be introduced Defiance, Disdain, and Rancour, with the most execrable troop of all evils, all impreca-tions, and all miseries. Whereupon you will think, and that not amiss, that Pandora had there spilt her unlucky bottle. Men unto men will be wolves, hobthrushers, and goblins, (as were Lycaon, Bellerophon, Nebuchodnosor,) plunderers, highway robbers, cut-throats, rapparees, murderers, poisoners, assassinators, lewd, wicked, malevolent, pernicious haters, set against every body, like to Ismael, Meta-bus, or Timon the Athenian, who for that cause was named Misanthropos; in such sort, that it would prove much more easy in nature to have fish entertained in the air, and bul-locks fed in the bottom of the ocean, than to support or tolerate a rascally rabble of people that will not lend. These fellows, I vow, do I hate with a perfect hatred; and if, conform to the pattern of this grievous, peevish, and per-verse world which lendeth nothing, you fig-ure and liken the little world, which is man, you will find in him a terrible justling coyle and clutter. The head will not lend the sight of his eyes to guide the feet and hands; the legs will refuse to bear up the body; the hands will leave off working any more for the

rest of the members; the heart will be weary of its continual motion for the beating of the pulse, and will no longer lend his assistance; the lungs will withdraw the use of their bel-lows; the liver will desist from convoying any more blood through the veins for the good of the whole; the bladder will not be indebted to the kidneys, so that the urine thereby will be totally stopped. The brains, in the interim, considering this unnatural course, will fall into a raving dotage, and withhold all feeling from the sinews, and motion from the mus-cles. Briefly, in such a world without order and array, owing nothing, lending nothing, and borrowing nothing, you would see a more dangerous conspiration than that which Æ-sop exposed in his *Apologue*. Such a world will perish undoubtedly; and not only perish, but perish very quickly. Were it Æsculapius himself, his body would immediately rot, and the chafing soul, full of indignation, take its flight to all the devils in hell after my money.

CHAPTER 4

Panurge continues his Discourse in the praise of Borrowers and Lenders

On the contrary, be pleased to represent unto your fancy another world, wherein every one lendeth, and every one oweth, all are debtors, and all creditors. O how great will that har-mony be, which shall thereby result from the regular motions of the heavens! Methinks I hear it every whit as well as ever Plato did. What sympathy will there be amongst the elements! O how delectable then unto na-ture will be her own works and productions! Whilst Ceres appeareth loaden with corn, Bacchus with wines, Flora with flowers, Po-mona with fruits, and Juno fair in a clear air, wholesome and pleasant. I lose myself in this high contemplation.

Then will among the race of mankind peace, love, benevolence, fidelity, tranquilli-ty, rest, banquets, feastings, joy, gladness, gold, silver, small money, chains, rings, with other ware, and chaffer of that nature, be found to trot from hand to hand. No suits at law, no wars, no strife, debate, nor wran-gling; none will be there an usurer, none will be there a pinch-penny, a scrape-good wretch, or churlish hard-heated refuser. Good God! Will not this be the golden age in the reign of Saturn? the true idea of the Olym-pic regions, wherein all other virtues ceasing, charity alone ruleth, governeth, domineereth, and triumpheth! All will be fair and goodly people there, all just and virtuous.

O happy world! O people of that world most happy! Yea, thrice and four times blessed is that people! I think in very deed that I am amongst them, and swear to you, by my good forsooth, that if this glorious aforesaid world had a Pope, abounding with Cardinals, that so he might have the association of a sacred college, in the space of very few years you should be sure to see the sancts much thicker in the roll, more numerous, wonder-working and mirific, more services, more vows, more staves, and wax-candles than are all those in the nine bishoprics of Britany, St. Yves only excepted. Consider, sir, I pray you, how the noble Patelin, having a mind to deify, and extol even to the third heavens the father of William Josseaume, said no more but this, And he did lend his goods to those who were desirous of them.

O the fine saying! Now let our microcosm be fancied conform to this model in all its members; lending, borrowing, and owing, that is to say, according to its own nature. For nature hath not to any other end created man, but to owe, borrow, and lend; no greater is the harmony amongst the heavenly spheres, than that which shall be found in its well ordered policy. The intention of the founder of this microcosm is, to have a soul therein to be entertained, which is lodged there, as a guest with its host, that it may live there for awhile. Life consisteth in blood; blood is the seat of the soul; therefore the chiefest work of the microcosm is, to be making blood continually.

At this forge are exercised all the members of the body; none is exempted from labour, each operates apart, and doth its proper office. And such is their hierarchy, that perpetually the one borrows from the other, the one lends the other, and the one is the other's debtor. The stuff and matter convenient, which nature giveth to be turned into blood, is bread and wine. All kind of nourishing victuals is understood to be comprehended in those two, and from hence in the Gothish tongue is called *companage*. To find out this meat and drink, to prepare and boil it, the hands are put to work, the feet do walk and bear up the whole bulk of the corporal mass; the eyes guide and conduct all; the appetite in the orifice of the stomach, by means of a little sourish black humour, called melancholy, which is transmitted thereto from the milt, giveth warning to shut in the food. The tongue doth make the first essay, and tastes it; the teeth to chaw it, and the stomach doth receive, digest, and chilify it. The mesaraic veins suck out of it what is good and fit, leaving behind the excrements, which are, through special conduits, for that purpose, voided by an expulsive faculty. Thereafter it is carried to the liver, where it being changed again, it by the virtue of that new transmutation becomes blood. What joy, conjecture you, will then be found amongst those officers, when they see this rivulet of gold, which is their sole restorative? No greater is the joy of alchymists, when, after long travail, toil, and expense, they see in their furnaces the transmutation. Then is it that every member doth prepare itself, and strive anew to purify and to refine this treasure. The kidneys, through the emulgent veins, draw that aquosity from thence, which you call urine, and there send it away through the ureters to be slipped downwards; where, in a lower receptacle and proper for it, to wit, the bladder, it is kept, and stayeth there until an opportunity to void it out in his due time. The spleen draweth from the blood its terrestrial part, *viz.* the grounds, lees, or thick substance settled in the bottom thereof, which you term melancholy. The bottle of the gall subtracts from thence all the superfluous choler; whence it is brought to another shop or work-house to be yet better purified and fined, that is, the heart, which by its agitation of diastolic and systolic motions so neatly subtiliseth and inflames it, that in the right side ventricle it is brought to perfection, and through the veins is sent to all the members. Each parcel of the body draws it then unto itself, and after its own fashion is cherished and alimented by it. Feet, hands, thighs, arms, eyes, ears, back, breasts, yea, all; and then it is, that who before were lenders, now become debtors. The heart doth in its left side ventricle so thinnify the blood, that it thereby obtains the name of spiritual; which being sent through the arteries to all the members of the body, serveth to warm and winnow the other blood which runneth through the veins. The lights never cease with its lappets and bellows to cool and refresh it; in acknowledgment of which good the heart, through the arterial vein, imparts unto it the choicest of its blood. At last it is made so fine and subtle within the *rete mirabile*, that thereafter those animal spirits are framed and composed of it; by means whereof the imagination, discourse, judgment, resolution, deliberation, ratiocination, and memory have their rise, actings, and operation.

Cops body, I sink, I drown, I perish, I wander astray, and quite fly out of my self, when I enter into the consideration of the profound abyss of this world, thus lending, thus owing. Believe me, it is a divine thing to lend; to owe, an heroic virtue. Yet is not this all. This little world thus lending, owing, and borrowing, is so good and charitable, that no sooner is the above-specified alimentation finished, but that it forthwith projecteth, and hath already forecast, how it shall lend to those who are not as yet born, and by that loan endeavour, what it may, to eternize itself, and multiply in images like the pattern, that is children. To this end every member doth of the choicest and most precious of its nourishment, pare and cut off a portion, then instantly dispatcheth it downwards to that place, where nature hath prepared for it very fit vessels and receptacles, through which descending to the genitories by long ambages, circuits, and flexuosities, it receiveth a competent form, and rooms apt enough both in the man and woman for the future conservation and perpetuating of human kind. All this is done by loans and debts of the one unto the other; and hence have we this word, the debt of marriage. Nature doth reckon pain to the refuser, with a most grievous vexation to his members, and an outrageous fury amidst his senses. But on the other part, to the lender a set reward accompanied with pleasure, joy, solace, mirth, and merry glee.

CHAPTER 5

How Pantagruel altogether abhorreth the Debtors and Borrowers

I UNDERSTAND you very well, quoth Pantagruel, and take you to be very good at topics, and thoroughly affectioned to your own cause. But preach it up, and patrocinate it, prattle on it, and defend it as much as you will, even from hence to the next Whitsuntide, if you please so to do, yet in the end will you be astonished to find how you shall have gained no ground at all upon me, nor persuaded me by your fair speeches and smooth talk to enter never so little into the thraldom of debt. You shall owe to none, said the Holy Apostle, anything save love, friendship, and a mutual benevolence.

You serve me here, I confess, with fine *Graphides* and *Diatyposes*, descriptions and figures, which truly please me very well. But

let me tell you, if you will represent unto your fancy an impudent blustering bully, and an importunate borrower, entering afresh and newly into a town already advertised of his manners, you shall find that at his ingress the citizens will be more hideously affrighted and amazed, and in a greater terror and fear, dread and trembling, than if the pest itself should step into it, in the very same garb and accoutrement wherein the Tyanean philosopher found it within the city of Ephesus. And I am fully confirmed in the opinion, that the Persians erred not, when they said, that the second vice was to lie, the first being that of owing money. For, in very truth, debts and lying are ordinarily joined together. I will nevertheless not from hence infer, that none must owe any thing, or lend any thing. For who so rich can be, that sometimes may not owe? or who can be so poor, that sometimes may not lend?

Let the occasion, notwithstanding, in that case, as Plato very wisely sayeth, and ordaineth in his *Laws*, be such, that none be permitted to draw any water out of his neighbour's well, until first they by continual digging and delving into their own proper ground shall have hit upon a kind of potter's earth, which is called Ceramite, and there had found no source or drop of water; for that sort of earth, by reason of its substance, which is fat, strong, firm and close, so retaineth its humidity, that it doth not easily evaporate it by any outward excursion or evaporation.

In good sooth, it is a great shame to choose rather to be still borrowing in all places from every one, than to work and win. Then only in my judgment should one lend, when the diligent, toiling, and industrious person is no longer able by his labour to make any purchase unto himself; or otherwise, when by mischance he hath suddenly fallen into an unexpected loss of his goods.

Howsoever let us leave this discourse, and from henceforward do not hang upon creditors, nor tie yourself to them. I make account for the time past to rid you freely of them, and from their bondage to deliver you. The least I should in this point, quoth Panurge, is to thank you, though it be the most I can do. And if gratitude and thanksgiving be to be estimated and prized by the affection of the benefactor, that is to be done infinitely and sempiternally; for the love which you bear me of your own accord and free grace, without any merit of mine, goeth far beyond the reach of any price or value. It transcends all weight, all number, all measure; it is endless and everlasting therefore, should I offer to commensurate and adjust it, either to the size and proportion of your own noble and gracious deeds or yet to the contentment and delight of the obliged receivers, I would come off but very faintly and flaggingly. You have verily done me a great deal of good, and multiplied your favours on me more frequently than was fitting to one of my condition. You have been more bountiful towards me than I have deserved, and your courtesies have by far surpassed the extent of my merits; I must needs confess it. But it is not, as you suppose, in the proposed matter. For there it is not where I itch, it is not there where it fretteth, hurts or vexeth me; for, henceforth being quit and out of debt, what countenance will I be able to keep? You may imagine that it will become me very ill for the first month, because I have never hitherto been brought up or accustomed to it. I am very much afraid of it. Furthermore, there shall not one hereafter, native of the country of Salmigondy, but he shall level the shot towards my nose. All the back-cracking fellows of the world, in discharging of their postern petarades, used commonly to say, *Voilà pour les quittes;* that is, For the quit. My life will be of very short continuance, I do foresee it. I recommend to you the making of my epitaph; for I perceive I will die confected in the very stench of farts. If at any time to come, by way of restorative to such good women as shall happen to be troubled with the grievous pain of the windcholic, the ordinary medicaments prove nothing effectual, the mummy of all my befarted body will straight be as a present remedy appointed by the physicians; whereof they, taking any small modicum, it will incontinently for their case afford them a rattle of bumshot, like a sal of muskets.

Therefore would I beseech you to leave me some few centuries of debts; as King Louis the Eleventh, exempting from suits in law the Reverend Miles d'Illiers, Bishop of Chartres, was by the said bishop most earnestly solicited to leave him some few for the exercise of his mind. I had rather give them all my revenue of the periwinkles, together with the other incomes of the locusts, albeit I should not thereby have any parcel abated from off the principal sums which I owe. Let us wave this matter, quoth Pantagruel, I have told it you over again.

CHAPTER 6

Why new married Men were privileged from going to the Wars

BUT, in the interim, asked Panurge, by what law was it constituted, ordained, and established, that such as should plant a new vineyard, those that should build a new house, and the new married men, should be exempted and discharged from the duty of warfare for the first year? By the law, answered Pantagruel, of Moses. Why, replied Panurge, the lately married? As for the vine-planters, I am now too old to reflect on them; my condition, at this present, induceth me to remain satisfied with the care of vintage, finishing, and turning the grapes into wine. Nor are these pretty new builders of dead stones written or pricked down in my Book of Life. It is all with live stones that I set up and erect the fabrics of my architecture, to wit, Men. It was, according to my opinion, quoth Pantagruel, to the end, first, that the fresh married folks should for the first year reap a full and complete fruition of their pleasures in their mutual exercise of the act of love, in such sort, that in waiting more at leisure on the production of posterity, and propagating of their progeny, they might the better increase their race, and make provision of new heirs. That, if in the years thereafter, the men should, upon their undergoing of some military adventure, happen to be killed, their names and coats of arms might continue with their children in the same families. And next, that the wives thereby coming to know whether they were barren or fruitful, (for one year's trial, in regard to the maturity of age, wherein, of old, they married, was held sufficient for the discovery,) they might pitch the more suitably, in case of their first husband's decease, upon a second match. The fertile women to be wedded to those who desire to multiply their issue; and the sterile ones to such other mates, as, misregarding the storing of their own lineage, choose them only for their virtues, learning, genteel behaviour, domestic consolation, management of the house, and matrimonial conveniences and comfort, and such like. The preachers of Varennes, saith Panurge, detest and abhor the second marriages, as altogether foolish and dishonest.

Foolish and dishonest? quoth Pantagruel. A plague take such preachers! Yea, but, quoth Panurge, the like mischief also befell the Friar Charmer, who in a full auditory making a sermon at Pareilly, and therein abominating the reiteration of marriage, and the entering again the bonds of a nuptial tie, did swear and heartily give himself to the swiftest devil in hell, if he had not rather choose, and would much more willingly undertake, the unmaidening or depucelating of a hundred virgins, than the simple drudgery of one widow. Truly I find your reason in that point right good, and strongly grounded.

But what would you think, if the cause why this exemption or immunity was granted, had no other foundation, but that, during the whole space of the said first year, they so lustily bobbed it with their female consorts, as both reason and equity require they should do, that they had drained and evacuated their spermatic vessels; and were become thereby altogether feeble, weak, emasculated, drooping and flaggingly pithless; yea, in such sort, that they, in the day of battle, like ducks which plunge over head and ears, would sooner hide themselves behind the baggage, than, in the company of valiant fighters and daring military combatants, appear where stern Bellona deals her blows, and moves a bustling noise of thwacks and thumps? Nor is it to be thought that, under the standards of Mars, they will so much as soon strike a fair stroke, because their most considerable knocks have been already jerked and whirrited within the curtains of his sweetheart Venus.

In confirmation whereof, amongst other relics and monuments of antiquity, we now as yet often see, that in all great houses, after the expiring of some few days, these young married blades are readily sent away to visit their uncles, that in the absence of their wives, reposing themselves a little, they may recover their decayed strength by the recruit of a fresh supply, the more vigorous to return again, and face about to renew the duelling shock and contact of an amorous dalliance: albeit for the greater part they have neither uncle nor aunt to go to.

Just so did the King Crackart, after the battle of the Cornets, not cashier us, (speaking properly,) I mean me and the quail-piper, but for our refreshment remanded us to our houses; and he is as yet seeking after his own. My grandfather's godmother was wont to say to me when I was a boy,

Patenostres et oraisons
Sont pout ceux-la qui les retiennent.

Ung fiffre allant en fenaisons
Est plus fort que deux qui en viennent.

Not orisons nor patenotres
  Shall ever disorder my brain.
One cadet, to the field as he flutters,
  Is worth two when they end the campaign.

That which prompteth me to that opinion is, that the vine-planters did seldom eat of the grapes, or drink of the wine of their labour, till the first year was wholly elapsed. During all which time also the builders did hardly inhabit their new-structured dwelling places, for fear of dying suffocated through want of respiration; as Galen hath most learnedly remarked, in the second book of the *Difficulty of Breathing*. Under favour, Sir, I have not asked this question without cause causing, and reason truly very ratiocinant. Be not offended, I pray you.

CHAPTER 7

How Panurge had a flea in his ear, and forbore to wear any longer his magnificent Codpiece

PANURGE, the day thereafter, caused pierce his right ear, after the Jewish fashion, and thereto clasped a little gold ring, of a ferny-like kind of workmanship, in the beazil or collet whereof was set and inchased a flea; and, to the end you may be rid of all doubts, you are to know that the flea was black. O what a brave thing it is, in every case and circumstance of a matter, to be thoroughly well informed! The sum of the expense hereof, being cast up, brought in, and laid down upon his council-board carpet, was found to amount to no more quarterly than the charge of the nuptials of a Hircanian tigress; even as you would say 609,000 maravedis. At these vast costs and excessive disbursements, as soon as he perceived himself to be out of debt, he fretted much; and afterwards, as tyrant and lawyers use to do, he nourished and fed her with the sweat and blood of his subjects and clients.

He then took four French ells of a coarse brown russet cloth, and therein apparelling himself, as with a long, plain-seemed, and single-stitched gown, left off the wearing of his breeches, and tied a pair of spectacles to his cap. In this equipage did he present himself before Pantagruel; to whom this disguise appeared the more strange, that he did not, as before, see that goodly, fair, and stately codpiece, which was the sole anchor of hope, wherein he was wonted to rely, and the last refuge he had amidst all the waves and boisterous billows, which a stormy cloud in a cross fortune would raise up against him. Honest Pantagruel, not understanding the mystery, asked him by way of interrogatory, what he did intend to personate in that new-fangled *Prosopopeia*?[27] I have, answered Panurge, a flea in mine ear, and have a mind to marry. In a good time, quoth Pantagruel, you have told me joyful tidings. Yet would not I hold a red-hot iron in my hand for all the gladness of them. But it is not the fashion of lovers to be accoutred in such dangling vestments, so as to have their shirts flagging down over their knees, without breeches, and with a long robe of a dark brown mingled hue, which is a colour never used in Talarian garments amongst any persons of honour, quality, or virtue. If some heretical persons and schismatical sectaries have at any time formerly been so arrayed and clothed, (though many have imputed such a kind of dress to cozenage, cheat, imposture, and an affectation of tyranny upon credulous minds of the rude multitude,) I will nevertheless not blame them for it, nor in that point judge rashly or sinistrously of them. Every one over-flowingly aboundeth in his own sense and fancy; yea, in things of a foreign consideration, altogether extrinsical and indifferent, which in and of themselves are neither commendable nor bad, because they proceed not from the interior of the thoughts and heart, which is the shop of all good and evil, of goodness, if it be upright, and that its affections be regulated by the pure and clean spirit of righteousness; and on the other side of wickedness, if its inclinations, straying beyond the bounds of equity, be corrupted and depraved by the malice and the suggestions of the devil. It is only the novelty and new fangledness thereof which I dislike, together with the contempt of common custom, and the fashion which is in use.

The colour, answered Panurge, is convenient, for it is conformable to that of my council-board carpet,—therefore will I henceforth hold me with it, and more narrowly and circumspectly than ever hitherto I have done, look to my affairs and business. Seeing I am once out of debt, you never yet saw man more unpleasing than I will be, if God help me not. Lo, here be my spectacles. To see me

afar off, you would readily say, that it were Friar John Burgess. I believe certainly, that in the next ensuing year, I shall once more preach the crusade, bounce buckram. Do you see this russet? Doubt not but there lurketh under it some hid property and occult virtue, known to very few in the world. I did not take it on before this morning; and nevertheless am already in a rage after lust, mad after a wife, and vehemently hot upon untying the codpiece-point: I itch, I tingle, I wriggle, and long exceedingly to be married, that, without the danger of cudgel-blows, I may labour my female copes-mate with the hard push of a bull-horned devil. O the provident and thrifty husband that I then will be! After my death, with all honour and respect due to my frugality, will they burn the sacred bulk of my body, of purpose to preserve the ashes thereof, in memory of the choicest pattern that ever was of a perfectly wary and complete house-holder. Cops-body, this is not the carpet whereon my treasurer shall be allowed to play false in his accounts with me, by setting down an X for a V, or an L for an S. For in that case should I make a hail of fisty-cuffs to fly into his face. Look upon me, Sir, both before and behind,—it is made after the manner of a toga, which was the ancient fashion of the Romans in time of peace. I took the mode, shape, and form thereof in Trajan's Column at Rome, as also in the Triumphal Arch of Septimus Severus. I am tired of the wars, weary of wearing buff-coats, cassocks, and hoquetons. My shoulders are pitifully worn, and bruised with the carrying of harness. Let armour cease, and the long robe bear sway! At least it must be so for the whole space of the succeeding year, if I be married; as yesterday, by the Mosaic law, you evidenced. In what concerneth the breeches, my great aunt Laurence did long ago tell me, that the breeches were only ordained for the use of the codpiece, and to no other end; which I, upon a no less forcible consequence, give credit to every whit, as well as to the saying of the fine fellow Galen, who, in his ninth book, *"Of the Use and Employment of our Members,"* allegeth, that the head was made for the eyes. For nature might have placed our heads in our knees or elbows, but having beforehand determined that the eyes should serve to discover things from afar, she for the better enabling them to execute their designed office, fixed them in the head, as on the top of a long pole, in the most eminent part of all the body: no otherwise than we see the phares, or high towers, erected in the mouths of havens, that navigators may the further off perceive with ease the lights of the nightly fires and lanterns. And because I would gladly, for some short while, (a year at least,) take a little rest and breathing time from the toilsome labour of the military profession, that is to say, be married, I have desisted from wearing any more a codpiece, and, consequently, have laid aside my breeches. For the codpiece is the principal and most especial piece of armour that a warrior doth carry; and therefore do I maintain even to the fire, (exclusively, understand you me,) that no Turks can properly be said to be armed men, in regard that codpieces are by their law forbidden to be worn.

CHAPTER 8

Why the Codpiece is held to be the chief piece of armour amongst Warriors

WILL you maintain, quoth Pantagruel, that the codpiece is the chief piece of a military harness? It is a new kind of doctrine, very paradoxical: for we say, at the spurs begins the arming of a man. Sir, I maintain it, answered Panurge, and not wrongfully do I maintain it. Behold how nature,—having a fervent desire after its production of plants, trees, shrubs, herbs, sponges, and plant-animals, to eternize, and continue them unto all succession of ages—in their several kinds or sorts, at least, although the individuals perish—unruinable, and in an everlasting being, —hath most curiously armed and fenced their buds, sprouts, shoots, and seeds, wherein the above-mentioned perpetuity consisteth, by strengthening, covering, guarding, and fortifying them with an admirable industry, with husks, cases, scarfs and swads, hulls, cods, stones, films, cartels, shells, ears, rinds, barks, skins, ridges, and prickles, which serve them instead of strong, fair, and natural codpieces. As is manifestly apparent in pease, beans, fasels, pomegranates, peaches, cottons, gourds, pumpions, melons, corn, lemons, almonds, walnuts, filberts, and chestnuts; as likewise in all plants, slips or sets whatsoever, wherein it is plainly and evidently seen, that the sperm and semence is more closely veiled, overshadowed, corroborated, and thoroughly harnessed, than any other part, portion, or parcel of the whole.

Nature, nevertheless, did not after that manner provide for the sempiternizing of the human race: but, on the contrary, created man naked, tender, and frail, without either offensive or defensive arms; and that in the estate of innocence, in the first age of all, which was the golden season; not as a plant, but living creature, born for peace, not war, and brought forth into the world with an unquestionable right and title to the plenary fruition and enjoyment of all fruits and vegetables, as also to a certain calm and gentle rule and dominion over all kinds of beasts, fowls, fishes, reptiles, and insects. Yet afterwards it happening in the time of the iron age, under the reign of Jupiter, when, to the multiplication of mischievous actions, wickedness and malice began to take root and footing within the then perverted hearts of men, that the earth began to bring forth nettles, thistles, thorns, briars, and such other stubborn and rebellious vegetables to the nature of man. Nor scarce was there any animal, which by a fatal disposition did not then revolt from him, and tacitly conspire, and covenant with one another, to serve him no longer, nor, in case of their ability to resist, to do him any manner of obedience, but rather, to the uttermost of their power, to annoy him with all the hurt and harm they could. The man, then, that he might maintain his primitive right and prerogative, and continue his sway and dominion over all, both vegetable and sensitive creatures; and knowing of a truth, that he could not be well accommodated, as he ought, without the servitude and subjection of several animals, bethought himself, that of necessity he must needs put on arms, and make provision of harness against wars and violence. By the holy Saint Babingoose, cried out Pantagruel, you are become, since the last rain, a great lifrelofre,—philosopher, I should say. Take notice, Sir, quoth Panurge, when Dame Nature had prompted him to his own arming, what part of the body it was, where, by her inspiration, he clapped on the first harness. It was forsooth by the double pluck of my little dog the ballock, and good Señor Don Priapos Stabostando,—which done, he was content, and sought no more. This is certified by the testimony of the great Hebrew captain and philosopher Moses, who affirmeth that he fenced that member with a brave and gallant codpiece, most exquisitely framed, and by right curious devices of a notably pregnant invention, made up and composed of fig-tree leaves, which, by reason of their solid stiffness, incisory notches, curled frisling, sleeked smoothness, large ampleness, together with their colour, smell, virtue, and faculty, were exceeding proper, and fit for the covering and arming of the sachels of generation, the hideously big Lorrain cullions being from thence only excepted; which swaggering down to the lowermost bottom of the breeches, cannot abide (for being quite out of all order and method,) the stately fashion of the high and lofty codpiece; as is manifest, by the noble Valentin Viardiere, whom I found at Nancy, on the first day of May—the more flauntingly to gallantise it afterwards—rubbing his ballocks spread out upon a table after the manner of a Spanish cloak. Wherefore it is, that none should henceforth say, who would not speak improperly, when any country bumpkin hieth to the wars, Have a care, my roister, of the wine-pot, that is, the scull; but, Have a care, my roister, of the milk-pot, that is the testicles. By the whole rabble of the horned fiends of hell, the head being cut off, that single person only thereby dieth. But, if the ballocks be marred, the whole race of human kind would forthwith perish, and be lost for ever.

This was the motive which incited the goodly writer Galen, *Lib.* 1. *De Spermate,* to aver with boldness, That it were better, that is to say, a less evil, to have no heart at all, than to be quite destitute of genitories: for in them is laid up, conserved and put in store, as in a secessive repository, and sacred warehouse, the semence and original source of the whole offspring of mankind. Therefore would I be apt to believe, for less than a hundred francs, that those are the very same stones, by means whereof Deucalion and Pyrrha restored the human race, in peopling with men and women the world, which a little before that had been drowned in the overflowing waves of a poetical deluge. This stirred up the valiant Justinian, *L.* 4. *De Cagotis Tollendis,* to collocate his *summum bonum in braguibus et braguetis.*[8] For this, and other causes, the Lord Humphry de Merville, following his king to a certain warlike expedition, whilst he was in trying upon his own person a new suit of armour, for of his old rusty harness he could make no more use, by reason that some few years since the skin of his belly was a great way removed from his kidneys; his lady thereupon, in the profound musing of a contemplative spirit, very maturely considering that he had but small care of the staff of love,

and packet of marriage, seeing he did no otherwise arm that part of the body, than with links of mail, advised him to shield, fence, and gabionate it with a big tilting helmet, which she had lying in her closet, to her otherways utterly unprofitable. On this lady were penned these subsequent verses, that are extant in the third book of the Shitbrena of Paultry Wenches.

When Yoland saw her spouse equipt for fight,
And, save the codpiece, all in armour dight,
My dear, she cry'd, Why, pray, of all the rest
Is that exposed, you know I love the best?
Was she to blame for an ill-manag'd fear,—
Or rather pious conscionable care?
Wise Lady, she! In hurly-burly fight,
Can any tell where random blows may light?

Leave off then, sir, from being astonished, and wonder no more at this new manner of decking and trimming up of myself as you now see me.

CHAPTER 9

How Panurge asketh counsel of Pantagruel whether he should marry, yea, or nay

To this Pantagruel replying nothing, Panurge prosecuted the discourse he had already broached, and therewithal fetching, as from the bottom of his heart, a very deep sigh, said, My lord and master, you have heard the design I am upon, which is to marry, if by some disastrous mischance all the holes in the world be not shut up, stopped, closed and bushed. I humbly beseech you, for the affection which of a long time you have borne me, to give me your best advice therein. Then, answered Pantagruel, seeing you have so decreed and taken deliberation thereon, and that the matter is fully determined, what need is there of any further talk thereof, but forthwith to put into execution what you have resolved? Yea, but, quoth Panurge, I would be loth to act anything therein without your counsel had thereto. It is my judgment also, quoth Pantagruel, and I advise you to it. Nevertheless, quoth Panurge, if I understood aright, that it were much better for me to remain a bachelor as I am, than to run headlong upon new hairbrained undertakings of conjugal adventure, I would rather choose not to marry. Quoth Pantagruel—Then do not marry. Yea, but quoth Panurge, would you have me so solitarily drag out the whole course of my life, without the comfort of a matrimonial consort? You know it is written: *Væ soli!*[9] and a single person is never seen to reap the joy and solace that is found with married folks. Then marry, in the name of God, quoth Pantagruel. But if, quoth Panurge, my wife should make me a cuckold; as it is not unknown unto you, how this hath been a very plentiful year in the production of that kind of cattle; I would fly off the hinges, and grow impatient beyond all measure and mean. I love cuckolds with all my heart, for they seem unto me to be of a right honest conversation, and I truly, do very willingly frequent their company: but should I die for it, I would not be one of their number. That is a point for me of a too-sore prickling point. Then do not marry, quoth Pantagruel, for without all controversy this sentence of Seneca is infallibly true, What thou to others shalt have done, others will do the like to thee. Do you, quoth Panurge, aver that without all exception? Yes, truly, quoth Pantagruel, without all exception. Ho, ho, says, Panurge, by the wrath of a little devil, his meaning is, either in this world, or in the other which is to come. Yet seeing I can no more do without a wife, than a blind man without his staff,—for the funnel must be in agitation, without which manner of occupation I cannot live,—were it not a great deal better for me to apply and associate myself to some one honest, lovely, and virtuous woman, than as I do, by a new change of females every day, run a hazard of being bastinadoed, or, (which is worse,) of the great pox, if not of both together. For never,—be it spoken, by their husbands' leave and favour,—had I enjoyment yet of an honest woman. Marry then, in God's name, quoth Pantagruel. But if, quoth Panurge, it were the will of God, and that my destiny did unluckily lead me to marry an honest woman, who should beat me, I would be stored with more than two third parts of the patience of Job, if I were not stark mad by it, and quite distracted with such rugged dealings. For it hath been told me, that those exceeding honest women have ordinarily very wicked headpieces; therefore is it, that their family lacketh not for good vinegar. Yet in that case should it go worse with me, if I did not then in such sort bang her back and breast, so thumpingly bethwack her gillets, to wit, her arms, legs, head, lights, liver, and milt, with her other entrails, and mangle, jag, and slash her coats, so after the cross billet fashion, that the greatest devil of

hell should wait at the gate for the reception of her damned soul. I could make a shift for this year to wave such molestation and disquiet, and be content to lay aside that trouble, and not to be engaged in it.

Do not marry then, answered Pantagruel. Yea, but, quoth Panurge, considering the condition wherein I now am, out of debt and unmarried; mark what I say, free from all debt, in an ill hour! for, where I deeply on the score, my creditors would be but too careful of my paternity, but being quit, and not married, nobody will be so regardful of me, or carry towards me a love like that which is said to be in a conjugal affection. And if by some mishap I should fall sick, I would be looked to very waywardly. The wise man saith, Where there is no woman, I mean, the mother of a family, and wife in the union of a lawful wedlock, the crazy and diseased are in danger of being ill used, and of having much brabbling and strife about them: as by clear experience hath been made apparent in the persons of popes, legates, cardinals, bishops, abbots, priors, priests, and monks: but there, assure yourself, you shall not find me. Marry, then, in the name of God, answered Pantagruel. But if, quoth Panurge, being ill at ease, and possibly through that distemper made unable to discharge the matrimonial duty that is incumbent to an active husband, my wife, impatient of that drooping sickness, and faint-fits of a pining languishment, should abandon and prostitute herself to the embraces of another man, and not only then not help and assist me in my extremity and need, but withal flout at, and make sport of that my grievous distress and calamity; or peradventure, which is worse, embezzle my goods, and steal from me, as I have seen it oftentimes befall unto the lot of many other men, it were enough to undo me utterly, to fill brimful the cup of my misfortune, and make me play the mad-pate reeks of Bedlam. Do not marry then, quoth Pantagruel. Yea, but, said Panurge, I shall never by any other means come to have lawful sons and daughters, in whom I may harbour some hope of perpetuating my name and arms, and to whom also I may leave and bequeath my inheritances and purchased goods, (of which latter sort you need not doubt, but that in some one or other of these mornings, I will make a fair and goodly show,) that so may I cheer up and make merry, when otherwise I should be plunged into a peevish sullen mood of pensive sullenness, as I do perceive daily by the gentle and loving carriage of your kind and gracious father towards you; as all honest folks use to do at their own homes, and private dwelling-houses. For being free from debt, and yet not married, if casually I should fret and be angry, although the cause of my grief and displeasure were never so just, I am afraid, instead of consolation, that I should meet with nothing else but scoffs, frumps, gibes, and mocks at my disastrous fortune. Marry then, in the name of God, quoth Pantagruel; and thus have I given you my advice.

CHAPTER 10

How Pantagruel representeth unto Panurge the difficulty of giving advice in the matter of marriage; and to that purpose mentioneth somewhat of the Homeric and Virgilian lotteries

YOUR counsel, quoth Panurge, under your correction and favour, seemeth unto me not unlike to the song of Gammer Yea-by-nay. It is full of sarcasms, mockeries, bitter taunts, nipping bobs, derisive quips, biting jerks, and contradictory iterations, the one part destroying the other. I know not, added Panurge, which of all your answers to lay hold on. Good reason why, quoth Pantagruel, for your proposals are so full of ifs and buts, that I can ground nothing on them, nor pitch upon any solid and positive determination satisfactory to what is demanded by them. Are not you assured within yourself of what you have a mind to? The chief and main point of the whole matter lieth there. All the rest is merely casual, and totally dependeth upon the fatal disposition of the heavens.

We see some so happy in the fortune of this nuptial encounter, that their family shineth, as it were, with the radiant effulgency of an idea, model, or representation of the joys of paradise; and perceive others, again, to be so unluckily matched in the conjugal yoke, that those very basest of devils, which tempt the hermits that inhabit the Deserts of Thebais and Montserrat, are not more miserable than they. It is therefore expedient, seeing you are resolved for once to make a trial of the state of marriage, that, with shut eyes, bowing your head, and kissing the ground, you put the business to a venture, and give it a fair hazard, in recommending the success of the residue to the disposure of Almighty God. It lieth not in my power to give you any

other manner of assurance, or otherwise to certify you of what shall ensue on this your undertaking. Nevertheless, if it please you, this you may do. Bring hither Virgil's poems, that after having opened the book, and with our fingers severed the leaves thereof three several times, we may, according to the number agreed upon between ourselves, explore the future hap of your intended marriage. For frequently, by a Homeric lottery, have many hit upon their destinies; as is testified in the person of Socrates, who, whilst he was in prison, hearing the recitation of this verse of Homer, said of Achilles in the Ninth of the *Iliads*,

Ἤματί κε τριτάτῳ Φθίην ἐρίβωλον ἱκοίμην·
We, the third day, to fertile Phthia came;

thereby foresaw that on the third subsequent day he was to die. Of the truth whereof he assured Æschines; as Plato, *in Critone*, Cicero *in primo, De Divinatione*, Diogenes, Laertius, and others, have to the full recorded in their works. The like is also witnessed by Opilius Macrinus, to whom, being desirous to know if he should be the Roman Emperor, befell by chance of lot, this sentence in the Eighth of the *Iliads*,

Ὦ γέρον, ἦ μάλα δή σε νέοι τείρουσι μαχηταί,
Σὴ δὲ βίη λέλυται, χαλεπὸν δέ σε γῆρας ὀπάζει·
Dotard, new warriors urge thee to be gone;
Thy life decays, and old age weighs thee
    down.

In fact he, being then somewhat ancient, had hardly enjoyed the sovereignty of the empire for the space of fourteen months, when by Heliogabulus, then both young and strong, he was dispossessed thereof, thrust out of all, and killed. Brutus doth also bear witness of another experiment of this nature, who, willing, through this exploratory way by lot, to learn what the event and issue should be of the Pharsalian battle, wherein he perished, he casually encountered on this verse, said of Patroclus in the Sixteenth of the *Iliads*,

Ἀλλά με μοῖρ' ὀλοὴ καὶ Λητῆς ἔκτανεν υἱός·
Fate, and Latona's son have shot me dead.

And accordingly Apollo was the field-word in the dreadful day of that fight. Divers notable things of old have likewise been foretold and known by casting of Virgilian lots; yea, in matters of no less importance than the obtaining of the Roman Empire, as it happened to Alexander Severus, who, trying his fortune at the said kind of lottery, did hit upon this verse written in the Sixth of the *Æneids,*

Tu regere imperio populos, Romane,
    memento.
Know, Roman, that thy business is to
    reign.

He within very few years thereafter was effectually and in good earnest created and installed Roman emperor. A semblable story thereto is related of Adrian, who, being hugely perplexed within himself out of a longing humour to know in what account he was with the emperor Trajan, and how large the measure of that affection was which he did bear unto him, had recourse, after the manner above specified, to the Maronian lottery, which by hap-hazard tendered him these lines out of the Sixth of the *Æneids,*

Quis procul ille autem ramis insignis olivæ,
Sacra ferens? Nosco crines, incanaque menta
Regis Romani;

But who is he, conspicuous from afar,
With olive boughs, that doth his offerings
    bear?
By the white hair and beard I know him plain
The Roman king.

Shortly thereafter was he adopted by Trajan and succeeded to him in the empire. Moreover to the lot of the praiseworthy emperor Claudius befell this line of Virgil, written in the First of his *Æneids,*

Tertia dum Latio regnantem viderit æstas,
Whilst the third summer saw him reign a
    king
In Latium.

And in effect he did not reign above two years. To the said Claudian also, inquiring concerning his brother Quintilius, whom he proposed as a colleague with himself in the empire, happened the response following, in the Sixth of the *Æneids,*

Ostendent terris hunc tantum fata,—
    Whom fate just let us see,
And would no longer suffer him to be.

And so it fell out; for he was killed on the seventeenth day after he had attained unto the management of the imperial charge. The very same lot also, with the like misluck, did betide the emperor Gordian the younger. To Claudius Albinus, being very solicitous to understand somewhat of his future adventures, did occur this saying, which is written in the Sixth of the *Æneids,*

Hic rem Romanam, magno turbante
    tumultu,
Sistet; eques sternet Pænos, Gallumque
    rebellem.

The Romans boiling with tumultuous
    rage,
This warrior shall the dangerous storm
    assuage;
With victories he the Carthaginian mauls,
And with strong hand shall crush the rebel
    Gauls.

Likewise when the emperor D. Claudius, Aurelian's predecessor, did with great eagerness research after the fate to come of his posterity, his hap was to alight on this verse in the First of the *Æneids,*

Hic ego nec metas rerum, nec tempora
    pono.
No bounds are to be set, no limits here.

Which was fulfilled by the goodly genealogical row of his race. When Mr. Peter Amy did in like manner explore and make trial, if he should escape the ambush of the hob-goblins, who lay in wait all-to-bemaul him, he fell upon this verse in the Third of the *Æneids,*

Heu! fuge crudeles terras, fuge littus
    avarum!
Ah flee the bloody land, the wicked shore!

Which counsel he obeying safe and sound, forthwith avoided all their ambuscades.

Were it not to shun prolixity, I could enumerate a thousand suchlike adventures, which, comformable to the dictate and verdict of the verse, have by that manner of lot-casting encounter befallen to the curious researchers of them. Do not you nevertheless imagine, lest you should be deluded, that I would upon this kind of fortune-flinging proof, infer an uncontrollable, and not to be gainsaid infallibility of truth.

CHAPTER 11

How Pantagruel sheweth the trial of one's fortune by the throwing of dice to be unlawful

It would be sooner done, quoth Panurge, and more expeditely, if we should try the matter at the chance of three fair dice. Quoth Pantagruel, That sort of lottery is deceitful, abusive, illicitous, and exceeding scandalous. Never trust in it. The accursed book of the *Recreation of Dice* was a great while ago excogitated in Achaia near Bourre, by that ancient enemy of mankind, the infernal calumniator, who, before the statue or massive image of the Bouraïc Hercules, did of old, and doth in several places of the world as yet, make many simple souls to err and fall into his snares. You know, how my father Gargantua hath forbidden it over all his kingdoms and dominions; how he hath caused to burn the moulds and draughts thereof, and altogether suppressed, abolished, driven forth, and cast it out of the land, as a most dangerous plague and infection to any well-polished state or commonwealth. What I have told you of dice, I say the same of the play at cockall. It is a lottery of the like guile and deceitfulness; and therefore, do not for convincing of me allege in opposition to this my opinion, or bring in the example of the fortunate cast of Tiberius, within the fountain of Aponus, at the oracle of Gerion. These are the baited hooks by which the devil attracts and draweth unto him the foolish souls of silly people into eternal perdition.

Nevertheless, to satisfy your humour in some measure, I am content you throw three dice upon this table, that, according to the number of the blots which shall happen to be cast up, we may hit upon a verse of that page, which in the setting open of the book you shall have pitched upon.

Have you any dice in your pocket? A whole bag-full, answered Panurge. That is provision against the devil, as is expounded by Merlin Coccaius, *Lib.* 2, *De Patria Diabolorum.* The devil would be sure to take me napping, and very much at unawares, if he should find me without dice. With this the three dice being taken out, produced, and thrown, they fell so pat upon the lower points, that the cast was five, six, and five. These are, quoth Panurge, sixteen in all. Let us take the sixteenth line of the page. The number pleaseth me very well; I hope we

shall have a prosperous and happy chance. May I be thrown amidst all the devils of hell, even as a great bowl cast athwart a set of nine pins, or cannon-ball shot among a battalion of foot, in case so many times I do not boult my future wife the first night of our marriage! Of that, forsooth, I make no doubt at all, quoth Pantagruel. You needed not have rapped forth such a horrid imprecation, the sooner to procure credit for the performance of so small a business, seeing possibly the first bout will be amiss, and that you know is usually at tennis called fifteen. At the next justling turn you may readily amend that fault, and so complete your reckoning of sixteen. Is it so, quoth Panurge, that you understand the matter? And must my words be thus interpreted? Nay, believe me, never yet was any solecism committed by that valiant champion, who often hath for me in Bellydale stood sentry at the hypogastrian cranny. Did you ever hitherto find me in the confraternity of the faulty? Never, I trow; never, nor ever shall, for ever and a day. I do the feat like a goodly friar, or father confessor, without default. And therein am I willing to be judged by the players. He had no sooner spoke these words, than the works of Virgil were brought in. But before the book was laid open, Panurge said to Pantagruel, My heart, like the furch of a hart in a rut, doth beat within my breast. Be pleased to feel and grope my pulse a little on this artery of my left arm. At its frequent rise and fall you would say that they swinge and belabour me after the manner of a probationer, posed and put to a peremptory trial in the examination of his sufficiency for the discharge of the learned duty of a graduate in some eminent degree in the college of the Sorbonists.

But would you not hold it expedient, before we proceed any further, that we should invocate Hercules and the Tenetian goddesses, who in the chamber of lots are said to rule, sit in judgment, and bear a presidential sway? Neither him nor them, answered Pantagruel, only open up the leaves of the book with your fingers, and set your nails at work.

CHAPTER 12

How Pantagruel doth explore by the Virgilian Lottery what fortune Panurge shall have in his marriage

Then at the opening of the book, in the sixteenth row of the lines of the disclosed page, did Panurge encounter upon this following verse:

Nec Deus hunc mensa, Dea nec dignata
  cubili est.
The god him from his table banished,
Nor would the goddess have him in her bed.

This response, quoth Pantagruel, maketh not very much for your benefit or advantage: for it plainly signifies and denoteth, that your wife shall be a strumpet, and yourself by consequence a cuckold. The goddess, whom you shall not find propitious nor favourable unto you, is Minerva, a most redoubtable and dreadful virgin, a powerful and fulminating goddess, an enemy to cuckolds, and effeminate youngsters, to cuckold-makers and adulterers. The god is Jupiter, a terrible and thunder-striking god from heaven. And withal it is to be remarked, that, conform to the doctrine of the ancient Hetrurians, the *manubes,* for so did they call the darting hurls, or slinging casts of the Vulcanian thunderbolts, did only appertain to her, and to Jupiter her father capital. This was verified in the conflagration of the ships of Ajax Oileus, nor doth this fulminating power belong to any other of the Olympic gods. Men, therefore, stand not in such fear of them. Moreover I will tell you, and you may take it as extracted out of the profoundest mysteries of mythology, that, when the giants had enterprised the waging of a war against the power of the celestial orbs, the gods at first did laugh at those attempts, and scorned such despicable enemies, who were, in their conceit, not strong enough to cope in feats of warfare with their pages; but when they saw by the gigantine labour, the high hill Pelion set on lofty Ossa, and that the mount Olympus was made shake, in order to be erected on the top of both; then did they all stand aghast.

Then was it that Jupiter held a parliament, or general convention, wherein it was unanimously resolved upon, and condescended to, by all the gods, that they should worthily and valiantly stand to their defence. And because they had often seen battles lost by the cumbersome lets and disturbing incumbrances of women, confusedly huddled in amongst armies, it was at that time decreed and enacted, That they should expel and drive out of heaven into Egypt, and the confines of Nile, that whole crew of goddesses disguised in the shapes of weasels, polecats, bats, shrew-mice, ferrets, fulmarts, and other such-like odd transformations, only Minerva was reserved to participate with Jupiter in the horrific fulminating power; as being the goddess both of war and learning, of arts and arms, of counsel and dispatch; a goddess armed from her birth, a goddess dreaded in heaven, in the air, by sea and land. By the belly of Saint Buff, quoth Panurge, should I be Vulcan, whom the poet blazons? Nay, I am neither a cripple, coiner of false money, nor smith as he was. My wife possibly will be as comely and handsome as ever was his Venus, but not a whore like her, nor I a cuckold like him. The crook-legged slovenly slave made himself to be declared a cuckold by a definite sentence and judgment, in the open view of all the gods. For this cause ought you to interpret the afore-mentioned verse quite contrary to what you have said. This lot importeth, that my wife will be honest, virtuous, chaste, loyal, and faithful; not armed, surly, wayward, cross, giddy, humorous, heady, hair-brained, or extracted out of brains, as was the goddess Pallas; nor shall this fair jolly Jupiter be my co-rival. He shall never dip his bread in my broth, though we should sit together at one table.

Consider his exploits and gallant actions. He was the most manifest ruffian, wencher, whoremonger, and most infamous cuckold-maker that ever breathed. He did always lecher it like a boar, and no wonder, for he was fostered by a sow in the Isle of Candia, if Agathocles the Babylonian be not a liar, and more rammishly lascivious than a buck; whence it is, that he is said by others to have been suckled and fed with milk of the Amalthæan goat. By the virtue of Acheron, he justled, bulled, and lastauriated in one day the third part of the world, beasts and people, floods and mountains; that was Europa. For this grand subagitatory achievement, the Ammonians caused draw, delineate, and paint him in the figure and shape of a ram ramming, and horned ram. But I know well enough how to shield and preserve myself from that horned champion. He will not, trust me, have to deal in my person with a sottish, dunsical Amphitryon, nor with a silly witless Argus, for all his hundred spectacles, nor yet with the cowardly meacock Acrisius,—the simple goosecap Lycus of Thebes, the doating blockhead Agenor, the phlegmatic pea-goose Asopus, rough-footed Lycaon, the luskish misshapen Corytus of Tuscany, nor with the large-backed and strong-reined Atlas. Let him alter, change, transform, and metamorphose himself into a hundred various shapes and figures, into a swan, a bull, a satyr, a shower of gold, or into a cuckoo, as he did when he unmaidened his sister Juno; into an eagle, ram or dove, as when he was enamoured of the virgin Phthia, who then dwelt in the Ægean territory; into fire, a serpent, yea, even into a flea, into epicurean and democratical atoms, or, more magistronostalistically, into those sly intentions of the mind, which in the schools are called second notions, I'll—catch him in the nick, and take him napping. And would you know what I would do unto him? Even that which to his father Cœlum, Saturn did,—Seneca foretold it of me, and Lactantius hath confirmed it—what the goddess Rhea did to Athis. I would make him two stone lighter, rid him of his Cyprian cymbals, and cut so close and neatly by the breech, that there should not remain thereof so much as one——, so cleanly would I shave him: and disable him for ever from being pope, for *Testiculos non habet*.[10] Hold there, said Pantagruel; ho, soft, and fair my lad! Enough of that,—cast up, turn over the leaves, and try your fortune for the second time. Then did he fall upon this ensuing verse.

Membra quatit, gelidusque coït formidine sanguis.
His joints and members quake, he becomes pale,
And sudden fear doth his cold blood congeal.

This importeth, quoth Pantagruel, that she will soundly bang your back and belly. Clean and quite contrary, answered Panurge, it is of me that he prognosticates, in saying that I will beat her like a tiger, if she vex me. Sir Martin Wagstaff will perform that office, and in default of a cudgel, the devil gulp him, if I should not eat her up quick, as Candaules the Lydian King did his wife, whom he ravened and devoured.

You are very stout, says Pantagruel, and courageous, Hercules himself durst hardly adventure to scuffle with you in this your raging fury. Nor is it strange; for a jan is worth two; and two in fight against Hercules are too strong. Am I a jan? quoth Panurge. No, no, answered Pantagruel. My mind was only running upon the lurch and trictrac. Thereafter

did he hit, at the third opening of the book, upon this verse:

Fœmineo prædæ, et spoliorum ardebat amore.
After the spoil and pillage, as in fire,
He burnt with a strong feminine desire.

This portendeth, quoth Pantagruel, that she will steal your goods and rob you. Hence this, according to these three drawn lots, will be your future destiny, I clearly see it,—you will be a cuckold, you will be beaten, and you will be robbed. Nay, it is quite otherwise, quoth Panurge, for it is certain that this verse presageth, that she will love me with a perfect liking. Nor did the satire-writing poet lie in proof hereof, when he affirmed, That a woman, burning with extreme affection, takes sometimes pleasure to steal from her sweetheart. And what I pray you? A glove, a point, or some such trifling toy of no importance, to make him keep a gentle kind of stirring in the research and quest thereof. In like manner, these small scolding debates, and petty brabbling contentions, which frequently we see spring up, and for a certain space boil very hot betwixt a couple of high-spirited lovers, are nothing else but recreative diversions for their refreshment, spurs to, and incentives of, a more fervent amity than ever. As, for example, we do sometimes see cutlers with hammers maul their finest whetstones, therewith to sharpen their iron tools the better. And therefore do I think, that these three lots make much for my advantage; which if not, I from their sentence totally appeal. There is no appealing, quoth Pantagruel, from the decrees of fate or destiny, of lot or chance: as is recorded by our ancient lawyers, witness Baldus, *Lib. ult. Cap. de Leg.* The reason hereof is, fortune doth not acknowledge a superior, to whom an appeal may be made from her, or any of her substitutes. And in this case the pupil cannot be restored to his right in full, as openly by the said author is alleged in *L. Ait Prætor, paragr. ult. ff. de minor.*

CHAPTER 13

How Pantagruel adviseth Panurge to try the future good or bad luck of his marriage by dreams

Now, seeing we cannot agree together in the manner of expounding or interpreting the sense of the Virgilian lots, let us bend our course another way, and try a new sort of divination. Of what kind? asked Panurge. Of a good ancient and authentic fashion, answered Pantagruel; it is by dreams. For in dreaming, such circumstances and conditions being thereto adhibited, as are clearly enough described by Hippocrates, in *Lib.* περὶ τῶν ἐνυπνίων, by Plato, Plotin, Iamblicus, Synesius, Aristotle, Xenophon, Galen, Plutarch, Artemidorus, Daldianus, Herophilus, Q. Calaber, Theocritus, Pliny, Athenæus, and others, the soul doth oftentimes foresee what is to come. How true this is, you may conceive by a very vulgar and familiar example; as when you see that at such a time as suckling babes, well nourished, fed and fostered with good milk, sleep soundly and profoundly, the nurses in the interim get leave to sport themselves, and are licentiated to recreate their fancies at what range to them shall seem most fitting and expedient, their presence, sedulity, and attendance on the cradle being, during all that space, held unnecessary. Even just so, when our body is at rest, that the concoction is every where accomplished, and that, till it awake, it lacks for nothing, our soul delighteth to disport itself, and is well pleased in that frolic to take a review of its native country, which is the heavens, where it receiveth a most notable participation of its first beginning, with an imbuement from its divine source, and in contemplation of that infinite and intellectual sphere, whereof the centre is every where, and the circumference in no place of the universal world, (to wit, God, according to the doctrine of Hermes Trismegistus,) to whom no new thing happeneth, whom nothing that is past escapeth, and unto whom all things are alike present; it remarketh not only what is *preterit*[11] and gone, in the inferior course and agitation of sublunary matters, but withal taketh notice what is to come; then bringing a relation of those future events unto the body by the outward senses and exterior organs, it is divulged abroad unto the hearing of others. Whereupon the owner of that soul deserveth to be termed a vaticinator, or prophet. Nevertheless, the truth is, that the soul is seldom able to report those things in such sincerity as it hath seen them, by reason of the imperfection and frailty of the corporeal senses, which obstruct the effectuating of that office; even as the moon doth not communicate unto this earth of ours that light which she receiveth from the sun with so much splendour, heat,

vigour, purity, and liveliness as it was given her. Hence it is requisite for the better reading, explaining, and unfolding of these somniatory vaticinations, and predictions, of that nature that a dexterous, learned, skilful, wise, industrious, expert, rational, and peremptory expounder or interpreter be pitched upon, such a one as by the Greeks is called *Onirocrit*, or *Oniropolist*. For this cause Heraclitus was wont to say, that nothing is by dreams revealed to us, that nothing is by dreams concealed from us, and that only we thereby have a mystical signification and secret evidence of things to come, either for our own prosperous or unlucky fortune, or for the favourable or disastrous success of another. The sacred Scriptures testify no less, and profane histories assure us of it, in both which are exposed to our view a thousand several kinds of strange adventures, which have befallen pat according to the nature of the dream, and that as well to the party dreamer, as to others. The Atlantic people, and those that inhabit the island of Thasos, one of the Cyclades, are of this grand commodity deprived; for in their countries none yet ever dreamed. Of this sort were Cleon of Daulia, Thrasymedes, and in our days the learned Frenchman Villanovanus, neither of all which knew what dreaming was.

Fail not therefore to morrow, when the jolly and fair Aurora with her rosy fingers draweth aside the curtains of the night to drive away the sable shades of darkness, to bend your spirits wholly to the task of sleeping sound, and thereto apply yourself. In the meanwhile you must denude your mind of every human passion or affection, such as are love and hatred, fear and hope; for as of old the great vaticinator, most famous and renowned prophet Proteus, was not able in his disguise or transformation into fire, water, a tiger, a dragon, and other such like uncouth shapes and visors, to presage anything that was to come, till he was restored to his own first natural and kindly form; just so doth man; for, at his reception of the art of divination, and faculty of prognosticating future things, that part in him which is the most divine, (to wit, the Νοῦς, or *Mens*,) must be calm, peaceable, untroubled, quiet, still, hushed, and not imbusied or distracted with foreign, soul-disturbing perturbations. I am content, quoth Panurge. But I pray you, sir, must I this evening, ere I go to bed, eat much or little? I do not ask this without cause. For if I sup not well, large, round, and amply, my sleeping is not worth a forked turnip. All the night long I then but doze and rave, and in my slumbering fits talk idle nonsense, my thoughts being in a dull brown study, and as deep in their dumps as is my belly hollow.

Not to sup, answered Pantagruel, were best for you, considering the state of your complexion, and healthy constitution of your body. A certain very ancient prophet, named Amphiaraus, wished such as had a mind by dreams to be imbued with any oracles, for four-and-twenty hours to taste no victuals, and to abstain from wine three days together. Yet shall not you be put to such a sharp, hard, rigorous, and extreme sparing diet. I am truly right apt to believe, that a man whose stomach is replete with various cheer, and in a manner surfeited with drinking, is hardly able to conceive aright of spiritual things; yet am not I of the opinion of those, who, after long and pertinacious fastings, think by such means to enter more profoundly into the speculation of celestial mysteries. You may very well remember how my father Gargantua (whom here for honour sake I name) hath often told us, that the writings of abstinent, abstemious, and long-fasting hermits were every whit as saltless, dry, jejune, and insipid, as were their bodies when they did compose them. It is a most difficult thing for the spirits to be in a good plight, serene and lively, when there is nothing in the body but a kind of voidness and inanity; seeing the philosophers with the physicians jointly affirm, that the spirits, which are styled animal, spring from, and have their constant practice in and through the arterial blood, refined, and purified to the life within the admirable net, which, wonderfully framed, lieth under the ventricles and tunnels of the brain. He gave us also the example of the philosopher, who, when he thought most seriously to have withdrawn himself unto a solitary privacy, far from the rustling clutterments of the tumultuous and confused world, the better to improve his theory, to contrive, comment and ratiocinate, was, notwithstanding his uttermost endeavours to free himself from all untoward noises, surrounded and environed about so with the barking of curs, bawling of mastiffs, bleating of sheep, prating of parrots, tattling of jack-daws, grunting of swine, girning of boars, yelping of foxes, mewing of cats, cheeping of mice, squeaking of weasels, croaking of frogs, crowing of cocks, cackling

of hens, calling of partridges, chanting of swans, chattering of jays, peeping of chickens, singing of larks, creaking of geese, chirping of swallows, clucking of moor-fowls, cucking of cuckoos, bumbling of bees, rammage of hawks, chirming of linnets, croaking of ravens, screeching of owls, whicking of pigs, gushing of hogs, curring of pigeons, grumbling of cushet-doves, howling of panthers, curkling of quails, chirping of sparrows, crackling of crows, nuzzing of camels, whining of whelps, buzzing of dromedaries, mumbling of rabbits, cricking of ferrets, humming of wasps, mioling of tigers, bruzzing of bears, sussing of kitlings, clamoring of scarfes, whimpering of fulmarts, booing of buffalos, warbling of nightingales, quavering of meavises, drintling of turkies, coniating of storks, trantling of peacocks, clattering of magpies, murmuring of stock-doves, crouting of cormorants, cigling of locusts, charming of beagles, guarring of puppies, snarling of messens, rantling of rats, guerieting of apes, snuttering of monkies, pioling of pelicans, quacking of ducks, yelling of wolves, roaring of lions, neighing of horses, barring of elephants, hissing of serpents, and wailing of turtles, that he was much more troubled, than if he had been in the middle of the crowd at the fair of Fontenay or Niort. Just so is it with those who are tormented with the grievous pangs of hunger. The stomach begins to gnaw, and bark as it were, the eyes to look dim, and the veins, by greedily sucking some refection to themselves from the proper substance of all the members of a fleshy consistence, violently pull down and draw back that vagrant, roaming spirit, careless and neglecting of his nurse and natural host, which is the body; as when a hawk upon the fist, willing to take her flight by a soaring aloft in the open spacious air, is on a sudden drawn back by a leash tied to her feet.

To this purpose also did he allege unto us the authority of Homer, the father of all philosophy, who said, that the Grecians did not put an end to their mournful mood for the death of Patroclus, the most intimate friend of Achilles, till hunger in a rage declared herself, and their bellies protested to furnish no more tears unto their grief. For from bodies emptied and macerated by long fasting, there could not be such supply of moisture and brackish drops, as might be proper on that occasion.

Mediocrity at all times is commendable;

nor in this case are you to abandon it. You may take a little supper, but thereat must you not eat of a hare, nor of any other flesh. You are likewise to abstain from beans, from the preak, by some called the polyp, as also from coleworts, cabbage, and all other such like windy victuals, which may endanger the troubling of your brains, and the dimming or casting a kind of mist over your animal spirits. For, as a looking glass cannot exhibit the semblance or representation of the object set before it, and exposed to have its image to the life expressed, if that the polished sleekedness thereof be darkened by gross breathings, dampish vapours, and foggy, thick, infectious exhalations,—even so the fancy cannot well receive the impression of the likeness of those things, which divination doth afford by dreams, if any way the body be annoyed or troubled with the fumish steam of meat, which it had taken in a while before; because, betwixt these two there still hath been a mutual sympathy and fellow-feeling of an indissolubly knit affection. You shall eat good Eusebian and bergamot pears, one apple of the short-shank pippin-kind, a parcel of the little plums of Tours, and some few cherries of the growth of my orchard. Nor shall you need to fear, that thereupon will ensue doubtful dreams, fallacious, uncertain, and not to be trusted to, as by some peripatetic philosophers hath been related; for that, say they, men do more copiously in the season of harvest feed on fruitages, than any other time. The same is mystically taught us by the ancient prophets and poets, who allege, that all vain and deceitful dreams lie hid and in covert, under the leaves which are spread on the ground: by reason that the leaves fall from the trees in the autumnal quarter. For the natural fervour, which abounding in ripe, fresh, recent fruits, cometh by the quickness of its ebullition to be with ease evaporated into the animal parts of the dreaming person—the experiment is obvious in most—is a pretty while before it be expired, dissolved, and evanished. As for your drink, you are to have it of the fair, pure water of my fountain.

The condition, quoth Panurge, is very hard. Nevertheless, cost what price it will, or whatsoever come of it, I heartily condescend thereto; protesting, that I shall to-morrow break my fast betimes, after my somniatory exercitations. Furthermore, I recommend myself to Homer's two gates, to Morpheus, to Iselon, to Phantasus, and unto Phobetor. If they in this my great need succour me, and grant me that assistance which is fitting, I will, in honour of them all, erect a jolly, genteel altar, composed of the softest down. If I were now in Laconia, in the temple of Juno, betwixt Œtile and Thalamis, she suddenly would disentangle my perplexity, resolve me of my doubts, and cheer me up with fair and jovial dreams in a deep sleep.

Then did he thus say unto Pantagruel. Sir, were it not expedient for my purpose to put a branch or two of curious laurel betwixt the quilt and bolster of my bed, under the pillow on which my head must lean? There is no need at all of that, quoth Pantagruel, for, besides that it is a thing very superstitious, the cheat thereof hath been at large discovered unto us in the writings of Serapion Ascalonites, Antiphon, Philochorus, Artemon, and Fulgentius Planciades. I could say as much to you of the left shoulder of a crocodile, as also of a cameleon, without prejudice be it spoken to the credit which is due to the opinion of old Democritus; and likewise of the stone of the Bactrians, called Eumetrides, and of the Hammonian horn; for so by the Æthiopians is termed a certain precious stone, coloured like gold, and in the fashion, shape, form and proportion of a ram's horn, as the horn of Jupiter Hammon is reported to have been: they over and above assuredly affirming, that the dreams of those who carry it about them are no less veritable and infallible, than the truth of the divine oracles. Nor is this much unlike to what Homer and Virgil wrote of these two gates of sleep; to which you have been pleased to recommend the management of what you have in hand. The one is of ivory, which letteth in confused, doubtful, and uncertain dreams; for through ivory, how small and slender soever it be, we can see nothing, the density, opacity, and close compactedness of its material parts hindering the penetration of the visual rays, and the reception of the species of such things as are visible. The other is of horn, at which an entry is made to sure and certain dreams, even as through horn, by reason of the diaphanous splendour, and bright transparency thereof, the species of all objects of the sight distinctly pass, and so without confusion appear, that they are clearly seen. Your meaning is, and you would thereby infer, quoth Friar John, that the dreams of all horned cuckolds, of which number Panurge, by the help of God, and his future wife, is without controversy to be one, are always true and infallible.

CHAPTER 14

Panurge's dream, with the interpretation thereof

At seven o'clock of the next following morning, Panurge did not fail to present himself before Pantagruel, in whose chamber were at that time Epistemon, Friar John of the Funnels, Ponocrates, Eudemon, Carpalim, and others, to whom, at the entry of Panurge, Pantagruel said, Lo, here cometh our dreamer. That word, quoth Epistemon, in ancient times cost very much, and was dearly sold to the children of Jacob. Then said Panurge, I have been plunged into my dumps so deeply, as if I had been lodged with Gaffer Noddycap. Dreamed indeed I have, and that right lustily; but I could take along with me no more thereof, that I did truly understand; save only, that I in my vision had a pretty, fair, young, gallant, handsome woman, who no less lovingly and kindly treated and entertained me, hugged, cherished, cockered, dandled, and made much of me, as if I had been another neat dilli-darling minion, like Adonis. Never was man more glad than I was then, my joy at that time was incomparable. She flattered me, tickled me, stroked me, groped me, frizzled me, curled me, kissed me, embraced me, laid her hands about my neck, and now and then made jestingly, pretty little horns above my forehead. I told her in the like disport, as I did play the fool with her, that she should rather place and fix them in a little below mine eyes, that I might see the better what I should stick at with them; for, being so situated, Momus then would find no fault therewith, as he did once with the position of the horns of bulls. The wanton, toying girl, notwithstanding any remonstrance of mine to the contrary, did always drive and thrust them further in: yet thereby, which to me seemed wonderful, she did not do me any hurt at all. A little after, though I know not how, I thought I was transformed into a tabor, and she into a chough, or madge-howlet.

My sleeping there being interrupted, I awaked in a start, angry, displeased, perplexed, chafing, and very wroth. There have you a large platter-full of dreams, make thereupon good cheer, and, if you please spare not to interpret them according to the understanding which you have in them. Come, Carpalim, let us to breakfast. To my

sense and meaning, quoth Pantagruel, if I have skill or knowledge in the art of divination by dreams, your wife will not really, and to the outward appearance of the world, plant, or set horns, and stick them fast in your forehead, after a visible manner, as satyrs use to wear and carry them; but she will be so far from preserving herself loyal in the discharge and observance of a conjugal duty, that, on the contrary she will violate her plighted faith, break her marriage oath, infringe all matrimonial ties, prostitute her body to the dalliance of other men, and so make you a cuckold. This point is clearly and manifestly explained and expounded by Artemidorus, just as I have related it. Nor will there be any metamorphosis, or transmutation made of you into a drum, or tabor, but you will surely be as soundly beaten as ever was tabor at a merry wedding. Nor yet will she be changed into a chough, but will steal from you, chiefly in the night, as is the nature of that thievish bird. Hereby may you perceive your dreams to be in every jot conform and agreeable to the Virgilian lots. A cuckold you will be, beaten and robbed. Then cried out Father John with a loud voice, He tells the truth; upon my conscience, thou wilt be a cuckold, an honest one, I warrant thee. O the brave horns that will be borne by thee! Ha, ha, ha! Our good Master de Cornibus. God save thee and shield thee! Wilt thou be pleased to preach but two words of a sermon to us, I will go through the parish-church to gather up alms for the poor.

You are, quoth Panurge, very far mistaken in your interpretation; for the matter is quite contrary to the sense thereof. My dream presageth, that I shall by marriage be stored with plenty of all manner of goods,—the hornifying of me showing, that I will possess a cornucopia, that Amalthæan horn, which is called the horn of abundance, whereof the fruition did still portend the wealth of the enjoyer. You possibly will say, that they are rather like to be satyr's horns; for you of these did make some mention. *Amen, amen, fiat, fiatur, ad differentiam papæ.*[12] Thus shall I have my touch-her-home still ready. My staff of love semipiternally in a good case, will, satyr-like be never toiled out; a thing which all men wish for, and send up their prayers to that purpose, but such a thing as nevertheless is granted but to few. Hence doth it follow by a consequence as clear as the sunbeams, that I will never be in the danger of being made a cuckold, for the defect hereof is *Causa sine qua non;* yea, the sole cause, as many think, of making husbands cuckolds. What makes poor scoundrel rogues to beg, I pray you? Is it not because they have not enough at home wherewith to fill their bellies and their pokes? What is it makes the wolves to leave the woods? Is it not the want of flesh meat? What maketh women whores? You understand me well enough. And herein may I very well submit my opinion to the judgment of learned lawyers, presidents, counsellors, advocates, procurers, attorneys, and other glossers and commentators on the venerable rubric, *De Frigidis et Maleficiatis.*[13] You are, in truth, sir, as it seems to me, (excuse my boldness, if I have transgressed,) in a most palpable and absurd error, to attribute my horns to cuckoldry. Diana wears them on her head after the manner of a crescent. Is she a cucquean for that? How the devil can she be cuckolded, who never yet was married? Speak somewhat more correctly, I beseech you, lest she, being offended, furnish you with a pair of horns, shapen by the pattern of those which she made for Actæon. The goodly Bacchus also carries horns,—Pan, Jupiter Hammon, with a great many others. Are they all cuckolds? If Jove be a cuckold, Juno is a whore. This follows by the figure metalepsis; as to call a child in the presence of his father and mother, a bastard, or whore's son, is tacitly and underboard, no less than if he had said openly, the father is a cuckold, and his wife a punk. Let our discourse come nearer to the purpose. The horns that my wife did make me are horns of abundance, planted and grafted in my head for the increase and shooting up of all good things. This will I affirm for truth, upon my word, and pawn my faith and credit both upon it. As for the rest, I will be no less joyful, frolic, glad, cheerful, merry, jolly, and gamesome, than a well-bended tabor in the hands of a good drummer at a nuptial feast, still making a noise, still rolling, still buzzing and cracking. Believe me, sir, in that consisteth none of my least good fortunes. And my wife will be jocund, feat, compt, neat, quaint, dainty, trim, tricked up, brisk, smirk, and smug, even as a pretty little Cornish chough. Who will not believe this, let hell or the gallows be the burden of his Christmas carol.

I remark, quoth Pantagruel, the last point or particle which you did speak of, and, having seriously conferred it with the first, find

that at the beginning you were delighted with the sweetness of your dream; but in the end and final closure of it you startingly awaked, and on a sudden were forthwith vexed in choler, and annoyed. Yea, quoth Panurge, the reason of that was, because I had fasted too long. Flatter not yourself, quoth Pantagruel; all will go to ruin. Know for a certain truth, that every sleep that endeth with a starting, and leaves the person irksome, grieved, and fretting, doth either signify a present evil, or otherwise presageth and portendeth a future imminent mishap. To signify an evil, that is to say, to show some sickness hardly curable, a kind of pestilentious or malignant bile, botch, or sore, lying and lurking hid, occult, and latent within the very centre of the body, which many times doth by the means of sleep, whose nature is to reinforce and strengthen the faculty and virtue of concoction, begin according to the theorems of physic to declare itself, and moves toward the outward superficies. At this sad stirring is the sleeper's rest and ease disturbed and broken, whereof the first feeling and stinging smart admonisheth, that he must patiently endure great pain and trouble, and thereunto provide some remedy: as when we say proverbially, to incense hornets, move a stinking puddle, and to awake a sleeping lion, instead of these more usual expressions, and of a more familiar and plain meaning, to provoke angry persons, to make a thing the worse by meddling with it, and to irritate a testy choleric man when he is at quiet. On the other part, to presage or foretel an evil, especially in what concerneth the exploits of the soul, in matter of somnial divinations, is as much as to say as that it giveth us to understand, that some dismal fortune or mischance is destinated and prepared for us, which shortly will not fail to come to pass. A clear and evident example hereof is to be found in the dream and dreadful awaking of Hecuba, as likewise in that of Euridice, the wife of Orpheus, neither of which was no sooner finished, saith Ennius, but that incontinently thereafter they awaked in a start, and were affrighted horribly. Thereupon these accidents ensued; Hecuba had her husband Priamus, together with her children, slain before her eyes, and saw then the destruction of her country; and Euridice died speedily thereafter in a most miserable manner. Æneas, dreaming that he spoke to Hector a little after his decease, did on a sudden on a great start, awake, and was afraid. How hereupon did follow this event; Troy that same night was spoiled, sacked, and burnt. At another time the same Æneas, dreaming that he saw his familiar Genii and Penates, in a ghastly fright and astonishment awaked, of which terror and amazement the issue was, that the very next day subsequent, by a most horrible tempest on the sea, he was like to have perished, and been cast away. Moreover, Turnus being prompted, instigated, and stirred up by the fantastic vision of an infernal fury, to enter into a bloody war against Æneas, awaked in a start much troubled and disquieted in spirit, in sequel whereof, after many notable and famous routs, defeats, and discomfitures in open field, he came at last to be killed in a single combat by the said Æneas. A thousand other instances I could afford, if it were needful, of this matter. Whilst I relate these stories of Æneas, remark the saying of Fabius Pictor, who faithfully averred, That nothing had at any time befallen unto, was done, or enterprised by him, whereof he had not previously had notice, and before-hand foreseen it to the full, by sure predictions altogether founded on the oracles of somnial divination. To this there is no want of pregnant reasons, no more than of examples. For if repose and rest in sleeping be a special gift and favour of the gods, as is maintained by the philosophers, and by the poet attested in these lines,

Then sleep, that heavenly gift, came to refresh
Of human labourers the wearied flesh;

such a gift or benefit can never finish or terminate in wrath and indignation, without portending some unlucky fate, and most disastrous fortune to ensue. Otherwise it were a molestation, and not an ease; a scourge, and not a gift; at least, not proceeding from the gods above, but from the infernal devils our enemies, according to the common vulgar saying.

Suppose the lord, father, or master of a family, sitting at a very sumptuous dinner, furnished with all manner of good cheer, and having at his entry to the table his appetite sharp set upon his victuals, whereof there was great plenty, should be seen rise in a start, and on a sudden fling out of his chair, abandoning his meat, frighted, appalled, and in a horrid terror, who should not know the cause hereof would wonder, and be aston-

ished exceedingly. But what? he heard his male servants cry, Fire, fire, fire, fire! his serving maids and women yell, Stop thief, stop thief! and all his children shout as loud as ever they could, Murder, O murder, murder! Then was it not high time for him to leave his banqueting, for application of a remedy in haste, and to give speedy order for succouring of his distressed household? Truly, I remember, that the Cabalists and Massorets, interpreters of the sacred Scriptures, in treating how with verity one might judge of evangelical apparitions, (because oftentimes the angel of Satan is disguised and transfigured into an angel of light,) said, That the difference of these two mainly did consist in this. The favourable and comforting angel useth in his appearance unto man at first to terrify and hugely affright him, but in the end he bringeth consolation, leaveth the person who hath seen him, joyful, well pleased, fully content, and satisfied. On the other side, the angel of perdition, that wicked, devilish, and malignant spirit, at his appearance unto any person, in the beginning cheereth up the heart of his beholder, but at last forsakes him, and leaves him troubled, angry, and perplexed.

CHAPTER 15

Panurge's excuse and exposition of the monastic mystery concerning powdered beef

THE Lord save those who see, and do not hear! quoth Panurge. I see you well enough, but know not what it is that you have said. The hunger-starved belly wanteth ears. For lack of victuals, before God, I roar, bray, yell, and fume, as in a furious madness. I have performed too hard a task to-day, an extraordinary work indeed. He shall be craftier, and do far greater wonders than ever did Mr. Mush, who shall be able any more this year to bring me on the stage of preparation for a dreaming verdict. Fie! not to sup at all, that is the devil. Pox take that fashion! Come, Friar John, let us go break our fast; for if I hit on such a round refection in the morning, as will serve thoroughly to fill the mill-hopper and hogs-hide of my stomach, and furnish it with meat and drink sufficient, then at a pinch, as in the case of some extreme necessity which presseth, I could make a shift that day to forbear dining. But not to sup! A plague rot that base custom, which is an error offensive to nature. That lady made the day for exercise, to travel, work, wait on, and labour in each his negotiation and employment; and, that we may with the more fervency and ardour prosecute our business, she sets before us a clear burning candle, to wit, the sun's resplendency; and at night, when she begins to take the light from us, she thereby tacitly implies no less, than if she would have spoken thus unto us: My lads and lasses, all of you are good and honest folks, you have wrought well to-day, toiled and turmoiled enough,—the night approacheth,—therefore cast off these moiling cares of yours, desist from all your swinking painful labours, and set your minds how to refresh your bodies in the renewing of their vigour with good bread, choice wine, and store of wholesome meats; then may you take some sport and recreation, and after that lie down and rest yourselves, that you may strongly, nimbly, lustily, and with the more alacrity to-morrow attend on your affairs as formerly.

Falconers in like manner, when they have fed their hawks, will not suffer them to fly on a full gorge, but let them on a perch abide a little, that they may rouse, bait, tower, and soar the better. That good pope, who was the first institutor of fasting, understood this well enough; for he ordained that our fast should reach but to the hour of noon; all the remainder of that day was at our disposure, freely to eat and feed at any time thereof. In ancient times there were but few that dined, as you would say, some churchmen, monks, and canons, for they have little other occupation. Each day is a festival unto them, who diligently heed the claustral proverb, *De missa ad mensam*.[14] They do not use to linger and defer their sitting down and placing of themselves at table, only so long as they have a mind in waiting for the coming of the abbot; so they fell to without ceremony, terms, or conditions; and every body supped, unless it were some vain, conceited, dreaming dotard. Hence was a supper called *Cæna*, which showeth that it is common to all sorts of people. Thou knowest it well, Friar John. Come, let us go, my dear friend, in the name of all the devils of the infernal regions, let us go. The gnawings of my stomach in this rage of hunger are so tearing, that they make it bark like a mastiff. Let us throw some bread and beef into his throat to pacify him, as once the sibyl did to Cerberus. Thou likest best monastical brewess, the prime, the flower of the pot. I am for the solid, principal verb that

comes after—the good brown loaf, always accompanied with a round slice of the Nine-lecture-powdered labourer. I know thy meaning, answered Friar John; this metaphor is extracted out of the claustral kettle. The labourer is the ox, that hath wrought and done the labour; after the fashion of nine lectures, that is to say, most exquisitely well and thoroughly boiled. These holy religious fathers, by a certain cabalistic institution of the ancients, not written, but carefully by tradition conveyed from hand to hand, rising betimes to go to morning prayers, were wont to flourish that their matutinal devotion with some certain notable preambles before their entry into the church, *viz.*, They dunged in the dungeries, pissed in the pisseries, spit in the spitteries, melodiously coughed in the cougheries, and doted in their doteries, that to the divine service they might not bring any thing that was unclean or foul. These things thus done, they very zealously made their repair to the Holy Chapel, for so was in their canting language termed the convent kitchen, where they with no small earnestness had care that the beef pot should be put on the crook for the breakfast of the religious brothers of our Lord and Saviour; and the fire they would kindle under the pot themselves. Now, the matins, consisting of nine lessons, were so incumbent on them, that they must have risen the earlier for the more expedite dispatching of them all. The sooner that they rose, the sharper was their appetite, and the barkings of their stomachs, and the gnawings increased in the like proportion, and consequently made these godly men thrice more a hungered and a thirst, than when their matins were hemmed over only with three lessons. The more betimes they rose, by the said cabal, the sooner was the beef pot put on; the longer that the beef was on the fire, the better it was boiled; the more it boiled, it was the tenderer; the tenderer that it was, the less it troubled the teeth, delighted more the palate, less charged the stomach, and nourished our good religious men the more substantially; which is the only end and prime intention of the first founders, as appears by this, That they eat, not to live, but live to eat, and in this world have nothing but their life. Let us go, Panurge.

Now have I understood thee, quoth Panurge, my plushcod friar, my caballine and claustral ballock. I freely quit the costs, interest, and charges, seeing you have so egregiously commented upon the most especial chapter of the culinary and monastic cabal. Come along, my Carpalim, and you, Friar John, my leather-dresser. Good morrow to you all, my good lords: I have dreamed enough to drink. Let us go. Panurge had no sooner done speaking, than Epistemon with a loud voice said these words. It is a very ordinary and common thing amongst men to conceive, foresee, know, and presage the misfortune, bad luck, or disaster of another; but to have the understanding, providence, knowledge, and prediction of a man's own mishap, is very scarce, and rare to be found any where. This is exceeding judiciously and prudently deciphered by Æsop in his *Apologues*, who there affirmeth, That every man in the world carrieth about his neck a wallet, in the fore-bag whereof are contained the faults and mischances of others, always exposed to his view and knowledge; and in the other scrip thereof, which hangs behind, are kept the bearer's proper transgressions, and inauspicious adventures, at no time seen by him, nor thought upon, unless he be a person that hath a favourable aspect from the heavens.

CHAPTER 16

How Pantagruel adviseth Panurge to consult with the Sibyl of Panzoust

A LITTLE while thereafter Pantagruel sent for Panurge, and said unto him, The affection which I bear you being now inveterate, and settled in my mind by a long continuance of time, prompteth me to the serious consideration of your welfare and profit; in order whereto, remark what I have thought thereon. It hath been told me that at Panzoust, near Crouly, dwelleth a very famous sibyl, who is endowed with the skill of foretelling all things to come. Take Epistemon in your company, repair towards her, and hear what she will say unto you. She is possibly, quoth Epistemon, some Canidia, Sagana, or Pythonissa, either whereof with us is vulgarly called a witch,—I being the more easily induced to give credit to the truth of this character of her, that the place of her abode is vilely stained with the abominable repute of abounding more with sorcerers and witches than ever did the plains of Thessaly. I should not, to my thinking, go thither willingly, for that it seems to me a thing unwarrantable, and altogether forbidden in the law of Moses. We are not Jews, quoth Pantagruel, nor is it a

matter judically confessed by her, nor authentically proved by others that she is a witch. Let us for the present suspend our judgment, and defer till after your return from thence the sifting and garbling of those niceties. How know we but that she may be an eleventh sibyl, or a second Cassandra? But although she were neither, and she did not merit the name or title of any of these renowned prophetesses, what hazard, in the name of God, do you run, by offering to talk and confer with her, of the instant perplexity and perturbation of your thoughts? Seeing especially, and which is most of all, she is, in the estimation of those that are acquainted with her, held to know more, and to be of a deeper reach of understanding, than is either customary to the country wherein she liveth, or to the sex whereof she is. What hindrance, hurt, or harm doth the laudable desire of knowledge bring to any man, were it from a sot, a pot, a fool, a stool, a winter mittain, a truckle for a pully, the lid of a goldsmith's crucible, an oil-bottle, or old slipper? You may remember to have read, or heard at least, that Alexander the Great, immediately after his having obtained a glorious victory over the King Darius at Arbela, refused, in the presence of the splendid and illustrious courtiers that were about him, to give audience to a poor certain despicable like fellow, who, through the solicitations and mediation of some of his royal attendants, was admitted humbly to beg that grace and favour of him. But sore did he repent, although in vain, a thousand and ten thousand times thereafter, the surly state which he then took upon him to the denial of so just a suit, the grant whereof would have been worth unto him the value of a brace of potent cities. He was indeed victorious in Persia, but withal so far distant from Macedonia, his hereditary kingdom, that the joy of the one did not expel the extreme grief, which through occasion of the other he had inwardly conceived; for not being able with all his power to find or invent a convenient mean and expedient, how to get or come by the certainty of any news from thence, both by reason of the huge remoteness of the places from one to another, as also because of the impeditive interposition of many great rivers, the interjacent obstacle of divers wild deserts, and obstructive interjection of sundry almost inaccessible mountains, —whilst he was in this sad quandary and solicitous pensiveness, which, you may suppose, could not be a small vexation to him, considering that it was a matter of no great difficulty to run over his whole native soil, possess his country, seize on his kingdom, instal a new king in the throne, and plant thereon foreign colonies, long before he could come to have any advertisement of it: for obviating the jeopardy of so dreadful inconveniency, and putting a fit remedy thereto, a certain Sidonian merchant of a low stature, but high fancy, very poor in shew, and, to the outward appearance of little or no account, having presented himself before him, went about to affirm and declare, that he had excogitated and hit upon a ready mean and way, by the which those of his territories at home should come to the certain notice of his Indian victories, and himself be perfectly informed of the state and condition of Egypt and Macedonia, within less than five days. Whereupon the said Alexander, plunged into a sullen animadvertency of mind, through his rash opinion of the improbability of performing a so strange and impossible-like undertaking, dismissed the merchant without giving ear to what he had to say, and vilified him. What could it have cost him to hearken unto what the honest man had invented and contrived for his good? What detriment, annoyance, damage, or loss could he have undergone to listen to the discovery of that secret, which the good fellow would have most willingly revealed unto him? Nature, I am persuaded, did not without a cause frame our ears open, putting thereto no gate at all, nor shutting them up with any manner of inclosures, as she hath done upon the tongue, the eyes, and other such out-jetting parts of the body. The cause as I imagine, is, to the end that every day and every night, and that continually, we may be ready to hear, and by a perpetual hearing apt to learn. For, of all the senses, it is the fittest for the reception of the knowledge of arts, sciences, and disciplines; and it may be, that man was an angel, that is to say, a messenger sent from God, as Raphael was to Tobit. Too suddenly did he contemn, despise, and misregard him; but too long thereafter, by an untimely and too late repentance, did he do penance for it. You say very well, answered Epistemon, yet shall you never for all that induce me to believe, that it can tend any way to the advantage or commodity of a man, to take advice and counsel of a woman, namely, of such a woman, and the woman of such a country. Truly I have found, quoth Panurge, a great deal of good in the counsel of women, chiefly in that of the old wives amongst them; for, every time I consult with them, I readily get a stool or two extraordinary, to the great solace of my bumgut passage. They are as sloth-hounds in the infallibillity of their scent, and in their sayings no less sententious than the rubrics of the law. Therefore in my conceit it is not an improper kind of speech to call them sage or wise women. In confirmation of which opinion of mine, the customary style of my language alloweth them the denomination of presage women. The epithet of sage is due unto them, because they are surpassing dexterous in the knowledge of most things. And I give them the title of presage for that they divinely foresee, and certainly foretell future contingencies, and events of things to come. Sometimes I call them not maunettes, but monettes, from their wholesome monitions. Whether it be so, ask Pythagoras, Socrates, Empedocles, and our master, Ortuinus. I furthermore praise and commend above the skies the ancient memorable institution of the pristine Germans, who ordained the responses and documents of old women to be highly extolled, most cordially reverenced, and prized at a rate in nothing inferior to the weight, test, and standard of the sanctuary. And as they were respectfully prudent in receiving of these sound advices, so by honouring and following them did they prove no less fortunate in the happy success of all their endeavours. Witness the old wife Aurinia, and the good mother Velleda, in the days of Vespasian. You need not any way doubt, but that feminine old age is always fructifying in qualities sublime, I would have said sibylline. Let us go, by the help, let us go, by the virtue of God, let us go. Farewell, Friar John, I recommend the care of my codpiece to you. Well, quoth Epistemon, I will follow you, with this protestation nevertheless, that if I happen to get a sure information, or otherwise find, that she doth use any kind of charm or enchantment in her responses, it may not be imputed to me for a blame to leave you at the gate of her house, without accompanying you any further in.

CHAPTER 17

How Panurge spoke to the Sibyl of Panzoust

THEIR voyage was six days journeying. On the seventh whereof, was shown unto them the house of the vaticinatress, standing on the knap or top of a hill, under a large and spacious walnut-tree. Without great difficulty they entered into that straw-thatched cottage, scurvily built, naughtily moveabled, and all besmoked. It matters not, quoth Epistemon; Heraclitus, the grand Scotist, and tenebrous darksome philosopher, was nothing astonished at his introit into such a coarse and paltry habitation; for he did usually show forth unto his sectators and disciples, that the gods made as cheerfully their residence in these mean homely mansions, as in sumptuous magnificent palaces, replenished with all manner of delight, pomp, and pleasure. I withal do really believe, that the dwelling-place of the so famous and renowned Hecate was just such another petty cell as this is, when she made a feast therein to the valiant Theseus; and that of no other better structure was the cot or cabin of Hyreus, or Œnopion, wherein Jupiter, Neptune, and Mercury were not ashamed, all three together, to harbour and sojourn a whole night, and there to take a full and hearty repast; and in payment of the shot they thankfully pissed Orion. They finding the ancient woman at a corner of her own chimney, Epistemon said, she is indeed a true sibyl, and the lively portrait of one represented by the Γρηῒ καμινοῖ of Homer. The old hag was in a pitiful bad plight and condition, in matter of the outward state and complexion of her body, the ragged and tattered equipage of her person, in the point of accoutrement, and beggarly poor provision of fare for her diet and entertainment; for she was ill apparelled, worse nourished, toothless, blear-eyed, crook-shouldered, snotty, her nose still dropping, and herself still drooping, faint, and pithless; whilst in this wofully wretched case she was making ready, for her dinner, porridge or wrinkled green coleworts, with a swerd of yellow bacon, mixed with a twice before cooked sort of waterish, unsavoury broth, extracted out of bare and hollow bones. Epistemon said, By the cross of a groat, we are to blame, nor shall we get from her any response at all, for we have not brought along with us the branch of gold. I have, quoth Panurge, provided pretty well for that, for here I have it within my bag, in the substance of a gold ring, accompanied with some fair pieces of small money. No sooner were these words spoken, when Panurge coming up towards her, after the ceremonial performance of a profound and humble salutation, presented

her with six neats' tongues dried in the smoke, a great butterpot full of fresh cheese, a boracho furnished with good beverage, and a ram's cod stored with single pence, newly coined. At last he, with a low courtesy, put on her medical finger a pretty handsome golden ring, whereinto was right artificially enchased a precious toadstone of Beausse. This done, in few words and very succinctly, did he set open and expose unto her the motive reason of his coming, most civilly and courteously entreating her, that she might be pleased to vouchsafe to give him an ample and plenary intelligence concerning the future good luck of his intended marriage.

The old trot for a while remained silent, pensive, and grinning like a dog; then, after she had set her withered breech upon the bottom of a bushel, she took into her hands three old spindles, which when she had turned and whirled betwixt her fingers very diversely, and after several fashions, she pryed more narrowly into, by the trial of their points, the sharpest whereof she retained in her hand, and threw the other two under a stone trough. After this she took a pair of yarn windles, which she nine times unintermittedly veered, and frisked about, then at the ninth revolution or turn, without touching them any more, maturely perpending the manner of their motion, she very demurely waited on their repose and cessation from any further stirring. In sequel whereof, she pulled off one of her wooden pattens, put her apron over her head, as a priest uses to do his amice, when he is going to sing mass, and with a kind of antic, gaudy, party-coloured string, knit it under her neck. Being thus covered and muffled, she whiffed off a lusty good draught out of the boracho, took three several pence forth of the ram-cod fob, put them into so many walnut shells, which she set down upon the bottom of a feather-pot, and then, after she had given them three whisks of a broom besom athwart the chimney, casting into the fire half a bevin of long heather, together with a branch of dry laurel, she observed with a very hush and coy silence, in what form they did burn, and saw, that, although they were in a flame, they made no kind of noise, or crackling din. Hereupon she gave a most hideous and horribly dreadful shout, muttering betwixt her teeth some few barbarous words, of a strange termination.

This so terrified Panurge that he forthwith said to Epistemon, The devil mince me into a gallimaufry, if I do not tremble for fear! I do not think but that I am now enchanted; for she uttereth not her voice in the terms of any Christian language. O look, I pray you, how she seemeth unto me to be by three full spans higher than she was when she began to hood herself with her apron. What meaneth this restless wagging of her slouchy chaps? What can be the signification of the uneven shrugging of her hulchy shoulders? To what end does she quaver with her lips, like a monkey in the dismembering of a lobster? My ears through horror glow; ah! how they tingle! I think I hear the shrieking of Proserpina; the devils are breaking loose to be all here. O the foul, ugly, and deformed beasts! Let us run away! by the hook of God I am like to die for fear! I do not love the devils; they vex me, and are unpleasant fellows. Now let us fly, and betake us to our heels. Farewell, Gammer, thanks and grammercy for your goods! I will not marry, no, believe me, I will not. I fairly quit my interest therein, and totally abandon and renounce it from this time forward, even as much as at present. With this, as he endeavoured to make an escape out of the room, the old crone did anticipate his flight, and make him stop. The way how she prevented him was this. Whilst in her hand she held the spindle, she hurried out to a back-yard close by her lodge, where, after she had peeled off the bark of an old sycamore three several times, she very summarily, upon eight leaves which dropped from thence, wrote with the spindle-point some curt and briefly-couched verses, which she threw into the air, then said unto them, Search after them if you will; find them if you can; the fatal destinies of your marriage are written in them.

No sooner had she done thus speaking than she did withdraw herself unto her lurking-hole, where on the upper seat of the porch she tucked up her gown, her coats and smock, as high as her arm-pits, and gave them a full inspection of the nockandroe: which being perceived by Panurge, he said to Epistemon, God's bodikins, I see the sibyl's hole, where many have perished, in seeing: let's fly this hole. She suddenly then bolted the gate behind her, and was never since seen any more. They jointly ran in haste after the fallen and dispersed leaves, and gathered them at last, though not without great labour and toil, for the wind had scattered them amongst the thorn-bushes of the valley. When they had

ranged them each after other in their due places, they found out their sentence, as it is metrified in this octastic.

> Thy fame upheld,
> Even so, so:
> And she with child
> Of thee: No.
>
> Thy good end
> Suck she shall,
> And flay thee, friend,
> But not all.

CHAPTER 18

How Pantagruel and Panurge did diversely expound the verses of the Sibyl of Panzoust

THE leaves being thus collected, and orderly disposed, Epistemon and Panurge returned to Pantagruel's court, partly well pleased, and other part discontented: glad for their being come back, and vexed for the trouble they had sustained by the way, which they found to be craggy, rugged, stony, rough, and ill adjusted. They made an ample and full relation of their voyage unto Pantagruel; as likewise of the estate and condition of the sibyl. Then having presented to him the leaves of the sycamore, they show him the short and twattle verses that were written in them. Pantagruel, having read and considered the whole sum and substance of the matter, fetched from his heart a deep and heavy sigh, then said to Panurge: You are now, forsooth, in a good taking, and have brought your hogs to a fine market. The prophecy of the sibyl doth explain and lay out before us the very same predictions which have been denoted, foretold, and presaged to us by the decree of the Virgilian lots, and the verdict of your own proper dreams; to wit, that you shall be very much disgraced, shamed, and discredited by your wife: for that she will make you a cuckold, in prostituting herself to others, being big with child by another than you,—will steal from you a great deal of your goods, and will beat you, scratch, and bruise you, even to plucking the skin in a part from off you;—will leave the print of her blows in some member of your body. You understand as much, answered Panurge, in the veritable interpretation and expounding of recent prophecies, as a sow in the matter of spicery. Be not offended, sir, I beseech you, that I speak thus boldly; for I find myself a little in choler, and that not without cause, seeing it is the contrary that is true. Take heed, and give attentive ear unto my words. The old wife said, that as the bean is not seen till first it be unhusked, and that its swad or hull be shaled, and peeled from off it, so it is that my virtue and transcendant worth will never come by the mouth of fame to be blazed abroad, proportionable to the height, extent, and measure of the excellency thereof, until preallably I get a wife, and make the full half of a married couple. How many times have I heard you say, that the function of a magistrate, and office of dignity, discovereth the merits, parts, and endowments of the person so advanced and promoted, and what is in him. That is to say, we are then best able to judge aright of the deservings of a man, when he is called to the management of affairs: for, when before he lived in a private condition, we could have no more certain knowledge of him, than of a bean within his husk. And thus stands the first article explained: Otherwise could you imagine, that the good fame, repute, and estimation of an honest man should depend upon the tail of a whore?

Now to the meaning of the second article! My wife will be with child, here lies the prime felicity of marriage, but not of me. Copsody, that I do believe indeed! It will be of a pretty little infant. O how heartily I shall love it! I do already dote upon it; for it will be my dainty feedle-darling, my genteel dillyminion. From thenceforth no vexation, care, or grief shall take such deep impression in my heart, how hugely great or vehement soever it otherwise appear, but that it shall vanish forthwith, at the sight of that my future babe, and at the hearing of the chat and prating of its childish gibberish. And blessed be the old wife. By my truly, I have a mind to settle some good revenue or pension upon her, out of the readiest increase of the lands of my Salmigondinois; not an inconstant, and uncertain rent-seek, like that of witless, giddy-headed bachelors, but sure and fixed, of the nature of the well-paid incomes of regenting doctors. If this interpretation doth not please you, think you my wife will bear me in her flanks, conceive with me, and be of me delivered, as women use in childbed to bring forth their young ones; so as that it may be said, Panurge is a second Bacchus, he hath been twice born; he is re-born, as was Hippolytus, —as was Proteus, one time of Thetis, and secondly, of the mother of the philosopher Apollonius, as were the two Palici, near the flood Simæthos in Sicily. His wife was big of child with him. In him is renewed and begun again the palintokis of the Megarians, and the palingenesis of Democritus. Fie upon such errors! To hear stuff of that nature rends mine ears.

The words of the third article are: She will suck me at my best end. Why not? That pleaseth me right well. You know the thing; I need not tell you, that it is my intercrural pudding with one end. I swear and promise, that in what I can, I will preserve it sappy, full of juice, and as well victualled for her use as may be. She shall not suck me, I believe, in vain, nor be destitute of her allowance; there shall her *justum*[15] both in peck and lippy be furnished to the full eternally. You expound this passage allegorically, and interpret it to theft and larceny. I love the exposition, and the allegory pleaseth me; but not according to the sense whereto you stretch it. It may be, that the sincerity of the affection which you bear me moveth you to harbour in your breast those refractory thoughts concerning me, with a suspicion of my adversity to come. We have this saying from the learned, That a marvellously fearful thing is love, and that true love is never without fear. But, Sir, according to my judgment, you do understand both of and by yourself, that here stealth signifieth nothing else, no more than in a thousand other places of Greek and Latin, old and modern writings, but the sweet fruits of amorous dalliance, which Venus liketh best when reaped in secret, and culled by fervent lovers filchingly. Why so? I prithee tell. Because, when the feat of the loose coat skirmish happeneth to be done under-hand and privily, between two well-disposed, athwart the steps of a pair of stairs lurkingly, and in covert, behind a suit of hangings, or close hid and trussed upon an unbound faggot, it is more pleasing to the Cyprian goddess and to me also,—I speak this without prejudice to any better, or more sound opinion,—than to perform that culbusting art, after the Cynic manner, in the view of the clear sunshine, or in a rich tent, under a precious stately canopy, within a glorious and sublime pavilion, or yet on a soft couch betwixt rich curtains of cloth of gold, without affrightment, at long intermediate respites, enjoying of pleasures and delights a bellyful, all at great ease, with a huge fly-flap fan of crimson satin, and a bunch of feathers of some East Indian ostrich, serving to give chase unto the flies all round about; whilst, in the interim, the female picks her teeth with a stiff straw, picked even then from out of the bottom of the bed she lies on. If you be not content with this my exposition, are you of the mind that my wife will suck and sup me up, as people use to gulp and swallow oysters out of the shell? or as the Cicilian women, according to the testimony of Dioscorides, were wont to do the grain of Alkermes? Assuredly that is an error. Who seizeth on it, doth neither gulch up, nor swill down, but takes away what hath been packed up, catcheth, snatcheth, and plies the play of hey-pass, repass.

The fourth article doth imply, that my wife will flay me, but not all. O the fine word! You interpret this to beating strokes and blows. Speak wisely. Will you eat a pudding? Sir, I beseech you to raise up your spirits above the low-sized pitch of earthly thoughts unto that height of sublime contemplation, which reacheth to the apprehension of the mysteries and wonders of dame Nature. And here be pleased to condemn yourself, by a renouncing of those errors which you have committed very grossly, and somewhat perversely, in expounding the prophetic sayings of the holy sibyl. Yet put the case, (albeit I yield not to it,) that, by the instigation of the devil, my wife should go about to wrong me, make me a cuckold down to my very breech, disgrace me otherways, steal my goods from me, yea, and lay violently her hands upon me;—she nevertheless should fail of her attempts and not attain to the proposed end of her unreasonable undertakings. The reason which induceth me hereto, is totally grounded on this last point, which is extracted from the profoundest privacies of a monastic pantheology, as good Friar Arthur Wagtail told me once upon a Monday morning, as we were, (if I have not forgot,) eating a bushel of trotter-pies; and I remember well it rained hard. God give him the good morrow! The women at the beginning of the world, or a little after, conspired to flay the men quick, because they found the spirit of mankind inclined to domineer it, and bear rule over them upon the face of the whole earth; and, in pursuit of this their resolution, promised, confirmed, swore, and covenanted amongst themselves by the pure faith they owe to the nocturnal Sanct Rogero. But O the vain enterprises of women! O the great fragility of that sex feminine! They did begin to flay the man, or peel him,

(as says Catullus,) at that member which of all the body they loved best, to wit, the nervous and cavernous cane, and that above five thousand years ago; yet have they not of that small part alone flayed any more till this hour but the head. In mere despite whereof the Jews snip off that parcel of the skin in circumcision, choosing far rather to be called clipyards, rascals, than to be flayed by women, as are other nations. My wife, according to this female covenant, will flay it to me, if it be not so already. I heartily grant my consent thereto, but will not give her leave to flay it at all. Nay, truly will I not, my noble king.

Yea, but, quoth Epistemon, you say nothing of her most dreadful cries and exclamations, when she and we both saw the laurel-bough burn without yielding any noise or crackling. You know it is a very dismal omen, an inauspicious sign, unlucky indice, and token formidable, bad, disastrous, and most unhappy, as is certified by Propertius, Tibullus, the quick philosopher Porphyrius, Eustathius on the *Iliads* of Homer, and by many others. Verily, verily, quoth Panurge, brave are the allegations which you bring me, and testimonies of two-footed calves. These men were fools, as they were poets; and dotards, as they were philosophers; full of folly, as they were of philosophy.

CHAPTER 19
How Pantagruel praiseth the counsel of dumb men

PANTAGRUEL, when this discourse was ended, held for a pretty while his peace, seeming to be exceeding sad and pensive, then said to Panurge, The malignant spirit misleads, beguileth and seduceth you. I have read, that in times past the surest and most veritable oracles were not those which either were delivered in writing, or uttered by word of mouth in speaking. For many times, in their interpretation, right witty, learned and ingenious men have been deceived through amphibologies, equivoques, and obscurity of words, no less than by the brevity of their sentences. For which cause Apollo, the god of vaticination, was surnamed Λοξίας. Those which were represented then by signs and outward gestures, were accounted the truest and the most infallible. Such was the opinion of Heraclitus. And Jupiter did himself in this manner give forth in Ammon frequently predictions. Nor was he single in this practice; for Apollo did the like amongst the Assyrians. His prophesying thus unto those people moved them to paint him with a large long beard, and clothes beseeming an old settled person, of a most posed, staid, and grave behaviour; not naked, young, and beardless, as he was pourtrayed most usually amongst the Grecians. Let us make trial of this kind of fatidicency; and go you, take advice of some dumb person without any speaking. I am content, quoth Panurge. But, says Pantagruel, it were requisite that the dumb you consult with be such as have been deaf from the hour of their nativity, and consequently dumb, for none can be so lively, natural, and kindly dumb, as he who never heard.

How is it, quoth Panurge, that you conceive this matter? If you apprehend it so, that never any spoke, who had not before heard the speech of other, I will from that antecedent bring you to infer very logically a most absurd and paradoxical conclusion. But let it pass; I will not insist on it. You do not then believe what Herodotus wrote of two children, who at the special command and appointment of Psammeticus king of Egypt, having been kept in a pretty country cottage, where they were nourished and entertained in a perpetual silence, did at last, after a certain long space of time, pronounce this word *Bec*, which in the Phrygian language signifieth Bread. Nothing less, quoth Pantagruel, do I believe, that it is a mere abusing of our understandings to give credit to the words of those, who say that there is any such thing as a natural language. All speeches have had their primary origin from the arbitrary institutions, accords and agreements of nations in their respective condescendments to what should be noted and betokened by them. An articulate voice, according to the dialecticians, hath naturally no signification at all; for that the sense and meaning thereof did totally depend upon the good will and pleasure of the first deviser and imposer of it. I do not tell you this without a cause, for Bartholus, *Lib.* 5. *de Verb. Oblig.*, very seriously reporteth, that even in his time there was in Eugubia one named Sir Nello de Gabrielis, who, although he, by a sad mischance, became altogether deaf, understood, nevertheless, every one that talked in the Italian dialect howsoever he expressed himself; and that only by looking on his external gestures, and casting an attentive eye upon the divers motions of his lips and chaps. I have read, I remember

also, in a very literate and eloquent author, that Tyridates, King of Armenia, in the days of Nero, made a voyage to Rome, where he was received with great honour and solemnity, and with all manner of pomp and magnificence. Yea, to the end there might be a sempiternal amity and correspondence preserved betwixt him and the Roman Senate, there was no remarkable thing in the whole city which was not shown unto him. At his departure the emperor bestowed upon him many ample donatives of an inestimable value: and besides, the more entirely to testify his affection towards him, heartily entreated him to be pleased to make choice of any whatsoever thing in Rome was most agreeable to his fancy; with a promise juramentally confirmed, that he should not be refused of his demand. Thereupon, after a suitable return of thanks for a so gracious offer, he required a certain Jack-pudding, whom he had seen to act his part most egregiously upon the stage, and whose meaning, albeit he knew not what it was he had spoken, he understood perfectly enough by the signs and gesticulations which he had made. And for this suit of his, in that he asked nothing else, he gave this reason,—That in the several wide and spacious dominions, which were reduced under the sway and authority of his sovereign government, there were sundry countries and nations much differing from one another in language, with whom, whether he was to speak unto them, or give any answer to their requests, he was always necessitated to make use of divers sorts of truchmen and interpreters. Now with this man alone, sufficient for supplying all their places, will that great inconveniency hereafter be totally removed; seeing he is such a fine gesticulator, and in the practice of chirology an artist so complete, expert and dexterous, that with his very fingers he doth speak. Howsoever, you are to pitch upon such a dumb one as is deaf by nature, and from his birth; to the end that his gestures and signs may be the more vividly and truly prophetic, and not counterfeit by the intermixture of some adulterate lustre and affectation. Yet whether this dumb person shall be of the male or female sex, is in your option, lieth at your discretion, and altogether dependeth on your own election.

I would more willingly, quoth Panurge, consult with and be advised by a dumb woman, were it not that I am afraid of two things. The first is,—That the greater part of women, whatever it be that they see, do always represent unto their fancies, think and imagine, that it hath some relation to the sugared entering of the goodly ithyphallos, and graffing in the cleft of the overturned tree the quick-set-imp of the pin of copulation. Whatever signs, shews, or gestures we shall make, or whatever our behaviour, carriage or demeanour shall happen to be in their view and presence, they will interpret the whole in reference to the act of androgynation, and the culbutizing exercise; by which means we shall be abusively disappointed of our designs, in regard that she will take all our signs for nothing else but tokens and representations of our desire to entice her unto the lists of a Cyprian combat, or catsenconny skirmish. Do you remember what happened at Rome two hundred and three-score years after the foundation thereof? A young Roman gentleman encountering by chance at the foot of Mount Celion with a beautiful Latin lady named Verona, who from her very cradle upwards had always been deaf and dumb, very civilly asked her, not without a chironomatic Italianising of his demand, with various jectigation of his fingers, and other gesticulations, as yet customary amongst the speakers of that country, What senators, in her descent from the top of the hill, she had met with going up thither. For you are to conceive, that he, knowing no more of her deafness than dumbness, was ignorant of both. She in the meantime, who neither heard nor understood so much as one word of what he said, straight imagined, by all that she could apprehend in the lively gesture of his manual signs, that what he then required of her was, what herself had a great mind to, even that which a young man doth naturally desire of a woman. Then was it, that by signs, which in all occurrences of venereal love are incomparably more attractive, valid and efficacious than words, she beckoned to him to come along with her to her house; which when he had done, she drew him aside to a privy room, and then made a most lively alluring sign unto him, to show that the game did please her. Whereupon, without any more advertisement, or so much as the uttering of one word on either side, they fell to, and bringuardised it lustily.

The other cause of my being averse from consulting with dumb women is,—That to our signs they would make no answer at all, but suddenly fall backwards in a divaricating posture, to intimate thereby unto us the reality of their consent to the supposed motion of our tacit demands. Or if they should chance to make any counter-signs responsory to our propositions, they would prove so foolish, impertinent, and ridiculous, that by them ourselves should easily judge their thoughts to have no excursion beyond the duffling academy. You know very well how at Brignoles, when the religious nun, sister Fatbum, was made big with child by the young Stifflystand-to't, her pregnancy came to be known, and she, cited by the abbess, and in a full convention of the convent, accused of incest. Her excuse was,—That she did not consent thereto, but that it was done by the violence and impetuous force of the Friar Stiffly-stand-to't. Hereto the abbess very austerely replying, Thou naughty wicked girl, why didst thou not cry—A rape, a rape? then should all of us have run to thy succour. Her answer was,—that the rape was committed in the dortor, where she durst not cry, because it was a place of sempiternal silence. But, quoth the abbess, thou roguish wench, why didst not thou then make some sign to those that were in the next chamber beside thee? To this she answered, That with her buttocks she made a sign unto them as vigorously as she could, yet never one of them did so much as offer to come to her help and assistance. But, quoth the abbess, thou scurvy baggage, why didst not thou tell it me immediately after the perpetration of the fact, that so we might orderly, regularly, and canonically have accused him? I would have done so, had the case been mine, for the clearer manifestation of mine innocency. I truly, madam, would have done the like with all my heart and soul, quoth sister Fatbum; but that fearing I should remain in sin, and in the hazard of eternal damnation, if prevented by a sudden death, I did confess myself to the father friar before he went out of the room, who, for my penance, enjoined me not to tell it, or reveal the matter unto any. It were a most enormous and horrid offence, detestable before God and the angels, to reveal a confession. Such an abominable wickedness would have possibly brought down fire from heaven, wherewith to have burnt the whole nunnery, and sent us all headlong to the bottomless pit, to bear company with Corah, Dathan, and Abiram.

You will not, quoth Pantagruel, with all your jesting, make me laugh. I know that all the monks, friars, and nuns, had rather violate and infringe the highest of the commandments of God, than break the least of their provincial statutes. Take you therefore Goatsnose, a man very fit for your present purpose; for he is, and hath been both dumb and deaf from the very remotest infancy of his childhood.

CHAPTER 20

How Goatsnose by signs maketh answer to Panurge

GOATSNOSE being sent for, came the day thereafter to Pantagruel's court; at his arrival to which Panurge gave him a fat calf, the half of a hog, two puncheons of wine, one load of corn, and thirty franks of small money: then having brought him before Pantagruel, in presence of the gentlemen of the bed-chamber, he made this sign unto him. He yawned a long time, and in yawning made, without his mouth, with the thumb of his right hand, the figure of the Greek letter *Tau*, by frequent reiterations. Afterwards he lifted up his eyes heavenwards, then turned them in his head, like a she-goat in the painful fit of an absolute birth, in doing whereof he did cough and sigh exceeding heavily. This done, after that he had made demonstration of the want of his codpiece, he from under his shirt took his placket-racket in a full gripe, making it therewith clack very melodiously betwixt his thighs: then, no sooner had he with his body stooped a little forwards, and bowed his left knee, but that immediately thereupon holding both his arms on his breast, in a loose faint-like posture, the one over the other, he paused awhile. Goatsnose looked wistly upon him, and having heedfully enough viewed him all over, he lifted up into the air his left hand, the whole fingers whereof he retained fist ways closed together, except the thumb and the fore-finger, whose nails he softly joined and coupled to one another. I understand, quoth Pantagruel, what he meaneth by that sign. It denotes marriage, and withal the number thirty, according to the profession of the Pythagoreans. You will be married. Thanks to you, quoth Panurge, in turning himself towards Goatsnose, my little sewer, pretty master's mate, dainty baily, curious serjeant-marshal, and jolly catchpole leader. Then did he lift higher up than before his said left hand, stretching out all the five fingers thereof, and severing them as wide from one another as he possibly could get done.

Here, says Pantagruel, doth he more amply and fully insinuate unto us, by the token which he showeth forth of the quinary number, that you shall be married. Yea, that you shall not only be affianced, betrothed, wedded, and married, but that you shall furthermore cohabit, and live jollily and merrily with your wife; for Pythagoras called five the nuptial number, which, together with marriage, signifieth the consummation of matrimony, because it is composed of a ternary, the first of the odd, and binary, the first of the even numbers, as of a male and female knit and united together. In very deed it was the fashion of old in the city of Rome at marriage festivals to light five wax tapers, nor was it permitted kindle any more at the magnific nuptials of the most potent and wealthy; nor yet any fewer at the penurious weddings of the poorest and most abject of the world. Moreover in times past, the heathen, or paynims, implored the assistance of five deities, or of one, helpful, at least, in five several good offices to those that were to be married. Of this sort were the nuptial Jove; Juno, president of the feast the fair Venus; Pitho, the goddess of eloquence and persuasion; and Diana, whose aid and succour was required to the labour of child-bearing. Then shouted Panurge, O the gentle Goatsnose, I will give him a farm near Cinais, and a wind-mill hard by Mirebalais! Hereupon the dumb fellow sneezeth with an impetuous vehemency, and huge concussion of the spirits of the whole body, withdrawing himself in so doing with a jerking turn towards the left hand. By the body of a fox new slain, quoth Pantagruel, what is that? This maketh nothing for your advantage; for he betokeneth thereby that your marriage will be inauspicious and unfortunate. This sneezing, according to the doctrine of Terpsion, is the Socratic demon. If done towards the right side, it imports and portendeth, that boldly, and with all assurance, one may go whither he will, and do what he listeth, according to what deliberation he shall be pleased to have thereupon taken: his entries in the beginning, progress in his proceedings, and success in the events, and issues, will be all lucky, good, and happy. The quite contrary thereto is thereby implied and presaged, if it be done towards the left. You, quoth Panurge, do take always the matter at the worst, and continually, like another Davus, cast in new disturbances and obstructions; nor ever yet did I know this old paltry Terpsion worthy of citation, but in points only of cozenage and imposture. Nevertheless, quoth Pantagruel, Cicero hath written I know not what to the same purpose in his Second Book of *Divination*.

Panurge then turning himself towards Goatsnose made this sign unto him. He inverted his eye-lids upwards, wrenched his jaws from the right to the left side, and drew forth his tongue half out of his mouth. This done, he posited his left hand wholly open, the mid-finger wholly excepted, which was perpendicularly placed upon the palm thereof, and set it just in the room where his codpiece had been. Then did he keep his right hand altogether shut up in a fist, save only the thumb, which he straight turned backwards directly under the right arm-pit, and settled it afterwards on that most eminent part of the buttocks, which the Arabs call the *Al-Katim*. Suddenly thereafter he made this inter-change; he held his right hand after the manner of the left, and posited it on the place wherein his codpiece sometime was, and retaining his left hand in the form and fashion of the right, he placed it upon his *Al-Katim*. This altering of hands did he reiterate nine several times; at the last whereof he reseated his eye-lids into their own first natural position. Then doing the like also with his jaws and tongue, he did cast a squinting look upon Goatsnose, diddering and shivering his chaps, as apes use to do now-a-days, and rabbits, whilst, almost starved with hunger, they are eating oats in the sheaf.

Then was it that Goatsnose, lifting up into the air his right hand wholly open and displayed, put the thumb thereof, even close unto its first articulation, between the two third joints of the middle and ring fingers, pressing about the said thumb thereof very hard with them both, and, whilst the remainent joints were contracted and shrunk in towards the wrist, he stretched forth with as much straitness as he could the fore and little fingers. That hand, thus framed and disposed of, he laid and posited upon Panurge's navel, moving withal continually the aforesaid thumb, and bearing up, supporting, or under-propping that hand upon the above-specified fore and little fingers, as upon two legs. Thereafter did he make in this posture his hand by little and little, and by degrees and pauses, successively to mount from athwart the belly to the stomach, from whence he made it to ascend to the breast, even upwards to Panurge's neck,

still gaining ground, till having reached his chin, he had put within the concave of his mouth his afore-mentioned thumb; then fiercely brandishing the whole hand which he made to rub and grate against the nose, he heaved it further up, and made the fashion, is if with the thumb thereof he would have put out his eyes. With this Panurge grew a little angry and went about to withdraw, and rid himself from this ruggedly untoward dumb devil. But Goatsnose, in the meantime, prosecuting the intended purpose of his prognosticatory response, touched very rudely, with the above-mentioned shaking thumb, now his eyes, then his forehead, and, after that, the borders and corners of his cap. At last Panurge cried out, saying, Before God, master-fool, if you do not let me alone, or that you will presume to vex me any more, you shall receive from the best hand I have a mask, wherewith to cover your rascally scoundrel face, you paltry shitten varlet. Then said Friar John, He is deaf and doth not understand what thou sayest unto him. Bulli-ballock, make sign to him of a hail of fisticuffs upon the muzzle.

What the devil, quoth Panurge, means this busy restless fellow? What is it, that this poly-pragmonetic Aliboron to all the fiends of hell doth aim at? He hath almost thrust out mine eyes, as if he had been to poach them in a skillet of butter and eggs. By God, *da jurandi*,[16] I will feast you with flirts and raps on the snout, interlarded with a double row of bobs and finger fillipings! Then did he leave him in giving him by way of salvo a volley of farts for his farewell. Goatsnose, perceiving Panurge thus to slip away from him, got before him, and, by mere strength enforcing him to stand, made this sign unto him. He let fall his right arm toward his knee on the same side as low as he could, and, raising all the fingers of that hand into a close fist, passed his dexter thumb betwixt the foremost and mid-fingers thereto belonging. Then scrubbing and swinging a little with his left hand alongst, and upon the uppermost in the very bough of the elbow of the said dexter arm, the whole cubit thereof, by leisure fair and softly, at these thumpatory warnings, did raise and elevate itself even to the elbow, and above it; on a sudden, did he then let it fall down as low as before, and after that, at certain intervals and such spaces of time raising and abasing it, he made a show thereof to Panurge. This so incensed Panurge, that he forthwith lifted his hand to have stricken him the dumb roister, and given him a sound whirret on the ear, but that the respect and reverence which he carried to the presence of Pantagruel restrained his choler, and kept his fury within bounds and limits. Then said Pantagruel, If the bare signs now vex and trouble you, how much more grievously will you be perplexed and disquieted with the real things, which by them are represented and signified. All truths agree, and are consonant with one another. This dumb fellow prophesieth and foretelleth that you will be married, cuckolded, beaten, and robbed. As for the marriage, quoth Panurge, I yield thereto, and acknowledge the verity of that point of his prediction; as for the rest I utterly abjure and deny it; and believe, Sir, I beseech you, if it may please you so to do, that in the matter of wives and horses never any man was predestinated to a better fortune than I.

CHAPTER 21

How Panurge consulteth with an old French poet, named Raminagrobis

I NEVER thought, said Pantagruel, to have encountered with any man so headstrong in his apprehensions, or in his opinions so wilful, as I have found you to be, and see you are. Nevertheless, the better to clear and extricate your doubts, let us try all courses, and leave no stone unturned, nor wind unsailed by. Take good heed to what I am to say unto you. The swans, which are fowls consecrated to Apollo, never chant but in the hour of their approaching death, especially in the Meander flood, which is a river that runneth along some of the territories of Phrygia. This I say, because Ælianus and Alexander Myndius write, that they had seen several swans in other places die, but never heard any of them sing or chant before their death. However, it passeth for current that the imminent death of a swan is presaged by his foregoing song, and that no swan dieth until preallably he have sung.

After the same manner poets, who are under the protection of Apollo, when they are drawing near their latter end, do ordinarily become prophets, and by the inspiration of that god sing sweetly, in vaticinating things which are to come. It hath been likewise told me frequently, that old decrepit men upon the brinks of Charon's banks do usher their decease with a disclosure, all at ease, to those that are desirous of such informations, of the determinate and assured truth of future accidents and contingencies. I remember also that Aristophanes, in a certain comedy of his, calleth the old folks Sibyls, Εἶθ' ὁ γέρων Σιβυλλιᾷ. For as when, being upon a pier by the shore, we see afar off mariners, seafaring men, and other travellers alongst the curled waves of azure Thetis within their ships, we then consider them in silence only, and seldom proceed any further than to wish them a happy and prosperous arrival: but, when they do approach near to the haven, and come to wet their keels within their harbour, then both with words and gestures we salute them, and heartily congratulate their access safe to the port wherein we are ourselves. Just so the angels, heroes, and good demons, according to the doctrine of the Platonics, when they see mortals drawing near unto the harbour of the grave, as the most sure and calmest port of any, full of repose, ease, rest, tranquillity, free from the troubles and solicitudes of this tumultuous and tempestuous world; then is it that they with alacrity hail and salute them, cherish and comfort them, and, speaking to them lovingly, begin even then to bless them with illuminations, and to communicate unto them the abstrusest mysteries of divination. I will not offer here to confound your memory by quoting antique examples of Isaac, of Jacob, of Patroclus towards Hector, of Hector towards Achilles, of Polymnestor towards Agamemnon, of Hecuba, of the Rhodian renowned by Posidonius, of Calanus the Indian towards Alexander the Great, of Orodes towards Mezentius, and of many others. It shall suffice for the present, that I commemorate unto you the learned and valiant knight and cavalier William of Bellay, late Lord of Langey, who died on the Hill of Tarara, the 10th of January, in the climacteric year of his age, and of our supputation 1543, according to the Roman account. The last three or four hours of his life he did employ in the serious utterance of a very pithy discourse, whilst with a clear judgment, and spirit void of all trouble, he did foretell several important things, whereof a great deal is come to pass, and the rest we wait for. Howbeit, his prophecies did at that time seem unto us somewhat strange, absurd, and unlikely; because there did not then appear any sign of efficacy enough to engage our faith to the belief of what he did prognosticate. We have here near to the town of Villaumere, a man that is both old and a poet, to wit, Raminagrobis, who to his second wife espoused my Lady Broad-sow, on whom he begot the fair Basoche. It hath been told me he is a dying, and so near unto his latter end, that he is almost upon the very last moment, point, and article thereof. Repair thither as fast as you can, and be ready to give an attentive ear to what he shall chant unto you. It may be, that you shall obtain from him what you desire, and that Apollo will be pleased by his means to clear your scruples. I am content, quoth Panurge. Let us go thither, Epistemon, and that both instantly and in all haste, lest otherwise his death prevent our coming. Wilt thou come along with us, Friar John? Yes, that I will, quoth Friar John, right heartily to do thee a courtesy, my billy-ballocks; for I love thee with the best of my milt and liver.

Thereupon, incontinently, without any further lingering, to the way they all three went, and quickly thereafter—for they made good speed—arriving at the poetical habitation, they found the jolly old man, albeit in the agony of his departure from this world, looking cheerfully, with an open countenance, splendid aspect, and behaviour full of alacrity. After that Panurge had very civilly saluted him, he in a free gift did present him with a gold ring, which he even then put upon the medical finger of his left hand, in the collet or bezle whereof was inchased an oriental sapphire, very fair and large. Then, in imitation of Socrates, did he make an oblation unto him of a fair white cock; which was no sooner set upon the tester of his bed, than that with a high raised head and crest, lustily shaking his feather-coat, he crowed stentoriphonically loud. This done, Panurge very courteously required of him, that he would vouchsafe to favour him with the grant and report of his sense and judgment touching the future destiny of his intended marriage. For answer hereto, when the honest old man had forthwith commanded pen, paper, and ink to be brought unto him, and that he was at the same call conveniently served with all the three, he wrote these following verses:

Take, or not take her,
    Off, or on:
Handy-dandy is your lot.
When her name you write, you blot.

'Tis undone, when all is done,
Ended e'er it was begun:
Hardly gallop, if you trot,

Set not forward when you run,
Nor be single, though alone,
    Take, or not take her.

Before you eat begin to fast;
For what shall be was never past.
Say, unsay, gainsay, save your breath:
Then wish at once her life and death.
    Take, or not take her.

These lines he gave out of his own hands unto them, saying unto them, Go, my lads, in peace,—the great God of the highest heavens be your guardian and preserver; and do not offer any more to trouble or disquiet me with this or any other business whatsoever. I have this same very day, which is the last both of May and of me, with a great deal of labour, toil, and difficulty, chased out of my house a rabble of filthy, unclean, and plaguily pestilentious rake-hells, black beasts, dusk, dun, white, ash-coloured, speckled, and a foul vermin of other hues, whose obtrusive importunity would not permit me to die at my own ease; for by fraudulent and deceitful pricklings, ravenous, harpy-like graspings, waspish stingings, and such-like unwelcome approaches, forged in the shop of I know not what kind of insatiabilities, they went about to withdraw, and call me out of those sweet thoughts, wherein I was already beginning to repose myself, and acquiesce in the contemplation and vision, yea, almost in the very touch and taste of the happiness and felicity which the good God hath prepared for his faithful saints and elect in the other life, and state of immortality. Turn out of their courses, and eschew them, step forth of their ways, and do not resemble them; meanwhile, let me be no more troubled by you, but leave me now in silence, I beseech you.

CHAPTER 22

How Panurge patrocinates and defendeth the order of the begging Friars

PANURGE, at his issuing forth of Raminagrobis's chamber said, as if he had been horribly affrighted, By the virtue of God, I believe that he is an heretic;—the devil take me, if I do not! he doth so villanously rail at the mendicant friars and Jacobins, who are the two hemispheres of the Christian world; by whose gyronomonic[17] circumbilivaginations, as by two celivagous[18] filopendulums,[19] all the autonomatic metagrobolism of the Rom-

ish church, when tottering and emblustricat-
ed with the gibble gabble gibberish of this
odious error and heresy, is homocentrically
poised. But what harm, in the devil's name,
have these poor devils the Capuchins and
Minims done unto him? Are not these beggarly devils sufficiently wretched already?
Who can imagine that these poor snakes, the
very extracts of Ichthyophagy, are not thoroughly enough besmoked and besmeared with
misery, distress, and calamity? Dost thou
think, Friar John, by thy faith, that he is in
the state of salvation? He goeth, before God,
as surely damned to thirty thousand baskets
full of devils, as a pruning-bill to the lopping
of a vine-branch. To revile with opprobrious
speeches the good and courageous props and
pillars of the church,—is that to be called a
poetical fury? I cannot rest satisfied with him,
he sinneth grossly, and blasphemeth against
the true religion. I am very much offended at
his scandalizing words and contumelious ob-
loquy. I do not care a straw, quoth Friar
John, for what he hath said; for although everybody should twit and jerk them, it were
but a just retaliation, seeing all persons are
served by them with the like sauce; therefore
do I pretend no interest therein. Let us see
nevertheless what he hath written. Panurge
very attentively read the paper which the old
man had penned, then said to his two fellow-
travellers, The poor drinker doteth. Howsoever, I excuse him, for that I believe he is
now drawing near to the end, and final closure of his life. Let us go make his epitaph.
By the answer which he hath given us, I am
not, I protest, one jot wiser than I was.
Hearken here, Epistemon, my little bully,
dost not thou hold him to be very resolute in
his responsory verdicts? He is a witty, quick,
and subtle sophister. I will lay an even wager, that he is a miscreant apostate. By the belly of a stalled ox, how careful he is not to be
mistaken in his words. He answered but by
disjunctives, therefore can it not be true
which he saith; for the verity of such like
propositions is inherent only in one of its two
members. O the cozening prattler that he is!
I wonder if Santiago of Bressure be one of
these cogging shirks. Such was of old, quoth
Epistemon, the custom of the grand vaticinator and prophet Tiresias, who used always, by
way of a preface, to say openly and plainly at
the beginning of his divinations and predictions,—That what he was to tell would either
come to pass or not. And such is truly the
style of all prudently presaging prognostica-
tors. He was nevertheless, quoth Panurge, so
unfortunately misadventurous in the lot of his
own destiny, that Juno thrust out both his
eyes.

Yes, answered Epistemon, and that merely
out of a spite and spleen for having pronounced his award more veritably than she,
upon the question which was merrily proposed by Jupiter. But, quoth Panurge, what
arch-devil is it, that hath possessed this Master Raminagrobis, that so unreasonably, and
without any occasion, he should have so snap-
pishly, and bitterly inveighed against these
poor honest fathers, Jacobins, minors, and
minims? It vexeth me grievously, I assure
you; nor am I able to conceal my indignation. He hath transgressed most enormously;
his soul goeth infallibly to thirty thousand
panniers full of devils. I understand you not,
quoth Epistemon, and it disliketh me very
much, that you should so absurdly and perversely interpret that of the friar mendicants,
which by the harmless poet was spoken of
black beasts, dun, and other sorts of other
coloured animals. He is not in my opinion
guilty of such a sophistical and fantastic allegory, as by that phrase of his to have
meaned the begging brothers. He in downright terms speaketh absolutely and properly
of fleas, punies, hand worms, flies, gnats, and
other such like scurvy vermin, whereof some
are black, some dun, some ash-coloured,
some tawny, and some brown and dusky, all
noisome, molesting, tyrannous, cumbersome,
and unpleasant creatures, not only to sick and
diseased folks, but to those also who are of a
sound, vigorous, and healthful temperament
and constitution. It is not unlike, that he may
have the ascarids, and the lumbrics, and
worms within the entrails of his body. Possibly doth he suffer, as it is frequent and usual
amongst the Egyptians, together with all
those who inhabit the Erythræan confines,
and dwell along the shores and coasts of the
Red Sea, some sour prickings, and smart
stingings in his arms and legs of those little
speckled dragons, which the Arabians call
Meden. You are to blame for offering to expound his words otherwise, and wrong the ingenious poet, and outrageously abuse and
miscall the said fraters, by an imputation of
baseness undeservedly laid to their charge.
We still should, in such like discourses of fatil-
oquent soothsayers, interpret all things to the
best. Will you teach me, quoth Panurge, how

to discern flies among milk, or show your father the way how to beget children? He is, by the virtue of god, an arrant heretic, a resolute formal heretic; I say, a rooted riveted combustible heretic, one as fit to burn as the little wooden clock at Rochel. His soul goeth to thirty thousand carts full of devils. Would you know whither? Cocks-body, my friend, straight under Proserpina's close stool, to the very middle of the self-same infernal pan, within which, she, by an excrementitious exacuation, voideth the fecal stuff of her stinking clysters, and that just upon the left side of the great cauldron of three fathom height, hard by the claws and talons of Lucifer, in the very darkest of the passage which leadeth towards the back chamber of Demogorgon. O the villain!

CHAPTER 23

How Panurge maketh a motion of a return to Raminagrobis

LET us return, quoth Panurge, not ceasing, to the uttermost of our abilities, to ply him with wholesome admonitions, for the furtherance of his salvation. Let us go back for God's sake, let us go in the name of God. It will be a very meritorious work, and of great charity in us to deal so in the matter, and provide so well for him, that albeit he come to lose both body and life, he may at least escape the risk and danger of the eternal damnation of his soul. We will by our holy persuasions bring him to a sense and feeling of his escapes, induce him to acknowledge his faults, move him to a cordial repentance of his errors, and stir up in him such a sincere contrition of heart for his offences, as will prompt him with all earnestness to cry mercy, and to beg pardon at the hands of the good fathers, as well of the absent, as of such as are present. Whereupon we will take instrument formally and authentically extended, to the end he be not, after his decease, declared an heretic, and condemned, as were the hobgoblins of the provost's wife of Orleans, to the undergoing of such punishments, pains, and tortures, as are due to, and inflicted on those that inhabit the horrid cells of the infernal regions: and withal incline, instigate, and persuade him to bequeath, and leave in legacy, (by way of an amends and satisfaction for the outrage and injury done to those good religious fathers, throughout all the convents, cloisters, and monasteries of this province,) many

pittances, a great deal of mass-singing, store of *obits,* and that sempiternally, on the anniversary day of his decease, every one of them all to be furnished with a quintuple allowance, and that the great borrachoe, replenished with the best liquor, trudge apace along the tables, as well of the young duckling monkitoes, lay-brothers, and lowermost degree of the abbey-lubbards, as of the learned priests, and reverend clerks,—the very meanest of the novices and mitiants unto the order being equally admitted to the benefit of those funerary and obsequial festivals, with the aged rectors, and professed fathers. This is the surest ordinary means, whereby from God he may obtain forgiveness.

Ho, ho, I am quite mistaken, I digress from the purpose, and fly out of my discourse, as if my spirits were a woolgathering. The devil take me if I go thither! Virtue God! the chamber is already full of devils. O what a swingeing, thwacking noise is now amongst them! O the terrible coil that they keep! Hearken, do you not hear the rustling, thumping bustle of their strokes and blows, as they scuffle one with another, like true devils indeed, who shall gulp up the Raminagrobis soul, and be the first bringer of it, whilst it is hot, to Monsieur Lucifer? Beware, and get you hence: for my part I will not go thither. The devil roast me if I go! Who knows but that these hungry mad devils may in the haste of their rage, and fury of their impatience, take a *qui* for a *quo,* and instead of Raminagrobis, snatch up poor Panurge frank and free? Though formerly when I was deep in debt, they always failed. Get you hence! I will not go thither. Before God, the very bare apprehension thereof is like to kill me. To be in the place where there are greedy, famished, and hunger-starved devils; amongst factious devils—amidst trading and trafficking devils—O the Lord preserve me! Get you hence, I dare pawn my credit on it, that no Jacobin, Cordelier, Carmelite, Capuchin, Theatin, or Minim, will bestow any personal presence at his interment. The wiser they because he hath ordained nothing for them in his latter will and testament. The devil take me, if I go thither. If he be damned, to his own loss and hindrance be it. What the deuce moved him to be so snappish and depravedly bent against the good fathers of the true religion? Why did he cast them off, reject them, and drive them quite out of his chamber, even in that very nick of time when he stood in greatest need of the aid, suffrage, and assistance of their devout prayers, and holy admonitions? Why did not he by testament leave them, at least, some jolly lumps and cantles of substantial meat, a parcel of cheek-puffing victuals, and a little belly-timber, and provision for the guts of these poor folks, who have nothing but their life in this world? Let him go thither who will; the devil take me, if I go; for, if I should, the devil would not fail to snatch me up. *Cancro.* Ho, the pox! Get you hence, Friar John, art thou content that thirty thousand wainload of devils should get away with thee at this same very instant? If thou be, at my request do these three things. First, give me thy purse; for besides that thy money is marked with crosses, and the cross is an enemy to charms, the same may befall to thee, which not long ago happened to John Dodin, collector of the excise of Coudray, at the ford of Vede, when the soldiers broke the planks. This monied fellow, meeting at the very brink of the bank of the ford with Friar Adam Crankcod, a Franciscan Observatin of Mirebeau, promised him a new frock, provided that, in the transporting of him over the water he would bear him upon his neck and shoulders, after the manner of carrying dead goats; for he was a lusty, strong-limbed sturdy rogue. The condition being agreed upon, Friar Crankcod trusseth himself up to his very ballocks, and layeth upon his back, like a fair little Saint Christopher, the load of the said supplicant Dodin, and so carried him gaily and with a good will, (as Æneas bore his father Anchises through the conflagration of Troy,) singing in the meanwhile a pretty *Ave Maris Stella.*[20] When they were in the very deepest place of all the ford, a little above the master-wheel of the water-mill, he asked if he had any coin about him. Yes, quoth Dodin, a whole bag full; and that he needed not to mistrust his ability in the performance of the promise, which he had made unto him, concerning a new frock. How? quoth Friar Crankcod, thou knewest well enough, that by the express rules, canons, and injunctions of our order, we are forbidden to carry about us any kind of money. Thou art truly unhappy, for having made me in this point to commit a heinous trespass. Why didst thou not leave thy purse with the miller? Without fail thou shalt presently receive thy reward for it; and if ever hereafter I may but lay hold on thee within the limits of our chancel at Mirebeau, thou shalt have the *Miserere* even

to the *Vitulos.*[21] With this, suddenly discharging himself of his burden, he throws me down your Dodin headlong. Take example by this Dodin, my dear friend, Friar John, to the end that the devils may the better carry thee away at thine own ease. Give me thy purse. Carry no manner of cross upon thee. Therein lieth an evident and manifestly apparent danger. For, if you have any silver coined with a cross upon it, they will cast thee down headlong upon some rocks, as the eagles use to do with the tortoises for the breaking of their shells, as the bald pate of the poet Æschylus can sufficiently bear witness. Such a fall would hurt thee very sore, my sweet bully, and I would be sorry for it. Or otherwise they will let thee fall, and tumble down into the high swollen waves of some capacious sea, I know not where; but, I warrant thee, far enough hence, as Icarus fell; which from thy name would afterwards get the denomination of the Funnelian sea.

Secondly, Be out of debt. For the devils carry a great liking to those that are out of debt. I have sore felt the experience thereof in mine own particular; for now the lecherous varlets are always wooing me, courting me, and making much of me, which they never did when I was all to pieces. The soul of one in debt is insipid, dry, and heretical altogether.

Thirdly, with thy cowl and *Domino de Grobis,*[22] return to Raminagrobis; and in case being thus qualified, thirty thousand boats full of devils forthwith come out to carry thee quite away, I shall be content to be at the charge of paying for the pint and faggot. Now, if for the more security thou wouldst have some associate to bear thee company, let not me be the comrade thou searchest for; think not to get a fellow-traveller of me,—nay, do not. I advise thee for the best. Get you hence; I will not go thither; the devil take me if I go. Notwithstanding all the fright that you are in, quoth Friar John, I would not care so much, as might possibly be expected I should, if I once had but my sword in my hand. Thou hast verily hit the nail on the head, quoth Panurge, and speakest like a learned doctor, subtle and well-skilled in the art of devilry. At the time when I was a student in the University of Toulouse, that same reverend father in the devil, Picatrix, rector of the Diabological Faculty, was wont to tell us, that the devils did naturally fear the bright glancing of swords, as much as the splendour and light of the sun. In confirmation of the verity whereof, he related this story, that Hercules, at his descent into hell to all the devils of those regions, did not by half so much terrify them with his club and lion's skin, as afterwards Æneas did with his clear shining armour upon him, and his sword in his hand well furbished and unrusted, by the aid, council, and assistance of the Sibylla Cumana. That was perhaps the reason why the senior John James Trivolse, whilst he was a dying at Chartres, called for his cutlass, and died with a drawn sword in his hand, laying about him alongst and athwart around the bed, and everywhere within his reach, like a stout, doughty, valorous, and knight-like cavalier; by which resolute manner of fence he scared away and put to flight all the devils that were then lying in wait for his soul at the passage of his death. When the Massorets and Cabalists are asked,—Why it is that none of all the devils do at any time enter into the terrestrial paradise? their answer has been, is, and will be still,—That there is a cherubim standing at the gate thereof with a flame-like glistering sword in his hand. Although, to speak in the true diabological sense or phrase of Toledo, I must needs confess and acknowledge, that veritably the devils cannot be killed, or die by the stroke of a sword: I do nevertheless avow and maintain, according to the doctrine of the said Diabology, that they may suffer a solution of continuity, (as if with thy shable thou shouldest cut athwart the flame of a burning fire, or the gross opacous exhalations of a thick and obscure smoke,) and cry out, like very devils, at their sense and feeling of this dissolution, which in real deed I must aver and affirm is devilishly painful, smarting, and dolorous.

When thou seest the impetuous shock of two armies, and vehement violence of the push in their horrid encounter with one another, dost thou think, Ballockasso, that so horrible a noise as is heard there, proceedeth from the voice and shouts of men? the dashing and jolting of harness? the clattering and clashing of armies? the hacking and slashing of battleaxes? the justling and crashing of pikes? the bustling and breaking of lances? the clamour and shrieks of the wounded? the sound and din of drums? the clangour and shrillness of trumpets? the neighing and rushing in of horses? with the fearful claps and thundering of all sorts of guns, from the double cannon to the pocket pistol inclusively? I cannot, goodly, deny, but that in these vari-

ous things which I have rehearsed there may be somewhat occasionative of the huge yell and tintamarre of the two engaged bodies. But the most fearful and tumultuous coil and stir, the terriblest and most boisterous garboil and hurry, the chiefest rustling Black Santus[23] of all, and most principal hurly burly, springeth from the grievously plangorous howling and lowing of devils, who, pell-mell, in a hand-over-head confusion, waiting for the poor souls of the maimed and hurt soldiery, receive unawares some strokes with swords, and so by those means suffer a solution of, and division in, the continuity of their aerial and invisible substances: as if some lackey, snatching at the lard-slices, stuck in a piece of roast meat on the spit, should get from Mr. Greasyfist a good rap on the knuckles with a cudgel. They cry out and shout like devils, even as Mars did, when he was hurt by Diomedes at the siege of Troy, who, as Homer testifieth of him, did then raise his voice more horrifically loud, and sonoriferously high, than ten thousand men together would have been able to do. What maketh all this for our present purpose? I have been speaking here of well-furbished armour and bright shining swords. But so is it not, Friar John, with thy weapon; for by a long discontinuance of work, cessation from labour, desisting from making it officiate, and putting it into that practice wherein it had been formerly accustomed, and, in a word, for want of occupation, it is, upon my faith, become more rusty than the key-hole of an old powdering-tub. Therefore it is expedient that you do one of these two things, either furbish your weapon bravely, and as it ought to be, or otherwise have a care, that, in the rusty case it is in, you do not presume to return to the house of Raminagrobis. For my part, I vow I will not go thither. The devil take me if I go.

CHAPTER 24

How Panurge consulteth with Epistemon

HAVING left the town of Villaumere, as they were upon their return towards Pantagruel, Panurge, in addressing his discourses to Epistemon, spoke thus. My most ancient friend and gossip, thou seest the perplexity of my thoughts, and knowest many remedies for the removal thereof; art thou not able to help and succour me? Epistemon, thereupon taking the speech in hand, represented unto Panurge, how the open voice and common fame of the whole country did run upon no other discourse, but the derision and mockery of his new disguise; whereof his counsel unto him was, that he would in the first place be pleased to make use of a little hellebore, for the purging of his brain of that peccant humour, which through that extravagant and fantastic mummery of his had furnished the people with a too just occasion of flouting and gibing, jeering and scoffing him, and that next he would resume his ordinary fashion of accoutrement, and go apparelled as he was wont to do. I am, quoth Panurge, my dear gossip Epistemon, of a mind and resolution to marry, but am afraid of being a cuckold, and to be unfortunate in my wedlock. For this cause have I made a vow to young St. Francis,—who at Plessis le Tours is much reverenced of all women, earnestly cried unto by them, and with great devotion; for he was the first founder of the confraternity of good men, whom they naturally covet, affect, and long for:—to wear spectacles in my cap, and to carry no codpiece in my breeches, until the present inquietude and perturbation of my spirits be fully settled.

Truly, quoth Epistemon, that is a pretty jolly vow, of thirteen to a dozen. It is a shame to you, and I wonder much at it, that you do not return unto yourself, and recall your senses from this their wild swerving and straying abroad, to that rest and stillness which becomes a virtuous man. This whimsical conceit of yours brings me to the remembrance of a solemn promise made by the shaghaired Argives, who, having in their controversy against the Lacedæmonians for the territory of Thyrea, lost the battle, which they hoped should have decided it for their advantage, vowed to carry never any hair on their heads, till preallably they had recovered the loss of both their honour and lands. As likewise to the memory of the vow of a pleasant Spaniard called Michael Doris, who vowed to carry in his hat a piece of the skin of his leg, till he should be revenged of him who had struck it off. Yet do not I know which of these two deserveth most to wear a green and yellow hood with a hare's ears tied to it, either the aforesaid vain-glorious champion, or that Enguerrant, who, having forgot the art and manner of writing histories, set down by the Samosatian philosopher, maketh a most tediously long narrative and relation thereof. For, at the first reading of such

a profuse discourse, one would think it had been broached for the introducing of a story of great importance and moment concerning the waging of some formidable war, or the notable change and mutation of potent states and kingdoms; but, in conclusion, the world laugheth at the capricious champion, at the Englishman who had affronted him, as also at their scribbler Enguerrant, more drivelling at the mouth than a mustard pot. The jest and scorn thereof is not unlike to that of the mountain of Horace, which by the poet was made to cry out and lament most enormously, as a woman in the pangs and labour of child-birth, at which deplorable and exorbitant cries and lamentations the whole neighbourhood being assembled in expectation to see some marvellous monstrous production, could at last perceive no other but the paltry ridiculous mouse.

Your mousing, quoth Panurge, will not make me leave my musing, why folks should be so frumpishly disposed, seeing I am certainly persuaded that some flout, who merit to be flouted at; yet, as my vow imports, so will I do. It is now a long time since, by Jupiter, we did swear faith and amity to one another. Give me your advice, billy, and tell me your own opinion freely, should I marry or no? Truly, quoth Epistemon, the case is hazardous, and the danger so eminently apparent, that I find myself too weak and insufficient to give you a punctual and peremptory resolution therein; and if ever it was true, that judgment is difficult in matters of the medicinal art, what was said by Hippocrates of Lango, it is certainly so in this case. True it is, that in my brain there are some rolling fancies, by means whereof somewhat may be pitched upon of a seeming efficacy to the disentangling your mind of those dubious apprehensions wherewith it is perplexed; but they do not thoroughly satisfy me. Some of the Platonic sect affirm, that whosoever is able to see his proper Genius, may know his own destiny. I understand not their doctrine, nor do I think that you adhere to them; there is a palpable abuse. I have seen the experience of it in a very curious gentleman of the country of Estangourre. This is one of the points. There is yet another not much better. If there were any authority now in the oracles of Jupiter Ammon; of Apollo in Lebadia, Delphos, Delos, Cyrra, Patara, Tegyres, Preneste, Lycia, Colophon, or in the Castilian Fountain; near Antiochia in Syria, between the Branchidians; of Bacchus in Dodona; of Mercury in Phares, near Patras; of Apis in Egypt; of Serapis in Canope; of Faunus in Menalia, and Albunea near Tivoli; of Tiresias in Orchomenus; of Mopsus in Cilicia; of Orpheus in Lesbos, and of Trophonius in Leucadia; I would in that case advise you, and possibly not, to go thither for their judgment concerning the design and enterprise you have in hand. But you know that they are all of them become as dumb as so many fishes, since the advent of that Saviour King, whose coming to this world hath made all oracles and prophecies to cease; as the approach of the sun's radiant beams expelleth goblins, bugbears, hob-thrushes, broams, screech owlmates, night-walking spirits, and tenebrions. These now are gone; but although they were as yet in continuance and in the same power, rule, and request that formerly they were, yet would not I counsel you to be too credulous in putting any trust in their responses. Too many folks have been deceived thereby. It stands, furthermore, upon record, how Agrippina did charge the fair Lollia with the crime of having interrogated the oracle of Apollo Clarius, to understand if she should be at any time married to the Emperor Claudius: for which cause she was at first banished, and thereafter put to a shameful and ignominious death.

But, saith Panurge, let us do better; the Ogygian Islands are not far distant from the haven of Sammalo. Let us, after that we shall have spoken to our king, make a voyage thither. In one of these four isles, to wit that which hath its primest aspect towards the sun setting, it is reported, and I have read in good antique and authentic authors, that there reside many soothsayers, fortune-tellers, vaticinators, prophets, and diviners of things to come; that Saturn inhabiteth that place, bound with fair chains of gold, and within the concavity of a golden rock, being nourished with divine ambrosia and nectar, which are daily in great store and abundance transmitted to him from the heavens, by I do not well know what kind of fowls,—it may be that they are the same ravens, which in the deserts are said to have fed St. Paul, the first hermit,—he very clearly foretelleth unto every one, who is desirous to be certified of the condition of his lot, what his destiny will be, and what future chance the fates have ordained for him; for the Parcæ, or Weird Sisters, do not twist, spin, or draw out a thread, nor yet

doth Jupiter perpend, project, or deliberate any thing, which the good old celestial father knoweth not to the full, even whilst he is asleep. This will be a very summary abbreviation of our labour, if we but hearken unto him a little upon the serious debate and canvassing of this my perplexity. That is, answered Epistemon, a gullery too evident, a plain abuse and fib too fabulous. I will not go, not I, I will not go.

CHAPTER 25
How Panurge consulteth with Her Trippa

NEVERTHELESS, quoth Epistemon, continuing his discourse, I will tell you what you may do, if you believe me, before we return to our king. Hard by here, in the Brown-wheat [Bouchart] Island, dwelleth Her Trippa. You know how by the arts of astrology, geomancy, chiromancy, metopomancy, and others of a like stuff and nature, he foretelleth all things to come; let us talk a little, and confer with him about your business. Of that, answered Panurge, I know nothing: but of this much concerning him I am assured, that one day, and that not long since, whilst he was prating to the great king, of celestial, sublime, and transcendent things, the lacqueys and footboys of the court, upon the upper steps of stairs between two doors, jummed, one after another, as often as they listed, his wife; who is passable fair, and a pretty snug hussy. Thus he who seemed very clearly to see all heavenly and terrestrial things without spectacles, who discoursed boldly of adventures passed, with great confidence opened up present cases and accidents, and stoutly professed the presaging of all future events and contingencies, was not able with all the skill and cunning that he had to perceive the bumbasting of his wife, whom he reputed to be very chaste; and hath not till this hour got notice of anything to the contrary. Yet let us go to him, seeing you will have it so; for surely we can never learn too much. They on the very next ensuing day came to Her Trippa's lodging. Panurge by way of donative, presented him with a long gown lined all through with wolf-skins, with a short sword mounted with a gilded hilt, and covered with a velvet scabbard, and with fifty good single angels: then in a familiar and friendly way did he ask of him his opinion touching the affair. At the very first Her Trippa, looking on him very wistly in the face, said unto him:—Thou hast the metaposcopy, and physiognomy of a cuck-old,—I say, of a notorious and infamous cuck-old. With this, casting an eye upon Panurge's right hand in all the parts thereof, he said, This rugged draught which I see here, just under the mount of Jove, was never yet but in the hand of a cuckold. Afterwards, he with a white lead pen swiftly and hastily drew a certain number of divers kinds of points, which by rules of geomancy he coupled and joined together, then said: Truth itself is not truer, than that it is certain, thou wilt be a cuckold, a little after thy marriage. That be-ing done, he asked of Panurge the horoscope of his nativity; which was no sooner by Pan-urge tendered unto him, than that, erecting a figure, he very promptly and speedily formed and fashioned a complete fabric of the houses of heaven, in all their parts, whereof when he had considered the situation and the aspects in their triplicities, he fetched a deep sigh, and said; I have clearly enough already dis-covered unto you the fate of your cuckoldry, which is unavoidable, you cannot escape it. And here have I got new and further assur-ance thereof, so that I may now hardly pro-nounce, and affirm without any scruple or hesitation at all, that thou wilt be a cuckold; that furthermore, thou wilt be beaten by thine own wife, and that she will purloin, filch, and steal of thy goods from thee; for I find the seventh house in all its aspects, of a mal-ignant influence, and every one of the planets threatening thee with disgrace, according as they stand seated towards one another, in re-lation to the horned signs of Aries, Taurus, and Capricorn. In the fourth house I find Jupi-ter in a decadence, as also in a tetragonal as-pect to Saturn, associated with Mercury. Thou wilt be soundly peppered, my good honest fellow, I warrant thee. I will be? answered Panurge. A plague rot thee, thou old fool, and doating sot, how graceless and unpleas-ant thou art! When all cuckolds shall be at a general rendezvous, thou shouldst be their standard-bearer. But whence comes this ci-ron-worm betwixt these two fingers? This Panurge said, putting the fore finger of his left hand betwixt the fore and mid finger of the right, which he thrust out towards Her Trippa, holding them open after the manner of two horns, and shutting into his fist his thumb with the other fingers. Then, in turn-ing to Epistemon, he said,—Lo here the true *Olus* of Martial, who addicted and devoted himself wholly to the observing the miseries,

crosses, and calamities of others, whilst his own wife, in the interim, did keep an open bawdy-house. This varlet is poorer than ever was Irus, and yet he is proud, vaunting, ar-rogant, self-conceited, over-weening, and more insupportable than seventeen devils; in one word, Πτωχαλάζων, which term of old was applied to the like beggarly strutting cox-combs. Come, let us leave this madpash bed-lam, this hair-brained fop, and give him leave to rave and doze his bellyfull, with his pri-vate and intimately acquainted devils; who, if they were not the very worst of all infernal fiends, would never have deigned to serve such a knavish, barking cur as this is. He hath not learnt the first precept of philosophy, which is, *Know thyself;* for, whilst he brag-geth and boasteth, that he can discern the least mote in the eye of another, he is not able to see the huge block that puts out the sight of both his eyes. This is such another Poly-pragmon, as is by Plutarch described. He is of the nature of the Lamian witches, who in foreign places, in the houses of strangers, in public and amongst the common people, had a sharper and more piercing inspection into their affairs than any lynx; but at home in their own proper dwelling-mansions were blinder than mold-warps, and saw nothing at all. For their custom was, at their return from abroad, when they were by themselves in pri-vate, to take their eyes out of their head, from whence they were as easily removable, as a pair of spectacles from their nose, and to lay them up into a wooden slipper, which for that purpose did hang behind the door of their lodging.

Panurge had no sooner done speaking, when Her Trippa took into his hand a tama-risk branch. In this, quoth Epistemon, he doth very well, right, and like an artist, for Nicander calleth it the Divinatory tree. Have you a mind, quoth Her Trippa, to have the truth of the matter yet more fully and amply disclosed unto you by pyromancy, by aero-mancy, whereof Aristophanes in his *Clouds* maketh great estimation, by hydromancy, by lecanomancy,[24] of old in prime request amongst the Assyrians, and thoroughly tried by Hermolaus Barbarus? Come hither, and I will show thee in this platter full of fair fountain water, thy future wife, lechering and sercroupierising it with two swaggering ruffians, one after another. Yea, but have a special care, quoth Panurge, when thou com-est to put thy nose within mine arse, that thou forget not to pull off thy spectacles. Her Trippa, going on in his discourse, said, By catoptromancy,[25] likewise held in such account by the Emperor Didius Julianus, that by means thereof he ever and anon foresaw all that which at any time did happen or befall unto him. Thou shalt not need to put on thy spectacles, for in a mirror thou wilt see her as clearly and manifestly nebrundiated, and billibodring it, as if I should show it in the fountain of the temple of Minerva, near Patras. By coscinomancy,[26] most religiously observed of old amidst the ceremonies of the ancient Romans. Let us have sieve and shears, and thou shalt see devils. By alphitomancy,[27] cried up by Theocritus in his *Pharmaceutria*. By aleuromancy, mixing the flower of wheat with oatmeal. By astragalomancy,[28] whereof I have the plots and models all at hand ready for the purpose. By tyromancy,[29] whereof we make some proof in a great Brehemont cheese, which I here keep by me. By gyromancy, if thou shouldest turn round circles, thou mightest assure thyself from me, that they would fall always on the wrong side. By sternomancy,[30] which maketh nothing for thy advantage, for thou hast an ill proportioned stomach. By libanomancy,[31] for the which we shall need but a little frankincense. By gastromancy, which kind of ventral fatiloquency was for a long time together used in Ferrara by Lady Giacoma Rodogina, the Engastrimythian prophetess. By cephalomancy, often practised amongst the High Germans, in their boiling of an ass's head upon burning coals. By ceromancy, where, by the means of wax dissolved into water, thou shalt see the figure, portrait, and lively representation of thy future wife, and of her fredin fredaliatory belly-thumping blades. By capnomancy,[32] O the gallantest and most excellent of all secrets! By axionomancy; we want only a hatchet and a jet-stone to be laid together upon a quick fire of hot embers. O how bravely Homer was versed in the practice hereof towards Penelope's suitors! By onychomancy, for that we have oil and wax. By tephromancy,[33] thou wilt see the ashes thus aloft dispersed, exhibiting thy wife in a fine posture. By botanomancy, for the nonce I have some few leaves in reserve. By sycomancy; O divine art in fig-tree leaves. By icthyomancy, in ancient times so celebrated, and put in use by Tiresias and Polydamus, with the like certainty of event as was tried of old at the Dina-ditch, within that grove conse-

crated to Apollo, which is in the territory of the Lycians. By chœromancy, let us have a great many hogs, and thou shalt have the bladder of one of them. By cleromancy,[34] as the bean is found in the cake at the Epiphany vigil. By anthropomancy,[35] practised by the Roman Emperor Heliogabalus. It is somewhat irksome, but thou wilt endure it well enough, seeing thou art destined to be a cuckold. By a sibylline stichomancy.[36] By onomatomancy.[37] How do they call thee? Chaw-turd, quoth Panurge. Or yet by alectryomancy. If I should here with a compass draw a round, and in looking upon thee, and considering thy lot divide the circumference thereof into four and twenty equal parts, then form a several letter of the alphabet upon every one of them; and lastly, posit a barley corn or two upon each of these so disposed letters, I durst promise upon my faith and honesty, that if a young virgin cock be permitted to range alongst and athwart them, he should only eat the grains which are set and placed upon these letters, A. C.u.c.k.o.l.d. T.h.o.u. S.h.a.l.t. B.e. And that as fatidically as under the Emperor Valens, most perplexedly desirous to know the name of him who should be his successor to the empire, the cock, vaticinating and alectryomantic, ate up the pickles that were deposited on the letters Θ. E. O. Δ. T.h.e.o.d. Or, for the more certainty, will you have a trial of your fortune by the art of aruspiciny?[38] By augury? Or by extispiciny?[39] By turdispiciny, quoth Panurge. Or yet by the mystery of necromancy? I will, if you please, suddenly set up again, and revive some one lately deceased, as Apollonius of Tyane did to Achilles, and the Pytheness in the presence of Saul; which body, so raised up and re-quickened, will tell us the sum of all you shall require of him: no more nor less than, at the invocation of Erictho, a certain defunct person foretold to Pompey the whole progress and issue of the fatal battle fought in the Pharsalian fields? Or, if you be afraid of the dead, as commonly all cuckolds are, I will make use of the faculty of sciomancy.[40]

Go, get thee gone, quoth Panurge, thou frantic ass, to the devil, and be buggered, filthy bardachio that thou art, by some Albanian, for a steeple-crowned hat. Why the devil didst not thou counsel me as well to hold an emerald, or the stone of a hyena under my tongue? Or to furnish and provide myself with tongues of whoops, and hearts of green frogs? Or to eat the liver and milt of some

dragon? To the end that by those means I
might, at the chanting and chirping of swans
and other fowls, understand the substance of
my future lot and destiny, as did of old the
Arabians in the country of Mesopotamia? Fifteen brace of devils seize upon the body and
soul of this horned renagado, miscreant,
cuckold, the enchanter, witch, and sorcerer
of antichrist; away to all the devils of hell?
Let us return towards our king, I am sure he
will not be well pleased with us, if he once
come to get notice that we have been in the
kennel of this muffled devil. I repent my being come hither. I would willingly dispense
with a hundred nobles, and fourteen yeomen,
on condition that he, who not long since did
blow in the bottom of my breeches, should
instantly with his squirting spittle inluminate
his moustaches. O Lord God now! how the
villain hath besmoked me with vexation and
anger, with charms and witchcraft, and with
a terrible coil and stir of infernal and Tartari-
an devils! The devil take him! Say *Amen,*
and let us go drink. I shall not have any appetite for my victuals, how good cheer soever I
make these two days to come,—hardly these
four.

CHAPTER 26

*How Panurge consulteth with Friar John of
the Funnels*

PANURGE was indeed very much troubled in
mind, and disquieted at the words of Her
Trippa, and therefore as he passed by the little village of Huymes, after he had made his
address to Friar John, in pecking at, rubbing
and scratching his own left ear, he said unto
him, Keep me a little jovial and merry, my
dear and sweet bully, for I find my brains altogether metagrabolized and confounded,
and my spirits in a most dunsical puzzle at
the bitter talk of this devilish, hellish,
damned, fool. Hearken my dainty cod.

Mellow c.	Mounted c.
Lead-coloured c.	Sleeked c.
Knurled c.	Diapred c.
Suborned c.	Spotted c.
Desired c.	Master c.
Stuffed c.	Seeded c.
Speckled c.	Lusty c.
Finely-metalled c.	Jupped c.
Arabian-like c.	Milked c.
Trussed up grey-	Calfeted c.
hound-like c.	Raised c.

Odd c.	Resolute c.
Steeled c.	Cabbage-like c.
Stale c.	Courteous c.
Orange-tawny c.	Fertile c.
Embroidered c.	Whizzing c.
Glazed c.	Neat c.
Interlarded c.	Common c.
Burgher-like c.	Brisk c.
Impowdered c.	Quick c.
Ebonized c.	Barelike c.
Brasiliated c.	Partitional c.
Organized c.	Patronymic c.
Passable c.	Cockney c.
Trunkified c.	Auromercuriated c.
Furious c.	Robust c.
Packed c.	Appetizing c.
Hooded c.	Succourable c.
Varnished c.	Redoubtable c.
Renowned c.	Affable c.
Matted c.	Memorable c.
Genetive c.	Palpaple c.
Gigantal c.	Barbable c.
Oval c.	Tragical c.
Claustral c.	Transpontine c.
Viril c.	Digestive c.
Stayed c.	Active c.
Massive c.	Vital c.
Manual c.	Magistral c.
Absolute c.	Monarchal c.
Well-set c.	Subtil c.
Gemel c.	Hammering c.
Turkish c.	Clashing c.
Burning c.	Tingling c.
Thwacking c.	Usual c.
Urgent c.	Exquisite c.
Handsome c.	Trim c.
Prompt c.	Succulent c.
Fortunate c.	Factious c.
Boxwood c.	Clammy c.
Latten c.	Fat c.
Unbridled c.	High-prized c.
Hooked c.	Requisite c.
Researched c.	Laycod c.
Encompassed c.	Hand-filling c.
Strouting out c.	Insuperable c.
Jolly c.	Agreeable c.
Lively c.	Formidable c.
Gerundive c.	Profitable c.
Franked c.	Notable c.
Polished c.	Musculous c.
Poudered Beef c.	Subsidiary c.
Positive c.	Satyric c.
Spared c.	Repercussive c.
Bold c.	Convulsive c.
Lascivious c.	Restorative c.
Gluttonous c.	Masculinating c.

Incarnative c.
Sigillative c.
Sallying c.
Plump c.
Thundering c.
Lechering c.
Fulminating c.
Sparkling c.
Ramming c.
Lusty c.
Household c.
Pretty c.
Astrolabian c.
Algebraical c.
Venust c.
Aromatizing c.
Trixy c.
Paillard c.
Gaillard c.
Broaching c.
Addle c.
Syndicated c.
Boulting c.
Snorting c.
Pilfering c.
Shaking c.
Bobbing c.
Chiveted c.
Fumbling c.
Topsyturvying c.
Raging c.
Piled up c.
Filled up c.
Manly c.
Idle c.
Membrous c.
Strong c.
Twin c.
Belabouring c.
Gentle c.
Stirring c.
Confident c.
Nimble c.
Roundheaded c.
Figging c.
Helpful c.
Spruce c.
Plucking c.
Ramage c.
Fine c.
Fierce c.
Brawny c.
Compt c.
Repaired c.
Soft c.
Wild c.

Renewed c.
Quaint c.
Starting c.
Fleshy c.
Auxiliary c.
New vamped c.
Improved c.
Malling c.
Sounding c.
Battled c.
Burly c.
Seditious c.
Wardian c.
Protective c.
Twinkling c.
Able c.
Algoristical c.
Odoriferous c.
Pranked c.
Jocund c.
Routing c.
Purloining c.
Frolic c.
Wagging c.
Ruffling c.
Jumbling c.
Rumbling c.
Thumping c.
Bumping c.
Cringeling c.
Berumpling c.
Jogging c.
Nobbing c.
Touzing c.
Tumbling c.
Fambling c.
Overturning c.
Shooting c.
Culeting c.
Jagged c.
Pinked c.
Arsiversing c.
Polished c.
Slasht c.
Hamed c.
Leisurely c.
Cut c.
Smooth c.
Depending c.
Independent c.
Lingering c.
Rapping c.
Reverend c.
Nodding c.
Disseminating c.
Affecting c.

Affected c.
Grappled c.
Stuffed c.
Well-fed c.
Flourished c.
Fallow c.
Sudden c.
Grasp-full c.
Swillpow c.
Crushing c.
Creaking c.
Dilting c.
Ready c.
Vigorous c.
Skulking c.

Superlative c.
Clashing c.
Wagging c.
Scriplike c.
Encremastered c.
Bouncing c.
Levelling c.
Fly-flap c.
Perinæ-tegminal c.
Squat couching c.
Short-hung c.
The hypogastrian c.
Witness-bearing c.
Testigerous c.
Instrumental c.

My harcabuzing cod, and buttock-stirring ballock, Friar John, my friend, I do carry a singular respect unto thee, and honour thee with all my heart. Thy counsel I hold for a choice and delicate morsel, therefore have I reserved it for the last bit. Give me thy advice freely, I beseech thee, Should I marry, or no? Friar John very merrily, and with a sprightly cheerfulness, made this answer to him. Marry, in the devil's name. Why not? What the devil else shouldst thou do, but marry? Take thee a wife and furbish her harness to some tune. Swinge her skin-coat, as if thou wert beating on a stock-fish; and let the repercussion of thy clapper from her resounding metal make a noise, as if a double peal of chiming-bells were hung at the cremasters of thy ballocks. As I say, marry, so do I understand, that thou shouldst fall to work, as speedily as may be: yea, my meaning is, that thou oughtest to be so quick and forward therein, as on this same very day, before sun-set, to cause proclaim thy banns of matrimony, and make provision of bedsteads. By the blood of a hog's-pudding, till when wouldst thou delay the acting of a husband's part? Dost thou not know, and is it not daily told unto thee, that the end of the world approacheth? We are nearer it by three poles, and half a fathom, than we were two days ago. The antichrist is already born, at least it is so reported by many. The truth is, that hitherto, the effects of his wrath have not reached further than to the scratching of his nurse and governesses. His nails are not sharp enough as yet, nor have his claws attained to their full growth, —he is little.

Crescat; nos qui vivimus, multiplicemur.[41]

It is written so, and it is holy stuff, I warrant you: the truth whereof is like to last as long as a sack of corn may be had for a penny, and a puncheon of pure wine for three-pence. Wouldst thou be content to be found with thy genitories full in the day of judgment? *Dum venerit judicare?*[42] Thou hast, quoth Panurge, a right clear, and neat spirit, Friar John, my metropolitan cod; thou speakst in very deed pertinently, and to purpose. That belike was the reason which moved Leander of Abydos, in Asia, whilst he was swimming through the Hellespontic sea, to make a visit to his sweetheart Hero of Sestus, in Europe, to pray unto Neptune and all the other marine gods, thus:

Now, whilst I go, have pity on me,
And at my back returning drown me.

He was loath, it seems, to die with his cods overgorged. He was to be commended: therefore do I promise, that from henceforth no malefactor shall by justice be executed within my jurisdiction of Salmigondinois, who shall not, for a day or two at least before, be permitted to culbut, and foraminate, onocrotal wise, so that there remain not in all his vessels, to write a Greek Υ. Such a precious thing should not be foolishly cast away. He will perhaps therewith beget a male, and so depart the more contentedly out of this life, that he shall have left behind him one for one.

CHAPTER 27

How Friar John merrily and sportingly counselleth Panurge

By Saint Rigomé, quoth Friar John, I do advise thee to nothing, my dear friend Panurge, which I would not do myself, were I in thy place. Only have a special care, and take good heed thou solder well together the joints of the double-backed, and two bellied beast, and fortify thy nerves so strongly, that there be no discontinuance in the knocks of the venerean thwacking, else thou art lost, poor soul. For, if there pass long intervals betwixt the priapising feats, and that thou make an intermission of too large a time, that will befall thee which betides the nurses, if they desist from giving suck to children,—they lose their milk; and if continually thou do not hold thy aspersory tool in exercise, and keep thy mentul going, thy lacticinian nectar will be gone, and it will serve thee only as a pipe to piss out at, and thy cods for a wallet of lesser value than a beggar's scrip. This is a certain truth I tell thee, friend, and doubt not of it; for myself have seen the sad experiment thereof in many, who cannot now do what they would, because before they did not what they might have done. *E desuetudine amittuntur privilegia:* non-usage oftentimes destroys one's right, say the learned doctors of the law; therefore, my billy, entertain as well as possibly thou canst, that hypogastrian lower sort of troglodytic people, that their chief pleasure may be placed in the case of sempiternal labouring. Give order that henceforth they live not, like idle gentlemen, idly upon their rents and revenues, but that they may work for their livelihood, by breaking ground within the Paphian trenches. Nay truly, answered Panurge, Friar John, my left ballock, I will believe thee, for thou dealest plain with me, and fallest downright square upon the business, without going about the bush with frivolous circumstances and unnecessary reservations. Thou with the splendour of a piercing wit hast dissipated all the louring clouds of anxious apprehensions and suspicions, which did intimidate and terrify me: therefore the heavens be pleased to grant to thee, at all she-conflicts, a stiff-standing fortune. Well then, as thou hast said, so will I do, I will, in good sooth, marry,—in that point there shall be no failing, I promise thee, —and shall have always by me pretty girls clothed with the name of my wife's waiting-maids, that lying under thy wings, thou mayest be night protector of their sisterhood, when thou comest to see me.

Let this serve for the first part of the sermon. Hearken, quoth Friar John, to the oracle of the bells of Varenes. What say they? I hear and understand them, quoth Panurge; their sound is, by my thirst, more uprightly fatidical, than that of Jove's great kettles in Dodona. Hearken! *Take thee a wife, take thee a wife, and marry, marry, marry: for if thou marry, thou shalt find good therein; here in a wife thou shalt find good; so marry, marry.* I will assure thee, that I shall be married:—all the elements invite and prompt me to it. Let this word be to thee a brazen wall, by diffidence not to be broken through. As for the second part of this our doctrine,—thou seemest in some measure to mistrust the readiness of my paternity, in the practising of my placket-racket within the Aphrodisian tennis-court at all times fitting, as if the stiff god of gardens were not favourable to me. I pray thee, favour me so much as to believe that I still have him at a beck, attending always my commandments, docile, obedient, vigorous, and active in all things, and everywhere, and never stubborn or refractory to my will or pleasure. I need no more, but to let go the reins, and slacken the leash, which is the belly-point, and when the game is shown unto him, say, Hey, Jack, to thy booty! he will not fail even then to flesh himself upon his prey, and tuzzle it to some purpose. Hereby you may perceive, although my future wife were as unsatiable and gluttonous in her voluptuousness, and the delights of venery, as ever was the Empress Messalina, or yet the Marchioness of Oincester, in England, yet I desire thee to give credit to it, that I lack not for what is requisite to overlay the stomach of her lust, but have wherewith aboundingly to please her. I am not ignorant that Solomon said, who indeed of that matter speaketh clerk-like, and learnedly,—as also how Aristotle after him declared for a truth, That, for the greater part, the lechery of a woman is ravenous and unsatisfiable. Nevertheless, let such as are my friends, who read those passages, receive from me for a most real verity, that I for such a Gill have a fit Jack; and that, if women's things cannot be satiated, I have an instrument indefatigable,—an implement as copious in the giving, as can in craving be their *vade mecums*. Do not here produce ancient examples of the paragons of Paillardice, and offer to match with my testiculatory ability the Priapæan prowess of the fabulous fornicators, Hercules, Proculus Cæsar, and Mahomet, who in his *Alchoran* doth vaunt, that in his cods he had the vigour of threescore bully ruffians; but let no zealous Christian trust the rogue,—the filthy ribald rascal is a liar. Nor shalt thou need to urge authorities, or bring forth the instance of the Indian prince, of whom Theophrastus, Plinius, and Athenæus testify, that, with the help of a certain herb, he was able, and had given frequent experiments thereof, to toss his sinewy piece of generation in the act of carnal concupiscence above threescore and ten times in the space of four and twenty hours. Of that I believe nothing, the number is supposititious, and too prodigally foisted in. Give no faith unto it, I beseech thee, but prithee trust me in this, and thy credulity therein shall not be wronged; for it is true, and *Probatum est*,[43] that my pioneer of nature,—the sacred ithy-phallian champion,—is of all stiff-intruding blades the primest. Come hither, my ballockette, and hearken. Didst thou ever see the monk of Castre's cowl? When in any house it was laid down, whether openly in the view of all, or covertly out of the sight of any, such was the ineffable virtue thereof for excitating and stirring up the people of both sexes unto lechery, that the whole inhabitants and indwellers, not only of that, but likewise of all the circumjacent places thereto, within three leagues around it, did suddenly enter into rut, both beasts and folks, men and women, even to the dogs and hogs, rats and cats.

I swear to thee, that many times heretofore I have perceived, and found in my codpiece a certain kind of energy, or efficacious virtue, much more irregular, and of a greater anomaly, than what I have related. I will not speak to thee either of house or cottage, nor of church or market, but only tell thee, that once at the representation of the Passion, which was acted at Saint Maxent's, I had no sooner entered within the pit of the theatre, but that forthwith, by the virtue and occult property of it, on a sudden all that were there, both players and spectators, did fall into such an exorbitant temptation of lust, that there was not angel, man, devil, nor deviless, upon the place, who would not then have bricollitched it with all their heart and soul. The prompter forsook his copy, he who played St. Michael's part came down from his perch, the devils issued out of hell, and carried along with them most of the pretty girls that were there, yea, Lucifer got out of his fetters; —in a word, seeing the huge disorder, I disparked myself forth of that inclosed place, in imitation of Cato the Censor, who perceiving, by reason of his presence, the Floralian festivals out of order, withdrew himself.

CHAPTER 28

How Friar John comforteth Panurge in the doubtful matter of cuckoldry

I UNDERSTAND thee well enough, said Friar John; but time makes all things plain. The most durable marble or porphyry is subject to old age and decay. Though for the present thou possibly be not weary of the exercise, yet is it like, I will hear thee confess a few years hence, that thy cods hang dangling downwards for want of a better truss. I see thee waxing a little hoar-headed already. Thy beard, by the distinction of grey, white, tawny, and black, hath to my thinking the resemblance of a map of the terrestrial globe, or geographical chart. Look attentively upon, and take inspection of what I shall show unto thee. Behold there Asia. Here are Tygris and Euphrates. Lo, there Africa. Here is the mountain of the moon,—yonder thou mayest perceive the fenny march of Nilus. On this side lieth Europe. Dost thou not see the Abbey of Theleme? This little tuft, which is altogether white, is the Hyperborean Hills. By the thirst of my throple, friend, when snow is on the mountains, I say the head and the chin, there is not then any considerable heat to be expected in the valleys and low-countries of the cod-piece. By the kibes of thy heels, quoth Panurge, thou dost not understand the topics. When snow is on the tops of the hills, lightning, thunder, tempest, whirlwinds, storms, hurricanes, and all the devils of hell rage in the valleys. Wouldst thou see the experience thereof, go to the territory of the Swiss, and earnestly perpend with thyself there the situation of the lake of Wunderberlich, about four leagues distant from Berne, on the Syonside of the land. Thou twittest me with my grey hairs, yet considerest not how I am of the nature of leeks, which with a white head carry a green, fresh, straight, and vigorous tail. The truth is, nevertheless, (why should I deny it?) that I now and then discern in myself some indicative signs of old age. Tell this, I prithee, to nobody, but let it be kept very close and secret betwixt us two; for I find the wine much sweeter now, more savoury to my taste, and unto my palate of a better relish than formerly I was wont to do; and withal, besides mine accustomed manner, I have a more dreadful apprehension than I ever heretofore have had, of lighting on bad wine. Note and observe that this doth argue and portend I know not what of the west and occident of my time, and signifieth that the south and meridian of mine age is past. But what then, my gentle companion? That doth but betoken that I will hereafter drink so much the more. That is not, the devil hale it, the thing that I fear; nor is it there where my shoe pinches. The thing that I doubt most, and have greatest reason to dread and suspect, is, that through some long absence of our King Pantagruel, (to whom I must needs bear company, should he go to all the devils of Barathrum,) my future wife shall make me a cuckold. This is, in truth, the long and short of it. For I am by all those

whom I have spoken to, menaced and threatened with a horned fortune; and all of them affirm, it is the lot to which from heaven I am predestinated. Every one, answered Friar John, that would be a cuckold, is not one. If it be thy fate to be hereafter of the number of that horned cattle, then may I conclude with an *Ergo,* thy wife will be beautiful, and *Ergo,* thou wilt be kindly used by her. Likewise with this *Ergo,* thou shalt be blessed with the fruition of many friends and well-willers. And finally with this other *Ergo,* thou shalt be saved, and have a place in paradise. These are monachal topics and maxims of the cloister. Thou mayst take more liberty to sin. Thou shalt be more at ease than ever. There will be never the less left for thee, nothing diminished, but thy goods shall increase notably. And if so be it was preordinated for thee, wouldst thou be so impious as not to acquiesce in thy destiny? Speak, thou jaded cod.

Faded c.	Cloyed c.
Mouldy c.	Squeezed c.
Musty c.	Resty c.
Paltry c.	Pounded c.
Senseless c.	Loose c.
Foundered c.	Coldish c.
Distempered c.	Pickled c.
Bewrayed c.	Churned c.
Inveigled c.	Filliped c.
Dangling c.	Singlifild c.
Stupid c.	Begrimed c.
Seedless c.	Wrinkled c.
Soaked c.	Fainted c.
Louting c.	Extenuated c.
Discouraged c.	Grim c.
Surfeited c.	Wasted c.
Peevish c.	Inflamed c.
Translated c.	Unhinged c.
Forlorn c.	Scurvy c.
Unsavoury c.	Straddling c.
Worm-eaten c.	Putrified c.
Overtoiled c.	Maimed c.
Miserable c.	Overlechered c.
Steeped c.	Druggerly c.
Kneaded-with-cold- water c.	Mitified c.
Appealant c.	Goat-ridden c.
Swaggering c.	Weakened c.
Withered c.	Ass-ridden c.
Broken-reined c.	Puff-pasted c.
Defective c.	St. Anthonified c.
Crestfallen c.	Untriped c.
Felled c.	Blasted c.
Fleeted c.	Cut off c.
	Beveraged c.

Scarified c.
Dashed c.
Slashed c.
Infeebled c.
Whore-hunting c.
Deteriorated c.
Chill c.
Scrupulous c.
Crazed c.
Tasteless c.
Hacked c.
Flaggy c.
Scrubby c.
Drained c.
Haled c.
Lolling c.
Drenched c.
Burst c.
Stirred up c.
Mitred c.
Peddlingly fur-
    nished c.
Rusty c.
Exhausted c.
Perplexed c.
Unhelved c.
Fizzled c.
Leprous c.
Bruised c.
Spadonic c.
Boughty c.
Mealy c.
Wrangling c.
Gangreened c.
Crustrissen c.
Ragged c.
Quelled c.
Bragodochio c.
Beggarly c.
Trepanned c.
Bedusked c.
Emasculated c.
Corked c.
Transparent c.
Vile c.
Antidated c.
Chopped c.
Pinked c.
Cup-glassified c.
Fruitless c.
Riven c.
Pursy c.
Fusty c.
Jadish c.
Fistulous c.
Languishing c.

Maleficiated c.
Hectic c.
Worn out c.
Ill-favoured c.
Duncified c.
Macerated c.
Paralytic c.
Degraded c.
Benumbed c.
Bat-like c.
Fart-shotten c.
Sunburnt c.
Pacified c.
Blunted c.
Rankling tasted c.
Rooted out c.
Costive c.
Hailed-on c.
Cuffed c.
Buffeted c.
Whirreted c.
Robbed c.
Neglected c.
Lame c.
Confused c.
Unsavoury c.
Overthrown c.
Boulted c.
Trode under c.
Desolate c.
Declining c.
Stinking c.
Sorrowful c.
Murdered c.
Matachin-like c.
Besotted c.
Customerless c.
Minced c.
Exulcerated c.
Patched c.
Stupified c.
Annihilated c.
Spent c.
Foiled c.
Anguished c.
Disfigured c.
Disabled c.
Forceless c.
Censured c.
Cut c.
Rifled c.
Undone c.
Corrected c.
Slit c.
Skittish c.
Spungy c.

Botched c.
Dejected c.
Jagged c.
Pining c.
Deformed c.
Mischieved c.
Cobbled c.
Imbased c.
Ransacked c.
Despised c.
Mangy c.
Abased c.
Supine c.
Mended c.
Dismayed c.
Harsh c.
Beaten c.
Barred c.
Abandoned c.
Confounded c.
Loutish c.
Borne down c.
Sparred c.
Abashed c.
Unseasonable c.
Oppressed c.
Grated c.
Falling away c.
Small cut c.
Disordered c.
Latticed c.
Ruined c.
Exasperated c.
Rejected c.
Belammed c.
Febricitant c.
Perused c.
Emasculated c.
Roughly handled c.
Examined c.
Cracked c.
Wayward c.
Hagled c.
Gleaning c.
Ill-favoured c.
Pulled c.
Drooping c.
Faint c.
Parched c.
Paltry c.
Cankered c.
Void c.
Vexed c.
Bestunk c.
Crooked c.
Brabbling c.

Rotten c.
Anxious c.
Clouted c.
Tired c.
Proud c.
Fractured c.
Melancholy c.
Coxcombly c.
Base c.
Bleaked c.
Detested c.
Diaphanous c.
Unworthy c.
Checked c.
Mangled c.
Turned over c.
Harried c.
Flawed c.
Froward c.
Ugly c.
Drawn c.
Riven c.
Distasteful c.
Hanging c.
Broken c.
Limber c.
Effeminate c.
Kindled c.
Evacuated c.
Grieved c.
Carking c.
Disorderly c.
Empty c.
Disquieted c.
Desisted c.
Confounded c.
Hooked c.
Divorous c.
Wearied c.
Sad c.
Cross c.
Vain-glorious c.
Poor c.
Brown c.
Shrunken c.
Abhorred c.
Troubled c.
Scornful c.
Dishonest c.
Reproved c.
Cocketed c.
Filthy c.
Shred c.
Chawned c.
Short-winded c.
Branchless c.

Chapped c.
Failing c.
Deficient c.
Lean c.
Consumed c.
Used c.
Puzzled c.
Allayed c.
Spoiled c.
Clagged c.
Palsy-strucken c.
Amazed c.
Bedunsed c.
Extirpated c.
Banged c.
Stripped c.
Hoary c.
Winnowed c.
Decayed c.
Disastrous c.
Unhandsome c.
Stummed c.
Barren c.
Wretched c.
Feeble c.
Cast down c.
Stopped c.
Kept under c.
Stubborn c.
Ground c.
Retchless c.
Weather-beaten c.
Flayed c.
Bald c.
Tossed c.
Flapping c.
Cleft c.
Meagre c.
Dumpified c.
Suppressed c.
Hagged c.
Jawped c.
Havocked c.
Astonished c.
Dulled c.
Slow c.
Plucked up c.
Constipated c.
Blown c.
Blockified c.
Pommeled c.
All-to-be-mauled c.
Fallen away c.
Unlucky c.
Sterile c.
Beshitten c.

Appeased c.
Caitiff c.
Woful c.
Unseemly c.
Heavy c.
Weak c.
Prostrated c.
Uncomely c.
Naughty c.
Laid flat c.
Suffocated c.
Held down c.
Barked c.
Hairless c.
Flamping c.
Hooded c.
Wormy c.
Besysted c.
Faulty c.
Bemealed c.
Mortified c.
Scurvy c.
Bescabbed c.
Torn c.
Subdued c.
Sneaking c.
Bare c.
Swart c.
Smutched c.
Raised up c.
Chopped c.
Flirted c.
Blained c.
Blotted c.
Sunk in c.
Gastly c.
Unpointed c.
Beblistered c.
Wizened c.
Beggar-plated c.
Douf c.
Clarty c.
Lumpish c.
Abject c.
Side c.
Choked up c.
Backward c.
Prolix c.
Spotted c.
Crumpled c.
Frumpled c.
Stale c.
Corrupted c.
Beflowered c.
Amated c.
Blackish c.

Underlaid c.
Loathing c.
Ill-filled c.
Bobbed c.
Mated c.
Tawny c.
Whealed c.
Besmeared c.
Hollow c.
Pantless c.
Guizened c.
Demiss c.
Refractory c.
Rensy c.
Frowning c.

Limping c.
Ravelled c.
Rammish c.
Gaunt c.
Beskimmered c.
Scraggy c.
Lank c.
Swashring c.
Moyling c.
Swinking c.
Harried c.
Tugged c.
Towed c.
Misused c.
Adamitical c.

Ballockatso to the devil, my dear friend Panurge, seeing it is so decreed by the gods, wouldst thou invert the course of the planets, and make them retrograde? Wouldst thou disorder all the celestial spheres? blame the intelligences, blunt the spindles, join the wherves, slander the spinning quills, reproach the bobbins, revile the clew-bottoms, and finally ravel and untwist all the threads of both the warp and the waft of the weird Sister-Parcæ? What a pox to thy bones dost thou mean, stony cod? Thou wouldst, if thou couldst, a great deal worse than the giants of old intended to have done. Come hither, billicullion. Whether wouldst thou be jealous without a cause, or be a cuckold and know nothing about it? Neither the one, nor the other, quoth Panurge, would I choose to be. But if I can get an inkling of the matter, I will provide well enough, or there shall not be one stick of wood within five hundred leagues about me, whereof to make a cudgel. In good faith, Friar John, I speak now seriously unto thee, I think it will be my best not to marry. Hearken to what the bells do tell me, now that we are nearer to them! *Do not marry, marry not, not, not, not, not; marry, marry not, not, not, not, not. If thou marry, thou wilt miscarry, carry carry; thou wilt repent it, resent it, sent it! If thou marry, thou a cuckold, a cou-cou-cuckoe, cou-cou-cuckold thou shalt be.* By the worthy wrath of God, I begin to be angry. This campanalian oracle fretteth me to the guts,—a March hare was never in such a chaff as I am. O how I am vexed! You monks and friars of the cowl-pated and hood-polled fraternity, have you no remedy nor salve against this malady of graffing horns in heads? Hath nature so abandoned human-kind, and of her help left us so destitute, that married men cannot know how to sail through the seas of this mortal life, and be safe from the whirlpools, quicksands, rocks, and banks, that lie alongst the coast of Cornwall?

I will, said Friar John, show thee a way, and teach thee an expedient, by means whereof thy wife shall never make thee a cuckold without thy knowledge, and thine own consent. Do me the favour, I pray thee, quoth Panurge, my pretty soft downy cod; now tell it, billy, tell it, I beseech thee. Take, quoth Friar John, Hans Carvel's ring upon thy finger, who was the King of Melinda's chief jeweller. Besides that this Hans Carvel had the reputation of being very skilful and expert in the lapidary's profession, he was a studious, learned, and ingenious man, a scientific person, full of knowledge, a great philosopher, of sound judgment, of a prime wit, good sense, clear-spirited, an honest creature, courteous, charitable, a giver of alms, and of a jovial humour, a boon companion, and a merry blade, if ever there was any in the world. He was somewhat gorbellied, had a little shake in his head, and was in effect unwieldy of his body. In his old age he took to wife the bailiff of Concordat's daughter, young, fair, jolly, gallant, spruce, frisk, brisk, neat, feat, smirk, smug, compt, quaint, gay, fine, trixy, trim, decent, proper, graceful, handsome, beautiful, comely, and kind,—a little too much—to her neighbours and acquaintance.

Hereupon it fell out, after the expiring of a scantling of weeks, that Master Carvel became as jealous as a tiger, and entered into a very profound suspicion, that his new-married gixy did keep a buttock-stirring with others. To prevent which inconveniency, he did tell her many tragical stories of the total ruin of several kingdoms by adultery; did read unto her the legend of chaste wives; then made some lectures to her in the praise of the choice virtue of pudicity, and did present her with a book in commendation of conjugal fidelity, wherein the wickedness of all licentious women was odiously detested; and withal he gave her a chain enriched with pure oriental sapphires. Notwithstanding all this, he found her always more and more inclined to the reception of her neighbour copes-mates, so that day by day his jealousy increased. In sequel whereof, one night as he was lying by her, whilst in his sleep the rambling fancies of the lecherous deportments of his wife did take up the cellules of his brain, he dreamt that he encountered with the devil, to whom he had discovered to the full the buzzing of his head, and suspicion that his wife did tread her shoe awry. The devil, he thought, in this perplexity, did for his comfort give him a ring, and therewithal did kindly put it on his middle finger, saying, Hans Carvel, I give thee this ring,—whilst thou carriest it upon that finger, thy wife shall never carnally be known by any other than thyself, without thy special knowledge and consent. Grammercy, quoth Hans Carvel, my Lord Devil, I renounce Mahomet, if ever it shall come off my finger. The devil vanished, as is his custom, and then Hans Carvel, full of joy awaking, found that his middle-finger was as far as it could reach within the what-do-you-call-it of his wife. I did forget to tell thee, how his wife, as soon as she had felt the finger there, said, in recoiling her buttocks, Off, yes, nay, tut, pish, tush, aye, lord, that is not the thing which should be put up in that place. With this Hans Carvel thought that some pilfering fellow was about to take the ring from him. Is not this an infallible, and sovereign antidote? Therefore, if thou wilt believe me, in imitation of this example never fail to have continually the ring of thy wife's commodity upon thy finger. When that was said, their discourse and their way ended.

CHAPTER 29

How Pantagruel convocated together a Theologian, Physician, Lawyer, and Philosopher, for extricating Panurge out of the perplexity wherein he was

No sooner were they come into the royal palace, but they, to the full, made report unto Pantagruel of the success of their expedition and showed him the response of Raminagrobis. When Pantagruel had read it over and over again, the oftener he perused it, being the better pleased therewith, he said, in addressing his speech to Panurge, I have not as yet seen any answer framed to your demand which affordeth me more contentment. For in this his succinct copy of verses, he summarily, and briefly, yet fully enough expresseth how he would have us to understand that every one, in the project and enterprise of marriage, ought to be his own carver, sole arbitrator of his proper thoughts, and from himself alone take counsel in the main and peremptory closure of what his determination should be, in either his assent to or dissent from it. Such always hath been my opinion to you, and when at first you spoke thereof to me, I truly told you this same very thing; but tacitly you scorned my advice, and would not harbour it within your mind. I know for certain, and therefore may I with the greater confidence utter my conception of it, that *Philauty,* or self love, is that which blinds your judgment and deceiveth you.

Let us do otherways, and that is this. Whatever we are, or have, consisteth in three things—the soul, the body, and the goods. Now, for the preservation of these three, there are three sorts of learned men ordained, each respectively to have care of that one which is recommended to his charge. Theologues are appointed for the soul, physicians for the welfare of the body, and lawyers for the safety of our goods. Hence it is, that it is my resolution to have on Sunday next with me at dinner a divine, a physician, and a lawyer, that with those three assembled thus together, we may in every point and particle confer at large of your perplexity. By Saint Picot, answered Panurge, we never shall do any good that way, I see it already. And you see yourself how the world is vilely abused, as when with a fox-tail one claps another's breech, to cajole him. We give our souls to keep to the theologues, who for the greater part are heretics. Our bodies we commit to the physicians, who never themselves take any physic. And then we intrust our goods to the lawyers, who never go to law against one another. You speak like a courtier, quoth Pantagruel. But the first point of your assertion is to be denied; for we daily see how good theologues make it their chief business, their whole and sole employment, by their deeds, their words, and writings, to extirpate errors and heresies out of the hearts of men, and in their stead profoundly plant the true and lively faith. The second point you spoke of I commend; for, in truth the professors of the art of medicine give so good order to the prophylactic, or conservative part of their faculty, in what concerneth their proper healths, that they stand in no need of making use of the other branch, which is the curative, or therapeutic, by medicaments. As for the third, I grant it to be true, for learned advocates and counsellors at law are so much taken up with the affairs of others in their consultations, pleadings, and such-like patrocinations of those who are their clients, that

they have no leisure to attend any controversies of their own. Therefore, on the next ensuing Sunday, let the divine be our goodly Father Hippothadeus, the physician our honest Master Rondibilis, and our legist our friend Bridlegoose. Nor will it be (to my thinking) amiss, that we enter into the pythagoric field, and choose for an assistant to the three aforenamed doctors our ancient faithful acquaintance, the philosopher, Trouillogan, especially seeing a perfect philosopher, such as is Trouillogan, is able positively to resolve all whatsoever doubts you can propose. Carpalim, have you a care to have them here all four on Sunday next to dinner, without fail.

I believe, quoth Epistemon, that throughout the whole country, in all the corners thereof, you could not have pitched upon such other four. Which I speak not so much in regard of the most excellent qualifications and accomplishments wherewith all of them are endowed for the respective discharge and management of each his own vocation and calling, (wherein without all doubt or controversy, they are the paragons of the land and surpass all others,) as for that Rondibilis, is married now, who before was not,—Hippothadeus was not before, nor is yet,—Bridlegoose was married once, but is not now,—and Trouillogan is married now, who wedded was to another wife before. Sir, if it may stand with your good liking, I will ease Carpalim of some parcel of his labour, and invite Bridlegoose myself, with whom I of a long time have had a very intimate familiarity, and unto whom I am to speak on the behalf of a pretty hopeful youth who now studieth at Tholouse, under the most learned, virtuous Doctor Boissonet. Do what you deem most expedient, quoth Pantagruel, and tell me, if my recommendation can in anything be steadable for the promoval of the good of that youth, or otherwise serve for bettering of the dignity and office of the worthy Boissonet, whom I do so love and respect for one of the ablest and most sufficient in his way, that anywhere are extant. Sir, I will use therein my best endeavours, and heartily bestir myself about it.

CHAPTER 30

How the theologue, Hippothadeus, giveth counsel to Panurge in the matter and business of his nuptial enterprise

THE dinner on the subsequent Sunday was no sooner made ready, than that the aforenamed invited guests gave thereto their appearance, all of them, Bridlegoose only excepted, who was the deputy-governor of Fonsbeton. At the ushering in of the second service, Panurge, making a low reverence, spake thus. Gentlemen, the question I am to propound unto you shall be uttered in very few words; Should I marry or no? If my doubt herein be not resolved by you, I shall hold it altogether insolvable, as are the *Insolubilia de Aliaco;*[44] for all of you are elected, chosen and culled out from amongst others, every one in his own condition and quality, like so many picked peas on a carpet.

The Father Hippothadeus, in obedience to the bidding of Pantagruel, and with much courtesy to the company, answered exceeding modestly after this manner. My friend, you are pleased to ask counsel of us; but first you must consult with yourself. Do you find any trouble or disquiet in your body by the importunate stings and pricklings of the flesh? That I do, quoth Panurge, in a hugely strong and almost irresistible measure. Be not offended, I beseech you, good father at the freedom of my expression. No truly, friend, not I, quoth Hippothadeus, there is no reason why I should be displeased therewith. But in this carnal strife and debate of yours, have you obtained from God the gift and special grace of continency? In good faith not, quoth Panurge. My counsel to you in that case, my friend, is that you marry, quoth Hippothadeus; for you should rather choose to marry once, than to burn still in fires of concupiscence. Then Panurge, with a jovial heart and a loud voice, cried out, That is spoke gallantly, without circumbilivaginating about and about, and never hitting it in its central point. Grammercy, my good father! In truth I am resolved now to marry, and without fail I shall do it quickly. I invite you to my wedding. By the body of a hen, we shall make good cheer, and be as merry as crickets. You shall wear the bridegroom's colours, and, if we eat a goose, my wife shall not roast it for me. I will intreat you to lead up the first dance of the bride's maids, if it may please you to do me so much favour and honour. There resteth yet a small difficulty, a little scruple, yea, even less than nothing, whereof I humbly crave your resolution. Shall I be a cuckold, father, yea or no? By no means, answered Hippothadeus, will you be a cuckold, if it please God. O the Lord help us now, quoth Panurge whither are we driven to,

good folks? To the conditionals, which, according to the rules and precepts of the dialectic faculty, admit of all contradictions and impossibilities. If my Transalpine mule had wings, my Transalpine mule would fly. If it please God, I shall not be a cuckold, but I shall be a cuckold, if it please him. Good God, if this were a condition which I knew how to prevent, my hopes should be as high as ever, nor would I despair. But you here send me to God's privy council, to the closet of his little pleasures. You, my French countrymen, which is the way you take to go thither?

My honest father, I believe it will be your best not to come to my wedding. The clutter and dingle dangle noise of marriage guests will but disturb you, and break the serious fancies of your brain. You love repose with solitude and silence; I really believe you will not come. And then you dance but indifferently, and would be out of countenance at the first entry. I will send you some good things to your chamber, together with the bride's favour, and there you may drink our health, if it may stand with your good liking. My friend, quoth Hippothadeus, take my words in the sense wherein I mean them, and do not misinterpret me. When I tell you,—if it please God,—do I to you any wrong therein? Is it an ill expression? Is it a blaspheming clause, or reserve any way scandalous unto the world? Do not we thereby honour the Lord God Almighty, Creator, Protector, and Conserver of all things? Is not that a mean, whereby we do acknowledge him to be the sole giver of all whatsoever is good? Do not we in that manifest our faith, that we believe all things to depend upon his infinite and incomprehensible bounty? and that without him nothing can be produced, nor after its production be of any value, force, or power, without the concurring aid and favour of his assisting grace? Is it not a canonical and authentic exception, worthy to be premised to all our undertakings? Is it not expedient that what we propose unto ourselves, be still referred to what shall be disposed of by the sacred will of God, unto which all things must acquiesce in the heavens as well as on the earth? Is not that verily a sanctifying of his holy name? My friend, you shall not be a cuckold, if it please God, nor shall we need to despair of the knowledge of his good will and pleasure herein, as if it were such an abstruse and mysteriously hidden secret, that for the clear understanding thereof it were necessary to consult with those of his celestial privy council, or expressly make a voyage unto the empyrean chamber, where order is given for the effectuating of his most holy pleasures. The great God hath done us this good, that he hath declared and revealed them to us openly and plainly, and described them in the Holy Bible. There will you find that you shall never be a cuckold, that is to say, your wife shall never be a strumpet, if you make choice of one of a commendable extraction, descended of honest parents, and instructed in all piety and virtue—such a one as hath not at any time haunted or frequented the company or conversation of those that are of corrupt and depraved manners, one loving and fearing God, who taketh a singular delight in drawing near to him by faith, and the cordial observing of his sacred commandments—and finally, one who, standing in awe of the Divine Majesty of the Most High, will be loth to offend him, and lose the favourable kindness of his grace, through any defect of faith, or transgression against the ordinances of his holy law, wherein adultery is most rigorously forbidden, and a close adherence to her husband alone, most strictly and severely enjoined; yea, in such sort, that she is to cherish, serve, and love him above any thing, next to God, that meriteth to be beloved. In the interim, for the better schooling of her in these instructions, and that the wholesome doctrine of a matrimonial duty may take the deeper root in her mind, you must needs carry yourself so on your part, and your behaviour is to be such that you are to go before her in a good example, by entertaining her unfeignedly with a conjugal amity, by continually approving yourself in all your words and actions a faithful and discreet husband; and by living, not only at home and privately with your own household and family, but in the face also of all men, and open view of the world, devoutly, virtuously, and chastely, as you would have her on her side to deport and to demean herself towards you, as becomes a godly, loyal, and respectful wife, who maketh conscience to keep inviolable the tie of a matrimonial oath. For as that looking-glass is not the best, which is most decked with gold and precious stones, but that which representeth to the eye the liveliest shapes of objects set before it, even so that wife should not be most esteemed who richest is, and of the noblest race, but she who, fearing God,

conforms herself nearest unto the humour of her husband.

Consider how the moon doth not borrow her light from Jupiter, Mars, Mercury, or any other of the planets, nor yet from any of those splendid stars which are set in the spangled firmament, but from her husband only, the bright sun, which she receiveth from him more or less, according to the manner of his aspect and variously bestowed eradiations. Just so should you be a pattern to your wife in virtue, goodly zeal, and true devotion, that by your radiance in darting on her the aspect of an exemplary goodness, she, in your imitation, may outshine the luminaries of all other women. To this effect you daily must implore God's grace to the protection of you both. You would have me then, quoth Panurge, twisting the whiskers of his beard on either side with the thumb and forefinger of his left hand, to espouse and take to wife the prudent frugal woman described by Solomon. Without all doubt she is dead, and truly to my best remembrance I never saw her; the Lord forgive me! Nevertheless I thank you, father. Eat this slice of marchpane, it will help your digestion; then shall you be presented with a cup of claret hypocras, which is right healthful and stomachal. Let us proceed.

CHAPTER 31

How the physician Rondibilis counselleth Panurge

PANURGE, continuing his discourse, said, The first word which was spoken by him who gelded the lubbardly quaffing monks of Saussiniac, after that he had unstoned Friar Cauldaureil, was this, Now for the rest. In like manner, I say, Now for the rest. Therefore, I beseech you, my good master Rondibilis, should I marry or not? By the raking pace of my mule, quoth Rondibilis, I know not what answer to make to this problem of yours.

You say that you feel in you the pricking stings of sensuality, by which you are stirred up to venery. I find in our faculty of medicine, and we have founded our opinion therein upon the deliberate resolution and final decision of the ancient Platonics, that carnal concupiscence is cooled and quelled five several ways.

First, by the means of wine. I shall easily believe that, quoth Friar John, for when I am well whittled with the juice of the grape, I care for nothing else, so I may sleep. When I say, quoth Rondibilis, that wine abateth lust, my meaning is, wine immoderately taken; for by intemperance proceeding from the excessive drinking of strong liquor, there is brought upon the body of such a swill-down bouser, a chillness in the blood, a slackening in the sinews, a disipation of the generative seed, a numbness and hebetation of the senses, with a persversive wryness and convulsion of the muscles; all which are great lets and impediments to the act of generation. Hence it is, that Bacchus, the god of bibbers, tipplers, and drunkards, is most commonly painted beardless, and clad in a woman's habit, as a person altogether effeminate, or like a libbed eunuch. Wine, nevertheless, taken moderately, worketh quite contrary effects, as is implied by the old proverb, which saith,—That Venus takes cold, when not accompanied with Ceres and Bacchus. This opinion is of great antiquity, as appeareth by the testimony of Diodorus the Sicilian, and confirmed by Pausanias, and universally held amongst the Lampsacians, that Don Priapus was the son of Bacchus and Venus.

Secondly, The fervency of lust is abated by certain drugs, plants, herbs, and roots, which make the taker cold, maleficiated, unfit for, and unable to perform the act of generation; as hath been often experimented in the water-lily, Heraclea, Agnus Castus, willow-twigs, hemp-stalks, woodbine, honeysuckle, tamarisk, chaste-tree, mandrake, bennet, keck-bugloss, the skin of a hippopotamus, and many other such, which, by convenient doses proportioned to the peccant humour and constitution of the patient, being duly and seasonably received within the body,— what by their elementary virtues on the one side, and peculiar properties on the other,— do either benumb, mortify, and beclumpse with cold the prolific semence, or scatter and disperse the spirits, which ought to have gone along with, and conducted sperm to the places destinated and appointed for its reception, —or lastly, shut up, stop, and obstruct the ways, passages, and conduits through which the seed should have been expelled, evacuated, and ejected. We have nevertheless of those ingredients, which, being of a contrary operation, heat the blood, bend the nerves, unite the spirits, quicken the senses, strengthen the muscles, and thereby rouse up, provoke, excite, and enable a man to the vigorous accomplishment of the feat of amorous dalliance. I have no need of these, quoth Pan-

urge, God be thanked, and you, my good master. Howsoever, I pray you, take no exception or offence at these my words; for what I have said was not out of any ill will I did bear to you, the Lord, he knows.

Thirdly, The ardour of lechery is very much subdued and check'd by frequent labour and continual toiling. For by painful exercises and laborious working, so great a dissolution is brought upon the whole body, that the blood, which runneth alongst the channels of the veins thereof, for the nourishment and alimentation of each of its members, hath neither time, leisure, nor power to afford the seminal resudation, or superfluity of the third concoction, which nature most carefully reserves for the conservation of the individual, whose preservation she more heedfully regardeth than the propagating of the species, and the multiplication of human kind. Whence it is, that Diana is said to be chaste, because she is never idle, but always busied about her hunting. For the same reason was a camp, or leaguer, of old called *Castrum,* as if they would have said *Castum;*[45] because the soldiers, wrestlers, runners, throwers of the bar, and other such like athletic champions, as are usually seen in a military circumvallation, do incessantly travail and turmoil, and are in perpetual stir and agitation. To this purpose Hippocrates also writeth in his book, *De Aere, Aqua, et Locis,* That in his time there was a people in Scythia, as impotent as eunuchs in the discharge of a venerean exploit; because that without any cessation, pause, or respite, they were never from off horseback, or otherwise assiduously employed in some troublesome and molesting drudgery.

On the other part, in opposition and repugnancy hereto, the philosophers say, That idleness is the mother of luxury. When it was asked Ovid, Why Ægisthus became an adulterer? he made no other answer but this, Because he was idle. Who were able to rid the world of loitering and laziness, might easily frustrate and disappoint Cupid of all his designs, aims, engines, and devices, and so disable and appal him that his bow, quiver, and darts should from thenceforth be a mere needless load and burthen to him: for that it could not then lie in his power to strike, or wound any of either sex, with all the arms he had. He is not, I believe, so expert an archer, as that he can hit the cranes flying in the air, or yet the young stags skipping through the thickets, as the Parthians knew well how to do: that is to say, people moiling, stirring, and hurrying up and down, restless, and without repose. He must have those hushed, still, quiet, lying at a stay, lither, and full of ease, whom he is able to pierce with all his arrows. In confirmation hereof, Theophrastus being asked on a time, What kind of beast or thing he judged a toyish, wanton love to be? he made answer, That it was a passion of idle and sluggish spirits. From which pretty description of tickling love-tricks, that of Diogenes's hatching was not very discrepant, when he defined lechery, The occupation of folks destitute of all other occupation. For this cause the Sicyonian sculptor Canachus, being desirous to give us to understand that sloth, drowsiness, negligence, and laziness were the prime guardians and governesses of ribaldry, made the statue of Venus, not standing, as other stone-cutters had used to do, but sitting.

Fourthly, The tickling pricks of incontinency, are blunted by an eager study; for from thence proceedeth an incredible resolution of the spirits, that oftentimes there do not remain so many behind as may suffice to push and thrust forwards the generative resudation to the places thereto appropriated, and there withal inflate the cavernous nerve, whose office is to ejaculate the moisture for the propagation of human progeny. Lest you should think it is not so, be pleased but to contemplate a little the form, fashion, and carriage of a man exceeding earnestly set upon some learned meditation, and deeply plunged therein, and you shall see how all the arteries of his brains are stretched forth, and bent like the string of a cross-bow, the more promptly, dexterously, and copiously to suppeditate, furnish, and supply him with store of spirits, sufficient to replenish and fill up the ventricles, seats, tunnels, mansions, receptacles, and cellules of common sense,— of the imagination, apprehension, and fancy, —of the ratiocination, arguing, and resolution,—as likewise of the memory, recordation, and remembrance; and with great alacrity, nimbleness, and agility to run, pass, and course from the one to the other, through those pipes, windings, and conduits, which to skilful anatomists are perceivable at the end of the wonderful net, where all the arteries close in a terminating point: which arteries, taking their rise and origin from the left capsule of the heart, bring through several circuits, ambages, and anfractuosities, the vital spirits, to subtilize and refine them to the ætherial purity of animal spirits. Nay, in such a studiously musing person, you may espy so extravagant raptures of one, as it were, out of himself, that all his natural faculties for that time will seem to be suspended from each their proper charge and office, and his exterior senses to be at a stand. In a word, you cannot otherwise choose than think, that he is by an extraordinary ecstacy quite transported of what he was, or should be; and that Socrates did not speak improperly, when he said, That philosophy was nothing else but a meditation upon death. This possibly is the reason why Democritus, deprived himself of the sense of seeing, prizing at a much lower rate the loss of his sight, than the diminution of his contemplations, which he frequently had found disturbed by the vagrant, flying-out strayings of his unsettled and roving eyes. Therefore is it, that Pallas, the goddess of wisdom, tutoress and guardianess of such as are diligently studious, and painfully industrious, is, and hath been still, accounted a virgin. The muses upon the same consideration are esteemed perpetual maids: and the graces for the like reason, have been held to continue in a sempiternal pudicity.

I remember to have read, that Cupid on a time being asked of his mother Venus, why he did not assault and set upon the Muses, his answer was, That he found them so fair, so sweet, so fine, so neat, so wise, so learned, so modest, so discreet, so courteous, so virtuous, and so continually busied and employed,— one in the speculation of the stars,—another in the supputation of numbers,—the third in the dimension of geometrical quantities,—the fourth in the composition of heroic poems,— the fifth in the jovial interludes of a comic strain,—the sixth in the stately gravity of a tragic vein,—the seventh in the melodious disposition of musical airs,—the eighth in the completest manner of writing histories, and books on all sorts of subjects,—and the ninth in the mysteries, secrets, and curiosities of all sciences, faculties, disciplines, and arts whatsoever, whether liberal or mechanic, that approaching near unto them he unbent his bow, shut his quiver, and extinguished his torch, through mere shame, and fear that by mischance he might do them some hurt or prejudice. Which done, he thereafter put off the fillet wherewith his eyes were bound, to look them in the face, and to hear their melody and poetic odes. There took he the greatest pleasure in the world, that many times he was transported with their beauty and pretty behaviour, and charmed asleep by the harmony; so far was he from assaulting them, or interrupting their studies. Under this article may be comprised what Hippocrates wrote in the afore-cited treatise concerning the Scythians; as also that in a book of his, entitled, *Of Breeding and Production,* where he hath affirmed all such men to be unfit for generation, as have their parotid arteries cut—whose situation is beside the ears—for the reason given already, when I was speaking of the resolution of the spirits, and of that spiritual blood whereof the arteries are the sole and proper receptacles; and that likewise he doth maintain a large portion of the parastatic liquor to issue and descend from the brains and backbone.

Fifthly, by the too frequent reiteration of the act of venery. There did I wait for you quoth Panurge, and shall willingly apply it to myself, whilst any one that pleaseth may, for me, make use of any of the four preceding. That is the very same thing, quoth Friar John, which Father Scyllino, Prior of Saint Victor at Marseilles, calleth by the name of maceration, and taming of the flesh. I am of the same opinion,—and so was the hermit of Saint Radegonde, a little above Chinon: for, quoth he, the hermits of Thebaide can no way more aptly or expediently macerate and bring down the pride of their bodies, daunt and mortify their lecherous sensuality, or depress and overcome the stubbornness and rebellion of the flesh, than by duffling and fanfreluching it five and twenty or thirty times a day. I see Panurge, quoth Rondibilis, neatly featured, and proportioned in all the members of his body, of a good temperament in his humours, well complexioned in his spirits, of a competent age, in an opportune time, and of a reasonably forward mind to be married. Truly, if he encounter with a wife of the like nature, temperament, and constitution, he may beget upon her children worthy of some transpontine monarchy; and the sooner he marry, it will be the better for him, and the more conducible for his profit, if he would see and have his children in his own time well provided for. Sir, my worthy master, quoth Panurge, I will do it, do not you doubt thereof; and that quickly enough, I warrant you. Nevertheless, whilst you were busied in the uttering of your learned discourse, this flea which I

have in mine ear hath tickled me more than ever. I retain you in the number of my festival guests, and promise you, that we shall not want for mirth, and good cheer enough, yea, over and above the ordinary rate. And, if it may please you, desire your wife to come along with you, together with her she-friends and neighbours—that is to be understood—and there shall be fair play.

CHAPTER 32

How Rondibilis declareth cuckoldry to be naturally one of the appendances of marriage

THERE remaineth, as yet, quoth Panurge, going on in his discourse, one small scruple to be cleared. You have seen heretofore, I doubt not, in the Roman standards, *S.P.Q.R.*[46] *Si, Peu, Que, Rien.* Shall not I be a cuckold? By the haven of safety, cried out Rondibilis, what is this you ask of me? If you shall be a cuckold? My noble friend, I am married, and you are like to be so very speedily; therefore be pleased, from my experiment in the matter, to write in your brain with a steel-pen this subsequent ditton, 'there is no married man who doth not run the hazard of being made a cuckold.' Cuckoldry naturally attendeth marriage. The shadow doth not more naturally follow the body, than cuckoldry ensueth after marriage, to place fair horns upon the husbands' heads.

And when you shall happen to hear any man pronounce these words—he is married—if you then say he is, hath been, shall be, or may be a cuckold, you will not be accounted an unskilful artist in framing of true consequences. Tripes and bowels of all the devils, cries Panurge, what do you tell me? My dear friend, answered Rondibilis, as Hippocrates on a time was in the very nick of setting forwards from Lango to Polistillo, to visit the philosopher Democritus, he wrote a familiar letter to his friend Dionysius, wherein he desired him, that he would, during the interval of his absence, carry his wife to the house of her father and mother, who were an honourable couple, and of good repute; because I would not have her at my home, said he, to make abode in solitude. Yet, notwithstanding this her residence beside her parents, do not fail, quoth he, with a most heedful care and circumspection, to pry into her ways, and to espy what places she shall go to with her mother, and who those be that shall repair unto her. Not, quoth he, that I do mistrust her virtue, or that I seem to have any diffidence of her pudicity, and chaste behaviour, —for of that I have frequently had good and real proofs,—but I must freely tell you, she is a woman. There lies the suspicion.

My worthy friend, the nature of women is set forth before our eyes, and represented to us by the moon in divers other things as well as in this, that they squat, skulk, constrain their own inclinations, and, with all the cunning they can, dissemble and play the hypocrite in the sight and presence of their husbands; who come no sooner to be out of the way, but that forthwith they take their advantage, pass the time merrily, desist from all labour, frolic it, gad abroad, lay aside their counterfeit garb, and openly declare and manifest the interior of their dispositions, even as the moon, when she is in conjunction with the sun, is neither seen in the heavens, nor on the earth, but in her opposition, when remotest from him shineth in her greatest fulness, and wholly appeareth in her brightest splendour whilst it is night. Thus women are but women.

When I say womankind, I speak of a sex so frail, so variable, so changeable, so fickle, inconstant, and imperfect, that, in my opinion, Nature, under favour nevertheless, of the prime honour and reverence which is due unto her, did in a manner mistake the road which she had traced formerly, and stray exceedingly from that excellence of providential judgment, by the which she had created and formed all other things, when she built, framed, and made up the woman. And having thought upon it a hundred and five times, I know not what else to determine therein, save only that in the devising, hammering, forging, and composing of the woman, she hath had a much tenderer regard, and by a great deal more respectful, heed to the delightful consortship, and sociable delectation of the man, than to the perfection and accomplishment of the individual womanishness or muliebrity. The divine philosopher Plato was doubtful in what rank of living creatures to place and collocate them, whether amongst the rational animals, by elevating them to an upper seat in the specifical classes of humanity; or with the irrational, by degrading them to a lower bench on the opposite side, of a brutal kind, and mere bestiality. For nature hath posited in a privy, secret and intestine place of their bodies, a sort of

member, by some not impertinently termed an animal, which is not to be found in men. Therein sometimes are engendered certain humours, so saltish, brackish, clammy, sharp, nipping, tearing, prickling, and most eagerly tickling, that by their stinging acrimony, rending nitrosity, figging itch, wriggling mordicancy, and smarting salsitude, (for the said member is altogether sinewy, and of a most quick and lively feeling,) their whole body is shaken and ebrangled their senses totally ravished and transported, the operations of their judgment and understanding utterly confounded, and all disordinate passions and perturbations of the mind throughly and absolutely allowed, admitted, and approved of; yea, in such sort, that if nature had not been so favourable unto them as to have sprinkled their forehead with a little tincture of bashfulness and modesty, you should see them in a so frantic mood run mad after lechery, and hie apace up and down with haste and lust, in quest of, and to fix some chamber-standard in their Paphian ground, that never did the Proëtides, Mimallonides, nor Lyæan Thyads deport themselves in the time of their Bacchanalian festivals more shamelessly, or with a so effronted and brazen-faced impudency; because this terrible animal is knit unto, and hath an union with all the chief and most principal parts of the body, as to anatomists is evident. Let it not here be thought strange that I should call it an animal, seeing therein I do no otherwise than follow and adhere to the doctrine of the academic and peripatetic philosophers. For if a proper motion be a certain mark and infallible token of the life and animation of the mover, as Aristotle writeth, and that any such thing as moveth of itself ought to be held animated, and of a living nature, then assuredly Plato with very good reason did give it the denomination of an animal, for that he perceived and observed in it the proper and self-stirring motions of suffocation, precipitation, corrugation, and of indignation, so extremely violent, that oftentimes by them is taken and removed from the woman all other sense and moving whatsoever, as if she were in a swounding lipothymy, benumbing syncope, epileptic, apoplectic palsy, and true resemblance of a pale-faced death.

Furthermore, in the said member there is a manifest discerning faculty of scents and odours very perceptible to women, who feel it fly from what is rank and unsavoury, and follow fragrant and aromatic smells. It is not un-known to me how Cl. Galen striveth with might and main to prove that these are not proper and particular notions proceeding in-trinsically from the thing itself, but acciden-tally, and by chance. Nor hath it escaped my notice, how others of that sect have laboured hardly, yea, to the utmost of their abilities, to demonstrate that it is not a sensitive discern-ing or perception in it of the difference of wafts and smells, but merely a various man-ner of virtue and efficacy, passing forth and flowing from the diversity of odoriferous sub-stances applied near unto it. Nevertheless, if you will studiously examine, and seriously ponder and weigh in Critolaus's balance the strength of their reasons and arguments, you shall find that they, not only in this, but in several other matters also of the like nature, have spoken at random, and rather out of an ambitious envy to check and reprehend their betters, than for any design to make inquiry into the solid truth.

I will not launch my little skiff any further into the wide ocean of this dispute, only will I tell you that the praise and commendation is not mean and slender which is due to those honest and good women, who living chastely and without blame, have had the power and virtue to curb, range, and subdue that unbri-dled, heady, and wild animal to an obedient, submissive, and obsequious yielding unto rea-son. Therefore here will I make an end of my discourse thereon, when I shall have told you, that the said animal being once satiated—if it be possible that it can be contented or satis-fied—by that aliment which nature hath pro-vided for it out of the epididymal storehouse of man, all its former and irregular and disor-dered motions are at an end, laid and as-suaged,—all its vehement and unruly longings lulled, pacified, and quieted,—and all the fur-ious and raging lusts, appetites, and desires thereof appeased, calmed, and extinguished. For this cause let it seem nothing strange un-to you, if we be in a perpetual danger of be-ing cuckolds, that is to say, such of us as have not wherewithal fully to satisfy the appetite and expectation of that voracious animal. Ods fish! quoth Panurge, have you no preventive cure in all your medicinal art for hindering one's head to be horny-graffed at home, whilst his feet are plodding abroad? Yes, that I have, my gallant friend, answered Rondibilis, and that which is a sovereign remedy, whereof I frequently make use myself; and, that you

may the better relish, it is set down and writ-ten in the book of a most famous author, whose renown is of a standing of two thou-sand years. Hearken and take good heed. You are, quoth Panurge, by cocks-hobby, a right honest man, and I love you with all my heart. Eat a little of this quince-pie; it is very proper and convenient for the shutting up of the orifice of the ventricle of the stomach, be-cause of a kind of astringent stypticity, which is in that sort of fruit, and is helpful to the first concoction. But what? I think I speak Latin before clerks. Stay till I give you somewhat to drink out of this Nestorian goblet. Will you have another draught of white hippocras? Be not afraid of the squinzy, no. There is neither squinanthus, ginger, nor grains in it; only a little choice cinnamon, and some of the best refined sugar, with the delicious white wine of the growth of that vine, which was set in the slips of the great sorb-apple, above the walnut tree.

CHAPTER 33

Rondibilis the Physician's cure of cuckoldry

At what time, quoth Rondibilis when Jupiter took a view of the state of his Olympic house and family, and that he had made the calen-dar of all the gods and goddesses, appointing unto the festival of every one of them its proper day and season, establishing certain fixed places and stations for the pronouncing of oracles, and relief of travelling pilgrims, and ordaining victims, immolations, and sac-rifices suitable and correspondent to the dig-nity and nature of the worshipped and adored deity. Did not he do, asked Panurge, therein, as Tinteville the bishop of Auxerre is said once to have done? This noble prelate loved entirely the pure liquor of the grape, as every honest and judicious man doth; therefore was it that he had an especial care and regard to the bud of the vine tree, as to the great grand-father of Bacchus. But so it is, that for sundry years together, he saw a most pitiful havoc, desolation, and destruction made amongst the sprouts, shootings, buds, blossoms, and scions of the vines, by hoary frost, dank fogs, hot mists, unseasonable colds, chill blasts, thick hail, and other calamitous chances of foul weather, happening, as he thought, by the dismal inauspiciousness of the Holy Days of St. George, St. Mary, St. Paul, St. Eutro-pius, Holy Rood, the Ascension, and other festivals, in that time when the sun passeth

under the sign of Taurus; and thereupon harboured in his mind this opinion, that the
aforenamed saints were Saint Hail-flingers,
Saint Frost-senders, Saint Fog-mongers, and
Saint Spoilers of the vine-buds. For which
cause he went about to have transmitted their
feasts from the spring to the winter, to be celebrated between Christmas and Epiphany, so
the mother of the three kings called it, allow-
ing them with all honour and reverence the
liberty then to freeze, hail, and rain as much
as they would; for that he knew that at such a
time frost was rather profitable than hurtful
to the vine-buds, and in their steads to have
placed the festivals of St. Christopher, St.
John the Baptist, St. Magdalene, St. Ann, St.
Domingo, and St. Lawrence; yea, and to have
gone so far as to collocate and transpose the
middle of August in and to the beginning of
May, because during the whole space of their
solemnity there was so little danger of hoary
frosts and cold mists, that no artificers are
then held in greater request, than the afford-
ers of refrigerating inventions, makers of
junkets, fit disposers of cooling shades, com-
posers of green arbours, and refreshers of
wine.

Jupiter, said Rondibilis, forgot the poor
devil Cuckoldry, who was then in the court at
Paris, very eagerly soliciting a piddling suit at
law for one of his vassals and tenants. Within
some few days thereafter, I have forgot how
many, when he got full notice of the trick,
which in his absence was done unto him, he
instantly desisted from prosecuting legal
processes in the behalf of others, full of solicitude to pursue after his own business, lest he
should be fore-closed, and thereupon he appeared personally at the tribunal of the great
Jupiter, displayed before him the importance
of his preceding merits, together with the acceptable services, which in obedience to his
commandments he had formerly performed;
and therefore, in all humility, begged of him
that he would be pleased not to leave him
alone amongst all the sacred potentates, destitute and void of honour, reverence, sacrifices, and festival ceremonies. To this petition
Jupiter's answer was excusatory, That all the
places and offices of his house were bestowed.
Nevertheless, so importuned was he by the
continual supplications of Monsieur Cuckoldry, that he, in fine, placed him in the rank,
list, toll, rubric, and catalogue, and appointed honours, sacrifices, and festival rites to be
observed on earth in great devotion, and ten-

dered to him with solemnity. The feast, because there was no void, empty, nor vacant
place in all the calendar, was to be celebrated
jointly with and on the same day that had
been consecrated to the goddess Jealousy.
His power and dominion should be over married folks, especially such as had handsome
wives. His sacrifices were to be suspicion, diffidence, mistrust, a lowering pouting sullenness, watchings, wardings, researchings, ply-
ings, explorations, together with the waylay-
ings, ambushes, narrow observations, and
malicious doggings of the husbands' scouts
and espials of the most privy actions of their
wives. Herewithal every married man was expressly and rigorously commanded to reverence, honour, and worship him, to celebrate
and solemnize his festival with twice more
respect than that of any other saint or deity,
and to immolate unto him, with all sincerity
and alacrity of heart, the above-mentioned
sacrifices and oblations, under pain of severe
censures, threatenings, and comminations of
these subsequent fines, mulcts, amercements,
penalties, and punishments to be inflicted on
the delinquents; that Monsieur Cuckoldry
should never be favourable nor propitious to
them,—that he should never help, aid, supply, succour, nor grant them any subventi-
tious furtherance, auxiliary, suffrage, or ad-
miniculary assistance,—that he should never
hold them in any reckoning, account, or estimation,—that he should never deign to enter
within their houses, neither at the doors, windows, nor any other place thereof;—that he
should never haunt nor frequent their companies or conversations, how frequently soever they should invocate him, and call upon
his name,—and that not only he should leave
and abandon them to rot alone with their
wives in a sempiternal solitariness, without
the benefit of the diversion of any copesmate
or corrival at all, but should withal shun and
eschew them, fly from them, and eternally
forsake and reject them as impious heretics
and sacrilegious persons, according to the accustomed manner of other gods, towards
such as are too slack in offering up the duties
and reverences which ought to be performed
respectively to their divinities; as is evidently
apparent in Bacchus towards negligent vine-
dressers; in Ceres, against idle ploughmen
and tillers of the ground; in Pomona, to unworthy fruiterers and costard-mongers; in
Neptune, towards dissolute mariners and seafaring men; in Vulcan towards loitering

smiths and forgemen; and so throughout the rest. Now, on the contrary, this infallible promise was added, that unto all those who should make a Holy Day of the above-recited festival, and cease from all manner of worldly work and negotiation, lay aside all their own most important occasions, and be so retchless, heedless, and careless of what might concern the management of their proper affairs, as to mind nothing else but a suspicious espying and prying into the secret deportments of their wives, and how to coop, shut up, hold at under, and deal cruelly and austerely with them, by all the harshness and hardships that an implacable and every way inexorable jealousy can devise and suggest, conform to the sacred ordinances of the afore-mentioned sacrifices and oblations, he should be continually favourable to them, should love them, sociably converse with them, should be day and night in their houses, and never leave them destitute of his presence. Now I have said, and you have heard my cure.

Ha, ha, ha, quoth Carpalim, laughing, this is a remedy yet more apt and proper than Hans Carvel's ring. The devil take me if I do not believe it! The humour, inclination, and nature of women is like the thunder, whose force in its bolt, or otherwise, burneth, bruiseth, and breaketh only hard, massive and resisting objects, without staying or stopping at soft, empty, and yielding matters. For it dasheth into pieces the steel sword, without doing any hurt to the velvet scabbard which insheatheth it. It crusheth also, and consumeth the bones, without wounding or endamaging the flesh, wherewith they are veiled and covered. Just so it is, that women for the greater part never bend the contention, subtlety, and contradictory disposition of their spirits, unless it be to do what is prohibited and forbidden. Verily, quoth Hippothadeus, some of our doctors aver for a truth, that the first woman of the world, whom the Hebrews call Eve, had hardly been induced or allured into the temptation of eating of the fruit of the tree of life, if it had not been forbidden her so to do. And that you may give the more credit to the validity of this opinion, consider how the cautelous and wily tempter did commemorate unto her, for an antecedent to his *enthymeme*,[47] the prohibition which was made to taste it; as being desirous to infer from thence, It is forbidden thee; therefore thou shouldest eat of it, else thou canst not be a woman.

CHAPTER 34

How women ordinarily have the greatest longing after things prohibited

When I was, quoth Carpalim, a whore-master at Orleans, the whole art of rhetoric, in all its tropes and figures, was not able to afford unto me a colour or flourish of greater force and value; nor could I by any other form or manner of elocution pitch upon a more persuasive argument for bringing young beautiful married ladies into the snares of adultery, through alluring and enticing them to taste with me of amorous delights, than with a lively sprightfulness to tell them in downright terms, and to remonstrate to them, (with a great show of detestation of a crime so horrid,) how their husbands were jealous. This was none of my invention. It is written, and we have laws, examples, reasons, and daily experiences confirmative of the same. If this belief once enter into their noodles, their husbands will infallibly be cuckolds; yea, by God, will they, without swearing, although they should do like Semiramis, Pasiphaë, Egesta, the women of the Isle Mandez in Egypt, and other such like queanish flirting harlots, mentioned in the writings of Herodotus, Strabo, and such like puppies.

Truly, quoth Ponocrates, I have heard it related, and it hath been told me for a verity, that Pope John XXII, passing on a day through the abbey of Toucherome, was in all humility required and besought by the abbess, and other discreet mothers of the said convent, to grant them an indulgence, by means whereof they might confess themselves to one another, alleging, That religious women were subject to some petty secret slips and imperfections, which would be a foul and burning shame for them to discover and to reveal to men, how sacerdotal soever their function were: but that they would freelier, more familiarly, and with greater cheerfulness, open to each other their offences, faults, and escapes, under the seal of confession. There is not anything, answered the pope, fitting for you to impetrate of me, which I would not most willingly condescend unto: but I find one inconvenience. You know, confession should be kept secret, and women are not able to do so. Exceeding well, quoth they, most holy father, and much more closely than the best of men.

The said pope on the very same day gave them in keeping a pretty box, wherein he purposely caused a little linnet to be put, willing them very gently and courteously to lock it up in some sure and hidden place, and promising them, by the faith of a pope, that he should yield to their request, if they would keep secret what was enclosed within that deposited box: enjoining them withal, not to presume one way nor other, directly or indirectly, to go about the opening thereof, under pain of the highest ecclesiastical censure, eternal excommunication. The prohibition was no sooner made, but that they did all of them boil with a most ardent desire to know and see what kind of thing it was that was within it. They thought it long already, that the pope was not gone, to the end they might jointly, with the more leisure and ease, apply themselves to the box-opening curiosity.

The holy father, after he had given them his benediction, retired and withdrew himself to the pontifical lodgings of his own palace. But he was hardly gone three steps from without the gates of their cloister, when the good ladies throngingly, and as in a huddled crowd, pressing hard on the backs of one another, ran thrusting and shoving who should be first at the setting open of the forbidden box, and descrying of the *Quod latitat*[48] within.

On the very next day thereafter, the pope made them another visit, of a full design, purpose, and intention, as they imagined, to dispatch the grant of their sought and wished for indulgence. But before he would enter into any chat or communing with them, he commanded the casket to be brought unto him. It was done so accordingly; but, by your leave, the bird was no more there. Then was it, that the pope did represent to their maternities, how hard a matter and difficult it was for them to keep secrets revealed to them in confession, unmanifested to the ears of others, seeing for the space of four-and-twenty hours they were not able to lay up in secret a box, which he had highly recommended to their discretion, charge, and custody.

Welcome, in good faith, my dear master, welcome! It did me good to hear you talk, the Lord be praised for all. I do not remember to have seen you before now, since the last time that you acted at Montpellier with our ancient friends, Anthony Saporta, Guy Bourguyer, Balthasar, Noyer, Tolet, John Quentin, Francis Robinet, John Perdrier, and Francis Rabelais, the moral comedy of him who had espoused and married a dumb wife. I was

there, quoth Epistemon. The good honest man, her husband, was very earnestly urgent to have the fillet of her tongue untied, and would needs have her speak by any means. At his desire, some pains were taken on her, and partly by the industry of the physician, other part by the expertness of the surgeon, the encyliglotte which she had under her tongue being cut, she spoke, and spoke again; yea, within a few hours she spoke so loud, so much, so fiercely, and so long, that her poor husband returned to the same physician for a receipt to make her hold her peace. There are, quoth the physician, many proper remedies in our art to make dumb women speak, but there are none that ever I could learn therein to make them silent. The only cure which I have found out is their husband's deafness. The wretch became within few weeks thereafter, by virtue of some drugs, charms, or enchantments, which the physician had prescribed unto him, so deaf, that he could not have heard the thundering of nineteen hundred cannons at a salvo. His wife perceiving that indeed he was as deaf as a door-nail, and that her scolding was but in vain, sith that he heard her not, she grew stark mad.

Some time after, the doctor asked for his fee of the husband; who answered, That truly he was deaf, and so was not able to understand what the tenour of his demand might be. Whereupon the leech bedusted him with a little, I know not what, sort of powder; which rendered him a fool immediately, so great was the stultificating virtue of that strange kind of pulverised dose. Then did this fool of a husband, and his mad wife, join together, and falling on the doctor and the surgeon, did so scratch, bethwack, and bang them, that they were left half dead upon the place, so furious were the blows which they received. I never in my lifetime laughed so much, as at the acting of that buffoonery.

Let us come to where we left off, quoth Panurge. Your words, being translated from the clapper-dudgeons to plain English, do signify, that it is not very inexpedient that I marry, and that I should not care for being a cuckold. You have there hit the nail on the head. I believe, master doctor, that on the day of my marriage you will be so much taken up with your patients, or otherwise so seriously employed, that we shall not enjoy your company. Sir, I will heartily excuse your absence.

Stercus et urina medici sunt prandia prima.
Ex aliis paleas, ex istis collige grana.[49]

You are mistaken, quoth Rondibilis, in the second verse of our distich; for it ought to run thus—

Nobis sunt signa, vobis sunt prandia digna.[50]

If my wife at any time prove to be unwell, and ill at ease, I will look upon the water which she shall have made in an urinal glass, quoth Rondibilis, grope her pulse, and see the disposition of her hypogaster, together with her umbilicary parts,—according to the prescript rule of Hippocrates, 2. *Aph.* 35,—before I proceed any further in the cure of her distemper. No, no, quoth Panurge, that will be but to little purpose. Such a feat is for the practice of us that are lawyers, who have the rubric, *De ventre inspiciendo.*[51] Do not therefore trouble yourself about it master doctor: I will provide for her a plaster of warm guts. Do not neglect your more urgent occasions otherwhere, for coming to my wedding. I will send you some supply of victuals to your own house, without putting you to the trouble of coming abroad, and you shall always be my special friend. With this, approaching somewhat nearer to him, he clapped into his hand, without the speaking of so much as one word, four rose nobles. Rondibilis did shut his fist upon them right kindly; yet, as if it had displeased him to make acceptance of such golden presents, he in a start, as if he had been wroth, said, He, he, he, he, he, there was no need of anything, I thank you nevertheless. From wicked folks I never get enough, and from honest people I refuse nothing. I shall be always, sir, at your command. Provided that I pay you well, quoth Panurge. That, quoth Rondibilis, is understood.

CHAPTER 35

How the philosopher Trouillogan handleth the difficulty of marriage

As this discourse was ended, Pantagruel said to the philosopher Trouillogan, Our loyal, honest, true, and trusty friend, the lamp from hand to hand is come to you. It falleth to your turn to give an answer, should Panurge, pray you, marry, yea, or no? He should do both, quoth Trouillogan. What say you, asked Panurge? That which you have heard, answered Trouillogan. What have I heard? replied Pan-

urge. That which I have said, replied Trouillogan. Ha, ha, ha, are we come to that pass? quoth Panurge. Let it go nevertheless, I do not value it at a rush, seeing we can make no better of the game. But howsoever tell me, should I marry or no? Neither the one nor the other, answered Trouillogan. The devil take me, quoth Panurge, if these odd answers do not make me dote, and may he snatch me presently away, if I do understand you. Stay awhile, until I fasten these spectacles of mine on this left ear, that I may hear you better. With this Pantagruel perceived at the door of the great hall, which was that day their dining room, Gargantua's little dog, whose name was Kyne; for so was Toby's dog called, as is recorded. Then did he say to these who were there present, Our king is not far off,—let us all rise.

That word was scarcely sooner uttered, than that Gargantua with his royal presence graced that banqueting and stately hall. Each of the guests arose to do their king that reverence and duty which became them. After that Gargantua had most affably saluted all the gentlemen there present, he said, Good friends, I beg this favour of you, and therein you will very much oblige me, that you leave not the places where you sate, nor quit the discourse you were upon. Let a chair be brought hither unto this end of the table, and reach me a cup full of the strongest and best wine you have, that I may drink to all the company. You are, in faith, all welcome, gentlemen. Now let me know, what talk you were about. To this Pantagruel answered, that at the beginning of the second service Panurge had proposed a problematic theme, to wit, Whether he should marry, or not marry? that Father Hippothadeus and Doctor Rondibilis had already dispatched their resolutions thereupon; and that, just as his majesty was coming in, the faithful Trouillogan in the delivery of his opinion hath thus far proceeded, that when Panurge asked,—whether he ought to marry, yea, or no?—at first he made this answer, Both together. When this same question was again propounded, his second answer was, Neither the one, nor the other. Panurge exclaimeth, that those answers are full of repugnancies and contradictions, protesting that he understands them not, nor what it is that can be meant by them. If I be not mistaken, quoth Gargantua, I understand it very well. The answer is not unlike to that which was once made by a philosopher in ancient time, who being interrogated, if he had a woman, whom they named him, to his wife? I have her, quoth he, but she hath not me,—possessing her, by her I am not possest. Such another answer, quoth Pantagruel, was once made by a certain bouncing wench of Sparta who being asked, if at any time she had had to do with a man? No, quoth she, but sometimes men have had to do with me. Well then, quoth Rondibilis, let it be a neuter in physic, —as when we say a body is neuter, when it is neither sick nor healthful,—and a mean in philosophy; *that,* by an abnegation of both extremes, and *this,* by the participation of the one and of the other. Even as when lukewarm water is said to be both hot and cold; or rather, as when time makes the partition, and equally divides betwixt the two, a while in the one, another while as long in the other opposite extremity. The holy apostle, quoth Hippothadeus, seemeth, as I conceive, to have more clearly explained this point, when he said, Those that are married, let them be as if they were not married; and those that have wives let them be as if they had no wives at all. I thus interpret, quoth Pantagruel, the having and not having of a wife. To have a wife, is to have the use of her in such a way as nature hath ordained, which is for the aid, society, and solace of man, and propagating of his race. To have no wife is not to be uxorious, play the coward, and be lazy about her, and not for her sake to distain the lustre of that affection which man owes to God; or yet for her to leave those offices and duties which he owes unto his country, unto his friends and kindred; or for her to abandon and forsake his precious studies, and other businesses of account, to wait still on her will, her beck, and her buttocks. If we be pleased in this sense to take having and not having of a wife, we shall indeed find no repugnancy nor contradiction in the terms at all.

CHAPTER 36

A continuation of the answers of the Ephectic and Pyrrhonian philosopher Trouillogan

You speak wisely, quoth Panurge, if the moon were green cheese. Such a tale once pissed my goose. I do not think but that I am let down into that dark pit, in the lowermost bottom where the truth was hid, according to the saying of Heraclitus. I see no whit at all, I hear nothing, understand as little, my senses are altogether dulled and blunted; truly I do very shrewdly suspect that I am enchanted. I will now alter the former style of my discourse, and talk to him in another strain. Our trusty friend, stir not, nor imburse any; but let us vary the chance, and speak without disjunctives. I see already, that these loose and ill-joined members of an enunciation do vex, trouble and perplex you.

Now go on, in the name of God! Should I marry?

Trouillogan. There is some likelihood therein.

Panurge. But if I do not marry?

Trouil. I see in that no inconvenience.

Pan. You do not?

Trouil. None, truly, if my eyes deceive me not.

Pan. Yea, but I find more than five hundred.

Trouil. Reckon them.

Pan. This is an impropriety of speech, I confess; for I do no more thereby, but take a certain for an uncertain number, and posit the determinate term for what is indeterminate. When I say therefore five hundred, my meaning is, many.

Trouil. I hear you.

Pan. Is it possible for me to live without a wife, in the name of all the subterranean devils?

Trouil. Away with these filthy beasts.

Pan. Let it be then in the name of God; for my Salmigondinish people used to say, To lie alone, without a wife, is certainly a brutish life. And such a life also was it assevered to be by Dido, in her lamentations.

Trouil. At your command.

Pan. By the pody cody, I have fished fair; where are we now? But will you tell me? Shall I marry?

Trouil. Perhaps.

Pan. Shall I thrive or speed well withal?

Trouil. According to the encounter.

Pan. But if in my adventure I encounter aright, as I hope I will, shall be I fortunate?

Trouil. Enough.

Pan. Let us turn the clean contrary way, and brush our former words against the wool: what if I encounter ill?

Trouil. Then blame not me.

Pan. But, of courtesy, be pleased to give me some advice. I heartily beseech you, what must I do?

Trouil. Even what thou wilt.

Pan. Wishy washy; trolly, lolly.

Trouil. Do not invocate the name of any thing, I pray you.

Pan. In the name of God, let it be so! My actions shall be regulated by the rule and square of your counsel. What is it that you advise and counsel me to do?

Trouil. Nothing.

Pan. Shall I marry?

Trouil. I have no hand in it.

Pan. Then shall I not marry?

Trouil. I cannot help it.

Pan. If I never marry, I shall never be a cuckold.

Trouil. I thought so.

Pan. But put the case that I be married.

Trouil. Where shall we put it?

Pan. Admit it be so then, and take my meaning, in that sense.

Trouil. I am otherwise employed.

Pan. By the death of a hog, and mother of a toad, O Lord, if I durst hazard upon a little fling at the swearing game, though privily and under thumb, it would lighten the burden of my heart, and ease my lights and reins exceedingly. A little patience, nevertheless, is requisite. Well then, if I marry, I shall be a cuckold.

Trouil. One would say so.

Pan. Yet if my wife prove a virtuous, wise, discreet, and chaste woman, I shall never be cuckolded.

Trouil. I think you speak congruously.

Pan. Hearken.

Trouil. As much as you will.

Pan. Will she be discreet and chaste? This is the only point I would be resolved in.

Trouil. I question it.

Pan. You never saw her?

Trouil. Not that I know of.

Pan. Why do you then doubt of that which you know not?

Trouil. For a cause.

Pan. And if you should know her?

Trouil. Yet more.

Pan. Page, my little pretty darling, take here my cap,—I give it to thee. Have a care you do not break the spectacles that are in it. Go down to the lower court. Swear there half an hour for me, and I shall in compensation of that favour swear hereafter for thee as much as thou wilt. But who shall cuckold me?

Trouil. Somebody.

Pan. By the belly of the wooden horse at Troy, Master Somebody, I shall bang, belam thee, and claw thee well for thy labour.

Trouil. You say so.

Pan. Nay, nay, that Nick in the dark cellar, who hath no white in his eye, carry me quite away with him, if, in that case, whensoever I go abroad from the palace of my domestic residence, I do not, with as much circumspection as they use to ring mares in our country to keep them from being sallied by stoned horses, clap a Bergamasco lock upon my wife.

Trouil. Talk better.

Pan. It is *bien chien, chié chanté,* well cacked, and cackled, shitten, and sung in matter of talk. Let us resolve on somewhat.

Trouil. I do not gainsay it.

Pan. Have a little patience. Seeing I cannot on this side draw any blood of you, I will try, if with the lancet of my judgment I be able to bleed you in another vein. Are you married, or are you not?

Trouil. Neither the one nor the other, and both together.

Pan. O the good God help us! By the death of a buffle-ox, I sweat with the toil and travail that I am put to, and find my digestion broke off, disturbed, and interrupted; for all my phrenes, metaphrenes, and diaphragms, back, belly, midrib, muscles, veins, and sinews, are held in a suspense, and for a while discharged from their proper offices, to stretch forth their several powers and abilities, for incornifistibulating, and laying up into the hamper of my understanding your various sayings and answers.

Trouil. I shall be no hinderer thereof.

Pan. Tush, for shame! Our faithful friend, speak, are you married?

Trouil. I think so.

Pan. You were also married before you had this wife.

Trouil. It is possible.

Pan. Had you good luck in your first marriage?

Trouil. It is not impossible.

Pan. How thrive you with this second wife of yours?

Trouil. Even as it pleaseth my fatal destiny.

Pan. But what in good earnest? Tell me— do you prosper well with her?

Trouil. It is likely.

Pan. Come on, in the name of God. I vow, by the burden of Saint Christopher, that I had rather undertake the fetching of a fart forth of the belly of a dead ass, than to draw out of you a positive and determinate resolution. Yet shall I be sure at this time to have a snatch at you, and get my claws over you. Our trusty friend, let us shame the devil of hell, and confess the verity. Were you ever a cuckold? I say you who are here, and not that other you, who playeth below in the tennis-court?

Trouil. No, if it was not predestinated.

Pan. By the flesh, blood, and body, I swear, reswear, forswear, abjure, and renounce: he evades and avoids, shifts and escapes me, and quite slips and winds himself out of my gripes and clutches.

At these words Gargantua arose, and said, Praised be the good God in all things, but especially for bringing the world into the height of refinedness beyond what it was when I first became acquainted therewith, that now the most learned and most prudent philosophers are not ashamed to be seen entering in at the porches and frontispieces of the schools of the Pyrrhonian, Aporrhetic, Sceptic, and Ephetic sects. Blessed be the holy name of God! Veritably, it is like henceforth to be found an enterprise of much more easy undertaking, to catch lions by the neck, horses by the mane, oxen by the horns, bulls by the muzzle, wolves by the tail, goats by the beard, and flying birds by the feet, than to entrap such philosophers in their words. Farewell, my worthy, dear, and honest friends.

When he had done thus speaking, he withdrew himself from the company. Pantagruel, and others with him would have followed and accompanied him, but he would not permit them so to do. No sooner was Gargantua departed out of the banqueting-hall, than that Pantagruel said to the invited guests; Plato's *Timæus*, at the beginning always of a solemn festival convention, was wont to count those that were called thereto. We, on the contrary, shall at the closure and end of this treatment, reckon up our number. One, two, three; where is the fourth? I miss my friend Bridlegoose. Was not he sent for? Epistemon answered,—That he had been at his house to bid and invite him, but could not meet with him; for that a messenger from the parliament of Myrelingois, in Myrelingues, was come to him, with a writ of summons, to cite and warn him personally to appear before the reverend senators of the High Court there, to vindicate and justify himself at the bar, of the crime of prevarication laid to his charge, and to be peremptorily instanced against him, in a certain decree, judgment, or sentence lately awarded, given, and pro-

nounced by him: and that, therefore, he had taken horse, and departed in great haste from his own house, to the end, that without peril or danger of falling into a default, or contumacy, he might be the better able to keep the prefixed and appointed time.

I will, quoth Pantagruel, understand how that matter goeth. It is now above forty years, that he hath been constantly the judge of Fonsbeton, during which space of time he hath given four thousand definitive sentences. Of two thousand three hundred and nine whereof, although appeal was made by the parties whom he had judicially condemned, from his inferior judicatory to the supreme court of the parliament of Myrelingois, in Myrelingues, they were all of them nevertheless confirmed, ratified, and approved of by an order, decree, and final sentence of the said sovereign court, to the casting of the appellants, and utter overthrow of the suits wherein they had been foiled at law, for ever and a day. That now, in his old age, he should be personally summoned, who in all the foregoing time of his life hath demeaned himself so unblameably in the discharge of the office and vocation he had been called unto, it cannot assuredly be, that such a change hath happened without some notorious misfortune and disaster. I am resolved to help and assist him in equity and justice to the uttermost extent of my power and ability. I know the malice, despite and wickedness of the world to be so much more now-a-days exasperated, increased, and aggravated by what it was not long since, that the best cause that is, how just and equitable soever it be, standeth in great need to be succoured, aided, and supported. Therefore presently, from this very instant forth, do I purpose, till I see the event and closure thereof, most heedfully to attend and wait upon it, for fear of some under-hand tricky surprisal, cavilling pettifoggery, or fallacious quirks in law, to his detriment, hurt, or disadvantage.

Then dinner being done, and the tables drawn and removed, when Pantagruel had very cordially and affectionately thanked his invited guests for the favour which he had enjoyed of their company, he presented them with several rich and costly gifts, such as jewels, rings set with precious stones, gold and silver vessels, with a great deal of other sort of plate besides, and lastly, taking of them all his leave, retired himself into an inner chamber.

CHAPTER 37

How Pantagruel persuaded Panurge to take counsel of a fool

WHEN Pantagruel had withdrawn himself, he, by a little sloping window in one of the galleries, perceived Panurge in a lobby not far from thence, walking alone, with the gesture, carriage, and garb of a fond dotard, raving, wagging, and shaking his hands, dandling, lolling, and nodding with his head, like a cow bellowing for her calf; and, having then called him nearer, spoke unto him thus. You are at this present, as I think, not unlike to a mouse entangled in a snare, who the more that she goeth about to rid and unwind herself out of the gin wherein she is caught, by endeavouring to clear and deliver her feet from the pitch whereto they stick, the fouler she is bewrayed with it, and the more strongly pestered therein. Even so is it with you. For the more that you labour, strive, and inforce yourself to disencumber, and extricate your thoughts out of the implicating involutions and fetterings of the grievous and lamentable gins and springs of anguish and perplexity, the greater difficulty there is in the relieving of you, and you remain faster bound than ever. Nor do I know for the removal of this inconveniency any remedy but one.

Take heed, I have often heard it said in a vulgar proverb, The wise may be instructed by a fool. Seeing the answers and responses of sage and injudicious men have no manner of way satisfied you, take advice of some fool, and possibly by so doing you may come to get that counsel which will be agreeable to your own heart's-desire and contentment. You know how by the advice and counsel and prediction of fools, many kings, princes, states, and commonwealths have been preserved, several battles gained, and divers doubts of a most perplexed intricacy resolved. I am not so diffident of your memory, as to hold it needful to refresh it with a quotation of examples; nor do I so far undervalue your judgment, but that I think it will acquiesce in the reason of this my subsequent discourse. As he who narrowly takes heed to what concerns the dexterous management of his private affairs, domestic businesses, and those adoes which are confined within the strait-laced compass of one family,—who is attentive, vigilant, and active in the economic rule of his own house,—whose frugal spirit never strays from home,—who loseth no occasion whereby he may purchase to himself more riches, and build up new heaps of treasure on his former wealth,—and who knows warily how to prevent the inconveniences of poverty, is called a worldly wise man, though perhaps in the second judgment of the intelligences which are above, he be esteemed a fool,—so, on the contrary is he most like, even in the thoughts of celestial spirits, to be not only sage, but to presage events to come by divine inspiration, who laying quite aside those cares which are conducible to his body, or his fortunes, and, as it were departing from himself, rids all his senses of terrene affections, and clears his fancies of those plodding studies which harbour in the minds of thriving men. All which neglects of sublunary things are vulgarly imputed folly. After this manner, the son of Picus, King of the Latins, the great soothsayer Faunus, was called Fatuus by the witless rabble of the common people. The like we daily see practised amongst the comic players, whose dramatic rolls, in distribution of the personages, appoint the acting of the fool to him who is the wisest of the troop. In approbation also of this fashion the mathematicians allow the very same horoscope to princes and to sots. Whereof a right pregnant instance by them is given in the nativities of Æneas and Chorœbus; the latter of which two is by Euphorion said to have been a fool; and yet had with the former the same aspects, and heavenly genethliac influences.

I shall not, I suppose, swerve much from the purpose in hand, if I relate unto you, what John Andrew said upon the return of a papal writ, which was directed to the mayor and burgesses of Rochelle, and after him by Panorme, upon the same Pontifical canon; Barbatias on the *Pandects*, and recently by Jason, in his *Councils*, concerning Seyny John, the noted fool of Paris, and Caillette's fore great grandfather. The case is this. At Paris, in the roast-meat cookery of the Petit-Chastelet, before the cook-shop of one of the roast-meat sellers of that lane, a certain hungry porter was eating his bread, after he had by parcels kept it a while above the reek and steam of a fat goose on the spit, turning at a great fire, and found it so besmoked with the vapour, to be savoury; which the cook observing, took no notice, till after having ravined his penny loaf, whereof no morsel had been unsmokified, he was about decamping and going away. But, by your leave, as the fellow thought to have departed thence shot-free, the master-cook laid hold upon him by the gorget, and demanded payment for the smoke of his roast-meat. The porter answered, That he had sustained no loss at all,—that by what he had done there was no diminution made of the flesh,—that he had taken nothing of his, and that therefore he was not indebted to him in anything. As for the smoke in question, that, although he had not been there, it would howsoever have been evaporated: besides, that before that time it had never been seen nor heard, that roast-meat smoke was sold upon the streets of Paris. The cook hereto replied, That he was not obliged nor any way bound to feed and nourish for nought a porter whom he had never seen before, with the smoke of his roast-meat, and thereupon swore, that if he would not forthwith content and satisfy him with present payment for the repast which he had thereby got, that he would take his crooked staves from off his back; which, instead of having loads thereafter laid upon them, should serve for fuel to his kitchen fires. Whilst he was going about so to do, and to have pulled them to him by one of the bottom rungs, which he had caught in his hand, the sturdy porter got out of his gripe, drew forth the knotty cudgel, and stood to his own defence. The altercation waxed hot in words, which moved the gaping hoydens of the sottish Parisians to run from all parts thereabouts, to see what the issue would be of that babbling strife and contention. In the interim of this dispute, to very good purpose Seyny John, the fool and citizen of Paris, happened to be there, whom the cook perceiving, said to the porter, Wilt thou refer and submit unto the noble Seyny John, the decision of the difference and controversy which is betwixt us? Yes, by the blood of a goose, answered the porter, I am content. Seyny John the fool, finding that the cook and porter had compromised the determination of their variance and debate to the discretion of his award and arbitrement, after that the reasons on either side, whereupon was grounded the mutual fierceness of their brawling jar, had been to the full displayed and laid open before him, commanded the porter to draw out of the fob of his belt a piece of money, if he had it. Whereupon the porter immediately without delay, in reverence to the authority of such a judicious umpire, put the tenth part of a silver Philip into his hand. This little Philip Seyny John took, then set it on his left shoulder, to try by feeling if it was of a sufficient weight. After that, laying it on the palm of his hand, he made it ring and tingle, to understand by the ear if it was of a good alloy in the metal whereof it was composed. Thereafter he put it to the ball or apple of his left eye, to explore by the sight, if it was well stamped and marked; all which being done, in a profound silence of the whole doltish people, who were the spectators of this pageantry, to the great hope of the cook's, and despair of the porter's prevalency in the suit that was in agitation, he finally caused the porter to make it sound several times upon the stall of the cook's shop. Then with a presidential majesty holding his bauble, sceptre-like, in his hand, muffling his head with a hood of marten skins, each side whereof had the resemblance of an ape's face, sprucified up with ears of pasted paper, and having about his neck a bucked ruff, raised, furrowed, and ridged, with pointing sticks of the shape and fashion of small organ pipes, he first with all the force of his lungs coughed two or three times, and then with an audible voice pronounced this following sentence. The Court declareth, that the porter, who ate his bread at the smoke of the roast, hath civilly paid the cook with the sound of his money. And the said Court ordaineth, that every one return to his own home, and attend his proper business, without costs and charges, and for a cause. This verdict, award, and arbitrement of the Parisian fool did appear so equitable, yea, so admirable to the aforesaid doctors, that they very much doubted, if the matter had been brought before the sessions for justice of the said place; or that the judges of the Rota at Rome had been umpires therein; or yet that the Areopagites themselves had been the deciders thereof; if by any one part, or all of them together, it had been so judicially sententiated and awarded. Therefore advise, if you will be counselled by a fool.

CHAPTER 38

How Triboulet is set forth and blazoned by Pantagruel and Panurge

By my soul, quoth Panurge, that overture pleaseth me exceedingly well. I will therefore lay hold thereon, and embrace it. At the very motioning thereof, my right entrail seemeth to be widened and enlarged, which was but just now hardbound, contracted, and costive. But as we have hitherto made choice of the purest and most refined cream of wisdom and sapience for our counsel, so would I now have to preside and bear the prime sway in our consultation as very a fool in the supreme degree. Triboulet, quoth Pantagruel, is completely foolish, as I conceive. Yes, truly, answered Panurge, he is properly and totally a fool, a

Pantagruel.	Panurge.
Fatal f.	Jovial f.
Natural f.	Mercurial f.
Celestial f.	Lunatic f.
Erratic f.	Ducal f.
Eccentric f.	Common f.
Ætherial and	Lordly f.
Junonian f.	Palatin f.
Arctic f.	Principal f.
Heroic f.	Pretorian f.
Genial f.	Elected f.
Inconstant f.	Courtly f.
Earthly f.	Primipilary f.
Salacious and	Triumphant f.
sporting f.	Vulgar f.
Jocund and wanton f.	Domestic f.
Pimpled f.	Exemplary f.
Freckled f.	Rare outlandish f.
Bell-tinging f.	Satrapal f.
Laughing and	Civil f.
lecherous f.	Popular f.
Nimming and	Familiar f.
filching f.	Notable f.
Unpressed f.	Favourized f.
First broached f.	Latinized f.
Augustal f.	Ordinary f.
Cæsarine f.	Transcendent f.
Imperial f.	Rising f.
Royal f.	Papal f.
Patriarchal f.	Consistorian f.
Original f.	Conclavist f.
Loyal f.	Bullist f.
Episcopal f.	Synodal f.
Doctoral f.	Doting and raving f.
Monachal f.	Singular and
Fiscal f.	surpassing f.
Extravagant f.	Special and
Writhed f.	excelling f.
Canonical f.	Metaphysical f.
Such another f.	Ecstatical f.
Graduated f.	Predicamental and
Commensal f.	categoric f.
Primolicentiated f.	Predicable and
Trainbearing f.	enunciatory f.
Supererogating f.	Decumane and
Collateral f.	superlative f.

Pantagruel.	Panurge.
Haunch and side f.	Dutiful and
Nestling, ninny, and	officious f.
youngling f.	Optical and
Flitting, giddy, and	perspective f.
unsteady f.	Algoristic f.
Brancher, novice, and	Algebraical f.
cockney f.	Cabalistical and
Haggard, cross, and	Massoretical f.
forward f.	Talmudical f.
Gentle, mild, and	Algamalized f.
tractable f.	Compendious f.
Mail-coated f.	Abbreviated f.
Pilfering and	Hyperbolical f.
purloining f.	Anatomastical f.
Tail-grown f.	Allegorical f.
Grey peckled f.	Tropological f.
Pleonasmical f.	Micher pincrust f.
Capital f.	Heteroclit f.
Hair-brained f.	Summist f.
Cordial f.	Abridging f.
Intimate f.	Morish f.
Hepatic f.	Leaden-sealed f.
Cupshotten and	Mandatory f.
swilling f.	Compassionate f.
Splenetic f.	Titulary f.
Windy f.	Crooching, showking,
Legitimate f.	ducking f.
Azymathal f.	Grim, stern, harsh,
Almicantarized f.	and wayward f.
Proportioned f.	Well-hung and tim-
Chinnified f.	bered f.
Swollen and puffed-	Ill-clawed, pounced,
up f.	and pawed f.
Overcockrilifedled	Well-stoned f.
and fied f.	Crabbed and unpleas-
Corollary f.	ing f.
Eastern f.	Winded and untaint-
Sublime f.	ed f.
Crimson f.	Kitchen-haunting f.
Ingrained f.	Lofty and stately f.
City f.	Spitrack f.
Basely-accoutred f.	Architrave f.
Mast-headed f.	Pedestal f.
Model f.	Tetragonal f.
Second notial f.	Renowned f.
Cheerful and	Rheumatic f.
buxom f.	Flaunting and brag-
Solemn f.	gadochio f.
Annual f.	Egregious f.
Festival f.	Humorous and capri-
Recreative f.	cious f.
Boorish and counter-	Rude, gross, and ab-
feit f.	surd f.
Pleasant f.	Large-measured f.
Privileged f.	Babble f.

Pantagruel.	Panurge.
Rustical f.	Down-right f.
Proper and peculiar f.	Broad-listed f.
Ever ready f.	Downsical-bearing f.
Diapasonal f.	Stale and over-worn f.
Resolute f.	Saucy and swagger-
Hieroglyphical f.	ing f.
Authentic f.	Full-bulked f.
Worthy f.	Gallant and vainglori-
Precious f.	ous f.
Fanatic f.	Gorgeous and gaudy
Fantastical f.	f.
Symphatic f.	Continual and inter-
Panic f.	mitting f.
Limbecked and dis-	Rebasing and round-
tilled f.	ling f.
Comportable f.	Prototypal and pre-
Wretched and heart-	cedenting f.
less f.	Prating f.
Fooded f.	Catechetic f.
Thick and threefold f.	Cacodoxical f.
Damasked f.	Meridional f.
Ferny f.	Nocturnal f.
Unleavened f.	Occidental f.
Barytonant f.	Trifling f.
Pink and spot-	Astrological and fig-
powdered f.	ure-flinging f.
Musket-proof f.	Genethliac and horo-
Pedantic f.	scopal f.
Strouting f.	Knavish f.
Wood f.	Idiot f.
Greedy f.	Blockish f.
Senseless f.	Beetle-headed f.
Godderlich f.	Grotesque f.
Obstinate f.	Impertinent f.
Contradictory f.	Quarrelsome f.
Pedagogical f.	Unmannerly f.
Daft f.	Captious and sophis-
Drunken f.	tical f.
Peevish f.	Soritic f.
Prodigal f.	Catholoproton f.
Rash f.	Hoti and Dioti f.
Plodding f.	Alphos and Catati f.

Pantagruel. If there was any reason why at Rome the Quirinal holiday of old was called the Feast of Fools; I know not, why we may not for the like cause institute in France the Tribouletic Festivals, to be celebrated and solemnized over all the land.

Panurge. If all fools carried cruppers.

Pant. If he were the god Fatuus, of whom we have already made mention, the husband of the goddess Fatua, his father would be Good Day, and his grand-mother Good Even.

Pan. If all fools paced, albeit he be some-what wry-legged, he would overlay at least a fathom at every rake. Let us go toward him without any further lingering or delay;—we shall have, no doubt, some fine resolution of him. I am ready to go, and long for the issue of our progress impatiently. I must needs, quoth Pantagruel, according to my former resolution therein, be present at Bridlegoose's trial. Nevertheless, whilst I shall be upon my journey towards Myrelingues, which is on the other side of the river of Loire, I will dispatch Carpalim to bring along with him from Blois the fool Triboulet. Then was Carpalim instantly sent away, and Pantagruel at the same time, attended by his domestics, Panurge, Epistemon, Ponocrates, Friar John, Gymnast, Ryzotomus, and others, marched forward on the high road to Myrelingues.

CHAPTER 39

How Pantagruel was present at the trial of Judge Bridlegoose, who decided causes and controversies in law by the chance and fortune of the dice

On the day following, precisely at the hour appointed, Pantagruel came to Myrelingues. At his arrival the presidents, senators, and counsellors prayed him to do them the honour to enter in with them, to hear the decision of all the causes, arguments, and reasons, which Bridlegoose in his own defence would produce, why he had pronounced a certain sentence, against the subsidy assessor, Toucheronde, which did not seem very equitable to that centumviral court. Pantagruel very willingly condescended to their desire, and accordingly entering in, found Bridlegoose sitting within the middle of the inclosure of the said court of justice; who immediately upon the coming of Pantagruel, accompanied with the senatorian members of that worshipful judicatory, arose, went to the bar, had his indictment read, and for all his reasons, defences, and excuses, answered nothing else, but that he was become old, and that his sight of late was very much failed, and become dimmer than it was wont to be; instancing therewithal many miseries and calamities, which old age bringeth along with it, and are concomitant to wrinkled elders; which *not. per Archid. d. l. lxxxvi. c. tanta.*[52] By reason of which infirmity he was not able so distinctly and clearly to discern the points and blots of the dice, as formerly he had been accustomed to do: whence it might very well have happened, said he, as old dim-sighted Isaac took Jacob for Esau, that I, after the same manner, at the decision of causes and controversies in law, should have been mistaken in taking a *quatre* for a *cinque*, or *trois* for a *deuce*. This, I beseech your worships, quoth he, to take into your serious consideration and to have the more favourable opinion of my uprightness, (notwithstanding the prevarication whereof I am accused, in the matter of Toucheronde's sentence,) for that at the time of that decree's pronouncing I only had made use of my small dice; and your worships, said he, knew very well, how by the most authentic rules of the law it is provided, That the imperfections of nature should never be imputed unto any for crimes and transgressions; as appeareth, *ff. de re milit. l. qui cum uno. ff. de reg. Jur. l. fere. ff. de ædil. edict. per totum. ff. de term. mod. l. Divus Adrianus,* resolved by *Lud. Rom. in l. si vero. ff. Sol. Matr.* And who would offer to do otherwise, should not thereby accuse the man, but nature, and the all-seeing providence of God, as is evident in *l. maximum vitium, c. de lib. prætor.*

What kind of dice, quoth Trinquamelle, grand president of the said court, do you mean, my friend Bridlegoose? The dice, quoth Bridlegoose, of sentences at law, decrees, and peremptory judgments, *Alea Judiciorum,*[53] whereof is written *Per Doct. 26. qu. 2. cap. sort. l. nec emptio ff. de contrahend. empt. l. quod debetur. ff. de pecul. et ibi Bartol.,* and which your worships do, as well as I, use, in this glorious sovereign court of yours. So do all other righteous judges in their decision of processes, and final determination of legal differences, observing that which hath been said thereof by D. Henri. Ferrandat, *et not. gl. in c. fin. de sortil. et l. sed cum ambo. ff. de jud. Ubi Docto.* Mark, that chance and fortune are good, honest, profitable, and necessary for ending of, and putting a final closure to dissensions and debates in suits at law. The same hath more clearly been declared by Bald. Bartol. et Alex. c. *communia de leg. l. si duo.* But how is it that you do these things? asked Trinquamelle. I very briefly, quoth Bridlegoose, shall answer you, according to the doctrine and instructions of *Leg. ampliorem in refutatoriis par. c. de appel.;* which is conformable to what is said in *Gloss. l. 1. ff. quod. met. causa Gaudent brevitate moderni.*[54] My practice is therein the same with that of your other wor-

ships, and as the custom of the judicatory requires, unto which our law commandeth us to have regard, and by the rule thereof still to direct and regulate our actions and procedures; *ut not. extra. de consuet. c. ex literis et ibi innoc.* For having well and exactly seen, surveyed, overlooked, reviewed, recognized, read, and read over again, turned and tossed over, seriously perused and examined the bills of complaint, accusations, impeachments, indictments, warnings, citations, summonings, comparitions, appearances, mandates, commissions, delegations, instructions, informations, inquests, preparatories, productions, evidences, proofs, allegations, depositions, cross speeches, contradictions, supplications, requests, petitions, inquiries, instruments of the deposition of witnesses, rejoinders, replies, confirmations of former assertions, duplies, triplies, answers to rejoinders, writings, deeds, reproaches, disabling of exceptions taken, grievances, salvation-bills, re-examination of witnesses, confronting of them together, declarations, denunciations, libels, certificates, royal missives, letters of appeal, letters of attorney, instruments of compulsion, declinatories, anticipatories, evocations, messages, dimissions, issues, exceptions, dilatory pleas, demurs, compositions, injunctions, reliefs, reports, returns, confessions, acknowledgements, exploits, executions, and other such like confects, and spiceries, both at the one and the other side, as a good judge ought to do, conform to what hath been noted thereupon. *Spec. de ordination. paragr. 3. et Tit. de Offi. omn. jud. paragr. fin. et de rescriptis præsentat. parag.* 1.—I posit on the end of a table in my closet, all the pokes and bags of the defendant, and then allow unto him the first hazard of the dice, according to the usual manner of your other worships. And it is mentioned, *l favorabiliores ff. de reg. jur. et in cap. cum sunt eod. tit. lib.* 6. which saith, *Quum sunt partium jura obscura, reo potius tavendum est quam actori.*[55] That being done, I thereafter lay down upon the other end of the same table the bags and sachels of the plaintiff, as your other worships are accustomed to do, *visum visu,* just over against one another: for, *Opposita juxta se posita clarius elucescunt:*[56] *ut not. in lib.* 1. *parag. Videamus. ff. de his qui sunt sui vel alieni juris, et in l. munerum § mixta ff. de mun. et hon.* Then do I likeways and semblably throw the dice for him, and forthwith liver him his chance. But quoth

Trinquamelle, my friend, how come you to know, understand and resolve, the obscurity of these various and seeming contrary passages, in law, which are laid claim to by the suitors and pleading parties? Even just, quoth Bridlegoose, after the fashion of your other worships: to wit, when there are many bags on the one side, and on the other, I then use my little small dice, after the customary manner of your other worships, in obedience to the law, *Semper in stipulationibus ff. de reg. jur.* and the law *versale* verifieth that *Eod. tit. semper in obscuris quod minimum est sequimur.*[57] canonized in *c. in obscuris, eod. tit. lib.* 6. I have other large great dice, fair and goodly ones, which I employ in the fashion that your other worships use to do, when the matter is more plain, clear, and liquid, that is to say, when there are fewer bags. But when you have done all these fine things, quoth Trinquamelle, how do you, my friend, award your decrees, and pronounce judgment? Even as your other worships, answered Bridlegoose; for I give out sentence in his favour unto whom hath befallen the best chance by dice, judiciary, tribunian, pretorial, what comes first. So our laws command, *ff. qui pot. in pign. l. creditor. c. de consul* 1. *Et de regul. jur. in* 6. *Qui prior est tempore potior est jure.*[58]

CHAPTER 40

How Bridlegoose giveth reasons, why he looked over those lawpapers which he decided by the chance of the dice

YEA, but, quoth Trinquamelle, my friend, seeing it is by the lot, chance, and throw of the dice that you award your judgments and sentences, why do not you deliver up these fair throws and chances, the very same day and hour, without any further procrastination or delay, that the controverting party-pleaders appear before you? To what use can those writings serve you, those papers, and other procedures contained in the bags and pokes of the law-suitors? To the very same use, quoth Bridlegoose, that they serve your other worships. They are behooful unto me, and serve my turn in three things very exquisite, and authentic. First, For formality-sake; the omission whereof, that it maketh all, whatever is done, to be of no force nor value, is excellently well proved, by *Spec. 1. tit. de instr. edit. et tit. de rescript. present.* Besides

that, it is not unknown to you, who have had many more experiments thereof than I, how oftentimes, in judicial proceedings, the formalities utterly destroy the materialities and substances of the causes and matters agitated; for *forma mutata, mutatur substantia.*[59] *ff. ad exhib. l. Julianus ff. ad leg. fals. l. si is qui quadraginta. Et extra, de decim. c. ad audientiam, et de celebrat. miss. c. in quadam.*

Secondly, They are useful and steadable to me, even as unto your other worships, in lieu of some other honest and healthful exercise. The late Master Othoman Vadat, [Vadere,] a prime physician, as you would say, *Cod. de commit. et archi. lib.* 12, hath frequently told me, That the lack and default of bodily exercise is the chief, if not the sole and only, cause of the little health and short lives of all officers of justice, such as your worships and I am. Which observation was singularly well, before him, noted and remarked by Bartholus in *lib.* 1. *c. de sent. quæ pro eo quod.* Therefore is it that the practice of such-like exercitations is appointed to be laid hold on by your other worships, and consequently not to be denied unto me, who am of the same profession; *Quia accessorium naturam sequitur principalis.*[60] *de reg. jur. l.* 7 *et l. cum principalis, et l. nihil dolo ff. eod. tit. ff. de fide-jus. l. fide-jus. et extra de officio de leg. cap.* I. Let certain honest and recreative sports and plays of corporeal exercises be allowed and approved of; and so far *ff. de al. lus. et aleat. l. solent. et authent. ut omnes obed. in princ. col.* 7. *et ff. de præscript. verb. l. si gratuitam; et l.* I. *cod. de spect. l.* II. Such also is the opinion of *D. Thomæ, in secunda, secundæ, Q.* I. 168. Quoted to very good purpose, by D. Albert de Rosa, who *fuit magnus practicus,*[61] and a solemn doctor, as Barbaria attesteth in *principiis consil.* Wherefore the reason is evidently and clearly deduced and set down before us in *gloss. in proæmio ff. par. ne autem tertii.*

Interpone tuis interdum gaudia curis.[62]

In very deed, once, in the year a thousand four hundred fourscore and nine, having a business concerning the portion and inheritance of a younger brother depending in the court and chamber of the four High Treasurers of France, whereinto as soon as ever I got leave to enter, by a pecuniary permission of the usher thereof,—as your other worships know very well, that *pecuniæ obediunt om-*

nia,[63] and there, says Baldus, in *l. singularia ff. si cert. pet. et Salic. in l. receptitia. Cod. de constit. pecuni. et Card. in Clem.* I. *de baptism.*—I found them all recreating and diverting themselves at the play called muss, either before or after dinner: to me, truly, it is a think altogether indifferent, whether of the two it was, provided that *hic not.,*[64] that the game of the muss is honest, healthful, ancient, and lawful, *a Muscho inventore, de quo cod. de petit. hæred. l. si post motam, et Muscarii.* Such as play and sport at the muss are excusable in and by law, *lib.* I. *c. de excus. artific. lib.* 10. And at the very same time was Master Tielman Piquet one of the players of that game of muss. There is nothing that I do better remember, for he laughed heartily, when his fellow-members of the aforesaid judicial chamber spoiled their caps in swingeing of his shoulders. He, nevertheless, did even then say unto them, that the banging and flapping of him to the waste and havoc of their caps, should not, at their return from the palace to their own houses, excuse them from their wives, *Per c. extra. de præsumpt. et ibi gloss.* Now, *resolutorie loquendo*[65] I should say, according to the style and phrase of your other worships, that there is no exercise, sport, game, play, nor recreation in all this palatine, palacial, or parliamentary world, more aromatizing and fragrant, than to empty and void bags and purses—turn over papers and writings—quote margins and backs of scrolls and rolls, fill panniers, and take inspection of causes *Ex Bart. et Joan. de Pra. in l. falsa de condit. et demonst. ff.*

Thirdly, I consider, as your own worships used to do, that time ripeneth and bringeth all things to maturity,—that by time everything cometh to be made manifest and patent,—and that time is the father of truth and virtue. *Gloss. in l.* I. *cod. de servit authent. de restit. et ea quæ pa. et spec. tit de requisit. cons.* Therefore is it, that after the manner and fashion of your other worships, I defer, protract, delay, prolong, intermit, surcease, pause, linger, suspend, prorogate, drive out, wire-draw, and shift off the time of giving a definitive sentence, to the end that the suit or process, being well fanned and winnowed, tossed and canvassed to and fro, narrowly, precisely, and nearly garbelled, sifted, searched, and examined, and on all hands exactly argued, disputed, and debated, may, by succession of time, come at last to its full ripeness and maturity. By means whereof, when

the fatal hazard of the dice ensueth thereupon, the parties cast or condemned by the said aleatory chance will with much greater patience, and more mildly and gently, endure and bear up the disastrous load of their misfortune, than if they had been sentenced at their first arrival unto the court, as *not. gl. ff. de excus. tut. l. tria onera.*

> *Portatur leviter quod portat quisque*
> *libenter.*[66]

On the other part, to pass a decree or sentence, when the action is raw, crude, green, unripe, and unprepared as at the beginning, a danger would ensue of a no less inconveniency than that which the physicians have been wont to say befalleth to him in whom an imposthume is pierced before it be ripe, or unto any other, whose body is purged of a strong predominating humour before its digestion. For as it is written, *in authent. hæc constit. in Innoc. de consist. princip.*—so is the same repeated *in gloss. in c. cæterum extra de jura. calumn. Quod medicamenta morbis exhibent, hoc jura negotiis.*[67] Nature furthermore admonisheth and teacheth us to gather and reap, eat and feed on fruits when they are ripe, and not before. *Instit. de rer. div. paragr. is ad quem. et ff. de action. empt. l. Julianus.* To marry likewise our daughters when they are ripe, and no sooner, *ff. de donation. inter vir. et uxor. l. cum. hic status. paragr. si quis sponsam et* 27 *qu.* I. *c. sicut dicit gloss.*

> *Jam matura thoro plenis adoleverat annis*
> *Virginitas.*[68]

And, in a word, she instructeth us to do nothing of any considerable importance, but in a full maturity and ripeness, 23 *q.* 2. § *ult. et* 23 *de c. ultimo.*

CHAPTER 41

How Bridlegoose relateth the history of the reconcilers of parties at variance in matters of law

I REMEMBER to the same purpose, quoth Bridlegoose, in continuing his discourse, that in the time when at Poictiers I was a student of law under Brocadium Juris,[69] there was at Semerve one Peter Dendin, a very honest man, careful labourer of the ground, fine singer in a church desk, of good repute and credit, and older than the most aged of all your worships, who was wont to say, that he had seen the great and goodly good man, the Council of Lateran, with his wide and broad-brimmed red hat. As also, that he had beheld and looked upon the fair and beautiful prag-matical sanction, his wife, with her huge ros-ary or patenotrian chapelet of jet beads, hanging at a large sky-coloured riband. This honest man compounded, attoned, and agreed more differences, controversies, and variances at law, than had been determined, voided, and finished during his time in the whole palace of Poictiers, in the auditory of Montmorillon, and in the town-house of the old Partenay. This amicable disposition of his rendered him venerable, and of great estimation, sway, power, and authority throughout all the neighboring places of Chauvigny, Nouaillé, Legugé, Vivonne, Mezeaux, Estables, and other bordering and circumjacent towns, vil-lages, and hamlets. All their debates were pa-cified by him; he put an end to their brabling suits at law, and wrangling differences. By his advice and counsels were accords and rec-oncilements no less firmly made, than if the verdict of a sovereign judge had been inter-posed therein, although, in very deed, he was no judge at all, but a right honest man, as you may well conceive,—*arg. in .l sed si unius ff. de jurejur. et de verbis obligatoriis l. con-tinuus.* There was not a hog killed within three parishes of him, whereof he had not some part of the haslet and puddings. He was almost every day invited either to a marriage-banquet, christening-feast, an uprising or women-churching treatment, a birthday's an-niversary, solemnity, a merry frolic gossiping, or otherwise to some delicious entertainment in a tavern, to make some accord and agree-ment between persons at odds, and in debate with one another. Remark what I say; for he never yet settled and compounded a differ-ence betwixt any two at variance, but he straight made the parties agreed and pacified to drink together, as a sure and infallible tok-en and symbol of a perfect and completely well-cemented reconciliation, a sign of a sound and sincere amity, and proper mark of a new joy and gladness to follow thereupon, —*Ut not. per doct. ff. de peric. et com. rei vend. l. i.* He had a son, whose name was Tenot Dendin, a lusty, young, sturdy, frisk-ing roister, so help me God, who likewise, in imitation of his peace-making father, would have undertaken and meddled with the mak-ing up of variances and deciding of contro-versies between disagreeing and contentious party-pleaders: as you know,

Sæpe solet similis filius esse patri,
Et sequitur leviter filia matris iter.[70]

Ut ait gloss. 6. quæst. i. c. Si quis, gloss. de cons. dist. 5. c. 2. fin. et est not. per Doct. cod. de impub. et aliis substit. l. ult. et l. legitime. ff. de stat. hom. gloss. in l. quod. si nolit. ff. de ædil. edict. l. quisquis c. ad leg. Jul. ma-jest. Excipio filios à moniali susceptos ex mon-acho. per gloss. in c. impudicas. 27. quæs-tione i. And such was his confidence to have no worse success than his father, that he as-sumed unto himself the title of Lawstrife-set-tler. He was likewise in these pacificatory ne-gotiations so active and vigilant,—for, *Vigi-lantibus jura subveniunt.*[71] *ex. l. pupillus. ff. quæ in fraud, cred, et ibid. l. non enim, et in-stit. in proæm.*—that when he had smelt, heard, and fully understood,—*ut ff. si quando paup. fec. l. Agaso. gloss. in verb. olfecit, id est, nasum ad culum posuit*—and found that there was anywhere in the country a debatea-ble matter at law, he would incontinently thrust in his advice, and so forwardly intrude his opinion in the business, that he made no bones of making offer, and taking upon him to decide it, how difficult soever it might hap-pen to be, to the full contentment and satis-faction of both parties. It is written, *Qui non laborat non manige ducat;*[72] and the said *gl. ff. de damn, infect. l. quamvis* and *Currere plus que le pas vetulam compellit egestas.*[73] *gloss. ff. de lib. agnosc. l. si quis pro qua facit. l. si plures. c. de condit. incert.* But so hugely great was his misfortune in this his undertak-ing, that he never composed any difference, how little soever you may imagine it might have been, but that, instead of reconciling the parties at odds, he did incense, irritate, and exasperate them to a higher point of dissension and enmity than ever they were at before. Your worships know, I doubt not that,

Sermo datur cunctis, animi sapientia paucis.[74]

Gl. ff. de alien. jud. mut. caus. fa. lib. 2. This administered unto the tavern-keepers, wine-drawers and vintners of Semerve an occasion to say, that under him they had not in the space of a whole year so much reconciliation-wine, for so were they pleased to called the good wine of Legugé, as under his father they had done in one half hour's time. It happened a little while thereafter, that he made a most heavy regret thereof to his father, attributing the causes of his bad success in pacificatory enterprizes to the perversity, stubbornness, froward, cross, and backward inclinations of the people of his time; roundly, boldly, and irreverently upbraiding, that if, but a score of years before the world had been so wayward, obstinate, previcacious, implacable, and out of all square, frame, and order, as it was then, his father had never attained to and acquired the honour and title of Strife-appeaser, so irrefragably, inviolably, and irrevocably as he had done. In doing whereof Tenot did heinously transgress against the law which prohibiteth children to the actions of their parents; *per gl. et Bart. l. 3. paragr. si quis. ff. de cond. ob caus. et authent. de nupt. par. sed quod sancitum. col.* 4. To this the honest old father answered thus. My son Dendin, when *Don Oportet*[75] taketh place, this is the course which we must trace. *gl. c. de appell. l. eos etiam.* For the road that you went upon was not the way to the fuller's mill, nor in any part thereof was the form to be found wherein the hare did sit. Thou hast not the skill and dexterity of settling and composing differences. Why? Because thou takest them at the beginning, in the very infancy and bud as it were, when they are green, raw, and indigestible. Yet I know, handsomely and featly, how to compose and settle them all. Why? Because I take them at their decadence, in their weaning, and when they are pretty well digested. So saith Gloss:

Dulcior est fructus post multa pericula ductus.[76]

L. non moriturus. c. de contrahend. et committ. stip. Didst thou ever hear the vulgar proverb, "Happy is the physician, whose coming is desired at the declension of a disease"? For the sickness being come to a crisis is then upon the decreasing hand, and drawing towards an end, although the physician should not repair thither for the cure thereof; whereby, though nature wholly do the work, he bears away the palm and praise thereof. My pleaders, after the same manner, before I did interpose my judgment in the reconciling of them, were waxing faint in their contestations. Their altercation heat was much abated, and, in declining from their former strife, they of themselves inclined to a firm accommodation of their differences; because there wanted fuel to that fire of burning rancour and despightful wrangling, whereof the lower sort of lawyers were the kindlers. That is to say, their purses were emptied of coin, they had not a win in their fob, nor penny in their bag, wherewith to solicit and present their actions.

Deficiente pecu, deficit omne, nia.[77]

There wanted then nothing but some brother to supply the place of a paranymph, braw-broker, proxenete, or mediator, who acting his part dexterously, should be the first broacher of the motion of an agreement, for saving both the one and the other party from that hurtful and pernicious shame, whereof he could not have avoided the imputation, when it should have been said, that he was the first who yielded and spoke of a reconcilement; and that, therefore, his cause not being good, and being sensible where his shoe did pinch him, he was willing to break the ice, and make the greater haste to prepare the way for a condescendment to an amicable and friendly treaty. Then was it that I came in pudding time, Dendin, my son, nor is the fat of bacon more relishing to boiled peas, than was my verdict then agreeable to them. This was my luck, my profit, and good fortune. I tell thee, my jolly son Dendin, that by this rule and method I could settle a firm peace, or at least clap up a cessation of arms, and truce for many years to come betwixt the Great King and the Venetian State,—the Emperor and the Cantons of Switzerland,—the English and the Scots, and betwixt the pope and the Ferrarians. Shall I go yet further? Yea, as I would have God to help me, betwixt the Turk and the Sophy, the Tartars and the Muscoviters. Remark well, what I am to say unto thee. I would take them at that very instant nick of time, when both those of the one and the other side should be weary and tired of making war, when they had voided and emptied their own cashes and coffers of all treasure and coin, drained and exhausted the purses and bags of their subjects, sold and mortgaged their domains and proper inheritances, and totally wasted, spent, and consumed the munition, furniture, provision, and victuals, that were necessary for the continuance of a military expedition. There I am sure, by God, or by his mother, that, would they, would they not, in spite of all teeth, they should be forced to take a little respite and breathing time to moderate the fury and cruel rage of their ambitious aims. This is the doctrine in *Gl. 37. d. c. si quando.*

Odero, si potero; si non, invitus amabo.[78]

CHAPTER 42

How suits at law are bred at first, and how they come afterwards to their perfect growth

FOR this cause, quoth Bridlegoose, going on in his discourse, I temporize and apply myself to the times, as your other worships use to do, waiting patiently for the maturity of the process, the full growth and perfection thereof in all its members, to wit, the writings and the bags. *Arg. in l. si major. c. commun. divid. et de cons. di.* 1. *c. solemnitates, et ibi gl.* A suit in law at its production, birth, and first beginning, seemeth to me, as unto your other worships, shapeless, without form or fashion, incomplete, ugly, and imperfect even as a bear, at his first coming into the world, hath neither hands, skin, hair, nor head, but is merely an inform, rude, and ill-favoured piece and lump of flesh, and would remain still so, if his dam, out of the abundance of her affection to her hopeful cub, did not with much licking put his members into that figure and shape which nature had provided for those of an arctic and ursinal kind; *ut not. Doct. ad. l. Aquil. l.* 2. *in fin.* Just so do I see, as your other worships do, processes and suits of law, at their first bringing forth to be numberless, without shape, deformed, and disfigured, for that then they consist only of one or two writings, or copies of instruments, through which defect they appear unto me, as to your other worships, foul, loathsome, filthy, and mis-shapen beasts. But when there are heaps of these legiformal papers packed, piled, laid up together, impoked, insacheled, and put up in bags, then is it that with a good reason we may term that suit, to which, as pieces, parcels, parts, portions, and members thereof, they do pertain, and belong, well-formed and fashioned, big-limbed, strong set, and in all and each of its dimensions most completely membered. Because *forma dat esse rei.*[79] *l. si is qui. ff. ad leg. Falcid. in c. cum dilecta de rescript. Barbat. concil.* 12. *lib.* 2. and before him Baldus, *in c. ult. extra de consuet. et l. Julianus ff. ad exhib. et. l. quæsitum ff. de leg.* 3. The manner is such

as is set down in *gl. p. quæst.* 1. *c. Paulus.*

Debile principium melior fortuna sequetur.[80]

Like your other worships also, the sergeants, catchpoles, pursuivants, messengers, summoners, apparitors, ushers, door-keepers, pettifoggers, attornies, proctors, commissioners, justices of the peace, judge delegates, arbitrators, overseers, sequestrators, advocates, inquisitors, jurors, searchers, examiners, notaries, tabellions, scribes, scriveners, clerks, prenotaries, secondaries, and expedanean judges, *de quibus tit. est. l.* 3. *c.,* by sucking very much, and that exceeding forcibly, and licking at the purses of the pleading parties, they, to the suits already begot and engendered, form, fashion, and frame head, feet, claws, talons, beaks, bills, teeth, hands, veins, sinews, arteries, muscles, humours, and so forth, through all the similary and dissimilary parts of the whole; which parts, particles, pendicles, and appurtenances, are the law pokes and bags, *gl. de cons. d.* 4. *accepisti.*

Qualis vestis erit, talia corda gerit.[81]

Hic notandum est,[82] that in this respect the pleaders, litigants, and law-suiters are happier than the officers, ministers, and administrators of justice, For *beatius est dare quam accipere,*[83] *ff. commun. l.* 3. *extra. de celebr. Miss. c. cum Marthæ. et* 24. *quæst.* 1. *cap. Od. gl.*

Affectum dantis pensat censura tonantis,[84]

Thus becometh the action or process, by their care and industry to be of a complete and goodly bulk, well-shaped, framed, formed, and fashioned, according to the canonical gloss.

Accipe, sume, cape, sunt verba placentia papæ.[85]

Which speech hath been more clearly explained by Albert de Ros, *in verbo Roma.*

Roma manus rodit, quas rodere non valet, odit.
Dantes custodit, non dantes spernit, et odit.[86]

The reason whereof is thought to be this:

Ad præsens ova, cras pullis sunt meliora.[87]

ut est gl. in l. quum hi. ff. de transact. Nor is this all; for the inconvenience of the contrary is set down in *gloss. c. de aliu. fin.*

Quum labor in damno est, crescit mortalis egestas.[88]

In confirmation whereof we find, that the true etymology and exposition of the word *process* is *purchase; viz.* of good store of money to the lawyers, and of many pokes,—*id est Prou Sacks,*—to the pleaders: upon which subject we have most celestial quips, gibes, and girds.

Litigando jura crescunt, litigando jus acquiritur.[89]

Item gl. in cap. illud extrem. de præsympt. et c. de prob. l. instrum. l. non epistolis. l. non nudis.

Et si non prosunt singula, multa juvant.[90]

Yea, but, asked Trinquamelle, how do you proceed, my friend, in criminal causes, the culpable and guilty party being taken and seized upon, *flagrante crimine?*[91] Even as your other worships use to do, answered Bridlegoose. First, I permit the plaintiff to depart from the court, enjoining him not to presume to return thither, till he preallably should have taken a good sound and profound sleep, which is to serve for the prime entry and introduction to the legal carrying on of the business. In the next place, a formal report is to be made to me of his having slept. Thirdly, I issue forth a warrant to convene him before me. Fourthly, He is to produce a sufficient and authentic attestation of his having thoroughly and entirely slept, conform to the *Gloss,* 32. *Quest.* 7. *c. Si quis cum.*

Quandoque bonus dormitat Homerus.[92]

Being thus far advanced in the formality of the process, I find that this consopiating act engendereth another act, whence ariseth the articulating of a member. That again produceth a third act, fashionative of another member; which third bringeth forth a fourth, procreative of another act. New members in a no fewer number are shapen and framed, one still breeding and begetting another—as link after link, the coat of mail at length is made—till thus piece after piece, by little and little, by information upon information, the

process be completely well-formed and perfect in all his members. Finally, having proceeded this length, I have recourse to my dice, nor is it to be thought, that this interruption, respite, or interpellation is by me occasioned without very good reason inducing me thereunto, and a notable experience of a most convincing and irrefragable force.

I remember, on a time, that in the camp at Stockholm, there was a certain Gascon named Gratianauld, native of the town of Saint Sever, who having lost all his money at play, and consecutively being very angry thereat—as you know, *Pecunia est alter sanguis,*[93] *ut ait Anto. de Burtio, in c. accedens. 2. extra ut lit. non contest. et Bald. in l. sis tuis. c. de opt. leg. per tot. in l. advocati. c. de advoc. div. jud. pecunia est vita hominis fideiussor in necessitatibus,*[94]—did, at his coming forth of the gaming-house in the presence of the whole company that was there, with a very loud voice, speak in his own language these following words: *"Pao cap de bious, hillots, que mau de pippe bous tresbire: ares que de pergudes sont les mies bingt, et quouatre baquettes, ta pla donnerien picz, trucz, et patactz; Sei degun de bous aulx, qui boille truquar ambe iou a bels embis."* Finding that none would make him any answer, he passed from thence to that part of the leaguer where the huff-snuff, honder-sponder, swash-buckling High Germans were, to whom he renewed these very terms, provoking them to fight with him; but all the return he had from them to his stout challenge was only, *"Der Gascongner thut sich ausz mit eim ieden zu schlagen, aber er ist geneigter zu stehlen; darum, liebe frauwen, habt sorg zu euerm hauszrath."* Finding also, that none of that band of Teutonic soldiers offered himself to the combat, he passed to that quarter of the leaguer where the French free-booting adventurers were encamped, and, reiterating unto them what he had before repeated to the Dutch warriors, challenged them likewise to fight with him, and therewithal made some pretty little Gasconado frisking gambols, to oblige them the more cheerfully and gallantly to cope with him in the lists of a duellizing engagement; but no answer at all was made unto him. Whereupon the Gascon, despairing of meeting with any antagonists, departed from thence, and laying himself down, not far from the pavilions of the grand Christian cavalier Crissé, fell fast asleep. When he had thoroughly slept an hour or two, another adventurous and all-hazarding blade of the forlorn hope of the lavishingly-wasting gamesters, having also lost all his monies, sallied forth with a sword in his hand, in a firm resolution to fight with the aforesaid Gascon, seeing he had lost as well as he.

Ploratur lachrymis amissa pecunia veris,[95]

saith the *Gl. de pænitent, distinct. 3. c. sunt plures.* To this effect having made inquiry and search for him throughout the whole camp, and in sequel thereof found him asleep, he said unto him, Up, ho, good fellow, in the name of all the devils of hell rise up, rise up, get up! I have lost my money as well as thou hast done, let us therefore go fight lustily together, grapple and scuffle it to some purpose. Thou mayest look and see that my tuck is no longer than thy rapier. The Gascon, altogether astonished at his unexpected provocation, without altering his former dialect, spoke thus: *"Cap de Sanct Arnaud, quau seys tu, qui me rebeilles? Que mau de taoverne te gire. Ho San Siobé, cap de Gasciogne, ta pla dormie iou, quand aquoest taquain me bingut estée."* The venturous roister inviteth him again to the duel, but the Gascon, without condescending to his desire, said only this. *"Hé pauvret, iou te esquinerio ares que son pla reposat. Vayne un pauque qui te posar comme iou, puesse truqueren."* Thus, in forgetting his loss, he forgot the eagerness which he had to fight. In conclusion, after that the other had likewise slept a little, they, instead of fighting, and possibly killing one another, went jointly to a sutler's tent, where they drank together very amicably, each upon the pawn of his sword. Thus by a little sleep was pacified the ardent fury of two warlike champions. There, gossip, comes the golden word of John Andr. *in cap. ult. de sent. et re judic. l. sexto.*

Sedendo et quiescendo fit anima prudens.[96]

CHAPTER 43

How Pantagruel excuseth Bridlegoose in the matter of sentencing actions at law by the chance of the dice

WITH this Bridlegoose held his peace. Whereupon Trinquamelle bid him withdraw from the court,—which accordingly was done,—and then directed his discourse to Pantagruel after this manner. It is fitting, most illustrious prince, not only by reason of the deep obligations wherein this present parliament, together with the whole Marquisate of Myrelingues, stand bound to your Royal Highness, for the innumerable benefits, which, as effects of mere grace, they have received from your incomparable bounty; but for that excellent wit also, prime judgment, and admirable learning wherewith Almighty God, the giver of all good things, hath most richly qualified and endowed you; that we tender and present unto you the decision of this new, strange, and paradoxical case of Bridlegoose; who, in your presence, to your both hearing and seeing, hath plainly confessed his final judging and determinating of suits of law, by the mere chance and fortune of the dice. Therefore do we beseech you, that you may be pleased to give sentence therein, as unto you shall seem most just and equitable. To this Pantagruel answered, Gentlemen, It is not unknown to you, how my condition is somewhat remote from the profession of deciding law controversies; yet, seeing you are pleased to do me the honour to put that task upon me, instead of undergoing the office of a judge, I will become your humble supplicant. I observe, gentlemen, in this Bridlegoose several things, which induce me to represent before you, that it is my opinion he should be pardoned. In the first place, his old age; secondly, his simplicity; to both which qualities our statute and common laws, civil and municipal together, allow many excuses for any slips or escapes, which, through the invincible imperfection of either, have been inconsiderably stumbled upon by a person so qualified. Thirdly, gentlemen, I must need display before you another case, which in equity and justice maketh much for the advantage of Bridlegoose, to wit, that this one, sole, and single fault of his ought to be quite forgotten, abolished, and swallowed up by that immense and vast ocean of just dooms and sentences, which heretofore he hath given and pronounced; his demeanours, for these forty years and upwards that he hath been a judge, having been so evenly balanced in the scales of uprightness, that envy itself, till now, could not have been so impudent as to accuse and twit him with any act worthy of a check or reprehension: as, if a drop of the sea were thrown into the Loire, none could perceive, or say, that by this single drop the whole river should be salt and brackish.

Truly, it seemeth unto me, that in the

whole series of Bridlegoose's juridical decrees there hath been I know not what of extraordinary savouring of the unspeakable benignity of God, that all these his preceding sentences, awards, and judgments, have been confirmed and approved of by ourselves, in this your own venerable and sovereign court. For it is usual, (as you know well,) with him whose ways are inscrutable, to manifest his own ineffable glory in blunting the perspicacity of the eyes of the wise, in weakening the strength of potent oppressors, in depressing the pride of rich extortioners, and in erecting, comforting, protecting, supporting, upholding, and shoring up the poor, feeble, humble, silly, and foolish ones of the earth. But, waving all these matters, I shall only beseech you, not by the obligations which you pretend to owe to my family, for which I thank you, but for that constant and unfeigned love and affection which you have always found in me, both on this and on the other side of the Loire, for the maintenance and establishment of your places, offices, and dignities, that for this one time you would pardon and forgive him upon these two conditions. First, That he satisfy, or posit sufficient surety for the satisfaction of the party wronged by the injustice of the sentence in question. For the fulfilment of this article, I will provide sufficiently. And, secondly, That for his subsidiary aid in the weighty charge of administrating justice, you would be pleased to appoint and assign unto him some virtuous counsellor, younger, learneder, and wiser than he, by the square and rule of whose advice he may regulate, guide, temper, and moderate in times coming all his judiciary procedures; or otherwise, if you intend totally to depose him from his office, and to deprive him altogether of the state and dignity of a judge, I shall cordially entreat you to make a present and free gift of him to me, who shall find in my kingdoms charges and employments enough wherewith to imbusy him, for the bettering of his own fortunes, and furtherance of my service. In the meantime, I implore the Creator, Saviour, and Sanctifier of all good things, in his grace, mercy, and kindness, to preserve you all, now and evermore, world without end.

These words thus spoken, Pantagruel, veiling his cap and making a leg with such a majestic grace as became a person of his paramount degree and eminency, farewelled Trinquamelle, the president and master

speaker of that Myrelinguesian parliament, took his leave of the whole court, and went out of the chamber: at the door whereof finding Panurge, Epistemon, Friar John, and others, he forthwith, attended by them, walked to the outer gate, where all of them immediately took horse to return towards Gargantua. Pantagruel by the way related to them from point to point the manner of Bridlegoose's sententiating differences at law. Friar John said, that he had seen Peter Dendin, and was acquainted with him at that time when he sojourned in the monastery of Fontaine le Comte, under the noble Abbot Ardillon. Gymnast likewise affirmed, that he was in the tent of the grand Christian cavalier de Crissé, when the Gascon, after his sleep, made an answer to the adventurer. Panurge was somewhat incredulous in the matter of believing that it was morally possible Bridlegoose should have been for such a long space of time so continually fortunate in that aleatory way of deciding law debates. Epistemon said to Pantagruel, Such another story, not much unlike to that in all the circumstances thereof, is vulgarly reported of the provost of Montlehery. In good sooth, such a perpetuity of good luck is to be wondered at. To have hit right twice or thrice in a judgment so given by hap-hazard might have fallen out well enough, especially in controversies that were ambiguous, intricate, abstruse, perplexed, and obscure.

CHAPTER 44

How Pantagruel relateth a strange history of the perplexity of human judgment

SEEING you talk, quoth Pantagruel, of dark, difficult, hard, and knotty debates, I will tell you of one controverted before Cneius Dolabella, Proconsul in Asia. The case was this.

A wife in Smyrna had of her first husband a child named Abecé. He dying, she, after the expiring of a year and a day, married again, and to her second husband bore a boy called Effegé. A pretty long time afterward it happened, as you know the affection of stepfathers and step-dames is very rare towards the children of the first fathers and mothers deceased, that this husband, with the help of his son Effegé, secretly, wittingly, willingly, and treacherously murdered Abecé. The woman came no sooner to get information of the fact, but, that it might not go unpunished, she caused kill them both, to revenge the death of her first son. She was apprehended and carried before Cneius Dolabella, in whose presence, she, without dissembling anything, confessed all that was laid to her charge; yet alleged, that she had both right and reason on her side for the killing of them. Thus was the state of the question. He found the business so dubious and intricate, that he knew not what to determine therein, nor which of the parties to incline to. On the one hand, it was an execrable crime to cut off at once both her second husband and her son. On the other hand, the cause of the murder seemed to be so natural, as to be grounded upon the law of nations, and the rational instinct of all the people of the world, seeing they two together had feloniously and murderously destroyed her first son;—not that they had been in any manner of way wronged, outraged, or injured by him, but out of an avaricious intent to possess his inheritance. In this doubtful quandary and uncertainty what to pitch upon, he sent to the Areopagites, then sitting at Athens, to learn and obtain their advice and judgment. That judicious senate, very sagely perpending the seasons of his perplexity, sent him word to summon her personally to compeer before him a precise hundred years thereafter, to answer to some interrogatories touching certain points, which were not contained in the verbal defence. Which resolution of theirs did import, that it was in their opinion so difficult and inextricable a matter, that they knew not what to say or judge therein. Who had decided that plea by the chance and fortune of the dice, could not have erred nor awarded amiss, on which side soever he had past his casting and condemnatory sentence. If against the woman, she deserved punishment for usurping sovereign authority, by taking that vengeance at her own hand, the inflicting whereof was only competent to the supreme power to administer justice in criminal cases. If for her, the just resentment of a so atrocious injury done unto her, in murdering her innocent son, did fully excuse and vindicate her of any trespass or offence about that particular committed by her. But this continuation of Bridlegoose for so many years, still hitting the nail on the head, never missing the mark, and always judging aright, by the mere throwing of the dice, and the chance thereof, is that which most astonisheth and amazeth me.

To answer, quoth Pantagruel, categorically to that which you wonder at, I must ingeniously confess and avow that I cannot; yet, conjecturally to guess at the reason of it, I would refer the cause of that marvellously long-continued happy success in the judiciary results of his definitive sentences, to the favourable aspect of the heavens, and benignity of the intelligences; who out of their love to goodness, after having contemplated the pure simplicity and sincere unfeignedness of Judge Bridlegoose in the acknowledgment of his inabilities, did regulate that for him by chance, which by the profoundest act of his maturest deliberation he was not able to reach unto. That, likewise, which possibly made him to diffide in his own skill and capacity, notwithstanding his being an expert and understanding lawyer, for anything that I know to the contrary, was the knowledge and experience which he had of the antinomies, contrarieties, antilogies, contradictions, traversings, and thwartings of laws, customs, edicts, statutes, orders, and ordinances, in which dangerous opposition, equity and justice being structured and founded on either of the opposite terms, and a gap being thereby opened for the ushering in of injustice and iniquity through the various interpretations of self-ended lawyers; being assuredly persuaded that the infernal calumniator, who frequently transformeth himself into the likeness of a messenger or angel of light, maketh use of these cross glosses and expositions in the mouths and pens of his ministers and servants, the perverse advocates, bribing judges, law-monging attorneys, prevaricating counsellors, and such other like law-wresting members of a court of justice, to turn by those means black to white, green to grey, and what is straight to a crooked ply. For the more expedient doing whereof, these diabolical ministers make both the pleading parties believe that their cause is just and righteous; for it is well known that there is no cause, how bad soever, which doth not find an advocate to patrocinate and defend it,—else would there be no process in the world, no suits at law, nor pleadings at the bar. He did in these extremities, as I conceive, most humbly recommend the direction of his judicial proceedings to the upright judge of judges, God Almighty,—did submit himself to the conduct and guideship of the blessed Spirit, in the hazard and perplexity of the definitive sentence,—and, by this aleatory lot, did as it were implore and explore the divine decree of his good will and pleasure, instead of that which we call the Final Judgment of a Court. To this effect, to the better attaining to his purpose, which was to judge righteously, he did, in my opinion, throw and turn the dice, to the end that by the providence aforesaid, the best chance might fall to him whose action was uprightest, and backed with greatest reason. In doing whereof he did not stray from the sense of the Talmudists, who say that there is so little harm in that manner of searching the truth, that in the anxiety and perplexedness of human wits, God oftentimes manifesteth the secret pleasure of his Divine Will.

Furthermore, I will neither think nor say, nor can I believe, that the unstraightness is so irregular, or the corruption so evident, of those of the Parliament of Myrelingois in Myrelingues, before whom Bridlegoose was arraigned for prevarication, that they will maintain it to be a worse practice to have the decision of a suit at law referred to the chance and hazard of a throw of the dice, hab nab, or luck as it will, then to have it remitted to, and past, by the determination of those whose hands are full of blood, and hearts of wry affections. Besides that, their principal direction in all law matters comes to their hands from one Tribonian, a wicked, miscreant, barbarous, faithless, and prefidious knave, so pernicious, unjust, avaricious, and perverse in his ways, that it was his ordinary custom to sell laws, edicts, declarations, constitutions, and ordinances, as at an outroop or putsale, to him who offered most for them. Thus did he shape measures for the pleaders, and cut their morsels to them by and out of these little parcels, fragments, bits, scantlings, and shreds of the law now in use, altogether concealing, suppressing, disannulling, and abolishing the remainder, which did make for the total law; fearing that, if the whole law were made manifest and laid open to the knowledge of such as are interested in it, and the learned books of the ancient doctors of the law upon the exposition of the Twelve Tables and Prætorian Edicts, his villanous pranks, naughtiness, and vile impiety should come to the public notice of the world. Therefore were it better, in my conceit, that is to say less inconvenient, that parties at variance in any juridical case should in the dark, march upon caltrops, than submit the determination of what is their right to such unhallowed sentences and horrible decrees: as Cato in his time wished and advised, that every judiciary court should be paved with caltrops.

CHAPTER 45

How Panurge taketh advice of Triboulet

On the sixth day thereafter, Pantagruel was returned home at the very same hour that Triboulet was by water come from Blois. Panurge, at his arrival, gave him a hog's bladder, puffed up with wind, and resounding, because of the hard peas that were within it. Moreover he did present him with a gilt wooden sword, a hollow budget made of a tortoise-shell, an osier-wattled wicker bottle full of Breton wine, and five and twenty apples of the orchard of Blandureau.

If he be such a fool, quoth Carpalim, as to be won with apples, there is no more wit in his pate than in the head of an ordinary cabbage. Triboulet girded the sword and scrip to his side, took the bladder in his hand, ate some few of the apples, and drunk up all the wine. Panurge very wistly and heedfully looking upon him said, I never yet saw a fool, and I have seen ten thousand franks worth of that kind of cattle, who did not love to drink heartily, and by good long draughts. When Triboulet had done with his drinking, Panurge laid out before him, and exposed the sum of the business wherein he was to require his advice, in eloquent and choicely-sorted terms, adorned with flourishes of rhetoric. But, before he had altogether done, Triboulet with his fist gave him a bouncing whirret between the shoulders, rendered back into his hand again the empty bottle, filipped and flirted him on the nose with the hog's bladder, and lastly, for a final resolution, shaking and wagging his head strongly and disorderly, he answered nothing else but this, By God, God, mad fool, beware the monk, Buzançay hornpipe! These words thus finished, he slipped himself out of the company, went aside, and, rattling the bladder, took a huge delight in the melody of the rickling, crackling, noise of the peas. After which time it lay not in the power of them all to draw out of his chaps the articulate sound of one syllable, insomuch that, when Panurge went about to interrogate him further, Triboulet drew his wooden sword, and would have struck him therewith. I have fished fair now, quoth Panurge, and brought my pigs to a fine market. Have I not got a brave determination of all my doubts, and a response in all things agreeable to the oracle that gave it? He is a great fool, that is not to be denied, yet he is a greater fool, who brought him hither to me,—but of the three I am the greatest fool, who did impart the secret of my thoughts to such an idiot ass and native ninny,—That bolt, quoth Carpalim, levels point blank at me.

Without putting ourselves to any stir or trouble in the least, quoth Pantagruel, let us maturely and seriously consider and perpend the gestures and speech which he hath made and uttered. In them, veritably, quoth he, have I remarked and observed some excellent and notable mysteries, yea, of such important worth and weight, that I shall never henceforth be astonished, nor think strange, why the Turks, with a great deal of worship and reverence, honour and respect natural fools equally with their primest doctors, mufties, divines, and prophets. Did not you take heed, quoth he, a little before he opened his mouth to speak, what a shogging, shaking, and wagging, his head did keep? By the approved doctrine of the ancient philosophers, the customary ceremonies of the most expert magicians, and the received opinions of the most learned lawyers, such a brangling agitation and moving should by us all be judged to proceed from, and be quickened and suscitated by, the coming and inspiration of the prophetizing and fatidical spirit, which, entering briskly and on a sudden into a shallow receptacle of a debil substance, (for, as you know, and as the proverb shows it, a little head containeth not much brains,) was the cause of that commotion. This is conform to what is avouched by the most skilful physicians, when they affirm, that shakings and tremblings fall upon the members of a human body, partly because of the heaviness and violent impetuosity of the burden and load that is carried, and other part, by reason of the weakness and imbecility that is in the virtue of the bearing organ. A manifest example whereof appeareth in those who, fasting, are not able to carry to their head a great goblet full of wine without a trembling and a shaking in the hand that holds it. This of old was accounted a prefiguration and mystical pointing out of the Pythian divineress, who used always, before the uttering of a response from the oracle, to shake a branch of her domestic laurel. Lampridius also testifieth, that the Emperor Heliogabalus, to acquire unto himself the reputation of a soothsayer, did, on several holy days, of prime solemnity, in the presence of the fanatic rabble,

make the head of his idol by some slight within the body thereof, publicly to shake. Plautus, in his *Asinaria*, declareth likewise, that Saurias, whithersoever he walked, like one quite distracted of his wits, kept such a furious lolling and mad-like shaking of his head, that he commonly affrighted those who casually met with him in their way. The said author in another place, showing a reason why Charmides shook and brangled his head, assevered that he was transported, and in an ecstasy. Catullus after the same manner maketh mention, in his *Berecynthia* and *Atys*, of the place wherein the Menades, Bacchical women, she priests of the Lyæan god, and demented prophetesses, carrying ivy boughs in their hands, did shake their heads. As in the like case, amongst the Galli, the gelded priests of Cybele were wont to do in the celebrating of their festivals. Whence, too, acceeding to the sense of the ancient theologues, she herself has her denomination; for κυβισ-ᾶν signifieth, to turn round, whirl about, shake the head, and play the part of one that is wry-necked.

Semblably Titus Livius writeth, that, in the solemnization time of the Bacchanalian holidays at Rome, both men and women seemed to prophetize and vaticinate, because of an affected kind of wagging of the head, shrugging of the shoulders, and jectigation of the whole body, which they used then most punctually. For the common voice of the philosophers, together with the opinion of the people, asserteth for an irrefragable truth, that vatication is seldom by the heavens bestowed on any, without the concomitancy of a little frenzy, and a head-shaking, not only when the said presaging virtue is infused, but when the person also therewith inspired, declareth and manifesteth it unto others. The learned lawyer Julian, being asked on a time, if that slave might be truly esteemed to be healthful and in a good plight, who had not only conversed with some furious, maniac, and enraged people, but in their company had also prophesied, yet without a noddleshaking concussion, answered, That seeing there was no head-wagging at the time of his predictions, he might be held for sound and competent enough. Is it not daily seen, how schoolmasters, teachers, tutors, and instructors of children, shake the heads of their disciples, as one would do a pot in holding it by the lugs, that by this erection, vellication, stretching and pulling their ears, which, according to the doctrine of the sage Egyptians, is a member consecrated to the memory, they may stir them up to recollect their scattered thoughts, bring home those fancies of theirs, which perhaps have been extravagantly roaming abroad upon strange and uncouth objects, and totally range their judgments, which possibly by disordinate affections have been made wild, to the rule and pattern of a wise, discreet, virtuous, and philosophical discipline. All which Virgil acknowledgeth to be true, in the branglement of Apollo Cynthius.

CHAPTER 46

How Pantagruel and Panurge diversely interpret the words of Triboulet

HE says you are a fool. And what kind of fool? A mad fool, who in your old age would enslave yourself to the bondage of matrimony, and shut your pleasures up within a wedlock, whose key some ruffian carries in his codpiece. He says furthermore, Beware of the monk. Upon mine honour, it gives me in my mind, that you will be cuckolded by a monk. Nay, I will engage mine honour, which is the most precious pawn I could have in my possession, although I were sole and peaceable dominator over all Europe, Asia, and Africa, that if you marry, you will surely be one of the horned brotherhood of Vulcan. Hereby may you perceive, how much I do attribute to the wise foolery of our morosoph Triboulet. The other oracles and responses did in the general prognosticate you a cuckold, without descending so near to the point of a particular determination, as to pitch upon what vocation amongst the several sorts of men, he should profess, who is to be the copesmate of your wife and hornifier of your proper self. Thus noble Triboulet tells it us plainly, from whose words we may gather with all ease imaginable, that your cuckoldry is to be infamous, and so much the more scandalous, that your conjugal bed will be incestuously contaminated with the filthiness of a monkery lecher. Moreover he says, that you will be the hornpipe of Buzançay,—that is to say, well horned, hornified, and cornuted. And, as Triboulet's uncle asked from Louis the Twelfth, for a younger brother of his own, who lived at Blois, the hornpipes of Buzançay, for the organ pipes, through the mistake of one word for another, even so, whilst you think to marry a wise, humble, calm, discreet, and honest wife, you shall unhappily stumble upon one, witless, proud, loud, obstreperous, bawling, clamorous, and more unpleasant than any Buzançay hornpipe. Consider withal, how he flirted you on the nose with the bladder, and gave you a sound thumping blow with his fist upon the ridge of the back. This denotes and presageth, that you shall be banged, beaten, and filipped by her, and that also she will steal of your goods from you, as you stole the hog's bladder from the little boys of Vaubreton.

Flat contrary, quoth Panurge;—not that I would impudently exempt myself from being a vassal in the territory of folly. I hold of that jurisdiction, and am subject thereto, I confess it. And why should I not? For the whole world is foolish. In the old Lorrain language, *fou* for *oou*; all and fool were the same thing. Besides, it is avouched by Solomon, that infinite is the number of fools. From an infinity nothing can be deducted or abated, nor yet, by the testimony of Aristotle, can anything thereto be added or subjoined. Therefore were I a mad fool, if, being a fool, I should not hold myself a fool. After the same manner of speaking, we may aver the number of the mad and enraged folks to be infinite. Avicenna maketh no bones to assert, that the several kinds of madness are infinite. Though this much of Triboulet's words tend little to my advantage, howbeit the prejudice which I sustain thereby be common with me to all other men, yet the rest of his talk and gesture maketh altogether for me. He said to my wife, Be weary of the monkey; that is as much as if she should be cheery, and take as much delight in a monkey, as ever did the Lesbia of Catullus in her sparrow; who will, for his recreation pass his time no less joyfully at the exercise of snatching flies, than heretofore did the merciless fly-catcher Domitian. Withal he meant by another part of his discourse, that she should be of a jovial country-like humour, as gay and pleasing as a harmonious hornpipe of Saulieu or Buzançay. The veridical Triboulet did therein hint at what I liked well, as perfectly knowing the inclinations and propensities of my mind, my natural disposition, and the bias of my interior passions and affections. For you may be assured, that my humour is much better satisfied and contented with the pretty, frolic, rural, dishevelled shepherdesses, whose bums through their coarse canvass smocks, smell of the clovergrass of the field, than with those great ladies in magnificent courts, with their flaunting top-knots and sultanas, their polvil, pastillos, and cosmetics. The homely sound, likewise, of a rustic hornpipe is more agreeable to my ears, than the curious warbling and musical quivering of lutes, theorbos, viols, rebecs, and violins. He gave me a lusty rapping thwack on my back,—what then? Let it pass, in the name and for the love of God, as an abatement of, and deduction from so much of my future pains in purgatory. He did it not out of any evil intent. He thought, belike, to have hit some of the pages. He is an honest fool, and an innocent changeling. It is a sin to harbour in the heart any bad conceit of him. As for myself, I heartily pardon him. He flirted me on the nose. In that there is no harm; for it importeth nothing else, but that betwixt my wife and me there will occur some toyish wanton tricks, which usually happen to all new married folks.

CHAPTER 47

How Pantagruel and Panurge resolved to make a visit to the oracle of the holy bottle

THERE is as yet another point, quoth Panurge, which you have not at all considered on, although it be the chief and principal head of the matter. He put the bottle in my hand and restored it me again. How interpret you that passage? What is the meaning of that? He possibly, quoth Pantagruel, signifieth thereby, that your wife will be such a drunkard as shall daily take in her liquor kindly, and ply the pots and bottles apace. Quite otherwise, quoth Panurge; for the bottle was empty. I swear to you, by the prickling brambly thorn of St. Fiacre in Brie, that our unique Morosoph, whom I formerly termed the lunatic Triboulet, referreth me, for attaining to the final resolution of my scruple, to the response-giving bottle. Therefore do I renew afresh the first vow which I made, and here in your presence protest and make oath by Styx and Acheron, to carry still spectacles in my cap, and never to wear a codpiece in my breeches, until upon the enterprise in hand of my nuptial undertaking, I shall have obtained an answer from the holy bottle. I am acquainted with a prudent, understanding, and discreet gentleman, and besides, a very good friend of mine, who knoweth the land, country, and place where its temple and oracle is built and posited. He will guide and conduct us thither sure and safely. Let us go thither, I beseech you. Deny me not, and say not, nay; reject

not the suit I make unto you, I entreat you. I will be to you an Achates, a Damis, and heartily accompany you all along in the whole voyage, both in your going forth and coming back. I have of a long time known you to be a great lover of peregrination, desirous still to learn new things, and still to see what you had never seen before.

Very willingly, quoth Pantagruel, I condescend to your request. But before we enter in upon our progress towards the accomplishment of so far a journey, replenished and fraught with imminent perils, full of innumerable hazards, and every way stored with evident and manifest dangers—What dangers? quoth Panurge, interrupting him. Dangers fly back, run from, and shun me whithersoever I go, seven leagues around,—as in the presence of the sovereign a subordinate magistracy is eclipsed; or as clouds and darkness quite vanish at the bright coming of a radiant sun; or as all sores and sicknesses did suddenly depart, at the approach of the body of St. Martin à Quande. Nevertheless, quoth Pantagruel, before we adventure to set forward on the road of our projected and intended voyage, some few points are to be discussed, expedited, and dispatched. First, let us send back Triboulet to Blois. Which was instantly done, after that Pantagruel had given him a frieze coat. Secondly, our design must be backed with advice and counsel of the king my father. And lastly, it is most needful and expedient for us, that we search for and find out some sibyl, to serve us for a guide, truchman, and interpreter. To this Panurge made answer, That his friend Xenomanes would abundantly suffice for the plenary discharge and performance of the sibyl's office; and that, furthermore, in passing through the Lanternatory revelling country, they should take along with them a learned and profitable Lanternesse, who would be no less useful to them in their voyage, than was the sibyl to Æneas, in his descent to the Elysian fields. Carpalim, in the interim, as he was upon the conducting away of Triboulet, in his passing by, hearkened a little to the discourse they were upon, then spoke out, saying, Ho, Panurge, master freeman, take my Lord Debitis at Calais, along with you, for he is goud-fallot, a good fellow. He will not forget those who have been debtors; these are Lanternes. Thus shall you not lack for both fallot and Lanterne. I may safely with the little skill I have, quoth Pantagruel, prognosticate, that by the way we shall engender no melancholy. I clearly perceive it already. The only thing that vexeth me is, that I cannot speak the Lanternatory language. I shall, answered Panurge, speak for you all. I understand it every whit as well as I do mine own maternal tongue; I have been no less used to it than to the vulgar French.

Br sz marg dalgotbric nubstzne zos,
Isquebsz prusq albork crinqs zacbac.
Misbe dilbarkz morp nipp stancz bos,
Strombtz, Panurge, walmap quost gruszbac.

Now guess, friend Epistemon, what is this? They are, quoth Epistemon, names of errant devils, passant devils, and rampant devils. These words of thine, dear friend of mine, are true, quoth Panurge, yet are they terms used in the language of the court of the Lanternish people. By the way, as we go upon our journey, I will make to thee a pretty little dictionary, which, notwithstanding, shall not last you much longer than a pair of new shoes. Thou shalt have learned it sooner than thou canst perceive the dawning of the next subsequent morning. What I have said in the foregoing tetrastic is thus translated out of the Lanternish tongue into our vulgar dialect.

All miseries attended me, whilst I
A lover was, and had no good thereby.
Of better luck the married people tell;
Panurge is one of those, and knows it well.

There is little more, then, quoth Pantagruel, to be done, but that we understand what the will of the king my father will be therein, and purchase his consent.

CHAPTER 48

How Gargantua sheweth, that the children ought not to marry without the special knowledge and advice of their fathers and mothers

No sooner had Pantagruel entered in at the door of the great hall of the castle, than that he encountered full butt with the good honest Gargantua coming forth from the council board, unto whom he made a succinct and summary narrative of what had passed and occurred, worthy of his observation, in his travels abroad, since their last interview; then, acquainting him with the design he had in hand, besought him that it might stand

with his good will and pleasure, to grant him leave to prosecute and go thorough-stitch with the enterprise which he had undertaken. The good man Gargantua, having in one hand two great bundles of petitions, indorsed and answered, and in the other some remembrancing notes and bills, to put him in mind of such other requests of supplicants, which, albeit presented, had nevertheless been neither read nor heard, he gave both to Ulrich Gallet, his ancient and faithful Master of Requests; then drew aside Pantagruel, and, with a countenance more serene and jovial than customary, spoke to him thus, I praise God, and have great reason so to do, my most dear son, that he hath been pleased to entertain in you a constant inclination to virtuous actions. I am well content that the voyage which you have motioned to me be by you accomplished, but withal I could wish you would have a mind and desire to marry, for that I see you are of competent years. [Panurge, in the meanwhile, was in a readiness of preparing and providing for remedies, salves, and cures against all such lets, obstacles, and impediments, as he could in the height of his fancy conceive might by Gargantua be cast in the way of their intinerary design.] Is it your pleasure, most dear father, that you speak? answered Pantagruel. For my part, I have not yet thought upon it. In all this affair I wholly submit and rest in your good liking and paternal authority. For I shall rather pray unto God that he would throw me down stark dead at your feet, in your pleasure, than that against your pleasure I should be found married alive. I never heard that by any law, whether sacred or profane, yea, amongst the rudest and most barbarous nations in the world, it was allowed and approved of, that children may be suffered and tolerated to marry at their own good will and pleasure, without the knowledge, advice, or consent asked and had thereto, of their fathers, mothers, and nearest kindred. All legislators, every where upon the face of the whole earth have taken away and removed this licentious liberty from children, and totally reserved it to the discretion of the parents.

My dearly beloved son, quoth Gargantua, I believe you, and from my heart thank God for having endowed you with the grace of having both a perfect notice of, and entire liking to, laudable and praiseworthy things; and that through the windows of your exterior senses he hath vouchsafed to transmit unto the interior faculties of your mind, nothing but what is good and virtuous. For in my time there hath been found on the continent a certain country, wherein are I know not what kind of Pastophorian mole-catching priests, who, albeit averse from engaging their proper persons into a matrimonial duty, like the potifical flamens of Cybele in Phrygia; as if they were capons, and not cocks; full of lasciviousness, salacity, and wantonness, who yet have, nevertheless, in the matter of conjugal affairs, taken upon them to prescribe laws and ordinances to married folks. I cannot goodly determine what I should most abhor, detest, loathe, and abominate,—whether the tyrannical presumption of those dreaded sacerdotal mole-catchers, who not being willing to contain and coop up themselves within the grates and trellises of their own mysterious temples, do deal in, meddle with, obtrude upon, and thrust their sickles into harvests of secular businesses, quite contrary and diametrically opposite to the quality, state, and condition of their callings, professions, and vocations; or the superstitious stupidity and senseless scrupulousness of married folks, who have yielded obedience, and submitted their bodies, fortunes, and estates to the discretion and authority of such odious, perverse, barbarous, and unreasonable laws. Nor do they see that, which is clearer than the light and splendour of the morning star,—how all these nuptial and connubial sanctions, statutes, and ordinances have been decreed, made, and instituted, for the sole benefit, profit, and advantage of the flaminal mysts and mysterious flamens, and nothing at all for the good, utility, or emolument of the silly hood-winked married people. Which administereth unto others a sufficient cause for rendering these churchmen suspicious of iniquity, and of an unjust and fraudulent manner of dealing, no more to be connived at nor countenanced, after that it be well weighed in the scales of reason, than if with a reciprocal temerity the laics, by way of compensation, would impose laws to be followed and observed by those mysts and flamens, how they should behave themselves in the making and performance of their rites and ceremonies, after what manner they ought to proceed in the offering up and immolating of their various oblations, victims, and sacrifices; seeing that, besides the edecimation and tithe-haling of their goods, they cut off and take parings, shreddings, and clippings of the gain proceeding from the labour of their hands, and sweat of their brows, therewith to entertain themselves the better. Upon which consideration, in my opinion, their injunctions and commands would not prove so pernicious and impertinent, as those of the ecclesiastic power, unto which they had tendered their blind obedience. For, as you have very well said, there is no place in the world, where, legally, a licence is granted to the children to marry without the advice and consent of their parents and kindred. Nevertheless, by those wicked laws, and mole-catching customs whereat there is a little hinted in what I have already spoken to you, there is no scurvy, measly, leprous, or pocky ruffian, pander, knave, rogue, scellum, robber, or thief, pilloried, whipped, and burn-marked in his own country for his crimes and felonies, who may not violently snatch away and ravish what maid soever he had a mind to pitch upon, how noble, how fair, how rich, honest, and chaste soever she be, and that out of the house of her own father, in his own presence, from the bosom of her mother, and in the sight and despite of her friends and kindred looking on a so woful spectacle, provided that the rascal villain be so cunning as to associate unto himself some mystical flamen, who, according to the covenant made betwixt them two, shall be in hope some day to participate of the prey.

Could the Goths, the Scythians, or Massagetæ do a worse or more cruel act to any of the inhabitants of a hostile city, when, after the loss of many of their most considerable commanders, the expense of a great deal of money, and a long siege, that they shall have stormed and taken it by a violent and impetuous assault? May not these fathers and mothers, think you, be sorrowful and heavy-hearted, when they see an unknown fellow, a vagabond stranger, a barbarous lout, a rude cur, rotten, fleshless, putrified, scraggy, boily, botchy, poor, a forlorn caitiff, and miserable sneak, by an open rapt, snatch away before their own eyes their so fair, delicate, neat, well-behavioured, richly provided for and healthful daughters, on whose breeding and education they had spared no cost nor charges, by bringing them up in an honest discipline to all the honourable and virtuous employments becoming one of their sex, descended of a noble parentage, hoping by those commendable and industrious means in an opportune and convenient time to bestow them on the worthy sons of their well-deserving neighbours and ancient friends, who had nourished, entertained, taught, instructed, and schooled their children with the same care and solicitude, to make them matches fit to attain to the felicity of a so happy marriage, that from them might issue an offspring and progeny no less heirs to the laudable endowments and exquisite qualifications of their parents, whom they every way resemble, than to their personal and real estates, moveables and inheritances? How doleful, trist, and plangorous would such a sight and pageantry prove unto them? You shall not need to think, that the collachrymation of the Romans and their confederates at the decease of Germanicus Drusus was comparable to this lamentation of theirs? Neither would I have you to believe that the discomfort and anxiety of the Lacedæmonians, when the Greek Helen, by the perfidiousness of the adulterous Trojan, Paris, was privily stolen away out of their country, was greater or more pitiful than this ruthful and deplorable collugency of theirs? You may very well imagine, that Ceres at the ravishment of her daughter Proserpine, was not more attristed, sad, nor mournful than they. Trust me, and your own reason, that the loss of Osiris was not so regrettable to Isis,—nor did Venus so deplore the death of Adonis,—nor yet did Hercules so bewail the straying of Hylas,—nor was the rapt of Polyxena more throbbingly resented and condoled by Priamus and Hecuba, than this aforesaid accident would be sympathetically bemoaned, grievous, ruthful, and anxious, to the wofully desolate and disconsolate parents.

Notwithstanding all this, the greater part of so vilely abused parents are so timorous and afraid of the devils and hobgoblins, and so deeply plunged in superstition, that they dare not gainsay nor contradict, much less oppose and resist, those unnatural and impious actions, when the mole-catcher hath been present at the perpetrating of the fact, and a party contractor and covenanter in that detestable bargain. What do they do then? They wretchedly stay at their own miserable homes, destitute of their well beloved daughters,—the fathers cursing the days and the hours wherein they were married,—and the mothers howling and crying, that it was not their fortune to have brought forth abortive issues, when they happened to be delivered of such unfortunate girls; and in this pitiful plight spend at best the remainder of their time, with tears and weeping for those their children, of and from whom they expected, (and, with good reason, should have obtained and reaped,) in these latter days of theirs, joy and comfort. Other parents there have been, so impatient of that affront and indignity put upon them, and their families, that, transported with the extremity of passion, in a mad and frantic mood, through the vehemency of a grievous fury and raging sorrow, they have drowned, hanged, killed, and otherwise put violent hands on themselves. Others, again, of that parental relation, have, upon the reception of the like injury, been of a more magnanimous and heroic spirit, who, in imitation and at the example of the children of Jacob, revenging upon the Sichemites the rapt of their sister Dina, having found the rascally ruffian in the association of his mystical mole-catcher, closely and in hugger-mugger conferring, and parleying, with their daughters, for the suborning, corrupting, depraving, perverting, and enticing these innocent unexperienced maids unto filthy lewdnesses, have without any further advisement on the matter, cut them instantly to pieces, and thereupon forthwith thrown out upon the fields their so dismembered bodies, to serve for food unto the wolves and ravens. Upon the chivalrous, bold, and courageous achievement of a so valiant, stout, and man-like act, the other mole-catching symmists have been so highly incensed, and have so chafed, fretted, and fumed thereat, that bills of complaint and accusations having been in a most odious and detestable manner put in before the competent judges, the arm of secular authority hath with much importunity and impetuosity been by them implored and required; they proudly contending, That the servants of God would become contemptible, if exemplary punishment were not speedily taken upon the persons of the perpetrators of such an enormous, horrid, sacrilegious, crying, heinous, and execrable crime.

Yet neither by natural equity, by the law of nations, nor by any imperial law whatsoever, hath there been found so much as one rubric, paragraph, point, or tittle, by the which any kind of chastisement or correction hath been adjudged due to be inflicted upon any for their delinquency in that kind. Reason opposeth, and nature is repugnant. For there is no virtuous man in the world, who both naturally and with good reason will not be more hugely troubled in mind, hearing of the news of the rape, disgrace, ignominy, and dishonour of his daughter, than of her death. Now any man, finding in hot blood one, who with a fore-thought felony hath murdered his daughter, may, without tying himself to the formalities and circumstances of a legal proceeding, kill him on a sudden, and out of hand, without incurring any hazard of being attainted and apprehended by the officers of justice for so doing. It is no wonder then if a lechering rogue, together with his molecatching abettor, be entrapped in the flagrant act of suborning his daughter, and, stealing her out of his house, though herself consent thereto, that the father in such a case of stain and infamy by them brought upon his family, should put them both to a shameful death, and cast their carcasses upon dunghills to be devoured and eaten up by dogs and swine, or otherwise, fling them a little further off to the direption, tearing and rending asunder of their joints and members by the wild beasts of the field, as being unworthy to receive the gentle, the desired, the last kind embraces of their great Alma Mater, the earth, commonly called burial.

Dearly beloved son, have an especial care, that after my decease none of these laws be received in any of your kingdoms; for whilst I breathe, by the grace and assistance of God, I shall give good order. Seeing, therefore, you have totally referred unto my discretion the disposure of you in marriage, I am fully of an opinion, that I shall provide sufficiently well for you in that point. Make ready and prepare yourself for Panurge's voyage. Take along with you Epistemon, Friar John, and such others as you will choose. Do with my treasures what unto yourself shall seem most expedient. None of your actions, I promise you, can in any manner of way displease me. Take out of my arsenal Thalasse whatsoever equipage, furniture, or provision you please, together with such pilots, mariners, and truchmen, as you have a mind to, and with the first fair and favourable wind set sail and make out to sea, in the name of God our Saviour. In the meanwhile, during your absence, I shall not be neglective of providing a wife for you, nor of those preparations, which are requisite to be made for the more sumptuous solemnizing of your nuptials with a most splendid feast, if ever there was any in the world.

CHAPTER 49

How Pantagruel did put himself in a readiness to go to sea; and of the herb named Pantagruelion

WITHIN very few days after that Pantagruel had taken his leave of the good Gargantua, who devoutly prayed for his son's happy voyage, he arrived at the sea-port, near to Sammalo, accompanied with Panurge, Epistemon, Friar John of the Funnels, Abbot of Theleme, and others of the royal house, especially with Xenomanes the great traveller, and thwarter of dangerous ways, who was to come at the bidding and appointment of Panurge, of whose Castlewick of Salmigondin he did hold some petty inheritance by the tenure of a mesne fee. Pantagruel, being come thither, prepared and made ready for launching a fleet of ships, to the number of those which Ajax of Salamine had of old equipped in convoy of the Grecian soldiery against the Trojan state. He likewise picked out for his use so many mariners, pilots, sailors, interpreters, artificers, officers, and soldiers, as he thought fitting, and therewithal made provision of so much victuals of all sorts, artillery, munition of divers kinds, clothes, monies, and other such luggage, stuff, baggage, chaffer, and furniture, as he deemed needful for carrying on the design of a so tedious, long, and perilous voyage. Amongst other things it was observed, how he caused some of his vessels to be fraught and loaded with a great quantity of an herb of his called Pantagruelion, not only of the green and raw sort of it, but of the confected also, and of that which was notably well befitted for present use, after the fashion of conserves. The herb Pantagruelion hath a little root, somewhat hard and rough, roundish, terminating in an obtuse and very blunt point, and having some of its veins, strings, or filaments coloured with some spots of white, never fixeth itself into the ground above the profoundness almost of a cubit, or foot and a half. From the root thereof proceedeth the only stalk, orbicular, cane-like, green without, whitish within, and hollow like the stem of smyrnium, *olus atrum*, beans, and gentian, full of long threads, straight, easy to be broken, jagged, snipped, nicked and notched a little after the manner of pillars and columns, slightly furrowed, chamfered, guttered and channelled and full of fibres, or hairs like strings, in which consisteth the chief value and dignity of the herb, especially in that part thereof which is termed *mesa*, as one would say the mean; and in that other, which had got the denomination of *milasea*. Its height is commonly five or six feet. Yet sometimes it is of such a tall growth, as doth surpass the length of a lance, but that is only when it meeteth with a sweet, easy, warm, wet, and well-soaked soil,—as is the ground of the territory of Olone, and that of Rasea, near to Preneste in Sabinia,—and that it want not for rain enough about the season of the fishers' holidays, and the æstival solstice. There are many trees whose height is by it very far exceeded, and you might call it *dendromalache* by the authority of Theophrastus. The plant every year perisheth,—the tree neither in the trunk, root, bark, or boughs, being durable.

From the stalk of this Pantagruelion plant there issue forth several large and great branches, whose leaves have thrice as much length as breadth, always green, roughish, and rugged like the orcanet, or Spanish bugloss, hardish, slit round about like unto a suckle, or as the saxifragum, as betony, and finally ending as it were in the points of a Macedonian spear, or of such a lancet as surgeons commonly make use of in their phlebotomizing tiltings. The figure and shape of the leaves thereof is not much different from that of those of the ash tree, or of agrimony; the herb itself being so like the Eupatorian plant, that many skilful herbalists have called it the Domestic Eupator, and the Eupator the Wild Pantagruelion. These leaves are in equal and parallel distances spread around the stalk, by the number in every rank either of five or seven, nature having so highly favoured and cherished this plant, that she hath richly adorned it with these two odd, divine, and mysterious numbers. The smell thereof is somewhat strong, and not very pleasing to nice, tender, and delicate noses. The seed inclosed therein mounteth up to the very top of its stalk, and a little above it.

This is a numerous herb: for there is no less abundance of it than of any other whatsoever. Some of these plants are spherical, some rhomboid, and some of an oblong shape, and all of these either black, bright-coloured, or tawny, rude to the touch, and mantled with a quickly-blasted-away coat, yet such a one as is of a delicious taste and savour to all shrill and sweetly singing birds, such as linnets, goldfinches, larks, canary birds, yellow hammers, and others of that airy chirping quire;

but it would quite extinguish the natural heat and procreative virtue of the semence of any man, who would eat much, and often of it. And although that of old amongst the Greeks there was certain kind of fritters and pancakes, buns and tarts, made thereof, which commonly for a liquorish daintiness were presented on the table after supper, to delight the palate and make the wine relish the better; yet is it of a difficult concoction, and offensive to the stomach. For it engendereth bad and unwholesome blood, and with its exorbitant heat woundeth them with grievous, hurtful, smart, and noisome vapours. And, as in divers plants and trees there are two sexes, male and female, which is perceptible in laurels, palms, cypresses, oaks, holmes, the daffodil, mandrake, fern, the agaric, mushroom, birthwort, turpentine, pennyroyal, peony, rose of the mount, and many other such like, even so in this herb there is a male which beareth no flower at all, yet it is very copious of and abundant in seed. There is likewise in it a female, which hath great store and plenty of whitish flowers, serviceable to little or no purpose, nor doth it carry in it seed of any worth at all, at least comparable to that of the male. It hath also a larger leaf, and much softer than that of the male, nor doth it altogether grow to so great a height. This Pantagruelion is to be sown at the first coming of the swallows, and is to be plucked out of the ground when the grasshoppers begin to be a little hoarse.

CHAPTER 50

How the famous Pantagruelion ought to be prepared and wrought

THE herb Pantagruelion in September, under the autumnal equinox, is dressed and prepared several ways, according to the various fancies of the people, and diversity of the climates wherein it groweth. The first instruction which Pantagruel gave concerning it was, to divest and despoil the stalk and stem thereof of all its flowers and seeds, to macerate and mortify it in stagnant, not running water, for five days together, if the season be dry, and the water hot; or for full nine or twelve days, if the weather be cloudish, and the water cold. Then must it be dried in the sun, till it be drained of its moisture. After this it is in the shadow where the sun shines not, to be peeled, and its rind pulled off. Then are the fibres and strings thereof to be parted, wherein, as we have already said, consisteth its prime virtue, price, and efficacy, and severed from the woody part thereof, which is unprofitable, and serveth hardly to any other use than to make a clear and glistering blaze, to kindle the fire, and for the play, pastime, and disport of little children, to blow up hogs' bladders, and make them rattle. Many times some use is made thereof by tippling sweet-lipped bibbers, who out of it frame quills and pipes, through which they with their liquor-attractive breath suck up the new dainty wine from the bung of the barrel. Some modern Pantagruelists, to shun and avoid that manual labour, which such a separating and partitional work would of necessity require, employ certain cataractic instruments, composed and formed after the same manner that the froward, pettish, and angry Juno, did hold the fingers of both her hands interwovenly clenched together, when she would have hindered the childbirth delivery of Alcmena, at the nativity of Hercules; and athwart those cataracts they break and bruise to very trash the woody parcels, thereby to preserve the better the fibres, which are the precious and excellent parts. In and with this sole operation do these acquiesce and are contented, who, contrary to the received opinion of the whole earth, and in a manner paradoxical to all philosophers, gain their livelihoods backwards, and by recoiling. But those that love to hold it at a higher rate, and prize it according to its value, for their own greater profit, do the very same which is told us of the recreation of the three fatal Sister-Parcæ, or of the nocturnal exercise of the noble Circe, or yet of the excuse which Penelope made to her fond wooing youngsters and effeminate courtiers, during the long absence of her husband Ulysses.

By these means is this herb put into a way to display its inestimable virtues, whereof I will discover a part;—for to relate all is a thing impossible to do. I have already interpreted and exposed before you the denomination thereof. I find that plants have their names given and bestowed upon them after several ways. Some got the name of him who first found them out, knew them, sowed them, improved them by culture, qualified them to a tractability, and appropriated them to the uses and subserviences they were fit for. As the Mercurialis from Mercury; Panacea from Panace, the daughter of Esculapius; Armois from Artemis, who is Diana; Eupatoria from

the king Eupator; Telephion from Telephus; Euphorbium from Euphorbus, King Juba's physician; Clymenos from Clymenus; Alcibiadium from Alcibiades; Gentian from Gentius, King of Sclavonia, and so forth, through a great many other herbs or plants. Truly, in ancient times, this prerogative of imposing the inventor's name upon an herb found out by him was held in a so great account and estimation, that, as a controversy arose betwixt Neptune and Pallas, from which of them two that land should receive its denomination, which had been equally found out by them both together; though thereafter it was called and had the appellation of Athens, from Athene, which is Minerva,—just so would Lynceus, King of Scythia, have treacherously slain the young Triptolemus whom Ceres had sent to show unto mankind the invention of corn, which until then had been utterly unknown; to the end that, after the murder of the messenger, whose death he made account to have kept secret, he might, by imposing, with the less suspicion of false dealing, his own name upon the said found out seed, acquire unto himself an immortal honour and glory for having been the inventor of a grain so profitable and necessary to and for the use of human life. For the wickedness of which treasonable attempt he was by Ceres transformed into that wild beast, which by some is called a lynx, and by others an ounce. Such also was the ambition of others upon the like occasion, as appeareth, by that very sharp wars, and of a long continuance have been made of old betwixt some residentiary kings in Cappadocia upon this only debate, of whose name a certain herb should have the appellation; by reason of which difference, so troublesome and expensive to them all, it was by them called Polemonion, and by us for the same cause termed Make-bate.

Other herbs and plants there are, which retain the names of the countries from whence they were transported; as the Median apples from Media, where they first grew; Punic apples from Punicia, that is to say, Carthage; Ligusticum, which we call Lovage, from Liguria, the coast of Genoa; Rhubarb from a flood in Barbary, as Ammianus attesteth, called Ru; Santonica from a region of that name; Fenugreek from Greece; Castanes from a country so called; Persicaria from Persia; Sabine from a territory of that appellation; Stœchas from the Stœchad Islands;

Spica Celtica from the land of the Celtic Gauls, and so throughout a great many other, which were tedious to enumerate. Some others, again, have obtained their denominations by way of antiphrasis, or contrariety; as Absinth, because it is contrary to Ψίντος, for it is bitter to the taste in drinking,—Holosteon, as if it were all bones, whilst on the contrary, there is no frailer, tenderer, nor brittler herb in the whole production of nature than it.

There are some other sorts of herbs, which have got their names from their virtues and operations; as Aristolochia, because it helpeth women in child-birth; Lichen, for that it cureth the disease of that name; Mallow, because it mollifieth; Callithricum, because it maketh the hair of a bright colour; Alyssum, Ephemerum, Bechium, Nasturtium, Henbane, and so forth through many more.

Other some there are, which have obtained their names from the admirable qualities that are found to be in them; as Heliotropium, which is the marigold, because it followeth the sun, so that at the sun rising it displayeth and spreads itself out, at his ascending it mounteth, at his declining it waneth, and when he is set, it is close shut; Adianton, because, although it grow near unto watery places, and albeit you should let it lie in water a long time, it will nevertheless retain no moisture nor humidity; Hierachia, Eringium, and so throughout a great many more. There are also a great many herbs and plants, which have retained the very same names of the men and women who have been metamorphosed and transformed in them; as from Daphne, the laurel is called also Daphne; Myrrh from Myrrha, the daughter of Cinarus; Pythis from Pythis; Cinara, which is the artichoke, from one of that name; Narcissus, with Saffron, Smilax, and divers others.

Many herbs, likewise, have got their names of those things which they seem to have some resemblance to; as Hippuris, because it hath the likeness of a horse's tail; Alopecuris, because it representeth in similitude the tail of a fox; Psyllion, from a flea which it resembleth; Delphinium, for that it is like the dolphin fish; Bugloss is so called, because it is an herb like an ox's tongue; Iris, so called, because in its flowers it hath some resemblance of the rainbow; Myosota, because it is like the ear of a mouse; Coronopus, for that it is of the likeness of a crow's foot. A great many other such there are, which here to recite were needless. Furthermore, as there are herbs and plants which have had their names from those of men, so by a reciprocal denomination have the surnames of many families taken their origin from them; as the Fabii, à fabis, beans; the Pisons, à pisis, peas; the Lentuli, from lentils; the Cicerons, à ciceribus vel ciceris, a sort of pulse called chickpeas, and so forth. In some plants and herbs, the resemblance or likeness hath been taken from a higher mark or object, as when we say Venus' navel, Venus' hair, Venus' tub, Jupiter's beard, Jupiter's eye, Mars' blood, the Hermodactyl or Mercury's fingers, which are all of them names of herbs, as there are a great many more of the like appellation. Others, again, have received their denomination from their forms; such as the trefoil, because it is three-leaved; Pentaphylon, for having five leaves; Serpolet, because it creepeth along the ground; Helxine, Petast, Myrobalon, which the Arabians called Been, as if you would say an acorn, for it hath a kind of resemblance thereto, and withal is very oily.

CHAPTER 51

Why it is called Pantagruelion, and of the admirable virtues thereof

By such like means of attaining to a denomination, the fabulous ways being only from thence expected; for, the Lord forbid, that we should make use of any fables in this a so very veritable history, is this herb called Pantagruelion; for Pantagruel was the inventor thereof. I do not say of the plant itself, but of a certain use which it serves for, exceeding odious and hateful to thieves and robbers, unto whom it is more contrarious and hurtful than the strangleweed and choke-fitch is to the flax, the cats-tail to the brakes, the sheavegrass to the mowers of hay, the fitches to the chickney-peas, the darnel to barley, the hatchet-fitch to the lentil-pulse, the antramium to the beans, tares to wheat, ivy to walls, the water-lily to lecherous monks, the birchenrod to the scholars of the college of Navarre in Paris, colewort to the vine-tree, garlic to the load-stone, onions to the sight, fernseed to women with child, willow-grain to vicious nuns, the yew-tree shade to those that sleep under it, wolfs-bane to wolves and libbards, the smell of fig-tree to mad bulls, hemlock to goslings, purslane to the teeth, or oil to trees. For we have seen many of those rogues, by virtue and right application of this herb, finish their lives short and long, after the manner of Phyllis, Queen of Thracia, of Benosus, Emperor of Rome, of Amata, King Latinus's wife, of Iphis, Autolycus, Lycambes, Arachne, Phædra, Leda, Achius, King of Lydia, and many thousands more; who were chiefly angry and vexed at this disaster therein, that, without being otherwise sick or evil disposed in their bodies, by a touch only of the Pantagruelion, they came on a sudden to have the passage obstructed, and their pipes, through which were wont to bolt so many jolly sayings, and to enter so many luscious morsels, stopped, more cleverly, than ever could have done the squinancy.

Others have been heard most woefully to lament at the very instant when Atropos was about to cut the thread of their life, that Pantagruel held them by the gorge. But, well-a-day, it was not Pantagruel; he never was an executioner. It was the Pantagruelion, manufactured and fashioned into an halter, and serving in the place and office of a cravat. In that, verily, they solecized and spoke improperly, unless you would excuse them by a trope, which alloweth us to posit the inventor in the place of the thing invented; as when Ceres is taken for bread, and Bacchus put instead of wine. I swear to you here, by the good and frolic words which are to issue out of that wine-bottle, which is a-cooling below in the copper vessel full of fountain water, that the noble Pantagruel never snatched any man by the throat, unless it was such a one as was altogether careless and neglective of those obviating remedies, which were preventive of the thirst to come.

It is also termed Pantagruelion by a similitude. For Pantagruel, at the very first minute of his birth, was no less tall than this herb is long, whereof I speak unto you,—his measure having been then taken the more easy, that he was born in the season of the great drought, when they were busiest in the gathering of the said herb, to wit, at that time when Icarus's dog, with his fiery bawling and barking at the sun, maketh the whole world troglodytic, and enforceth people everywhere to hide themselves in dens and subterranean caves. It is likewise called Pantagruelion, because of the notable and singular qualities, virtues, and properties thereof. For as Pantagruel hath been the idea, pattern, prototype, and exemplary of all jovial perfection and accomplishment—in the truth whereof I believe there is none of you, gentlemen drinkers, that putteth any question—so in this Pantagruelion have I found so much efficacy and energy, so much completeness and excellency, so much exquisiteness and rarity, and so many admirable effects and operations of a transcendent nature, that, if the worth and virtue thereof had been known, when those trees, by the relation of the prophet, made election of a wooden king to rule and govern over them, it without doubt would have carried away from all the rest the plurality of votes and suffrages.

Shall I yet say more? If Oxilus, the son of Orius, had begotten this plant upon his sister Hamadryas, he had taken more delight in the value and perfection of it alone, than in all his eight children, so highly renowned by our ablest mythologians, that they have sedulously recommended their names to the never-failing tuition of an eternal remembrance. The eldest child was a daughter, whose name was Vine; the next born was a boy, and his name was Fig-tree; the third was called Walnut-tree; the fourth Oak; the fifth Sorbapple-tree; the sixth Ash; the seventh Poplar; and the last had the name of Elm, who was the greatest surgeon in his time. I shall forbear to tell you, how the juice or sap thereof, being poured and distilled within the ears, killeth every kind of vermin, that by any manner of putrefaction cometh to be bred and engendered there, and destroyeth also any whatsoever other animal that shall have entered in thereat. If, likewise, you put a little of the said juice with a pail or bucket full of water, you shall see the water instantly turn and grow thick therewith, as if it were milk curds, whereof the virtue is so great, that the water thus curded is a present remedy for horses subject to the cholic, and such as strike at their own flanks. The root thereof well boiled mollifieth the joints, softeneth the hardness of shrunk-in sinews, is every way comfortable to the nerves, and good against all cramps and convulsions, as likewise all cold and knotty gouts. If you would speedily heal a burning, whether occasioned by water or fire, apply thereto a little raw Pantagruelion, that is to say, take it so as it cometh out of the ground, without bestowing any other preparation or composition upon it; but have a special care to change it for some fresher, in lieu thereof, as soon as you shall find it waxing dry upon the sore.

Without this herb, kitchens would be detested, the tables of dining-rooms abhorred, although there were great plenty and variety of most dainty and sumptuous dishes of meat set down upon them—and the choicest beds also, how richly soever adorned with gold, silver, amber, ivory, porphyry, and the mixture of most precious metals, would without it yield no delight or pleasure to the reposers in them. Without it millers could neither carry wheat, nor any other kind of corn, to the mill, nor would they be able to bring back from thence flour, or any other sort of meal whatsoever. Without it, how could the papers and writs of lawyers' clients be brought to the bar? Seldom is the mortar, lime, or plaister brought to the workhouse without it. Without it, how should the water be got out of a draw-well; in what case would tabellions, notaries, copyists, makers of counterpanes, writers, clerks, secretaries, scriveners, and suchlike persons be without it? Were it not for it, what would become of the toll-rates and rent-rolls? Would not the noble art of printing perish without it? Whereof could the chassis or paper windows be made? How should the bells be rung? The altars of Isis are adorned therewith, the Pastophorian priests are therewith clad and accoutred, and whole human nature covered and wrapped therein, at its first position and production in and into this world. All the lanific trees of Seres, the bumbast and cotton bushes in the territories near the Persian sea, and Gulf of Bengala; the Arabian swans, together with the plants of Malta, do not all of them clothe, attire, and apparel so many persons as this one herb alone. Soldiers are now-a-days much better sheltered under it, than they were in former times, when they lay in tents covered with skins. It overshadows the theatres and amphitheatres from the heat of a scorching sun. It begirdeth and encompasseth forests, chases, parks, copses, and groves, for the pleasure of hunters. It descendeth into the salt and fresh of both sea and river waters, for the profit of fishers. By it are boots of all sizes, buskins, gamashes, brodkins, gambados, shoes, pumps, slippers, and every cobbled ware wrought and made steadable for the use of man. By it the butt and rover bows are strung, the crossbows bended, and the slings made fixed. And, as if it were an herb every whit as holy as the vervain, and reverenced by ghosts, spirits, hobgoblins, fiends, and phantoms, the bodies of deceased men are never buried without it.

I will proceed yet further. By the means of this fine herb, the invisible substances are visibly stopped, arrested, taken, detained, and prisoner-like committed to their receptive gaols. Heavy and ponderous weights are by it heaved, lifted up, turned, veered, drawn, carried, and every way moved quickly, nimbly and easily, to the great profit and emolument of human kind. When I perpend with myself these and such like marvellous effects of this wonderful herb, it seemeth strange unto me, how the invention of so useful a practice did escape through so many by-past ages the knowledge of the ancient philosophers, considering the inestimable utility which from thence proceeded, and the immense labour, which, without it, they did undergo in their pristine lucubrations. By virtue thereof, through the retention of some aerial gusts, are the huge barges, mighty galleons, the large floats, the Chiliander, the Myriander ships launched from their stations, and set agoing at the pleasure and arbitrement of their rulers, conders, and steersmen. By the help thereof those remote nations, whom nature seemed so unwilling to have discovered to us, and so desirous to have kept them still *in abscondito*[97] and hidden from us, that the ways through which their countries were to be reached unto, were not only totally unknown, but judged also to be altogether impermeable and inaccessible, are now arrived to us, and we to them.

Those voyages outreached the flights of birds, and far surpassed the scope of feathered fowls, how swift soever they had been on the wing, and notwithstanding that advantage which they have of us, in swimming through the air. Taproban hath seen the heaths of Lapland, and both the Javas, the Riphæan mountains; wide distant Phebol shall see Theleme, and the Islanders drink of the flood of Euphrates. By it the chillmouthed Boreas hath surveyed the parched mansions of the torrid Auster, and Eurus visited the regions which Zephyrus hath under his command; yea, in such sort have interviews been made, by the assistance of this sacred herb, that, maugre longitudes and latitudes, and all the variations of the zones, the Peræcian people, and Anteocian, Amphiscian, Heteroscian, and Periscian have oft rendered and received mutual visits to and from other, upon all the climates. These strange exploits bred such astonishment to the celestial intelligences, to all the marine and terrestrial gods, that they were on a sudden all afraid. From which amazement, when they saw, how, by means of this blest Pantagruelion, the Arctic people looked upon the Antarctic, scoured the Atlantic Ocean, passed the tropics, pushed through the torrid zone, measured all the zodiac, sported under the equinoctial, having both poles level with their horizon; they judged it high time to call a council for their own safety and preservation.

The Olympic gods, being all and each of them affrighted at the sight of such achievements, said, Pantagruel hath shapen work enough for us, and put us more to a plunge, and nearer our wit's end, by this sole herb of his, than did of old the Aloidæ by overturning mountains. He very speedily is to be married, and shall have many children by his wife. It lies not in our power to oppose this destiny; for it hath passed through the hands and spindles of the Fatal Sisters, necessity's inexorable daughters. Who knows but by his sons may be found out an herb of such another virtue and prodigious energy, as that by the aid thereof in using it aright according to their father's skill, they may contrive a way for human kind to pierce into the high aërian clouds, get up unto the spring-head of the hail, take an inspection of the snowy sources, and shut and open as they please the sluices from whence proceed the floodgates of the rain; then prosecuting their etherial voyage, they may step in unto the lightning workhouse and shop, where all the thunderbolts are forged, where, seizing on the magazine of heaven, and storehouse of our warlike fire munition, they may discharge a bouncing peal or two of thundering ordnance, for joy of their arrival to these new supernal places; and, charging those tonitrual guns afresh, turn the whole force of that artillery wherein we most confided against ourselves. Then is it like, they will set forward to invade the territories of the moon, whence, passing through both Mercury and Venus, the Sun will serve them for a torch, to show the way from Mars to Jupiter and Saturn. We shall not then be able to resist the impetuosity of their intrusion, nor put a stoppage to their entering in at all, whatever regions, domiciles, or mansions of the spangled firmament they shall have any mind to see, to stay in, or to travel through for their recreation. All the celestial signs together, with the constellations of the fixed stars, will jointly be at their devotion then. Some will take up their lodging at the Ram, some at the Bull, and others at the Twins; some at the Crab, some at the Lion Inn, and others at the sign of the Virgin; some at the Balance, others at the Scorpion, and others will be quartered at the Archer; some will be harboured at the Goat, some at the Water-pourer's sign, some at the Fishes: some will lie at the Crown, some at the Harp, some at the Golden Eagle and the Dolphin; some at the Flying Horse, some at the Ship, some at the great, some at the little Bear, and so throughout the glistening hostelries of the whole twinkling asteristic welkin. There will be sojourners come from the earth, who, longing after the taste of the sweet cream, of their own skimming off, from the best milk of all the dairy of the Galaxy, will set themselves at table down with us, drink of our nectar and ambrosia, and take to their own beds at night for wives and concubines, our fairest goddesses, the only means whereby they can be deified. A junto hereupon being convocated, the better to consult upon the manner of obviating so dreadful a danger, Jove, sitting in his presidential throne, asked the votes of all the other gods, which, after a profound deliberation amongst themselves on all contingencies, they freely gave at last, and then resolved unanimously to withstand the shocks of all whatsoever sublunary assaults.

CHAPTER 52

How a certain kind of Pantagruelion is of that nature that the fire is not able to consume it

I HAVE already related to you great and admirable things; but, if you might be induced to adventure upon the hazard of believing some other divinity of this sacred Pantagruelion, I very willingly would tell it you. Believe it, if you will, or, otherwise, believe it not, I care not which of them you do, they are both alike to me. It shall be sufficient for my purpose to have told you the truth, and the truth I will tell you. But to enter in thereat, because it is of a knaggy, difficult, and rugged access, this is the question which I ask of you. If I had put within this bottle two pints, the one of wine, and the other of water, thoroughly and exactly mingled together, how would you unmix them? After what manner would you go about to sever them, and separate the one liquor from the other, in such sort, that you render me the water apart, free from the wine, and the wine also pure, without the intermixture of one drop of water, and both of them in the same measure;

quantity, and taste, that I had embottled them? Or, to state the question otherwise. If your carmen and mariners, entrusted for the provision of your houses with the bringing of a certain considerable number of tuns, puncheons, pipes, barrels, and hogsheads of *Graves* wine, or of the wine of Orleans, Beaune, and Mirevaux, should drink out the half, and afterwards with water fill up the other empty halves of the vessels as full as before; as the Limosins use to do, in their carriages by wains and carts, of the wines of Argenton and Sangaultier, after that, how would you part the water from the wine, and purify them both in such a case? I understand you well enough. Your meaning is, that I must do it with an ivy funnel. That is written, it is true, and the verity thereof explored by a thousand experiments; you have learned to do this feat before, I see it. But those that have never known it, nor at any time have seen the like, would hardly believe that it were possible. Let us nevertheless proceed.

But put the case, we were now living in the age of Sylla, Marius Cæsar, and other such Roman emperors, or that we were in the time of our ancient Druids, whose custom was to burn and calcine the dead bodies of their parents and lords, and that you had a mind to drink the ashes or cinders of your wives or fathers, in the infused liquor of some good white-wine, as Artemisia drunk the dust and ashes of her husband Mausolus; or, otherwise, that you did determine to have them reserved in some fine urn, or reliquary pot; how would you save the ashes apart, and separate them from those other cinders and ashes into which the fuel of the funeral and bustuary fire hath been converted? Answer, if you can. By my figgings, I believe it will trouble you so to do.

Well, I will dispatch, and tell you, that, if you take of this celestial Pantagruelion so much as is needful to cover the body of the defunct, and after that you shall have enwrapped and bound therein, as hard and closely as you can, the corps of the said deceased person, and sewed up the folding-sheet, with thread of the same stuff, throw it into the fire, how great or ardent soever it be, it matters not a straw, the fire through this Pantagruelion will burn the body and reduce to ashes the bones thereof, and the Pantagruelion shall be not only not consumed nor burnt, but also shall neither lose one atom of the ashes enclosed within it, nor receive one

atom of the huge bustuary heap of ashes resulting from the blazing conflagration of things combustible laid round about it, but shall at last, when taken out of the fire, be fairer, whiter, and much cleaner than when you did put it in first. Therefore it is called *Asbeston*, which is as much as to say incombustible. Great plenty is to be found thereof in Caprasia, as likewise in the climate Dia Cyenes, at very easy rates. O how rare and admirable a thing it is, that the fire, which devoureth, consumeth, and destroyeth all such things else, should cleanse, purge, and whiten this sole Pantagruelion Carpasian Asbeston! If you mistrust the verity of this relation, and demand for further confirmation of my assertion a visible sign, as the Jews, and such incredulous infidels use to do, take a fresh egg, and orbicularly, or rather, ovally, enfold it within this divine Pantagruelion. When it is so wrapped up, put it in the hot embers of a fire, how great or ardent soever it be, and, having left it there as long as you will, you shall at last, at your taking it out of the fire, find the egg roasted hard, and as it were burnt, without any alteration, change, mutation, or so much as a calefaction of the sacred Pantagruelion. For less than a million of pounds sterling, modified, taken down and amoderated to the twelfth part of one four pence half-penny farthing, you are to put it to a trial, and make proof thereof.

Do not think to overmatch me here, by paragoning with it in the way of a more eminent comparison the Salamander. That is a fib; for, albeit a little ordinary fire, such as is used in dining-rooms and chambers, gladden, cheer up, exhilarate and quicken it, yet may I warrantably enough assure, that in the flaming fire of a furnace it will, like any other animated creature, be quickly suffocated, choked, consumed, and destroyed. We have seen experiment thereof, and Galen many ages ago hath clearly demonstrated and confirmed it, *lib*. 3. *De Temperamentis*. and Dioscorides maintaineth the same doctrine, *lib*. 2. Do not here instance, in competition with this sacred herb, the feather alum, or the wooden tower of Piræus, which Lucius Sylla was never able to get burnt; for that Archelaus, governor of the town for Mithridates King of Pontus, had plastered it all over on the outside with the said allum. Nor would I have you to compare therewith the herb, which Alexander Cornelius called Eonem, and said, that it had some resemblance with that oak which bears the mistletoe, and that it could neither be consumed, nor receive any manner of prejudice by fire, nor by water, no more than the mistletoe, of which was built, said he, the so renowned ship Argos. Search where you please for those that will believe it. I in that point desire to be excused. Neither would I wish you to parallel therewith,—although I cannot deny, but that it is of a very marvellous nature,—that sort of tree which groweth along the mountains of Briançon and Ambrun, which produceth out of its root the good Agaric. From its body it yieldeth unto us a so excellent rosin, that Galen hath been bold to equal it unto the turpentine. Upon the delicate leaves thereof it retaineth for our use that sweet heavenly honey, which is called the manna; and, although it be of a gummy, oily, fat and greasy substance, it is notwithstanding unconsumable by any fire. It is in the Greek and Latin called *Larix*. The Alpinese name is *Melze*. The Anternorides and Venetians term it *Larége;* which gave occasion to that castle in Piedmont to receive the denomination of Larignum, by putting Julius Cæsar to a stand at his return from amongst the Gauls.

Julius Cæsar commanded all the yeomen, boors, hinds, and other inhabitants in, near unto, and about the Alps and Piedmont to bring all manner of victuals and provision for an army to those places, which on the military road he had appointed to receive them for the use of his marching soldiery. To which ordinance all of them were obedient, save only those as were within the garrison of Larignum, who, trusting in the natural strength of the place, would not pay their contribution. The emperor, purposing to chastise them for their refusal, caused his whole army to march straight towards that castle, before the gate whereof was erected a tower built of huge big spars and rafters of the larch tree, fast bound together with pins and pegs of the same wood, and interchangeably laid on one another, after the fashion of a pile or stack of timber, set up in the fabric thereof to such an apt and convenient height that from the parapet above the portcullis they thought with stones and levers to beat off and drive away such as should approach thereto.

When Cæsar had understood, that the chief defence of those within the castle did consist in stones and clubs, and that it was not an easy matter to sling, hurl, dart, throw, or cast them so far as to hinder the approaches, he forthwith commanded his men to throw great store of bavins, faggots, and fascines round about the castle; and, when they had made the heap of a competent height, to put them all in a fair fire, which was thereupon incontinently done. The fire put amidst the faggots was so great and so high, that it covered the whole castle, that they might well imagine the tower would thereby be altogether burnt to dust and demolished. Nevertheless, contrary to all their hopes and expectations, when the flame ceased, and that the faggots were quite burnt and consumed, the tower appeared as whole, sound, and entire as ever. Cæsar, after a serious consideration had thereof, commanded a compass to be taken without the distance of a stone's cast from the castle round about it; there, with ditches and entrenchments to form a blockade; which when the Larignans understood, they rendered themselves upon terms. And then, by a relation from them, it was, that Cæsar learned the admirable nature and virtue of this wood, which of itself produceth neither fire, flame, nor coal, and would, therefore, in regard of that rare quality of incombustibility, have been admitted into this rank and degree of a true Pantagruelion plant; and that so much the rather, for that Pantagruel directed that all the gates, doors, angiports, windows, gutters, frettized, and embowed ceilings, cans, and other whatsoever wooden furniture in the abbey of Theleme, should be all materiated of this kind of timber. He likewise caused to cover therewith the sterns, stems, cook-rooms or laps, hatchets, decks, courses, bends and walls of his carricks, ships, galleons, galleys, brigantines, foysts, frigates, crears, barks, floyts, pinks, pinnaces, hoys, catches, capers, and other vessels of his Thalassian arsenal; were it not that the wood or timber of the larchtree being put within a large and ample furnace, full of huge vehemently flaming fire proceeding from the fuel of other sorts and kinds of wood, cometh at last to be corrupted, consumed, dissipated, and destroyed, as are stones in a lime-kiln. But this Pantagruelion Asbeston is rather by the fire renewed and cleansed, than by the flames thereof consumed or changed. Therefore,

Arabians, Indians, Sabæans,
Sing not, in hymns and Io Pæans,
Your incense, myrrh, or ebony.

Come here, a nobler plant to see,
And carry home, at any rate,
Some seed, that you may propagate.
If in your soil it takes, to heaven
A thousand thousand thanks be given;

And say, with France it goodly goes,
Where the Pantagruelion grows.

[Sir Thomas Urquhart's part of the translation ends here, and that of Motteux begins.]

BOOK FOUR

TREATING OF THE HEROIC DEEDS AND SAYINGS OF THE GOOD PANTAGRUEL

THE AUTHOR'S EPISTLE DEDICATORY

To the Most Illustrious Prince, and Most Reverend Lord Odet, Cardinal de Chastillon

You are not unacquainted, most illustrious prince, how often I have been, and am daily pressed and required by great numbers of eminent persons, to proceed in the Pantagruelian fables: they tell me that many languishing, sick and disconsolate persons, perusing them, have deceived their grief, passed their time merrily, and been inspired with new joy and comfort. I commonly answer, that I aimed not at glory and applause, when I diverted myself with writing; but only designed to give by my pen, to the absent who labour under affliction, that little help which at all times I willingly strive to give to the present that stand in need of my art and service. Sometimes I at large relate to them, how Hippocrates in several places, and particularly in *lib.* 6. *Epidem.*, describing the institution of the physician his disciple, and also Soranus of Ephesus, Oribasius, Galen, Hali Abbas, and other authors, have descended to particulars, in the prescription of his motions, deportment, looks, countenance, gracefulness, civility, cleanliness of face, clothes, beard, hair, hands, mouth, even his very nails; as if he were to play the part of a lover in some comedy, or enter the lists to fight some potent enemy. And indeed the practice of physic is properly enough compared by Hippocrates to a fight, and also to a farce acted between three persons, the patient, the physician, and the disease. Which passage has sometimes put me in mind of Julia's saying to Augustus her father. One day she came before him in a very gorgeous, loose, lascivious dress, which very much displeased him, though he did not much discover his discontent. The next day she put on another, and in a modest garb, such as the chaste Roman ladies wore, came into his presence. The kind father could not then forbear expressing the pleasure which he took to see her so much altered, and said to her: Oh! how much more this garb becomes, and is commendable in the daughter of Augustus. But she, having her excuse ready, answered: This day, sir, I dressed myself to please my father's eye; yesterday, to gratify that of my husband. Thus disguised in looks and garb, nay even, as formerly was the fashion, with a rich and pleasant gown with four sleeves, which was called *philonium* according to Petrus Alexandrinus in 6. *Epidem.*, a physician might answer to such as might find the metamorphosis indecent: Thus have I accoutred myself, not that I am proud of appearing in such a dress; but for the sake of my patient, whom alone I wholly design to please, and no ways offend or dissatisfy. There is also a passage in our father Hippocrates, in the book I have named, which causes some to sweat, dispute, and labour: not indeed to know whether the physician's frowning, discontented, and morose Catonian look render the patient sad, and his joyful, serene, and pleasing countenance rejoice him; for experience teaches us that this is most certain; but whether such sensations of grief, or pleasure, are produced by the apprehension of the patient observing his motions and qualities in his physician and drawing from thence conjectures of the end and catastrophe of his disease; as, by his pleasing look, joyful and desirable events, and by his sorrowful and unpleasing air, sad and dismal consequences; and whether those sensations be produced by a transfusion of the serene or gloomy, aerial or terrestrial, joyful or melancholic spirits of the physician,

232

into the person of the patient, as is the opinion of Plato and Averroes.

Above all things, the fore-cited authors have given particular directions to physicians about the words, discourse, and converse, which they ought to have with their patients; every one aiming at one point, that is, to rejoice them without offending God, and in no ways whatsoever to vex or displease them. Which causes Herophilus much to blame the physician Callianax, who, being asked by a patient of his, Shall I die? impudently made him this answer:

Patroclus died, whom all allow,
By much a better man than you.

Another, who had a mind to know the state of his distemper, asking him, after our merry Patelin's way; Well, doctor, does not my water tell you I shall die? He foolishly answered, No; if Latona, the mother of those lovely twins, Phœbus and Diana, begot thee. Galen, *lib.* 4, *Comment.* 6. *Epidem.*, blames much also Quintus his tutor, who, a certain nobleman of Rome, his patient, saying to him, You have been at breakfast, my master, your breath smells of wine; answered arrogantly, Yours smells of fever: which is the better smell of the two, wine or a putrid fever? But the calumny of certain cannibals, misanthropes, perpetual eavesdroppers, has been so foul and excessive against me, that it had conquered my patience, and I had resolved not to write one jot more. For the least of their detractions were, that my books are all stuffed with various heresies, of which, nevertheless, they could not show one single instance: much, indeed, of comical and facetious fooleries, neither offending God nor the king; (and truly I own they are the only subject, and only theme of these books) but of heresy, not a word, unless they interpreted wrong, and against all use of reason, and common language, what I had rather suffer a thousand deaths, if it were possible than have thought: as you should make bread to be stone, a fish to be a serpent, and an egg to be a scorpion. This, my lord, emboldened me once to tell you, as I was complaining of it in your presence, that if I did not esteem myself a better Christian, than they show themselves towards me, and if my life, writings, words, nay thoughts, betrayed to me one single spark of heresy, or I should in a detestable manner fall into the snares of the spirit of detraction,

Διάβολος, who, by their means, raises such crimes against me; I would then, like the phœnix, gather dry wood, kindle a fire, and burn myself in the midst of it. You were then pleased to say to me, that King Francis, of eternal memory, had been made sensible of those false accusations; and that having caused my books (mine, I say, because several, false and infamous, have been wickedly laid to me) to be carefully and distinctly read to him by the most learned and faithful anagnost in this kingdom, he had not found any passage suspicious; and that he abhorred a certain envious, ignorant, hypocritical informer, who grounded a mortal heresy on an *n* put instead of an *m* by the carelessness of the printers.

As much was done by his son, our most gracious, virtuous, and blessed sovereign, Henry, whom Heaven long preserve: so that he granted you his royal privilege, and particular protection for me, against my slandering adversaries.

You kindly condescended since, to confirm me these happy news at Paris; and also lately, when you visited my Lord Cardinal du Bellay, who, for the benefit of his health, after a lingering distemper, was retired to St. Maur, that place (or rather paradise) of salubrity, serenity, conveniency, and all desirable country pleasures.

Thus, my lord, under so glorious a patronage, I am emboldened once more to draw my pen, undaunted now and secure; with hopes that you will still prove to me, against the power of detraction, a second Gallic Hercules in learning, prudence, and eloquence; an Alexicacos in virtue, power, and authority: you, of whom I may truly say what the wise monarch Solomon saith of Moses, that great prophet and captain of Israel, *Ecclesiast.* 45. A man fearing and loving God, who found favour in the sight of all flesh, well-beloved both of God and man; whose memorial is blessed. God made him like to the glorious saints, and magnified him so, that his enemies stood in fear of him; and for him made wonders; made him glorious in the sight of kings, gave him a commandment for his people, and by him showed his light: he sanctified him in his faithfulness, and meekness, and chose him out of all men. By him he made us to hear his voice, and caused by him the law of life and knowledge to be given.

Accordingly, if I shall be so happy as to hear any one commend those merry composures, they shall be adjured by me to be obliged, and pay their thanks to you alone, as also to offer their prayers to Heaven, for the continuance and increase of your greatness; and to attribute no more to me, than my humble and ready obedience to your commands; for by your most honourable encouragement, you at once have inspired me with spirit, and with invention; and without you my heart had failed me, and the fountain-head of my animal spirits had been dry. May the Lord keep you in his blessed mercy.

My Lord,

Your Most Humble, and

Most Devoted Servant,

FRANCIS RABELAIS, *Physician*

Paris, *this 28th of January*, MDLII

THE AUTHOR'S PROLOGUE

GOOD people. God save and keep you! Where are you? I can't see you: stay—I'll saddle my nose with spectacles—oh, oh! it will be fair anon, I see you. Well, you have had a good vintage, they say: this is no bad news to Frank, you may swear. You have got an infallible cure against thirst: rarely performed of you, my friends! You, your wives, children, friends, and families are in as good case as hearts can wish; it is well, it is as I would have it: God be praised for it, and if such be his will, may you long be so. For my part, I am thereabouts, thanks to his blessed goodness; and by the means of a little Pantagruelism, (which you know is a certain jollity of mind, pickled in the scorn of fortune,) you see me now hale and cheery, as sound as a bell, and ready to drink, if you will. Would you know why I'm thus, good people? I will even give you a positive answer—Such is the Lord's will, which I obey and revere; it being said in his word, in great derision to the physician neglectful of his own health, Physician, heal thyself.

Galen had some knowledge of the Bible, and had conversed with the Christians of his time, as appears *lib.* II. *De Usu Partium; lib.* 2. *De Differentiis Pulsuum, cap.* 3, and *ibid. lib.* 3. *cap* 2. and *lib. De Rerum Affectibus* (if it be Galen's). Yet it was not for any such veneration of holy writ that he took care of his own health. No, it was for fear of being twitted with the saying so well known among physicians.

Ἰατρὸς ἄλλων αὐτὸς ἕλκεσι βρύων.

He boasts of healing poor and rich,
Yet is himself all over itch.

This made him boldly say, that he did not desire to be esteemed a physician, if from his twenty-eighth year to his old age he had not lived in perfect health, except some ephemer-ous fevers, of which he soon rid himself: yet he was not naturally of the soundest temper, his stomach being evidently bad. Indeed, as, he saith, *lib.* 5, *De Sanitate Tuenda,* that physician will hardly be thought very careful of the health of others, who neglects his own. Asclepiades boasted yet more than this; for he said that he had articled with fortune not to be reputed a physician, if he could be said to have been sick, since he began to practise physic, to his latter age, which he reached, lusty in all his members, and victorious over fortune; till at last the old gentleman unluckily tumbled down from the top of a certain ill-propt and rotten staircase, and so there was an end of him.

If by some disaster health is fled from your worships to the right or to the left, above or below, before or behind, within or without, far or near, on this side or the other side, wheresoever it be, may you presently, with the help of the Lord, meet with it. Having found it, may you immediately claim it, seize it, and secure it. The law allows it: the king would have it so: nay, you have my advice for it. Neither more not less than the law makers of old did fully impower a master to claim and seize his runaway servant, wherever he might be found. Odsbodikins, is it not written and warranted by the ancient customs of this so noble, so rich, so flourishing realm of France, that the dead seizes the quick? See what has been declared very lately in that point by that learned, wise, courteous, humane and just civilian, Andrew Tiraqueau, counsellor of the great victorious, and triumphant Henry II, in the most honourable court of Parliament at Paris. Health is our life, as Ariphron the Sicyonian wisely has it; without health life is not life, it is not living life: ἈΒΙ'ΟΣ ΒΙ'ΟΣ, ΒΙ'ΟΣ'ΑΒΙ'ΩΤΟΣ. Without health life is only a languishment, and an image of death. Therefore, you that want your health, that is to say, that are dead, seize the quick; secure life to yourselves, that is to say, health.

I have this hope in the Lord, that he will hear our supplications, considering with what faith and zeal we pray, and that he will grant this our wish, because it is moderate and mean. Mediocrity was held by the ancient sages to be golden, that is to say precious, praised by all men, and pleasing in all places. Read the sacred Bible, you will find, the prayers of those who asked moderately were never unanswered. For example, little dapper Zaccheus, whose body and reliques the monks of St. Garlick, near Orleans, boast of having, and nicknamed him St. Sylvanus, he only wished to see our blessed Saviour near Jerusalem. It was but a small request and no more than anybody then might pretend to. But alas! he was but low-built; and one of so diminutive a size, among the crowd, could not so much as get a glimpse of him. Well then he struts, stands on tip-toes, bustles, and bestirs his stumps, shoves and makes way, and with much ado clambers up a sycamore. Upon this, the Lord, who knew his sincere affection, presented himself to his sight, and was not only seen by him, but heard also; nay, what is more, he came to his house, and blessed his family.

One of the sons of the prophets in Israel felling wood near the river Jordan, his hatchet forsook the helve, and fell to the bottom of the river: so he prayed to have it again, (it was but a small request, mark ye me,) and having a strong faith, he did not throw the hatchet after the helve, as some spirits of contradiction say by way of scandalous blunder, but the helve after the hatchet, as you all properly have it. Presently two great miracles were seen: up springs the hatchet from the bottom of the water, and fixes itself to its old acquaintance the helve. Now had he wished to coach it to heaven in a fiery chariot like Elias, to multiply in seed like Abraham, be as rich as Job, strong as Sampson, and beautiful as Absalom, would he have obtained it, do ye think? In troth, my friends, I question it very much.

Now I talk of moderate wishes in point of hatchet, (but harkee me, be sure you do not forget when we ought to drink,) I will tell you what is written among the apologues of wise Æsop the Frenchman. I mean the Phrygian and Trojan, as Max. Planudes makes him; from which people, according to the most faithful chronicles, the noble French are descended. Ælian writes that he was of Thrace; and Agathias, after Herodotus, that he was of Samos; it is all one to Frank.

In his time lived a poor honest country fellow of Gravot, Tom Wellhung by name, a wood-cleaver by trade, who in that low drudgery made shift so to pick up a sorry livelihood. It happened that he lost his hatchet. Now tell me who ever had more cause to be vexed than poor Tom? Alas, his whole estate and life depended on his hatchet; by his hatchet he earned many a fair penny of the best wood-mongers or log-merchants, among whom he went a jobbing; for want of his hatchet he was like to starve; and had death but met with him six days after without a hatchet, the grim fiend would have mowed him down in the twinkling of a bed-staff. In this sad case he began to be in a heavy taking, and called upon Jupiter with the most eloquent prayers—for you know necessity was the mother of eloquence. With the whites of his eyes turned up towards heaven, down on his marrow-bones, his arms reared high, his fingers stretched wide, and his head bare, the poor wretch without ceasing was roaring out, by way of litany, at every repetition of his supplications, My hatchet, lord Jupiter, my hatchet! my hatchet! only my hatchet, O Jupiter, or money to buy another, and nothing else! alas, my poor hatchet!

Jupiter happened then to be holding a grand council, about certain urgent affairs, and old gammer Cybele was just giving her opinion, or, if you would rather have it so, it was young Phœbus the beau; but, in short, Tom's outcries and lamentations were so loud, that they were heard with no small amazement at the council-board, by the whole consistory of the gods. What a devil have we below, quoth Jupiter, that howls so horridly? By the mud of Styx, have not we had all along, and have not we here still enough to do, to set to rights a world of damned puzzling businesses of consequence? We made an end of the fray between Presthan, King of Persia, and Soliman the Turkish Emperor; we have stopped up the passages between the Tartars and the Muscovites; answered the Xeriff's petition; done the same to that of Golgots Rays; the state of Parma's dispatched; so is that of Maydenburg that of Mirandola, and that of Africa, that town on the Mediterranean which we call Aphrodisium; Tripoli by carelessness has got a new master; her hour was come.

Here are the Gascons cursing and damning, demanding the restitution of their bells.

In yonder corner are the Saxons, Easterlings, Ostrogoths, and Germans, nations formerly invincible, but now aberkeids, bridled, curbed, and brought under by a paltry diminutive crippled fellow: they ask us revenge, relief, restitution of their former good sense, and ancient liberty.

But what shall we do with this same Ramus and this Galland, with a pox to them, who surrounded with a swarm of their scullions, blackguard ragamuffins, sizers, vouchers, and stipulators, set together by the ears the whole university of Paris? I am in a sad quandary about it, and for the heart's blood of me cannot tell yet with whom of the two to side.

Both seem to me notable fellows, and as true cods as ever pissed. The one has rosenobles, I say fine and weighty ones; the other would gladly have some too. The one knows something; the other is no dunce. The one loves the better sort of men; the other is beloved by them. The one is an old cunning fox; the other with tongue and pen, tooth and nail, falls foul of the ancient orators and philosophers, and barks at them like a cur.

What thinkest thou of it, say, thou bawdy Priapus? I have found thy council just before now, *et habet tua mentula mentem*.[1]

King Jupiter, answered Priapus, standing up and taking off his cowl, his snout uncased and reared up, fiercely and stiffly propt, since you compare the one to a yelping snarling cur, and the other to sly Reynard the fox, my advice is, with submission, that without fretting or puzzling your brains any further about them, without any more ado, even serve them both as, in the days of yore, you did the dog and the fox. How? asked Jupiter; when? who were they? where was it? You have a rare memory, for aught I see, returned Priapus! This right worshipful father Bacchus, whom we have here nodding with his crimson phiz, to be revenged on the Thebans, had got a fairy fox, who whatever mischief he did, was never to be caught or wronged by any beast that wore a head.

The noble Vulcan here present had framed a dog of Monesian brass, and with long puffing and blowing, put the spirit of life into him: he gave it to you, you gave it your Miss Europa, Miss Europa gave it Minos, Minos gave it Procris, Procris gave it Cephalus. He was also of the fairy kind; so that, like the lawyers of our age, he was too hard for all other sorts of creatures; nothing could escape the dog. Now who should happen to meet but these two? What do you think they did? Dog by his destiny was to take fox, and fox by his fate was not to be taken.

The case was brought before your council: you protested that you would not act against the fates; and the fates were contradictory. In short, the end and result of the matter was, that to reconcile two contradictions was an impossibility in nature. The very pang put you into a sweat; some drops of which happening to light on the earth, produceth what the mortals call cabbage. All our noble consistory, for want of a categorical resolution, were seized with such a horrid thirst, that above seventy-eight hogsheads of nectar were swilled down at that sitting. At last you took my advice, and transmogrified them into stones; and immediately got rid of your perplexity, and a truce with thirst was proclaimed through this vast Olympus. This was the year of flabby cods, near Teumessus, between Thebes and Chalcis.

After this manner, it is my opinion, that you should petrify this dog and this fox. The metamorphosis will not be incongruous: for they both bear the name of Peter. And because, according to the Limosin proverb, to make an oven's mouth there must be three stones, you may associate them with master Peter du Coignet, whom you formerly petrified for the same cause. Then those three dead pieces shall be put in an equilateral trigone, somewhere in the great temple at Paris; in the middle of the porch, if you will; there to perform the office of extinguishers, and with their noses put out the lighted candles, torches, tapers, and flambeaux; since, while they lived, they still lighted, ballock-like, the fire of faction, division, ballock sects, and wrangling among those idle bearded boys, the students. And this will be an everlasting monument to show, that those puny self-conceited pedants, ballock-framers, were rather contemned than condemned by you. *Dixi*, I have said my say.

You deal too kindly by them, said Jupiter, for aught I see, Monsieur Priapus. You do not use to be so kind to every body, let me tell you; for as they seek to eternize their names, it would be much better for them to be thus changed into hard stones, than to return to earth and putrefaction. But now to other matters. Yonder behind us, towards the

Tuscan sea, and the neighbourhood of Mount Apennine, do you see what tragedies are stirred up by certain topping ecclesiastical bullies? This hot fit will last its time, like the Limosins' ovens, and then will be cooled, but not so fast.

We shall have sport enough with it; but I foresee one inconveniency: for methinks we have but little store of thunder ammunition, since the time that you, my fellow gods, for your pastime, lavished them away to bombard new Antioch, by my particular permission; as since, after your example, the stout champions, who had undertaken to hold the fortress of Dindenarois against all comers, fairly wasted their powder with shooting at sparrows; and then, not having wherewith to defend themselves in time of need, valiantly surrendered to the enemy, who were already packing up their awls, full of madness and despair, and thought on nothing but a shameful retreat. Take care this be remedied, son Vulcan: rouse up your drowsy Cyclopes, Asteropes, Brontes, Arges, Polyphemus, Steropes, Pyracmon, and so forth; set them at work, and make them drink as they ought.

Never spare liquor to such as are at hot work. Now let us dispatch this bawling fellow below. You Mercury, go see who it is, and know what he wants. Mercury looked out at heaven's trap-door, through which as I am told, they hear what is said here below. By the way, one might well enough mistake it for the scuttle of a ship; though Icaromenippus said it was like the mouth of a well. The light-heeled deity saw that it was honest Tom, who asked for his lost hatchet; and accordingly he made his report to the synod. Marry, said Jupiter, we are finely helped up, as if we had now nothing else to do here but to restore lost hatchets. Well, he must have it then for all this, for so it is written in the book of fate, (do you hear?) as well as if it was worth the whole duchy of Milan. The truth is, the fellow's hatchet is as much to him as a kingdom to a king. Come, come, let no more words be scattered about it, let him have his hatchet again.

Now, let us make an end of the difference betwixt the levites and mole-catchers of Landerousse. Whereabouts were we? Priapus was standing in the chimney-corner, and having heard what Mercury had reported, said in a most courteous and jovial manner: King Jupiter, while by your order and particular favour, I was garden-keeper-general on earth,

I observed that this word hatchet is equivocal to many things: for it signifies a certain instrument, by the means of which men fell and cleave timber. It also signifies (at least I am sure it did formerly) a female soundly and frequently thumpthumppriggletickletwiddletobyed. Thus I perceived that every cock of the game used to call his doxy his hatchet; for with that same tool (this he said lugging out and exhibiting his nine-inch knocker) they so strongly and resolutely shove and drive in their helves, that the females remain free from a fear epidemical amongst their sex, viz., that from the bottom of the male's belly the instrument should dangle at his heel for want of such feminine props. And I remember, for I have a member, and a memory too, ay, and a fine memory, large enough to fill a (butter-firkin:) I remember, I say, that one day of tubilustre [horn-fair] at the festivals of good-man Vulcan in May, I heard Josquin Des Prez, Olkegan, Hobrethe, Agricola, Brumel, Camelin, Vigoris, de la Fage, Bruyer, Prioris, Seguin, de la Rue, Midy, Moulu, Mouton, Gascogne, Loyset, Compere, Penet, Fevin, Rousée, Richard Fort, Rousseau, Consilion, Constantio Festi, Jacquet Bercan, melodiously singing the following catch on a pleasant green.

Long John to bed went to his bride,
And laid a mallet by his side:
What means this mallet, John, saith she?
Why! it is to wedge thee home, quoth he.
Alas! cried she, the man's a fool:
What need you use a wooden tool?
When lusty John does to me come,
He never shoves but with his bum.

Nine Olympiads, and an intercalary year after (I have a rare member, I would say memory; but I often make blunders in the symbolization and colligance of those two words) I heard Adrian Villart, Gombert, Janequin, Arcadet, Claudin, Certon, Manchicourt, Auxerre, Villiers, Sandrin, Sohier, Hesdin, Morales, Passereau, Maille, Maillart, Jacotin, Heurteur, Vardelot, Carpentras, l'Heritier, Cadéac, Doublet, Vermont, Bouteiller, Lupi, Pagnier, Millet, du Moulin, Alaire, Maraut, Morpain, Gendre, and other merry lovers of music, in a private garden, under some fine shady trees, round about a bulwark of flagons, gammons, pasties, with several coated quails, and laced mutton, waggishly singing:

Since tools without their hafts are useless lumber,
And hatchets without helves are of that number;
That one may go in t'other, and may match it,
I'll be the helve, and thou shalt be the hatchet.

Now would I know what kind of hatchet this bawling Tom wants? This threw all the venerable gods and goddesses into a fit of laughter, like any microcosm of flies; and even set limping Vulcan a hopping and jumping smoothly three or four times for the sake of his dear. Come, come, said Jupiter to Mercury, run down immediately and cast at the poor fellow's feet three hatchets; his own, another of gold, and a third of massy silver, all of one size: then having left it to his will to take his choice, if he take his own, and be satisfied with it, give him the other two: if he take another, chop his head off with his own: and henceforth serve me all those losers of hatchets after that manner. Having said this, Jupiter, with an awkward turn of his head, like a jackanapes swallowing of pills, made so dreadful a phiz, that all the vast Olympus quaked again. Heaven's foot messenger, thanks to his low-crowned narrow-brimmed hat, his plume of feathers, heel-pieces, and running stick with pigeon wings, flings himself out of heaven's wicket, through the empty deserts of the air, and in a trice nimbly alights on the earth, and throws at friend Tom's feet the three hatchets, saying unto him; Thou hast bawled long enough to be a-dry: thy prayers and request are granted by Jupiter; see which of these three is thy hatchet, and take it away with thee. Wellhung lifts up the golden hatchet, peeps upon it, and finds it very heavy: then staring on Mercury, cries, Codszouks this is none of mine; I will not have it: the same he did with the silver one, and said, it is not this neither, you may even take them again. At last, he takes up his own hatchet, examines the end of the helve, and finds his mark there; then, ravished with joy, like a fox that meets some straggling poultry, and sneering from the tip of his nose, he cried, By the mass, this is my hatchet, master god; if you will leave it me, I will sacrifice to you a very good and huge pot of milk, brim full, covered with fine strawberries, next ides, i.e. the 15th of May.

Honest fellow, said Mercury, I leave it thee; take it; and because thou hast wished and chosen moderately, in point of hatchet,

by Jupiter's command, I give thee those two others; thou hast now wherewith to make thyself rich: be honest. Honest Tom gave Mercury a whole cartload of thanks, and revered the most great Jupiter. His old hatchet he fastens close to his leathern girdle, and girds it above his breech like Martin of Cambray: the two others, being more heavy, he lays on his shoulder. Thus he plods on, trudging over the fields, keeping a good countenance amongst his neighbours and fellowparishioners, with one merry saying or other after Patelin's way. The next day, having put on a clean white jacket, he takes on his back the two precious hatchets, and comes to Chinon, the famous city, noble city, ancient city, yea the first city in the world, according to the judgment and assertion of the most learned Massorets. At Chinon he turned his silver hatchet into fine testons, crown-pieces, and other white cash; his golden hatchet into fine angels, curious ducats, substantial ridders, spankers, and rose nobles: then with them purchases a good number of farms, barns, houses, out-houses, thatched-houses, stables, meadows, orchards, fields, vineyards, woods, arable lands, pastures, ponds, mills, gardens, nurseries, oxen, cows, sheep, goats, swine, hogs, asses, horses, hens, cocks, capons, chickens, geese, ganders, ducks, drakes, and a world of all other necessaries, and in a short time became the richest man in the country, nay even richer than that limping scrapegood Maulevrier. His brother bumpkins, and the other yeomen and country-puts thereabouts, perceiving his good fortune, were not a little amazed, insomuch that their former pity of Tom was soon changed into an envy of his so great and unexpected rise; and as they could not for their souls devise how this came about, they made it their business to pry up and down, and lay their heads together, to inquire, seek, and inform themselves by what means, in what place, on what day, what hour, how, why, and wherefore, he had come by his great treasure.

At last, hearing it was by losing his hatchet, Ha, ha! said they, was there no more to do but to lose a hatchet to make us rich? Mum for that; it is as easy as pissing a bed, and will cost but little. Are then at this time the revolutions of the heavens, the constellations of the firmament and aspects of the planets such, that whosoever shall lose a hatchet, shall immediately grow rich? Ha, ha, ha! by Jove, you shall even be lost, and it please you, my dear hatchet. With this they all fairly lost their hatchets out of hand. The devil of one that had a hatchet left: he was not his mother's son, that did not lose his hatchet. No more was wood felled or cleaved in that country, through want of hatchets. Nay, the Æsopian apologue even saith, that certain petty country gents, of the lower class, who had sold Wellhung their little mill and little field, to have wherewithal to make a figure at the next muster, having been told that his treasure was come to him by this only means, sold the only badge of their gentility, their swords, to purchase hatchets to go lose them, as the silly clodpates did, in hopes to gain store of chink by that loss.

You should have truly sworn they had been a parcel of your petty spiritual usurers, Rome-bound, selling their all, and borrowing of others to buy store of mandates, a pennyworth of a new-made pope.

Now they cried out and brayed, and prayed and bawled, and invoked Jupiter: My hatchet! my hatchet! Jupiter, my hatchet! on this side, my hatchet! on that side, my hatchet! ho, ho, ho, ho, Jupiter, my hatchet! The air round about rung again with the cries and howlings of these rascally losers of hatchets.

Mercury was nimble in bringing them hatchets; to each offering that which he had lost, as also another of gold, and a third of silver.

Every he still was for that of gold, giving thanks in abundance to the great giver, Jupiter; but in the very nick of time, that they bowed and stooped to take it from the ground, whip, in a trice, Mercury lopped off their heads, as Jupiter had commanded; and of heads, thus cut off, the number was just equal to that of the lost hatchets.

You see how it is now; you see how it goes with those, who in the simplicity of their hearts wish and desire with moderation. Take warning by this, all you greedy, fresh-water shirks, who scorn to wish for anything under ten thousand pounds: and do not for the future run on impudently, as I have sometimes heard you wishing, Would to God, I had now one hundred seventy-eight millions of gold! Oh! how I should tickle it off. The deuce on you, what more might a king, an emperor, a pope wish for? For that reason, indeed, you see that after you have made such hopeful wishes, all the good that comes to you of it is the itch or the scab, and not a cross in your breeches to scare the devil that tempts you to make these wishes: no more than those two mumpers, wishers after the custom of Paris; one of whom only wished to have in good old gold as much as hath been spent, bought, and sold in Paris, since its first foundations were laid, to this hour; all of it valued at the price, sale, and rate of the dearest year in all that space of time. Do you think the fellow was bashful? Had he eaten sour plums unpeeled? Were his teeth on edge, I pray you? The other wished our lady's church brim-full of steel needles, from the floor to the top of the roof, and to have as many ducats as might be crammed into as many bags as might be sewed with each and every one of these needles, till they were all either broke at the point or eye. This is to wish with a vengeance! What think you of it? What did they get by it, in your opinion? Why at night both my gentlemen had kibed-heels, a tetter in the chin, a church-yard cough in the lungs, a catarrh in the throat, a swingeing boil at the rump, and the devil of one musty crust of a brown George the poor dogs had to scour their grinders with. Wish therefore for mediocrity, and it shall be given unto you, and over and above yet; that is to say, provided you bestir yourself manfully, and do your best in the meantime.

Ay, but say you, God might as soon have given me seventy-eight thousand as the thirteenth part of one half: for he is omnipotent, and a million of gold is no more to him than one farthing. Oh, oh! pray tell me who taught you to talk at this rate of the power and predestination of God, poor silly people? Peace, tush, st, st, st! fall down before his sacred face, and own the nothingness of your nothing.

Upon this, O ye that labour under the affliction of the gout, I ground my hopes; firmly believing, that if it so pleases the divine goodness, you shall obtain health, since you wish and ask for nothing else, at least for the present. Well, stay yet a little longer with half an ounce of patience.

The Genose do not use, like you, to be satisfied with wishing health alone, when after they have all the live-long morning been in a brown study, talked, pondered, ruminated, and resolved in the counting-house, of whom and how they may squeeze the ready, and who by their craft must be hooked in, wheedled, bubbled, sharped, over-reached, and choused; they go to the exchange, and greet one another with a *Sanità et guadagno messer;* health and gain to you, sir. Health alone will not go down with the greedy curmudgeons: they over and above must wish for gain, with a pox to them; ay, and for the fine crowns, or *scudi di Guadaigne:* whence, heaven be praised, it happens many a time, that the silly wishers and woulders are baulked, and get neither.

Now, my lads, as you hope for good health, cough once aloud with lungs of leather; take me off three swingeing bumpers; prick up your ears; and you shall hear me tell wonders of the noble and good Pantagruel.

CHAPTER 1

How Pantagruel went to sea to visit the oracle of Bacbuc, alias the Holy Bottle

In the month of June on Vesta's Holiday, the very numerical day on which Brutus, conquering Spain, taught its strutting dons to truckle under him, and that niggardly miser Crassus was routed and knocked on the head by the Parthians, Pantagruel took his leave of the good Gargantua, his royal father. The old gentleman, according to the laudable custom of the primitive Christians, devoutly prayed for the happy voyage of his son and his whole company, and then they took shipping at the port of Thalassa. Pantagruel had with him Panurge, Friar John des Entomeures, *alias* of the Funnels, Epistemon, Gymnast, Euthenes, Rhizotomus, Carpalim, *cum multis aliis,*[2] his ancient servants and domestics: also Xenomanes, the great traveller, who had crossed so many dangerous roads, dikes, ponds, seas, and so forth, and was come some time before, having been sent for by Panurge.

For certain good causes and considerations him thereunto moving, he had left with Gargantua, and marked out, in his great and universal hydrographical chart, the course which they were to steer to visit the Oracle of the Holy Bottle Bacbuc. The number of ships were such as I described in the third book, convoyed by a like number of triremes, men of war, galleons, and feluccas, well-rigged, caulked, and stored with a good quantity of Pantagruelion.

All the officers, dragomen, (interpreters,) pilots, captains, mates, boatswains, midshipmen, quartermasters, and sailors, met in the *Thalamege*, Pantagruel's principle flag-ship, which had in her stern, for her ensign, a huge large bottle, half silver, well polished, the other half gold, enamelled with carnation; whereby it was easy to guess that white and red were the colours of the noble travellers, and that they went for the word of the Bottle.

On the stern of the second was a lantern, like those of the ancients, industriously made with diaphanous stone, implying that they were to pass by Lanternland. The third ship had for her device a fine deep China ewer. The fourth, a double-handed jar of gold, much like an ancient urn. The fifth, a famous can made of sperm of emerald. The sixth, a monk's mumping bottle made of the four metals together. The seventh, an ebony funnel, all embossed and wrought with gold after the tauchic manner. The eighth, an ivy goblet, very precious, inlaid with gold. The ninth a cup of fine obriz gold. The tenth, a tumbler of aromatic agoloch (you call it *lignum aloes*) edged with Cyprian gold, after the Azemine make. The eleventh, a golden vine-tub of mosaic work. The twelfth, a runlet of unpolished gold, covered with a small vine of large Indian pearl of topiarian work. Insomuch that there was not a man, however in the dumps, musty, sourlooked, or melancholic he were, not even excepting that blubbering whiner Heraclitus, had he been there, but seeing this noble convoy of ships and their devices, must have been seized with present gladness of heart, and smiling at the conceit, have said, that the travellers were all honest topers, true-pitcher men; and have judged by a most sure prognostication, that their voyage both outward and homeward-bound, would be performed in mirth and perfect health.

In the *Thalamege*, where was the general meeting, Pantagruel made a short but sweet exhortation, wholly backed with authorities from Scripture upon navigation; which being ended, with an audible voice prayers were said in the presence and hearing of all the burghers of Thalassa, who had flocked to the mole to see them take shipping. After the prayers, was melodiously sung a psalm of the holy King David, which begins, *When Israel went out of Egypt;* and that being ended, tables were placed upon deck, and a feast speedily served up. The Thalassians, who had also borne a chorus in the psalm, caused store of bellytimber and vinegar to be brought out of their houses. All drank to them: they drank to all: which was the cause that none of the whole company gave up what they had eaten, nor were sea-sick, with a pain at the head and stomach; which inconveniency they could not so easily have prevented by drinking, for some time before, salt water, either alone or mixed with wine; using quinces, citron peel, juice of pomegranates, sourish sweet-meats, fasting a long time, covering their stomachs with paper, or following such other idle remedies, as foolish physicians prescribe to those that go to sea.

Having often renewed their tipplings, each mother's son retired on board his own ship, and set sail all so fast with a merry gale at south east; to which point of the compass the chief pilot, James Brayer by name, had shaped his course, and fixed all things accordingly. For seeing that the Oracle of the Holy Bottle lay near Cathay, in the Upper India, his advice, and that of Xenomanes also, was not to steer the course which the Portuguese use, while sailing through the torrid zone, and Cape Bona Speranza, at the south point of Africa, beyond the equinoctial line, and losing sight of the northern pole, their guide, they make a prodigious long voyage; but rather to keep as near the parallel of the said India as possible, and to tack to the westward of the said pole, so that winding under the north, they might find themselves in the latitude of the port of Olone, without coming nearer it for fear of being shut up in the frozen sea; whereas, following this canonical turn, by the said parallel, they must have that on the right to the eastward, which at their departure was on their left.

This proved a much shorter cut; for without shipwreck, danger or loss of men, with uninterrupted good weather, except one day near the island of the Macreons, they performed in less than four months the voyage of Upper India, which the Portuguese, with a thousand inconveniences and innumerable dangers, can hardly complete in three years. And it is my opinion, with submission to better judgments, that this course was perhaps steered by those Indians who sailed to Germany, and were honourably received by the King of the Swedes, while Quintus Metellus Celer was proconsul of the Gauls; as Cornelius Nepos, Pomponius Mela, and Pliny after them tell us.

CHAPTER 2

How Pantagruel bought many rarities in the island of Medamothy

THAT day and the two following they neither discovered land nor anything new; for they had formerly sailed that way: but on the fourth they made an island called Medamothy, of a fine and delightful prospect, by reason of the vast number of lighthouses, and high marble towers in its circuit, which is not less than that of Candia. Pantagruel, inquiring who governed there, heard that it was King Philophanes, absent at that time upon account of the marriage of his brother Philotheamon with the infanta of the kingdom of Engys.

Hearing this, he went ashore in the harbour, and while every ship's crew watered, passed his time in viewing divers pictures, pieces of tapestry, animals, fishes, birds, and other exotic and foreign merchandises, which were along the walks of the mole, and in the markets of the port. For it was the third day of the great and famous fair of the place, to which the chief merchants of Africa and Asia resorted. Out of these Friar John bought him two rare pictures; in one of which, the face of a man that brings in an appeal (or that calls out to another) was drawn to the life; and in the other a servant that wants a master, with every needful particular, action, countenance, look, gait, feature, and deportment, being an original, by Master Charles Charmois, principal painter to King Megistus; and he paid for them in the court fashion, with *congé* and grimace. Panurge bought a large picture, copied and done from the needle-work formerly wrought by Philomela, showing to her sister Progne how her brother-in-law Tereus had by force hand-selled her copyhold, and then cut out her tongue, that she might not (as women will) tell tales. I vow and swear by the handle of my paper lantern, that it was a gallant, a mirific, nay, a most admirable piece.

Nor do you think, I pray you, that in it was the picture of a man playing the beast with two backs with a female; this had been too silly and gross: no, no; it was anotherguise thing, and much plainer. You may, if you please, see it at Theleme, on the left hand, as you go into the high gallery. Epistemon bought another, wherein were painted to the life, the Ideas of Plato, and the Atoms of Epicurus. Rhizotomus purchased another, wherein Echo was drawn to the life. Pantagruel caused to be bought, by Gymnast, the life and deeds of Achilles, in seventy-eight pieces of tapestry, four fathoms long, and three fathoms broad, all of Phrygian silk, embossed with gold and silver; the work beginning of the nuptials of Peleus and Thetis, continuing to the birth of Achilles: his youth, described by Statius Papinius; his warlike achievements, celebrated by Homer; his death and obsequies, written by Ovid and Quintus Calaber; and ending at the appearance of his ghost, and Polyxena's sacrifice, rehearsed by Euripides.

He also caused to be bought three fine young unicorns; one of them a male of a chesnut colour, and two grey dappled females; also a tarand, whom he bought of a Scythian of the Gelone's country.

A tarand is an animal as big as a bullock, having a head like a stag, or a little bigger, two stately horns with large branches, cloven feet, hair long like that of a furred Muscovite, I mean a bear, and a skin almost as hard as steel armour. The Scythian said that there are but few tarands to be found in Scythia, because it varieth its colour according to the diversity of the places where it grazes and abides, and represents the colour of the grass, plants, trees, shrubs, flowers, meadows, rocks, and generally of all things near which it comes. It hath this common with the sea-pulp, or polypus, with the thoes, with the wolves of India, and with the chameleon; which is a kind of a lizard so wonderful, that Democritus hath written a whole book of its figure, and anatomy, as also of its virtue and property in magic. This I can affirm, that I have seen it change its colour, not only at the approach of things that have a colour, but by its own voluntary impulse, according to its fear or other affections: as for example, upon a green carpet, I have certainly seen it become green; but having remained there some time, it turned yellow, blue, tanned, and purple, in course, in the same manner as you see a turkey-cock's comb change colour according to its passions. But what we find most surprising in this tarand is, that not only its face and skin, but also its hair could take whatever colour was about it. Near Panurge with his kersey coat, its hair used to turn gray: near Pantagruel with his scarlet mantle, its hair and skin grew red; near the pilot, dressed after the fashion of the Isiaci of Anubis, in Egypt, its hair seemed all white; which two last colours the chameleon cannot borrow.

When the creature was free from any fear or affection, the colour of its hair was just such as you see that of the asses of Meung.

CHAPTER 3

How Pantagruel received a letter from his father Gargantua, and of the strange way to have speedy news from far distant places

WHILE Pantagruel was taken up with the purchase of these foreign animals, the noise of ten guns and culverins, together with a loud and joyful cheer of all the fleet, was heard from the mole. Pantagruel looked towards the haven, and perceived that this was occasioned by the arrival of one of his father Gargantua's celoces, or advice-boats, named the *Chelidonia;* because on the stern of it was carved in Corinthian brass, a sea swallow; which is a fish as large as a dare-fish of Loire, all flesh, without scale, with cartilaginous wings, (like a bat's,) very long and broad, by the means of which, I have seen them fly a fathom above water, about a bow-shot. At Marseilles this flying fish is called lendole. And indeed that ship was as light as a swallow; so that it rather seemed to fly on the sea than to sail. Malicorne, Gargantua's esquire carver, was come in her, being sent expressly by his master to have an account of his son's health and circumstances, and to bring him credentials. When Malicorne had saluted Pantagruel, and the prince had embraced him about the neck, and showed him a little of the cap-courtesy, before he opened the letters, the first thing he said to him was, Have you here the Gozal, the heavenly messenger? Yes, sir, said he, here it is swaddled up in this basket. It was a grey pigeon, taken out of Gargantua's dove-house, whose young ones were just hatched when the advice-boat was going off.

If any ill fortune had befallen Pantagruel, he would have fastened some black riband to his feet; but because all things had succeeded happily hitherto, having caused it to be undressed, he tied to its feet a white riband, and, without any further delay, let it loose. The pigeon presently flew away, cutting the air with an incredible speed; as you know that there is no flight like a pigeon's, especially when it hath eggs or young ones, through the extreme care which nature hath fixed in it to relieve and be with its young; insomuch, that in less than two hours it compassed in the air the long tract which the advice-boat, with all her diligence, with oars and sails, and a fair wind, could not go through in less than three days and three nights, and was seen as it was going into the dove-house to its nest.

Whereupon the worthy Gargantua, hearing that it had the white riband on, was joyful and secure of his son's welfare. This was the custom of the noble Gargantua and Pantagruel, when they would have speedy news of something of great concern; as the event of some battle, either by sea or land; the surrendering or holding out of some strong place; the determination of some difference of moment; the safe or unhappy delivery of some queen or great lady; the death or recovery of their sick friends or allies, and so forth. They used to take the gozal, and had it carried from one to another by the post, to the places whence they desired to have news. The gozal, bearing either a black or white riband, according to the occurrences and accidents, used to remove their doubts at its return, making, in the space of one hour, more way through the air, than thirty post-boys could have done in one natural day. May not this be said to redeem and gain time with a vengeance, think you? For the like service, therefore, you may believe, as a most true thing, that, in the dove-houses of their farms, there were to be found, all the year long, store of pigeons hatching eggs, or rearing their young. Which may be easily done in aviaries and voleries, by the help of saltpetre and the sacred herb vervain.

The gozal being let fly, Pantagruel perused his father Gargantua's letter, the contents of which were as followeth:

MY DEAREST SON, The affection that naturally a father bears to a beloved son, is so much increased in me, by reflecting on the particular gifts which by the divine goodness have been heaped on thee, that since thy departure it hath often banished all other thoughts out of my mind; leaving my heart wholly possessed with fear, lest some misfortune has attended thy voyage: for thou knowest that fear was ever the attendant of true and sincere love. Now because, as Hesiod sayeth, A good beginning of any thing is the half of it; or, Well begun is half done, according to the old saying; to free my mind from this anxiety, I have expressly dispatched Malicorne, that he may give me a true account of thy health at the beginning of thy voyage. For if it be good, and such as I wish it, I shall easily foresee the rest.

I have met with some diverting books, which the bearer will deliver thee; thou mayest read them when thou wantest to unbend

and ease thy mind from thy better studies. He will also give thee at large the news at court. The peace of the Lord be with thee. Remember me to Panurge, Friar John, Epistemon, Xenomanes, Gymnast, and the other principal domestics, my good friends. Dated at our paternal seat, this 13th day of June.

Thy father and friend, GARGANTUA.

CHAPTER 4

How Pantagruel writ to his father Gargantua, and sent him several curiosities

PANTAGRUEL, having perused the letter, had a long conference with the esquire Malicorne; insomuch, that Panurge at last interrupting them, asked him, Pray, sir, when do you design to drink? when shall we drink? When shall the worshipful esquire drink? What a devil! have you not talked long enough to drink? It is a good motion, answered Pantagruel; go, get us something ready at the next inn; I think it is the Satyr on horseback. In the meantime he writ to Gargantua as followeth, to be sent by the aforesaid esquire.

MOST GRACIOUS FATHER, As our senses and animal faculties are more discomposed at the news of events unexpected, though desired (even to an immediate dissolution of the soul from the body), than if those accidents had been foreseen; so the coming of Malicorne hath much surprised and disordered me. For I had no hopes to see any of your servants, or to hear from you, before I had finished our voyage; and contented myself with the dear remembrance of your august majesty, deeply impressed in the hindmost ventricle of my brain, often representing you to my mind.

But since you have made me happy beyond expectation, by the perusal of your gracious letter, and the faith I have in your esquire hath revived my spirits by the news of your welfare; I am, as it were, compelled to do what formerly I did freely, that is, first to praise the Blessed Redeemer, who by his divine goodness preserves you in this long enjoyment of perfect health; then to return you eternal thanks for the fervant affection which you have for me your most humble son and unprofitable servant.

Formerly a Roman, named Furnius, said to Augustus, who had received his father into favour, and pardoned him after he had sided with Anthony, that by that action the emperor had reduced him to this extremity, that for want of power to be grateful, both while he lived and after it, he should be obliged to be taxed with ingratitude. So I may say, that the excess of your fatherly affection drives me into such a straight, that I should be forced to live and die ungrateful; unless that crime be redressed by the sentence of the stoics, who say, that there are three parts in a benefit, the one of the giver, the other of the receiver, the third of the remunerator; and that the receiver rewards the giver, when he freely recieves the benefit, and always remembers it; as on the contrary, that man is most ungrateful who despises and forgets a benefit. Therefore, being overwhelmed with infinite favours, all proceeding from your extreme goodness, and on the other side wholly incapable of making the smallest return, I hope, at least, to free myself from the imputation of ingratitude, since they can never be blotted out of my mind; and my tongue shall never cease to own, that, to thank you as I ought, transcends my capacity.

As for us, I have this assurance in the Lord's mercy and help, that the end of our voyage will be answerable to its beginning, and so it will be entirely performed in health and mirth. I will not fail to set down in a journal a full account of our navigation, that, at our return, you may have an exact relation of the whole.

I have found here a Scythian tarand, an animal strange and wonderful for the variations of colour on its skin and hair, according to the distinction of neighbouring things: it is as tractable and easily kept as a lamb; be pleased to accept of it.

I also send you three young unicorns, which are the tamest of creatures.

I have conferred with the esquire, and taught him how they must be fed. These cannot graze on the ground, by reason of the long horn on their forehead, but are forced to browse on fruit trees, or on proper racks, or to be fed by hand, with herbs, sheaves, apples, pears, barley, rye, and other fruits and roots, being placed before them.

I am amazed that ancient writers should report them to be so wild, furious, and dangerous, and never seen alive: far from it, you will find that they are the mildest things in the world, provided they are not maliciously offended. Likewise I send you the life and deeds of Achilles, in curious tapestry; assuring you whatever rarities of animals, plants,

birds, or precious stones, and others, I shall be able to find and purchase in our travels, shall be brought to you, God willing, whom I beseech, by his blessed grace, to preserve you.

From Medamothy, *this 15th of June.* Panurge, Friar John, Epistemon, Xenomanes, Gymnast, Eusthenes, Rhizotomus, and Carpalim, having most humbly kissed your hand, return your salute a thousand times.

Your most dutiful son and servant,
PANTAGRUEL.

While Pantagruel was writing this letter, Malicorne was made welcome with a thousand goodly good-morrows and howd'ye's: they clung about him so, that I cannot tell you how much they made of him, how many humble services, how many from my love and to my love were sent with him. Pantagruel, having writ his letters, sat down at table with him, and afterwards presented him with a large chain of gold, weighing eight hundred crowns; between whose septenary links, some large diamonds, rubies, emeralds, turquoise stones, and unions were alternately set in. To each of his bark's crew, he ordered to be given five hundred crowns. To Gargantua, his father, he sent the tarand covered with a cloth of satin, brocaded with gold: and the tapestry containing the life and deeds of Achilles, with the three unicorns in frized cloth of gold trappings: and so they left Medamothy; Malicorne, to return to Gargantua; and Pantagruel, to proceed in his voyage: during which, Epistemon read to him the books which the esquire had brought; and because he found them jovial and pleasant, I shall give you an account of them, if you earnestly desire it.

CHAPTER 5

How Pantagruel met a ship with passengers returning from Lanternland

ON the fifth day, beginning already to wind by little and little about the pole, going still farther from the equinoctial line, we discovered a merchant-man to the windward of us. The joy for this was not small on both sides; we in hopes to hear news from sea, and those in the merchantman from land. So we bore upon them, and coming up with them we hailed them: and finding them to be Frenchmen of Xaintonge, backed our sails and lay by to talk to them. Pantagruel heard that they came from Lanternland; which added to his joy, and that of the whole fleet. We inquired about the state of that country, and the way of living of the Lanterns: and were told, that about the latter end of the following July, was the time prefixed for the meeting of the general chapter of the Lanterns; and that if we arrived there at that time, as we might easily, we should see a handsome, honourable, and jolly company of Lanterns; and that great preparations were making, as if they intended to lanternise there to the purpose. We were told also, that if we touched at the great kingdom of Gebarim, we should be honourably received and treated by the sovereign of that country, King Ohabé, who, as well as all his subjects, speaks Touraine French.

While we were listening to this news, Panurge fell out with one Dingdong, a drover or sheep merchant of Taillebourg. The occasion of the fray was thus.

This same Dingdong, seeing Panurge without a codpiece, with his spectacles fastened to his cap, said to one of his comrades, Prithee, look, is there not a fine medal of a cuckold? Panurge, by reason of his spectacles, as you may well think, heard more plainly by half with his ears than usually; which caused him (hearing this) to say to the saucy dealer in mutton, in a kind of a pet:

How the devil should I be one of the hornified fraternity, since I am not yet a brother of the marriage-noose, as thou art; as I guess by thy ill-favoured phiz?

Yea, verily, quoth the grazier, I am married, and would not be otherwise for all the pairs of spectacles in Europe; nay, not for all the magnifying gim-cracks in Africa; for I have got me the cleverest, prettiest, handsomest, properest, neatest, tightest, honestest, and soberest piece of woman's flesh for my wife, that is in all the whole country of Xaintonge; I will say that for her, and a fart for all the rest. I bring her home a fine eleven-inch-long branch of red coral for her Christmas-box. What hast thou to do with it? what is that to thee? who art thou? whence comest thou, O dark lanthorn of antichrist? Answer, if thou art of God. I ask thee, by the way of question, said Panurge to him very seriously, if with the consent and countenance of all the elements, I had gingumbob'd, codpieced, and thumpthumpriggledtickledtwiddled thy so clever, so pretty, so handsome, so proper, so neat, so tight, so honest,

and so sober female importance, insomuch that the stiff deity that has no forecast, Priapus, (who dwells here at liberty, all subjection of fastened codpieces, or bolts, bars, and locks, abdicated,) remained sticking in her natural Christmas-box in such a lamentable manner, that it were never to come out, but eternally should stick there, unless thou didst pull it out with thy teeth; what wouldst thou do? Wouldst thou everlastingly leave it there, or wouldst thou pluck it out with thy grinders? Answer me, O thou ram of Mahomet, since thou art one of the devil's gang. I would, replied the sheepmonger, take thee such a woundy cut on this spectacle-bearing lug of thine, with my trusty bilbo, as would smite thee dead as a herring. Thus, having taken pepper in the nose, he was lugging out his sword, but alas! cursed cows have short horns; it stuck in the scabbard; as you know that at sea, cold iron will easily take rust, by reason of the excessive and nitrous moisture. Panurge, so smitten with terror, that his heart sunk down to his midriff, scoured off to Pantagruel for help: but Friar John laid hand on his flashing scymitar that was new ground, and would certainly have dispatched Dingdong to rights, had not the skipper, and some of his passengers, beseeched Pantagruel not to suffer such an outrage to be committed on board his ship. So the matter was made up, and Panurge and his antagonist shaked fists, and drank in course to one another, in token of a perfect reconciliation.

CHAPTER 6

How the fray being over, Panurge cheapened one of Dingdong's sheep

THIS quarrel being hushed, Panurge tipped the wink upon Epistemon and Friar John, and taking them aside,—Stand at some distance out of the way, said he, and take your share of the following scene of mirth: you shall have rare sport anon, if my cake be not dough, and my plot do but take. Then addressing himself to the drover, he took off to him a bumper of good lantern wine. The other pledged him briskly and courteously. This done, Panurge earnestly entreated him to sell him one of his sheep.

But the other answered him, Is it come to that, friend and neighbour? Would you put tricks upon travellers? Alas, how finely you love to play upon poor folk! Nay, you seem a rare chapman, that is the truth on it. Oh, what a mighty sheep merchant you are! In good faith, you look liker one of the diving trade, than a buyer of sheep. Adzookers, what a blessing it would be to have one's purse, well lined with chink, near your worship at a tripe-house, when it begins to thaw! Humph, humph, did not we know you well, you might serve one a slippery trick! Pray do but see, good people, what a mighty conjuror the fellow would be reckoned. Patience, said Panurge: but waving that, be so kind as to sell me one of your sheep. Come, how much? What do you mean, master of mine? answered the other. They are long-woolled sheep: from these did Jason take his golden fleece. The order of the house of Burgundy was drawn from them. Zwoons, man, they are oriental sheep, topping sheep, fatted sheep, sheep of quality. Be it so, said Panurge: but sell me one of them, I beseech you, and that for a cause, paying you ready money upon the nail, in good and lawful occidental current cash. Wilt say how much? Friend, neighbour, answered the seller of mutton, hark ye me a little, on the ear.

Panurge. On which side you please; I hear you.

Dingdong. You are going to Lantern-land, they say.

Pan. Yea, verily.

Ding. To see fashions?

Pan. Yea, verily.

Ding. And be merry?

Pan. Yea, verily.

Ding. Your name is, as I take it, Robin Mutton?

Pan. As you please for that, sweet sir.

Ding. Nay, without offence.

Pan. So I understand it.

Ding. You are, as I take it, the king's jester; are not you?

Pan. Yea, verily.

Ding. Give me your hand—humph, humph, you go to see fashions, you are the king's jester, your name is Robin Mutton! Do you see this same ram? His name, too, is Robin. Here Robin, Robin, Robin! Baea, baea, baea. Hath he not a rare voice?

Pan. Ay, marry has he, a very fine and harmonious voice.

Ding. Well, this bargain shall be made between you and me, friend and neighbour; we will get a pair of scales, then you Robin Mutton shall be put into one of them, and Tup Robin into the other. Now I will hold you a peck of Busch oysters, that in weight, value,

and price, he shall outdo you, and you shall be found light in the very numerical manner, as when you shall be hanged and suspended.

Patience, said Panurge: but you would do much for me, and your whole posterity, if you would chaffer with me for him, or some other of his inferiors. I beg it of you; good your worship, be so kind. Hark ye, friend of mine, answered the other, with the fleece of these, your fine Rouen cloth is to be made; your Leominster superfine wool is mine arse to it; mere flock in comparison. Of their skins the best cordovan will be made, which shall be sold for Turkey and Montelimart, or for Spanish leather at least. Of the guts shall be made fiddle and harp strings, that will sell as dear as if they came from Munican or Aquileia. What do you think of it, hah? If you please, sell me one of them, said Panurge, and I will be yours for ever. Look, here is ready cash. What's the price? This he said, exhibiting his purse stuffed with new Henricuses.

CHAPTER 7

Which if you read, you will find how Panurge bargained with Dingdong

NEIGHBOUR, my friend, answered Dingdong, they are meat for none but kings and princes: their flesh is so delicate, so savoury, and so dainty, that one would swear it melted in the mouth. I bring them out of a country where the very hogs, God be with us, live on nothing but myrobalans. The sows in the styes, when they lie-in (saving the honour of this good company) are fed only with orange-flowers. But, said Panurge, drive a bargain with me for one of them, and I will pay you for it like a king, upon the honest word of a true Trojan: come, come, what do you ask? Not so fast, Robin, answered the trader, these sheep are lineally descended from the very family of the ram that wafted Phryxus and Helle over the sea, since called the Hellespont. A pox on it, said Panurge, you are *clericus vel addiscens!*[3] *Ità*[4] is a cabbage, and *verè*[5] a leek, answered the merchant. But rr, rrr, rrrr, rrrrr, hoh Robin, rr, rrr, rrrr, you do not understand that gibberish do you? Now I think of it, over all the fields, where they piss, corn grows as fast as if the Lord had pissed there; they need neither be tilled nor dunged. Besides, man, your chemists extract the best saltpetre in the world out of their urine. Nay, with their very dung (with reverence be it spoken) the doctors in our country make pills that cure seventy-eight kinds of diseases, the least of which is the evil of St. Eutropius of Xaintes, from which, good Lord deliver us! Now what do you think on't, neighbour, my friend? The truth is, they cost me money, that they do. Cost what they will, cried Panurge, trade with me for one of them, paying you well. Our friend, quoth the quack-like sheep man, do but mind the wonders of nature that are found in those animals, even in a member which one would think were of no use. Take me but these horns, and bray them a little with an iron pestle, or with an andiron, which you please, it is all one of me; then bury them wherever you will, provided it be where the sun may shine, and water them frequently; in a few months I will engage you will have the best asparagus in the world not even excepting those of Ravenna. Now, come and tell me whether the horns of you other knights of the bull's feather have such a virtue and wonderful propriety?

Patience, said Panurge. I do not know whether you be a scholar or no, pursued Dingdong: I have seen a world of scholars, I say great scholars, that were cuckolds, I'll assure you. But hark you me, if you were a scholar, you should know that in the most inferior members of those animals—which are the feet—there is a bone—which is the heel—the astragalus, if you will have it so, wherewith, and with that of no other creature breathing, except the Indian ass, and the dorcades of Libya, they used in old times to play at the royal game of dice, whereat Augustus the emperor won above fifty thousand crowns one evening. Now such cuckolds as you will be hanged ere you get half so much at it. Patience, said Panurge; but let us dispatch. And when, my friend and neighbour, continued the canting sheep-seller, shall I have duly praised the inward members, the shoulders, the legs, the knuckles, the neck, the breast, the liver, the spleen, the tripes, the kidneys, the bladder, wherewith they make footballs; the ribs, which serve in Pigmyland to make little cross-bows, to pelt the cranes with cherry-stones; the head, which with a little brimstone serves to make a miraculous decoction to loosen and ease the belly of costive dogs? A turd on it, said the skipper to his preaching passenger, what a fiddle-faddle have we here? There is too long a lecture by half: sell him if thou wilt; if thou wilt not, do not let the man lose more time. I hate a gibble-gabble, and a rimble-ramble talk. I am for a man of brevity. I will, for your sake, replied the holder forth; but then he shall give me three livres, French money, for each pick and choose. It is a woundy price, cried Panurge; in our country, I could have five, nay six, for the money: see that you do not overreach me, master. You are not the first man whom I have known to have fallen, even sometimes to the endangering, if not breaking, of his own neck, for endeavouring to rise all at once. A murrain seize thee for a blockheaded booby, cried the angry seller of sheep; by the worthy vow of our lady of Charroux, the worst in this flock is four times better than those which in days of yore the Coraxians in Tuditania, a country of Spain, used to sell for a gold talent each; and how much dost thou think, thou Hibernian fool, that a talent of gold was worth? Sweet sir, you fall into a passion, I see, returned Panurge: well hold, here is your money. Panurge, having paid his money, chose him out of all the flock a fine topping ram; and as he was hauling it along, crying out and bleating, all the rest, hearing and bleating in concert, stared to see whither their brother ram should be carried. In the meanwhile the drover was saying to his shepherds: Ah! how well the knave could choose him out a ram; the whore-son has skill in cattle. On my honest word, I reserved that very piece of flesh for the Lord of Cancale, well knowing his disposition: for the good man is naturally overjoyed when he holds a good-sized handsome shoulder of mutton instead of a left-handed racket, in one hand, with a good sharp carver in the other: got wot how he bestirs himself then.

CHAPTER 8

How Panurge caused Dingdong and his sheep to be drowned in the sea

ON a sudden, you would wonder how the thing was so soon done; for my part I cannot tell you, for I had not leisure to mind it; our friend Panurge, without any further tittle-tattle, throws you his ram overboard into the middle of the sea, bleating and making a sad noise. Upon this all the other sheep in the ship, crying and bleating in the same tone, made all the haste they could to leap nimbly into the sea, one after another; and great was the throng who should leap in first after their leader. It was impossible to hinder them: for you know that it is the nature of sheep always to follow the first, wheresoever it goes; which makes Aristotle, *lib.* 9. *De Hist. Animal.*, mark them for the most silly and foolish animals in the world. Dingdong, at his wit's end, and stark staring mad, as a man who saw his sheep destroy and drown themselves before his face, strove to hinder and keep them by might and main; but all in vain: they all, one after the other frisked and jumped into the sea, and were lost. At last he laid hold on a huge sturdy one by the fleece, upon the deck of the ship, hoping to keep it back, and so save that and the rest; but the ram was so strong that it proved too hard for him, and carried its master into the herring pond in spite of his teeth; where it is supposed he drank somewhat more than his fill; so that he was drowned, in the same manner as one-eyed Polyphemus' sheep carried out of the den Ulysses and his companions. The like happened to the shepherds and all their gang, some laying hold on their beloved tup, this by the horns, the other by the legs, a third by the rump, and others by the fleece; till in fine they were all of them forced to sea, and drowned like so many rats. Panurge on the gunnel of the ship, with an oar in his hand, not to help them you may swear, but to keep them from swimming to the ship, and saving themselves from drowning, preached and canted to them all the while, like any little Friar Oliver Maillard, or another Friar John Burgess; laying before them rhetorical common-places concerning the miseries of this life, and the blessings and felicity of the next; assuring them that the dead were much happier than the living in this vale of misery, and promising to erect a stately cenotaph and honorary tomb to every one of them, on the highest summit of Mount Cenis, at his return from Lantern-land; wishing them, nevertheless, in case they were not disposed to shake hands with this life, and did not like their salt liquor, they might have the good luck to meet with some kind whale which might set them ashore safe and sound, on some land of Gotham, after a famous example.

The ship being cleared of Dingdong and his tups: Is there ever another sheepish soul left lurking on board? cried Panurge. Where are those of Toby Lamb, and Robin Ram, that sleep whilst the rest are a feeding? Faith I cannot tell myself. This was an old coaster's trick. What thinkest of it, Friar John, hah? Rarely performed, answered Friar John: only methinks that as formerly in war, on the day

of battle, a double pay was commonly promised the soldiers for that day: for if they overcome, there was enough to pay them; and if they lost, it would have been shameful for them to demand it, as the cowardly foresters did after the battle of Cerizoles: so likewise, my friend, you ought not to have paid your man, and the money had been saved. A fart for the money, said Panurge: have I not had above fifty thousand pounds worth of sport? Come now, let us be gone; the wind is fair. Hark you me, my friend John: never did man do me a good turn, but I returned, or at least acknowledged it; no, I scorn to be ungrateful; I never was, nor ever will be: never did man do me an ill one without rueing the day that he did it, either in this world or the next. I am not yet so much a fool neither. Thou damnest thyself like any old devil, quoth Friar John: it is written, *Mihi vindictam, &c.*[6] Matter of breviary, mark ye me.

CHAPTER 9

How Pantagruel arrived at the island of Ennasin, and of the strange ways of being akin in that country

WE had still the wind at south-south-west, and had been a whole day without making land. On the third day, at the flies up rising, (which, you know, is some two or three hours after the sun's,) we got sight of a triangular island, very much like Sicily for its form and situation. It was called the Island of Alliances.

The people there are much like your carrot-pated Poitevins, save only that all of them, men, women, and children, have their noses shaped like an ace of clubs. For that reason the ancient name of the country was Ennasin. They were all akin, as the mayor of the place told us, at least they boasted so.

You people of the other world esteem it a wonderful thing, that, out of the family of the Fabii at Rome, on a certain day, which was the 13th of February, at a certain gate, which was the Porta Carmentalis, since named Scelerata, formerly situated at the foot of the Capitol, between the Tarpeian rock and the Tiber, marched out against the Veientes of Etruria, three hundred and six men bearing arms, all related to each other, with five thousand other soldiers, every one of them their vassals, who were all slain near the river Cremera, that comes out of the lake of Beccano. Now from this same country of Ennasin, in case of need, above three hundred thousand, all relations, and of one family, might march out. Their degrees of consanguinity and alliance are very strange: for being thus akin and allied to one another, we found that none was either father or mother, brother or sister, uncle or aunt, nephew or niece, son-in-law, or daughter-in-law, godfather or godmother, to the other; unless, truly, a tall flat-nosed old fellow, who, as I perceived, called a little shitten arsed girl, of three or four years old, father, and the child called him daughter.

Their distinction of degrees of kindred was thus: a man used to call a woman, my lean bit; the woman called him, my porpoise. Those, said Friar John, must needs stink damnably of fish, when they have rubbed their bacon one with the other. One smiling on a young buxom baggage, said, Good morrow, dear currycomb. She, to return him his civility, said, The like to you, my steed. Ha! ha! ha! said Panurge, that is pretty well in faith; for indeed it stands her in good stead to currycomb this steed. Another greeted his buttock with a Farewell, my case. She replied, Adieu, trial. By St. Winifred's placket, cried Gymnast, this case has been often tried. Another asked a she-friend of his, How is it, hatchet? She answered him, At your service, dear helve. Odds belly, saith Carpalim, this helve and this hatchet are well matched. As we went on, I saw one who, calling his she-relation, styled her my crum, and she called him, my crust.

Quoth one to a brisk, plump, juicy female, I am glad to see you, dear tap. So am I to find you so merry, sweet spiggot, replied she. One called a wench, his shovel; she called him, her peal: one named his, my slipper: and she my foot: another, my boot; she, my shasoon.

In the same degree of kindred, one called his, my butter; she called him, my eggs; and they were akin just like a dish of buttered eggs. I heard one call his, my tripe, and she called him, my faggot. Now I could not, for the heart's blood of me, pick out or discover what parentage, alliance, affinity, or consanguinity was between them, with reference to our custom; only they told us that she was faggot's tripe. [*Tripe de fagot,* means the smallest sticks in a faggot.] Another complimenting his convenient, said, Yours, my shell: she replied, I was yours before, sweet oyster. I reckon, said Carpalim, she hath gutted his oyster. Another long-shanked ugly rogue, mounted on a pair of high-heeled wooden slippers, meeting a strapping, fusty, squobbed dowdy, says he to her, How is it, my top? She was short upon him, and arrogantly replied, Never the better for you, my whip. By St. Anthony's hog, said Xenomanes, I believe so; for how can this whip be sufficient to lash this top?

A college professor, well provided with cod, and powdered and prinked up, having a while discoursed with a great lady, taking his leave, with these words, Thank you, sweet-meat; she cried, There needs no thanks, sour-sauce. Saith Pantagruel, This is not altogether incongruous, for sweet meat must have sour sauce. A wooden loggerhead said to a young wench, It is long since I saw you, bag: All the better, cried she, pipe. Set them together, said Panurge, then blow in their arses, it will be a bagpipe. We saw, after that, a diminutive humpback gallant, pretty near us, taking leave of a she-relation of his, thus: Fare thee well, friend hole: she reparteed, Save thee, friend peg. Quoth Friar John, What could they say more, were he all peg and she all hole? But now would I give something to know if every cranny of the hole can be stopped up with that same peg.

A bawdy bachelor, talking with an old trout, was saying, Remember, rusty gun. I will not fail, said she, scourer. Do you reckon these two to be akin? said Pantagruel to the mayor: I rather take them to be foes: in our country a woman would take this as a mortal affront. Good people of the other world, replied the mayor, you have few such and so near relations as this gun and scourer are to one another; for they both come out of one shop. What, was the shop their mother? quoth Panurge. What mother, said the mayor, does the man mean? That must be some of your world's affinity; we have here neither father nor mother: your little paltry fellows, that live on the other side the water, poor rogues, booted with whisps of hay, may indeed have such; but we scorn it. The good Pantagruel stood gazing and listening; but at those words he had like to have lost all patience.

Having very exactly viewed the situation of the island, and the way of living of the Ennaséd nation, we went to take a cup of the creature at a tavern, where there happened to be a wedding after the manner of the country. Bating that shocking custom, there was special good cheer.

While we were there, a pleasant match was

struck up betwixt a female called Pear (a
tight thing, as we thought, but by some
who knew better things, said to be quaggy
and flabby,) and a young soft male, called
Cheese, somewhat sandy. (Many such
matches have been, and they were formerly
much commended.) In our country we say, •
*Il ne fut ocques tel mariage, qu'est de la
poire et du fromage;* there is no match like
that made between the pear and the cheese:
and in many other places good store of such
bargains have been driven. Besides, when
the women are at their last prayers, it is to
this day a noted saying, that after cheese
comes nothing.

In another room I saw them marrying an
old greasy boot to a young pliable buskin.
Pantagruel was told, that young buskin took
old boot to have and to hold, because she was
of special leather, in good case, and waxed,
seared, liquored, and greased to the purpose,
even though it had been for the fisherman
that went to bed with his boots on. In another
room below, I saw a young brogue taking a
young slipper for better for worse: which,
they told us, was neither for sake of her piety,
parts, or person, but for the fourth compre-
hensive p, portion; the spankers, spur-royals,
rose-nobles, and other coriander seed with
which she was quilted all over.

CHAPTER 10

*How Pantagruel went ashore at the island of
Chely, where he saw King St. Panigon*

WE sailed right before the wind, which we
had at west, leaving those odd alliancers with
their ace-of-clubs snouts, and having taken
height by the sun, stood in for Chely, a large,
fruitful, wealthy, and well-peopled island.
King St. Panigon, first of the name, reigned
there, and, attended by the princes, his sons,
and the nobles of his court, came as far as the
port to receive Pantagruel, and conducted
him to his palace; near the gate of which, the
queen, attended by the princesses her daughters, and the court ladies, received us. Panigon directed her and all her retinue to salute
Pantagruel and his men with a kiss; for such
was the civil custom of the country: and they
were all fairly bussed accordingly, except
Friar John, who stepped aside, and sneaked
off among the king's officers. Panigon used
all the entreaties imaginable to persuade Pantagruel to tarry there that day and the next:
but he would needs be gone, and excused

himself upon the opportunity of wind and
weather, which being oftener desired than
enjoyed, ought not to be neglected when it
comes. Panigon, having heard these reasons,
let us go, but first made us take off some five
and twenty or thirty bumpers each.

Pantagruel, returning to the port, missed
Friar John, and asked why he was not with
the rest of the company? Panurge could not
tell how to excuse him, and would have gone
back to the palace to call him, when Friar
John overtook them, and merrily cried, Long
live the noble Panigon! As I love my belly, he
minds good eating, and keeps a noble house
and a dainty kitchen. I have been there, boys.
Every thing goes about by dozens. I was in
good hopes to have stuffed my puddings
there like a monk. What! always in a kitchen,
friend? said Pantagruel. By the belly of St.
Crampacon, quoth the Friar, I understand
the customs and ceremonies which are used
there, much better than all the formal stuff,
antic postures, and nonsensical fiddle-faddle
that must be used with those women, *magni
magna, shitten cumshita,* cringes, grimaces,
scrapes, bows, and congees; double honours
this way, triple salutes that way, the embrace, the grasp, the squeeze, the hug, the
leer, the smack, *beso las manos de vostra mer-
cé de vostra maestá.* You are most *tarabin,
tarabas, Stront;* that is downright Dutch.
Why all this ado? I do not say but a man
might be for a bit by the bye and away, to be
doing as well as his neighbours; but this little
nasty cringing and courtesying made me as
mad as any March devil. You talk of kissing
ladies; by the worthy and sacred frock I wear,
I seldom venture upon it, lest I be served as
was the Lord of Guyercharois. What was it?
said Pantagruel; I know him; he is one of the
best friends I have.

He was invited to a sumptuous feast, said
Friar John, by a relation and neighbour of
his, together with all the gentlemen and ladies in the neighbourhood. Now some of the
latter [the ladies] expecting his coming,
dressed the pages in women's clothes, and
finified them like any babies; then ordered
them to meet my lord at his coming near the
draw-bridge; so the complimenting monsieur
came, and there kissed the petticoated lads
with great formality. At last the ladies, who
minded passages in the gallery, burst out with
laughing, and made signs to the pages to take
off their dress; which the good lord having
observed, the devil a bit he durst make up to

the true ladies to kiss them, but said, that since they had disguised the pages, by his great grandfather's helmet, these were certainly the very footmen and grooms still more cunningly disguised. Odds fish, *da jurandi*,[7] why do not we rather remove our humanities into some good warm kitchen of God, that noble laboratory; and there admire the turning of the spits, the harmonious rattling of the jacks and fenders, criticise on the position of the lard, the temperature of the pottages, the preparation for the dessert, and the order of the wine service? *Beati immaculati in via*.[8] Matter of breviary, my masters.

CHAPTER 11

Why monks love to be in kitchens

THIS, said Epistemon, is spoke like a true monk: I mean like a right monking monk, not a bemonked monastical monkling. Truly you put me in mind of some passages that happened at Florence, some twenty years ago, in a company of studious travellers, fond of visiting the learned, and seeing the antiquities of Italy, among whom I was. As we viewed the situation and beauty of Florence, the structure of the dome, the magnificence of the churches and palaces, we strove to outdo one another in giving them their due; when a certain monk of Amiens, Bernard Lardon by name, quite angry, scandalized, and out of all patience, told us, I do not know what the devil you can find in this same town, that is so much cried up: for my part I have looked and pored and stared as well as the best of you; I think my eyesight is as clear as another body's; and what can one see after all? There are fine houses, indeed, and that is all. But the cage does not feed the birds. God and Monsieur St. Bernard, our good patron, be with us! in all this same town I have not seen one poor lane of roasting cooks; and yet I have not a little looked about, and sought for so necessary a part of a commonwealth: ay, and I dare assure you that I have pried up and down with the exactness of an informer; as ready to number both to the right and left, how many, and on what side, we might find most roasting cooks, as a spy would be to reckon the bastions of a town. Now at Amiens, in four, nay five times less ground than we have trod in our contemplations, I could have shown you above fourteen streets of roasting cooks, most ancient, savoury, and aromatic. I cannot imagine what kind of pleasure you can have taken in gazing on the lions and Africans, (so methinks you call their tigers,) near the belfry; or in ogling the porcupines and ostriches in the Lord Philip Strozzi's palace. Faith and truth I had rather see a good fat goose at the spit. This porphyry, those marbles are fine; I say nothing to the contrary: but our cheesecakes at Amiens are far better in my mind. These ancient statues are well made; I am willing to believe it: but by St. Ferreol of Abbeville, we have young wenches in our country, which please me better a thousand times.

What is the reason, asked Friar John, that monks are always to be found in kitchens; and kings, emperors, and popes are never there? Is there not, said Rhizotomus, some latent virtue and specific property hid in the kettles and pans, which, as the loadstone attracts iron, draws the monk there, and cannot attract emperors, popes, or kings? Or is it a natural induction and inclination, fixed in the frocks and cowls, which of itself leads and forceth those good religious men into kitchens, whether they will or no? He means, forms, following matter, as Averroës calls them, answered Epistemon. Right, said Friar John.

I will not offer to solve this problem, said Pantagruel; for it is somewhat ticklish, and you can hardly handle it without coming off scurvily; but I will tell you what I have heard. Antigonus, King of Macedon, one day coming to one of his tents, where his cooks used to dress his meat, and finding there poet Antagoras frying a conger, and holding the pan himself, merrily asked him, Pray, Mr. Poet, was Homer frying congers when he wrote the deeds of Agamemnon? Antagoras readily answered, But do you think, sir, that when Agamemnon did them, he made it his business to know if any in his camp were frying congers? The king thought it an indecency that a poet should be thus a frying in a kitchen; and the poet let the king know, that it was a more indecent thing for a king to be found in such a place. I will clap another story upon the neck of this, quoth Panurge, and will tell you what Breton Villandry answered one day to the Duke of Guise.

They were saying that at a certain battle of King Francis, against the Emperor, Charles the Fifth, Breton, armed *cap-a-pé* to the teeth, and mounted like St. George; yet sneaked off, and played least in sight during the engagement. Blood an'ouns, answered

Breton, I was there, and can prove it easily; nay, even where you, my lord, dared not have been. The duke began to resent this as too rash and saucy: but Breton easily appeased him, and set them all a laughing. I gad, my lord, quoth he, I kept out of harm's way; I was all the while with your page Jack, skulking in a certain place where you had not dared hide your head, as I did. Thus discoursing, they got to their ships, and left the island of Chely.

CHAPTER 12

How Pantagruel passed through the land of Pettifogging, and of the strange way of living among the Catchpoles

STEERING our course forwards the next day, we passed through Pettifogging, a country all blurred and blotted, so that I could hardly tell what to make on it. There we saw some pettifoggers and catchpoles, rogues that will hang their father for a groat. They neither invited us to eat or drink; but, with a multiplied train of scrapes and cringes, said they were all at our service, for a consideration.

One of our interpreters related to Pantagruel their strange way of living, diametrically opposite to that of our modern Romans; for at Rome a world of folks get an honest livelihood by poisoning, drubbing, lambasting, stabbing, and murdering; but the catchpoles earn theirs by being thrashed; so that if they were long without a tight lambasting, the poor dogs with their wives and children would be starved. This is just, quoth Panurge, like those who, as Galen tells us, cannot erect the cavernous nerve towards the equinoctial circle, unless they are soundly flogged. By St. Patrick's slipper, whoever should jirk me so, would soon, instead of setting me right, throw me off the saddle, in the devil's name.

The way is this, said the interpreter. When a monk, levite, close-fisted usurer, or lawyer owes a grudge to some neighbouring gentleman, he sends to him one of those catchpoles, or apparitors, who nabs, or at least cites him, serves a writ or warrant upon him, thumps, abuses, and affronts him impudently by natural instinct, and according to his pious instructions: insomuch, that if the gentleman hath but any guts in his brains, and is not more stupid than a gyrin frog, he will find himself obliged either to apply a faggot-stick or his sword to the rascal's jobbernol, give him the gentle lash, or make him cut a caper

out of the window, by way of correction. This done, Catchpole is rich for four months at least, as if bastinadoes were his real harvest: for the monk, levite, usurer, or lawyer, will reward him roundly; and my gentleman must pay him such swingeing damages, that his acres must bleed for it, and he be in danger of miserably rotting within a stone doublet, as if he had struck the king.

Quoth Panurge, I know an excellent remedy against this; used by the Lord of Basché. What is it? said Pantagruel. The Lord of Basché, said Panurge, was a brave, honest, noble-spirited gentleman, who, at his return from the long war, in which the Duke of Ferrara, with the help of the French, bravely defended himself against the fury of Pope Julius the Second, was every day cited, warned, and prosecuted at the suit, and for the sport and fancy of the fat prior of St. Louant.

One morning as he was at breakfast with some of his domestics (for he loved to be sometimes among them) he sent for one Loire his baker, and his spouse, and for one Oudart, the vicar of his parish, who was also his butler, as the custom was then in France; then said to them before his gentleman and other servants: You all see how I am daily plagued with these rascally catchpoles: truly if you do not lend me your helping hand, I am finally resolved to leave the country, and go fight for the sultan, or the devil, rather than be thus eternally teazed. Therefore to be rid of their damned visits, hereafter, when any of them come here, be ready you baker and your wife, to make your personal appearance in my great hall, in your wedding clothes, as if you were going to be affianced. Here take these ducats, which I give you to keep you in a fitting garb. As for you, Sir Oudart, be sure you make your personal appearance there in your fair surplice and stole, not forgetting your holy water, as if you were to wed them. Be you there also, Trudon, said he to his drummer, with your pipe and tabour. The form of matrimony must be read, and the bride kissed at the beat of the tabour; then all of you, as the witnesses used do in this country, shall give one another the remembrance of the wedding,—which you know is to be a blow with your fist, bidding the party struck, remember the nuptials by that token. This will but make you have the better stomach to your supper; but when you come to the catchpole's turn, thrash him thrice and threefold, as you would a sheaf of green corn; do not spare him; maul him, drub him, lambast him, swinge him off, I pray you. Here, take these steel gauntlets, covered with kid. Head, back, belly, and sides, give him blows innumerable: he that gives him most, shall be my best friend. Fear not to be called to an account about it; I will stand by you: for the blows must seem to be given in jest, as it is customary among us at all weddings.

Ay, but how shall we know the catchpole, said the man of God? All sorts of people daily resort to this castle. I have taken care of that, replied the lord. When some fellow, either on foot, or on a scurvy jade, with a large broad silver ring on his thumb, comes to the door, he is certainly a catchpole: the porter, having civilly let him in, shall ring the bell; then be all ready, and come into the hall, to act the tragi-comedy, whose plot I have now laid for you.

That numerical day, as chance would have it, came an old fat ruddy catchpole. Having knocked at the gate, and then pissed, as most men will do, the porter soon found him out, by his large greasy spatterdashes, his jaded hollow-flanked mare, his bag full of writs and informations dangling at his girdle, but, above all, by the large silver hoop on his left thumb.

The porter was civil to him, admitted him kindly, and rung the bell briskly. As soon as the baker and his wife heard it, they clapped on their best clothes, and made their personal appearance in the hall, keeping their gravities like a new-made judge. The dominie put on his surplice and stole, and as he came out of his office, met the catchpole, had him in there, and made him suck his face a good while, while the gauntlets were drawing on all hands; and then told him, You are come just in pudding-time; my lord is in his right cue: we shall feast like kings anon, here is to be swingeing doing; we have a wedding in the house; here, drink and cheer up; pull away.

While these two were at hand-to-fist, Basché seeing all his people in the hall in their proper equipages, sends for the vicar. Oudart comes with the holy water pot, followed by the catchpole, who, as he came into the hall, did not forget to make good store of awkward cringes, and then served Basché with a writ. Basché gave him grimace for grimace, slipped an angel into his mutton fist, and prayed him to assist at the contract and ceremony: which he did. When it was ended, thumps and fisticuffs began to fly about among the assistants; but when it came to the catchpole's turn, they all laid on him so unmercifully with their gauntlets, that they at last settled him, all stunned and battered, bruised and mortified, with one of his eyes black and blue, eight ribs bruised, his brisket sunk in, his omoplates in four quarters, his under jawbone in three pieces; and all this in jest, and no harm done. God wot how the levite belaboured him, hiding within the long sleeve of his canonical shirt his huge steel gauntlet lined with ermine: for he was a strong built ball, and an old dog at fisticuffs. The catchpole, all of a bloody tiger-like stripe, with much ado crawled home to L'Isle Bouchart, well pleased and edified however with Basché kind reception; and, with the help of the good surgeons of the place, lived as long as you would have him. From that time to this, not a word of the business; the memory of it was lost with the sound of the bells that rung with joy at his funeral.

CHAPTER 13

How, like Master Francis Villon, the Lord of Basché commended his servants

THE catchpole being packed off on blind Sorrel,—so he called his one-eyed-mare,—Basché sent for his lady, her women, and all his servants, into the arbour of his garden; had wine brought, attended with good store of pasties, hams, fruit, and other table-ammunition, for a nunchion; drank with them joyfully, and then told them this story.

Master Francis Villon, in his old age, retired to St. Maxent, in Poictou, under the patronage of a good honest abbot of the place. There to make sport for the mob, he undertook to get "The Passion" acted, after the way, and in the dialect of the country. The parts being distributed, the play having been rehearsed, and the stage prepared, he told the mayor and aldermen, that the mystery would be ready after Niort fair, and that there only wanted properties and necessaries, but chiefly clothes fit for the parts: so the mayor and his brethren took care to get them.

Villon, to dress an old clownish father greybeard, who was to represent G—d the father, begged of Friar Stephen Tickletoby, sacristan to the Franciscan friars of the place, to lend him a cope and a stole. Tickletoby refused him, alleging, that by their provincial statutes, it was rigorously forbidden to give or lend anything to players. Villon replied, that the statute reached no farther than farces, drolls, antics, loose and dissolute games, and that he asked no more than what he had seen allowed at Brussels and other places. Tickletoby, notwithstanding, peremptorily bid him provide himself elsewhere if he would, and not to hope for any thing out of his monastical wardrobe. Villon gave an account of this to the players, as of a most abominable action; adding, that God would shortly revenge himself, and make an example of Tickletoby.

The Saturday following, he had notice given him, that Tickletoby, upon the filly of the convent—so they call a young mare that was never leaped yet—was gone a mumping to St. Ligarius, and would be back about two in the afternoon. Knowing this, he made a cavalcade of his devils of "The Passion" through the town. They were all rigged with wolves', calves', and rams' skins, laced and trimmed with sheep's heads, bulls' feathers, and large kitchen tenterhooks, girt with broad leathern girdles; whereat hanged dangling huge cowbells and horsebells, which made a horrid din. Some held in their claws black sticks full of squibs and crackers: others had long lighted pieces of wood, upon which, at the corner of every street, they flung whole handfuls of rosin-dust, that made a terrible fire and smoke. Having thus led them about, to the great diversion of the mob, and the dreadful fear of little children, he finally carried them to an entertainment at a summer-house, without the gate that leads to St. Ligarius.

As they came near to the place, he espied Tickletoby afar off, coming home from mumping, and told them in macaronic verse.

Hic est de patria, natus, de gente belistra,
Qui solet antiquo bribas portare bisacco.[9]

A plague on his friarship, said the devils then; the lousy beggar would not lend a poor cope to the fatherly father; let us fright him. Well said, cried Villon; but let us hide ourselves till he comes by, and then charge him home briskly with your squibs and burning sticks. Tickletoby being come to the place, they all rushed on a sudden into the road to meet him, and in a frightful manner threw fire from all sides upon him and his filly foal, ringing and tingling their bells, and howling like so many real devils, Hho, hho, hho, hho,

brrou, rrou, rrourrs, rrrourrs, hoo, hou, hho, hho, hhoi. Friar Stephen, don't we play the devils rarely? The filly was soon scared out of her seven senses, and began to start, to funk it, to squirt it, to trot it, to fart it, to bound it, to gallop it, to kick it, to spurn it, to calcitrate it, to wince it, to frisk it, to leap it, to curvet it, with double jerks, and bum-motions; insomuch that she threw down Tickletoby, though he held fast by the tree of the packsaddle with might and main. Now his straps and stirrups were of cord; and on the right side, his sandals were so entangled and twisted, that he could not for the heart's blood of him get out his foot. Thus he was dragged about by the filly through the road, scratching his bare breech all the way; she still multiplying her kicks against him, and straying for fear over hedge and ditch; insomuch that she trepanned his thick skull so, that his cockle brains were dashed out near the Osanna or high-cross. Then his arms fell to pieces, one this way, and the other that way; and even so were his legs served at the same time. Then she made a bloody havoc with his puddings; and being got to the convent, brought back only his right foot and twisted sandal, leaving them to guess what had become of the rest.

Villon, seeing that things had succeeded as he intended, said to his devils, You will act rarely, gentlemen devils, you will act rarely; I dare engage you will top your parts. I defy the devils of Saumur, Douay, Montmorillon, Langez, St. Espain, Angers; nay, by gad, even those of Poictiers, for all their bragging and vapouring to match you.

Thus, friends, said Basché, I forsee, that hereafter you will act rarely this tragical farce, since the very first time you have so skilfully hampered, bethwacked, belammed, and bebumped the catchpole. From this day I double your wages. As for you, my dear, said he to his lady, make your gratifications as you please; you are my treasurer, you know. For my part, first and foremost, I drink to you all. Come on, box it about, it is good and cool. In the second place, you, Mr. Steward, take this silver basin, I give it you freely. Then you, my gentlemen of the horse, take these two silver gilt cups, and let not the pages be horse-whipped these three months. My dear, let them have my best white plumes of feathers, with the gold buckles to them. Sir Oudart, this silver flagon falls to your share: this other I give to the cooks. To the valets de chambre I give this silver basket; to the grooms, this silver gilt boat; to the porter, these two plates, to the hostlers, these ten porringers. Trudon, take you these silver spoons and this sugar box. You, footman, take this large salt. Serve me well, and I will remember you. For on the word of a gentleman, I had rather bear in war one hundred blows on my helmet in the service of my country, than be once cited by these knavish catchpoles, merely to humour this same gorbellied prior.

CHAPTER 14

A further account of Catchpoles who were drubbed at Basché's house

FOUR days after, another, young, long-shanked, raw-boned catchpole, coming to serve Basché with a writ at the fat prior's request, was no sooner at the gate, but the porter smelt him out and rung the bell; at whose second pull, all the family understood the mystery. Loire was kneading his dough; his wife was sifting meal; Oudart was toping in his office; the gentlemen were playing at tennis; the Lord Basché at in and out with my lady; the waiting-men and gentlewomen at push-pin; the officers at lanterlue, and the pages at hot-cockles, giving one another smart bangs. They were all immediately informed that a catchpole was housed.

Upon this, Oudart put on his sacerdotal, and Loire and his wife their nuptial badges: Trudon piped it, and then taboured it like mad; all made haste to get ready, not forgetting the gauntlets. Basché went into the outward yard: there the catchpole meeting him fell on his marrow-bones, begged of him not to take it ill, if he served him with a writ at the suit of the fat prior; and in a pathetic speech, let him know that he was a public person, a servant to the monking tribe, apparitor to the abbatial mitre, ready to do as much for him, nay, for the least of his servants, whensoever he would employ and use him.

Nay, truly, said the lord, you shall not serve your writ till you have tasted some of my good quinquenays wine, and been a witness to a wedding which we are to have this very minute. Let him drink and refresh himself, added he, turning towards the levitical butler, and then bring him into the hall. After which, Catchpole, well stuffed and moistened, came with Oudart to the place where

all the actors in the farce stood ready to begin. The sight of their game set them a laughing, and the messenger of mischief grinned also for company's sake. Then the mysterious words were muttered to and by the couple, their hands joined, the bride bussed, and all besprinkled with holy water. While they were bringing wine and kickshaws, thumps began to trot about by dozens. The catchpole gave the levite several blows. Oudart, who had his gauntlet hid under his canonical shirt, draws it on like a mitten, and then, with his clenched fist, souse he fell on the catchpole, and mauled him like a devil: the junior gauntlets dropped on him likewise like so many battering rams. Remember the wedding by this, by that, by these blows, said they. In short they stroked him so to the purpose, that he pissed blood out at mouth, nose, ears, and eyes, and was bruised, thwackt, battered, bebumped, and crippled at the back, neck, breast, arms, and so forth. Never did the bachelors at Avignon, in carnival time, play more melodiously at raphe, than was then played on the catchpole's microcosm: at last down he fell.

They threw a great deal of wine on his snout, tied round the sleeve of his doublet a fine yellow and green favour, and got him upon his snotty beast, and God knows how he got to L'Isle Bouchart; where I cannot truly tell you whether he was dressed and looked after or no, both by his spouse and the able doctors of the country; for the thing never came to my ears.

The next day they had a third part to the same tune, because it did not appear by the lean catchpole's bag, that he had served his writ. So the fat prior sent a new catchpole at the head of a brace of bums, for his *garde du corps*, to summon my lord. The porter ringing the bell, the whole family was overjoyed, knowing that was another rogue. Basché was at dinner with his lady and the gentlemen; so he sent for the catchpole, made him sit by him, and the bums by the women, and made them eat till their bellies cracked with their breeches unbuttoned. The fruit being served, the catchpole arose from table and before the bums cited Basché. Basché kindly asked him for a copy of the warrant, which the other had got ready: he then takes witness, and a copy of the summons. To the catchpole and his bums he ordered four ducats for civility money. In the meantime all were withdrawn for the farce. So Trudon gave the alarm with his tabour. Basché desired the catchpole to stay and see one of his servants married, and witness the contract of marriage, paying him his fee. The catchpole slap dash was ready, took out his ink-horn, got paper immediately, and his bums by him.

Then Loire came into the hall at one door, and his wife with the gentlewomen at another, in nuptial accoutrements. Oudart, *in pontificalibus,*[10] takes them both by their hands, asketh them their will, giveth them the matrimonial blessing, and was very liberal of holy water. The contract written, signed, and registered, on one side was brought wine and comfits; on the other, white and orange-tawny-coloured favours were distributed: on another, gauntlets privately handed about.

CHAPTER 15

How the ancient custom at nuptials is renewed by the Catchpole

THE catchpole, having made shift to get down a swingeing sneaker of Breton wine, said to Basché, Pray, Sir, what do you mean? You do not give one another the memento of the wedding. By St. Joseph's wooden shoe, all good customs are forgot. We find the form, but the hare is scampered; and the nest, but the birds are flown. There are no true friends now-a-days. You see how, in several churches, the ancient laudable custom of tippling, on account of the blessed saints O O, at Christmas, is come to nothing. The world is in its dotage, and doomsday is certainly coming all so fast. Now come on; the wedding, the wedding, the wedding; remember it by this. This he said, striking Basché and his lady; then her women and the levite. Then the tabour beat a point of war, and the gauntlets began to do their duty: insomuch that the catchpole had his crown cracked in no less than nine places. One of the bums had his right arm put out of joint, and the other his upper jawbone or mandibule dislocated; so that it hid half his chin, with a denudation of the uvula, and sad loss of the molar, masticatory, and canine teeth. Then the tabour beat a retreat; the gauntlets were carefully hid in a trice, and sweetmeats afresh distributed to renew the mirth of the company. So they all drank to one another, and especially to the catchpole and his bums. But Oudart cursed and damned the wedding to the pit of hell, complaining that one of the bums had

utterly disincornifistibulated his nether shoulder-blade. Nevertheless, he scorned to be thought a flincher, and made shift to tope to him on the square.

The jawless bum shrugged up his shoulders, joined his hands, and by signs begged his pardon; for speak he could not. The sham bridegroom made his moan, that the crippled bum had struck him such a horrid thump with his shoulder-of-mutton fist on the nether elbow, that he was grown quite esperruquanchuzelubleouzerireliced down to his very heel, to the no small loss of mistress bride.

But what harm had poor I done? cried Trudon, hiding his left eye with his kerchief, and showing his tabour cracked on one side: they were not satisfied with thus poaching, black and blueing, and morrambouzevezengouzequoquemorgasacbaquevezinemaffreliding my poor eyes, but they have also broke my harmless drum. Drums indeed are commonly beaten at weddings,—and it is fit they should; but drummers are well entertained, and never beaten. Now let Belzebub even take the drum, to make his devilship a nightcap. Brother, said the lame catchpole, never fret thyself; I will make thee a present of a fine, large, old patent, which I have here in my bag, to patch up thy drum and for Madame St. Ann's sake I pray thee forgive us. By Our Lady of Riviere, the blessed dame, I meant no more harm than the child unborn. One of the equerries who hopping and halting like a mumping cripple, mimicked the good limping Lord de la Roche Posay, directed his discourse to the bum with the pouting jaw, and told him, What, Mr. Manhound, was it not enough thus to have morcrosastebesasteverestegrigeligoscopapopondrillated us all in our upper members with your botched mittens, but you must also apply such morderegripippiatabirofreluchamburelurecaquelurintimpaniments on our shin-bones with the hard tops and extremities of your cobbled shoes. Do you call this children's play? By the mass, it is no jest. The bum, wringing his hands, seemed to beg his pardon, muttering with his tongue, mon, mon, mon, vrelon, von, von, like a dumb man. The bride crying laughed, and laughing cried, because the catchpole was not satisfied with drubbing her without choice or distinction of members, but had also rudely roused and toused her; pulled off her topping, and not having the fear of her husband before his eyes, treacherously trepignemanpenillorifrizonoufresterfumbledtumbled and squeezed her lower parts. The devil go with it, said Basché; there was much need indeed that this same Master King (this was the catchpole's name) should thus break my wife's back: however, I forgive him now; these are little nuptial caresses. But this I plainly perceive, that he cited me like an angel, and drubbed me like a devil. He hath something in him of Friar Thumpwell. Come, for all this, I must drink to him, and to you likewise his trusty esquires. But, said his lady, why hath he been so very liberal of his manual kindness to me, without the least provocation? I assure you, I by no means like it: but this I dare say for him, that he hath the hardest knuckles that ever I felt on my shoulders. The steward held his left arm in a scarf, as if it had been rent and torn in twain: I think it was the devil, said he, that moved me to assist at these nuptials; shame on ill luck; I must needs be meddling with a pox, and now see what I have got by the bargain, both my arms are wretchedly engoulevezinemassed and bruised. Do you call this a wedding? By St. Bridget's tooth I had rather be at that of a Tom T——dman. This is, on my word, even just such another feast as was that of the Lapithæ described by the philosopher of Samosata. One of the bums had lost his tongue. The two other, though they had more need to complain, made their excuse as well as they could, protesting that they had no ill design in this dumbfounding; begging that, for goodness sake, they would forgive them; and so, though they could hardly budge a foot, or wag along, away they crawled. About a mile from Basché's seat the catchpole found himself somewhat out of sorts. The bums got to L'Isle Bouchard, publicly saying, that since they were born, they had never seen an honester gentleman than the Lord of Basché, or civiller people than his, and that they had never been at the like wedding (which I verily believe); but that it was their own faults if they had then tickled off, and tossed about from post to pillar, since themselves had begun the beating. So they lived I cannot exactly tell you how many days after this. But from that time to this it was held for a certain truth, that Basché's money was more pestilential, mortal, and pernicious to the catchpoles and bums, than were formerly the *aurum Tholosanum*[11] and the Sejan horse to those that possessed them. Ever since this, he lived quietly, and Basché's wedding grew into a common proverb.

CHAPTER 16

How Friar John made trial of the nature of the Catchpoles

THIS story would seem pleasant enough, said Pantagruel, were we not to have always the fear of God before our eyes. It had been better, said Epistemon, if those gauntlets had fallen upon the fat prior. Since he took a pleasure in spending his money partly to vex Basché, partly to see those catchpoles banged, good lusty thumps would have done well on his shaven crown, considering the horrid concussions now-a-days among those puny judges. What harm had done those poor devils the catchpoles? This puts me in mind, said Pantagruel, of an ancient Roman named L. Neratius. He was of noble blood, and for some time was rich; but had this tyrannical inclination, that whenever he went out of doors, he caused his servants to fill their pockets with gold and silver, and meeting in the street your spruce gallants and better sort of beaux, without the least provocation, for his fancy, he used to strike them hard on the face with his fist; and immediately after that, to appease them, and hinder them from complaining to the magistrates, he would give them as much money as satisfied them according to the law of the twelve tables. Thus he used to spend his revenue, beating people for the price of his money. By St. Bennet's sacred boot, quoth Friar John, I will know the truth of it presently.

This said, he went on shore, put his hand in his fob, and took out twenty ducats; then said with a loud voice, in the hearing of a shoal of the nation of catchpoles, Who will earn twenty ducats, for being beaten like the devil? Io, Io, Io, said they all: you will cripple us for ever, sir, that is most certain; but the money is tempting. With this they were all thronging who should be first, to be thus preciously beaten. Friar John singled him out of the whole knot of these rogues in grain, a red-snouted catchpole, who upon his right thumb wore a thick broad silver hoop, wherein was set a good large toad-stone. He had no sooner picked him out from the rest, but I perceived that they all muttered and grumbled; and I heard a young thin-jawed catchpole, a notable scholar, a pretty fellow at his pen, and, according to public report, much cried up for his honesty at Doctors-Commons, making his complaint, and muttering, because this same crimson phiz carried away all the practice;

and that if there were but a score and a half of bastinadoes to be got, he would certainly run away with eight and twenty of them. But all this was looked upon to be nothing but mere envy.

Friar John so unmercifully thrashed, thumped, and belaboured Red-snout, back and belly, sides, legs, and arms, head, feet, and so forth, with the home and frequently repeated application of one of the best members of a faggot, that I took him to be a dead man: then he gave him the twenty ducats; which made the dog get on his legs, pleased like a little king or two. The rest were saying to Friar John, Sir, sir, brother devil, if it please you to do us the favour to beat some of us for less money, we are all at your devil-ship's command, bags, papers, pens, and all. Red-snout cried out against them, saying, with a loud voice, Body of me, you little prigs, will you offer to take the bread out of my mouth? will you take my bargain over my head; would you draw and inveigle from me my clients and customers? Take notice, I summon you before the official this day sevennight; I will law and claw you like any old devil of Vauverd, that I will——Then turning himself towards Friar John, with a smiling and joyful look, he said to him, Reverend father in the devil, if you have found me a good hide, and have a mind to divert yourself once more, by beating your humble servant, I will bate you half in half this time, rather than lose your custom: do not spare me, I beseech you: I am all, and more than all yours, good Mr. Devil; head, lungs, tripes, guts, and garbage; and that at a pennyworth, I'll assure you. Friar John never heeded his proffers, but even left them. The other catchpoles were making addresses to Panurge, Epistemon, Gymnast, and others, entreating them charitably to bestow upon their carcasses a small beating, for otherwise they were in danger of keeping a long fast: but none of them had a stomach to it. Some time after, seeking fresh water for the ship's company, we met a couple of old female catchpoles of the place, miserably howling and weeping in concert. Pantagruel had kept on board, and already had caused a retreat to be sounded. Thinking that they might be related to the catchpole that was bastinadoed, we asked them the occasion of their grief. They replied, that they had too much cause to weep; for that very hour from an exalted triple tree, two of the honestest gentlemen in Catchpole-land had

been made to cut a caper on nothing. Cut a caper on nothing; said Gymnast; my pages use to cut capers on the ground: to cut a caper on nothing, should be hanging and choking, or I am out. Ay, ay, said Friar John, you speak of it like St. John de la Palisse.

We asked them why they treated these worthy persons with such a choking hempen sallad. They told us they had only borrowed, *alias* stolen, the tools of the mass, and hid them under the handle of the parish. This is a very allegorical way of speaking, said Epistemon.

CHAPTER 17

How Pantagruel came to the islands of Tohu and Bohu; and of the strange death of Widenostrils, the swallower of Windmills

THAT day Pantagruel came to the two islands of Tohu and Bohu, where the devil a bit we could find any thing to fry with. For one Widenostrils, a huge giant, had swallowed every individual pan, skillet, kettle, frying-pan, dripping-pan, and brass and iron pot in the land, for want of windmills, which were his daily food. Whence it happened, that somewhat before day, about the hour of his digestion, the greedy churl was taken very ill, with a kind of a surfeit, or crudity of stomach, occasioned, as the physicians said, by the weakness of the concocting faculty of his stomach, naturally disposed to digest whole windmills at a gust, yet unable to consume perfectly the pans and skillets; though it had indeed pretty well digested the kettles and pots; as they said, they knew by the hypostases and eneoremes of four tubs of second-hand drink which he had evacuated at two different times that morning. They made use of divers remedies according to art, to give him ease: but all would not do; the distemper prevailed over the remedies, insomuch that the famous Widenostrils died that morning, of so strange a death, that, I think you ought no longer to wonder at that of the poet Æschylus. It had been foretold him by the soothsayers, that he would die on a certain day, by the ruin of something that should fall on him. That fatal day being come in its turn, he removed himself out of town, far from all houses, trees, rocks, or any other things that can fall, and endanger by their ruin; and strayed in a large field, trusting himself to the open sky; there, very secure, as he thought, unless, indeed, the sky should happen to fall, which he held to be impossible. Yet, they say, that the larks are much afraid of it; for if it should fall, they must all be taken.

The Celts that once lived near the Rhine—they are our noble valiant French—in ancient times were also afraid of the sky's falling: for being asked by Alexander the Great, what they feared most in this world, hoping well they would say that they feared none but him, considering his great achievements; they made answer, that they feared nothing but the sky's falling: however, not refusing to enter into a confederacy with so brave a king; if you believe Strabo, *lib.* 7, and Arrian, *lib.* 1.

Plutarch also, in his book of the face that appears on the body of the moon, speaks of one Pharnaces, who very much feared the moon should fall on the earth, and pitied those that live under that planet, as the Æthiopians and Taprobanians, if so heavy a mass ever happened to fall on them; and would have feared the like of heaven and earth, had they not been duly propped up and borne by the atlantic pillars as the ancients believed, according to Aristotle's testimony, *lib.* 5, *Metaphys.* Notwithstanding all this, poor Æschylus was killed by the fall of the shell of a tortoise, which falling from betwixt the claws of an eagle high in the air, just on his head, dashed out his brains.

Neither ought you to wonder at the death of another poet, I mean old jolly Anacreon, who was choked with a grapestone. Nor at that of Fabius the Roman prætor, who was choked with a single goat's hair, as he was supping up a porringer of milk. Nor at the death of that bashful fool, who by holding in his wind, and for want of letting out a bumgunshot, died suddenly in the presence of the Emperor Claudius. Nor at that of the Italian, buried in the *Via Flaminia* at Rome, who, in his epitaph, complains that the bite of a she puss on his little finger was the cause of his death. Nor of that of Q. Lecanius Bassus, who died suddenly of so small a prick with a needle on his left thumb, that it could hardly be discerned. Nor of Quenelault, a Norman physician, who died suddenly at Montpellier, merely for having side-ways took a worm out of his hand with a penknife. Nor of Philomenes, whose servant having got him some new figs for the first course of his dinner, whilst he went to fetch wine, a straggling well-hung ass got into the house, and seeing the figs on the table, without further invita-

tion soberly fell to. Philomenes coming into the room, and nicely observing with what gravity the ass eat its dinner, said to his man, who was come back, Since thou hast set figs here for this reverend guest of ours to eat, methinks it is but reason thou also give him some of this wine to drink. He had no sooner said this, but he was so excessively pleased, and fell into so exorbitant a fit of laughter, that the use of his spleen took that of his breath utterly away, and he immediately died. Nor of Spurius Saufeius, who died supping up a soft boiled egg as he came out of a bath. Nor of him who, as Boccacio tells us, died suddenly by picking his grinders with a sage-stalk. Nor of Phillipot Placut, who being brisk and hale, fell dead as he was paying an old debt; which causes, perhaps, many not to pay theirs, for fear of the like accident. Nor of the painter Zeuxis, who killed himself with laughing at the sight of the antic jobbernol of an old hag drawn by him. Nor, in short, of a thousand more of which authors write; as Varrius, Pliny, Valerius, J. Bapista Fulgosus, and Bacabery the elder. In short, Gaffer Widenostrils choked himself with eating a huge lump of fresh butter at the mouth of a hot oven, by the advice of physicians.

They likewise told us there, that the King of Cullan in Bohu had routed the grandees of King Mecloth, and made sad work with the fortresses of Belima.

After this, we sailed by the islands of Nargues and Zargues; also by the islands of Teleniabin and Geleniabin, very fine and fruitful in ingredients for clysters; and then by the islands of Enig and Evig, on whose account formerly the Landgrave of Hesse was swinged off with a vengeance.

CHAPTER 18

How Pantagruel met with a great storm at sea

THE next day we espied nine sail that came spooning before the wind: they were full of Dominicans, Jesuits, Capuchins, Hermits, Austins, Bernardins, Egnatins, Celestins, Theatins, Amadeans, Cordeliers, Carmelites, Minims, and the devil and all of other holy monks and friars, who were going to the Council of Chesil, to sift and garble some new articles of faith against the new heretics. Panurge was overjoyed to see them, being most certain of good luck for that day, and a long train of others. So having courteously saluted the blessed fathers, and recommended the salvation of his precious soul to their devout prayers and private ejaculations, he caused seventy-eight dozen of Westphalia hams, units of pots of caviare, tens of Bolonia sausages, hundreds of botargoes, and thousands of fine angels, for the souls of the dead, to be thrown on board their ships. Pantagruel seemed metagrabolized, dozing, out of sorts, and as melancholic as a cat. Friar John, who soon perceived it, was inquiring of him whence should come this unusual sadness? when the master, whose watch it was, observing the fluttering of the ancient above the poop, and seeing that it began to overcast, judged that we should have wind; therefore he bid the boatswain call all hands upon deck, officers, sailors, foremast-men, swabbers, and cabin-boys, and even the passengers; made them first settle their top-sails, take in their sprit-sail; then he cried, In with your top-sails, lower the foresail, tallow under the parrels, brade up close all them sails, strike your top-masts to the cap, make all sure with your sheeps-feet, lash your guns fast. All this was nimbly done. Immediately it blowed a storm; the sea began to roar, and swell mountain high; the rut of the sea was great, the waves breaking upon our ship's quarter; the north-west wind blustered and overblowed; boisterous gusts, dreadful clashing and deadly scuds of wind whistled through our yards, and made our shrouds rattle again. The thunder grumbled so horridly, that you would have thought heaven had been tumbling about our ears; at the same time it lightened, rained, hailed, the sky lost its transparent hue, grew dusky, thick, and gloomy, so that we had no other light than that of the flashes of lightning, and rending of the clouds: the hurricanes, flaws, and sudden whirlwinds began to make a flame about us, by the lightnings, fiery vapours, and other aerial ejaculations. Oh how our looks were full of amazement and trouble, while the saucy winds did rudely lift up above us the mountainous waves of the main! Believe me, it seemed to us a lively image of the chaos, where fire, air, sea, land, and all the elements were in a refractory confusion. Poor Panurge having, with the full contents of the inside of his doublet, plentifully fed the fish, greedy enough of such odious fare, sat on the deck all in a heap, with his nose and arse together, most sadly cast down, moping and half dead; invoked and called to his assistance all the blessed he and she saints he could muster up;

swore and vowed to confess in time and place convenient, and then bawled out frightfully, Steward, *maître d'hôtel*, see hoe! my friend, my father, my uncle, prithee let us have a piece of powdered beef or pork; we shall drink but too much anon, for aught I see. Eat little and drink the more, will hereafter be my motto, I fear. Would to our dear Lord, and to our blessed, worthy, and sacred Lady, I were now, I say, this very minute of an hour, well on shore, on *terra firma,* hale and easy. O twice and thrice happy those that plant cabbages! O Destinies, why did you not spin me for a cabbage-planter? O how few are there to whom Jupiter hath been so favourable, as to predestinate them to plant cabbages! They have always one foot on the ground, and the other not far from it. Dispute who will of felicity, and *summum bonum,*[12] for my part, whosoever plants cabbages, is now, by my decree, proclaimed most happy; for as good a reason as the philosopher Pyrrho, being in the same danger, and seeing a hog near the shore, eating some scattered oats, declared it happy in two respects; first, because it had plenty of oats, and besides that, was on shore. Ha, for a divine and princely habitation, commend me to the cow's floor.

Murder! This wave will sweep us away, blessed Saviour! O my friends! a little vinegar. I sweat again with mere agony. Alas, the mizen sail is split, the gallery is washed away, the masts are sprung, the main-top-mast-head dives into the sea; the keel is up to the sun; our shrouds are almost all broke, and blown away. Alas! alas! where is our main course? *Al is verlooren, by Godt;* our top-mast is run adrift. Alas! who shall have this wreck? Friend, lend me here behind you one of these whales. Your lanthorn is fallen, my lads. Alas! do not let go the main tack nor the bowlin. I hear the block crack; is it broke? For the Lord's sake, let us have the hull, and let all the rigging be damned. Be, be, be, bous, bous, bous. Look to the needle of your compass, I beseech you, good Sir Astrophil, and tell us, if you can, whence comes this storm. My heart's sunk down below my midriff. By my troth, I am in a sad fright, bou, bou, bou, bous, bous, I am lost forever. I conskite myself for mere madness and fear. Bou, bou, bou, bou, Otto to to to to ti. Bou, bou, bou, ou, ou, ou, bou, bou, bous. I sink, I am drowned, I am gone, good people, I am drowned.

CHAPTER 19

What countenances Panurge and Friar John kept during the storm

PANTAGRUEL, having first implored the help of the great and Almighty Deliverer, and prayed publicly with fervent devotion, by the pilot's advice held tightly the mast of the ship. Friar John had stripped himself to his waistcoat, to help the seamen. Epistemon, Ponocrates, and the rest did as much. Panurge alone sat on his breech upon deck, weeping and howling. Friar John espied him going on the quarter-deck, and said to him, Odzoons! Panurge the calf, Panurge the whiner, Panurge the brayer, would it not become thee much better to lend us here a helping hand, than to lie lowing like a cow, as thou dost, sitting on thy stones like a bald-breeched baboon? Be, be, be, bous, bous, bous, returned Panurge; Friar John, my friend, my good father, I am drowning, my dear friend! I drown! I am a dead man, my dear father in God, I am a dead man, my friend: your cutting hanger cannot save me from this: alas! alas! we are above *e la*. Above the pitch, out of tune, and off the hinges. Be, be, be, bou, bous. Alas! we are now above *g sol re ut*. I sink, I sink, ha, my father, my uncle, my all. The water is got into my shoes by the collar; bous, bous, bous, paish, hu, hu, hu, he, he, he, ha, ha, ha, I drown. Alas! alas! Hu, hu, hu, hu, hu, hu, hu, be, be, bous, bous, bobous, bobous, ho, ho, ho, ho, alas! alas! Now I am like your tumblers, my feet stand higher than my head. Would to heaven I were now with those good holy fathers bound for the council, whom we met this morning, so godly, so fat, so merry, so plump, and comely. Holos, nolos, holas, holas, alas! This devilish wave, (*mea culpa Deus*,)[13] I mean this wave of God, will sink our vessel. Alas, Friar John, my father, my friend, confession. Here I am down on my knees; *confiteor*;[14] your holy blessing. Come hither and be damned, thou pitiful devil, and help us, said Friar,—who fell a swearing and cursing like a tinker,—in the name of thirty legions of black devils, come; will you come? Do not let us swear, at this time, said Panurge; holy father, my friend, do not swear, I beseech you; to-morrow as much as you please, Holos, holos, alas, our ship leaks. I drown, alas, alas! I will give eighteen hundred thousand crowns to any one that will set me on shore, all bewrayed and bedaubed as I am now. If ever

there was a man in my country in the like pickle. *Confiteor*, alas! a word or two of testament or codicil at least. A thousand devils seize the cuckoldy cow-hearted mongrel, cried Friar John. Ods belly, art thou talking here of making thy will, now we are in danger, and it behoveth us to bestir our stumps lustily, or never? Wilt thou come, ho devil? Midshipman, my friend; O the rare lieutenant; here Gymnast, here on the poop. We are, by the mass, all beshit now, our light is out. This is hastening to the devil as fast as it can. Alas, bou, bou, bou, bou, bou, alas, alas, alas, alas, said Panurge, was it here we were born to perish? Oh! ho! good people I drown, I die. *Consummatum est*.[15] I am sped—*Magna, gna, gna*, said Friar John. Fie upon him, how ugly the shitten howler looks. Boy, younker, see hoyh. Mind the pumps, or the devil choke thee. Hast thou hurt thyself? Zoons, here fasten it to one of these blocks. On this side, in the devil's name, hay—so my boy. Ah, Friar John, said Panurge, good ghostly father, dear friend, do not let us swear, you sin. Oh, ho, oh, ho, be be be bous, bous, bhous, I sink, I die, my friends. I die in charity with all the world. Farewell, *in manus*.[16] Bohus, bohous, bhousowauswaus. St. Michael of Aure! St. Nicholas! now, now or never, I here make you a solemn vow, and to our Saviour, that if you stand by me this time, I mean if you set me ashore out of this danger, I will built you a fine large little chapel or two, between Candé and Monsoreau, where neither cow nor calf shall feed. Oh ho, oh ho. Above eighteen pailfuls or two of it are got down my gullet; bous, bhous, bhous, bhous, how damned bitter and salt it is! By the virtue, said Friar John, of the blood, the flesh, the belly, the head, if I hear thee again howling, thou cuckoldy cur, I will maul thee worse than any sea wolf. Ods fish, why do not we take him up by the lugs and throw him overboard to the bottom of the sea? Here, sailor, ho honest fellow. Thus, thus, my friend, hold fast above. In truth here is a sad lightning and thundering; I think that all the devils are got loose; it is holiday with them; or else Madame Proserpine is in child's labour: all the devils dance a morrice.

CHAPTER 20

How the Pilots were forsaking their ships in the greatest stress of weather

OH, said Panurge, you sin, Friar John, my former crony! former, I say, for at this time I am no more, you are no more. It goes against my heart to tell it you: for I believe this swearing doth your spleen a great deal of good; as it is a great ease to a wood cleaver to cry hem at every blow; and as one who plays at nine pins is wonderfully helped, if, when he hath not thrown his bowl right, and is like to make a bad cast, some ingenious stander by leans and screws his body half way about, on that side which the bowl should have took to hit the pin. Nevertheless you offend, my sweet friend. But what do you think of eating some kind of cabirotadoes? Would not this secure us from this storm? I have read, that in a storm at sea no harm ever befel the ministers of the gods Cabiri, so much celebrated by Orpheus, Apollonius, Pherecides, Strabo, Pausanias, and Herodotus. He dotes, he raves, the poor devil! A thousand, a million, nay, a hundred million of devils seize the hornified doddipole. Lend us a hand here, hoh, tiger, wouldst thou? Here, on the starboard side. Ods me, thou buffalo's head stuffed with relics, what ape's paternoster art thou muttering and chattering here between thy teeth? That devil of a sea calf is the cause of all this storm, and is the only man who doth not lend a helping hand. By G—, if I come near thee, I'll fetch thee out by the head and ears with a vengeance, and chastise thee like any tempestative devil. Here mate, my lad, hold fast, till I have made a double knot. O brave boy! Would to heaven thou wert abbot of Talemouze, and that he that is were guardian of Croullay. Hold, brother Ponocrates, you will hurt yourself man. Epistemon, pray thee stand off out of the hatchway. Methinks I saw the thunder fall there but just now. Con the ship, so ho—Mind your steerage. Well said, thus, thus, steady, keep her thus, get the long boat clear—steady. Ods fish, the beak-head is staved to pieces. Grumble, devils, fart, belch, shite, a turd on the wave. If this be weather, the devil is a ram. Nay, by G—, a little more would have washed me clear away into the current. I think all the legions of devils hold here their provincial chapter, or are polling, canvassing, and wrangling for the election of a new rector. Starboard; well said. Take heed; have a care of your noddle, lad, in the devil's name So ho, starboard, starboard. Be be, be, bous, bous, bous, cried Panurge, bous, bous, be, be, be, bous, bous, I am lost. I see neither heaven nor earth; of the four elements we have here only fire and water left. Bou, bou, bou, bous, bous,

bous. Would it were the pleasure of the worthy divine bounty, that I were at this present hour in the close at Sevillé, or at Innocent's, the pastry-cook, over against the painted wine vault at Chinon, though I were to strip to my doublet, and bake the pettipasties myself.

Honest man, could not you throw me ashore? you can do a world of good things, they say I give you all Salmigondinois, and my large shore full of whilks, cockles, and periwinkles, if, by your industry, I ever set foot on firm ground. Alas, alas, I drown. Harkee, my friends, since we cannot get safe into port, let us come to an anchor into some road, no matter whither. Drop all your anchors; let us be out of danger, I beseech you. Here honest tar, get you into the chains, and heave the lead, if it please you. Let us know how many fathom water we are in. Sound, friend, in the Lord Harry's name. Let us know whether a man might here drink easily, without stooping. I am apt to believe one might. Helm a-lee, hoh, cried the pilot. Helm-a lee; a hand or two at the helm; about ships with her; helm a-lee; helm a-lee. Stand off from the leech of the sail. Hoh! belay, here make fast below; hoh, helm a-lee, lash sure the helm a-lee, and let her drive. Is it come to that? said Pantagruel: our Saviour then help us. Let her lie under the sea, cried James Brahier, our chief mate, let her drive. To prayers, to prayers, let all think on their souls, and fall to prayers; nor hope to escape but by a miracle. Let us, said Panurge, make some good pious kind of vow: alas, alas, alas! bou, bou, be, be, be, bous, bous, bous, oho, oho, oho, oho, let us make a pilgrim: come, come, let every man club his penny towards it, come on. Here, here, on this side, said Friar John, in the devil's name. Let her drive, for the Lord's sake unhang the rudder: hoh, let her drive, let her drive, and let us drink, I say, of the best and most cheering; do you hear, steward, produce, exhibit; for, do you see this, and all the rest will as well go to the devil out of hand. A pox on that wind-broker Æolus, with his fluster-blusters. Sirrah, page, bring me here my drawer (for so he called his breviary); stay a little here, haul, friend, thus. Odzoons, here is a deal of hail and thunder to no purpose. Hold fast above, I pray you. When have we All-saints day? I believe it is the unholy holiday of all the devil's crew. Alas, said Panurge, Friar John damns himself here as black as buttermilk for the nonce. Oh what a good friend I lose in him. Alas, alas, this is another gats-bout than last year's. We are falling out of Scylla into Charybdis. Oho! I drown. *Confiteor;* one poor word or two by way of testament, Friar John, my ghostly father; good Mr. Abstractor, my crony, my Achates, Xenomanes, my all. Alas! I drown; two words of testament here upon this ladder.

CHAPTER 21

A continuation of the storm, with a short discourse on the subject of making testaments at sea

To make one's last will, said Epistemon, at this time that we ought to bestir ourselves and help our seamen, on the penalty of being drowned, seems to me as idle and ridiculous a maggot as that of some of Cæsar's men, who, at their coming into the Gauls, were mightily busied in making wills and codicils; bemoaned their fortune, and the absence of their spouses and friends at Rome; when it was absolutely necessary for them to run to their arms, and use their utmost strength against Ariovistus their enemy.

This also is to be as silly, as that jolt-headed loblolly of a carter, who, having laid his waggon fast in a slough, down on his marrow-bones, was calling on the strong-backed deity, Hercules, might and main, to help him at a dead lift, but all the while forgot to goad on his oxen, and lay his shoulder to the wheels, as it behoved him: as if a Lord have mercy upon us, alone, would have got his cart out of the mire.

What will it signify to make your will now? for either we shall come off or drown for it. If we escape, it will not signify a straw to us; for testaments are of no value or authority, but by the death of the testators. If we are drowned, will it not be drowned too? Pr'ythee who will transmit it to the executors? Some kind wave will throw it ashore, like Ulysses, replied Panurge; and some king's daughter, going to fetch a walk in the fresco, on the evening, will find it, and take care to have it proved and fulfilled; nay, and have some stately cenotaph erected to my memory, as Dido had to that of her good man Sichæus; Æneas to Deiphobus, upon the Trojan shore, near Rhœte! Andromache to Hector, in the city of Buthrotus; Aristotle to Hermias and Eubulus; the Athenians to the poet Euripides; the Romans to Drusus in Germany,

and to Alexander Severus, their emperor, in the Gauls; Argentier to Callaischre; Xenocrates to Lysidices; Timares to his son Teleutagoras; Eupolis and Aristodice to their son Theotimus; Onestus to Timocles; Callimachus to Sopolis, the son of Dioclides; Catullus to his brother; Statius to his father; Germain of Brie to Hervé, the Breton tarpaulin. Art thou mad, said Friar John, to run on at this rate? Help, here, in the name of five hundred thousand millions of cart-loads of devils, help! may a shanker gnaw thy moustachios, and the three rows of pock-royals and cauliflowers cover thy bum and turd-barrel, instead of breeches and cod-piece. Codsooks our ship is almost overset. Ods death, how shall we clear her? it is well if she do not founder. What a devilish sea there runs! She will neither try nor hull; the sea will overtake her, so we shall never escape; the devil escape me. Then Pantagruel was heard to make a sad exclamation, saying, with a loud voice, Lord save us, we perish; yet not as we would have it, but thy holy will be done. The Lord and the blessed Virgin be with us, said Panurge. Holos, alas, I drown; be be be bous, be bous, bous: *in manus.* Good heavens, send me some dolphin to carry me safe on shore, like a pretty little Arion. I shall make shift to sound the harp, if it be not unstrung. Let nineteen legions of black devils seize me, said Friar John, (the Lord be with us, whispered Panurge, between his chattering teeth.) If I come down to thee, I will show thee to some purpose, that the badge of thy humanity dangles at a calf's breech, thou ragged, horned, cuckoldy booby: mgna, mgnan, mgnan: come hither and help us, thou great weeping calf, or may thirty millions of devils leap on thee. Wilt thou come, sea-calf? Fie! how ugly the howling whelp looks. What, always the same ditty? Come on now, my bonny drawer. This he said, opening his breviary. Come forward, thou and I must be somewhat serious for a while; let me peruse thee stiffly. *Beatus vir qui non abiit.*[17] Pshaw, I know all this by heart; let us see the legend of Mons. St. Nicholas.

Horrida tempestas montem turbavit acutum. [18]

Tempeste was a mighty flogger of lads, at Mountaigu College. If pendants be damned for whipping poor little innocent wretches their scholars, he is, upon my honour, by this time fixed within Ixion's wheel, lashing the crop-eared, bob-tailed cur that gives it motion. If they are saved for having whipped innocent lads, he ought to be above the——

CHAPTER 22

An end of the storm

SHORE, shore! cried Pantagruel. Land ho, my friends, I see land! Pluck up a good spirit, boys, it is within a kenning. So! we are not far from a port.—I see the sky clearing up to the northwards.—Look to the south-east! Courage, my hearts, said the pilot; now she will bear the hullock of a sail: the sea is much smoother; some hands aloft to the main top. Put the helm a-weather. Steady! steady! Haul your after mizen bowlings. Haul, haul, haul! Thus, thus, and no near. Mind your steerage; bring your main tack aboard Clear your sheets; clear your bowlings; port, port. Helm a-lee. Now to the sheet on the starboard side, thou son of a whore. Thou art mightily pleased, honest fellow, quoth Friar John, with hearing make mention of thy mother. Luff, luff, cried the quartermaster that conned the ship, keep her full, luff the helm. Luff. It is, answered the steersman. Keep her thus. Get the bonnets fixed. Steady, steady.

That is well said, said Friar John; now, this is something like a tansey. Come, come, come, children, be nimble. Good. Luff, luff, thus. Helm a-weather. That is well said and thought on. Methinks the storm is almost over. It was high time, faith: however, the Lord be thanked. Our devils begin to scamper. Out with all your sails. Hoist your sails. Hoist. That is spoke like a man, hoist, hoist. Here, a God's name, honest Ponocrates; thou art a lusty fornicator; the whoreson will get none but boys. Eusthenes, thou art a notable fellow. Run up to the fore-top sail. Thus, thus. Well said, i' faith; thus, thus. I dare not fear anything all this while, for it is holiday. Vea, vea, vea! huzza! This shout of the seaman is not amiss, and pleases me, for it is holiday. Keep her full thus. Good. Cheer up my merry mates, all, cried out Epistemon; I see already Castor on the right. Be, be, bous, bous, bous, said Panurge, I am much afraid it is the bitch Helen. It is truly Mixarchagenas, returned Epistemon, if thou likest better that denomination, which the Argives give him. Ho, ho! I see land too; let her bear in with the harbour: I see a good many people on the beach: I see a light on an obeliscolychny.

Shorten your sails, said the pilot; fetch the sounding line; we must double that point of land, and mind the sands. We are clear of them, said the sailors. Soon after, Away she goes, quoth the pilot, and so doth the rest of our fleet; help came in good season.

By St. John, said Panurge, this is spoke somewhat like: O the sweet word! there is the soul of music in it. Mgna, mgna, mgna, said Friar John; if ever thou taste a drop of it, let the devil's dam taste me, thou ballocky devil. Here, honest soul, here is a full sneaker of the very best. Bring the flagons: dost hear, Gymnast? and that same large pasty jambic, or gammonic, even as you will have it. Take heed you pilot her in right.

Cheer up, cried out Pantagruel; cheer up my boys: let us be ourselves again. Do you see yonder, close by our ship, two barks, three sloops, five ships, eight pinks, four yawls, and six frigates, making towards us, sent by the good people of the neighbouring island to our relief? But who is this Ucalegon below, that cried, and makes such a sad moan? Were it not that I hold the mast firmly with both my hands, and keep it straighter than two hundred tacklings—I would——It is, said Friar John, that poor devil, Panurge, who is troubled with a calf's ague; he quakes for fear when his belly is full. If, said Pantagruel, he hath been afraid during this dreadful hurricane and dangerous storm, provided he hath done his part like a man, I do not value him a jot the less for it. For as, to fear in all encounters, is the mark of a heavy and cowardly heart; as Agamemnon did, who, for that reason, is ignominiously taxed by Achilles with having dog's eyes, and a stag's heart: so, not to fear when the case is evidently dreadful, is a sign of want or smallness of judgment. Now, if anything ought to be feared in this life, next to offending God, I will not say it is death. I will not meddle with the disputes of Socrates and the academics, that death of itself is neither bad nor to be feared; but, I will affirm, that this kind of shipwreck is to be feared, or nothing is. For, as Homer saith, it is a grievous, dreadful, and unnatural thing, to perish at sea. And, indeed, Æneas, in the storm that took his fleet near Sicily, was grieved that he had not died by the hand of the brave Diomedes; and said that those were three, nay four times happy, who perished in the conflagration at Troy. No man here hath lost his life, the Lord our Saviour be eternally praised for it: but in truth here is a ship sadly out of order. Well, we must take care to have the damage repaired. Take heed we do not run aground and bulge her.

CHAPTER 23

How Panurge played the good fellow when the storm was over

WHAT cheer, ho, fore and aft? quoth Panurge. Oh ho! all is well, the storm is over. I beseech ye, be so kind as to let me be the first that is sent on shore; for I would by all means a little untruss a point. Shall I help you still? Here, let me see, I will coil this rope; I have plenty of courage, and of fear as little as may be. Give it me yonder, honest tar. No, no, I have not a bit of fear. Indeed, that same decumane wave, that took us fore and aft, somewhat altered my pulse. Down with your sails; well said. How now, Friar John? you do nothing. Is it time for us to drink now? Who can tell but St. Martin's running footman may still be hatching us some further mischief? shall I come and help you again? Pork and peas choke me, if I do heartily repent, though too late, not having followed the doctrine of the good philosopher, who tells us that to walk by the sea, and to navigate by the shore, are very safe and pleasant things: just as it is to go on foot, when we hold our horse by the bridle. Ha! ha! ha! by G— all goes well. Shall I help you here too? Let me see, I will do this as it should be, or the devil is in it.

Epistemon, who had the inside of one of his hands all flayed and bloody, having held a tackling with might and main, hearing what Pantagruel had said, told him: You may believe me, lord, I had my share of fear as well as Panurge; yet I spared no pains in lending my helping hand. I considered, that since by fatal and unavoidable necessity, we must all die, it is the blessed will of God that we die this or that hour, and this or that kind of death: nevertheless we ought to implore, invoke, pray, beseech, and supplicate him: but we must not stop there; it behoveth us also to use our endeavours on our side, and, as the holy writ saith, to co-operate with him.

You know what C. Flaminius, the consul said, when by Hannibal's policy he was penned up near the lake of Peruse, alias Thrasymene. Friends, said he to his soldiers, you must not hope to get out of this place

barely by vows or prayers to the gods; no, it is by fortitude and strength we must escape and cut ourselves a way with the edge of our swords through the midst of our enemies.

Sallust likewise makes M. Portius Cato say this: The help of the gods is not obtained by idle vows and womanish complaints; it is by vigilance, labour, and repeated endeavours, that all things succeed according to our wishes and designs. If a man, in time of need and danger, is negligent, heartless, and lazy, in vain he implores the gods; they are then justly angry and incensed against him. The devil take me, said Friar John (I'll go his halves, quoth Panurge), if the close of Sevillé had not been all gathered, vintaged, gleaned, and destroyed, if I had only sung *contra hostium insidias*[19] (matter of breviary) like all the rest of the monkish devils, and had not bestirred myself to save the vineyard as I did, dispatching the truant picaroons of Lerné with the staff of the cross.

Let her sink or swim a God's name, said Panurge, all's one to Friar John; he doth nothing; his name is Friar John Dolittle; for all he sees me here sweating and puffing to help with all my might this honest tar, first of the name.—Hark you me, dear soul, a word with you,—but pray be not angry. How thick do you judge the planks of our ship to be? Some two good inches and upwards, returned the pilot; don't fear. Odskilderkins, said Panurge, it seems then we are within two fingers' breadth of damnation.

Is this one of the nine comforts of matrimony? Ah, dear soul, you do well to measure the danger by the yard of fear. For my part, I have none on't; my name is William Dreadnought. As for my heart, I have more than enough on't; I mean none of your sheep's heart; but of wolf's heart; the courage of a bravo. By the pavilion of Mars, I fear nothing but danger.

CHAPTER 24

How Panurge was said to have been afraid without reason, during the storm

GOOD morrow, gentlemen said Panurge, good morrow to you all: you are in very good health, thanks to heaven and yourselves; you are all heartily welcome, and in good time. Let us go on shore.—Here cockswain, get the ladder over the gunnel; man the sides: man the pinnace, and get her by the ship's side. Shall I lend you a hand here? I am stark mad for want of business, and would work like any two yokes of oxen. Truly this is a fine place, and these look like a very good people. Children, do you want me still in anything? do not spare the sweat of my body, for God's sake. Adam—this is man—was made to labour and work, as the birds were made to fly. Our Lord's will is, that we get our bread with the sweat of our brows, not idling and doing nothing, like this tatterdamallion of a monk here, this Friar Jack, who is fain to drink to hearten himself up, and dies for fear.—Rare weather.—I now find the answer of Anacharsis, the noble philosopher, very proper: being asked what ship he reckoned the safest? he replied, That which is in the harbour. He made yet a better repartee, said Pantagruel, when somebody inquiring which is greater, the number of the living or that of the dead? he asked them, amongst which of the two they reckoned those that are at sea? ingeniously implying, that they are continually in danger of death, dying live, and living die. Portius Cato also said, that there were but three things of which he would repent; if ever he had trusted his wife with his secret, if he had idled away a day, and if he had ever gone by sea to a place which he could visit by land. By this dignified frock of mine, said Friar John to Panurge, friend, thou hast been afraid during the storm, without cause or reason: for thou wert not born to be drowned, but rather to be hanged, and exalted in the air, or to be roasted in the midst of a jolly bonfire. My lord, would you have a good cloak for the rain; leave me off your wolf and badger-skin mantle: let Panurge but be flayed, and cover yourself with his hide. But do not come near the fire, nor near your blacksmith's forges, a God's name; for in a moment you will see it in ashes. Yet be as long as you please in the rain, snow, hail, nay by the devil's maker, throw yourself, or dive down to the very bottom of the water, I'll engage you'll not be wet at all. Have some winter boots made of it, they'll never take in a drop of water: make bladders of it to lay under boys, to teach them to swim, instead of corks, and they will learn without the least danger. His skin, then, said Pantagruel, should be like the herb called true maiden's hair, which never takes wet nor moistness, but still keeps dry, though you lay it at the bottom of the water as long as you please; and for that reason is called *Adiantos*.

Friend Panurge, said Friar John, I pray thee never be afraid of water: thy life for mine thou art threatened with a contrary element. Ay, ay, replied Panurge, but the devil's cooks dote sometimes, and are apt to make horrid blunders as well as others: often putting to boil in water, what was designed to be roasted on the fire: like the head cooks of our kitchen, who often lard partridges, queests, and stock-doves, with intent to roast them, one would think; but it happens sometimes, that they even turn the partridges into the pot, to be boiled with cabbages, the queests with leek pottage, and the stock-doves with turnips. But hark you me, good friends, I protest before this noble company, that as for the chapel which I vowed to Mons. St. Nicholas, between, Candé and Monsoreau, I honestly mean that it shall be a chapel of rose-water, which shall be where neither cow nor calf shall be fed: for between you and I, I intend to throw it to the bottom of the water. Here is a rare rogue for you, said Eusthenes: here is a pure rogue, a rogue in grain, a rogue enough, a rogue and a half. He is resolved to make good the Lombardic proverb, *Passato il pericolo, gabbato il santo.*

The devil was sick, the devil a monk would be
The devil was well, the devil a monk was he.

CHAPTER 25

How, after the storm, Pantagruel went on shore in the Island of the Macreons

IMMEDIATELY after, he went ashore at the port of an island which they called the island of the Macreons. The good people of the place received us very honourably. An old Macrobius (so they called their eldest elderman) desired Pantagruel to come to the town-house to refresh himself, and eat something: but he would not budge a foot from the mole till all his men were landed. After he had seen them, he gave order that they should all change clothes, and that some of all the stores in the fleet should be brought on shore, that every ship's crew might live well: which was accordingly done, and God wot how well they all toped and caroused. The people of the place brought them provisions in abundance. The Pantagruelists returned them more: as the truth is their's were somewhat damaged by the late storm. When they had well-stuffed the insides of their doublets, Pantagruel desired every one to lend their help to repair the damage; which they readily did. It was easy enough to refit there; for all the inhabitants of the island were carpenters, and all such handicrafts as are seen in the arsenal at Venice. None but the largest island was inhabited, having three ports and ten parishes; the rest being overrun with wood, and desert, much like the forest of Arden. We entreated the old Macrobius to show us what was worth seeing in the island; which he did; and in the desert and dark forest we discovered several old ruined temples, obelisks, pyramids, monuments, and ancient tombs, with divers inscriptions and epitaphs; some of them in hieroglyphic characters; others in the Ionic dialect; some in the Arabic, Agarenian, Sclavonian, and other tongues; of which Epistemon took an exact account. In the interim, Panurge said to Friar John, Is this the island of the Macreons? Macreon signifies in Greek an old man, or one much stricken in years. What is that to me, said Friar John, how can I help it? I was not in the country when they christened it. Now I think on it, quoth Panurge, I believe the name of mackerel (that is a bawd in French) was derived from it: for procuring is the province of the old, as buttock-riggling is that of the young. Therefore I do not know but this may be the bawdy or Mackerel island, the original and prototype of the island of that name at Paris. Let us go and dredge for cock-oysters. Old Macrobius asked, in the Ionic tongue, How, and by what industry and labour, Pantagruel got to their port that day, there having been such blustering weather, and such a dreadful storm at sea. Pantagruel told him that the Almighty Preserver of mankind had regarded the simplicity and sincere affection of his servants, who did not travel for gain or sordid profit; the sole design of their voyage being a studious desire to know, see, and visit the Oracle of Bacbuc, and take the word of the Bottle upon some difficulties offered by one of the company: nevertheless this had not been without great affliction, and evident danger of shipwreck. After that, he asked him what he judged to be the cause of that terrible tempest, and if the adjacent seas were thus frequently subject to storms; as in the ocean are the Ratz of Sammaieu, Maumusson, and in the Mediterranean sea the gulph of Sataly, Montargentan, Piombino, Capo Melio in Laconia, the Straits of Gibraltar, Faro di Messina, and others.

CHAPTER 26

How the good Macrobius gave us an account of the Mansion and Decease of the Heroes

THE good Macrobius then answered,— Friendly strangers, this island is one of the Sporades; not of your Sporades that lie in the Carpathian sea, but one of the Sporades of the ocean: in former times rich, frequented, wealthy, populous, full of traffic, and in the dominions of the rulers of Britain, but now, by course of time, and in these latter ages of the world, poor and desolate, as you see. In this dark forest, above seventy-eight thousand Persian leagues in compass, is the dwelling-place of the demons and heroes, that are grown old, and we believed that some one of them died yesterday; since the comet, which we saw for three days before together, shines no more: and now it is likely, that at his death there arose this horrible storm; for while they are alive all happiness attends both this and the adjacent islands, and a settled calm and serenity. At the death of every one of them, we commonly hear in the forest, loud and mournful groans, and the whole land is infested with pestilence, earthquakes, inundations, and other calamities; the air with fogs and obscurity, and the sea with storms and hurricanes. What you tell us, seems to me likely enough, said Pantagruel. For, as a torch or candle, as long as it hath life enough and is lighted, shines round about, disperses its light, delights those that are near it, yields them its service and clearness, and never causes any pain or displeasure; but as soon as it is extinguished, its smoke and evaporation infect the air, offend the by-standers, and are noisome to all: so, as long as those noble and renowned souls inhabit their bodies, peace, profit, pleasure, and honour never leave the places where they abide; but as soon as they leave them, both the continent and adjacent islands are annoyed with great commotions; in the air fogs, darkness, thunder, hail; tremblings, pulsations, agitations of the earth; storms and hurricanes at sea; together with sad complaints amongst the people, broaching of religions, changes in governments, and ruins of commonwealths.

We had a sad instance of this lately, said Epistemon, at the death of that valiant and learned knight, William du Bellay; during whose life France enjoyed so much happiness, that all the rest of the world looked upon it with envy, sought friendship with it, and stood in awe of its power; but now, after his decease, it hath for a considerable time been the scorn of the rest of the world.

Thus, said Pantagruel, Anchises being dead at Drepani, in Sicily, Æneas was dreadfully tossed and endangered by a storm; and perhaps for the same reason, Herod, that tyrant and cruel King of Judea, finding himself near the passage of a horrid kind of death,—for he died of a phthiriasis, devoured by vermin and lice; as before him died L. Sylla, Pherecydes, the Syrian, the preceptor of Pythagoras, the Greek poet Alcmæon, and others,—and foreseeing that the Jews would make bonfires at his death, caused all the nobles and magistrates to be summoned to his seraglio, out of all the cities, towns, and castles of Judea, fraudulently pretending that he had some things of moment to impart to them. They made their personal appearance; whereupon he caused them all to be shut up in the hippodrome of the seraglio; then said to his sister Salome, and Alexander her husband: I am certain that the Jews will rejoice at my death; but if you will observe and perform what I tell you, my funeral shall be honourable, and there will be a general mourning. As soon as you see me dead, let my guards, to whom I have already given strict commission to that purpose, kill all the noblemen and magistrates that are secured in the hippodrome. By these means, all Jewry shall, in spite of themselves, be obliged to mourn and lament, and foreigners will imagine it to be for my death, as if some heroic soul had left her body. A desperate tyrant wished as much when he said, When I die, let earth and fire be mixed together; which was as good as to say, let the whole world perish. Which saying the tyrant Nero altered, saying, While I live, as Suetonius affirms it. This detestable saying, of which Cicero, *lib. De Finib.* and Seneca, *lib.* 2, *De Clementia*, make mention, is ascribed to the Emperor Tiberius, by Dion Nicæus and Suidas.

CHAPTER 27

Pantagruel's discourse of the decease of heroic souls; and of the dreadful prodigies that happened before the death of the late Lord de Langey

I would not, continued Pantagruel, have missed the storm that hath thus disordered us, were I also to have missed the relation of these things told us by this good Macrobius.

Neither am I unwilling to believe what he said of a comet that appears in the sky some days before such a decease. For some of these souls are so noble, so precious, and so heroic that heaven gives us notice of their departing some days before it happens. And as a prudent physician, seeing by some symptoms that his patient draws towards his end, some days before, gives notice of it to his wife, children, kindred, and friends, that, in that little time he hath yet to live, they may admonish him to settle all things in his family, to tutor and instruct his children as much as he can, recommend his relict to his friends in her widowhood, and declare what he knows to be necessary about a provision for the orphans; that he may not be surprised by death without making his will, and may take care of his soul and family: in the same manner the heavens, as it were, joyful for the approaching reception of those blessed souls, seem to make bonfires by those comets and blazing meteors, which they at the same time kindly design should prognosticate to us here, that in a few days one of those venerable souls is to leave her body, and this terrestrial globe. Not altogether unlike this was what was formerly done at Athens, by the judges of the Areopagus. For when they gave their verdict to cast or clear the culprits that were tried before them, they used certain notes according to the substance of the sentences; by Θ, signifying sentence to death; by T, absolution; by A, ampliation or a demur, when the case was not sufficiently examined. Thus having publicly set up those letters, they eased the relations and friends of the prisoners, and such others as desired to know their doom, of their doubts. Likewise by these comets, as in ætherial characters, the heavens silently say to us, Make haste mortals, if you would know or learn of the blessed souls any thing concerning the public good, or your private interest; for their catastrophe is near, which being past, you will vainly wish for them afterwards.

The good-natured heavens still do more: and that mankind may be declared unworthy of the enjoyment of those renowned souls, they fright and astonish us with prodigies, monsters, and other foreboding signs, that thwart the order of nature.

Of this we had an instance several days before the decease of the heroic soul of the learned and valiant Chevalier de Langey, of whom you have already spoken. I remember it, said Epistemon; and my heart still trembles within me, when I think on the many dreadful prodigies that we saw five or six days before he died. For the Lords D'Assier, Chemant, one-eyed Mailly, St. Ayl, Villeneufve-la-Guart, Master Gabriel, physician of Savillan, Rabelais, Cohuau, Massuau, Majorici, Ballou, Cercu alias Bourgmaistre, Francis Proust, Ferron, Charles Girard, Francis Bourré, and many other friends and servants to the deceased, all dismayed, gazed on each other without uttering one word; yet not without foreseeing that France would in a short time be deprived of a knight so accomplished, and necessary for its glory and protection, and that heaven claimed him again as its due. By the tufted tip of my cowl, cried Friar John, I am even resolved to become a scholar before I die. I have a pretty good head-piece of my own, you must confess. Now pray give me leave to ask a civil question. Can these same heroes or demigods you talk of, die? May I never be damned, if I was not so much a lobcock as to believe they had been immortal, like so many fine angels. Heaven forgive me! but this most reverend father, Macrobius, tells us they die at last. Not all, returned Pantagruel.

The stoics held them all to be mortal, except one, who alone is immortal, impassable, invisible. Pindar plainly saith, that there is no more thread, that is to say, no more life, spun from the distaff and flax of the hard-hearted fates for the goddesses Hamadryades, than there is for those trees that are preserved by them, which are good, sturdy, downright oaks; whence they derived their original, according to the opinion of Callimachus, and Pausanias *in Phoci.* With whom concurs Martianus Capella. As for the demigods, fauns, satyrs, sylvans, hobgoblins, ægipanes, nymphs, heroes, and demons, several men have, from the total sum, which is the result of the divers ages calculated by Hesiod, reckoned their life to be 9720 years: that sum consisting of four special numbers orderly arising from one, the same added together, and multiplied by four every way, amounts to forty; these forties, being reduced into triangles by five times, make up the total of the aforesaid number. See Plutarch, in his book about the *Cessation of Oracles.*

This, said Friar John, is not matter of breviary; I may believe as little or as much of it as you and I please. I believe, said Pantagruel, that all intellectual souls are exempted

from Atropos's scissors. They are all immortal, whether they be of angels, of demons, or human: yet I will tell you a story concerning this, that is very strange, but is written and affirmed by several learned historians.

CHAPTER 28

How Pantagruel related a very sad story of the Death of the Heroes

EPITHERSES, the father of Æmilian the rhetorician, sailing from Greece to Italy, in a ship freighted with divers goods and passengers, at night the wind failed them near the Echinades, some islands that lie between the Morea and Tunis, and the vessel was driven near Paxos. When they got thither, some of the passengers being asleep, others awake, the rest eating and drinking, a voice was heard that called aloud, Thamous! which cry surprised them all. This same Thamous was their pilot, an Egyptian by birth, but known by name only to some few travellers. The voice was heard a second time, calling Thamous, in a frightful tone; and none making answer, but trembling, and remaining silent, the voice was heard a third time, more dreadful than before.

This caused Thamous to answer: Here am I; what dost thou call me for? What wilt thou have me do? Then the voice, louder than before, bid him publish, when he should come to Palodes, that the great god Pan was dead.

Epitherses related that all the mariners and passengers, having heard this, were extremely amazed and frighted; and that consulting among themselves, whether they had best conceal or divulge what the voice had enjoined; Thamous said, his advice was, that if they happened to have a fair wind, they should proceed without mentioning a word of it, but if they chanced to be becalmed, he would publish what he had heard. Now when they were near Palodes, they had no wind, neither were they in any current. Thamous then getting up on the top of the ship's forecastle and casting his eyes on the shore, said that he had been commanded to proclaim that the great god Pan was dead. The words were hardly out of his mouth, when deep groans, great lamentations, and doleful shrieks, not of one person, but of many together, were heard from the land.

The news of this—many being present— was soon spread at Rome; insomuch that Tiberius, who was then emperor, sent for this

Thamous, and having heard him, gave credit to his words. And inquiring of the learned in his court, and at Rome, who was that Pan? he found by their relation that he was the son of Mercury and Penelope, as Herodotus and Cicero in his third book of *The Nature of the Gods* had written before.

For my part, I understand it of that great Saviour of the faithful, who was shamefully put to death at Jerusalem, by the envy and wickedness of the doctors, priests, and monks of the Mosaic law. And methinks, my interpretation is not improper; for he may lawfully be said in the Greek tongue to be *Pan,* since he is our *all.* For all that we are, all that we live, all that we have, all that we hope, is him, by him, from him, and in him. He is the god Pan, the great shepherd, who, as the loving shepherd Corydon affirms, hath not only a tender love and affection for his sheep, but also for their shepherds. At his death, complaints, sighs, fears, and lamentations were spread through the whole fabric of the universe, whether heavens, land, sea or hell.

The time also concurs with this interpretation of mine; for this most good, most mighty Pan, our only Saviour, died near Jerusalem, during the reign of Tiberius Cæsar.

Pantagruel, having ended this discourse, remained silent, and full of contemplation. A little while after, we saw the tears flow out of his eyes as big as ostrich's eggs. God take me presently, if I tell you one single syllable of a lie in the matter.

CHAPTER 29

How Pantagruel sailed by the Sneaking Island, where Shrovetide reigned

THE jovial fleet being refitted and repaired, new stores taken in, the Macreons over and above satisfied and pleased with the money spent there by Pantagruel, our men in better humour than they used to be, if possible, we merrily put to sea the next day, near sunset, with a delicious fresh gale.

Xenomanes showed us afar off the Sneaking Island, where reigned Shrovetide of whom Pantagruel had heard much talk formerly: for that reason he would gladly have seen him in person, had not Xenomanes advised him to the contrary: first, because this would have been much out of our way: and then for the lean cheer, (*manger maigre,*) which he told us was to be found at that prince's court, and indeed all over the island.

You can see nothing there for your money, said he, but a huge greedy guts, a tall woundy swallower of hot wardens and muscles; a long-shanked mole-catcher; an overgrown bottler of hay; a mossy-chinned demi-giant, with a double shaven crown, of lantern breed; a very great loitering noddy-peaked youngster, banner-bearer to the fish-eating tribe, dictator of mustard land, flogger of little children, calciner of ashes, father and foster-father to physicians; swarming with pardons, indulgences, and stations; a very honest man; a good catholic, and as brimful of devotion as ever he can hold.

He weeps the three-fourth parts of the day, and never assists at any weddings; but, give the devil his due, he is the most industrious larding-stick and skewer-maker in forty kingdoms.

About six years ago, as I passed through Sneaking-land, I brought home a large skewer from thence, and made a present of it to the butchers of Quande, who set a great value upon them, and that for a cause. Some time or other, if ever we live to come back to our own country, I will show you two of them fastened on the great church porch. His usual food is pickled coats of mail, salt helmets and headpieces, and salt sallads; which sometimes makes him piss pins and needles. As for his clothing, it is comical enough of conscience, both for make and colour; for he wears grey and cold, nothing before, and nought behind, with the sleeves of the same.

You will do me a kindness, said Pantagruel, if, as you have described his clothes, food, actions, and pastimes, you will also give me an account of his shape and disposition in all its parts. Prithee do, dear cod, said Friar John, for I have found him in my breviary, and then follows the moveable holy-days. With all my heart, answered Xenomanes; we may chance to hear more of him as we touch at the Wild Island, the dominions of the squab Chitterlings, his enemies; against whom he is eternally at odds: and were it not for the help of the noble Carnival, their protector, and good neighbour, this meagre-looking Shrovetide would long before this have made sad work among them, and rooted them out of their habitation. Are these same Chitterlings, said Friar John, male or female, angels, or mortals, women or maids? They are, replied Xenomanes, females in sex, mortal in condition, some of them maids, others not. The devil have me, said Friar John, if I be not for them. What a shameful disorder in nature, is it not, to make war against women? Let us go back, and hack the villain to pieces.—What! meddle with Shrovetide? cried Panurge, in the name of Belzebub, I am not yet so weary of my life. No, I am not yet so mad as that comes to. *Quid juris?*[20] Suppose we should find ourselves pent up between the Chitterlings and Shrovetide? between the anvil and the hammers? Shankers and buboes stand off! godzooks, let us make the best of our way. I bid you good night, sweet Mr. Shrovetide; I recommend to you the Chitterlings, and pray don't forget the puddings.

CHAPTER 30

How Shrovetide is anatomized and described by Xenomanes

As for the inward parts of Shrovetide, said Xenomanes; his brain is (at least it was in my time) in bigness, colours, substance, and strength, much like the left cod of a he hand-worm.

The ventricles of his said brain like an auger.
The worm-like excrescence, like a christmas-box.
The membranes, like a monk's cowl.
The funnel, like a mason's chisel.
The fornix, like a casket.
The glandula pinealis, like a bag-pipe.
The rete mirabile, like a gutter.
The dug-like processes, like a patch.
The tympanums, like a whirly-gig.
The rocky bones, like a goose-wing.
The nape of the neck, like a paper lantern.
The nerves, like a pipkin.
The uvula, like a sackbut.
The palate, like a mitten.
The spittle, like a shuttle.
The almonds, like a telescope.
The bridge of his nose, like a wheelbarrow.
The head of the larynx, like a vintage-basket.
The stomach, like a belt.
The pylorus, like a pitchfork.
The wind-pipe, like an oyster-knife.
The throat, like a pincushion stuffed with oakum.
The lungs, like a prebend's furgown.
The heart, like a cope.
The mediastine, like an earthen cup.
The pleura, like a crow's bill.
The arteries, like a watch-coat.
The midriff, like a montero-cap.
The liver, like a double-tongued mattock.

The veins, like a sash-window.
The spleen, like a catcall.
The guts, like a trammel.
The gall, like a cooper's adze.
The entrails, like a gantlet.
The mesentery, like an abbot's mitre.
The hungry-gut, like a button.
The blind gut like a breast-plate.
The colon like a bridle.
The arse-gut like a monk's leathern bottle.
The kidneys, like a trowel.
The loins, like a padlock.
The ureters, like a pot-hook.
The emulgent veins, like two gilli-flowers.
The spermatic vessels, like a cully-mully-puff.
The parastata, like an ink-pot.
The bladder, like a stone-bow.
The neck, like a mill-clapper.
The mirach, or lower parts of the belly, like a high-crowned hat.
The siphach, or its inner rind, like a wooden cuff.
The muscles, like a pair of bellows.
The tendons, like a hawking-glove.
The ligaments, like a tinker's budget.
The bones, like three-cornered cheese-cakes.
The marrow, like a wallet.
The cartilages, like a field-tortoise, alias a mole.
The glandules in the mouth, like a pruning-knife.
The animal spirits, like swingeing fisty-cuffs.
The blood-fermenting, like a multiplication of flirts on the nose.
The urine, like a fig-pecker.
The sperm, like a hundred tenpenny nails.

And his nurse told me, that being married to Mid-lent, he only begot a good number of local adverbs, and certain double fasts.

His memory he had like a scarf.
His common sense, like a buzzing of bees.
His imagination, like the chime of a set of bells.
His thoughts, like a flight of starlings.
His conscience, like the unnestling of a parcel of young herons.
His deliberations, like a set of organs.
His repentance, like the carriage of a double cannon.
His undertakings, like the ballast of a galleon.
His understanding, like a torn breviary.
His notions, like snails crawling out of strawberries.

His will, like three filberts in a porringer.
His desire, like six trusses of hay.
His judgment, like a shoeing horn.
His discretion, like the truckle of a pully.
His reason, like a cricket stool.

CHAPTER 31
Shrovetide's outward parts anatomized

SHROVETIDE, continued Xenomanes, is somewhat better proportioned in his outward parts, excepting the seven ribs which he had over and above the common shape of men.

His toes, were like a virginal on an organ.
His nails, like a gimlet.
His feet, like a guitar.
His heels, like a club.
The soles of his feet like a crucible.
His legs, like a hawk's lure.
His knees, like a joint-stool.
His thighs, like a steel cap.
His hips, like a wimble.
His belly as big as a tun, buttoned after the old fashion, with a girdle riding over the middle of his bosom.
His navel, like a cymbal.
His groin, like a minced pie.
His member, like a slipper.
His purse, like an oil cruet.
His genitals, like a joiner's plainer.
Their erecting muscles, like a racket.
The perineum, like a flageolet.
His arse-hole, like a crystal looking-glass.
His bum, like a harrow.
His loins, like a butter-pot.
The peritonæum, or caul, wherein his bowels were wrapped, like a billiard-table.
His back, like an overgrown rack-bent cross-bow.
The vertebræ, or joints of his back-bone, like a bagpipe.
His ribs, like a spinning-wheel.
His brisket, like a canopy.
His shoulder-blades, like a mortar.
His breast, like a game at nine-pins.
His paps, like a horn-pipe.
His arm-pits, like a chequer.
His shoulders like a hand-barrow.
His arms, like a riding-hood.
His fingers, like a brotherhood's andirons.
The fibulæ, or lesser bones of his legs, like a pair of stilts.
His shin-bones, like sickles.
His elbows, like a mouse-trap.
His hands, like a curry-comb.
His neck, like a talboy.

His throat, like a felt to distil hippocras.
The knob in his throat, like a barrel, where hanged two brazen wens, very fine and harmonious, in the shape of an hour-glass.
His beard, like a lantern.
His chin, like a mushroom.
His ears, like a pair of gloves.
His nose, like a buskin.
His nostrils, like a forehead cloth.
His eye-brows, like a dripping-pan.
On his left brow was a mark of the shape and bigness of an urinal.
His eye-lids, like a fiddle.
His eyes, like a comb-box.
His optic nerves, like a tinder-box.
His forehead, like a false cup.
His temples, like the cock of a cistern.
His cheeks, like a pair of wooden shoes.
His jaws, like a caudle cup.
His teeth, like a hunter's staff. Of such colt's teeth as his, you will find one at Colonges les Royaux in Poictou, and two at la Brosse in Xaintonge, on the cellar door.
His tongue, like a jew's harp.
His mouth, like a horse-cloth.
His face embroidered like a mule's pack saddle.
His head contrived like a still.
His skull, like a pouch.
The suturæ, or seams of his skull, like the annulus piscatoris, or the fisher's signet.
His skin, like a gabardine.
His epidermis, or outward skin, like a bolting-cloth.
His hair, like a scrubbing-brush.
His fur, such as above said.

CHAPTER 32
A continuation of Shrovetide's countenance, postures, and way of behaving

IT is a wonderful thing, continued Xenomanes, to hear and see the state of Shrovetide.

If he chanced to spit, it was whole baskets full of goldfinches.
If he blowed his nose, it was pickled grigs.
When he wept, it was ducks with onion sauce.
When he trembled, it was large venison pasties.
When he did sweat, it was old ling with butter sauce.
When he belched, it was bushels of oysters.
When he sneezed, it was whole tubs full of mustard.

When he coughed, it was boxes of marmalade.

When he sobbed, it was watercresses.

When he yawned, it was pots full of pickled
pease.

When he sighed, it was dried neats' tongues.

When he whistled, it was a whole scuttle full
of green apes.

When he snored, it was a whole pan full of
fried beans.

When he frowned, it was soused hogs' feet.

When he spoke, it was coarse brown russet
cloth; so little it was like crimson silk, with
which Parisatis desired that the words of
such as spoke to her son Cyrus, King of
Persia, should be interwoven.

When he blowed, it was indulgence money-
boxes.

When he winked, it was buttered buns.

When he grumbled, it was March cats.

When he nodded, it was iron-bound waggons.

When he made mouths, it was broken staves.

When he muttered, it was lawyers' revels.

When he hopped about, it was letters of licence and protections.

When he stepped back, it was sea cockle-
shells.

When he slabbered, it was common ovens.

When he was hoarse, it was an entry of mor-
rice-dancers.

When he broke wind, it was dun cows' leather spatterdashes.

When he funcked, it was washed-leather
boots.

When he scratched himself, it was new proclamations.

When he sung, it was peas in cods.

When he evacuated, it was mushrooms and
morilles.

When he puffed, it was cabbages with oil,
alias caules amb'olif.

When he talked, it was the last year's snow.

When he dreamt, it was of a cock and a
bull.

When he gave nothing, so much for the bearer.

If he thought to himself, it was whimsies and
maggots.

If he dozed, it was leases of lands.

What is yet more strange, he used to work
doing nothing, and did nothing though he
worked; caroused sleeping, and slept carousing, with his eyes open, like the hares in our
country, for fear of being taken napping by
the Chitterlings, his inveterate enemies; biting he laughed, and laughing bit; eat nothing
fasting, and fasted eating nothing; mumbled
upon suspicion, drank by imagination, swam
on the tops of high steeples, dried his clothes
in ponds and rivers, fished in the air, and
there used to catch decumane lobsters; hunted at the bottom of the herring-pond, and
caught there ibices, stamboucs, chamois, and
other wild goats; used to put out the eyes of
all the crows which he took sneakingly;
feared nothing but his own shadow, and the
cries of fat kids; used to gad abroad some
days, like a truant school-boy; played with
the ropes of bells on festival days of saints;
made a mallet of his fist, and writ on hairy
parchment prognostications and almanacks
with his huge pin-case.

Is that the gentleman? said Friar John: he
is my man: this is the very fellow I looked
for; I will send him a challenge immediately.
This is, said Pantagruel, a strange and monstrous sort of man, if I may call him a man.
You put me in mind of the form and looks of
Amodunt and Dissonance. How were they
made, said Friar John? May I be peeled like
a raw onion, if ever I heard a word of them.
I'll tell you what I read of them in some ancient apologues, replied Pantagruel.

Physis—that is to say Nature—at her first
burthen begat Beauty and Harmony, without
carnal copulation, being of herself very fruitful and prolific. Antiphysis, who ever was the
antagonist of Nature, immediately, out of a
malicious spite against her for her beautiful
and honourable productions, in opposition
begot Amodunt and Dissonance, by copulation with Tellumon. Their heads were round
like a football, and not gently flatted on both
sides, like the common shape of men. Their
ears stood pricked up like those of asses; their
eyes, as hard as those of crabs, and without
brows, stared out of their heads, fixed on
bones like those of our heels; their feet were
round, like tennis-balls; their arms and hands
turned backwards towards the shoulders;
and they walked on their heads, continually
turning round like a ball, topsy-turvy, heels
over head.

Yet—as you know that apes esteem their
young the handsomest in the world—Antiphysis extolled her offspring, and strove to
prove, that their shape was handsomer and
neater than that of the children of Physis:
saying, that thus to have spherical heads and
feet, and walk in a circular manner, wheeling

round, had something in it of the perfection of the divine power, which makes all beings eternally turn in that fashion; and that to have our feet uppermost, and the head below them, was to imitate the Creator of the universe; the hair being like the roots, and the legs like the branches of man: for trees are better planted by their roots, than they could be by their branches. By this demonstration she implied, that her children were much more to be praised for being like a standing tree, than those of Physis, that made a figure of a tree upside down. As for the arms and hands, she pretended to prove that they were more justly turned towards the shoulders, because that part of the body ought not to be without defence, while the forepart is duly fenced with teeth, which a man cannot only use to chew, but also to defend himself against those things that offend him. Thus by the testimony and astipulation of the brute beasts, she drew all the witless herd and mob of fools into her opinion, and was admired by all brainless and nonsensical people.

Since that, she begot the hypocritical tribes of eaves-dropping dissemblers, superstitious pope-mongers, and priest-ridden bigots, the frantic Pistolets, the demoniacal Calvins, impostors of Geneva, the scrapers of benefices, apparitors with the devil in them, and other grinders and squeezers of livings, herb-stinking hermits, gulligutted dunces of the cowl, church vermin, false zealots, devourers of the substance of men, and many more other deformed and ill-favoured monsters, made in spite of nature.

CHAPTER 33

How Pantagruel discovered a monstrous physeter, or whirlpool, near the Wild Island

ABOUT sunset, coming near the Wild Island, Pantagruel spied afar off a huge monstrous physeter,—a sort of whale, which some call a whirlpool,—that came right upon us, neighing, snorting, raised above the waves higher than our main-tops, and spouting water all the way into the air, before itself, like a large river falling from a mountain: Pantagruel showed it to the pilot, and to Xenomanes.

By the pilot's advice, the trumpets of the *Thalamege* were sounded, to warn all the fleet to stand close, and look to themselves. This alarm being given, all the ships, gal-leons, frigates, brigantines,—according to their naval discipline,—placed themselves in the order and figure of a Greek upsilon, (Υ) the letter of Pythagoras, as cranes do in their flight; and like an acute angle, in whose cone and basis the *Thalamege* placed herself ready to fight smartly. Friar John, with the grenadiers, got on the forecastle.

Poor Panurge began to cry and howl worse than ever: Babillebabou, said he, shrugging up his shoulders, quivering all over with fear, there will be the devil upon dun. This is a worse business than that the other day. Let us fly, let us fly; old Nick take me if it is not Leviathan, described by the noble prophet Moses, in the life of patient Job. It will swallow us all, ships and men, shag, rag, and bob-tail, like a dose of pills. Alas, it will make no more of us, and we shall hold no more room in its hellish jaws, than a sugar-plum in an ass's throat. Look, look, it is upon us; let us wheel off, whip it away, and get ashore. I believe it is the very individual sea monster that was formerly designed to devour Andromeda: we are all undone. Oh! for some valiant Perseus here now to kill the dog.

I'll do its business presently said Pantagruel; fear nothing. Odd's belly, said Panurge, remove the cause of my fear then. When the devil would you have a man be afraid, but when there is so much cause? If your destiny be such, as Friar John was saying a while ago, replied Pantagruel, you ought to be afraid of Pyroeis, Eous, Æthon, and Phlegon, the sun's coach horses, that breathe fire at the nostrils; and not of physeters, that spout nothing but water at the snout and mouth. Their water will not endanger your life; and that element will rather save and preserve than hurt or endanger you.

Ay, ay, trust to that, and hang me, quoth Panurge: yours is a very pretty fancy. Odd's fish: did I not give you a sufficient account of the element's transmutation, and the blunders that are made of roast for boiled, and boiled for roast? Alas, here it is; I'll go hide myself below. We are dead men, every mother's son of us; I see upon our main-top that merciless hag Atropos, with her scissors new ground, ready to cut our threads all at one snip. Oh! how dreadful and abominable thou art; thou hast drowned a good many beside us, who never made their brags of it. Did it but spout good, brisk, dainty, delicious white wine, instead of this damned bitter salt water, one might better bear with it, and there would be some cause to be patient; like that English lord, who being doomed to die, and had leave to choose what kind of death he would, chose to be drowned in a butt of malmsey. Here it is.—Oh, oh! devil! Sathanas! Leviathan! I cannot abide to look upon thee, thou art so abominably ugly.—Go to the bar, go take the pettifoggers.

CHAPTER 34

How the monstrous physeter was slain by Pantagruel

THE physeter, coming between the ships and the galleons, threw water by whole tuns upon them, as if it had been the cataracts of the Nile in Ethiopia. On the other side, arrows, darts, gleaves, javelins, spears, harping-irons, and partizans, flew upon it like hail. Friar John did not spare himself in it. Panurge was half dead for fear. The artillery roared and thundered like mad, and seemed to gall it in good earnest, but did but little good: for the great iron and brass cannon-shot, entering its skin, seemed to melt like tiles in the sun.

Pantagruel then, considering the weight and exigency of the matter, stretched out his arms, and showed what he could do. You tell us, and it is recorded, that Commodus, the Roman emperor, could shoot with a bow so dexterously, that at a good distance he would let fly an arrow through a child's fingers, and never touch them. You also tell us of an Indian archer, who lived when Alexander the Great conquered India, and was so skilful in drawing the bow, that at a considerable distance he would shoot his arrows through a ring, though they were three cubits long, and their iron so large and weighty, that with them he used to pierce steel cutlasses, thick shields, steel breastplates, and generally what he did hit, how firm, resisting, hard, and strong soever it were. You also tell us wonders of the industry of the ancient Franks, who were preferred to all others in point of archery; and when they hunted either black or dun beasts, used to rub the head of their arrows with hellebore, because the flesh of the venison, struck with such an arrow, was more tender, dainty, wholesome, and delicious—paring off, nevertheless, the part that was touched round about. You also talk of the Parthians, who used to shoot backwards, more dexterously than other nations forwards; and also celebrate the skill of the Scythians in that art, who sent once to Dari-

us, King of Persia, an ambassador, that made him a present of a bird, a frog, a mouse, and five arrows, without speaking one word; and being asked what those presents meant, and if he had commission to say anything, answered, that he had not: which puzzled and gravelled Darius very much, till Gobrias, one of the seven captains that had killed the magi, explained it, saying to Darius: By these gifts and offerings the Scythians silently tell you, that except the Persians, like birds, fly up to heaven, or like mice, hide themselves near the centre of the earth, or, like frogs, dive to the very bottom of ponds and lakes, they shall be destroyed by the power and arrows of the Scythians.

The noble Pantagruel was, without comparison, more admirable yet in the art of shooting and darting: for with his dreadful piles and darts, nearly resembling the huge beams that support the bridges of Nantes, Saumur, Bergerac, and at Paris the millers' and the changers' bridges, in length, size, weight, and iron-work, he at a mile's distance, would open an oyster, and never touch the edges; he would snuff a candle, without putting it out; would shoot a magpie in the eye; take off a boot's undersole, or, a riding-hood's lining, without soiling them a bit; turn over every leaf of Friar John's breviary, one after another, and not tear one.

With such darts, of which there was good store in the ship, at the first blow he ran the physeter in at the forehead so furiously, that he pierced both its jaws and tongue: so that from that time to this it no more opened its guttural trap-door, nor drew and spouted water. At the second blow he put out its right eye, and at the third its left: and we had all the pleasure to see the physeter bearing those three horns in its forehead, somewhat leaning forwards in an equilateral triangle.

Meanwhile it turned about to and fro, staggering and straying like one stunned, blinded, and taking his leave of the world. Pantagruel, not satisfied with this, let fly another dart, which took the monster under the tail likewise sloping; then with three other on the chine, in a perpendicular line, divided its flank from the tail to the snout at an equal distance: then he larded it with fifty on one side, and after that, to make even work, he darted as many on its other side: so that the body of the physeter seemed like the hulk of a galleon with three masts, joined by a competent dimension of its beams, as if they had been the ribs and chain-wales of the keel; which was a pleasant sight. The physeter then giving up the ghost, turned itself upon its back, as all dead fishes do; and being thus overturned, with the beams and darts upside down in the sea, it seemed a scolopendra or centipede, as that serpent is described by the ancient sage Nicander.

CHAPTER 35

How Pantagruel went on shore in the Wild Island, the ancient abode of the Chitterlings

THE boat's crew of the ship *Lantern* towed the physeter ashore on the neighbouring shore, which happened to be the Wild Island, to make an anatomical dissection of its body, and save the fat of its kidneys, which, they said, was very useful and necessary for the cure of a certain distemper, which they called want of money. As for Pantagruel, he took no manner of notice of the monster; for he had seen many such, nay, bigger, in the Gallic ocean. Yet he condescended to land in the Wild Island, to dry and refresh some of his men, (whom the physeter had wetted and bedaubed,) at a small desert sea-port, towards the south, seated near a fine pleasant grove, out of which flowed a delicious brook of fresh, clear, and purling water. Here they pitched their tents, and set up their kitchens; nor did they spare fuel.

Every one having shifted, as they thought fit, Friar John rang the bell, and the cloth was immediately laid, and supper brought in. Pantagruel eating cheerfully with his men, much about the second course, perceived certain little sly Chitterlings clambering up a high tree near the pantry, as still as so many mice. Which made him ask Xenomanes, what kind of creatures these were; taking them for squirrels, weazels, martins, or ermines. They are Chitterlings, replied Xenomanes. This is the Wild Island, of which I spoke to you this morning: there hath been an irreconcilable war, this long time, between them and Shrovetide, their malicious and ancient enemy. I believe that the noise of the guns, which we fired at the physeter, hath alarmed them, and made them fear their enemy hath come with his forces to surprise them, or lay the island waste; as he hath often attempted to do, though he still came off but bluely; by reason of the care and vigilance of the Chitterlings, who, (as Dido said to Æneas's com-panions, that would have landed at Carthage without her leave or knowledge,) were forced to watch and stand upon their guard, considering the malice of their enemy, and the neighbourhood of his territories.

Pray, dear friend, said Pantagruel, if you find that by some honest means we may bring this war to an end, and reconcile them together, give me notice of it; I will use my endeavours in it, with all my heart, and spare nothing on my side to moderate and accommodate the points in dispute between both parties.

This is impossible at this time, answered Xenomanes. About four years ago, passing incognito by this country, I endeavoured to make a peace, or at least a long truce among them; and I certainly had brought them to be good friends and neighbours, if both one and the other parties would have yielded to one single article. Shrovetide would not include in the treaty of peace, the wild puddings, nor the highland sausages, their ancient gossips and confederates. The Chitterlings demanded, that the fort of Cacques might be under their government, as is the Castle of Sullouoir, and that a parcel of I don't know what stinking villains, murderers, robbers, that held it then, should be expelled. But they could not agree in this, and the terms that were offered seemed too hard to either party. So the treaty broke off, and nothing was done. Nevertheless, they became less severe, and gentler enemies than they were before; but since the denunciation of the national Council of Chesil, whereby they—the Chitterlings—were roughly handled, hampered, and cited; whereby also Shrovetide was declared filthy, beshitten, and bewrayed, in case he made any league, or agreement with them; they are grown wonderfully inveterate, incensed, and obstinate against one another, and there is no way to remedy it. You might sooner reconcile cats and rats or hounds and hares together.

CHAPTER 36

How the wild Chitterlings laid an ambuscade for Pantagruel

WHILE Xenomanes was saying this, Friar John spied twenty or thirty young slender-shaped Chitterlings, posting as fast as they could towards their town, citadel, castle, and fort of Chimney, and said to Pantagruel, I smell a rat: there will be here the devil upon two sticks, or I am much out. These worship-ful Chitterlings may chance to mistake you for Shrovetide, though you are not a bit like him. Let us once in our lives leave our junket-ing for a while, and put ourselves in a pos-ture to give them a bellyful of fighting, if they would be at that sport. There can be no false Latin in this, said Xenomanes: Chitter-lings are still Chitterlings, always double-hearted and, treacherous.

Pantagruel then arose from table, to visit and scour the thicket, and returned presently; having discovered, on the left, an ambuscade of squab Chitterlings; and on the right, about half a league from thence, a large body of huge giant-like armed Chitterlings, ranged in battalia along a little hill, and marching furiously towards us at the sound of bag-pipes, sheep's paunches, and bladders, the merry fifes and drums, trumpets, and clari-ons, hoping to catch us as Moss caught his mare. By the conjecture of seventy-eight standards, which we told, we guessed their number to be two and forty thousand, at a modest computation.

Their order, proud gait, and resolute looks, made us judge that they were none of your raw, paltry links, but old war-like Chitter-lings and Sausages. From the foremost ranks to the colours they were all armed *cap-à-pié* with small arms, as we reckoned them at a distance: yet, very sharp, and case-hardened. Their right and left wings were lined with a great number of forest puddings, heavy pat-tipans, and horse sausages, all of them tall and proper islanders, banditti, and wild.

Pantagruel was very much daunted, and not without cause; though Epistemon told him that it might be the use and custom of the Chitterlingonians to welcome and receive thus in arms their foreign friends, as the no-ble kings of France are received and saluted at their first coming into the chief cities of the kingdom, after their advancement to the crown. Perhaps, said he, it may be the usual guard of the queen of the place; who, having notice given her, by the junior Chitterlings of the forlorn hope whom you saw on the tree, of the arrival of your fine and pompous fleet, hath judged that it was, without doubt, some rich and potent prince, and is come to visit you in person.

Pantagruel, little trusting to this, called a council, to have their advice at large in this doubtful case. He briefly showed them how this way of reception, with arms, had often,

under colour of compliment and friendship, been fatal. Thus, said he, the Emperor Anto-nius Caracalla, at one time, destroyed the cit-izens of Alexandria, and at another time, cut off the attendants of Artabanus, King of Per-sia, under colour of marrying his daughter: which, by the way, did not pass unpunished: for, a while after, this cost him his life.

Thus Jacob's children destroyed the Siche-mites, to revenge the rape of their sister Di-nah. By such another hypocritical trick, Gal-lienus the Roman emperor, put to death the military men in Constantinople. Thus, under colour of friendship, Antonius enticed Ar-tavasdes, King of Armenia; then, having caused him to be bound in heavy chains, and shackled, at last put him to death.

We find a thousand such instances in his-tory; and King Charles VI is justly commend-ed for his prudence to this day, in that, com-ing back victorious over the Ghenters and other Flemings, to his good city of Paris, and when he came to Bourget, a league from thence, hearing that the citizens with their mallets—whence they got the name of Maillo-tins—were marched out of town in battalia, twenty thousand strong, he would not go into the town, till they had laid down their arms, and retired to their respective homes; though they protested to him, that they had taken arms with no other design than to receive him with the greater demonstration of hon-our and respect.

CHAPTER 37

How Pantagruel sent for Colonel Maul-Chit-terling, and Colonel Cut-Pudding; with a discourse well worth your hearing, about the names of places and persons

THE resolution of the council was, that, let things be how they would, it behoved the Pantagruelists to stand upon their guard. Therefore Carpalim and Gymnast were or-dered by Pantagruel to go for the soldiers that were on board the *Cup* galley, under the com-mand of Colonel Maul-chitterling, and those on board the *Vine-tub* frigate, under the com-mand of Colonel Cut-pudding the younger. I will ease Gymnast of that trouble, said Pan-urge, who wanted to be upon the run: you may have occasion for him here. By this worthy frock of mine, quoth Friar John, thou hast a mind to slip thy neck out of the collar, and absent thyself from the fight, thou white-livered son of a dunghill! upon my virginity thou wilt never come back. Well, there can be no great loss in thee; for thou wouldst do nothing here but howl, bray, weep, and dishearten the good soldiers. I will certainly come back, said Panurge, Friar John, my ghostly father, and speedily too: do but take care that these plaguy Chitterlings do not board our ships. All the while you will be a fighting, I will pray heartily for your victory, after the example of the valiant captain and guide of the people of Israel, Moses. Having said this, he wheeled off.

Then said Epistemon to Pantagruel, The denomination of these two colonels of yours, Maul-chitterling and Cut-pudding, promiseth us assurance, success, and victory, if those Chitterlings should chance to set upon us. You take it rightly, said Pantagruel, and it pleaseth me to see you foresee and prognosticate our victory by the name of our colonels.

This way of foretelling by names is not new; it was in old times celebrated, and religiously observed by the Pythagoreans. Several great princes and emperors have formerly made use of it. Octavianus Augustus, second emperor of the Romans, meeting on a day a country fellow named Eutychus,—that is, fortunate,—driving an ass named Nicon—that is in Greek, victorious,—moved by the signification of the ass's and ass-driver's names, remained assured of all prosperity and victory.

The Emperor Vespasian, being once all alone at prayers, in the temple of Serapis, at the sight and unexpected coming of a certain servant of his, named Basilides,—that is, royal,—whom he had left sick a great way behind, took hopes and assurance of obtaining the empire of the Romans. Regilian was chosen emperor, by the soldiers, for no other reason, but the signification of his name. See the *Cratylus* of the divine Plato. (By my thirst I will read him, said Rhizotomus; I hear you so often quote him.) See how the Pythagoreans, by reason of the names and numbers, conclude that Patroclus was to fall by the hand of Hector; Hector by Achilles; Achilles by Paris; Paris by Philoctetes. I am quite lost in my understanding, when I reflect upon the admirable invention of Pythagoras, who by the number, either even or odd, of the syllables of every name, would tell you of what side a man was lame, hunch-backed, blind, gouty, troubled with the palsy, pleurisy, or any other distemper incident to human kind; allotting even numbers to the left, and odd ones to the right side of the body.

Indeed, said Epistemon, I saw this way of syllabising tried at Xaintes, at a general procession, in the presence of that good, virtuous, learned, and just president, Brian Vallée, Lord of Douhait. When there went by a man or woman that was either lame, blind of one eye, or hump-backed, he had an account brought him of his or her name; and if the syllables of the name were of an odd number, immediately, without seeing the persons, he declared them to be deformed, blind, lame, or crooked of the right side; and of the left, if they were even in number; and such indeed we ever found them.

By this syllabical invention, said Pantagruel, the learned have affirmed, that Achilles kneeling, was wounded by the arrow of Paris in the right heel; for his name is of odd syllables; (here we ought to observe that the ancients used to kneel the right foot:) and that Venus was also wounded before Troy in the left hand; for her name in Greek is Ἀφροδίτη, of four syllables; Vulcan lamed of his left foot for the same reason; Philip, King of Macedon, and Hannibal, blind of the right eye; not to speak of sciaticas, broken bellies, and hemicranias, which may be distinguished by this Pythagorean reason.

But returning to names: do but consider how Alexander the Great, son of King Philip, of whom we spoke just now, compassed his undertaking, merely by the interpretation of a name. He had besieged the strong city of Tyre, and for several weeks battered it with all his power: but all in vain. His engines and attempts were still baffled by the Tyrians, which made him finally resolve to raise the siege, to his great grief; foreseeing the great stain which such a shameful retreat would be to his reputation. In this anxiety and agitation of mind he fell asleep, and dreamed that a satyr was come into his tent, capering, skipping, and tripping it up and down, with his goatish hoofs, and that he strove to lay hold on him. But the satyr still slipt from him, till at last, having penned him up into a corner, he took him. With this he awoke, and telling his dream to the philosophers and sages of his court, they let him know that it was a promise of victory from the gods, and that he should soon be master of Tyre; the word *satyros,* divided in two, being *sa Tyros,* and signifying Tyre is thine; and in truth, at the next onset, he took the town by storm, and, by a complete victory, reduced that stubborn people to subjection.

On the other hand, see how, by the signification of one word, Pompey fell into despair. Being overcome by Cæsar at the battle of Pharsalia, he had no other way left to escape but by flight; which, attempting by sea, he arrived near the island of Cyprus, and perceived on the shore, near the city of Paphos, a beautiful and stately palace: now asking the pilot what was the name of it, he told him, that it was called Κακοβασιλέα, that is, evil king; which struck such a dread and terror in him, that he fell into despair, as being assured of losing shortly his life; insomuch that his complaints, sighs, and groans were heard by the mariners and other passengers. And indeed, a while after, a certain strange peasant, called Achillas, cut off his head.

To all these examples might be added what happened to L. Paulus Emilius, when the senate elected him imperator, that is, chief of the army which they sent against Perses, King of Macedon. That evening returning home to prepare for his expedition, and kissing a little daughter of his called Trasia, she seemed somewhat sad to him. What is the matter, said he, my chicken? Why is my Trasia thus sad and melancholy? Daddy, replied the child, Persa is dead. This was the name of a little bitch, which she loved mightily. Hearing this, Paulus took assurance of a victory over Perses.

If time would permit us to discourse of the sacred Hebrew writ, we might find a hundred noted passages, evidently showing how religiously they observed proper names and their significations.

He had hardly ended this discourse, when the two colonels arrived with their soldiers, all well armed and resolute. Pantagruel made them a short speech, entreating them to behave themselves bravely, in case they were attacked; for he could not yet believe that the Chitterlings were so treacherous: but he bad them by no means to give the first offence; giving them carnival for the watch-word.

CHAPTER 38

How Chitterlings are not to be slighted by men

You shake your empty noddles now, jolly topers, and do not believe what I tell you here, any more than if it were some tale of a tub. Well, well, I cannot help it. Believe it if you will; if you will not, let it alone. For my part, I very well know what I say. It was in the

Wild Island, in our voyage to the Holy Bottle; I tell you the time and place; what would you have more? I would have you call to mind the strength of the ancient giants, that undertook to lay the high mountain Pelion, on the top of Ossa, and set among those the shady Olympus, to dash out the gods' brains, unnestle them, and scour their heavenly lodgings. Theirs was no small strength, you may well think, and yet they were nothing but Chitterlings from the waist downwards, or, at least, serpents, not to tell a lie for the matter.

The serpent that tempted Eve, too, was of the Chitterling kind, and yet it is recorded of him, that he was more subtle than any beast of the field. Even so are Chitterlings. Nay, to this very hour they hold in some universities, that this same tempter was the Chitterling called Ithyphallus, into which was transformed bawdy Priapus, arch-seducer of females in paradise, that is, a garden, in Greek.

Pray now tell me, who can tell but that the Swiss, now so bold and warlike, were formerly Chitterlings? For my part I would not take my oath to the contrary. The Himantopodes, a nation very famous in Ethiopia, according to Pliny's description, are Chitterlings, and nothing else. If all this will not satisfy your worships, or remove your incredulity, I would have you forthwith (I mean drinking first, that nothing be done rashly) visit Lusignan, Parthenay, Vouant, Mervant, and Ponzauges in Poictou. There you will find a cloud of witnesses, not of your affidavit men of the right stamp, but credible, time out of mind, that will take their corporal oath, on Rigomé's knuckle-bone, that Melusina, their founder, or foundress, which you please, was woman from the head to the prick-purse, and thence downwards was a serpentine Chitterling, or if you will have it otherwise, a Chitterlingdized serpent. She nevertheless had a genteel and noble gait, imitated to this very day by your hop-merchants of Britanny, in their *paspié* and country dances.

What do you think was the cause of Erichthonius's being the first inventor of coaches, litters, and chariots? Nothing but because Vulcan had begot him with Chitterlingdized legs; which to hide, he chose to ride in a litter, rather than on horseback; for Chitterlings were not yet in esteem at that time.

The Scythian nymph, Ora, was likewise half woman and half Chitterling; and yet seemed so beautiful to Jupiter, that nothing could serve him but he must give her a touch of his godship's kindness; and accordingly he had a brave boy by her, called Colaxes; and therefore I would have you leave off shaking your empty noddles at this, as if it were a story, and firmly believe that nothing is truer than the gospel.

CHAPTER 39

How Friar John joined with the cooks to fight the Chitterlings

FRIAR JOHN, seeing these furious Chitterlings thus boldly march up, said to Pantagruel, Here will be a rare battle of hobby-horses, a pretty kind of puppet-show fight, for aught I see. Oh! what mighty honour and wonderful glory will attend our victory! I would have you only be a bare spectator of this fight, and for any thing else, leave me and my men to deal with them. What men? said Pantagruel. Matter of breviary, replied Friar John. How came Potiphar, who was head cook of Pharaoh's kitchens, he that bought Joseph, and whom the said Joseph might have made a cuckold, if he had not been a Joseph; how came he, I say, to be made general of all the horse in the kingdom of Egypt? Why was Nabuzardan, King Nebuchadnezzar's head cook, chosen, to the exclusion of all other captains, to besiege and destroy Jerusalem. I hear you, replied Pantagruel. By St. Christopher's whiskers, said Friar John, I dare lay a wager that it was because they had formerly engaged Chitterlings, or men as little valued; whom to rout, conquer, and destroy, cooks are, without comparison, more fit, than cuirassiers and *gens d'armes* armed at all points, or all the horse and foot in the world.

You put me in mind, said Pantagruel, of what is written amongst the facetious and merry sayings of Cicero. During the more than civil wars between Cæsar and Pompey, though he was much courted by the first, he naturally leaned more to the side of the latter. Now one day, hearing that the Pompeyians, in a certain rencontre, had lost a great many men, he took a fancy to visit their camp. There he perceived little strength, less courage, but much disorder. From that time, forseeing that things would go ill with them, as it since happened, he began to banter now one and then another, and be very free of his cutting jests: so some of Pompey's captains, playing the good fellows, to show their assurance, told him, Do you see how many eagles we have yet? (They were then the device of the Romans in war.) They might be of use to you, replied Cicero, if you had to do with magpies.

Thus seeing we are to fight Chitterlings, pursued Pantagruel, you infer thence that it is a culinary war, and have a mind to join with the cooks. Well, do as you please, I will stay here in the meantime, and wait for the event of the rumpus.

Friar John went that very moment among the sutlers, into the cooks' tents, and told them in a pleasing manner; I must see you crowned with honour and triumph this day, my lads; to your arms are reserved such achievements as never yet were performed within the memory of man. Odd's belly, do they make nothing of the valiant cooks? let us go fight yonder fornicating Chitterlings! I will be your captain. But first let us drink, boys,—come on—let us be of good cheer. Noble captain, returned the kitchen tribe, this was spoken like yourself; bravely offered: huzza! we are all at your excellency's command, and will live and die by you. Live, live, said Friar John, a God's name: but die by no means. That is the Chitterlings' lot; they shall have their bellyful of it: come on then, let us put ourselves in order; Nabuzardan's the word.

CHAPTER 40

How Friar John fitted up the sow; and of the valiant cooks that went into it

THEN, by Friar John's order, the engineers and their workmen fitted up the great sow that was in the ship *Leathern-Bottle*. It was a wonderful machine, so contrived, that, by means of large engines that were round about in rows, it threw forked iron bars, and foursquare steel-bolts; and in its hold two hundred men at least could easily fight, and be sheltered. It was made after the model of the sow of Riole, by the means of which Bergerac was re-taken from the English, in the reign of Charles the Sixth.

Here are the names of the noble and valiant cooks who went into the sow, as the Greeks did into the Trojan horse.

Sour-sauce.	Cock-broth.
Sweet-meat.	Slipslop.
Greedy-gut.	Crisp-pig.
Liquorice-chops.	Greasy-slouch.
Soused-pork.	Fat-gut.
Slap-sauce.	Bray-mortar.

Lick-sauce.
Hog's-foot.
Hodge-podge.
Carbonadoe.
Sop-in-pan.

Pick-fowl.
Mustard-pot.
Hog's-haslet.
Chopt-phiz.
Gallimaufrey.

All these noble cooks, in their coat of arms, did bear, in a field gules, a larding-pin vert, charged with a chevron argent.

Lard, hog's-lard.
Nibble-lard.
Filch-lard.
Fat-lard.
Pinch-lard.
Top-lard.

Pick-lard.
Save-lard.
Snatch-lard.
Gnaw-lard.
Scrape-lard.
Chew-lard.

Gaillardon (by syncope) born near Rambouillet. The culinary doctor's name was Gaillardlardon, in the same manner as you use to say idolatrous for idololatrous.

Stiff-lard.
Dainty-lard.
Watch-lard.
Sweet-lard.
Eat-lard.
Snap-lard.
Catch-lard.
Cut-lard.

Mince-lard.
Fresh-lard.
Rusty-lard.
Waste-lard.
Ogle-lard.
Weigh-lard.
Gulch-lard.
Eye-lard.

Names unknown among the Marranes and Jews.

Ballocky.
Pick-sallad.
Broil-rasher.
Cony-skin.
Dainty-chops.
Pie-wright.
Pudding-pan.
Save-dripping.
Water-cress.
Scrape-turnip.
Trivet.
Monsieur-Ragout.
Snail-dresser.
Soup-monger.
Brewis-belly.
Chine-picker.

Crack-pipkin.
Scrape-pot.
Porridge-pot.
Lick-dish.
Toss-pot.
Mustard-sauce.
Claret-sauce.
Swill-broth.
Thirsty.
Kitchen-stuff.
Verjuice.
Salt-gullet.
Suck-gravy.
Macaroon.
Skewer-maker.

Smell-smock; he was afterwards taken from the kitchen, and removed to chamber-practice, for the service of the noble Cardinal Hunt-venison.

Rot-roast.
Dish-clout.
Save-suet.
Fire-fumbler.
Pillicock.
Long-tool.
Prick-pride.
Prick-madam.
Pricket.
Flesh-smith.
Cram-gut.
Tuzzy-mussy.
Jacket-liner.

Guzzle-drink.
Fox-tail.
Fly-flap.
Old-Grizzle.
Ruff-belly.
Sirloin.
Spit-mutton.
Fritter-fryer.
Hog's-gullet.
Saffron-sauce.
Strutting-tom.
Slashed-snout.
Smutty-face.

Mondam, that first invented madam's sauce, and for that discovery, was thus called in the Scotch-French dialect.

Loblolly.
Slabber-chops.
Scampot.
Gully-guts.
Rinse-pot.
Goodman Goosecap.
Munch-turnip.
Sloven.

Swallow-pitcher.
Wafer-monger.
Snap-gobbet.
Scurvy-phiz.
Trencher-man.
Pudding-bag.
Pig-sticker.

Robert: he invented Robert's sauce, so good and necessary for roasted conies, ducks, fresh pork, poached eggs, salt fish, and a thousand other such dishes.

Cold-eel.
Thornback.
Gurnard.
Grumbling-gut.
Alms-scrip.
Taste-all.
Scrap-merchant.
Belly-timberman.
Hashee.
Frig-palate.
Powdering-tub.
Frying-pan.
Man of dough.
Sauce-doctor.
Waste-butter.
Shitbreech.

Thick-brawn.
Tom T—d.
Mouldy-crust.
Hasty.
Red-herring.
Cheesecake.
Big-snout.
Lick-finger.
Tit-bit.
Sauce-box.
All fours.
Whimwham.
Baste-roast.
Gaping-Hoyden.
Calf's pluck.
Leather breeches.

All these noble cooks went into the sow, merry, cheery, hale, brisk, old dogs at mischief, and ready to fight stoutly. Friar John, ever and anon waving his huge scimitar, brought up the rear, and double-locked the doors on the inside.

CHAPTER 41

How Pantagruel broke the Chitterlings at the knees

THE Chitterlings advanced so near, that Pantagruel perceived that they stretched their arms, and already began to charge their lances; which caused him to send Gymnast to know what they meant, and why they thus, without the least provocation, came to fall upon their old trusty friends, who had neither said nor done the least ill thing to them. Gymnast being advanced near their front, bowed very low, and said to them, as loud as ever he could: We are friends, we are friends; all, all of us your friends, yours, and at your command; we are for Carnival, your old confederate. Some have since told me, that he mistook, and said cavernal instead of carnival.

Whatever it was, the word was no sooner out of his mouth, but a huge little squab Sausage, starting out of the front of their main body, would have griped him by the collar. By the helmet of Mars, said Gymnast, I will swallow thee; but thou shalt only come in, in chips and slices; for, big as thou art, thou couldest never come in whole. This spoke, he lugs out his trusty sword, Kiss-mine-arse, (so he called it,) with both his fists, and cut the sausage in twain. Bless me, how fat the foul thief was! it puts me in mind of the huge bull of Berne, that was slain at Marignan, when the drunken Swiss were so mauled there. Believe me, it had little less than four inches lard on its paunch.

The Sausage's job being done, a crowd of others flew upon Gymnast, and had most scurvily dragged him down, when Pantagruel with his men came up to his relief. Then began the martial fray, higgledy piggledy. Maul-chitterling did maul Chitterlings; Cut-pudding did cut puddings; Pantagruel did break the Chitterlings at the knees; Frair John play'd at least in sight within his sow, viewing and observing all things; when the pattipans, that lay in ambuscade, most furiously sallied out upon Pantagruel.

Friar John, who lay snug all this while, by that time perceiving the route and hurly-burly, set open the doors of his sow, and sallied out with his merry Greeks, some of them armed with iron-spits, others with handirons, racks, fire-shovels, frying-pans, kettles, gridirons, oven forks, tongs, dripping pans, brooms, iron pots, mortars, pestles, all in battle array, like so many house-breakers, hallooing and roaring out altogether most frightfully, Nabuzardan, Nabuzardan, Nabuzardan. Thus shouting and hooting, they fought like dragons, and charged through the pattipans and sausages. The Chitterlings perceiving this fresh reinforcement, and that the others would be too hard for them, betook themselves to their heels, scampering off with full speed, as if the devil had come for them. Friar John, with an iron crow, knocked them down as fast as hops: his men too were not sparing on their side. O! what a woeful sight it was! the field was all over strewed with heaps of dead or wounded Chitterlings; and history relates, that had not heaven had a hand in it, the Chitterling tribe had been totally routed out of the world, by the culinary champions. But there happened a wonderful thing, you may believe as little or as much of it as you please.

From the north flew towards us a huge, fat, thick, grizzly swine, with long and large wings, like those of a windmill; its plumes red crimson, like those of a phenicoptere (which in Languedoc they call *Flaman;*) its eyes were red, and flaming like a carbuncle; its ears green like a Prasin emerald; its teeth like a topaz; its tail long and black like jet; its feet white, diaphanous, and transparent like a diamond, somewhat broad, and of the splay kind, like those of geese, and as Queen Dick's used to be at Thoulouse, in the days of yore. About its neck it wore a gold collar, round which were some Ionian characters, whereof I could pick out but two words, ΤΣ'ΑΘΗΝΑΝ : hog teaching Minerva.

The sky was clear before; but at that monster's appearance, it changed so mightily for the worse, that we were all amazed at it. As soon as the Chitterlings perceived the flying hog, down they all threw their weapons, and fell on their knees, lifting up their hands, joined together without speaking one word, in a posture of adoration. Friar John and his party kept on mincing, felling, braining, mangling, and spitting the Chitterlings like mad: but Pantagruel sounded a retreat, and all hostility ceased.

The monster having several times hovered backwards and forwards between the two armies, with a tail-shot voided above twenty-seven butts of mustard on the ground; then flew away through the air, crying all the while, Carnival, Carnival, Carnival.

CHAPTER 42

How Pantagruel held a treaty with Niphle-
seth, Queen of the Chitterlings

THE monster being out of sight, and the two
armies remaining silent, Pantagruel demanded a parley with the Lady Niphleseth, Queen
of the Chitterlings, who was in her chariot, by
the standards; and it was easily granted. The
queen alighted, courteously received Pantagruel, and was glad to see him. Pantagruel
complained to her of this breach of peace:
but she civilly made her excuse, telling him
that a false information had caused all this
mischief; her spies having brought her word,
that Shrovetide their mortal foe, was landed,
and spent his time in examining the urine of
physeters.

She, therefore, entreated him to pardon
them their offence; telling him that sir-reverence was sooner found in Chitterlings than
gall; and offering, for herself and all her successors, to hold of him, and his, the whole island and country; to obey him in all his commands, be friends to his friends, and foes to
his foes; and also to send every year, as an acknowledgment of their homage, a tribute of
seventy-eight thousand Chitterlings, to serve
him at his first course at table, six months in
the year; which was punctually performed.
For the next day she sent the aforesaid quantity of royal Chitterlings to the good Gargantua, under the conduct of young Niphleseth,
infanta of the island.

The good Gargantua made a present of
them to the great King of Paris. But by
change of air, and for want of mustard, (the
natural balsam and restorer of Chitterlings,)
most of them died. By the great king's particular grant, they were buried in heaps in a part
of Paris, to this day called, *La Rue pavée d'*
Andouilles; the street paved with Chitterlings. At the request of the ladies at his court,
young Niphleseth, was preserved, honourably used, and since that married to her
heart's content; and was the mother of many
fine children, for which heaven be praised.

Pantagruel civilly thanked the queen, for-
gave all offences, refused the offer she had
made of her country, and gave her a pretty
little knife. After that he asked her several
nice questions concerning the apparition of
that flying hog. She answered, that it was the
idea of Carnival, their tutelary god in time of
war, first founder, and original of all the
Chitterling race; for which reason he resem-

bled a hog; for Chitterlings drew their extraction from hogs.

Pantagruel asking for what purpose, and
curative indication, he had voided so much
mustard on the earth, the queen replied, that
mustard was their *sang-réal,* and celestial balsam, of which, laying but a little in the
wounds of the fallen Chitterlings, in a very
short time the wounded were healed, and the
dead restored to life. Pantagruel held no further discourse with the queen, but retired on
shipboard. The like did all the boon companions, with their implements of destruction,
and their huge sow.

CHAPTER 43

How Pantagruel went into the Island of
Ruach

Two days after, we arrived at the Island of
Ruach; and I swear to you, by the celestial
hen and chickens, that I found the way of living of the people so strange and wonderful,
that I cannot, for the heart's blood of me, half
tell it you. They live on nothing but wind, eat
nothing but wind, and drink nothing but
wind. They have no other houses but weath-
ercocks. They sow no other seeds but the
three sorts of wind-flowers, rue, and herbs
that make one break wind to the purpose:
these scour them off charmingly. The common sort of people, to feed themselves, make
use of feather, paper, or linen fans, according
to their abilities. As for the rich, they live by
the means of windmills.

When they would have some noble treat,
the tables are spread under one or two windmills. There they feast as merry as beggars,
and during the meal, their whole talk is commonly of the goodness, excellency, salubrity,
and rarity of winds; as you, jolly topers, in
your cups, philosophize and argue upon
wines. The one praises the south-east, the
other the south-west, this the west and by
south, and this the east and by north; another
the west, and another the east; and so of the
rest. As for lovers and amorous sparks, no gale
for them like a smock-gale. For the sick they
use bellows, as we use clysters among us.

Oh! (said to me a little diminutive swollen
bubble) that I had now but a bladder-full of
that same Languedoc wind which they call
Cierce. The famous physician, Scurron, passing one day by this country, was telling us,
that it is so strong, that it will make nothing
of overturning a loaded waggon. Oh! what

good would it not do my œdipodic leg. The biggest are not the best; but, said Panurge, rather would I had here a large butt of that same good Languedoc wine, that grows at Mirevaux, Canteperdrix, and Frontignan.

I saw a good likely sort of a man there, much resembling Ventrose, tearing and fuming in a grievous fret, with a tall burly groom, and a pimping little page of his, laying them on, like the devil, with a buskin. Not knowing the cause of his anger, at first I thought that all this was by the doctor's advice, as being a thing very healthy to the master to be in a passion, and to his man to be banged for it. But at last I heard him taxing his man with stealing from him like a rogue as he was, the better half of a large leathern bag of an excellent southerly wind, which he had carefully laid up, like a hidden reserve, against the cold weather.

They neither exonerate, dung, pis, nor spit in that island; but, to make amends, they belch, fizzle, funk, and give tail shots in abundance. They are troubled with all manner of distempers: and, indeed, all distempers are engendered, and proceed from ventosities, as Hippocrates demonstrates, *lib. De Flatibus*. But the most epidemical among them is the wind-cholic. The remedies which they use are large clysters, whereby they void store of windiness. They all die of dropsies and tympanies; the men farting, and the women fizzling: so that their soul takes her leave at the back-door.

Some time after, walking in the island, we met three hair-brained airy fellows, who seemed mightily puffed up, and went to take their pastime, and view the plovers, who live on the same diet as themselves, and abound in the island. I observed that as your true topers, when they travel, carry flasks, leathern bottles, and small runlets along with them, so each of them had at his girdle a pretty little pair of bellows. If they happened to want wind, by the help of those pretty bellows they immediately drew some, fresh and cool, by attraction and reciprocal expulsion: for, as you well know, wind essentially defined, is nothing but fluctuating and agitated air.

Awhile after, we were commanded, in the king's name, not to receive, for three hours, any man or woman of the country, on board our ships; some having stolen from him a rousing fart, of the very individual wind which old goodman Æolus, the snorer, gave Ulysses, to conduct his ship, whenever it should happen to be becalmed. Which fart the king kept religiously, like another *sangréal*, and performed a world of wonderful cures with it, in many dangerous diseases, letting loose, and distributing to the patient, only as much of it as might frame a virginal fart; which is, if you must know, what our sanctimonials, alias nuns, in their dialect, call ringing backwards.

CHAPTER 44

How small rain lays a high wind

PANTAGRUEL commended their government and way of living, and said to their hypenemian mayor, If you approve Epicurus's opinion, placing the *summum bonum* in pleasure, (I mean pleasure that is easy and free from toil,) I esteem you happy; for your food being wind, costs you little or nothing, since you need but blow. True, sir, returned the mayor, but, alas! nothing is perfect here below: for too often, when we are at table, feeding on some good blessed wind of God, as on celestial manna, merry as so many friars, down drops on a sudden some small rain, which lays our wind, and so robs us of it. Thus many a meal is lost for want of meat.

Just so, quoth Panurge, Jenin Toss-pot, of Quinquenais, evacuating some wine of his own burning [urine] on his wife's posteriors, laid the ill-fumed wind that blowed out of their centre, as out of some magisterial æolipile. Here is a kind of a whim on that subject, which I made formerly:

One evening when Toss-pot had been at his butts,
And Joan, his fat spouse, crammed with turnips her guts,
Together they pigg'd, nor did drink so besot him,
But he did what was done when his daddy begot him.
Now, when to recruit, he'd fain have been snoring,
Joan's back-door was filthily puffing and roaring:
So for spite he bepiss'd her, and quickly did find.
That a small rain lays a very high wind.

We are also plagued yearly with a very great calamity, cried the mayor, for a giant, call Widenostrils, who lives in the Island of Tohu, comes hither every spring to purge, by the advice of his physicians, and swallows us, like so many pills, a great number of wind-mills, and of bellows also, at which his mouth waters exceedingly.

Now this is a sad mortification to us here, who are fain to fast over three or four whole Lents every year for this, besides certain pet-ty Lents, ember weeks, and other orison and starving tides. And have you no remedy for this? asked Pantagruel. By the advice of our Mezarims, replied the mayor, about the time that he uses to give us a visit, we garrison our windmills with good store of cocks and hens. The first time that the greedy thief swallowed them, they had like to have done his business at once: for they crowed and cackled in his maw, and fluttered up and down athwart and along in his stomach, which threw the glutton into a lipothymy cardiac passion, and dread-ful and dangerous convulsions, as if some ser-pent, creeping in at his mouth, had been frisking in his stomach.

Here is a comparative *as*, altogether incon-gruous and impertinent, cried Friar John, in-terrupting them; for I have formerly heard, that if a serpent chance to get into a man's stomach, it will not do him the least hurt, but will immediately get out, if you do but hang the patient by the heels, and lay a pan full of warm milk near his mouth. You were told this, said Pantagruel, and so were those who gave you this account; but none ever saw or read of such a cure. On the contrary, Hippocrates, in his fifth book of *Epidem.*, writes, that such a case happening in his time, the patient presently died of a spasm and convulsion.

Besides the cocks and hens, said the may-or, continuing his story, all the foxes in the country whipped into Widenostrils' mouth, posting after the poultry; which made such a stir with Reynard at their heels, that he griev-vously fell into fits each minute of an hour. At last, by the advice of a Baden enchan-ter, at the time of the paroxysm, he used to flay a fox, by way of antidote and counter-poison. Since that he took better advice, and eases himself with taking a clyster made with a decoction of wheat and barley corns, and of livers of goslings; to the first of which the poultry run, and the foxes to the latter. Be-sides, he swallows some of your badgers or fox-dogs, by the way of pills and boluses. This is our misfortune.

Cease to fear, good people, cried Pantag-ruel, this huge Widenostrils, this same swal-lower of Windmills, is no more, I will assure

you: he died, being stifled and choked with a lump of fresh butter at the mouth of a hot oven, by the advice of his physicians.

CHAPTER 45

How Pantagruel went ashore in the Island of Pope-Figland

THE next morning we arrived at the Island of Pope-figs; formerly a rich and free people, called the Gaillardets; but now, alas! miser-ably poor, and under the yoke of the Papi-men. The occasion of it was this.

On a certain yearly high holiday, the bur-gomaster, syndics, and topping rabbies of the Gaillardets, chanced to go into the neighbour-ing island Papimany to see the festival, and pass away the time. Now one of them having espied the pope's picture, (with the sight of which, according to a laudable custom, the people were blessed on high-offering holi-days,) made mouths at it, and cried, A fig for it! as a sign of manifest contempt and deri-sion. To be revenged of this affront, the Papi-men, some days after, without giving the oth-ers the least warning, took arms, and sur-prised, destroyed, and ruined the whole is-land of the Gaillardets; putting the men to the sword, and sparing none but the women and children; and those too only on condition to do what the inhabitants of Milan were con-demned to, by the Emperor Frederick Bar-barossa.

These had rebelled against him in his ab-sence, and ignominiously turned the empress out of the city, mounting her a horseback on a mule called Thacor, with her breech fore-most towards the old jaded mule's head, and her face turned towards the crupper. Now Frederick being returned, mastered them, and caused so careful a search to be made, that he found out and got the famous mule Thacor. Then the hangman, by his order, clapped a fig into the mule's jimcrack, in the presence of the enslaved cits that were brought into the middle of the great market-place, and proclaimed, in the emperor's name, with trumpets, that whosoever of them would save his own life, should publicly pull the fig out with his teeth, and after that, put it in again in the very individual cranny whence he had drawn it, without using his hands, and that whoever refused to do this, should presently swing for it, and die in his shoes. Some sturdy fools, standing upon their punctillio, chose honourably to be hanged, rather than submit to so shameful and abominable a disgrace; and others, less nice in point of ceremony, took heart of grace, and even resolved to have at the fig, and a fig for it, rather than make a worse figure with a hempen collar, and die in the air, at so short warning: accordingly when they had neatly picked out the fig with their teeth, from old Thacor's snatch-blatch, they plainly showed it the head's-man, saying, *Ecco lo fico,* behold the fig.

By the same ignominy the rest of these poor distressed Gaillardets saved their bacon, becoming tributaries and slaves, and the name of Pope-figs was given them, because they said, A fig for the pope's image. Since this, the poor wretches never prospered, but every year the devil was at their doors, and they were plagued with hail, storms, famine, and all manner of woes, as an everlasting punishment for the sin of their ancestors and relations. Perceiving the misery and calamity of that generation, we did not care to go further up into the country; contenting ourselves with going into a little chapel near the haven, to take some holy water. It was dilapidated and ruined, wanting also a cover—like Saint Peter at Rome. When we were in, as we dipped our fingers in the sanctified cistern, we spied in the middle of that holy pickle, a fellow muffled up with stoles, all under water, like a diving duck, except the tip of his snout to draw his breath. About him stood three priests, true shavelings, clean shorn, and polled, who were muttering strange words to the devils out of a conjuring book.

Pantagruel was not a little amazed at this, and, inquiring what kind of sport these were at, was told, that, for three years last past, the plague had so dreadfully raged in the island, that the better half of it had been utterly depopulated, and the lands lay fallow and unoccupied. Now, the mortality being over, this same fellow, who had crept into the holy tub, having a large piece of ground, chanced to be sowing it with white winter wheat, at the very minute of an hour that a kind of a silly sucking devil, who could not yet write or read, or hail and thunder, unless it were on parsley or coleworts, had got leave of his master Lucifer to go into this Island of Pope-figs, where the devils were very familiar with the men and women, and often went to take their pastime.

This same devil got thither, directed his discourse to the husbandman, and asked him what he was doing. The poor man told him, that he was sowing the ground with corn, to help him to subsist the next year. Ay, but the ground is none of thine, Mr. Plough-jobber, cried the devil, but mine; for since the time that you mocked the pope, all this land has been proscribed, adjudged, and abandoned to us. However, to sow corn is not my province: therefore I will give thee leave to sow the field, that is to say, provided we share the profit. I will, replied the farmer. I mean, said the devil, that of what the land shall bear, two lots shall be made, one of what shall grow above ground, the other of what shall be covered with earth: the right of choosing belongs to me; for I am a devil of noble and ancient race; thou art a base clown. I therefore chose what shall lie under ground, take thou what shall be above. When dost thou reckon to reap, hah? About the middle of July, quoth the farmer. Well, said the devil, I'll not fail thee then: in the meantime, slave as thou oughtest. Work, clown, work: I am going to tempt to the pleasing sin of whoring, the nuns of Dryfart, the sham saints of the cowl, and the gluttonish crew: I am more than sure of these. They need but meet, and the job is done: true fire and tinder, touch and take: down falls nun and up gets friar.

CHAPTER 46

How a junior devil was fooled by a husbandman of Pope-Figland

In the middle of July, the devil came to the place aforesaid, with all his crew at his heels, a whole choir of the younger fry of hell; and having met the farmer, said to him, Well, clodpate, how hast thou done, since I went? Thou and I must share the concern. Ay, master devil, quoth the clown, it is but reason we should. Then he and his men began to cut and reap the corn: and, on the other side, the devil's imps fell to work, grubbing up and pulling out the stubble by the root.

The countryman had his corn thrashed, winnowed it, put it into sacks, and went with it to market. The same did the devil's servants, and sat them down there by the man to sell their straw. The countryman sold off his corn at a good rate, and with the money filled an old kind of a demi-buskin, which was fastened to his girdle. But the devil a sou the devils took: far from taking handsel, they were flouted and jeered by the country louts.

Market being over, quoth the devil to the

farmer, Well, clown, thou hast choused me once, it is thy fault; chouse me twice, it will be mine. Nay, good sir devil, replied the farmer, how can I be said to have choused you, since it was your worship that chose first? The truth is, that, by this trick, you thought to cheat me, hoping that nothing would spring out of the earth for my share, and that you should find whole under ground the corn which I had sowed, and with it tempt the poor and needy, the close hypocrite, or the covetous griper; thus making them fall into your snares. But troth, you must even go to school yet: you are no conjuror, for aught I see: for the corn that was sown is dead and rotten, its corruption having caused the generation of that which you saw me sell: so you chose the worst, and therefore are cursed in the gospel. Well, talk no more of it, quoth the devil: what canst thou sow our field with for next year? If a man would make the best of it, answered the ploughman, it were fit he sow it with radishes. Now, cried the devil, thou talkest like an honest fellow, bumpkin: well, sow me good store of radishes, I will see and keep them safe from storms, and will not hail a bit on them. But harkye me, this time I bespeak for my share what shall be above ground; what is under shall be thine. Drudge on, looby, drudge on. I am going to tempt heretics; their souls are dainty victuals, when broiled in rashers, and well powdered. My Lord Lucifer has the griping in the guts; they will make a dainty warm dish for his honour's maw.

When the season of radishes was come, our devil failed not to meet in the field, with a train of rascally underlings, all waiting devils, and finding there the farmer and his men, he began to cut and gather the leaves of the radishes. After him the farmer with his spade dug up the radishes, and clapped them up into pouches. This done, the farmer, and their gangs, hied them to market, and there the farmer presently made good money of his radishes: but the poor devil took nothing; nay, what was worse, he was made a common laughing stock by the gaping hoydons. I see thou hast played me a scurvy trick, thou villanous fellow, cried the angry devil: at last I am fully resolved even to make an end of the business betwixt thee and myself, about the ground, and these shall be the terms: we will clapperclaw each other, and whoever of us two shall first cry, Hold, shall quit his share of the field, which shall wholly belong to the conqueror. I fix the time for this trial of skill, on this day seven-night: assure thyself that I will claw thee off like a devil. I was going to tempt your fornicators, bailiffs, perplexers of causes, scriveners, forgers of deeds, two-handed councillors, prevaricating solicitors, and other such vermin; but they were so civil as to send me word by an interpreter, that they are all mine already. Besides our master Lucifer is so cloyed with their souls, that he often sends them back to the smutty scullions, and slovenly devils of his kitchen, and they scarce go down with them, unless now and then, when they are high-seasoned.

Some say there is no breakfast like a student's, no dinner like a lawyer's, no afternoon's nunchion like a vinedresser's, no supper like a tradesman's, no second supper like a serving wench's, and none of these meals equal to a frockified hobgoblin's. All this is true enough. Accordingly, at my Lord Lucifer's first course, hobgoblins, alias imps in cowls, are a standing dish. He willingly used to breakfast on students; but, alas, I do not know by what ill luck they have of late years joined the Holy Bible to their studies: so the devil a one we can get down among us; and I verily believe that unless the hypocrites of the tribe of Levi help us in it, taking from the enlightened book-mongers their St. Paul, either by threats, revilings, force, violence, fire, and faggot, we shall not be able to hook in any more of them, to nibble at below. He dines commonly on councillors, mischief-mongers, multipliers of law suits, such as wrest and pervert right and law, and grind and fleece the poor: he never fears to want any of these. But who can endure to be wedded to a dish?

He said, the other day, at a full chapter, that he had a great mind to eat the soul of one of the fraternity of the cowl, that had forgot to speak for himself, in his sermon; and he promised double pay, and a large pension, to any one that should bring him such a tit-bit piping hot. We all went a hunting after such a rarity, but came home without the prey: for they all admonish the good women to remember their convent. As for afternoon nunchions, he has left them off, since he was so woefully griped with the cholic; his fosterers, sutlers, charcoal-men, and boiling cooks having been sadly mauled and peppered off in the northern countries.

His high devilship sups very well on tradesmen, usurers, apothecaries, cheats, coiners, and adulterers of wares. Now and then, when he is on the merry pin, his second supper is of serving wenches; who, after they have, by stealth, soaked their faces with their master's good liquor, fill up the vessel with it at second hand, or with other stinking water.

Well, drudge on, boor, drudge on; I am going to tempt the students of Trebisonde, to leave father and mother, forego for ever the established and common rule of living, disclaim and free themselves from obeying their lawful sovereign's edicts, live in absolute liberty, proudly despise every one, laugh at all mankind, and taking the fine jovial little cap of poetic licence, become so many pretty hobgoblins.

CHAPTER 47

How the Devil was deceived by an old woman of Pope-Figland

THE country lob trudged home very much concerned and thoughtful, you may swear; insomuch that his good woman, seeing him thus look moping, weened that something had been stolen from him at market: but when she had heard the cause of his affliction, and seen his budget well lined with coin, she bade him be of good cheer, assuring him that he would be never the worse for the scratching bout in question; wishing him only to leave her to manage that business, and not trouble his head about it; for she had already contrived how to bring him off cleverly. Let the worst come to the worst, said the husbandman, it will be but a scratch; for I'll yield at the first stroke, and quit the field. Quit a fart, replied the wife; he shall have none of the field: rely upon me, and be quiet; let me alone to deal with him, You say he is a pimping little devil, that is enough; I will soon make him give up the field, I will warrant you. Indeed, had he been a great devil, it had been somewhat.

The day that we landed in the island happened to be that which the devil had fixed for the combat. Now the countryman, having, like a good Catholic, very fairly confessed himself and received, betimes in the morning, by the advice of the vicar, had hid himself, all but the snout, in the holy water pot, in the posture in which we found him; and just as they were telling us this story, news came that the old woman had fooled the devil, and gained the field. You may not be sorry, perhaps, to hear how this happened.

The devil, you must know, came to the poor man's door, and rapping there, cried, So ho! ho the house! ho, clodpate! where art thou! Come out with a vengeance; come out with a wannion; come out and be damned: now for clawing. Then briskly and resolutely entering the house, and not finding the countryman there, he spied his wife lying on the ground piteously weeping and howling. What is the matter? asked the devil. Where is he? what does he? Oh! that I knew where he is, replied threescore and five, the wicked rogue, the butcherly dog, the murderer. He has spoiled me; I am undone; I die of what he has done to me. How, cried the devil, what is it? I will tickle him off for you by and by. Alas, cried the old dissembler, he told me, the butcher, the tyrant, the tearer of devils, told me, that he had made a match to scratch with you this day, and to try his claws, he did but just touch me with his little finger, here betwixt the legs, and has spoiled me for ever. Oh! I am a dead woman; I shall never be myself again: do but see! Nay, and besides, he talked of going to the smith's, to have his pounces sharpened and pointed. Alas! you are undone, Mr. Devil; good sir, scamper quickly, I am sure he won't stay; save yourself, I beseech you. While she said this, she uncovered herself up to the chin, after the manner in which the Persian women met their children who fled from the fight, and plainly showed her what do ye call it. The frighten'd devil, seeing the enormous solution of the continuity in all its dimensions, blessed himself, and cried out, Mahon, Demiourgon, Megæra, Alecto, Persephone; 'slife, catch me here when he comes! I am gone: 'sdeath, what a gash! I resign him the field.

Having heard the catastrophe of the story, we retired a shipboard, not being willing to stay there any longer. Pantagruel gave to the poor's box of the fabric of the church, eighteen thousand good royals, in commiseration of the poverty of the people, and the calamity of the place.

CHAPTER 48

How Pantagruel went ashore at the Island of Papimany

HAVING left the desolate Island of the Pope-figs, we sailed, for the space of a day, very fairly and merrily, and made the blessed Island Papimany. As soon as we had dropt anchor in the road, before we had well moored our ship with ground-tackle, four persons, in different garbs, rowed towards us in a skiff. One of them was dressed like a monk in his frock, draggle-tailed, and booted: the other like a falconer, with a lure, and a long-winged hawk on his fist: the third like a solici-tor, with a large bag, full of informations, subpœnas, breviates, bills, writs, cases and other implements of pettifogging. The fourth looked like one of your vine barbers about Orleans, with a jantee pair of canvass trou-sers, a dosser, and a pruning knife at his gir-dle.

As soon as the boat had clapped them on board, they all with one voice asked, Have you seen him, good passengers, have you seen him?—Who? asked Pantagruel. You know, answered they. Who is it? asked Friar John. 'Sblood and 'ounds, I'll thrash him thick and threefold. This he said, thinking that they inquired after some robber, murderer, or church-breaker. Oh wonderful, cried the four, do not you foreign people know the one? Sirs, replied Epistemon, we do not understand those terms: but if you will be pleased to let us know who you mean, we will tell you the truth of the matter, without any more ado. We mean, said they, He that is. Did you ever see him? He that is, returned Pantagruel, ac-cording to our theological doctrine, is God, who said to Moses, I am that I am. We never saw him, nor can he be beheld by mortal eyes. We mean nothing less than that su-preme God, who rules in heaven, replied they; we mean the god on earth. Did you ever see him? Upon my honour, replied Carpalim, they mean the pope. Ay, ay, answered Pan-urge: yea verily, gentlemen, I have seen three of them, whose sight has not much bettered me. How! cried they, our sacred decretals in-form us, that there never is more than one living. I mean successively, one after the oth-er, returned Panurge: otherwise I never saw more than one at a time.

O thrice and four times happy people! cried they, you are welcome, and more than double welcome! They then kneeled down before us and would have kissed our feet, but we would not suffer it, telling them that, should the pope come thither in his own per-son, it is all they could do to him. No, certain-ly, answered they, for we have already re-solved upon the matter. We would kiss his bare arse, without boggling at it, and eke his two pounders: for he has a pair of them, the holy father, that he has; we find it so by our five decretals, otherwise he could not be

pope. So that, according to our subtile decre-talin philosophy, this is a necessary conse-quence: he is pope; therefore, he has geni-tories (genitals) and should genitories no more be found in the world, the world could no more have a pope.

While they were talking thus, Pantagruel inquired of one of the coxswain's crew, who those persons were? He answered, that they were the four estates of the realm; and added, that we should be made as welcome as prin-ces, since we had seen the pope. Panurge hav-ing been acquainted with this by Pantagruel, said to him in his ear, I swear and vow, sir, it is even so; he that has patience may compass any thing. Our seeing the pope hath done us no good; now, in the devil's name, it will do us a great deal. We then went ashore, and the whole country, men, women, and children, came to meet us as in a solemn procession. Our four estates cried out to them with a loud voice, They have seen him! they have seen him! they have seen him! That proclamation being made, all the mob kneeled before us, lifting up their hands towards heaven, and crying, O happy men! O most happy! and this acclamation lasted about a quarter of an hour.

Then came the school-master of the place, with all his ushers, and school-boys, whom he magisterially flogged, as they used to whip children in our country formerly, when some criminal was hanged, that they might remem-ber it. This displeased Pantagruel, who said to them, Gentlemen, if you do not leave off whipping these poor children, I am gone. The people were amazed, hearing his stento-rian voice; and I saw a little hump with long fingers, say to the hypodidascal, What! in the name of wonder do all those that see the pope grow as tall as yon huge fellow that threatens us! Ah! how I shall think time long till I have seen him too, that I may grow and look as big. In short, the acclamations were so great, that Homenas (so they called their bishop) has-tened thither, on an unbridled mule, with green trappings, attended by his apposts (as they said) and his supposts, or officers, bear-ing crosses, banners, standards, canopies, torches, holy water-pots, etc. He too wanted to kiss our feet, (as the good Christian Val-finier did to Pope Clement,) saying, that one of their hypothetes, that is, one of the scaven-gers, scourers, and commentators of their holy decretals, had written that, in the same manner as the Messiah, so long and so much expected by the Jews, at last appeared among them; so, on some happy day of God, the pope would come into that island; and that, while they waited for that blessed time, if any who had seen him at Rome, or elsewhere, chanced to come among them, they should be sure to make much of them, feast them plentifully, and treat them with a great deal of reverence. However, we civilly desired to be excused.

CHAPTER 49

How Homenas, Bishop of Papimany, showed us the Uranopet decretals

HOMENAS then said to us: It is enjoined us by our holy decretals to visit churches first, and taverns after. Therefore, not to decline that fine institution, let us go to church; we will afterwards go and feast ourselves. Man of God, quoth Friar John, do you go before, we will follow you: you spoke in the matter properly, and like a good Christian; it is long since we saw any such. For my part this rejoices my mind very much, and I verily believe that I shall have the better stomach after it. Well it is a happy thing to meet with good men! Being come near the gate of the church, we spied a huge thick book, gilt, and covered all over with precious stones, as rubies, emeralds, diamonds, and pearls, more, or at least as valuable as those which Augustus consecrated to Jupiter Capitolinus. This book hung in the air, being fastened with two thick chains of gold to the zoophore of the porch. We looked on it, and admired it. As for Pantagruel, he handled it, and dandled it, and turned it as he pleased, for he could reach it without straining; and he protested, that whenever he touched it, he was seized with a pleasant tickling at his finger's end, new life and activity in his arms, and a violent temptation in his mind to beat one or two serjeants, or such officers, provided they were not of the shaveling kind. Homenas then said to us, The law was formerly given to the Jews by Moses, written by God himself. At Delphos, before the portal of Apollo's temple, this sentence, ΓΝΩΘΙ ΣΕ ΑΥΤΟΝ was found written with a divine hand. And some time after it, E I was also seen and as divinely written and transmitted from heaven. Cybele's image was brought out of heaven, into a field called Pessinunt, in Phrygia; so was that of Diana to Tauris, if you will believe Euripides; the oriflamb, or holy standard,

was transmitted out of heaven to the noble and most Christian kings of France, to fight against the unbelievers. In the reign of Numa Pompilius, second King of the Romans, the famous copper buckler called Ancile, was seen to descend from heaven. At Acropolis, near Athens, Minerva's statue formerly fell from the imperial heaven. In like manner the sacred decretals, which you see, were written with the hand of an angel, of the cherubim kind. You outlandish people will hardly believe this, I fear, Little enough of conscience, said Panurge.—And then, continued Homenas, they were miraculously transmitted to us here from the very heaven of heavens; in the same manner as the river Nile is called *Diipetes* by Homer, the father of all philosophy, (the holy decretals always excepted.) Now, because you have seen the pope, their evangelist and everlasting protector, we will give you leave to see and kiss them on the inside, if you think meet. But then you must fast three days before, and canonically confess; nicely and strictly mustering up, and inventorising your sins great and small, so thick that one single circumstance of them may not escape you; as our holy decretals, which you see direct. This will take up some time. Man of God, answered Panurge, we have seen and descried decrees, and eke decretals enough of conscience; some on paper, others on parchment, fine and gay like any painted paper lantern, some on vellum, some in manuscript, and others in print: so you need not take half these pains to show these. We will take the good-will for the deed, and thank you as much as if we had. Ay, marry, said Homenas, but you never saw those that are angelically written. Those in your country are only transcripts from ours; as we find it written by one of our old decretaline scholiasts. For me, do not spare me; I do not value the labour; so I may serve you: do but tell me whether you will be confessed, and fast only three short little days of God? As for confessing, answered Panurge, there can be no great harm in it; but this same fasting, master of mine, will hardly down with us at this time, for we have so very much overfasted ourselves at sea, that the spiders have spun their cobwebs over our grinders. Do but look on this good Friar John des Entomeures, (Homenas then courteously demy-clipped him about the neck) some moss is growing in his throat, for want of bestirring and exercising his chaps. He speaks the truth, vouched Friar John; I have so much fasted that I am almost grown hump-shouldered. Come, then, let us go into the church, said Homenas; and pray forgive us if for the present, we do not sing you a fine high mass. The hour of mid-day is past, and after it our sacred decretals forbid us to sing mass, I mean your high and lawful mass. But I will say a low and dry one, for you. I had rather have one moistened with some good Anjou wine, cried Panurge; fall to, fall to your low mass, and dispatch. Odd's-boddi-kins, quoth Friar John, it frets me to the guts that I must have an empty stomach at this time of day. For, had I eaten a good breakfast and fed like a monk, if he should chance to sing us the *Requiem æternam dona eis, Domine,*[21] I had then brought thither bread and wine for the *traits passez,* (those that are gone before.) Well, patience; pull away, and save tide: short and sweet, I pray you, and this for a cause.

CHAPTER 50

How Homenas showed us the Arch-type, or representation of a pope

Mass being mumbled over, Homenas took a huge bundle of keys out of a trunk near the head altar, and put thirty-two of them into so many key-holes; put back so many springs; then with fourteen more mastered so many padlocks, and at last opened an iron window strongly barred above the said altar. This being done, in token of great mystery, he covered himself with wet sackcloth, and drawing a curtain of crimson satin, showed us an image daubed over, coarsely enough, to my thinking: then he touched it with a pretty long stick, and made us all kiss the part of the stick that had touched the image. After this he said unto us, What think you of this image? It is the likeness of a pope, answered Pantagruel: I know it by the triple crown, his furred amice, his rochet, and his slipper. You are in the right, said Homenas; it is the idea of that same good god on earth, whose coming we devoutly await, and whom we hope one day to see in this country. O happy, wished for, and much expected day! and happy, most happy you, whose propitious stars have so favoured you, as to let you see the living and real face of this good god on earth! by the single sight of whose picture we obtain full remission of all the sins which we remember that we have committed, as also a third part, and eighteen quarantaines of the

sins which we have forgot: and indeed we only see it on high annual holidays.

This caused Pantagruel to say, that it was a work like those which Dædalus used to make, since, though it were deformed and ill drawn, nevertheless some divine energy, in point of pardons, lay hid and concealed in it. Thus, said Friar John, at Sevillé, the rascally beggars being one evening on a solemn holiday at supper in the spital, one bragged of having got six blancs, or two-pence half-penny; another eight liards, or two-pence; a third, seven caroluses, or six-pence; but an old mumper made his vaunts of having got three testons, or five shillings. Ah, but, cried his comrades, thou hast a leg of God; as if, continued Friar John, some divine virtue could lie hid in a stenching ulcerated rotten shank. Pray, said Pantagruel, when you are for telling us some such nauseous tale, be so kind as not to forget to provide a bason, Friar John: I'll assure you, I had much ado to forbear bringing up my breakfast. Fie! I wonder a man of your coat is not ashamed to use thus the sacred name of God, in speaking of things so filthy and abominable! fie, I say. If among your monking tribes such an abuse of words is allowed, I beseech you leave it there, and do not let it come out of the cloisters. Physicians, said Epistemon, thus attribute a kind of divinity to some diseases: Nero also extolled mushrooms, and, in a Greek proverb, termed them divine food, because with them he had poisoned Claudius his predecessor. But methinks, gentlemen, this same picture is not over like our late pope's. For I have seen them, not with their pallium, amice, or rochet on, but with helmets on their heads, more like the top of a Persian turban; and while the Christian commonwealth was in peace, they alone were most furiously and cruelly making war. This must have been then, returned Homenas, against the rebellious, heretical Protestants; reprobates, who are disobedient to the holiness of this good god on earth. It is not only lawful for him to do so, but it is enjoined him by the sacred decretals; and if any dare transgress one single iota against their commands, whether they be emperors, kings, dukes, princes, or commonwealths, he is immediately to pursue them with fire and sword, strip them of all their goods, take their kingdoms from them, proscribe them, anathematize them, and destroy not only their bodies, those of their children, relations, and others, but damn also their souls to the very bottom of the most hot and burning cauldron in hell. Here, in the devil's name, said Panurge, the people are no heretics; such as was our Raminagrobis, and as they are in Germany and England. You are Christians of the best edition, all picked and culled, for aught I see. Ay, marry are we, returned Homenas, and for that reason we shall all be saved. Now let us go and bless ourselves with holy-water, and then to dinner.

CHAPTER 51

Table-talk in praise of the decretals

Now, topers, pray observe that while Homenas was saying his dry mass, three collectors, or licensed beggars of the church, each of them with a large bason, went round among the people with a loud voice; Pray remember the blessed men who have seen his face. As we came out of the temple, they brought their basons brim full of papimany chink to Homenas, who told us that it was plentifully to feast with; and that, of this contribution and voluntary tax, one part should be laid out in good drinking, another in good eating, and the remainder in both: according to an admirable exposition hidden in a corner of their holy decretals; which was performed to a T, and that at a noted tavern not much unlike that of Will's at Amiens. Believe me, we tickled it off there with copious cramming, and numerous swilling.

I made two notable observations at that dinner: the one, that there was not one dish served up, whether of cabrittas, capons, hogs, (of which latter there is great plenty in Papimany,) pigeons, conies, leverets, turkeys, or others, without abundance of magistral stuffing: the other, that every course, and the fruit also, were served up by unmarried females of the place, tight lasses, I will assure you, waggish, fair, good-conditioned, and comely, spruce, and fit for business. They were all clad in fine long white albs, with two girdles; their hair interwoven with narrow tape and purple riband, stuck with roses, gilly-flowers, marjoram, daffidown-dillies, thyme, and other sweet flowers.

At every cadence, they invited us to drink and bang it about, dropping us neat and genteel courtesies: nor was the sight of them unwelcome to all the company; and as for Friar John, he leered on them sideways, like a cur that steals a capon. When the first course was

taken off, the females melodiously sung us an epode in the praise of the sacrosant decretals; and then the second course being served up, Homenas, joyful and cheery, said to one of the she butlers, Light here, Clerica. Immediately one of the girls brought him a tall-boy brim-full of extravagant wine. He took fast hold of it, and fetching a deep sigh, said to Pantagruel, My lord, and you my good friends, here's to ye, with all my heart: you are all very welcome. When he had tipped that off, and given the tall-boy to the pretty creature, he lifted up his voice and said, O most holy decretals, how good is good wine found through your means! This is the best jest we have had yet, observed Panurge. But it would still be better, said Pantagruel, if they could turn bad wine into good.

O seraphic *Sextum!* continued Homenas, how necessary are you not to the salvation of poor mortals! O cherubic *Clementinæ!* how perfectly the perfect institution of a true Christian is contained and described in you! O angelical *Extravagantes!*[22] how many poor souls that wander up and down in mortal bodies, through this vale of misery, would perish, were it not for you! When, ah! when shall this special gift of grace be bestowed on mankind, as to lay aside all other studies and concerns, to use you, to peruse you, to understand you, to know you by heart, to practise you, to incorporate you, to turn you into blood, and incentre you into the deepest ventricles of their brains, the inmost marrow of their bones, and most intricate labyrinth of their arteries? Then, ah, then! and no sooner than then, nor otherwise than thus, shall the world be happy! While the old man was thus running on, Epistemon rose and softly said to Panurge, For want of a close stool, I must even leave you for a moment or two: this stuff has unbunged the orifice of my mustard-barrel: but I'll not tarry long.

Then, ah then! continued Homenas, no hail, frost, ice, snow, overflowing, or *vis major:* then plenty of all earthly goods here below. Then uninterrupted and eternal peace through the universe, an end of all wars, plunderings, drudgeries, robbing, assassinates, unless it be to destroy these cursed rebels the heretics. Oh, then, rejoicing, cheerfulness, jollity, solace, sports, and delicious pleasures, over the face of the earth. Oh! what great learning, inestimable erudition, and god-like precepts, are knit, linked, riveted, and mortised in the divine chapters of these eternal decretals!

Oh! how wonderfully, if you read but one demy canon, short paragraph, or single observation of these sacrosanct decretals, how wonderfully, I say, do you not perceive to kindle in your hearts a furnace of divine love, charity towards your neighbour, (provided he be no heretic,) bold contempt of all casual and sublunary things, firm content in all your affections, and ecstatic elevation of soul even to the third heaven.

CHAPTER 52

A continuation of the miracles caused by the decretals

SPOKE like an organ, quoth Panurge; but for my part, I believe as little of it as I can. For, one day by chance I happened to read a chapter of them at Poictiers, at the most decretalipotent Scotch doctor's, and old Nick turn me into bumfodder, if this did not make me so hide-bound and costive, that for four or five days I hardly scumbered one poor butt of sir-reverence; and that, too, was full as dry and hard, I protest, as Catullus tells us were those of his neighbour Furius:

Nec toto decies cacas in anno,
Atque id durius est fabâ, et lapillis:
Quod tu si manibus teras, fricesque,
Non unquam digitum inquinare possis.[23]

Oh, ho, cried Homenas, by our lady, it may be you were then in a state of mortal sin, my friend. Well turned, cried Panurge, this was a new strain egad.

One day, said Friar John, at Sevillé I had applied to my posteriors, by way of hind-towel, a leaf of an old *Clementinæ* which our rent-gatherer, John Guimard, had thrown out into the green of our cloister; now the devil broil me like a black pudding, if I was not so abominably plagued with chaps, chawns, and piles at the fundament, that the orifice of my poor nockandroe was in a most woeful pickle for I do not know how long. By our lady, cried Homenas, it was a plain punishment of God, for the sin that you had committed in bewraying that sacred book, which you ought rather to have kissed and adored; I say with an adoration of *latria*, or of *hyperdulia*[24] at least: the Panormitan never told a lie in the matter.

Saith Ponocrates: At Montpelier, John Choüart having bought of the monks of St. Olary a delicate set of decretals, written on fine large parchment of Lamballe, to beat gold between the leaves, not so much as a piece that was beaten in them came to good, but all were dilacerated and spoiled. Mark this, cried Homenas; it was a divine punishment and vengeance.

At Mans, said Eudemon, Francis Cornu, apothecary, had turned an old set of *Extravagantes* into waste paper: may I never stir, if whatever was lapped up in them was not immediately corrupted, rotten, and spoiled; incense, pepper, cloves, cinnamon, saffron, wax, cassia, rhubarb, tamarinds, all drugs and spices, were all lost without exception. Mark, mark, quoth Homenas, an effect of divine justice! This comes of putting the sacred Scriptures to such profane uses.

At Paris, said Carpalim, snip Groignet the tailor had turned an old *Clementinæ* into patterns and measures, and all the clothes that were cut on them were utterly spoiled and lost; gowns, hoods, cloaks, cassocks, jerkins, jackets, waistcoats, capes, doublets, petticoats, *corps de robes,* farthingales, and so forth. Snip, thinking to cut a hood, would cut you out a codpiece; instead of a cassock, he would make you a high-crowned hat; for a waistcoat, he would shape you out a rochet; on the pattern of a doublet, he would make you a thing like a frying-pan; then his journeymen having stitched it up, did jag it and pink it at the bottom, and so it looked like a pan to fry chesnuts. Instead of a cape, he made a buskin; for a farthingale, he shaped a montero cap; and thinking to make a cloak, he would cut out a pair of our big out-strouting Swiss breeches, with panes like the outside of a tabour. Insomuch that Snip was condemned to make good the stuffs to all his customers; and to this day poor cabbage's hair grows through his hood, and his arse through his pocket-holes. Mark, an effect of heavenly wrath and vengeance! cried Homenas.

At Cahusac, said Gymnast, a match being made by the lords of Estissac and Viscount Lausun to shoot at a mark, Perotou had taken to pieces a set of decretals, and set one of the leaves for the white to shoot at: now I sell, nay I give and bequeath for ever and aye, the mould of my doublet to fifteen hundred hampers full of black devils, if ever any archer in the country (though they are singular marksmen in Guienne) could hit the white. Not the least bit of the holy scribble was contaminated or touched: nay, and Sansornin the elder, who held stakes, swore to us, *figues dioures,* hard figs, (his greatest oath,) that he had openly, visibly, and manifestly seen the bolt of Carquelin moving right to the round circle in the middle of the white; and that just on the point, when it was going to hit and enter, it had gone aside above seven foot and four inches wide of it towards the bakehouse.

Miracle! cried Homenas, miracle! miracle! *Clerica,* come wench, light, light here. Here's to you all, gentlemen; I vow you seem to me very sound Christians. While he said this, the maidens began to snicker at his elbow, grinning, giggling, and twittering among themselves. Friar John began to paw, neigh, and whinny at the snout's end, as one ready to leap, or at least to play the ass, and get up and ride tantivy to the devil, like a beggar on horseback.

Methinks, said Pantagruel, a man might have been more out of danger near the white of which Gymnast spoke, than was formerly Diogenes near another. How is that? asked Homenas; what was it? Was he one of our decretalists? Rarely fallen in again egad, said Epistemon, returning from stool; I see he will hook his decretals in, though by the head and shoulders.

Diogenes, said Pantagruel, one day, for pastime, went to see some archers that shot at butts, one of whom was so unskilful, that, when it was his turn to shoot, all the bystanders went aside, lest he should mistake them for the mark. Diogenes had seen him shoot extremely wide of it: so when the other was taking aim a second time, and the people removed at a great distance to the right and left of the white, he placed himself close by the mark; holding that place to be the safest, and that so bad an archer would certainly rather hit any other.

One of the Lord d'Estissac's pages at last found out the charm, pursued Gymnast, and by his advice Perotin put in another white made up of some papers of Pouillac's lawsuit, and then every one shot cleverly.

At Landerousse, said Rhizotomus, at John Delif's wedding were very great doings, as it was then the custom of the country. After supper, several farces, interludes, and comical scenes were acted: they had also several morris-dancers with bells and tabours; and divers sorts of masks and mummers were let

in. My school-fellows and I, to grace the festival to the best of our power, (for fine white and purple liveries had been given to all of us in the morning) contrived a merry mask with store of cockle-shells, shells of snails, periwinkles, and such other. Then for want of cuckoo pintle, or priest-pintle, lousebur, clote, and paper, we made ourselves false faces with the leaves of an old *Sextum,* that had been thrown by, and lay there for any one that would take it up: cutting out holes for the eyes, nose, and mouth. Now, did you ever hear the like since you were born? when we had played out little boyish antic tricks, and came to take off our sham faces, we appeared more hideous and ugly than the little devils that acted the "Passion" at Douay: for our faces were utterly spoiled at the places which had been touched by those leaves: one had there the small-pox; another, God's token, or the plague-spot; a third, the crinckums; a fourth, the measles; a fifth, botches, pushes, and carbuncles; in short, he came off the least hurt, who only lost his teeth by the bargain. Miracle! bawled out Homenas, miracle!

Hold, hold, cried Rhizotomus, it is not yet time to clap. My sister Kate, and my sister Ren, had put the crepines of their hoods, their ruffles, snuffekins, and neck-ruffs new washed, starched, and ironed, into that very book of decretals; for, you must know, it was covered with thick boards, and had strong clasps. Now by the virtue of God— Hold, interrupted Homenas, what God do you mean? There is but one, answered Rhizotomus. In heaven, I grant, replied Homenas; but we have another here on earth, do you see. Ay, marry have we, said Rhizotomus; but on my soul I protest I had quite forgot it. Well then, by the virtue of god the pope, their pinners, neck-ruffs, bibs, coifs, and other linen, turned as black as a charcoal-man's sack. Miracle! cried Homenas. Here, *Clerica,* light me here; and pr'ythee, girl, observe these rare stories. How comes it to pass then, asked Friar John, that people say,

Ever since decrees had tails,
And *gens d'armes* lugged heavy mails,
Since each monk would have a horse,
All went here from bad to worse.

I understand you, answered Homenas: this is one of the quirks and little satires of the newfangled heretics.

CHAPTER 53

How by the virtue of the decretals, gold is subtilely drawn out of France to Rome

I WOULD, said Epistemon, it had cost me a pint of the best tripe that ever can enter into gut, so we had but compared with the original the dreadful chapters, *Execrabilis, De multa, Si plures, De annatis per totum, Nisi essent, Cum ad monasterium, Quod delectio, Mandatum;*[25] and certain others, that draw every year out of France to Rome, four hundred thousand ducats and more.

Do you make nothing of this? asked Homenas. Though, methinks, after all, it is but little, if we consider that France, the most Christian, is the only nurse the see of Rome has. However, find me in the whole world a book, whether of philosophy, physic, law, mathematics, or other human learning, nay, even, by my God, of the Holy Scripture itself, will draw as much money thence? None, none, pshaw, tush, blurt, pish; none can. You may look till your eyes drop out of your head, nay, till doomsday in the afternoon, before you can find another of that energy; I will pass my word for that.

Yet these devilish heretics refuse to learn and know it. Burn them, tear them, nip them with hot pincers, drown them, hang them, spit them at the bunghole, pelt them, paut them, bruise them, beat them, cripple them, dismember them, cut them, gut them, bowel them, paunch them, thrash them, slash them, gash them, chop them, slice them, slit them, carve them, saw them, bethwack them, pare them, hack them, hew them, mince them, flea them, boil them, broil them, roast them, toast them, bake them, fry them, crucify them, crush them, squeeze them, grind them, batter them, burst them, quarter them, unlimb them, behump them, bethump them, belump them, belabour them, pepper them, spitchcock them, and carbonade them on gridirons, these wicked heretics! decretalifuges, decretalicides, worse than homicides, worse than patricides, decretalictiones of the devil of hell.

As for you other good people, I must earnestly pray and beseech you to believe no other thing, to think on, say, undertake, or do no other thing, than what's contained in our sacred decretals, and their corollaries, this fine *Sextum*, these fine *Clementinæ*, these fine *Extravagants*. O deific books! So shall you enjoy glory, honour, exaltation, wealth, dignities, and preferments in this world; be revered, and dreaded by all, preferred, elected, and chosen, above all men.

For, there is not under the cope of heaven a condition of men, out of which you will find persons fitter to do and handle all things, than those who by divine prescience, eternal predestination, have applied themselves to the study of the holy decretals.

Would you choose a worthy emperor, a good captain, a fit general in time of war, one that can well foresee all inconveniences, avoid all dangers, briskly and bravely bring his men on to a breach or attack, still be on sure grounds, always overcome without loss of his men, and know how to make a good use of his victory? Take me a decretist.—No, no, I mean a decretalist. Ho, the foul blunder, whispered Epistemon.

Would you, in time of peace, find a man capable of wisely governing the state of a commonwealth, of a kingdom, of an empire, of a monarchy; sufficient to maintain the clergy, nobility, senate, and commons in wealth, friendship, unity, obedience, virtue, and honesty? Take a decretalist.

Would you find a man, who, by his exemplary life, eloquence, and pious admonitions, may in a short time, without effusion of human blood, conquer the Holy Land, and bring over to the holy church the misbelieving Turks, Jews, Tartars, Muscovites, Mamelukes, and Sarrabonites? Take me a decretalist.

What makes, in many countries, the people rebellious and depraved, pages saucy and mischievous, students sottish and duncical? Nothing but that their governors, and tutors were not decretalists.

But what, on your conscience, was it, do you think, that established, confirmed, and authorised those fine religious orders, with whom you see the Christian world every where adorned, graced, and illustrated, as the firmament is with its glorious stars? The holy decretals.

What was it that founded, underpropped, and fixed, and now maintains, nourishes, and feeds the devout monks, and friars in convents, monasteries, and abbeys; so that did they not daily and nightly pray without ceasing, the world would be in evident danger of returning to its primitive chaos? The sacred decretals.

What makes and daily increases the famous and celebrated patrimony of St. Peter in plenty of all temporal, corporeal, and spiritual blessings? The holy decretals.

What made the holy apostolic see and pope of Rome, in all times, and at this present, so dreadful in the universe, that all kings, emperors, potentates, and lords, willing, nilling, must depend upon him, hold of him, be crowned, confirmed, and authorised by him, come thither to strike sail, buckle, and fall down before his holy slipper, whose picture you have seen? The mighty decretals of God.

I will discover you a great secret. The universities of your world have commonly a book either open or shut in their arms, and devices: what book do you think it is? Truly, I do not know, answered Pantagruel; I never read it. It is the decretals, said Homenas, without which the privileges of all universities would soon be lost. You must own, that I have taught you this; ha, ha, ha, ha, ha!

Here Homenas began to belch, to fart, to funk, to laugh, to slaver, and to sweat; and then he gave his huge greasy four-cornered cap to one of the lasses, who clapt it on her pretty head with a great deal of joy, after she had lovingly bussed it, as a sure token that she should be first married. *Vivat*, cried Epistemon, *fifat, bibat, pipat.*[26]

O apocalyptic secret! continued Homenas; light, light, Clerica, light here with double lanterns. Now for the fruit, virgins.

I was saying then, that giving yourselves thus wholly to the study of the holy decretals, you will gain wealth and honour in this world: I add, that in the next you will infallibly be saved in the blessed kingdom of heaven, whose keys are given to our good god and decretaliarch. O my good god, whom I adore and never saw, by thy special grace open unto us, at the point of death at least, this most sacred treasure of our holy mother church, whose protector, preserver, butler, chief larder, administrator, and disposer thou art; and take care, I beseech thee, O lord, that the precious works of supererogation, the goodly pardons, do not fail us in time of need: so that the devils may not find an opportunity to gripe our precious souls, and the dreadful jaws of hell may not swallow us. If we must pass through purgatory, thy will be done. It is in thy power to draw us out of it when thou pleasest. Here Homenas began to shed huge hot briny tears, to beat his breast, and kiss his thumbs in the shape of a cross.

CHAPTER 54

How Homenas gave Pantagruel some bon-Christian pears

EPISTEMON, Friar John, and Panurge, seeing this doleful catastrophe, began, under the cover of their napkins, to cry, meeow, meeow, meeow; feigning to wipe their eyes all the while as if they had wept. The wenches were doubly diligent, and brought brimmers of Clementine wine to every one, besides store of sweetmeats; and thus the feasting was revived.

Before we arose from table, Homenas gave us a great quantity of fair large pears; saying, Here, my good friends, these are singular good pears; you will find none such any where else, I dare warrant. Every soil bears not every thing, you know; India alone boasts black ebony; the best incense is produced in Sabæa; the sphragitid earth at Lemnos: so this island is the only place where such fine pears grow. You may, if you please, make nurseries with their kernels in your country.

I like their taste extremely, said Pantagruel. If they were sliced, and put into a pan on the fire with wine and sugar, I fancy they would be very wholesome meat for the sick, as well as for the healthy. Pray what do you call them? No otherwise than you have heard, replied Homenas. We are a plain downright sort of people, as God would have it, and call figs, figs; plums, plums; and pears, pears. Truly, said Pantagruel, if I live to go home,—which I hope will be speedily, God willing,—I'll set off and graff some in my garden in Touraine, by the banks of the Loire, and will call them bon-Christian or good-Christian pears: for I never saw better Christians than are these good Papimans. I would like him two to one better yet, said Friar John, would he but give us two or three cartloads of yon buxom lasses. Why, what would you do with them? cried Homenas. Quoth Friar John, No harm, only bleed the kind-hearted souls straight between the two great toes, with certain clever lancets of the right stamp: by which operation good Christian children would be inoculated upon them, and the breed be multiplied in our country, in which there are not many over good, the more's the pity.

Nay verily, replied Homenas, we cannot do this; for you would make them tread their shoes awry, crack their pipkins, and spoil their shapes: you love mutton, I see, you will run at sheep; I know you by that same nose and hair of yours, though I never saw your face before. Alas! alas! how kind you are! And would you indeed damn your precious soul? Our decretals forbid this. Ah, I wish you had them at your finger-end. Patience, said Friar John; but, *si tu vis dare, præsta, quæsumus.*[27] Matter of breviary. As for that, I defy all the world, and I fear no man that wears a head and a hood, though he were a chrystallin, I mean a decretalin doctor.

Dinner being over, we took our leave of the right reverend Homenas, and of all the good people, humbly giving thanks; and, to make them amends for their kind entertainment, promised them that, at our coming to Rome, we would make our applications so effectually to the pope, that he would speedily be sure to come to visit them in person. After this we went on board.

Pantagruel, by an act of generosity, and as an acknowledgment of the sight of the pope's picture, gave Homenas nine pieces of double frized cloth of gold, to be set before the grates of the window. He also caused the church box, for its repairs and fabric, to be quite filled with double crowns of gold; and ordered nine hundred and fourteen angels to be delivered to each of the lasses, who had waited at table, to buy them husbands when they could get them.

CHAPTER 55

How Pantagruel, being at sea, heard various unfrozen words

WHEN we were at sea, junketting, tippling, discoursing, and telling stories, Pantagruel rose and stood up to look out: then asked us, Do you hear nothing, gentlemen? Methink I hear some people talking in the air, yet I can see nobody. Hark! According to his command we listened, and with full ears sucked in the air, as some of you suck oysters, to find if we could hear some sound scattered through the sky; and to lose none of it, like the Emperor Antoninus, some of us laid their hands hollow next to their ears; but all this would not do, nor could we hear any voice. Yet Pantagruel continued to assure us he heard various voices in the air, some of men, and some of women.

At last we began to fancy that we also heard something, or at least that our ears tingled; and the more we listened, the plainer we discerned the voices, so as to distin-

guish articulate sounds. This mightily frightened us, and not without cause; since we could see nothing, yet heard such various sounds and voices of men, women, children, horses, etc., insomuch that Panurge cried out, Cods belly, there is no fooling with the devil; we are all beshit, let us fly. There is some ambuscade hereabouts. Friar John, art thou here, my love? I pray thee, stay by me, old boy. Hast thou got thy swingeing tool? See that it do not stick in thy scabbard; thou never scourest it half as it should be. We are undone. Hark! They are guns, gad judge me: let us fly, I do not say with hands and feet, as Brutus said at the Battle of Pharsalia; I say, with sails and oars: let us whip it away: I never find myself to have a bit of courage at sea; in cellars, and elsewhere, I have more than enough. Let us fly and save our bacon. I do not say this for any fear that I have; for I dread nothing but danger, that I do not; I always say it, that should not. The free archer of Baignolet said as much. Let us hazard nothing therefore, I say, lest we come off bluely. Tack about, helm a lee, thou son of a bachelor. Would I were now well in Quinquenois, though I were never to marry. Haste away, let us make all the sail we can; they will be too hard for us; we are not able to cope with them; they are ten to our one; I will warrant you; nay, and they are on their dunghill, while we do not know the country. They will be the death of us. We will lose no honour by flying: Demosthenes saith, that the man that runs away, may fight another day. At least, let us retreat to the leeward. Helm a lee; bring the main tack aboard, hawl the bowlins, hoist the topgallants; we are all dead men; get off, in the devil's name, get off.

Pantagruel, hearing the sad outcry which Panurge made, said, Who talks of flying? Let us first see who they are; perhaps they may be friends: I can discover nobody yet, though I can see a hundred miles round me. But let us consider a little: I have read that a philosopher, named Petron, was of opinion, that there were several worlds, that touched each other in an equilateral triangle; in whose centre, he said, was the dwelling of truth: and that the words, ideas, copies, and images of all things past, and to come, resided there; round which was the age; and that with success of time part of them used to fall on mankind, like rheums and mildews; just as the dew fell on Gideon's fleece, till the age was fulfilled.

I also remember, continued he, that Aristotle affirms Homer's words to be flying, moving, and consequently animated. Besides, Antiphanes said, that Plato's philosophy was like words, which, being spoken in some country during a hard winter are immediately congealed, frozen up, and not heard: for what Plato taught young lads, could hardly be understood by them when they were grown old. Now continued he, we should philosophize and search whether this be not the place where those words are thawed.

You would wonder very much, should this be the head and lyre of Orpheus. When the Thracian women had torn him to pieces, they threw his head and lyre into the river Hebrus; down which they floated to the Euxine sea, as far as the island of Lesbos; the head continually uttering a doleful song, as it were, lamenting the death of Orpheus, and the lyre, with the wind's impulse, moving its strings, and harmoniously accompanying the voice. Let us see if we cannot discover them hereabouts.

CHAPTER 56

How among the frozen words Pantagruel found some odd ones

THE skipper made answer: Be not afraid, my lord, we are on confines of the Frozen Sea, on which, about the beginning of last winter, happened a great and bloody fight between the Arimaspians and the Nephelibates. Then the words and cries of men and women, the hacking, slashing, and hewing of battleaxes, the shocking, knocking, and jolting of armours and harnesses, the neighing of horses, and all other martial din and noise, froze in the air; and now, the rigour of the winter being over, by the succeeding serenity and warmth of the weather, they melt and are heard.

By jingo, quoth Panurge, the man talks somewhat like; I believe him: but could not we see some of them? I think I have read, that, on the edge of the mountain on which Moses received the Judaic law, the people saw the voices sensibly.—Here, here, said Pantagruel, here are some that are not yet thawed. He then threw us on the deck whole handfuls of frozen words, which seemed to us like your rough sugar plums, of many colours, like those used in heraldry; some words gules, (this means also jests and merry sayings,) some vert, some azure, some black,

some or, (this means fair words;) and when we had somewhat warmed them between our hands, they melted like snow, and we really heard them, but could not understand them, for it was a barbarous gibberish. One of them, only, that was pretty big, having been warmed between Friar John's hands, gave a sound much like that of chesnuts when they are thrown into the fire, without being first cut, which made us all start. This was the report of a field piece in its time, cried Friar John.

Panurge prayed Pantagruel to give him some more; but Pantagruel told him, that to give words was the part of a lover. Sell me some then, I pray you, cried Panurge. That is the part of a lawyer, returned Pantagruel. I would sooner sell you silence, though at a dearer rate; as Demosthenes formerly sold it by the means of his *argentangina,* or silver quinsey.

However, he threw three or four handfuls of them on the deck; among which I perceived some very sharp words, and some bloody words, which, the pilot said, used sometimes to go back, and recoil to the place whence they came, but it was with a slit weasand: we also saw some terrible words, and some others not very pleasant to the eye.

When they had been all melted together, we heard a strange noise, hin, hin, hin, hin, his, tick, tock, taack, bredelin-brededack, frr, frr, frr, bou, bou, bou, bou, bou, bou, track, track, trr, trr, trr, trrr, trrrr; on, on, on, on, ouououououon, gog, magog, and I do not know what other barbarous words; which, the pilot said, were the noise made by the charging squadrons, the shock and neighing of horses.

Then we heard some large ones go off like drums and fifes, and others like clarions and trumpets. Believe me we had very good sport with them. I would fain have saved some merry odd words, and have preserved them in oil, as ice and snow are kept, and between clean straw. But Pantagruel would not let me, saying, that it is a folly to hoard up what we are never like to want, or have always at hand; odd, quaint, merry, and fat words of gules, never being scarce among all good and jovial Pantagruelists.

Panurge somewhat vexed Friar John, and put him in the pouts; for he took him at his word, while he dreamed of nothing less. This caused the friar to threaten him with such a piece of revenge as was put upon G. Jousseaume, who having taken the merry Patelin at his word, when he had overbid himself in some cloth, was afterwards fairly taken by the horns like a bullock, by his jovial chapman, whom he took at his word like a man. Panurge, well knowing that threatened folks live long, bobbed, and made mouths at him, in token of derision, then cried, Would I had here the word of the Holy Bottle, without being thus obliged to go further in pilgrimage to her.

CHAPTER 57

How Pantagruel went ashore at the dwelling of Gaster, the first master of arts in the world

THAT day Pantagruel went ashore in an island, which, for situation and governor, may be said not to have its fellow. When you just come into it, you find it rugged, craggy, and barren, unpleasant to the eye, painful to the feet, and almost as inaccessible as the mountain of Dauphiné, which is somewhat like a toad-stool, and was never climbed, as any can remember, by any but Doyac, who had the charge of King Charles the Eighth's train of artillery.

This same Doyac, with strange tools and engines, gained that mountain's top, and there he found an old ram. It puzzled many a wise head to guess how it got thither. Some said that some eagle, or great horn-coot, having carried it thither while it was yet a lambkin, it had got away, and saved itself among the bushes.

As for us, having with much toil and sweat overcome the difficult ways at the entrance, we found the top of the mountain so fertile, healthful, and pleasant, that I thought I was then in the true garden of Eden, or earthly paradise, about whose situation our good theologues are in such a quandary, and keep such a pother.

As for Pantagruel, he said, that there was the seat of Areté—that is as much as to say, virtue—described by Hesiod. This, however, with submission to better judgments. The ruler of this place was one Master Gaster, the first master of arts in the world. For, if you believe that fire is the great master of arts, as Tully writes, you very much wrong him and yourself: alas, Tully never believed this. On the other side, if you fancy Mercury to be the first inventor of arts, as our ancient Druids believed of old, you are mightily beside the mark. The satirist's sentence, that affirms master Gaster to be the master of all arts, is true. With him peacefully resided old goody Penia, alias Poverty, the mother of the ninety-nine Muses, on whom Porus, the lord of Plenty, formerly begot Love, that noble child, the mediator of heaven and earth, as Plato affirms *in Symposio.*

We were all obliged to pay our homage, and swear allegiance to that mighty sovereign; for he is imperious, severe, blunt, hard, uneasy, inflexible: you cannot make him believe, represent to him, or persuade him anything.

He does not hear: and, as the Egyptians said that Harpocrates, the god of silence, named Sigalion in Greek, was *astomé,* that is, without a mouth; so Gaster was created without ears, even like the image of Jupiter in Candia.

He only speaks by signs: but those signs are more readily obeyed by every one, than the statutes of senates, or commands of monarchs: neither will he admit the least let or delay in his summons. You say, that when a lion roars, all the beasts at a considerable distance round about, as far as his roar can be heard, are seized with a shivering. This is written, it is true; I have seen it. I assure you, that at master Gaster's command, the very heavens tremble, and all the earth shakes: his command is called, Do this or die. Needs must when the devil drives; there's no gainsaying of it.

The pilot was telling us how, on a certain time, after the manner of the members that mutinied against the belly, as Æsop describes it, the whole kingdom of the Somates went off into a direct faction against Gaster, resolving to throw off his yoke: but they soon found their mistake, and most humbly submitted; for otherwise they had all been famished.

What company soever he is in, none dispute with him for precedence or superiority; he still goes first, though kings, emperors, or even the pope, were there. So he held the first place at the council of Basle; though some will tell you that the council was tumultuous, by the contention and ambition of many for priority.

Every one is busied, and labours to serve him; and, indeed, to make amends for this, he does this good to mankind, as to invent for them all arts, machines, trades, engines, and crafts: he even instructs brutes in arts which are against their nature, making poets of ravens, jackdaws, chattering jays, parrots, and starlings, and poetesses of magpies, teaching them to utter human language, speak and sing; and all for the gut. He reclaims and tames eagles, gerfalcons, falcons gentle, sakers, lanners, goshawks, sparrow-hawks, merlins, hagards, passengers, wild rapacious birds; so that setting them free in the air, whenever he thinks fit, as high and as long as he pleases, he keeps them suspended, straying, flying, hovering, and courting him above the clouds: then on a sudden he makes them stoop, and come down amain from heaven next to the ground; and all for the gut.

Elephants, lions, rhinoceroses, bears, horses, mares, and dogs, he teaches to dance, prance, vault, fight, swim, hide themselves, fetch and carry what he pleases; and all for the gut.

Salt and fresh-water fish, whales, and the monsters of the main, he brings them up from the bottom of the deep; wolves he forces out of the woods, bears out of the rocks, foxes out of their holes, and serpents out of the ground; and all for the gut.

In short, he is so unruly, that in his rage he devours all men and beasts: as was seen among the Vascons, when Q. Metellus besieged them in the Sertorian wars; among the Saguntines besieged by Hannibal; among the Jews besieged by the Romans, and six hundred more; and all for the gut. When his regent Penia takes a progress, wherever she moves, all senates are shut up, all statutes repealed, all orders and proclamations vain; she knows, obeys, and has no law. All shun her, in every place choosing rather to expose themselves to shipwreck at sea, and venture through fire, rocks, caves, and precipices, than be seized by that most dreadful tormentor.

CHAPTER 58

How, at the court of the Master of Ingenuity, Pantagruel detested the Engastrimythes and the Gastrolaters

AT the court of that great master of ingenuity, Pantagruel observed two sorts of troublesome and too officious apparitors, whom he very much detested. The first were called Engastrimythes; the others, Gastrolaters.

The first pretended to be descended of the ancient race of Eurycles; and for this brought the authority of Aristophanes, in his comedy called *The Wasps:* whence of old they were called Euryclians, as Plato writes, and Plutarch in his book of the *Cessation of Oracles.* In the holy decrees, 26, *qu.* 3, they are styled *Ventriloqui:* and the same name is given them in Ionian by Hippocrates, in his fifth book of *Epid.,* as men who speak from the belly. Sophocles calls them *Sternomantes.* These were soothsayers, enchanters, cheats, who gulled the mob, and seemed not to speak and give answers from the mouth, but from the belly.

Such a one, about the year of our Lord 1513, was Jacoba Rodogina, an Italian woman of mean extract: from whose belly, we, as well as an infinite number of others at Ferrara, and elsewhere, have often heard the voice of the evil spirit speak; low, feeble, and small, indeed; but yet very distinct, articulate, and intelligible, when she was sent for, out of curiosity, by the lords and princes of the Cisalpine Gaul. To remove all manner of doubt, and be assured that this was not a trick, they used to have her stripped stark naked, and caused her mouth and nose to be stopped. This evil spirit would be called Curledpate, or Cincinnatulo, seeming pleased when any called him by that name; at which, he was always ready to answer. If any spoke to him of things past or present, he gave pertinent answers, sometimes to the amazement of the hearers: but if of things to come, then the devil was gravelled, and used to lie as fast as a dog can trot. Nay, sometimes he seemed to own his ignorance; instead of an answer, letting out a rousing fart, or muttering some words with barbarous and uncouth inflexions, and not to be understood.

As for the Gastrolaters, they stuck close to one another in knots and gangs. Some of them merry, wanton, and soft as so many milksops; others louring, grim, dogged, demure, and crabbed; all idle, mortal foes to business, spending half their time in sleeping, and the rest in doing nothing, a rent-charge and dead unnecessary weight on the earth, as Hesiod saith; afraid, as we judged, of offending or lessening their paunch. Others were masked, disguised, and so oddly dressed, that it would have done you good to have seen them.

There's a saying, and several ancient sages write, that the skill of nature appears wonderful in the pleasure which she seems to have taken in the configuration of sea-shells, so great is their variety in figures, colours, streaks, and inimitable shapes. I protest the variety we perceived in the dresses of the gastrolatrous coquillons was not less. They all owned Gaster for their supreme god, adored him as a god, offered him sacrifices as to their omnipotent deity, owned no other god, served, loved, and honoured him above all things.

You would have thought that the holy apostle spoke of those, when he said, *Phil.* chap. 3, "Many walk, of whom I have told you often, and now tell you even weeping, that they are enemies of the cross of Christ: whose end is destruction, whose God is their belly." Pantagruel compared them to the cyclops Polyphemus, whom Euripides brings in speaking thus: I only sacrifice to myself (not to the gods) and to this belly of mine the greatest of all gods.

CHAPTER 59

Of the ridiculous statue Manduce; and how, and what the Gastrolaters sacrifice to their ventripotent god

WHILE we fed our eyes with the sight of the phyzzes and actions of these lounging gulli-gutted Gastrolaters, we on a sudden heard the sound of a musical instrument called a bell; at which all of them placed themselves in rank and file, as for some mighty battle, every one according to his office, degree, and seniority.

In this order, they moved towards master Gaster, after a plump, young, lusty, gorbellied fellow, who, on a long staff, fairly gilt, carried a wooden statue, grossly carved, and as scurvily daubed over with paint; such a one as Plautus, Juvenal, and Pomp. Festus described it. At Lyons, during the Carnival, it is called Maschecroute, or Gnaw-crust; they call this Manduce.

It was a monstrous, ridiculous, hideous figure, fit to fright little children: its eyes were bigger than its belly, and its head larger than all the rest of its body: well mouth-cloven however, having a goodly pair of wide, broad jaws, lined with two rows of teeth, upper tier and under tier, which, by the magic of a small twine hid in the hollow part of the golden staff, were made to clash, clatter, and rattle dreadfully one against another; as they do at Metz, with St. Clement's dragon.

Coming near the Gastrolaters, I saw they were followed by a great number of fat waiters and tenders, laden with baskets, dossers, hampers, dishes, wallets, pots, and kettles.

Then under the conduct of Manduce, and singing I do not know what dithyrambics, crepalocomes, and epenons, opening their baskets and pots, they offered their god,

White hippocras, with dry toasts.	Soft bread. Household bread.
White bread.	Capirotades.
Brown bread.	Cold loins of veal, with spice.
Carbonadoes, six sorts.	Zinziberine.
Brawn.	Beatille pies.
Sweet-breads.	Brewis.
Fricassees, nine sorts.	Marrow-bones, toast, and cabbage.
Monastical brewis.	Hashes.
Gravy soup.	
Hotch-pots.	

Eternal drink intermixed. Brisk delicate white wine led the van; claret and champaign followed, cool, nay, as cold as the very ice, I say; filled and offered in large silver cups. Then they offered,

Chitterlings garnished with mustard.	Carvelats. Bolognia sausages.
Hams.	Chines and peas.
Hung beef.	Hogs' haslets.
Sausages.	Brawn heads.
Neats' tongues.	Powdered venison with turnips.
Scotch collops.	Pickled olives.
Puddings.	

All this associated with sempiternal liquor. Then they housed within his muzzle,

Legs of mutton with shalots.	Curlews. Wood-hens.
Olias.	Coots, with leeks.
Lumber pies with hot sauce.	Fat-kids. Shoulders of mutton with capers.
Ribs of pork with onion sauce.	Sirloins of beef.
Roast capons, basted with their own dripping.	Breasts of veal. Pheasants and pheasant poots.
Caponets.	Fried pasty-crust.
Caviare and toast.	Forced capons.
Fawns, deer.	Parmesan cheese.
Hares, leverets.	Red and pale hippocras.
Partridges and young partridges.	Gold-peaches.
Plovers.	Artichokes.
Dwarf-herons.	Dry and wet sweetmeats, seventy-eight sorts.
Teals.	
Duckers.	
Bitterns.	Boiled hens, and fat capons marinated.
Shovelers.	

Pullets with eggs.
Chickens.
Rabbits, and sucking rabbits.
Quails, and young quails.
Pigeons, squabs, and squeakers.
Herons, and young herons.
Fieldfares.
Olives.
Thrushes.
Young sea-ravens.
Geese, goslings.
Queests.
Widgeons.
Souced hog's feet.
Mavises.
Grouse.
Turtles.
Doe-conies.
Peacocks.
Storks.
Woodcocks.
Snipes.
Ortolans.
Turkey cocks, hen turkeys, and turkey poots.
Stock-doves, and woodculvers.
Pigs, with wine sauce.
Blackbirds, ousels, and rayles.
Moor-hens.
Bustards, and bustard poots.

Fig-peckers.
Young Guinea hens.
Flamingoes.
Cygnets.
A reinforcement of vinegar intermixed.
Venison pasties.
Lark-pies.
Dormice-pies.
Cabretto pasties.
Roe-buck pies.
Pigeon pies.
Kid pasties.
Capon-pies.
Bacon pies.
Hedgehogs.
Snites.
Then large puffs.
Thistle-finches.
Whores' farts.
Fritters.
Cakes, sixteen sorts.
Crisp wafers.
Quince tarts.
Curds and cream.
Whipped cream.
Preserved myrabolans.
Jellies.
Welsh barrapyclids.
Macaroons.
Tarts, twenty sorts.
Lemon-cream, raspberry cream, etc.
Comfits, one hundred colours.
Cream wafers.
Cream-cheese.

Vinegar brought up the rear to wash the mouth, and for fear of the squinsy: also toasts to scour the grinders.

CHAPTER 60

What the Gastrolaters sacrificed to their god on interlarded fish-days

PANTAGRUEL did not like this pack of rascally scoundrels, with their manifold kitchen sacrifices, and would have been gone, had not Epistemon prevailed with him to stay and see the end of the farce. He then asked the skipper, what the idle lobcocks used to sacrifice to their gorbellied god on interlarded fish-days? For his first course, said the skipper, they give him:

Caviare.
Botargoes.
Fresh butter.
Pease soup.
Spinage.
Fresh herrings, full roed.
Salads, a hundred varieties, of cresses, sodden, hop-tops, bishop's-cods, celery, chives, rampions, jew's-ears (a sort of mushrooms that sprout out of old elders) asparagus, wood-bine, and a world of others.
Red herrings.
Pilchards.
Anchovies.
Fry of tunny.
Cauliflowers.
Beans.
Salt salmon.
Pickled griggs.
Oysters in the shell.

Then he must drink, or the devil would gripe him at the throat: this, therefore, they take care to prevent, and nothing is wanting. Which being done, they give him lampreys with hippocras sauce:

Gurnards.
Salmon-trouts.
Barbels, great and small.
Roaches.
Cockerells.
Minnows.
Thornbacks.
Sleeves.
Sturgeons.
Sheath-fish.
Mackerels.
Maids.
Plaice.
Fried oysters.
Cockles.
Prawns.
Smelts.
Rock-fish.
Gracious lords.
Sword-fish.
Skate-fish.
Lamprels.
Jegs.
Pickerells.
Golden carps.
Burbates.
Salmons.
Salmon-peels.
Dolphins.
Barn trouts.
Millers'-thumbs.
Precks.
Bret fish.

Flounders.
Sea-nettles.
Mullets.
Gudgeons.
Dabs and sandings.
Haddocks.
Carps.
Pikes.
Bottitoes.
Rochets.
Sea-bears.
Sharplings.
Tunnies.
Silver-eels.
Chevins.
Cray-fish.
Pallours.
Shrimps.
Congers.
Porpoises.
Bases.
Shads.
Murenes, a sort of lampreys.
Craylings.
Smys.
Turbots.
Trout, not above a foot long.
Salmon.
Meagers.
Sea breams.
Halibuts.
Soles.

Dog's tongue, or kind fool.

Mussels.

Lobsters.

Great prawns.

Dace.

Bleaks.

Tenches.

Ombres.

Fresh cods.

Dried melwels.

Darefish.

Fausens, and grigs.

Eelpouts.

Tortoises.

Serpents, i.e. wood-
eels.

Dorees.

Moor-game.

Perches.

Loaches.

Crab-fish.

Snails and whelks.

Frogs.

If, when he had crammed all this down his guttural trapdoor, he did not immediately make the fish swim again in his paunch, death would pack him off in a trice. Special care is taken to antidote his godship with vine-tree syrup. Then is sacrificed to him, haberdines, poor-jack, minglemangled mismashed, etc.

Eggs fried, beaten, buttered, poached, hardened, boiled, broiled, stewed, sliced, roasted in the embers, tossed

in the chimney, etc.
Stock-fish.
Green-fish.
Sea-batts.
Cods' sounds.
Sea-pikes.

Which to concoct and digest the more easily, vinegar is multiplied. For the latter part of their sacrifices they offer,

Rice milk, and hasty pudding.

Buttered, wheat, and flummery.

Water-gruel, and milk porridge.

Frumenty and bonny clamber.

Stewed prunes, and baked bullace.

Pistachios, or fistic nuts.

Figs.

Almond-butter.

Skirret-root.

White-pot.

Raisins.

Dates.

Chestnuts and wal-
nuts.

Filberts.

Parsnips.

Artichokes.

Perpetuity of soaking with the whole.

It was none of their fault, I will assure you, if this same god of theirs was not publicly, preciously, and plentifully served in the sacrifices, better yet than Heliogabalus's idol; nay, more than Bel and the Dragon in Babylon, under King Belshazzar. Yet Gaster had the manners to own that he was no god, but a poor, vile, wretched creature. And as King Antigonus, first of the name, when one Hermodotus, (as poets will flatter, especially princes,) in some of his fustian dubbed him a god, and made the sun adopt him for his son, said to him; My lasanophore (or in plain English my groom of the close-stool), can give thee the lie; so master Gaster very civilly used to send back his bigoted worshippers to his close-stool, to see, smell, taste, philosophise, and examine what kind of divinity they could pick out of his sir-reverence.

CHAPTER 61

How Gaster invented means to get and pre-serve corn

THOSE gastrolatrous hobgoblins being withdrawn, Pantagruel carefully minded the famous master of arts, Gaster. You know that, by the institution of nature, bread has been assigned him for provision and food; and that, as an addition to this blessing, he should never want the means to get bread.

Accordingly, from the beginning he invented the smith's art, and husbandry to manure the ground, that it might yield him corn; he invented arms, and the art of war, to defend corn; physic and astronomy, with other parts of mathematics, which might be useful to keep corn a great number of years in safety from the injuries of the air, beasts, robbers, and purloiners: he invented water, wind, and handmills, and a thousand other engines to grind corn, and to turn it into meal; leaven to make the dough ferment, and the use of salt to give it a savour; for he knew that nothing bred more diseases than heavy, unleavened, unsavoury bread.

He found a way to get fire to bake it; hourglasses, dials, and clocks to mark the time of its baking; and as some countries wanted corn, he contrived means to convey it out of one country into another.

He had the wit to pimp for asses and mares, animals of different species, that they might copulate for the generation of a third, which we call mules, more strong and fit for hard service than the other two. He invented carts and waggons, to draw him along with greater ease: and as seas and rivers hindered his progress, he devised boats, gallies, and ships (to the astonishment of the elements) to waft him over to barbarous, unknown, and far distant nations, thence to bring, or thither to carry corn.

Besides, seeing that, when he had tilled the ground, some years the corn perished in it for want of rain in due season, in others rotted, or was drowned by its excess, sometimes spoiled by hail, shook out by the wind, or beaten down by storms, and so his stock was destroyed on the ground; we are told that ever since the days of yore, he has found out a way to conjure the rain down from heaven only with cutting certain grass, common enough in the field, yet known to very few, some of which was then shown us. I took it to be the same as the plant, one of whose boughs being dipped by Jove's priest in the Agrian fountain, on the Lycian mountain in Arcadia, in time of drought, raised vapours which gathered into clouds, and then dissolved into rain, that kindly moistened the whole country.

Our master of arts was also said to have found a way to keep the rain up in the air, and make it to fall into the sea; also to annihilate the hail, suppress the winds, and remove storms as the Methanensians of Trœzene used to do. And as in the fields thieves and plunderers sometimes stole, and took by force the corn and bread which others had toiled to get, he invented the art of building towns, forts, and castles, to hoard and secure that staff of life. On the other hand, finding none in the fields, and hearing that it was stored up and secured in towns, forts, and castles, and watched with more care than ever were the golden pippins of the Hesperides, he turned engineer, and found ways to beat, storm, and demolish forts and castles, with machines and warlike thunderbolts, battering-rams, ballistas, and catapults, whose shapes were shown us, not over-well understood by our engineers, architects, and other disciples of Vitruvius; as master Philibert de l'Orme, King Megistus's principal architect, has owned to us.

And seeing that sometimes all these tools of destruction were baffled by the cunning subtilty or the subtle cunning (which you please) of fortifiers, he lately invented cannons, field-pieces, culverins, mortar-pieces, basilisks, murdering instruments that dart iron, leaden, and brazen balls, some of them outweighing huge anvils. This by the means of a most dreadful powder, whose hellish compound and effect has even amazed nature, and made her own herself out-done by art; the Oxydracian thunders, hails, and storms, by which the people of that name immediately destroyed their enemies in the field, being but mere popguns to these. For, one of our great guns, when used is more dreadful, more terrible, more diabolical, and maims, tears, breaks, slays, mows down, and sweeps away more men, and causes a greater consternation and destruction, than a hundred thunderbolts.

CHAPTER 62

How Gaster invented an art to avoid being hurt or touched by cannon balls

GASTER having secured himself with his corn within strongholds, has sometimes been attacked by enemies; his fortresses, by that thrice three-fold cursed instrument, levelled and destroyed: his dearly beloved corn and bread snatched out of his mouth, and sacked by a tyrannic force; therefore he then sought means to preserve his walls, bastions, rampiers, and sconces from cannon-shot, and to hinder the bullets from hitting him, stopping them in their flight, or at least from doing him or the besieged walls any damage. He showed us a trial of this, which has been since used by Fronton, and is now common among the pastimes and harmless recreations of the Thelemites. I will tell you how he went to work, and pray for the future be a little more ready to believe what Plutarch affirms to have tried. Suppose a herd of goats were all scampering as if the devil drove them, do but put a bit of eringo into the mouth of the hindmost nanny, and they will all stop stock still, in the time you can tell three.

Thus Gaster, having caused a brass falcon to be charged with a sufficient quantity of gunpowder, well purged from its sulphur, and curiously made up with fine camphor; he then had a suitable ball put into the piece, with twenty-four little pellets like hail-shot, some round, some pearl fashion: then taking his aim, and levelling it at a page of his, as if he would have hit him on the breast; about sixty strides off the piece, half-way between it and the page in a right line, he hanged on a gibbet by a rope a very large siderite, or iron-like stone, otherwise called herculean, formerly found on Ida in Phrygia by one Magnes, as Nicander writes, and commonly called load-stone; then he gave fire to the prime on the piece's touch-hole, which in an instant consuming the powder, the ball and hail-shot were with incredible violence and swiftness hurried out of the gun at its muzzle, that the air might penetrate to its chamber, where otherwise would have been a vacuum; which nature abhors so much, that this universal machine, heaven, air, land, and sea would sooner return to the primitive chaos, than admit the least void any where. Now the ball and small shot, which threatened the page with no less than quick destruction, lost their impetuosity, and remained suspended and hovering round the stone: nor did any of them, notwithstanding the fury with which they rushed, reach the page.

Master Gaster could do more than all this yet, if you will believe me: for he invented a way how to cause bullets to fly backwards, and recoil on those that sent them, with as great a force, and in the very numerical parallel for which the guns were planted. And indeed, why should he have thought this difficult, seeing the herb ethiopis opens all locks whatsoever; and an echinus or remora, a silly weakly fish, in spite of all the winds that blow from the thirty-two points of the compass, will in the midst of a hurricane make you the biggest first-rate remain stock still, as if she were becalmed, or the blustering tribe had blown their last: nay, and with the flesh of that fish, preserved with salt, you may fish gold out of the deepest well that was ever sounded with a plummet; for it will certainly draw up the precious metal. Since, as Democritus affirmed, and Theophrastus believed and experienced, that there was an herb at whose single touch an iron wedge, though never so far driven into a huge log of the hardest wood that is, would presently come out; and it is this same herb your hickways, alias woodpeckers, use, when with some mighty axe any one stops up the hole of their nests, which they industriously dig and make in the trunk of some sturdy tree. Since stags and hinds, when deeply wounded with darts, arrows, and bolts, if they do but meet the herb called dittany, which is common in Candia, and eat a little of it, presently the shafts came out, and all is well again; even as kind Venus cured her beloved by-blow Æneas, when he was wounded on the right thigh with an arrow by Juturna, Turnus's sister. Since the very wind of laurels, fig-trees, or sea claves, makes the thunder sheer off insomuch that it never strikes them. Since at the sight of a ram, mad elephants recover their former senses. Since mad bulls coming near wild fig-trees, called caprifici, grow tame, and will not budge a foot, as if they had the cramp. Since the venomous rage of vipers is assuaged if you but touch them with a beechen bough. Since also Euphorion writes, that

in the Isle of Samos, before Juno's temple was built there, he has seen some beasts called neades, whose voice made the neighbouring places gape and sink into a chasm and abyss. In short, since elders grow of a more pleasing sound, and fitter to make flutes, in such places where the crowing of cocks is not heard, as the ancient sages have writ, and Theophrastus relates: as if the crowing of a cock dulled, flattened, and perverted the wood of the elder, as it is said to astonish and stupify with fear that strong and resolute animal, a lion. I know that some have understood this of wild elder, that grows so far from towns or villages, that the crowing of cocks cannot reach near it; and doubtless that sort ought to be preferred to the stenching common elder, that grows about decayed and ruined places; but others have understood this in a higher sense, not literal, but allegorical, according to the method of the Pythagoreans: as when it was said that Mercury's statue could not be made of every sort of wood; to which sentence they gave this sense; that God is not to be worshipped in a vulgar form, but in a chosen and religious manner. In the same manner by this elder, which grows far from places where cocks are heard, the ancients meant, that the wise and studious ought not to give their minds to trivial or vulgar music, but to that which is celestial, divine, angelical, more abstracted, and brought from remoter parts, that is, from a region where the crowing of cocks is not heard: for, to denote a solitary and unfrequented place, we say, cocks are never heard to crow there.

CHAPTER 63

How Pantagruel fell asleep near the Island of Chaneph, and of the problems proposed to be solved when he waked

THE next day, merrily pursuing our voyage, we came in sight of the Island of Cheneph, where Pantagruel's ship could not arrive, the wind chopping about, and then failing us so that we were becalmed, and could hardly get ahead, tacking about from starboard to larboard, and larboard to starboard, though to our sails we added drabblers.

With this accident we were all out of sorts, moping, drooping, metagrabolized, as dull as dun in the mire, in C *sol fa ut* flat, out of tune, off the hinges, and I-don't-know-how-ish, without caring to speak one single syllable to each other.

Pantagruel was taking a nap, slumbering
and nodding on the quarter deck, by the cuddy, with an Heliodorus in his hand; for still
it was his custom to sleep better by book than
by heart.

Epistemon was conjuring, with his astrolabe, to know what latitude we were in.

Friar John was got into the cook-room, examining, by the ascendant of the spirits, and
the horoscope of ragouts and fricassees, what
time of day it might then be.

Panurge (sweet baby!) held a stalk of
Pantagruelion, alias hemp, next his tongue,
and with it made pretty bubbles and bladders.

Gymnast was making tooth pickers with
lentisk.

Ponocrates, dozing, dozed, and dreaming,
dreamed; tickled himself to make himself
laugh, and with one finger scratched his noddle where it did not itch.

Carpalim, with a nut-shell, and a trencher
of verne, (that's a card in Gascony,) was
making a pretty little merry windmill, cutting
the card longways into four slips, and fastening them with a pin to the convex of the nut,
and its concave to the tarred side of the gunnel of the ship.

Eusthenes, bestriding one of the guns, was
playing on it with his fingers, as if it had been
a trump-marine.

Rhizotomus, with the soft coat of a field
tortoise, alias ycleped a mole, was making
himself a velvet purse.

Xenomanes was patching up an old weather-beaten lantern, with a hawk's jesses.

Our pilot (good man!) was pulling maggots out of the seamen's noses.

At last Friar John, returning from the forecastle, perceived that Pantagruel was awake.
Then breaking this obstinate silence, he
briskly and cheerfully asked him how a man
should kill time, and raise good weather, during a calm at sea?

Panurge, whose belly thought his throat
cut, backed the motion presently, and asked
for a pill to purge melancholy.

Epistemon also came on, and asked how a
man might be ready to bepiss himself with
laughing, when he has no heart to be merry?

Gymnast, arising, demanded a remedy for
a dimness of eyes.

Ponocrates, after he had a while rubbed
his noddle, and shaken his ears, asked, how

one might avoid dog-sleep? Hold, cried Pantagruel, the Peripatetics have wisely made a
rule, that all problems, questions, and doubts,
which are offered to be solved, ought to be
certain, clear, and intelligible. What do you
mean by dog's-sleep? I mean, answered Ponocrates, to sleep fasting in the sun at noonday as the dogs do.

Rhizotomus, who lay stooping on the
pump, raised his drowsy head, and lazily
yawning, by natural sympathy, set almost every one in the ship ayawning too: then he
asked for a remedy against oscitations and
gapings.

Xenomanes, half puzzled, and tired out
with new vamping his antiquated lantern,
asked, how the hold of the stomach might be
so well ballasted and freighted from the keel
to the main hatch, with stores well stowed,
that our human vessels might not heel, or be
walt, but well trimmed and stiff?

Carpalim, twirling his diminutive windmill, asked how many motions are to be felt
in nature, before a gentleman may be said to
be hungry?

Eusthenes, hearing them talk, came from
between decks, and from the capstern called
out to know why a man that is fasting bit by
a serpent also fasting, is in greater danger of
death, than when man and serpent have eat
their breakfasts? Why a man's fasting-spittle
is poisonous to serpents and venomous creatures?

One single solution may serve for all your
problems, gentlemen, answered Pantagruel,
and one single medicine for all such symptoms and accidents. My answer shall be short,
not to tire you with a long needless train of
pedantic cant. The belly has no ears, nor is it
to be filled with fair words: you shall be answered to content by signs and gestures. As
formerly at Rome, Tarquin the proud, its
last king, sent an answer by signs to his son
Sextus, who was among the Gabii at Gabii.
(Saying this, he pulled the string of a little
bell, and Friar John hurried away to the
cookroom.) The son having sent his father a
messenger to know how he might bring the
Gabii (Gabini) under a close subjection; the
king, mistrusting the messenger, made him
no answer, and only took him into his privy
garden, and in his presence, with his sword,
lopped off the heads of the tall poppies that
were there. The express returned without any
other dispatch: yet having related to the
prince what he had seen his father do, he eas-

ily understood that by those signs he advised him to cut off the heads of the chief men in the town, the better to keep under the rest of the people.

CHAPTER 64

How Pantagruel gave no answer to the problems

PANTAGRUEL then asked what sort of people dwelt in that damned island? They are, answered Xenomanes, all hypocrites, holy mountebanks, tumblers of *Ave Marias,* spiritual comedians, sham saints, hermits, all of them poor rogues, who like the hermit of Lormont between Blaye and Bordeaux, live wholly on alms given them by passengers. Catch me there if you can, cried Panurge! may the devil's head-cook conjure my bumgut into a pair of bellows, if ever you find me among them. Hermits, sham saints, living forms of mortification, holy mountebanks, avaunt, in the name of your father Satan, get out of my sight: when the devil's a hog, you shall eat bacon. I shall not forget yet awhile our fat Concilipetes of Chesil. O that Beelzebub and Astorath had counselled them to hang themselves out of the way, and they had done it! we had not then suffered so much by devilish storms as we did for having seen them. Hark ye me, dear rogue, Xenomanes, my friend, I prithee are these hermits, hypocrites, and eaves-droppers, maids or married? Is there anything of the feminine gender among them? Could a body hypocritically take there a small hypocritical touch? Will they lie backwards, and let out their forerooms? There's a fine question to be asked, cried Pantagruel. Yes, yes, answered Xenomanes; you may find there many goodly hypocritesses, jolly spiritual actresses, kind hermitesses, women that have a plaguy deal of religion: then there's the copies of them, little hypocritillons, sham sanctitos, and hermetillons. Foh! away with them, cried Friar John; a young saint, an old devil! (Mark this, an old saying, and as true a one as a young whore an old saint.) Were there not such, continued Xenomanes, the Isle of Chaneph, for want of a multiplication of progeny, had long ere this been desert and desolate.

Pantagruel sent them by Gymnast, in the pinnace, seventy-eight thousand fine pretty little gold half-crowns, of those that are marked with a lantern. After this he asked, What's o'clock? Past nine, answered Episte-

mon. It is then the best time to go to dinner, said Pantagruel: for the sacred line, so celebrated by Aristophanes in his play called *Concionatores,* is at hand, never failing when the shadow is decempedal.

Formerly, among the Persians, dinner time was at a set hour only for kings: as for all others, their appetite and their belly was their clock; when that chimed, they thought it time to go to dinner. So we find in Plautus a certain parasite making a heavy do, and sadly railing at the inventors of hour-glasses and dials, as being unnecessary things, there being no clock more regular than the belly.

Diogenes, being asked at what times a man ought to eat, answered, The rich when he is hungry, the poor when he has anything to eat. Physicians more properly say, that the canonical hours are,

To rise at five, to dine at nine,
To sup at five, to sleep at nine.

The famous king Petosiris's magic was different,—Here the officers for the gut came in, and got ready the tables and cupboards; laid the cloth, whose sight and pleasant smell were very comfortable; and brought plates, napkins, salts, tankards, flagons, tall-boys, ewers, tumblers, cups, goblets, basons, and cisterns.

Friar John, at the head of the stewards, sewers, yeomen of the pantry, and of the mouth, tasters, carvers, cup-bearers, and cupboard-keepers, brought four stately pasties so huge, that they put me in mind of the four bastions at Turin. Odsfish, how manfully did they storm them! What havoc did they make with the long train of dishes that came after them! How bravely did they stand to their pan-puddings, and paid off their dust! How merrily did they soak their noses!

The fruit was not yet brought in, when a fresh gale at west and by north began to fill the main course, missen-sail, foresail, tops, and top-gallants: for which blessing they all sung divers hymns of thanks and praise.

When the fruit was on the table, Pantagruel asked: Now tell me, gentlemen, are your doubts fully resolved or no? I gape and yawn no more, answered Rhizotomus. I sleep no longer like a dog, said Ponocrates. I have cleared my eyesight, said Gymnast. I have broke my fast, said Eusthenes: so that for this whole day shall be secure from the danger of my spittle:

Asps.
Amphisbenes.
Amerudutes.
Abedissimons.
Alhartafs
Ammobates.
Apimaos.
Alhatrabans.
Aractes.
Asterions.
Alcharates.
Arges.
Spiders.
Starry lizards.
Attelabes.
Ascalabotes.
Hæmorrhoids.
Basilisks.
Fitches.
Sucking water-
    snakes.
Black wag-leg flies.
Spanish flies.
Catoblepes.
Horned snakes.
Caterpillars.
Crocodiles.
Toads.
Night-mares.
Mad dogs.
Colotes.
Cychriodes.
Cafezates.
Cauhares.
Snakes.
Cuhersks, two-
    tongued adders.
Amphibious serpents.
Cenchres.
Cockatrices.
Dipsades.
Domeses.
Dryinades.
Dragons.
Elopes.
Enhydrides.
Falvises.
Galeotes.

Harmenes.
Handons.
Icles.
Jarraries.
Ilicines.
Pharoah's mice.
Kesudures.
Sea-hares.
Chalcidic newts.
Footed serpents.
Manticores.
Molures.
Mouse-serpents.
Shrew-mice.
Miliares.
Megalaunes.
Spitting-asps.
Porphyri.
Pareades.
Phalanges.
Penphredons.
Pine-tree-worms.
Rutulæ.
Worms.
Rhagions.
Rhaganes.
Salamanders.
Slow-worms.
Stellions.
Scorpenes.
Scorpions.
Horn-worms.
Scalavotins.
Solofuidars.
Deaf-asps.
Horse-leeches
Salt-haters.
Rot-serpents.
Stink-fish.
Stuphes.
Sabrins.
Blood-sucking flies.
Hornfretters.
Scolopendres.
Tarantulas.
Blind worms.
Tetragnathias.
Teristales.
Vipers, etc.

CHAPTER 65

How Pantagruel passed the time with his servants

IN what hierarchy of such venomous creatures do you place Panurge's future spouse?

asked Friar John. Art thou speaking ill of women, cried Panurge, thou mangy scoundrel, thou sorry, noddy-peaked shaveling monk? By the cenomanic paunch and gixie, said Epistemon, Euripides has written, and makes Andromache say it, that by industry, and the help of the gods, men had found remedies against all poisonous creatures; but none was yet found against a bad wife.

This flaunting Euripides, cried Panurge, was gabbling against women every foot, and therefore was devoured by dogs, as a judgment from above; as Aristophanes observes. —Let us go on. Let him speak that is next. I can leak now like any stone-horse, said then Epistemon. I am, said Xenomanes, full as an egg and round as a hoop; my ship's hold can hold no more, and will now make shift to bear a steady sail. Said Carpalim, A truce with thirst, a truce with hunger; they are strong, but wine and meat are stronger. I am no more in the dumps, cried Panurge; my heart is a pound lighter. I am in the right cue now, as brisk as a body-louse, and as merry as a beggar. For my part, I know what I do when I drink; and it is a true thing (though it is in your Euripides) that is said by that jolly toper Silenus of blessed memory, that

The man's emphatically mad,
Who drinks the best, yet can be sad.

We must not fail to return our humble and hearty thanks to the Being, who, with this good bread, this cool delicious wine, these good meats and rare dainties, removes from our bodies and minds these pains and perturbations, and at the same time fills us with pleasure and with food.

But methinks, sir, you did not give an answer to Friar John's question; which, as I take it, was how to raise good weather? Since you ask no more than this easy question, answered Pantagruel, I will strive to give you satisfaction; some other time we will talk of the rest of the problems if you will.

Well then, Friar John asked how good weather might be raised. Have we not raised it? Look up and see our full top-sails: Hark! how the wind whistles through the shrouds, what a stiff gale it blows; observe the rattling of the tacklings, and see the sheets, that fasten the mainsail behind; the force of the wind puts them upon the stretch. While we passed our time merrily, the dull weather also passed away; and while we raised the glasses to our mouths, we also raised the wind by a secret sympathy in nature.

Thus Atlas and Hercules clubbed to raise and underprop the falling sky, if you will believe the wise mythologists; but they raised it some half an inch too high; Atlas, to entertain his guest Hercules more pleasantly, and Hercules to make himself amends for the thirst which sometimes before had tormented him in the deserts of Africa.—Your good father, said Friar John, interrupting him, takes care to free many people from such an inconveniency; for I have been told by many venerable doctors, that his chief butler, Turelupin, saves above eighteen hundred pipes of wine yearly, to make servants, and all comers and goers, drink before they are a-dry.—As the camels and dromedaries of a caravan, continued Pantagruel, used to drink for the thirst that is past, for the present, and for that to come; so did Hercules: and being thus excessively raised, this gave new motion to the sky, which is that of titubation and trepidation, about which our crack-brained astrologers make such a pother.—This, said Panurge, makes the saying good,

While jolly companions carouse it together,
A fig for the storm, it gives way to good
  weather.

Nay, continued Pantagruel, some will tell you, that we have not only shortened the time of the calm, but also much disburthened the ship; not like Æsop's basket, by easing it of the provisions, but by breaking our fasts; and that a man is more terrestrial and heavy when fasting, than when he has eaten and drank, even as they pretend that he weighs more dead than living. However it is, you will grant they are in the right, who take their morning's draught, and breakfast before a long journey; then say that the horses will perform the better, and that a spur in the head is worth two in the flank; or, in the same horse dialect,

That a cup in the pate
Is a mile in the gate.

Don't you know that formerly the Amycleans worshipped the noble Bacchus above all other gods, and gave him the name of Psila,

which in the Doric dialect signifies wings: for, as the birds raise themselves by a towering flight with their wings above the clouds; so, with the help of soaring Bacchus, the powerful juice of the grape, our spirits are exalted to a pitch above themselves, our bodies are more sprightly, and their earthly parts become soft and pliant.

CHAPTER 66

*How, by Pantagruel's order, the Muses were
saluted near the Isle of Ganabim*

This fair wind and as fine talk brought us in the sight of a high land, which Pantagruel discovering afar off, showed it Xenomanes, and asked him, Do you see yonder to the leeward a high rock, with two tops much like Mount Parnassus in Phocis? I do plainly, answered Xenomanes; it is the Isle of Ganabim. Have you a mind to go ashore there? No, returned Pantagruel. You do well indeed, said Xenomanes; for there is nothing worth seeing in the place. The people are all thieves: yet there is the finest fountain in the world, and a very large forest towards the right top of the mountain. Your fleet may take in wood and water there.

He that spoke last, spoke well, quoth Panurge; let us not by any means be so mad as to go among a parcel of thieves and sharpers. You may take my word for it, this place is just such another as, to my knowledge, formerly were the islands of Sark and Herm, between the smaller and the greater Britain; such as was the Poneropolis of Philip in Thrace; islands of thieves, banditti, picaroons, robbers, ruffians, and murderers, worse than raw-head and bloody-bones, and full as honest as the senior fellows of the college of iniquity, the very outcasts of the county gaol's commonside. As you love yourself, do not go among them: if you go, you will come off but bluely, if you come off at all. If you will not believe me, at least believe what the good and wise Xenomanes tells you: for may I never stir if they are not worse than the very cannibals: they would certainly eat us alive. Do not go among them, I pray you; it were safer to take a journey to hell. Hark, by cod's body, I hear them ringing the alarm bell most dreadfully as the Gascons about Bordeaux used formerly to do against the commissaries and officers for the tax on salt, or my ears tingle. Let's sheer off.

Believe me, sir, said Friar John, let's rather land; we will rid the world of that vermin, and inn there for nothing. Old Nick go with thee for me, quoth Panurge. This rash hair-brained devil of a friar fears nothing, but ventures and runs on like a mad devil as he is, and cares not a rush what becomes of others; as if every one was a monk, like his friarship.

A pox on grinning honour, say I. Go to, returned the friar, thou mangy noddy-peak! thou forlorn druggle-headed sneaksby! and may a million of black devils anatomize thy cockle brain. The hen-hearted rascal is so cowardly, that he bewrays himself for fear every day. If thou art so afraid, dunghill, do not go, stay here and be hanged, or go and hide thy loggerhead under Madam Proserpine's petticoat.

Panurge hearing this, his breach began to make buttons: so he slunk in, in an instant, and went to hide his head down in the bread-room among the musty biscuits, and the orts and scraps of broken bread.

Pantagruel in the meantime said to the rest, I feel a pressing retraction, in my soul, which like a voice admonishes me not to land there. Whenever I have felt such a motion within me, I have found myself happy in avoiding what it directed me to shun, or in undertaking what it prompted me to do; and never had occasion to repent following its dictates.

As much, said Epistemon, is related of the dæmon of Socrates, so celebrated among the Academics. Well then, sir, said Friar John, while the ship's crew water, have you a mind to have good sport? Panurge is got down somewhere in the hold, where he is crept into some corner, and lurks like a mouse in a cranny; let them give the word for the gunner to fire yon gun over the round-house on the poop: this will serve to salute the Muses of this Anti-parnassus: besides, the powder does but decay in it. You are in the right, said Pantagruel: here, give the word for the gunner.

The gunner immediately came, and was ordered by Pantagruel to fire the gun, and then charge it with fresh powder; which was soon done. The gunners of the other ships, frigates, galleons and galleys of the fleet, hearing us fire, gave every one a gun to the island: which made such a horrid noise, that you would have sworn heaven had been tumbling about our ears.

CHAPTER 67

How Panurge bewrayed himself for fear; and of the huge cat Rodilardus, which he took for a puny devil

PANURGE, like a wild, addle-pated, giddy goat, sallies out of the bread-room in his shirt, with nothing else about him but one of his stockings, half on half off, about his heel, like a rough footed pigeon; his hair and beard all be-powdered with crumbs of bread, in which he had been over head and ears, and a huge and mighty puss partly wrapped up in his other stocking. In this equipage, his chops moving like a monkey's who is a louse-hunting, his eyes staring like a dead pig's, his teeth chattering, and his bum quivering, the poor dog fled to Friar John, who was then sitting by the chain-wales of the starboard side of the ship, and prayed him heartily to take pity on him, and keep him in the safe-guard of his trusty bilbo; swearing, by his share of Papimany, that he had seen all hell broke loose.

Woe is me, my Jacky, cried he, my dear Johnny, my old crony, my brother, my ghostly father! all the devils keep holiday, all the devils keep their feast to-day, man: pork and peas choke me, if ever thou sawest such preparations in thy life for an infernal feast. Dost thou see the smoke of hell's kitchens? (This he said, showing him the smoke of the gunpowder above the ships.) Thou never sawest so many damned souls since thou wast born; and so fair, so bewitching they seem, that one would swear they are Stygian ambrosia. I thought at first, God forgive me, that they had been English souls; and I don't know, but that this morning the Isle of Horses, near Scotland, was sacked, with all the English who had surprised it, by the lords of Termes and Essay.

Friar John, at the approach of Panurge, was entertained with a kind of smell that was not like that of gunpowder, nor altogether so sweet as musk; which made him turn Panurge about, and then he saw that his shirt was dismally bepawed and bewrayed with fresh sir-reverence. The retentive faculty of the nerve, which restrains the muscle called sphincter (it is the arse-hole, and it please you) was relaxated by the violence of the fear which he had been in during his fantastic visions. Add to this, the thundering noise of the shooting, which seems more dreadful between decks than above. Nor ought you to wonder at such a mishap; for one of the symptoms and accidents of fear is, that it often opens the wicket of the cupboard wherein second-hand meat is kept for a time. Let us illustrate this noble theme with some examples.

Messer Pantolfe de la Cassina, of Sienna, riding post from Rome, came to Chamberry, and alighting at honest Vinet's, took one of the pitchforks in the stable; then turning to the inn-keeper, said to him, *"Da Roma in qua, io non son andato del corpo. Di gratia piglia in mano questa forcha, et fa mi paura."* I have not had a stool since I left Rome. I pray thee take this pitchfork, and fright me. Vinet took it, and made several offers, as if he would in good earnest have hit the signore, but did not; so the Sienese said to him, *"Si tu non fai altramente, tu non fai nulla: pero sforzati di adoperarli più guagliardamente."* If thou dost not go another way to work, thou hadst as good do nothing: therefore try to bestir thyself more briskly. With this, Vinet lent him such a swinging stoater with the pitchfork souce between the neck and the collar of his jerkin, that down fell signore on the ground arsyversy, with his spindle shanks wide straggling over his pole. Then mine host sputtering, with a full-mouthed laugh, said to his guest, By Beelzebub's bum-gut, much good may it do you, Signore Italiano. Take notice this is *datum Camberiaci,* given at Chamberry. It was well the Sienese had untrussed his points, and let down his drawers: for this physic worked with him as soon as he took it; and as copious was the evacuation, as that of nine buffaloes and fourteen missificating arch-lubbers. Which operation being over, the mannerly Sienese courteously gave mine host a whole bushel of thanks, saying to him, *"Io ti ringratio, bel messere; così facendo tu m'ai esparmiata la speza d'un servitiale."* I thank thee, good landlord; by this thou hast even saved me the expense of a clyster.

I will give you another example of Edward V, king of England. Master Francis Villon, being banished France, fled to him, and got so far into his favour, as to be privy to all his household affairs. One day the king, being on his close stool, showed Villon the arms of France, and said to him, Dost thou see what respect I have for thy French kings? I have none of their arms any where but in this backside, near my close stool. Odd's life, said the buffoon, how wise, prudent, and careful of your health, your highness is! How carefully your learned doctor, Thomas Linacer,

looks after you! He saw that, now you grow old, you are inclined to be somewhat costive, and every day were fain to have an apothecary; I mean, a suppository or clyster thrust into your royal nockandroe; so he has, much to the purpose, induced you to place here the arms of France; for the very sight of them puts you into such a dreadful fright, that you immediately let fly, as much as would come from eighteen squattering *bonasi* of Pæonia. And if they were painted in other parts of your house, by jingo, you would presently conskite yourself wherever you saw them. Nay, had you but here a picture of the great oriflamb of France, odds bodikins, your tripes and bowels would be in no small danger of dropping out at the orifice of your posteriors. But henh, henh, *atque iterum*[28] henh.

A silly cockney am I not,
  As ever did from Paris come?
And with a rope and sliding knot
  My neck shall know what weighs my bum.

A cockney of short reach, I say, shallow of judgment, and judging shallowly, to wonder, that you should cause your points to be untrussed in your chamber before you come into this closet. By our lady, at first I thought your close stool had stood behind the hangings of your bed; otherwise it seemed very odd to me you should untruss so far from the place of evacuation. But now I find I was a gull, a wittal, a woodcock, a mere ninny, a dolt-head, a noddy, a changeling, a calf-lolly, a doddipole. You do wisely, by the mass, you do wisely; for had you not been ready to clap your hind face on the mustard-pot as soon as you came within sight of these arms, mark ye me, cop's body, the bottom of your breeches had supplied the office of a close stool.

Friar John, stopping the handle of his face with his left hand, did, with the fore-finger of the right, point out Panurge's shirt to Pantagruel, who, seeing him in this pickle, scared, appalled, shivering, raving, staring, bewrayed, and torn with the claws of the famous cat Rodilardus, could not choose but laugh, and said to him, Prythee what wouldst thou do with this cat? With this cat, quoth Panurge, the devil scratch me, if I did not think it had been a young soft-chinned devil, which, with this same stocking instead of mitten, I had snatched up in the great hutch of hell, as thievishly as any sizar of Montague college could have done. The devil take Tybert: I feel it has all be-pinked my poor hide, and drawn on it to the life I do not know how many lobsters' whiskers. With this he threw his boar-cat down.

Go, go, said Pantagruel, be bathed and cleaned, calm your fear, put on a clean shift, and then your clothes. What! do you think I am afraid cried Panurge. Not I, I protest: by the testicles of Hercules, I am more hearty, bold, and stout, though I say it that should not, than if I had swallowed as many flies as are put into plum-cakes, and other paste at Paris, from Midsummer to Christmas. But what is this? hah! oh, ho! how the devil came I by this? Do you call this what the cat left in the malt, filth, dirt, dung, dejection, fæcal matter, excrement, stercoration, sir-reverence, ordure, second-hand meats, fumets, stronts, scybal, or spyrathe? 'Tis Hibernian saffron, I protest. Hah, hah, hah! it is Irish saffron, by Shaint Pautrick, and so much for this time. Selah. Let us drink.

NOTES

The following notes are intended in the main to clear up the frequent Latin expressions which occur throughout the text. The Dalibon edition of the works of Rabelais has been used, with its annotations by Le Duchat, Bernier, Motteux, the Abbé de Marsy, Voltaire, Ginguené, and others. The editor has also consulted the more up to date researches of scholars like Lefranc and Boulenger; also the *Revue des études rabelaisiennes* and the *Revue du seizième siècle*.

In translations from the Scriptures, the King James version of the Bible has been used. OED = Oxford English Dictionary.

BOOK ONE

1. Virgil, *Eclogues*, iv. 61. *Matri longa decem tulerunt fastidia menses*: Ten months have brought long weariness to your mother.

2. The reference is to the codification of ancient laws called the Digest, or Pandects, of Justinian. At the time of Rabelais *ff* was the sign used to designate the Digest, *l* the sign for law. Although Rabelais' citations are usually accurate, they are intended only as a show of erudition in mockery of the pedantry of the time. Since they seldom add to the meaning of the text, no attempt will be made to interpret the frequent references.

3. Aulus Gellius, the second-century author of the *Noctes Atticæ*, and one of the many authors frequently quoted in the Digest. The law referred to deals with seven-month children.

4. Privation presupposes something had.

5. Who has failed to experience the eloquence which comes from the flowing cup?

6. As a bridegroom (with a play on the word *spongia*, sponge); Ps. 19. 5.

7. As a thirsty land. Ps. 143. 6.

8. Have a care for the person, pour for two; *bus* is not in use. (*Bus* refers to the use of *duos* where *duobus* should be used. *Bus*, however, besides being a Latin case ending, has the same sound as *bu*, the past participle of *boire*, to drink, and "to drink" can be used only in the present, since there is never any end to drinking.)

9. I thirst. John, 19. 28.

10. And he poured out of the same. Ps. 75. 8.

11. Nature abhors a vacuum.

12. An addition of the translator. The expression is used with reference to the practice of turning the emptied cup upside down on the left thumb-nail to show that all the liquor has been drunk. From the German, *auf den Nagel*, "on to the nail." Cf. OED.

13. The French text reads. *"Que grand tu as,* (supple *le gousier*)!"* How great a (supply the word *throat*) you have!

14. Male and Female joined together are nearest to Man. (An addition of the translator.)

15. Light is good.

16. *Magnificat,* the opening word of the Canticle of the Blessed Virgin (Cf. Luke, 1. 46-55), is sung at Vespers rather than at Matins, the morning prayer of the Church.

17. Each lesson of the Divine Office is followed by the prayer: *Tu autem, Domine, miserere nobis,* But thou, O Lord, have mercy on us.

18. . . . . . That there was no science of the modes of signification.

19. *Dormi securè:* Sleep soundly (a collection of sermons popular in the sixteenth century).

20. May it profit. (The term used to signify a gift given—especially to bishops—in token of welcome. Cf. OED.)

21. *A Treatise on the Abundance of Things Venerable,* by John of Barrauco. (Work and author are apparently inventions of Rabelais.)

22. An artificial word from the mnemonic formula which sums up the valid moods and figures of the syllogism. The formula was invented by Peter of Spain (afterwards Pope John XXI). The opening line gives the valid moods of the first figure: *Barbara, celarent, darii, ferio*—artificial words in which vowels symbolize the type of proposition and certain consonants the proper method of conversion to the first, or perfect, figure. Bragmardo, a coined word, resembles the designation of an impossible syllogism.

23. And he that is wise will not abhor them. Ecclus. 38. 4.

24. Render unto Caesar the things which be Caesar's and unto God the things which be God's. Luke, 20. 25. *Ibi jacet lepus:* Here lies the hare (i.e., here is the main argument).

25. We will make good cheer in the Charity-

room (the guest room). I have killed a pig and I have good wine.

26. For God's sake, give us our bells. (Rabelais has *clochas*—with a pun on *cloaca*, sewer?—which he makes up from the French word *cloche*, bell.)

27. Would that.

28. Do you want pardons too? By the sun, you shall have them, and they won't cost you anything. (Janotus cautiously swears *per diem*, by day, rather than *per Deum*, by God.)

29. Give us our bells; they belong to the city.

30. "Man that is in honour, and understandeth not, is like the beasts that perish," which Psalm I know not. (Ps. 49. 20.)

31. And it is a good Achilles. (An Achilles is an argument which cannot be overthrown.)

32. The expression used to end an argument which does not prove anything.

33. The key word for the third mood of the first figure of the syllogism. Cf. note 22.

34. A meaningless collection of rhetorical tags.

35. *Valete et plaudite*: Farewell and applaud (used at the conclusion of a Latin play). *Calepinus recensui*: I, Calepinus, have finished the text (the formula used to conclude manuscripts).

36. "Thou dost not conclude in mood and figure [of the syllogism]." Supposition is a term from logic, and refers to the way in which a term may substitute for a thing in discourse. The *parva logicalia* form part of the *Summulæ Logicales*, a logical work by Peter of Spain. The passage continues: "The cloth, now what is its supposition?—Indeterminately and distributively. —I did not ask thee . . . . in *what way* does it substitute for the thing, but *for what* does it stand?—It is, Blockhead, substituting for my shins, and therefore I will carry it, I myself, as the supposition carries the apposition."

37. And all things rise and fall, grow and decline. Sallust, *Bellum Jugurthinum*, ii. 13.

38. It is vain for you to rise up early. Ps. 77. 2.

39. To the Chapter, all who have the right to be there.

40. Against the snares of the enemy.

41. For peace.

42. Give me drink.

43. Lick a villain, he will kick you; kick a villain, and he will lick you.

44. Make haste slowly.

45. Drinkable gold, a panacea. (Moses ground the golden calf into powder and made his followers drink it. Exod. 32, 20.)

46. O Holy God. (From the Good Friday ceremony of the unveiling of the Cross.)

47. From the wicked enemy deliver us, O Lord.

48. *The Supplement to the Supplement to the Chronicles*.

49. "The snare is broken" by Fourniller, "and we are escaped. Our help is in the name of the Lord." (Ps. 74. 7, 8.)

50. The rubric indicating the place where the celebrant at divine service removes his cope.

51. In the statutes of the Order (to which the monk belonged).

52. The root of Jesse has sprung up.

53. The greatest clerics are not the wisest.

54. The drones, sluggish creatures, they keep away from the hives. Virgil, *Georgics*, iv. 168.

55. Why? Because.

56. The shape of the nose reveals the *Ad te levavi* (Unto thee . . . do I lift up. Ps. 25. 1).

57. A short prayer pierces the skies, and a long drink empties the cup.

58. Come, let us drink. (A parody on *Venite adoremus*: Come, let us adore.)

59. One of the Decretals, or papal decrees: On the Frigid and those who have been made Impotent through Witchcraft.

60. *On Despising the World and Fleeing the Times*.

61. A monk on the inside of the cloister is worth less than a couple eggs, but on the outside he is well worth thirty.

62. In time and place.

BOOK TWO

1. Quack powder.

2. But excluding it.

3. We testify that we have seen. John, 3. 11.

4. The belly almighty.

5. Remember not. (Cf. Tob. 3. 3.) Rabelais is punning on the words *ne* and *nez*. *Ne*, the Latin particle used to introduce a negative, is pronounced in the same way as the French word *nez* (nose).

6. Dried-up bodies.

7. The Milky Way.

8. From one side and the other.

9. According to mood and figure (of the syllogism).

10. *Da jurandi=Da veniam jurandi:* Pardon me for swearing.

11. And Og, the king of Bashan (Cf. Deut. 3).

12. In the discard.

13. Poets and painters have equal freedom to attempt whatever they dare. Horace, *Ars Poetica*, 9-10.

14. We cross the Seine at daybreak and at dusk; we stroll about the intersections and crossroads of the city; we spout Latin.

15. To eat in a tavern.

16. Some fine shoulders of mutton sprinkled with parsley.

17. Scarcity of money in our purses.

18. To pawn (from *oppignerare*).

19. Await.

20. Messengers.

21. Most willingly, as soon as the first small light of day appears, I betake myself to one of these well-built churches, and then, sprinkling myself with holy water, I mutter some priestly

Mass prayer. And murmuring my prayers for each hour, I elevate and purify my soul of its nocturnal soilings. I revere those who are in heaven. I venerate with divine worship the Ruler of the Stars. I love and cherish my neighbours. I keep the Ten Commandments; and according to the small strength of my powers I do not depart from them the breadth of a finger-nail. Nevertheless, it is also true that because Mammon does not cough up anything into my pockets, it is seldom and slowly that I give alms to those needy ones who beg from door to door.

22. My genius is not so naturally apt as this scoundrelly rascal says, to flay our vernacular French, but contrariwise I strive with might and main [literally, with oars and sails] to enrich it with the same redundancy that marks Latin.

23. Where rests the body of the most saintly Saint Martial.

24. In some far-off place.

25. Decree of the University of Paris which permits young ladies to bare their throats at will.

26. *On the Worthy Art of Genteel Farting*, by Marcus Orthuinus.

27. *The Ant-Heap of the Arts.*

28. *On the Use of Soups and on the Worthiness of Tippling*, by Sylvester de Priero, Jacobin.

29. The original text reads *Decrotatorium scholarium: On the Brushing Up of Scholars.* (Rabelais intends a pun on *Decrotatorium* and Decretal.)

30. Tartaret, *On the Ways of Going to Stool.*

31. Bricot, *On the Variations within Soups.*

32. Three books of the Reverend Father, Brother Lubin, Provincial of Chatter-land, *On Gobbling Up Rashers of Bacon.*

33. Pasquin, the marble doctor, *On Eating Kids prepared with Artichokes, during the Ecclesiastically Proscribed Papal Season.* (*Pasquin* refers to a statue in Rome, to which were affixed lampoons against prominent persons, from which our word *pasquinade*.)

34. Major, *On How to Make Puddings.*

35. Bede, *On the Absolute Perfection of Tripes.*

36. The overwhelmingly clear exposition, by the most renowned Doctor of Laws, Master Pilotus Scrapfarthing, *Of the Patching Up of the Fiddle-faddle of the Gloss of Accursius.*

37. *The Wiles of the Franc-Archers* of Baniolet.

38. *Military Manual*, with diagrams by Tevot.

39. *Treatise on the Custom and Benefit of Flaying Horses and Mares*, written by Our Master of Quebec.

40. Fourteen books by Master Rostocostjambedanesse, *On Serving Mustard after Dinner;* annotated by Master Vaurillon.

41. Jabolenus, *The Cosmography of Purgatory.*

42. On the most subtle question: *Whether a Chimæra, humming in the Void, is able to eat Second Intentions* [the Reflex Universal], debated over a period of ten weeks by the Council of Constance.

43. The mumblings of Scotus.

44. One hundred and ten volumes by Master Alberic, *On the Art of Keeping your Spurs clear of the Horse's Flanks.*

45. Three books by the same author, *On Camping in the Hair* (*Criminibus* should read *crinibus*).

46. Treatise of Marforio, Bachelor of Arts, who rests at Rome: *On the Manner of Adorning and Rigging-out the Cardinals' Mules.* (Marforio's statue lies on the ground in one of the courts of the ancient Capitol.)

47. *A Forecast*, which begins *Silvii triquebille*, bleated out by Our Master Songecreux.

48. Bishop Boudarin: Ninety-one books, *On the Profits of Milking* [Indulgences], with a Papal privilege limited to three years.

49. *On Giving the Canonical Hours the Once Over*, forty books by Professor Lickdish.

50. *The Overthrow of the Confraternities*, author unknown.

51. *The Torpor of Italian Affairs*, by Master Brûlefer. The original text reads *Poltronismus.*

52. Raymond Lullus, *On the Trivial Occupations of Princes.*

53. *Calebistris*: the female sexual organs; *caffardiæ*: canting; Master Jacob Hoogstraaten, "expert in taking the measure of heretics."

54. Eight very elegant books by Codtickler: *On the Tap-rooms of the Doctors of Theology and Doctoral Candidates.*

55. *On How to Sweep Out Chimneys*, by Master Eccius.

56. Blockhead's treatise, *On the Life and Worthiness of Fops.*

57. *Moral Reflections of a Liripoop of the Sorbonne*, by Master Lupoldus. (*Liripoop*: a graduate's hood.)

58. *Uproar by the Doctors of Cologne against Reuchlin.*

59. Gerson, *On the Right of the Church to Depose the Pope.*

60. *On the Frightfulness of Excommunication*, a short treatise without a Preface, by John Ditebrodius. (*Acephalos*: without a head; i.e., brainless.)

61. *On the Art of Calling Up He-Devils and She-Devils*, by Guingolfus.

62. Sutor: *Against a certain person who called him a Slabsauce-eater, and that Slabsauce-eaters are not condemned by the Church.*

63. *The Doctors' Chamber-pot.*

64. *The Fields of Enemas*, by S. C. (Symphorien Champier).

65. Justinian, *On the Suppression of White Leprosy.* (The original text reads, *On the Suppression of Bigots.*)

66. *The Pharmacopæia of the Soul.*

67. *On the Devil's Homeland*, by Merlin Coccaius.

68. Many times already I have conjured you, by things sacred, by the gods and goddesses, that if any respect for things holy affects you to solace my need; but my cries and lamentations are to no avail. Allow me, I beseech you, allow me, wicked men, to go where my destiny calls me. Weary me no longer with your empty questionings but remember the old proverb, that a hungry stomach has no ears.

69. Blessed are the dunces, for they have stumbled.

70. He who falls wisely will never fall off the bridge.

71. For *in verbo sacerdotis*: On the word of a priest.

72. See Book 1, note 17.

73. Summation of facts.

74. The artificial word standing for one of the forms of the fourth (or indirect first) figure of the syllogism. See Book II, note 22.

75. The original reads *grenoillibus*: Despising the frogs.

76. What law is there for minors?

77. By oracle of living voice.

78. With a single voice.

79. Now as before.

80. O Holy and Immortal God. (From the Good Friday ceremony of the unveiling of the Cross.)

81. Brother Lubin, in the *Treatise on the Beverages of the Mendicant Orders*.

82. And where will you find them?

83. The first two words of grace after meals: May God grant us His peace.

84. The words of the priest at the close of Mass: Go, the Mass is ended.

85. Thank you, sirs.

86. And Bartholus quotes it.

87. To the limit of speech (i.e., to the point of silence).

88. And, behold, a greater than Solomon is here. Matt. 22. 42.

89. The disciple is not above his master. Matt. 10. 24.

90. As a thirsty land. Ps. 143. 6.

91. He that is able to receive it, let him receive it. Matt. 19. 12.

92. They pretend to be Curii, but they live like Bacchanals. Juvenal, *Satires*, II. 3. (Curius was a consul of Rome, famous for his frugality and sobriety.)

BOOK THREE

1. "The introduction of a pretended speaker." —OED.

2. *Lapathium acutum* is a plant of uncertain identity mentioned by Pliny. A pun on the word *passion* is intended.

3. And victorious, dispensed laws to the not-unwilling nations. *Georgics*, IV. 5, 61.

4. According to the saying: Things ill-gotten wither away.

5. According to the saying: Things ill-gotten will last scarcely to the third generation.

6. It is finished. John, 19. 30.

7. See above, note 1.

8. Justinian, in his treatise *On the Suppression of Bigots*, put the *summum bonum* [highest good] in the breeches.

9. Woe to him that is alone. Eccles. 4. 10.

10. He has no testicles.

11. Past and gone.

12. *Fiat* was used to close petitions favourably received. *Fiatur* is bad Latin, which the Pope would not use in official documents.

13. On the Frigid and those who have been made Impotent through Witchcraft.

14. Straight from the Mass to the dinner-table.

15. Due.

16. See Book II, note 10.

17. A word constructed by Rabelais from *gyrus* and *gnomen*: the shadow of the sun turning on the sun-dial.

18. Another word coined by Rabelais: coming from the sky.

19. Counterweight.

20. Hail, Star of the Sea (a hymn to the Blessed Virgin, sung at Vespers).

21. The first and last words of the Penetential Psalms, the Psalms chanted by the monks while administering the Discipline.

22. Tom-cat's hood.

23. A kind of burlesque hymn. To sing the Black Sanctus: to lament. OED.

24. Reading images in water.

25. Reading the signs in mirrors.

26. Divination by the turning of a sieve.

27. Divination by means of barley-meal.

28. Reading the dice.

29. Divination by means of the holes in cheese.

30. Divination by means of the "wish-bone."

31. Reading the smoke of incense.

32. Smoke-reading.

33. Divination by means of ashes thrown up in the air.

34. Divination by means of pigs.

35. Divination by means of the human body. (The Emperor Heliogabalus is reported to have consulted the entrails of children.)

36. Divination by lines of verse taken at random.

37. Divination by names.

38. The examination of the flesh of sacrificed animals.

39. The same as in the preceding note.

40. Divination by means of the shades of the departed.

41. The original text: *Crescite:* Be fruitful; we who live, let us multiply. (A mixture of Scriptural tags; cf. Gen. 1. 28; II Cor. 4. 11.)

42. When he shall have come to judge.

43. It has been proved.

44. *Unsolvable Problems*, by Peter d'Ailly.

45. Chaste.

46. *SPQR* stands for *senatus populusque romanus*: the Senate and People of Rome.

47. A truncated syllogism.

48. What is hidden.

49. *Excrement and urine are the meals of medics; from everything else gather straw, but from these grain.*

50. *To us they are signs, to you they are fitting food.*

51. On Inspecting the Belly.

52. . . . Which are noted by the Archdeacon; the references that follow relate to the codes of law.

53. Judgement by lot.

54. The man of today loves brevity.

55. When the rights of the disputants are obscure, the defendant is to be favoured over the accuser.

56. When things opposed are set side by side they become more clear.

57. When the situation is obscure, take the course of least consequence.

58. The first-comer has the benefit in law.

59. If the form is changed, the substance is changed.

60. Because what is secondary conforms to the nature of the principal.

61. Who was a great practitioner.

62. Vary your cares from time to time with pleasures.

63. Money rules everything.

64. *Hic nota*: observe here that.

65. Speaking by way of resolution.

66. A voluntary burden is a light burden.

67. The law is to business what medicines are to the sick.

68. Now Virginity, ready for marriage, had been maturing over the years.

69. Legal axioms are called *Brocards*. From this Rabelais invents the name of a professor.

70. The son is often like the father, and the daughter follows easily in her mother's path.

71. To the vigilant the laws are a help.

72. If any would not work, neither should he eat. II Thess. 3. 10.

73. Need makes the old lady run faster than a trot.

74. The word is given to all, wisdom of the soul to few.

75. What is needful.

76. Gloss: sweeter is the fruit plucked from danger.

77. If money is lacking, everything is lacking.

78. I will hate if I can; otherwise I will love against my will.

79. Form gives being to a thing.

80. Better fortune will follow a poor beginning.

81. As the outward garb is, so is the heart.

82. This is to be observed.

83. It is more blessed to give than to receive. Acts, 20. 35.

84. The disposition of the giver counterbalances the judgement of him who thunders.

85. Receive, take up, hold: these are words pleasing to the Pope.

86. Rome eats up the hand within reach, hates the hand she cannot consume; she protects those who give, casts aside those who do not give.

87. An egg in the hand is better than a chicken tomorrow.

88. When the fruits of labour are lost, mortal poverty increases.

89. Through the courts, laws increase; through the courts, a new law is gained.

90. And when things taken one by one fail, taken all together they prosper.

91. Red-handed.

92. Sometimes even good Homer nods (Horace, *Ars Poetica*, 359).

93. Money is a second blood.

94. Money is the life of man and his most dependable prop in need.

95. Lost money is wept for with real tears. Juvenal, *Satires*, XIII. 134.

96. Through calm and repose the soul becomes wise.

BOOK FOUR

1. And your *mentula* has spirit. (Rabelais is punning on the word *mentula*, which is at the same time the word for the male organ and the diminutive of *mens*, mind or spirit.)

2. Along with many others.

3. You are either a clerk (i.e., a clever fellow) or learning to be one.

4. *Ita*: yes.

5. *Vere*: truly.

6. Vengeance is mine; I will repay, saith the Lord. Rom. 12. 19.

7. See Book II, note 10.

8. Blessed are the undefiled in the way. Ps. 119. 1.

9. Here is a man of the country, sprung from the race of hoboes, who is used to carrying bread in his old sack.

10. In full pontificals.

11. The gold of Toulouse. (The reference is to temple gold, gained through warfare, which until it was disposed of brought misfortune to the inhabitants of the city.)

12. See Book III, note 8.

13. From the *Confiteor*: Through my fault, O Lord.

14. I confess.

15. See Book III, note 6.

16. The beginning of the prayer, "Into thy hands, O Lord, I commend my spirit," which always occurs at the conclusion of the Office of Compline.

17. Blessed is the man that walketh not (in the counsel of the ungodly). Ps. 1. 1.

18. A terrible Tempest swirled about the sharp peak. (*Tempest* was the name of the Principal of the College of Montaigu [*montem acutum*].)

19. Against the snares of the enemy.

20. What law is there (for us).

21. From the Introit of the Mass for the Dead: Eternal rest give to them, O Lord.

22. *Sextum*: To the original five books of the Decretals Boniface VIII, in 1298, added a sixth volume in which were gathered together the Constitutions of the Popes subsequent to the year 1234. This sixth volume was called the *Sextum*.

Clementinæ: A further addition to the preceding collections of the Decretals. It consisted of the Constitutions of Clement V and the Council of Vienne.

Extravagantes: Papal decrees not contained in the above collections.

23. Nor do you crap ten times throughout the year, and then it is tougher than beans or a stone; take it and grind it and crumble it in your hands and you will not be able to dirty a single finger. *Carmina*, xxiii. 20-3.

24. *Latria* is the term used to designate the kind of veneration given to God alone; *hyperdulia* designates the kind of veneration accorded to the Blessed Virgin.

25. The chapter-headings of the Decretals which deal with the payment of revenues to Rome.

26. Long may he live, long may he drink. (*Fifat* and *pipat* are *vivat* and *bibat* pronounced with a German accent.)

27. If you do not wish to give, then lend, we beseech you. (*Præsta quæsumus* are the introductory words of a large number of prayers.)

28. And again.